A HOUSE FULL

and

THE STRAWBE

Helen Upshall has been interested in writing fiction since she was a teenager. She has published twenty novels, including several written under pseudonyms.

She is married, with a son, and lives in Bournemouth, where she combines her career as an author with researching her family history.

A HOUSE FULL OF WOMEN

and

THE STRAWBERRY GIRL

Helen Upshall

PAN BOOKS

A House Full of Women first published 1991 by Judy Piatkus (Publishers) Ltd
The Strawberry Girl first pubished 1993 by Judy Piatkus (Publishers) Ltd

This omnibus edition published 2002 by Pan Books
an imprint of Pan Macmillan Ltd
Pan Macmillan, 20 New Wharf Road, London N1 9RR
Basingstoke and Oxford
Associated companies throughout the world
www.panmacmillan.com

ISBN 0 330 40054 1

1 3 5 7 9 8 6 4 2

A CIP catalogue record for this book is available from the British Library.

Printed and bound in Great Britain by
Mackays of Chatham plc, Chatham, Kent

A HOUSE FULL OF WOMEN

For my sisters, Eileen, Ruth and Beryl,
with love, and remembering with affection
the sad and happy times we spent together
at No. 51, our special House full of Women

Chapter One

Fran rolled away from Henry, but with a grab he brought her back into the circle of his arm.

'No,' he whispered, 'today is your day and you're going to have an extra lie-in. Babe is still fast asleep and Katie won't be here for another hour at least.'

'There isn't time, Henry,' Fran protested as he slid his hand beneath her winceyette nightdress. 'Babe is going to stir any minute and you know I don't like a late start on Sundays.'

'Just a cuddle then,' he persuaded. He held her fast, his work-worn fingers rough against the smooth skin of her rounded belly. Fran knew by the moistness of his lips and the rising pulses of passion that he wouldn't give up until . . . After bearing him five children she was weary of this part of marriage, but Henry Sheldon was an ardent and persistent lover. He knew how to make her weaken and in spite of her protests her body quickly reacted to his fondling. Her breasts were soft but firm and the nipples hardened. Then she was breathing quickly, arching her body to mate with his . . .

'Now, Henry,' she begged. '*Now* – As he reached his climax, and she was gasping with ecstasy, he pulled free, spilling his unwanted seed where it could do no harm – and from the large cot on the other side of the room came a small voice, urgent in its appeal.

'Mummy, Mummy! I want to get up now, Daddy.'

A moment of fumbling, some ragged breathing from Henry, a guilty sigh from Fran as she slid from the huge double bed and the comfort of the feather mattress.

'What you doing?' Babe demanded, on the verge of tears.

'Just trying to wake up, dear,' Fran said. She put the side of the cot down, lifted the small four-year-old auburn-haired girl into her arms and carried her into the next bedroom, where Ruby and Hilda slept in another double bed.

'You stay here with Hilda while I get washed and dressed. And you, Ruby, up, there's jobs to be done. You can clean the grate while Daddy gets the breakfast going.'

When Fran returned to her own room again, contented snores indicated that Henry had gone back to sleep. She stood looking down at him with a loving gaze. His dark hair was tousled against the starched white pillowcase, his weather-beaten cheeks relaxed with just hint of a smile – a smile that was so very dear to her. In sleep he looked younger than his forty-six years. She didn't often have time to stand still and reflect, but now memories of their youth flipped the years backwards to another time, another place, and a very different, younger – she had to admit it – a more handsome face. She felt herself colour guiltily as she hastened to get washed and dressed ready for church.

She chivvied Ruby to hurry along with the chores, clearing out the dead ash from the kitchen range before relighting the fire. Henry was soon down, whistling contentedly as he fried bacon and bread in the huge iron pan. By the time Fran had dressed the two youngest girls, eggs too were splattering noisily in the pan.

Kate, the eldest of the family, arrived before breakfast was over, and the mill house soon echoed to the sound of a happy family gathering on this special Sunday, Mothering Sunday 1931.

Kate was in service at Sherbrook House, where the Maitland family lived. They owned the village and acres of the surrounding land, including a stretch of the river Sher which flowed along the bottom of the mill-house garden. Not so many years ago the huge mill wheel had been driven by water from a tributary of the river which ran alongside the house. Weeks of wet weather meant that river and stream were running high, occasionally spilling over on to the garden and paths, making the ground soggy, but today winter had abated and there was the promise of spring in the bright morning sunshine.

Fran noticed how smart Kate was looking in a brown check skirt and patterned blouse. At sixteen she was attractive, her rich auburn-coloured hair coiled neatly in earphones, reminding Fran of herself at that age. Memories stirred, and Fran could feel again the excitement of all the staff as they made new dresses or remodelled old ones, ready for the annual servants' ball held every Christmas in the great hall at Lady Hinckley's where she had been Nanny. Such pleasant memories of doing a job she loved, with few worries. All that had changed since her marrying Henry. It was no easy task keeping four girls well-dressed. She was always making do and mending, as well as cleaning and cooking. There were never enough hours in the day to do all that was necessary for a large family.

On their way to church Fran called at the small cottage next door to the mill house to take a cake to her mother, Gran Brown. Her father, the estate's shepherd, was out on the Dorset hills tending his sheep.

'The meat's in the oven, Ma,' Fran said. 'I don't expect to be much later than usual, though, so it should be all right, but when you're ready go round and baste the potatoes and joint if you will. I hope Pa will get in from the fields in time for dinner, being that Kate is home today. We'll have a nice family get-together.'

'He was out early this morning,' Gran said. 'Expecting the last of the lambs to drop. He's quite pleased with his flock, but I reckon he's getting past working all hours at lambing time.'

'Then he must tell Mr Maitland, Ma,' Fran said, a trifle impatiently. 'As long as Pa goes on doing it all by himself, they'll expect him to. He's sixty-eight, after all, time they started to think about the future.'

'Don't you say that to your father, Fran! He'll keep going till the rheumatics won't let him get up of a morning.'

'He looks so pale and gets so tired. He ought to be easing up.'

'But he won't want his sheep tended by anyone else, you know that.'

'Yes, he'll be stubborn to the last, I suppose, in spite of Dr Gibbs telling him that his blood is poor and he needs more rest.'

'Nice bit of raw liver'll do him good when the butcher calls next week,' Sara Brown said. ''Twill be a bit easier when the weather gets warmer and lambing's done with. Now you get on or you'll be late for church. I'll see to the dinner.'

Fran turned and left the small cottage. She knew that her mother would go to the window and watch Henry proudly leading his family down the lane to the bridge and out of sight. Although a short, dapper little man, Henry stood tall with dignified self-esteem. Farm labourer he might be but he had been to Canada logging, and would have returned there but Fran wouldn't leave her parents to accompany him. She was grateful that he had settled down in Sherbrook, though he was more in love with his shire horses than with his family, she sometimes thought. But he was a good man, hard-working, God-fearing, and although they were poor financially, they had much to be thankful for.

The service was a happy one, but when the vicar spoke of a mother's role as the pillar of the family unit, Fran felt a lump in her throat. She tried to do the best she could for them all but sometimes she was guilty of impatience. The atmosphere became warm, and the very fact that Fran was completely relaxed made her drowsy. The vicar's voice grew distant, monotonous, and her thoughts strayed back to the time just before she was married. She supposed it was seeing Kate looking so grown up that sparked off her reminiscences.

It was at Christmas in a distant past that the plans for her marriage to Henry were at last complete.

Henry had left his job at the brewery several months earlier to take up his work as carter on the Sherbrook House estate. He was living in the old mill house, preparing it for his new wife. Fran should have been at home in Sherbrook long before this, living with her parents in the small shepherd's cottage, getting everything ready for a summer wedding and helping Henry next door. But Lady Hinckley was determined to hang on to Fran for as long as she could. 'Just another week, my dear,' she kept saying, and one week had grown into six months. When the time actually came for her to leave the staff had decided to make Fran's departure a memorable one.

It was her last night at Hinckley Hall, and in four days' time, on Boxing Day, she would become Mrs Henry Sheldon. Music and laughter reached her ears as she descended the back stairs. She was late going to the servants' hall, having had some difficulty settling the children. Halfway down the dimly lit staircase she caught the sound of the door at the top opening. She turned, expecting to see one of the other servants. Instead, a tall, lean figure gazed down at her. She recognised him as one of the house guests, a friend of Mr Jonathan.

'This leads to the servants' quarters, sir,' she said politely. 'You've come down one flight too many.'

The man raised his eyebrows questioningly. He had been a frequent visitor to the house of late.

'I don't think so,' he said. 'This party sounds more exciting than the one upstairs.'

'But this is only for the staff, sir.'

His long legs brought him down to stand one step above her, and his haunting eyes mesmerised her.

'Forget the "Sir",' he whispered. 'I shan't be missed. What's your name?'

'Frances Brown, sir. Fran to most people.'

'You're Nanny, aren't you? I've heard them talking about you. Leaving to get married, I understand?'

Fran lowered her gaze to the dainty, blue dancing slippers that just peeped beneath her long, turquoise-blue dress.

'I . . . I gave Lady Hinckley plenty of warning. In fact, we should have been married back in the summer.'

'My name is Luke,' he introduced himself, holding out his hand. 'Luke Hammond. Her ladyship tried to hang on to you, didn't she? Can't say I blame her.'

Fran blushed at his implication. His dark eyes seemed to bore right into her soul.

'Having trouble in replacing you, and young Andrew and the twins are loath to part with you, so I believe.'

'I realise it's difficult, but Andrew will be going away to school after next summer, and the twins will soon get used to someone new.'

Fran felt uneasy at the young man's scrutiny, as well as at holding a conversation on the back stairs with a guest who should be upstairs. She carried on down to the bottom with Luke Hammond following.

'Mind if I join the party?' he asked. 'I know it isn't the done thing, but it is your farewell one, isn't it?'

Fran didn't know how to answer. She was well used to house guests eyeing her inquisitively on the occasions when she had to take the children to the drawing room to say goodnight. This young man was no exception although he was so devilishly handsome that he had been the focus of servant gossip for several days. Fran had been pumped by the other girls to find out what she could, but all she had been able to glean was that he was a fellow officer in the Royal Navy, and a friend of Mr Jonathan.

'I really don't think it would be your kind of party,' she managed to say in a nervous whisper. Whatever would the others think if she arrived escorted by this young man?

He towered above her and, with a compelling hand at her waist, ushered her through the door. Fran was immediately drawn into the centre of her circle of friends, who showered her with confetti and petals made from crepe paper. They put them down her neck, and when she was pushed to the floor one of the bolder young men, with the help of Bessie the parlourmaid, with whom he was walking out, lifted Fran's petticoats and shook confetti into the tops of her stockings and up her knicker legs. Fran's screams brought Talbot, the butler, so they pulled Fran to her feet quickly and she was waltzed round the room in time to music provided by an old Pianola. She went quite dizzy, and her long hair, so carefully arranged in her usual attractive style on top of her head, came loose until it fell about her neck and shoulders in a cascade of red-gold silk. They plied her with mulled wine and goodness knows what else. By the time she was thrown into the air six times, once for every year she had been with the Hinckleys, she hardly felt a thing. Her head spun and her feet were light as strong arms propelled her round the servants' hall. She felt as if she were floating on magical wings in time to a Viennese waltz.

Luke then took her to the long trestle table where a variety of food and drink was waiting to be consumed.

'I think it's probably time you had something to eat,' he said with a wry smile.

Fran had to cling to his arm for support, but nothing was going to stop her from enjoying the festivities.

No one questioned Luke Hammond's presence but his youthful, dashing appearance added lustre to the occasion, and Fran felt light-headed when he insisted she should partner him for ever dance.

After a rumbustious rendition of the Gay Gordons she was laughing up at him as if she had known him all her life. She saw him through a spider's web of fantasy as he picked her up and carried her to the nursery floor of the vast house. He set her down on the side of her bed, his eyes bright with anticipation.

Fran waved a finger at him. 'Sssch. Musschn't wake the children.'

Luke crossed the floor with a mere two strides to close and lock the communicating door. Fran watched, but his intentions didn't register so she made no protest. She giggled a great deal as he removed her clothes. Then her cheeks grew warm and her eyes burned. She lay back, looking into Luke's admiring expression as he scanned her nakedness.

'Mm,' he muttered. 'Such white skin – feels like porcelain.' He fingered her hipbone tenderly. Somewhere in the back of her mind she knew she was being outrageously brazen, but ever since the last time she and Henry had been together her body craved a man's touch. She was no longer a virgin. Once Henry had gone to live in Sherbrook their meetings had been infrequent, but increasing in passion, until Henry's impatience could not be supressed. Fran had been consumed with guilt but Henry had pacified her, excusing their impetuosity by blaming Lady Hinckley.

Luke's hands caressed with tantalising delicacy. Cupping her breasts, he lowered his face until his mouth met hers. A hesitant, gentle kiss at first until he realised that Fran was as eager as he.

She remembered little else except the height their passion reached, and then there was no going back. She recalled whispered promises and a declaration of love, but did it really ever happen?

The heat was stifling, probably because the sun was coming through the window directly on to the pew where Fran was sitting beside Henry. She moved slightly and opened her coat at the neck, her cheeks flushed. She sensed that Henry glanced down at her and then took her hand in his. He squeezed reassuringly while she wrestled with emotions she had tried to put behind her over the past nineteen years. The thought of how different her life might have been charged her with disloyalty to Henry.

During the singing of the last hymn the children all went up to the front of the church, where they were given a bunch of daffodils to take to their mothers. Ruby took Babe with her, and when they emerged into the sunlight outside Fran was holding three bunches of flowers.

'Good morning, Mrs Sheldon,' the vicar said, giving her a limp handshake. 'You've done well this morning, I see,' he added, nodding towards the daffodils.

'I'm going to take them to Lennie's grave, vicar,' Fran replied demurely, and walked on with Henry following. Conversation wasn't easy with the sound of church bells hanging in the valley, but when they were a little distance away she turned to Henry.

'You go on home with the girls and I'll put these on Lennie's grave.'

'Wouldn't it be nice to have them in the house, just for today?' Henry suggested gently.

'There's plenty coming on in the garden,' she said. 'And it would only mean I'd have to traipse down here tomorrow, and I've got enough to do with wash-day as it is.'

Henry recognised the signs of emotional uncertainty. For the most part Fran was a strong woman, but grief for her first-born, her only son, was always there just below the surface. In spite of her love for the girls, her obsessive love for Lennie seemed almost unnatural. He had tried to woo her back to reality. 'Life is for the living,' he told her on more than one occasion. He had tried to keep his own hurt private so as not to distress the girls. Fran's sorrowing had become an indulgence, but who was he to question a mother's love?

He patted her arm understandingly. 'Don't be long then, my dear.'

'Can I come with you?' Ruby chanted, and soon all the girls were hanging on their mother's arm.

'No,' Fran said firmly. 'Kate can come, she doesn't get the chance to visit her brother's grave very often. The rest of you go home with Daddy and see to the dinner.'

Fran wove a pathway through the headstones, glancing at the inscriptions and remembering villagers who had passed on long ago, including members of the Brown family. She came to a small mound beneath a holly bush.

'Mum,' Kate said in a perplexed tone. 'There's no room for any more flowers. The vase is full. You must have known . . .'

Fran felt herself go cold. She stiffened and clenched her gloved fist. Then with a shrug she pulled off her gloves, bent down and fussed with the beautiful bouquet of tulips and daffodils that did indeed fill the vase. She kept her face hidden, not wanting her daughter to see the guilt that she knew must be evident in her expression. *He* had visited Sherbrook again. Why couldn't he leave her alone and let the past die with Lennie? It was embarrassing. How could she explain away the expensive blooms obviously bought at a florist's shop? Was he deliberately reminding her of a brief lapse of fidelity? She wished Luke Hammond had never come into her life. She took some of the flowers out of the vase and said to Kate:

'Someone must have put these here by mistake. How could I afford such an extravagance?'

'You can't throw them away, Mum. They're too fresh and lovely.'

Fran nodded to the other side of the path. 'Take them to your great-grandparents' grave, then,' she said shortly.

She was grateful for a few moments in which to recover from the shock. It wasn't the first time she had found flowers here, but each time she experienced a strange tightening in her breast. On the first occasion, some months after Lennie's death seven years ago, a card had been attached to the flowers. No message, just a scrawled L.H. beneath the printed 'In Deepest Sympathy', reminding her of that brief interlude which should never have happened. As time passed she was to discover that Luke Hammond was not only a friend of Jonathan Hinckley but also of Nicholas Maitland, and the young naval officers sometimes came to Sherbrook House to spend a few days of their leave together. When Fran was aware of Luke's presence in the vicinity she remained at home, making

excuses for not going down to the church or village. Now she hoped Kate hadn't noticed her agitation, and she prayed that she might be spared from ever coming face to face with him.

She set the pace on the homeward journey, a pace that Kate recognised as being fast and furious, and she knew better than to question the reason. She wondered about her mother's change of attitude, though. It seemed quite illogical to her that a few flowers mistakenly placed on her brother's grave could cause such annoyance.

Fran felt an underlying impatience with everyone and everything for the remainder of the day. But Henry's happy-go-lucky nature eventually relieved the tension, and they all enjoyed a peaceful Sunday as a united family.

Three weeks after Mothering Sunday, Easter was celebrated and the girls eagerly enjoyed a holiday from school. It was a Monday morning and Fran was back in the usual routine of wash-day. As she pegged several blue-white petticoats on the line, she glanced up at the sky. After the long, wet winter it was something of a change to have a dry wash-day, but even as she looked she noticed that the sky was thickening, and over the Dorset hills dark clouds were lingering menacingly.

Gran Brown staggered over the damp grass with a wicker basket laden with clean washing.

'You should have left that for me, Ma,' Fran said.

'My feet are bad,' the old lady moaned. 'I wish I could get around like you do, but I can't and that's that.'

'That's why I suggested that you did the mangling instead. If we don't hurry up I reckon that storm's going to beat us to it.'

'It'll dry quickly while the sun's out,' Gran Brown mumbled as she picked her way across the uneven garden back to the outhouse where Ruby was helping. Together they folded the sheets, and then, while Gran fed them through the heavy wooden rollers, Ruby turned the big iron handle with one hand and caught the sheet with the other.

'Your mother thinks there's going to be a storm so we'd best hurry up,' Gran said.

Ruby smiled at her Gran sympathetically. Her mother's temper was short, especially on wash-day when there was so much to do. It was usually poor old Gran who received the butt end of her mother's tongue. Not that any of them escaped, except the two little ones, Hilda and Babe. Today, with the promise of warmer weather, her mother seemed in happier fettle, and the line, which stretched right down the long garden at the back of the old mill house almost to the river bank, was soon filled to capacity with sparkling washing, billowing in the wind. Even when Gran had returned to her small cottage next door to get dinner for herself and Grandad, Ruby could hear her mother singing softly as she put the cold meat out ready for Dad to carve when he came in from the fields, and waited for the potatoes to boil.

While they ate their dinner, Fran kept a close watch on the weather through the window.

'I don't like the look of those clouds out there, Henry,' she said. 'I do believe the weather's on the change.'

''Tis early for the weather to be so warm, but the ground underfoot is still very wet and the wind's getting mighty strong. River's running pretty high, too, so I'd best get the sluice boards open before we go to bed tonight.'

After Ruby had helped with the washing-up, she was allowed out to play. She skipped off down the lane to a row of terraced cottages where a small group of children were playing on the grass verge. A tall girl of eleven came to greet her and together they went off round to the back garden to do what they considered were more grown-up things, like combing each other's hair into different styles, while they talked about the boys in the village.

'Can't do much with your hair,' Marion Belmont said. 'It's too long, Ruby. Why don't you get your mother to cut it off?'

'I keep asking her to, but she won't. We've all got to have long hair. Even our Kate has had to put hers up into earphones since she went to the big house to work. It isn't fair,' Ruby grumbled. 'And all because the children Mum was nanny to in service had long hair.'

They had been in the garden a little while when the wind suddenly seemed to whip up into a frenzy. The distant rumble of thunder could be heard, so they went up to Marion's bedroom. Mrs Belmont was a happy-go-lucky woman with much less stringent house rules than Fran, which made visiting Ruby's school friend a happy adventure. They got carried away with enthusiasm over Ruby's lovely long blonde hair. Without thinking of the consequences, Ruby allowed Marion to snip a bit here and there with some rather blunt scissors. When she looked on the bedroom lino she saw to her horror great locks of curly hair blowing about as the draught swept underneath the door.

'Marion!' she exclaimed fearfully. 'Whatever's our Mum going to say? And Dad? I'll get into terrible trouble.'

'Don't expect she'll notice,' Marion said nonchalantly. 'It'll soon grow again, anyway.' She stood back to admire her handiwork. Ruby, forgetting about the consequences for the moment, gazed into the mirror on the dressing table, feeling quite proud of the shoulder-length ringlets. The two girls giggled a great deal, and Ruby managed to put visions of her parents' fiery wrath out of her mind until Mrs Belmont suddenly opened the door.

'Think you'd best run home, Rub – Oh, my goodness, what *have* you two been up to? Marion, have you done this?' Her face was a mask of disbelief. 'Whatever is your mother going to say, Ruby?' Her pale cheeks turned pink with anger as she looked down at the hair lying on the lino. She lashed out at her daughter, cuffing round the girl's head while Marion shrieked in protest.

The wild wind howled in protest too, which reminded Prue Belmont why she had rushed up to Marion's bedroom. If only she had been ten minutes sooner, she thought in despair.

'Ruby, you get off home. There's going to be a nasty storm and your mother will be looking for you to help get the washing in.'

'Yes, Mrs Belmont,' Ruby said politely. How ever was she going to face her mother looking like this? The hour of reckoning had come sooner than she had anticipated but she did as she was told, said a hurried goodbye to her friend and ran back up the lane. Already large spots of rain were spewing out of the big black cloud. Through the garden gate she went, and round the side of the old mill house where water from the stream was seeping over the banks and spilling on to the path.

Fran saw her coming and called, 'Hurry up, Ruby! Help me, there's going to be such a downpour.' Even as she spoke it seemed as if the heavens opened and a deluge descended on them, the mighty roaring wind tearing the washing out of her hands and nearly pulling her away with it.

The line snapped and one end tore through the air, taking with it several petticoats. Fran and Ruby looked on helplessly as line and washing ended up in the swollen river. Ruby heard her mother's anxious voice carried away on the wind as she followed her gaze towards the swirl of water back upriver. A wall of dirty brown froth was cascading towards them at tremendous speed.

'Get in the house!' Fran screamed. Stopping just long enough to grab the basket overflowing with laundry, she chased Ruby into the mill house scullery. She had just slammed the door shut behind them when they heard the enormous roar of water as it tore along, bursting the riverbank, covering everything in its wake. Ruby went to stand on tiptoe at the stone sink to watch as the garden was turned into a lake in seconds.

By now the two little ones had come running from the kitchen into the scullery and were crying with fright. 'Come along,' Fran said. ''Tis all right. A bad spring tide – no worse than we've had in the past. Let's go next door to see Gran.' But water was seeping underneath the back door. 'Help me, Ruby. Fetch that pile of newspapers in the box by the range. Hilda, give me the old towel on the copper.'

Together they rolled newspapers up and laid them along the floor and on top of that placed towels and old sheets kept for the purpose. Fran went to the front door, which was seldom used except when the vicar called. Lifting the letter box from inside, she saw that the path was just about visible in the front where the ground rose slightly.

'We'll have to put galoshes on, and our macs,' she said, trying to sound calm, but Ruby detected a croakiness in her voice which warned of her mother's fear.

They dressed up against the wind and rain before Fran dared to open the front door. When she did, it was almost ripped from its hinges. She held on as firmly as she could to Hilda and Babe, then gave Ruby a push so that she could pull the door behind her.

'Ruby, you go on ahead while I bring the little ones with me. Hold on tightly to the front wall. The wind is that strong, it'll blow you over if you don't take care.'

Hilda was crying, and Babe's frightened screams could be heard above the roar of the storm. They clung frantically to Fran's mac as she inched her way along the low garden wall behind Ruby. She must be mad to bring the children out in this, Fran thought, but her mother needed her as well. Normally, the short journey next door took a few steps, but now the little terrified party took three steps forward and were blown back two. Gasping for breath, soaked to the skin, and with water swirling round their galoshes, they finally reached the cottage door. Fran banged noisily, shouting: 'It's me, Ma. Let us in, we're like drowned rats.'

They heard the bolts being slid back and Gran opened the door, pale-faced and frightened.

'Fran! Oh, Fran, whatever's going to happen? Your father and Henry – they were going to try to get the stock up to the top field. Pray God they got up there in time.'

'Now don't fret, Ma. They'll have got up there all right. But it's a bad storm and no mistake.' Fran hurried the children inside and with her back heaved against the door to get it shut. 'We may as well stay with you till it calms a bit. I'll put the kettle on.'

They carried their dripping galoshes and macs through to the scullery and then Fran filled the kettle with water from the single cold-water tap. With Babe still clinging to her skirt she carried it to the fire in the back kitchen. The rain beat against the small windows and the wind howled round the chimneys. She joined Gran at the window and watched the trees swaying crazily.

'I never ever saw anything like it before,' Gran Brown said with a tremble in her voice. 'I've seen the river rise and known gusts of wind howl round the cottage like a pack of angry wolves – but I ain't never seen a wall of water like that afore.'

'Spring tides, I suppose,' Fran said, but her thoughts were out on the land with the men. Cattle and sheep were most likely frightened out of their wits. Goodness knows where they'd end up if they started to panic and run this way and that. At sixty-eight, Pa wasn't as nimble as he used to be. He'd have his work cut out to control his flock with only the help of old Sukey, the sheep dog. Perhaps the other men on the estate would go to give him a hand. There was all the livestock to get to shelter and Henry would have his own job to do. But they were well used to the elements, she consoled herself. Her father knew no other way of life than here on the Dorset hills, and Henry had plenty of experience, having been raised on a big estate near Blandford where at the age of twelve he had been put to work in the stables. Fran tried not to dwell on her fears but she silently prayed for the men's safety.

When they could tear themselves away from the window, Fran got out the Halma board and the packet of Snap cards to amuse the children. Unable to concentrate, she left them to their own devices while she sat by the fireplace opposite her mother, sipping some much needed tea. They seldom spoke as they gazed into the red coals, each with her private anxiety, both too frightened to voice their alarm.

Fran got up hurriedly and lit the lamp on the table. Darkness had thrown a shadowy blanket round the cottage, shutting out the ferocious winds and the blinding rain from view. But nothing could blot out the noise of the storm. The children liked being in Gran's cottage but soon tired of playing games. Ruby watched at the window until it was too dark to see any more, then she let the curtain drop disconsolately. 'Daddy ought to be home soon, didn't he?' she questioned. 'And Granddad. Whatever can he be doing with sheep at this hour?'

Fran tried to motion her to silence, and by the unspoken fear that each saw in the other's eyes they acknowledged some sort of understanding. As they made fresh tea and set out the cups, Fran suddenly noticed Ruby's hair. After getting a soaking it had become plastered to her head, but now that it had dried and fluffed up it was curly and unmanageable, barely reaching her shoulders.

'Why you . . . you *naughty* girl – you've cut your hair!' she raged. 'Now what'll your father say? You'll be for it, my girl. No play for you and twice as many jobs.' Anger afforded an outlet to her worry.

Ruby began to sob. 'Marion did it. I didn't mean her to cut so much off.'

'Don't make excuses, I dare say you were equally to blame.' Fran turned to her mother. 'That wretched girl! Still, I suppose I can understand Prue Belmont, not having any children of her own. Trouble is, when you adopt a child you can't know what sort of background its real parents had. Prue's a good sort and she loves children so I suppose it's only natural that she's spoilt Marion – quite uncontrollable she is, but Prue only laughs.' Fran was red-faced with indignation.

Gran wasn't really listening, and after more reproach from her mother Ruby remained subdued. Even though the storm hurled its fury on the land, bringing down trees and old wooden buildings as well as the river torrents rushing over the landscape, she was too frightened of what her father was going to say about her hair to worry about the storm any more. He was so proud of the girls' hair and of the way Fran groomed and cared for it. Babe and Kate both had rich auburn-coloured hair like Fran's, but Hilda's, while jet black like Henry's and Lennie's, had a softer and silkier texture.

Suddenly there was a loud banging on Gran's front door.

'That'll be Henry and Dad,' Fran said, rushing out into the front parlour. 'I expect the water's too deep to get in at the back.'

Ruby felt quite sick at the prospect of what her father was going to say once he set eyes on her. And he'd notice – nothing ever escaped his keen, observant eyes. The sound of hushed voices wafted into the kitchen, where Gran pulled herself out of the armchair near the fire. She suffered from corns and calluses, which made her feet painful to walk on, so she couldn't hurry anywhere. Then Fran's voice echoed louder and with deep consternation. Ruby forgot about her hair. Dad! Granddad! Something was wrong.

It was the estate manager who brought Fran back into the room and looked at Gran with a solemn expression.

'Mrs Brown, we're all so sorry . . . Henry did everything he could to save Edwin, but the sheep panicked and ran towards the rope bridge. Edwin was faithful to the last, trying to save the silly creatures, but they were swept away in the current and Edwin with them. Henry dived in after him but the river's a cruel force to reckon with during a spring tide.'

'You mean – oh, you can't mean – not both of them! They'll cling on somehow, they'll swim for survival – surely?' Gran gasped, clutching the bib of her apron. Her pale cheeks turned quite pink and then back to an ashen colour.

Ruby knew by the grave look on Mr Fry's rugged features that it was too late for her dad and granddad. Poor Gran, she was desperately fighting for self-control, and when Ruby looked at her mother, she saw that her chin was trembling as she too tried to take in the awful news.

The cottage and the old mill house, no longer used for grinding corn, but a dwelling place for Henry, Fran and their children for the past eighteen years, became a silent shrine of mourning. Throughout the night Fran did her best to console her mother while she struggled with the pain within her own breast. The past seven years had taken their toll as she had been forced to come to terms with her son's death. It wasn't fair, her heart cried out, to lose her only boy, and now her father and husband in one day. She couldn't bear it. Wasn't it more than a body could stand? For hours she paced the floor, going to the girls when they cried out in their sleep, brewing tea to try to ease their sorrow. Ruby had taken it the hardest. She had screamed hysterically at the realisation of what had happened to her father. Mr and Mrs Maitland from Sherbrook House had visited and brought Kate home with them. They had spent time talking with Gran, while Fran had explained to the girls what had happened. Eventually she had persuaded them to go to bed. Fran felt as if her insides had been gouged out of her body. The emptiness was indescribable – yet the house was full of sickened, heart-broken women.

Chapter Two

It was a cloudy morning when Fran went into the back bedroom to pull back the floral curtains.

'Draw them along again when you've dressed,' she said in a quiet voice and the two older girls remembered that today was the day of the funeral. 'Ruby, you'll have to wear Katie's old dark-blue coat – I know it's still a bit long for you but we must make do. Mrs Maitland has given me a grey coat of her mother's for you, Katie dear, and I've sewn the black diamonds on the sleeves for both of you. Now hurry up, and when we've had a cup of tea we'll all go and say goodbye to Daddy and Granddad.' Her voice broke and she hurried downstairs.

There was no conversation between any of them, only a still, silent thickness which seemed as if it would choke them.

Fran had her work cut out to get Gran ready. She wept and wailed persistently until Fran lost patience with her.

'We *must* get ready, Ma!' she shouted. 'The others will be here in a minute and you don't want Eric and Annie to get here and find you still in your petticoats.' Cruel though she knew it was, Fran realised that to mention her brother was the only way to make her mother move, and when she had fastened the row of buttons on her long serge jacket which nearly covered her full-length black skirt, she brushed her mother's white hair and rolled it into a bun before setting her black felt hat on the top.

'Make sure you've got a clean handkerchief in your bag, Ma, and you just sit quiet until Eric and Annie get here. The train should just about be getting into Blandford station now. Mr Maitland has kindly sent cars for all the family. I can't imagine how Henry's mother has taken it. After losing three sons in the war, now Henry – it only leaves Nathan and Sissie . . .' She had to rush away to hide her own grief. If only she could get away somewhere by herself and give way to her pent-up emotions, which she felt she must bottle up for the sake of the children. She had to be strong for the rest of them.

As soon as the cars arrived, bringing the relatives, Fran was caught up in the event, feeling as if it was happening to someone else. She did all that was required of her, feeling numb. Sherbrook and the surrounding villages were a close-knit community and stood by one another in times of trouble. Everything looked black as they prepared to take Henry and her father on their last journey. There were no motor-drawn hearses for Edwin Brown and Henry Sheldon, whose lives had been so dedicated to the land and farm animals, even though Mr Maitland had offered to arrange it. The local undertaker, a distant cousin of Edwin Brown, had been only too glad to offer his services with horses and carriages. The dark horses, their black plumes waving in the breeze, started the slow descent down the hill. Only the beautiful floral wreaths covering the two coffins, and on top of the large hearse, afforded colourful relief from the sombreness. When someone mentioned rain, Fran looked up and saw purple clouds in the angry heavens, and she wondered what could possibly have made God so displeased with her that he had taken two devoted men from the same family at the same time.

Tears fell unhindered during the emotional service and then the sorrowful procession made its way to the open graves in the churchyard. Fran was glad that her brother Eric was there to support their mother, and Nathan and Sissie to show compassion to Henry's parents, while she gave and found comfort with her arms around Kate and Ruby.

She felt a sob catch in her throat as the gravel fell on the coffins.

'Dust to dust, earth to earth, ashes to ashes . . .'

Life seemed to have stopped for Fran, and yet it continued. The weeks passed with much weeping; both she and her mother had a lifetime of memories to sort out. Fran had of necessity to be the strong one and make unpleasant decisions, but she was able to vent her bitterness on much of the old worm-eaten furniture she had grown up with, which ended up on a bonfire in the garden. She guessed that some of the villagers would think she was a heartless creature, but she knew she couldn't afford to rent a large enough house in Brimdene to take the contents of two homes.

The Maitlands were kind, promising that there was no urgency for them to move, but Fran knew that the mill house and the shepherd's cottage were required for the new men and their families. She tackled the problem philosophically, grateful for the help given by Henry's parents and brother Nathan, who found the house they were to rent in Brimdene. It was the girls' future she had to consider now. Jobs would be easier for them to find in a town than here in the countryside. It was what Henry had always wanted for his beloved girls, but Fran had been reluctant on account of her elderly parents. Now here she was having to uproot her mother as well as herself and the girls.

No one would ever know how difficult each day was. Some days when she found herself alone she just sat and wept.

One Saturday morning, on a perfect June day, the sun brilliant in a cloudless sky, Fran looked out of the scullery window down the long garden towards the river where Babe was playing. It was difficult to believe that this was the scene of such a dreadful event only a couple of months earlier. She could still hear the roar and see the frothy wall of water as it coursed its treacherous avenue of greed. The only difference was that Ma's curtains were fluttering in a gentle breeze on the line today instead of the girls' petticoats, and the river was meandering along as if it was incapable of causing so much havoc. They were all going to miss it, as well as the peaceful sounds and smells of the countryside.

Fran strolled out into the sunshine and down the path to the water's edge. Babe was sitting in the long grass entwining reeds together, chattering non-stop as if she hadn't a care in the world. Fran couldn't understand why she hadn't wanted to go with Ruby and Hilda to play with Marion Belmont, but she had been adamant that she wanted to stay at home. Fran wondered what was going on in her mind. She had shown little reaction to her father's and grandfather's deaths. Come to that, so had Hilda. Perhaps they were too young. Nature had its own way of softening blows for those too weak to accept life's knocks. Ruby had taken it badly. She had nightmares as well as periods of hysterical screaming. Fran felt the wave of nausea churning in her stomach again. It crept up on her just when she thought she was getting the better of it, with the realisation that she had to shoulder all the responsibility alone, and that the change in circumstances would alter their whole lives.

The children had been Henry's life. He had adored each of them, and now he was no more . . . swallowed up by the merciless tide and carried away, every breath sucked out of his lungs to be replaced by dirty water. Fran felt herself swaying at the picture, which refused to fade. She'd be glad to get away from the river, whose cruel force tormented her, drew her into its very depths. Faces, not quite manifesting themselves in the ripples of water, blurred, disappeared, taunted her again . . . In the distance she heard footsteps crunch on the nearby gravel path, then strong hands gently guided her backwards, away from the water's edge.

Strange flutterings murmured in her stomach and she blinked away torturous memories of the past weeks and months as she looked up at the stranger supporting her.

'Are you all right, Fran?' he asked with concern.

She stared in disbelief. 'Luke?' she managed to say, then laughed nervously. 'Heavens! Where did you spring from? I wasn't going to – do anything silly.' She tore herself from his grasp. 'I was daydreaming,' she said hurriedly. 'It's so lovely this morning, and the river is so calm – it's hard to believe that it can change its moods so quickly.'

'Fran.' His voice was gently scolding. 'I'm so dreadfully sorry. I know what you've been going through, but this isn't the answer.'

Babe placed herself between Luke and Fran, holding her mother tightly as if protecting her from this tall, arrogant stranger.

Fran faced Luke, embarrassed and indignant. 'Can't a woman stand and stare in her own back garden without some busybody thinking she's going to . . . to . . . run away from her responsibilities?' she said. 'I've got four girls who depend on me.'

'I'm aware of your situation, Fran, and that's why I came: to ask if there's anything I can do to help.'

Flushed and upset at his insinuations, but at the same time impressed that he should visit her, she said quietly: 'You'd best come inside.'

Luke followed her along the path and in through the back door. Fran went straight to the window to check that Babe hadn't followed too, then she led the way into the kitchen, where she turned on Luke. 'You shouldn't have come here,' she said heatedly. 'Whatever will people think?'

Luke looked nonplussed. 'That I've come to pay my respects in the very sad loss of your husband and father, Fran, I should think.' He took a step nearer her, but she placed her hands on the back of one of the high-backed dining chairs, indicating that he keep his distance. 'Fran,' he said, with genuine concern in his tone, 'I am *so* very sorry. It was a terrible tragedy for you and the children, and your mother.'

Fran gulped awkwardly, playing for time. 'A tragedy it certainly was,' she conceded, then covered her face with her hands, trying to shut out the mental picture. 'I've never seen anything like it before,' she said in a trembling voice.

'The Maitlands told me about it. The elements can be so cruel, but I imagine it's not the first time you've been flooded here at the mill house?'

'We've had it lapping at the doors a few times and in a bad winter it saturates the garden, but I've never seen such fury in a tide before. Henry had just said that the river was running high, and as soon as he'd gone back to work the heavens opened and a wall of water came rushing down into the valley. It was like a bad dream.'

'You've had a rough time. And all the clearing-up to do when the river subsided.'

'I can't remember much about the clearing-up,' Fran said slowly. 'There's always silt left after a flooding. I . . . I just don't recall who . . .' She passed her hand over her brow, her eyes filling with salty tears.

'I'm sorry if I've brought it all back, Fran. The memory of that day must be horrifying. The water soon went down, according to Mr Maitland. It was a freak tide.' She hadn't thought to ask him to sit down but he pulled out a dining chair from under the whitewood table. 'My ship was due to sail a week ago, but more maintenance work needed to be done in dock so it gave me the chance to visit you. As soon as I heard of the tragedy I knew I had to come.' He sat down as if he meant to prolong his visit. 'I hope you won't think it's in bad taste to approach you so soon after Henry's death? Time is never on my side as I'm away more than I'm in this country.' He paused before saying: 'My thoughts are always with you, though, and what might have been – what should have been.'

'In poor taste!' Fran almost screamed the words at him. What was he suggesting? 'I'm grateful for your sympathy,' she acknowledged. 'But how can you dare to presume that I'd ever want to see you again after what you did?'

'That was years ago now – eighteen, nineteen – and we've both matured since then. I found it difficult to forgive you for marrying Henry and bearing his children after what we experienced that night. I thought you might at least have postponed your marriage to him until we had time to talk.'

'There was nothing to talk about then, and there's nothing to talk about now,' Fran said adamantly. 'I'm sick of you stalking me – yes, stalking me. Every time I go to the churchyard to place flowers on my son's grave you've been there before me. Why?'

'Why shouldn't I? Lennie was my son, not Henry's, and well you know it.'

'*Your* son?' she questioned. 'Don't flatter yourself, Luke. He was every bit Henry's son, dark-haired like Henry, with brown eyes.'

'But Henry had a sallow skin, and Lennie was pale-skinned like me. I have brown eyes too – he could easily have been mine.'

'I can't think why you haven't married and had children of your own,' she retorted impatiently. 'Why must you be so obsessed with my son?'

'Because I just know he was mine too.'

'I thought you had more intelligence than to build up such a fantasy, coveting what doesn't belong to you,' she said angrily, 'Lennie's been dead for seven years, and now my life is in a turmoil and you have the audacity to come here to torment me even further.'

'Fran, you know that isn't true. I came here to offer my heartfelt sympathy, and I mean that sincerely.'

'Now go, then,' she snapped.

'I realise how hard things are going to be for you,' he continued patiently. 'You have your mother to consider, as well as bringing up four girls by yourself – I only want to help.'

'You'll do that best by leaving me in peace. We're moving to Brimdene to be near my in-laws.'

'Then let me keep in touch,' he pleaded, crossing his knees, indicating that he had no intention of leaving just yet.

'I don't know where we'll be living. It's early days, and there's still a lot to be arranged.'

'Isn't there any way I can help you before I go back to sea?' he begged.

Fran gripped the chair-back with renewed ferocity. 'Go back to sea and forget me – that's what would help me most of all. Forget, Luke, *forget*!' she shouted, her voice trembling.

He gazed with deep affection into her beautiful blue eyes. God, how the memory of this petite, high-spirited woman had taunted him over the past few years. He admired her sense of loyalty, and he loved her all the more for her rejection of him now. It was surface rejection. The expression in her eyes told him that she wasn't averse to his attention although she would never admit it.

'I shall never forget you, Fran,' he said calmly. 'I'm sorry about Henry, of course I am, but hasn't fate intervened?'

'No!' Fran's voice was alarmingly loud. 'Just because of what happened when we were young and silly doesn't mean you can walk in here –'

'I have every right to walk in here and claim what's mine,' he interrupted. 'You were mine, Fran, before you were Henry's wife, and Lennie was proof of that.'

Fran's cheeks were bright red. She felt so angry she was sure she could have strangled him with ease. Yet the manner of the man was such that she knew she could turn to him for comfort.

'Indeed he was not,' she argued. 'Lennie belonged to Henry and me. You should never have come here, you have no claim on me at all.'

'It's sad that you'll be moving away from here, but I shall continue to place flowers on Lennie's grave whenever I visit Sherbrook. At least it proves my love and devotion to you and my son.'

'Don't you realise the embarrassment it causes? Haven't you any discretion? People notice things and are quick to gossip.'

'I'm not ashamed of my feelings for you. Maybe I am being too previous, but I want you to consider letting me look after you and the girls. I can give you more than Henry ever could – and I want to, Fran, I really want to.' Luke stood up suddenly and went to her, placing long elegant fingers on her shoulders as he looked deep into her eyes. Then Babe appeared from nowhere and leapt forward to get between them again.

'Hullo, Copperknob,' Luke said kindly, ruffling her curls. 'It's all right, I'm not going to hurt your mother.' He laughed sardonically, which only made Babe cling to her mother.

'You'd better go before the others come back,' Fran said in a low voice. 'It was kind of you to pay your respects.' She placed her arms loosely round her youngest daughter's shoulders. 'Times will be hard but we shall get used to managing alone.' She made her way pointedly to the front door.

Luke walked slowly behind her. He looked down at the red-headed child and jingled the coins in his pocket before offering some pennies to Babe. She smiled shyly, doubtfully.

'Go on, Copperknob, take them and share them with your sisters.'

Fran nodded, so Babe took the money while Luke searched his other pocket and found some sixpences.

'Here's one each for your money boxes. If you go to Brimdene to live you'll be able to buy ice creams at the seaside.' He took a step nearer Fran, but she countered by stepping back a pace. He smiled as he held out his hand, and when Fran hesitantly placed hers into his he kept hold of it tightly while he tried to pull her closer. Babe jammed herself against her mother's stomach and with a laugh Luke let go.

'You're well protected, Fran. But this isn't goodbye. I'll find you sooner or later, wherever you go. I suppose your brother will have your mother to stay with them once or twice a year?'

'I doubt that,' Fran said. 'Annie didn't want to have her now. Their lives mustn't be upset.' She sighed. 'We shall be all right. Ma will be a help with the girls.'

'And together your pensions will pay the rent? Is that the plan?'

'I dare say we shall manage our financial affairs satisfactorily. Mr Maitland has been very kind to us, but no amount of money will make up for the loss of my husband and my father,' she said. 'My task now is to do the best I can for my girls, to bring them up as their father would have liked. I worry about moving to Brimdene, of course I do,' she confessed. 'This is my home, where Henry and I have been happy – and had our sadness, too.' She sighed, finding comfort in being able to talk to someone other than the girls. 'If only I could have stayed on for a year or two . . . But I appreciate the situation Mr Maitland is in. He needs the house for the new farmhand and Ma's cottage for a shepherd. It's just that . . . well, this was one situation we could never have anticipated.' Fran groped in her pinafore pocket for her handkerchief. 'The hand of God . . . and all that . . . I suppose it could be His justice – although I didn't want – God knows!'

'That night, Fran, you wanted me as much as I wanted you,' Luke said slowly with emotion. 'If only we had met sooner! But you can't expect me to forget what happened between us now, any more than I have done all these years. You've been beside me in my dreams as well as in my waking thoughts.'

'There's such a thing as love, Luke Hammond. All you wanted was my body. There's also such a thing as class difference. There was never any question of a match between us.'

'Obviously not you you – but I went away and dreamed that one day we would belong to each other.'

Fran's cheeks were scarlet with fury. How dare he come here and talk so brazenly? And in front of Babe, too! Still, she was too young, thank goodness, to understand what he was saying.

'I think it's time you went.' Her voice was low, yet indicated the anger she felt.

Luke inclined his head. He was getting to her. He recognised all the signs of her weakening just as she had done before her wedding. If only he had been able to stop her marrying Henry! He didn't doubt for one moment that she had loved the good-looking little man from the brewery much more than she had ever loved him – then . . . There was a lifetime, though, for him to make her change her mind. 'Please promise me that if ever I can be of assistance to you, Fran, you'll contact me. You've suffered enough – it grieves me to think of you having to struggle financially.'

'I told you, Luke, we'll manage. In the town the girls will have a good education and the opportunity to earn a decent living.'

'And you? What will you do? Go out to work?'

'At my age? What could I do? I can sew, and it will help if I just continue to make all the girls' clothes as I have done in the past. I'm forty-two years old, for goodness sake, and not always in the best of health.'

'You're very pale. Make sure you see a good doctor as soon as you settle in Brimdene. I shall find you, Fran, never fear.' He looked down at the small child clinging to Fran's apron. 'This one is a miniature of you. Her hair is a superb colour, and she has an abundance of it. As she grows older it'll get darker in shade similar to yours. Have none of the children eyes as blue as yours?'

Fran shook her head. 'No, they all have dark-brown eyes like Henry's' Her throat went tight and she felt herself swaying. She gave Babe a gentle push. 'Go out in the garden to play, Babe, it'll soon be dinnertime.'

The little girl seemed unwilling to leave her mother alone with the stranger, but she knew better than to argue, and after hesitating she skipped away, her lovely hair dancing down her back.

'I'll be staying overnight with the Maitlands.' Luke explained. 'Nicholas Maitland is coming from Portsmouth to visit his parents so I shall return there with him. It's been most fortuitous to have a close friend here at Sherbrook and I have been very discreet always, Fran. No one has ever seen me place the flowers on Lennie's grave. People sleep most deeply between one and three in the morning. I suppose I might have been in danger of being caught as a poacher, but sleeping ashore doesn't come easily after months away at sea.'

'Find yourself a nice woman from your own class who'll make you a good wife,' Fran scolded, reasserting herself. 'You're still in your prime, Luke, but you're deluding yourself if you imagine there was anything lasting between us, so go away and forget about me. Let me get on with the job of bringing up my children and looking after Ma.'

Luke shook his head sadly. 'If only you'd let me help – I really want to, Fran. I mean everything I say.'

'*No*! No, no, *no*!' Fran shouted in a sudden fit of temper.

Luke opened the door and left without another word. Fran sat down on the chaise longue – one that had seen better days, given to her by her previous employer, Lady Hinckley. She buried her head in her hands and wept as if her heart would break. For weeks now she had bottled up the real deep-rooted grief. Why should it have been Luke Hammond who caused the floodgates to open? She had suffered immense pain because she tried to hide the anguish of her loneliness. Even when she wept silent tears in the dead of night Babe would stir, sometimes cry out and cling to Fran as if she knew the awful despair she was experiencing. Now her tears were not only for Henry and her father, who, she could scarcely realise, would never be coming home again, but for the wrong she had done nineteen years ago. One night of lying beside Luke Hammond, did it really warrant such a ransom? Almost everything she loved had been taken from her now except her four girls. Her atonement must be to care for them, bring them up to love God and respect their fellow beings, to make something of themselves and to obey God's commandments. Tears and recriminations drained her, but she got up, dried her sore eyes and went out into the garden to fold the washing and peg it over the line to air in the warm summer sunshine.

Chapter Three

The move was arranged to take place at the beginning of the summer holiday when the school term ended. Ruby, Hilda and Babe were all excited at the prospect of going to live in a seaside resort but Fran's dread grew daily. She fretted for her mother, knowing the heartache such an upheaval would inevitably cause. There was Kate, too. It just wasn't wise to take her away from a secure position with the Maitlands until Fran was sure that work was available in Brimdene. She slept hardly at all from worry, and then only from sheer exhaustion. Night after night she stood at the bedroom window in her long nightdress, her hair in a plait hanging over one shoulder, her eyes filled with tears as she stared at the stars in the summer sky. Why should this terrible thing have happened to them?

The moonbeams glistened across the black water of the river and it seemed as if she could see Henry's face in one of the bramble bushes on the far bank. She knew it had to be a figment of her imagination, but he often came in the darkness of night, smiling his loving smile with arms outstretched to her. She regretted the times when she had rejected him. It was strange how, after all these years, she now experienced nights of longing, wanting to feel Henry's strong arms holding her, his exploring fingers arousing her latent passion. It was difficult to comprehend that she would never know such intimate union again. And it was even more difficult to realise that in another two days she would be gone from here for ever. She wanted to savour these memories. She clutched the front of her nightdress and drew in great gasps of breath, fighting for control. She mustn't give way, she must be strong for the sake of her children, but oh, the pain, the anguish, yes, and the bitterness. Wasn't taking her first-born enough? she demanded of God. Hadn't she suffered enough grief already? She clung to the brass knob at the foot of the bed and her body shook with violent sobs. No longer could she restrain them so she went in bare feet round the bed to the door where a shaft of moonlight guided her to the spiral staircase. Babe had stirred and she didn't want to waken her so she tiptoed down to the kitchen where she sat at the scrubbed whitewood table, rested her head on her trembling hands and let the tears flow in an unhindered stream. It seemed in her distorted vision as if they ran down the long garden, over the bank and into the river where they were caught up in the same current that had swept Henry and her father away from them for ever. Chilled, and weary with emptiness, she watched the pale pink dawn rise across the meadows and only then could she bear to go upstairs and lie beside the sleeping Babe.

Gran Brown watched the preparations for the move with trepidation. Moving from Sherbrook was going to be a dreadful wrench to her. She had lived in the village all her life, and her forebears had been faithful workers for the Maitland family over several generations. The girls all thought it was an adventure, but the mere thought of living in a town filled Gran Brown with fear. She tried not to let it show, but she wept many a silent tear during the lonely days following Edwin's death.

People were kind during these difficult days. Kate was allowed the day off to help Fran and Ruby as packing cases and furniture were removed from the two houses and put in the removal van. At sixteen Kate was old enough to experience a great deal of emotion at all that had happened recently. She was deeply hurt that she wasn't allowed to go with the rest of the family. It was all right at the Maitlands' and she had some good friends in the village but, like her dad, she yearned for a more exciting life in town. She was afraid for her own future as well as her mother's. Whispered conversations about her mother and what fate might have in store gave Kate cause for concern. Her worst fear was that having been left behind she would quickly be forgotten.

Fran placed an arm round Kate's shoulders as they watched the loaded van set off down the hill. 'Seems like the end of everything,' she said solemnly.

'A new beginning, Mum,' Kate said bravely. 'That's the way Mrs Maitland said we must look at it – but oh, Mum, you will let me come too, as soon as you can, won't you?' Kate's tears would not be suppressed any longer. She clung to Fran, crying hysterically, burying her face in her mother's bosom. Fran allowed this display of emotion to last a few seconds and then she pushed Kate away from her.

'Come on now, dear, this won't do. Prue will be expecting us for dinner. Wasn't it thoughtful of her to give us a meal before we go off to catch the train? After we've eaten I'll walk down as far as the church with you and visit Lennie one last time.'

'But you'll come back here sometimes, surely?' Kate asked with bloodshot, puffy eyes.

'Of course, whenever I can, but there won't be much money to spare, dear. Besides, Gran is the last of the Browns. There's no family left except us, and once we're gone the Brown family will be forgotten.'

Kate hadn't realised the wider implications of 'family' before. Now she vowed that she didn't ever want to be married and have family if it meant goodbyes. Splitting up like this was too painful. She couldn't bear it, and when they reached Prue Belmont's cottage, one on each side of Gran to help her along over the rough ground, she turned to her mother. 'I think I'll go on, Mum. Say goodbye to Hilda and Babe for me.' She turned to hug Ruby. 'You help Mum, mind, Ruby. I'll miss you all so much.' She kissed Gran and her mother, and without a backward glance hurried on down to the bridge. There she turned. They were all standing at the gate. She picked up the skirt of her coarse grey dress and wiped her eyes, then waved with both hands before continuing on her way.

Prue was sympathetic to Fran's plight. She was a cheery woman whom everyone loved, the local midwife. Now she did her best to comfort Fran and her mother, and later, after dinner, when the taxi came to take them to the station, she hugged her friend.

'Take care, Fran, and don't worry about Kate. I'll keep my eye on her. She can always come down to us on her day off. Brimdene's only twenty miles away. 'Tisn't the other side of the world. She'll have to get herself a bicycle. That way she won't have to spend out on train fares when she visits you.'

'We're going to miss you,' Fran sobbed. 'And . . . and . . . everyone . . . and Lord knows how I'm going to manage with rent to pay and everything so much more expensive in the town.' She pulled away, her heartstrings taut with the strain of parting, but Prue held on to her hands.

'Sam and me, we meant what we said, Fran. If there's ever anything we can to to help, you know we will. Babe would be happy here with us if things get rough. You know we'd be good to her – it won't be easy for you until the girls leave school and get work.'

'But we'll stick together,' Fran said, bravely. 'Henry would expect that of me. The girls were Henry's life and now 'tis my job to raise them the best way I can. His dream was to move to the town, and we'll have Kate with us as soon as it's possible.'

As the taxi drove past the big house, Fran looked for some sign of Kate. Leaving one of Henry's girls behind was enough. She'd never part willingly with any of them.

Fran was agreeably surprised at the house her in-laws had found for them, but it took days to get it into good shape. It was modern with a lavatory and bathroom inside. Open grates instead of the usual kitchen range meant no more black-leading but she scarcely thought about the benefits. Would she ever get used to this being 'home'? It was as if she was on an extended holiday and any minute she would find herself going home to Sherbrook.

The roads were all well-kept, the houses neat with tidy gardens full of flowers and shrubs, and she knew that Henry would approve of the high position of the house even if the hill leading to it was a drag. She supposed her in-laws had remembered the flooding at the mill house when they chose this particular spot. They had been so good to her and at least she had been relieved of the worry of finding somewhere to live. Granddad Sheldon had even paid the first month's rent so that Fran could get herself and her finances sorted out.

It was amazing how quickly they drifted into a routine. Ma seemed to have accepted that her one room upstairs at the back of the house overlooking the garden was her final abode. She seldom complained except about her feet, and once she came downstairs in the morning she stayed there until after dinner was over and the washing-up done, and then she returned to her own room for a nap and quiet time. The break was not without distressing moments and Fran knew that she took some of the bitterness out on her mother, but she also knew that she couldn't manage without her. She was always on hand to help with the dishes and preparing vegetables, and in the evenings she sat and mended socks and repaired tears in the girls' underwear, while Fran cut out and stitched, tacked and fitted so that the girls were well-dressed. But the pain for each one of them remained. Ma wept openly when she was unable to hide it any longer. Fran could only give way when she was alone in her bedroom after a hard day's work when nothing seemed to have gone right.

The girls settled down in Brimdene quickly. August remained hot and dry and they were able to visit the beach on their own. Fran only accompanied them on rare occasions. While they were out of the way she could spend the afternoons sewing, making gymslips and blouses ready for the autumn term at their new school. But on the last bank holiday of the year they were all up early, packing bathing costumes and caps, food and drink to enjoy a day at the seaside with Prue and Marion Belmont, who were coming with Kate. They were all to meet at the Pier Approach and Fran felt a measure of excitement that Kate would be home for a whole week.

The day was bright with colour and seeing Kate again helped to put Sherbrook with all its past tragedies out of Fran's mind. Ruby and Marion were soon gossiping like a couple of hens while Kate was overjoyed to have Babe and Hilda skipping along at her side.

They walked along the promenade, away from the crowded pier, to where there were fewer people. When they found a nice clean space on the sandy beach, the girls dug a large hole in which to dangle their legs as they sat round the edge to eat sandwiches and drink lemonade, while Fran and Prue sat in deck chairs, catching up on all the latest news over a cup of tea.

'You won't be able to go into the water straight after eating,' Fran warned. 'Ruby, you and Marion can take the two little ones along to find the Punch and Judy show. It's near the pier. Babe will enjoy that. Here's a penny to put in the box, unless you can come away before the man comes round.'

Prue delved into her bag. 'Here you are, Marion, here's a penny for you as well, and on the way back buy ice creams for yourselves, and bring one back for Katie.' She put a shilling into a small cloth bag which Marion was wearing round her neck, and the girls set off.

Fran and Prue talked about everyday matters until Katie went down to the water's edge, and then Prue asked: 'How have the girls settled down, Fran?'

'Babe and Hilda don't seem too bad, but I can't do much with Ruby. She's persistently naughty, and aggravating beyond endurance.'

'She's the middle one, Fran. She'll grow out of these tantrums in time. She wants to grow up too quickly, like Marion. Poor mites, I think of you all so often, and Kate has looked so forlorn when I've seen her in the village. She was that excited today I thought she'd burst.'

'Any news from Sherbrook? I suppose our house is occupied?'

Prue fell silent and looked out to sea at the mist which hung on the horizon. She sighed. 'Yes, the new families settled in just a week ago. They seem nice enough folk. The shepherd is in his early forties, I should think, with two children, the girl is fourteen and the boy is seventeen. They say they're both clever, especially the boy.'

'The age to start work, then.'

'The boy helps his father during the school holidays, otherwise he's at some college or other. Haven't found out yet what he's studying for.'

'What about the girl?'

'They're trying to get her in at the big house. From what I've seen of them they think they're above letting her go into service, but what else is there?'

'I do want to have Kate come to live with us, Prue. She might be a good influence on Ruby. At least she'd be a help to me.'

'Have you made enquiries about work in the town?'

'There's always shop work, of course,' Fran said slowly. 'Then there's domestic work. Sissy works for the Neale family. They're the owners of the main shop in Brimdene, and they own a hotel as well. Sissy's going to put a few feelers out to see if there's any suitable job going for Kate, but don't say anything to her just yet. I don't want to build her hopes up if nothing comes of it.'

'I hope it does for her sake. She feels so left out.'

'I suppose boys will be the next problem with her. With Henry to take the responsibility it wasn't such a worry, but now I can't imagine how I'm going to cope with four of them.'

At that moment Kate came running up from the water's edge, waving to the other girls returning from the Punch and Judy show. On such a hot day the ice cream in the cornets they had bought was melting fast, dripping down their fingers as they quickly licked at each one in turn.

'I've had to lick some of yours up, Katie,' Ruby said, handing it over.

'You should know better than to do that,' Fran said sharply. 'Don't you understand we all have germs?'

'It's all right, Mum,' Kate soothed. 'If she hadn't I wouldn't have an ice cream left at all.'

Babe screamed as a wasp buzzed round her head.

'Kate, get her into the sea quickly. All of you, go on down to the water's edge and finish those messy things before you get stung.'

Prue got to her feet and helped Babe hurry down the sand and into the water. She had removed her shoes and stockings and was delighted to have an excuse to paddle with Babe, while Fran looked on somewhat disapprovingly. After that, the girls changed into bathing costumes with much giggling as they wriggled beneath large towels, and then they ran into the sea.

'Now you watch the little ones, Ruby and Kate,' Fran called, and at last she was able to relax in a deck chair to chat to Prue about Sherbrook, old friends, neighbours and memories.

Ruby and Marion returned to fill buckets with sand and water in order to make a sand castle, while Kate wandered off looking for shells. Fran and Prue dozed in the afternoon sun but woke with a start when Hilda started to shake her mother.

'We can't find our Babe,' she said. 'Mummy, wake up! Auntie Prue, Auntie Prue, Babe's gone!'

The two women were up in an instant, shading their eyes from the heat haze as they scoured the beach for any sign of the small red-headed child.

'Kate, you go left towards the small rowing-boat jetty, and you, Ruby, run along to the pier. She might have gone back to look for the Punch and Judy man again,' Fran said.

'Don't worry, Fran, she can't have gone far,' Prue consoled. 'I'll walk along too, and ask round among the people sitting on the beach.'

'Supposing she went out too far – out of her depth . . .' Fran panicked. 'It's all Ruby's fault, I told her to watch out for the little ones.'

Her heart thumped anxiously against her chest and she felt as if she would explode. Henry would never forgive her if anything happened to his Babe. But there was no Henry. Fran caught her breath. Dear Henry, please find my baby, she begged, and then, feeling guilty, she found herself pleading to God. Waiting seemed like an eternity, and she dared not move in case Babe returned. Besides, there were their things to look after. Other people who had been sitting nearby joined in the search and Fran lost sight of Prue and the girls. It was amazing how quickly they merged into the kaleidoscope of colour and activity on the beach. Surely Babe would be quickly spotted by her hair? But there were several red-headed children playing on the sand.

Ruby ran, frantically looking this way and that. There was no sign of the Punch and Judy show and she stood gazing round, searching for the place where it had been. She was on the verge of tears.

'The Punch and Judy show man packed up and moved along to the Chines.' The delicate voice came from nowhere. Then Ruby found herself grasping the side of a long wicker carriage, something like a large pram. It took her a few moments to comprehend that in it lay a girl of about her own age who had spoken. 'And if you're looking for a little girl with bright auburn hair, she's just gone investigating beneath the awning round the pierrots' stage.'

Ruby couldn't help staring. How awful to be confined to one of these things, she thought, forgetting about Babe.

'Didn't you ought to go and fish her out?' the girl said with a bright smile. 'Don't look so worried. Children go missing all the time on the beach.'

'Thank you very much,' Ruby mumbled and went to where the pierrots' theatre was set up on the sand.

The man wouldn't let her go in the entrance without paying.

'I think my little sister's got in underneath,' she explained.

'Blinkin' kids,' the big man grumbled. 'Go on then, you can take a quick look, but be sharp, mind.'

Ruby felt acute embarrassment as she stood behind the row of canvas chairs set out for the audience. There, down by the stage, stood Babe, looking up in wonderment at the performance in progress. Outside, with the noise of people on the beach, it had been impossible to hear the out-of-tune piano that accompanied the pierrots, who sang and danced in their all-in-one costumes of white material, decorated with huge coloured pom-poms. Their tall dunce's hats bobbed, making the pom-pom at the end look as if at any moment it would fall off. Ruby was spellbound, too.

'Get a move on, missie. Is she there or ain't she?' the man asked roughly.

'Yes, but she's right down in the front,' Ruby whispered in a frightened voice.

'Just wait until this act has finished, then you can get her – but don't make a habit of this, mind. Next time you'll have to pay like honest folk do.'

If Ruby hadn't been so scared of the man, she would have enjoyed watching the pierrots, but she was thankful when the song ended and she could run down to grab Babe.

'Mum's ever so cross with you,' she chided. 'You mustn't go off by yourself.' As the big man held the rope aside for them to go out, he smiled and patted Babe on the head. Ruby pulled Babe along hurriedly to return to face her mother's anger. They passed the spinal carriage again and the occupant smiled cheerily.

'Thanks very much,' Ruby stopped to say.

'That's OK. You'd be surprised what I see from this position. Can you come back for a chat? I get lonely with no one to talk to, and people think I'm dumb, stuck in this thing.'

'I'll ask Mummy,' Ruby said, and she kept a firm hold on Babe as they ran back along the beach.

Fran didn't know whether to cry with relief or lash out at both Babe and Ruby.

'She was watching the pierrots, Mummy,' Ruby explained apologetically.

'You naughty girl,' Fran scolded. 'Don't you ever go off by yourself again. And you just keep a watch on your sisters better in future, Ruby.'

'She's found, and that's all that matters,' Prue said calmly. 'Nothing like getting a free view, is there, Babe?'

Ruby went on to explain about the girl in the spinal carriage who had watched where Babe went.

'I hope you thanked her properly,' Fran said, shading her eyes against the sun to look along the beach. 'Poor girl! It must be awful to have to spend a lovely day like this in one of those things.'

'I wonder what's wrong with her,' Prue said. 'Might be disease, or even a spinal injury caused through an accident.'

'She asked, could I go back to talk to her.' Ruby broached the subject hesitantly. She thought she knew by her mother's expression what the answer would be, but when Fran looked down at her she managed to smile faintly.

'Well, just for a little while. It must be so frustrating to watch other girls playing in the water and on the sand, and not be able to join in yourself. Mind your manners now, Ruby. Just for quarter of an hour and then come back. We don't want to have to go looking for you as well.'

Ruby could hardly believe her luck to be allowed to go away by herself and not have to look after the younger ones. So far, since they had lived in Brimdene, they were hardly allowed outside the front gate except when they went to visit the grandparents, or to go shopping. Ruby got the impression that her mother thought all kinds of danger lurked round each and every corner in the suburban area of Brimdene where they lived. She retraced her steps to where the carriage had been placed, just at the foot of a slope down to the silver-white sand. To her surprise the girl was now lying on her back.

'Hullo,' Ruby said. 'Can you turn yourself over, then?'

'No, my nurse or parents have to do it. I have to have an hour on my front every four hours. I prefer it on my front as I can manage to lift my head to watch what people are doing, but this way up all I can see is the sky. Come up this end so that I can see you. Did you get into terrible trouble or something? You looked scared to death.'

'No. I do usually get blamed for everything, but we were all anxious this time.'

'What's your name?'

'Ruby Sheldon. What's yours?'

'Anita Feltham. I'm thirteen, how old are you?'

'Ten, nearly eleven.'

'I expect you're wondering what on earth I'm doing in this thing – everyone does, but you're too polite to ask, so I'll tell you. I have a disease of the spine, which is why I have to live almost entirely out of doors. I have to lie flat all the time – but I am getting better, and soon, I hope, I'm going to learn to walk again.'

'How long have you been like this then?' Ruby asked, wide-eyed with curiosity.

'Six months. They thought I was going to die at first.'

'How awful!'

'I don't remember much about the beginning, I just found myself in hospital. I'll be half afraid to walk again, but it would be lovely to be able to swim and play ball on the sand like other girls.'

'Gosh! Can you really swim?'

'Of course, silly. Can't you? Whatever school do you go to?'

'We've only just moved here from Sherbrook. We went to the village school there, but here we're going to Cumberland Road Elementary School for Girls.'

'Then you must live quite near us. I started at the Infant's School in Cumberland Road.'

They exchanged details about each other and were joined by two women who had been sitting in deck chairs on the promenade.

'Hullo,' Mrs Feltham said, with a warm smile. 'It's so nice of you to come to talk to Anita. But I'm afraid we're going to have to go home now, dear.'

'This is Ruby, Mum. They've moved here from Sherbrook and she's going to Cumberland School. She lives a few roads away from us so can she come and visit, please?'

'Of course, dear – if her parents agree.'

'She hasn't got a dad. He was drowned in that dreadful spring tide we read about.'

Ruby began to feel awkward, but Mrs Feltham, who had appeared somewhat aloof to begin with, suddenly put her arm round Ruby's shoulders.

'Oh, you poor dear! It was a terrible tragedy – you're one of four girls then?' Ruby nodded. 'I'd like to meet your mother one day when you've settled down in Brimdene. Of course you can visit any time you like. You'll be good company for Anita until school starts.'

The other woman, who Ruby could see was a nurse, started to push the carriage up the ramp.

'Do come to my house soon, Ruby,' Anita begged.

'I will if I can, but I have my two young sisters to look after and I have to help Mummy too.' Ruby waved and skipped off down to the sandy beach again and back to where Fran, Prue and the others were packing up.

'Oh, have we got to go home already?' she asked.

'Afraid so, dear. Auntie Prue mustn't miss the train. I expect the trams will be crowded it being bank holiday.'

They started the long trail back along the promenade to the pier-head again.

'It's been lovely to see you all, Fran dear,' Prue said, kissing her friend lightly on the cheek. 'Everyone in Sherbrook will be anxious to know how you are. You must come and visit us very soon.'

Fran sighed, and her chin trembled. 'It's a bit soon, Prue. I know I'll have to make the effort but I haven't got the courage just yet. There's still a fair bit to do in the house, and there's the girls' clothes to get ready for school. I don't like to leave Ma on her own for long, but thanks for the invitation.'

'Sam said I must be sure to invite you. You'll always be welcome at any time, and I know you'll want to visit the graves.'

'That's been the worst part of moving, leaving my family behind, but it gives me a reason for wanting to go back to Sherbrook – eventually.' They waved Prue and Marion off on the tram to go back to the railway station, and boarded another tram which took them nearest to where they lived.

This was the tiring part, Fran thought, when they reached the terminus. The children were very tired and hot, and the walk seemed endless, especially up the last hill. Their footsteps began to drag and Fran was forced to keep stopping to urge on Ruby and Babe who lagged behind while Kate and Hilda were way out in front. At last they reached the garden gate and Fran recognised her brother-in-law Nathan's bicycle propped up against the wall outside. He was a constant source of support, ever ready to advise. Just being able to discuss problems with him was a comfort.

The girls found extra energy when they realised that Uncle Nathan was there. They hoped he had brought one of their cousins with him on the seat attached to the crossbar, but when they went inside he was sitting on the sofa alone, talking to Gran Brown.

Nathan was Henry's double in many ways. He was a stockier

man and slightly taller, but his eyes always held the same magical, mischievous expression and the girls loved him dearly. It was the next best thing to having their dad back again, and he was quickly surrounded by them.

'Where's Sybil and Jenny?' Ruby asked.

'Has Andrew come with you, Uncle Nathan?' Hilda and Babe chorused.

'No, Andrew's in bed, and Sybil and Jenny have gone to a church picnic – they should be home by now. Kate, let me look at you – my, you're as pretty as a picture! 'Tis nice to have you home. Have you all had a good time at the beach? You're as brown as berries.'

Nathan enjoyed a playful frolic with them before Fran sent them off to bed, while Kate put her small case down and stood and stared. There was so much for her to explore, the house and garden – even the garden shed. 'Whose bike is this?' she asked enviously.

Nathan went out to the yard and looked lovingly at her. 'Yours, Katie. A present from your grandparents and me, to make up for not being able to come home to live just yet.'

'For me?' she questioned in disbelief. 'I . . . I can't believe it! Mum, is it true?'

'Yes, Kate – aren't you lucky?'

Kate thought there was a hint of disapproval in her mother's tone, and the frown prompted her to respond quickly with: 'Oh, *thank you*, Uncle Nathan. But I can't ride – will you teach me?'

'That's why we got it now, so that you can learn this week while you're home. It'll be up to your mother whether you take it back to Sherbrook or not. You can always take it on the train and it'll save you that long walk at the other end.'

'It's lovely – and it's really mine!' she breathed proudly.

Nathan helped her to sit on it and adjusted the saddle to suit her height. 'You must be able to reach the ground with your toe in case of emergency,' he said. 'I'll probably have to go on adjusting it until you've finished growing. I'll come and take you out each evening this week until you feel confident. Haven't you ridden at all before?'

'Only on that little bike your Sybil and Jenny had.'

'You'll soon get the hang of it.'

Her determination helped, and a few days later she was popping to visit her grandparents and going to do the shopping on her bicycle. She taught Ruby to ride as well, but the saddle was too high so she could only manage standing up. But that was good enough to get her to Anita's house in the mornings when she had finished the jobs in the house, and their friendship blossomed.

The week's holiday passed much too quickly for Kate. If only she didn't have to go back to Sherbrook. But she knew it was no use to plead with her mother. Everything was different. She envied her sisters living in the town. Being parted from them all made her feel isolated, and she had to fight back the tears on Sunday at teatime when Uncle Nathan went with her to the railway station to see her off.

Nathan went straight back to Fran to reassure her.

'I just thought I'd look in on my way home to tell you that I put the bike in the guard's van, and saw Katie safely in a carriage with two elderly ladies,' he said. 'She'll be fine, Fran – don't worry.'

The tears began then, and Nathan gathered her in his arms. His jacket smelt as Henry's had done, of horses, hay and earth, and when the crying lessened she could feel his warm breath on the side of her wet cheek. He held her fast and she was grateful for the comfort of his embrace.

'I . . . I'm sorry, Nathan – I shouldn't have . . .'

'Isn't that what brothers-in-law are for?' he whispered softly.

She gave a small, weak laugh and pulled away, dabbing at her eyes furiously. 'It's just that I feel so guilty at having to send Kate back. Bad enough Henry and Pa missing without Kate not being able to stay here with us. I do hope Sissy will soon hear of something for her in town.'

'There's plenty of time, love. You've hardly had time to get your thoughts together yet, and at least Kate is safe enough with the Maitlands.'

'Sometimes it all comes over me like a great black monster,' Fran said. 'How on earth am I going to manage without Henry? I'm just not strong enough, Nathan.'

''Course you are, Fran, and we're always here to help. That's what families are for. We all miss Henry, but we'll stand by his wife and kids, that's for sure.' He kissed her tenderly, gave her a really warm hug and then turned and hurried out of the back door.

Fran stood there for several seconds. Poor Nathan, he had lost the last of his brothers, and his duty, after caring for his own wife and children, was to his ageing parents. There was Sissy, but Nathan was now the only man in the family to bear the family's burdens. He would have to be guide, comforter, even protector for Fran and her girls as well. It was good to know that he was thoughtful enough to be available whenever she needed him.

She didn't hurry to bed, although Sunday was the one night she normally did. Knitting, sewing and mending were all put out of sight on the Sabbath and she hated Sundays of all the days of the week. It used to be the one day Henry had been able to spend with his family, so that day she missed him most of all, and the day of rest became a day of silent mourning. She eventually locked the doors, put out the gas lights and, with a candle to light her way, went upstairs. She knocked lightly on Ma's door and opened it a crack. ''Night, Ma. Sleep well.'

There was a pause and then a shaky voice answered: ''Night, Fran – and you, my dear.'

Another lump restricted Fran's throat. She knew she ought to go in and apologise for the harsh words she had spoken on so many occasions throughout the week, but she wasn't one to show affection easily. She closed the door softly and peeped in on each of the girls. At last she stood in front of her dressing table and peered at herself in the flickering candlelight. Her eyes were red, her cheeks pale and drawn.

So many cruel thoughts invaded her mind at times like this. Her mother might fall ill, or one of the girls, and what would happen to them if she should be taken ill? She turned to look at the sleeping baby of the family. She didn't like the idea of Babe occupying Henry's place in the big double bed, and she had tried to persuade her to sleep in the small room, which was really Kate's, but Babe had only stayed there for a couple of hours and then stealthily crept back to the comfort of her mother's arms. It was too soon for all of them to adjust to life without Henry. She had never thought what life would be like without the support of her man, but what wife did? Only perhaps a wife who was treated cruelly by her husband, and now she realised how very fortunate she had been. So often she had taken the decisions, cajoled Henry into doing things her way, and been the dominant one, but, oh, what wouldn't she give to have her man back to head the family as was his right? She had taken everything for granted and now regretted it. She undressed and lay on the top of the bed. It was a hot night, too hot to sleep, and she wondered how Kate had fared on her return journey. So much responsibility with so many of them dependent on her.

Sleep came in fits and starts, every sound magnified to startle her – the town sounds were vastly different from country noises. People would soon get to know that there was no man in this home. What would she do if an intruder forced his way in? A house full of women – it was a demoralising thought.

Chapter Four

The girls found the large town school awe-inspiring, but they soon settled down and within a few days Babe announced that she wasn't going to answer to 'Babe' any longer.

'My teacher says Barbara is much too nice to be shortened,' she said to Fran. 'You can call be Babs if you like, but at school I'm Barbara.'

Fran turned away with an amused expression. She remembered how besotted Henry had been with his darling Babe from the moment she was born. Now, here she was going to school and he would miss her growing up.

Hilda was the only one who appeared not to like school very much and she knew she could easily play on her mother's sympathy with imaginary aches and pains. Fran indulged her. She was the baby who had taken Lennie's place in her affections at the time of his death. Dark-haired, dark-eyed, she was so much like Lennie that Fran doted on her, and during the autumn months when loneliness overwhelmed her she was glad of any excuse to keep Hilda home.

Christmas was drawing near and Fran dreaded it. She wished she could go away somewhere and forget that it was the festive season, but she must do the best for her family just as Henry would have wanted.

'You seem a bit preoccupied, Fran,' Nathan said to her one evening. He had made a habit of calling in to see if everything was all right once or twice each week and Fran was grateful for his concern.

Hilda and Babs were in bed and asleep. Gran Brown and Ruby were finishing their Ovaltine. They said good night and went upstairs, leaving Fran and Nathan alone.

'There's a lot to think about,' she admitted. 'Ruby's in the Christmas play and needs a costume made, and Babs is going to be a cracker so we've got to concoct a crepe-paper outfit for her.'

'You'll manage, I dare say. You always do; in fact, you thrive on having plenty of sewing to do. You don't get out enough, Fran. It's good that you can make the girls' clothes but it gives you time to sit and brood. You should get out and about more.'

'Doing what, for goodness sake?'

'There's the pictures – that's all the rage nowadays.'

'Pictures!' Fran exclaimed. 'Nathan Sheldon, are you out of your mind? Can you imagine Henry allowing such a thing? He considered they'd be the downfall of this country.'

'Henry would have come round to it in time. He wasn't one to let the world pass him by, Fran. He loved life and everyone in it.'

'I don't need you to lecture me about Henry's likes and dislikes,' she said pointedly. 'Henry had strong principles, and we shall go on observing them just the same as he would have done.'

It wasn't the first time she and Nathan had disagreed. It seemed to lessen the tension that Fran could sense often existed between them. A long silence ensued before Nathan stood up, saying: 'Henry wouldn't have wanted you to fret, love. We must do what we can to give the girls a happy life, but you're still young enough to enjoy yourself too.' He squeezed her affectionately and made her prick herself.

'Oh, Nathan, careful,' she grumbled.

Nathan pulled the sewing out of her hands and tucked his fingers in the hollow of her armpit until she was wriggling helplessly.

'I can still make you laugh, Fran. Never forget that.' He kissed her cheek lightly, his dark-brown eyes boring into Fran's blue ones with an intensity that made her look away. He reached out and held her chin, forcing her to look back at him. 'We're kinsfolk, aren't we?'

Fran couldn't bear the expression in his face, which reminded her so much of Henry. She experienced a moment of unease, so she got up and went to the kitchen to make some hot chocolate, and they chatted about the Christmas preparations and arrangements for family gatherings. Nathan stayed on, sitting in the armchair opposite her. It was almost like being back at the mill house with Henry giving her his special persuasive smile. Fran tried to shut the memory out by glancing up at the clock. She noticed that Nathan followed her glance, his smile deepening. She wished that he would make a move to go home.

'Better think about bed, I suppose,' she said.

There was an intense silence. 'Then we'd better get on with it.'

Nathan's face was wreathed in smiles, his eyes a reflection of his thoughts. 'You must miss Henry, Fran,' he suggested.

'You know I do,' she answered shortly.

'I don't mean like that,' he said. 'I mean – well – you know . . .' Suddenly he was kneeling down on the floor in front of her, his hands on her knees, pinching and groping. 'A lovely little woman like you, Fran, was made to be loved. I get all I want from Laura, but there's more to spare – let's call it comfort.'

'Nathan! Stop! For pity's sake, *stop*!'

'Ssh, your ma'll hear. Just a little harmless fun, Fran. Come on, you know you like it . . .' He pushed her dress up to her thighs and struggled to get to her knickers. She fought wildly but somehow he found his way up inside the elasticated leg and with a snap the elastic gave way. There was no stopping him. He buried his head on her stomach to keep her still and with the other hand he pulled her knickers down. He was incensed with desire, urged on by the fact that she was unable to prevent him from thrusting his fat fingers inside her. No matter how much she cried out he refused to let her go. With every attempt she made to get out of the huge leather armchair his passion increased. She pushed against his massive shoulders but, like Henry, he had such power in his masculine body that she made no impression.

'Henry . . . Henry . . .' she implored on the verge of tears. Nathan paused, his breathing irregular as he stared up at her stupefied.

'Fran, 'tis me, Nathan – Henry's gone, love . . .'

There were several seconds of anguished silence.

Fran, realising that her mistake had been a fortuitous one, pushed her skirt down and stood up so that Nathan's hands fell away. She gave him a contemptuous shove. 'Get up, you foolish man, and don't you dare try anything like that on again.' She calmly went to the couch where he had placed his overcoat and held it out to him.

'Go home to your wife, Nathan,' she said huskily. 'I just can't imagine what got into you, but you hadn't better try that on again.'

Nathan looked suitably rebuked as he took the overcoat and placed it over his arm. 'Fran, Fran,' he said penitently. 'Aren't we as good as related?'

'Only husbands and wives do what you had in mind. Where's your discretion, for goodness sake? My marriage was sacred to me, and Henry's memory will last much longer than a few months, a year, two years – for ever, I hope.'

He smiled as only a Sheldon man could. It would have been so easy ... For a second she had believed that it was Henry up to his old tricks, and her reaction was justified. First, the protests, then the surrender ... Dear God, how would she ever survive?

'I ... I thought you must be near crazy for it by now,' Nathan said half apologetically. 'And – if you ever feel the need ...'

'I shan't betray my sister-in-law's trust, that's for sure, Nathan Sheldon. You just get off home to her and realise how lucky you are. I had a good husband, and I bore him five children. These days, I've got too much else to think about to hanker after *that*!'

Nathan fingered the cloth of his heavy coat. 'You won't tell Laura, will you, Fran?' he asked sheepishly.

'I ought to, but as long as you behave yourself in future and be good to her as you've always been in the past, as far as I know, no one will ever hear anything from me.' She grabbed his coat from his hands, and held it out so that he could put his arms through the heavy sleeves. He took ages to do up the buttons, by which time Fran had gone to the scullery and was turning the handle of the back door. Nathan walked past her, barely touching her arm by way of acknowledgement. She closed the door after him and turned the key. She listened for the crunch of Nathan's boots on the gravel outside and after they had died away there was an eerie nothingness. She was trembling, partly with rage, partly with fear. She put the guard round the fire, intending to prepare for bed. If only Nathan knew how much her body did crave a man's touch, but not in that coarse, illicit, clumsy way. She needed to be loved tenderly for herself. To have someone share the burdens of everyday living. Someone to talk to in the evenings when the girls and Ma were all in bed. How could she feel so unutterably lonely in this house full of women?

Preparing for Christmas was little different from previous years. Only the surroundings had changed. Everyone rolled up their sleeves and gathered round the kitchen table skinning almonds, chopping cherries, picking over washed currants and sultanas, and seeding the raisins. Babs was doing the job she loved best, that of rubbing bread between her small hands to make the breadcrumbs. When she tired of being helpful she crawled beneath the table and secretly begged a currant from Gran Brown, who sat down to do her share.

In the midst of the activity there was a loud knock at the front door and Ruby was sent to answer it. Immediately the door was open, the sound of the Salvation Army band filled the house and all except Gran rushed into the hallway to sing along with the carols, while Fran cleaned her hands on her apron and hurried to find her purse for a few coppers. This was a new experience for the girls and they loved it. Fran was apprehensive about the new experience for her of baking the large fruitcake in the gas oven.

'Won't be such a good cake, having to cook in that thing,' Gran Brown said, disparagingly.

'We've managed not to ruin anything since we came here, Ma, so I expect the cake will turn out all right,' Fran said.

To everyone's delight it did, in spite of Fran having to sit up until nearly midnight waiting for it to cook through. With the delicious smells that pervaded the house during the following days, and the buying and surreptitious wrapping of presents, the spirit of Christmas affected the entire household. Fran was kept so busy she had no time for self-pity or concerns for the future. The costumes were completed in time and the school concert, which took place on the last day of term, was a great event. Fran was quite proud of Ruby's performance, and Babe's too.

On Christmas Eve Fran took the girls into town. They visited the large stores crammed with people enjoying a spending spree and admiring the sparkling Christmas lights. Granddad Sheldon had given each of the girls the required sixpence to visit Father Christmas's grotto in make-believe Lapland, and they came away with small gifts.

If Fran felt a hollow emptiness at Henry's and Kate's absence over the festive days, she didn't let the others see it. She even bought a clockwork clown to hang on Ma's doorknob for Christmas morning just as Henry had always done. It was a small gesture of fun to please the children, and to carry on the tradition of Father Christmas visiting everyone. Thanks to Nathan, Fran found a net stocking at the foot of her bed containing some scent and soap, secretly placed there by Ruby who was taking on the role of elder daughter and trying her best to please her mother.

It was a happy occasion when Kate arrived home on Sunday morning just before morning service. Her cheeks were rosy but chafed, and her fingers were frozen after the long cycle ride from Sherbrook. Fran insisted on a drink of hot cocoa before they set out.

'I suppose they've kept you busy all over Christmas,' she said. 'Never mind, perhaps this will be the last Christmas you'll be there.'

'Oh, Mum, I do hope so,' Kate said eagerly.

'You mustn't bank on anything, though, Kate. There aren't too many jobs going at present, but Aunt Sissy is keeping her eye and ear open just in case. Now we'd best be off or we'll be late. There'll be a full church this morning, I expect. You can tell me all the news as we go along.'

Fran wondered about Luke Hammond and whether he would be home on leave at the Maitlands' for Christmas. She recalled treating him rather harshly when he had visited her after Henry's death, but it had been too soon – much too soon. Nathan had revived emotions and feelings of frustration, and the fact that she was still attractive to men brought a faint glow to her cheeks.

'I quite enjoyed the cycle ride,' Kate was saying. 'It was a bit cold this morning, but better than waiting about for trains. It's much quicker and I can go back whatever time I like.'

'But you mustn't leave it until it's dark, Kate. I don't want you about in the lanes late at night. You don't have to cycle back to Sherbrook. You can go back by train after tomorrow when they're back to running normally. Put your bike on the train, like you did when Uncle Nathan first got the bike.'

'I've only just got home, Mum.' Kate laughed. 'Don't let's think about having to leave just yet.' She pushed her gloved hand through Fran's arm and squeezed reassuringly.

Kate's time at home passed by all too quickly, and as a special treat Fran took the other girls to the station to see her off on the train. When they had waved her out of sight they went for a walk along the clifftop before going home through the park.

By the time the girls returned to school, the weather had become more severe with heavy overnight frosts, and often when Fran got up in the morning the mains water was frozen. Candles were lit and placed beneath the pipes to thaw them out, and small oil stoves helped to increase the temperature in the bedrooms. Fran's first job every morning, after a cup of tea to warm her up, was to clean the grate and light the fire downstairs. At least winter in the town didn't seem quite so bleak as in the country, and yet Fran missed being able to look across the river at the white-sheeted meadows. Icicles, like Christmas decorations, hung from gutters, and Jack Frost left delicately drawn patterns on windows everywhere, but the scenes were not as picturesque as in the Dorset countryside, where trees wore their winter-whites and tapering fingers of ice dripped tears in the weak midday sun.

Fran often woke in the mornings convinced that she heard the cows mooing as they went in for milking. It was usually five o' clock, the exact time when country people would be stirring to start the day's work. Somewhere inside her lurked the timetable she had been brought up with and every now and then it served to remind her of a pattern she was no longer part of. Whenever she saw the corporation cart horses going back to the depot or setting off pulling ash carts, she thought of Henry and his love of horses. Not that she needed reminders; Henry was beside her wherever she went, whatever she did. She felt his influence and constantly used it to correct the children, but Sherbrook was slowly receding into the deepest crevices of her mind. She missed the river, and often imagined she could hear the rush of water on a rough day, yet at the same time she felt aggressive towards it, even hating it. She had felt tied to the gentry's way of life and had longed to be free of it, but there were times now when she wished she could go to the big house and ask for some minor repair to be done, or seek advice over some legal matter.

There was always Sissy, though, a tower of strength, more like a close friend than a sister-in-law. When one of the girls went down with a fever it was Sissy who came to her aid.

In spite of everything, Fran realised that she had a great deal to be thankful for, a nice home and a good family.

At last the dark days of winter began to give way to brighter mornings. While the wintry weather had given her a valid excuse not to return to Sherbrook, Fran knew that both she and her mother must find the courage to visit the churchyard on the anniversary of the tragedy.

It was a time of mixed emotions, each mile taking them back ... back in time to the day of the awful storm and freak tide. Fran worried that it would be too much of a strain for Ma, but Prue and Sam Belmont welcomed them warmly, and over dinner they never stopped talking.

Later, when they walked down to the graveyard, Fran felt a strange emptiness envelop her at the sight of the bare grass covering the mounds of dry earth. Previously she had experienced antagonism when finding evidence of Luke Hammond's visits to Sherbrook, but now it was as if even he had forsaken both her and Lennie.

There was nothing to remind anyone that any of them had ever been a part of this village except the black lettering on cold marble. LENNIE SHELDON, aged 10 years. HENRY SHELDON, aged 46 years. EDWIN BROWN, aged 68 years.

Some might say that Edwin Brown had lived the best years of his life, but sixty-eight wasn't old. Some country folk lived to be ninety and more. Forty-six was too young to die. It was cruel to take a man when he had his wife and children to provide for. And ten-year-old Lennie ... Fran openly wept as she savoured memories of her first-born, her only son. A tall lad for his age. Pale-skinned and dark-haired, quick-witted like his father, but a deep thinker. In solemn emotional moments Fran was almost glad that he had been spared the world's crude experiences. He had been too delicate, too caring to withstand the harshness of a cruel world.

When the fresh flowers were in position, brightening up the family corner of the churchyard, Fran suggested that they all stood in a circle round the graves, holding hands, vowing never to forget.

Inevitably some things had changed, but the visit was not as traumatic as Fran had feared. She could appreciate now that her town house in Brimdene was a vast improvement on the old mill house. She knew it was harder for her mother to accept, but even she must be grateful for the amenities of town dwelling. Fran and the girls were young enough to adapt to the new way of life – something Henry had hankered after. It was a sobering thought that through his death she now had what he had sought.

While the girls took themselves off to meet old friends, Fran was glad of the opportunity to ask after her eldest daughter.

'Is Kate well, Prue?' she said. 'Has she got over the fact that she had to stay in Sherbrook, d'you think?'

Prue made a grimace of doubt. 'She seems happy enough, but I fancy she harbours a grudge, Fran, which is only natural, poor child. Bad enough to lose her dad without the rest of her folks deserting her as well. It hasn't been easy for her.'

Fran wished with all her heart that circumstances and miles hadn't distanced them from one another. Kate was maturing rapidly. Of necessity she had become independent and Fran felt concerned for her and what effects the separation might have. She was the eldest and, with Henry gone and Gran's years advancing, Fran needed Kate as a friend now as much as a daughter. Kate must feel she didn't belong anywhere. She wasn't a schoolgirl any more but she wasn't really adult either. Where did she fit in?

'Does Kate visit you sometimes, Prue?' Fran asked.

'Quite often, and we see her in the village and at church. She misses you all. She's had no one to share her grief with.'

Fran sighed and went to stand outside the back door, watching the girls take turns on the swing at the end of Prue's garden.

How could anyone share their grief? It was a torment for each of them in a different way. She had to try to keep the hurt she felt from the girls, while at the same time understanding her mother's deep sorrow. The two little ones didn't seem to care, and that worried her as much as Ruby's rebellion or Kate's silence. It all seemed to fall on her shoulders. How she wished that she could demonstrate her love to each of them better, to make up for their father's love as well.

Prue joined her in the doorway, and they strolled down the garden and across the meadow, still exchanging local news and remembering old times, until it was time to return and prepare tea.

Kate had come down from the big house on her bicycle so she set off immediately after tea so that she reached the station before the taxi bringing the rest of the family.

'You shouldn't have come all this way, Katie,' Gran said as they stood on the platform.

'I wanted to see you off,' Kate said. 'I like riding my bike and I shall be able to cycle all the way to Brimdene now that the weather is getting better and the lighter evenings are coming.'

'Everything all right up at Sherbrook House?' Fran asked Kate. 'We don't seem to have had much time to talk, dear, but now that we've been once we'll come again soon.'

Kate hugged her mother when they heard the train coming. 'I do want to come to Brimdene to live, Mum.' She had the distinct impression that her mother had shelved that idea for good. 'But it was nice that you all came to Aunty Prue's. Nothing's the same here, though. Mrs Maitland is very kind to me but I'd rather be with you. I'd like to get a proper job.'

'You've got a job, Kate, and that's important. You're much luckier than many of the town girls. I shall find it difficult to place Ruby when the time comes.'

With that Kate had to be satisfied. She kissed her sisters goodbye and waved the train out of sight. She didn't weep any more. It only made her feel thoroughly wretched, but she hated being the only one left in Sherbrook. Now the two-mile cycle ride gave her time to think.

She felt the separation acutely. It had been hard enough when the rest of the family lived at the old mill house, but now twenty miles seemed to isolate her completely. She knew she was lucky to have Aunty Prue, Uncle Sam and Marion, but they weren't real family, even though their cottage was the happiest place in the world. Aunty Prue was lenient with Marion, but they enjoyed a different type of friendship and were more like sisters, Kate thought. Kate wanted desperately to be close to her mother, to ease her pain and help her with family problems, but she only commanded obedience and respect, which kept Kate at arm's length.

Dusk was falling as she left the outskirts of Blandford to take the lonely country road that led to Sherbrook, and before long she had to get off her bicycle to switch on the front and rear lamps. To her dismay the rear one wouldn't work. The battery must have run out. Had she left it on inadvertently? The view of the deserted lane ahead of her was disconcerting. She didn't fancy walking; besides, it would make her late reaching Sherbrook House and both Mrs Maitland and Mrs Sturmey would be concerned. Despite the bangs she gave the lamp, twisting the knobs and removing the battery before trying it yet again, it still wouldn't work, so there was nothing for it but to ride on regardless of the consequences. The village policeman wasn't likely to be out at this time of the evening. He usually did his cycle round when the pubs and local inns closed, so she felt fairly safe to pedal away.

She hadn't gone far when she heard a hiss, the front tyre seemed to disintegrate and she realised the rim of the wheel was crunching on the ground. A puncture! It was her first experience of one. She gallantly pumped up the tyre with her pump and rode on for a few yards, but it quickly went flat again so there was nothing for it but to walk.

The lane became eerie. The leaves on the tall trees on either side of the lane, except where she passed an isolated cottage, rustled mischievously and occasionally the wind howled as if to torment her. She walked on, keeping in the centre of the road, all the while watching for hopeful signs of life where lighted lamps shone from cottage windows. She had never needed to be out alone during the hours of darkness when her father was alive. He had escorted her to and from Sherbrook House, but now she had to be brave and try not to be scared.

Surely the end must be in sight. The lane had never seemed quite so long as it did tonight. Then, out of the darkness, she heard the soft sound of movement behind her. Before she could look round, bicycles drew up, one on either side of her. She prayed that it would be the police constable, at worst a lad from the village, but she found herself looking at two boys with unfamiliar faces.

'What have we here then? Pretty little maid out on the prowl at this hour?' one of them jested.

'My rear lamp won't work, and I've got a puncture as well,' Kate said. She hoped that her voice didn't indicate her fear.

'What a stroke of luck, Maurice,' the other boy said. 'She can't escape and if she runs we can catch her easily on our bikes. You should make sure your bicycle is roadworthy before you go off to meet your boyfriend late at night.'

'If you must know,' she said hotly, 'I've been in to Blandford to see my family off on the train back to Brimdene.'

The boys laughed. 'A likely story! So why haven't you gone with them?'

'Because I work at Sherbrook House – that's why!' she declared impatiently. 'And they'll come out looking for me if I don't soon arrive there.'

'Another likely story.' They started to circle round and round her. 'Gentry folk don't pay too much attention to what their servants get up to. If you go out looking for trouble they can get rid of you and find someone else.'

'The Maitlands aren't like that,' Kate protested. 'They've been good to me and my family, especially when my father and grandfather drowned in the river.'

This seemed to silence the young men, but they still persisted in circling round her, getting as close to her as they dared. One of them tipped her hat forward, the other caught her back wheel and held her back.

'Oh, please, do stop,' she pleaded, trying to keep her voice steady. 'I don't even know you, so why can't you go on your way and leave me alone?'

One of them dismounted. He was very tall and lean with rugged features. He peered into her face. Kate tried to keep her bicycle between herself and him. 'Because we ought to get to know you better, miss. No girl who values her reputation would be out alone after dark. Come on, how about a roll in the hay? 'Course I can't pay you but I bet your boyfriend didn't pay for it either.' He leered towards her and laughed sadistically.

'You're only silly schoolboys,' she said crossly. 'What would you know about such things?'

'O-oh? What an invitation, Maurice! Let's show her, shall we? I'll hold her down while you get in, and then I'll have a go.'

'Don't be so coarse!' Kate snapped, but inside she was trembling, and in a moment she knew tears would be evident. She mustn't give way. She must show strength even if all she possessed wasn't sufficient to fight off these two burly farm labourers. The boy threw down his bicycle and made a grab for Kate, but she pushed her bicycle into his stomach.

'Come on, Maurice, let's get her down. What the devil are you waiting for?'

'No, Felix, *no*!' The other boy put himself between his friend and Kate. By his broad back Kate knew that he was the stockier of the two, but by his voice he sounded much less aggressive. 'Sorry, miss. We didn't mean to frighten you. Felix doesn't hold his drink very well. I'm sorry we can't help you with your bike, but it isn't far now to the big house.' He picked up his friend's bicycle and by his actions demanded that they should continue on their way, much to the disgust of Felix.

Kate just remained standing where she was. Her heart was thumping with fright when she considered what might have happened. She felt very alone and vulnerable, but thankful that one of them had come to his senses in time. She couldn't imagine who they were or where they were going, but the one called Maurice had mentioned the 'big house', which must mean he had connections locally.

After that each sound, each whisper of wind caused her to panic inside. However much she tried to hurry, her legs were wooden, refusing to be pushed at a faster pace. She didn't believe that the lane could stretch so far, but at last she was passing the woods that skirted the big house on three sides. Home was in sight somewhere beyond the trees. Suddenly she thought she saw a dim light in the distance. Perhaps it was the policeman going home after his round. In case it wasn't, she put a spurt on to reach the entrance to Sherbrook House before the rider, coming towards her quite speedily, did. The light grew brighter, and Kate caught her breath, fearful that it was this Felix returning to get what he had been denied before. No way now could she reach the entrance before the cyclist. Should she hide close up to the hedge? Would she be lucky enough to find a gap through which she could squeeze? Fear gripped her with such ferocity that she found she couldn't go another step. She just stood still and waited as the man emerged out of the darkness and skidded to a halt in front of her.

'Look, miss, I know just how scared you must be.' She almost sighed with relief that it was the young man called Maurice who had returned and not Felix. 'I'm sorry about Felix – sorry that we behaved so badly. I want to make it up to you by escorting you to Sherbrook House, if I may?'

'Humph!' she retorted. 'And what makes you think I trust you?'

'I realise how damning our behaviour was and I'm truly sorry. It's one thing to play a prank – but I've got a sister a bit younger than you, only fourteen in fact, and I would throttle anyone who did to her what Felix and I just did to you. It was unforgivable – you all alone on such an isolated road. I'll walk in front of you, or behind, whichever you prefer, but at least I'll be company for the rest of the way.'

'Not *my* company! Please yourself where you walk or ride, but I want nothing to do with you at all. Just keep your distance.'

He chose to walk on the other side of Kate's machine. She was breathing quite rapidly, and he must surely be aware of her fear.

They walked in silence, each with their own thoughts. Kate was wondering who he was, with his rather posh way of talking. He couldn't be of Dorset stock, she thought.

'My name is Maurice Lambert and my father is the new shepherd on the Sherbrook estate,' he said after a while, as if he had read her thoughts. 'I believe we live in your grandparents' cottage; well, my parents do with my sister. I'm away at college for most of the time. I'm still on Easter holiday at present.' He paused, evidently hoping that Kate would say something, but she remained mute until they reached the entrance to Sherbrook House. He placed his bicycle across her path.

'I've said I'm sorry and I meant it,' he said with hurt in his tone. 'You must be Kate Sheldon; I've seen you once or twice in church, though I would rather you'd introduced yourself. It may be a poor effort, but really, I am trying to make amends for myself and Felix. He's not so bad once you get to know him and as long as he hasn't been drinking.'

'I don't have anything to do with young men who drink,' Kate said haughtily.

'But we were out celebrating, in a mild sort of way. Felix lives in Croydon. We're mates at college in London, and he came home with me for a couple of days as we've just heard that we've passed the last set of tests we took before the vacation. It's been jolly hard work, I can tell you. Only natural that we were on the look-out for a bit of fun. There was no one interesting at the King's Head so I suppose we drank one to many – or at least Felix did.'

'I'm really not interested. What you do for fun is no concern of mine – or hadn't better be. The Maitlands are my guardians as well as Aunt Prue and Uncle Sam – and if *he* should hear about this you'll get a good hiding, most likely.'

Maurice didn't reply, but in the night light Kate could see two sparkling eyes which seemed to be laughing at her. She tried to push the bicycle round him but he moved with her.

'There is one thing I can do to make amends, and that is repair your puncture and get you a new battery for your rear light. Felix goes back to Croydon tomorrow so I'll be at a loose end. Please let me, Kate?'

His plea sounded so genuinely earnest that she was tempted to give in. 'Uncle Sam will soon fix it for me,' she said quietly.

'No, I want to. I insist, *and* I'll tell Sam Belmont how we met. If he gives me a good hiding, then so be it. I reckon I most probably deserve it, but knowing Sam, he'll understand. Oh, he'll rant and rave, but Sam knows I wouldn't be party to hurting any girl, much less do what Felix was suggesting. You're a pretty girl. Can't we at least part friends? I'll mend your bike and bring it up to the house tomorrow or the next day.'

Kate reluctantly allowed him to wheel her bicycle away alongside his own. At least she knew now who he was, and if he didn't return it in two days as promised, she'd tell Uncle Sam.

When she went in through the back entrance, Mrs Sturmey quickly accosted her with a few harsh words, but when she heard of the puncture she showed some sympathy. Kate went up to her small room in the attic and prepared for bed. After the fright came the anticlimax, and with it a strange feeling she hadn't experienced before. She washed her face and brushed her teeth at the small marble-topped wash-stand in the corner. She was getting so tall that she was outgrowing the little attic room, but it was the place she thought of as her own home. Here there was no one to spy on her. No one to know that when she took all her clothes off at night she stood before the cracked mirror on the back of the door to learn about her own body. She didn't need anyone to tell her that it was shapely. Her rich red hair, when let down from the earphones, fell over her naked shoulders and almost covered her firm, round breasts. Her dark-brown eyes burned uncomfortably as she found herself ruminating on Maurice Lambert while she brushed through her thick tresses. Why was she thinking about a young man who might have been excited enough through drink to take advantage of her? She began to think less angrily about him. He had, after all, returned to make sure she got home safely. He had a pleasant voice, he was nice looking ... Kate jumped happily into bed, curling up inside her winceyette nightgown, and enjoyed dreaming dreams ...

Chapter Five

The next day Kate found herself singing softly as she went about her work in the large mansion house. She didn't notice that Mrs Sturmey and one or two of the other servants eyed her suspiciously. She hadn't even been aware of how unhappy she had been over the past year, but now, all of a sudden, it seemed to the other staff that Kate Sheldon had shed her grief, or come to terms with the loss of her father, and had decided to make the best of her life. Perhaps, they thought, the fact that her mother, grandmother and sisters had paid a long-awaited visit to Sherbrook had made all the difference and they were pleased for Kate. A few days later, though, when a respectable young man knocked on the door of the servants' entrance and asked if he might see Kate for a few minutes, speculation changed.

'Only five minutes, Kate,' Mrs Sturmey said sternly.

Kate slid shyly through the door and closed it. 'You shouldn't have asked for me,' she whispered frantically. 'You could have left my bike at the Belmonts'.' She dared to face him and liked what she saw. He had a fresh complexion and was well-dressed, not spotty and dishevelled like so many of the estate boys. He was hatless, revealing a shock of black wavy hair with a high forehead – sign of intelligence, her mother would say.

'I've cleaned and polished it all up.' Maurice seemed to be nervous too, and for a few seconds they remained motionless, staring straight into each other's eyes. 'What time do you have off?' he blurted.

'Not much,' she said.

'I'm only home for the rest of this week. I'd like to meet you when you finish work tonight. We could go for a walk, couldn't we? I realise it can't be very nice for you, knowing that my family live in your grandparents' cottage, but I'd like you to come home with me. Mum would make us cocoa.'

Kate shook her head. 'Mrs Sturmey doesn't like us to go out after dark,' she said.

'Then this afternoon. You get some time off, don't you?'

Kate didn't answer immediately. Then, throwing caution to oblivion, she said quickly, 'I must get back to work. This afternoon when I've written to my mum I shall go down to the post office in the village.'

She opened the door. They heard the crackle of a starched apron inside and Maurice whispered: 'What time?'

'Three o'clock. Thank you very much for mending my bike.' She shut the door decisively.

'And what did that young man want with you, may I ask?' Mrs Sturmey asked.

'He stopped last night to see if there was anything he could do to help. He walked me home, and then took my bicycle away to mend it, Mrs Sturmey.' The housekeeper grunted disapprovingly. 'He's the boy from the family who live in Granddad's cottage,' Kate explained.

'I know well enough who he is. Not the boy for you to associate with, young lady. He's a college lad. No good hobnobbing with clever folk who soon get above themselves. Don't do anything your father wouldn't like, Kate.'

'He only brought my bike back, Mrs Sturmey,' Kate replied indignantly.

'Good. Now you can get back to work, then.'

For a while Kate felt downcast at the housekeeper's attitude, but who was she to advise her about the choice of friends? The prospect of a further meeting with Maurice helped the morning along, and when the luncheon things were cleared away and the staff had eaten their own dinner, Kate went up to her room to write to her mother. In her neat, round handwriting Kate quickly filled a whole sheet, giving graphic details of her encounter with Maurice and Felix, until she came to the part where the unsavoury suggestions had been made. With flushed cheeks she tore the letter into shreds and began again. She mustn't say anything to upset her mother, so she related the incident in a casual way, explaining that she had a puncture on the way home and that the young man from Gran's old cottage had mended it for her.

Kate took special care with her appearance as she put on her warm coat and felt hat to walk down the road to the village. Even before she reached the bridge she could see Maurice waiting for her there, and as soon as he saw her coming he began to walk towards her.

His smile was full of genuine warmth as he greeted her. 'Hullo, Kate. I'm glad you came. I thought you might not.'

'I had to write to Mum so I had to come to the post,' she said indifferently.

'It's quite a nice day. Could we walk by the river?'

Kate shrugged. 'I s'pose so.'

'Oh! Was that thoughtless of me, Kate? It's a year since the accident. You must hate the river.'

'I often walk by the river because I can feel Dad with me.'

'You're very brave. I think I'd die if anything happened to my dad,' Maurice admitted honestly.

'It's a terrible experience – but you just have to get on with living. I thought I'd never get over it. I wanted so much to move to Brimdene with Mum – but I had to stay here. I shall eventually go when they can find me a job to do.'

'The Maitlands can't take my sister Carol yet. They told my parents that you might be moving away and then Carol could have your job.'

'Well, I'm sorry, I'm sure, if my staying interferes with your family's plans.'

'No, no, I didn't mean it like that, Kate. Gosh, you are touchy! It's just that Mum doesn't like her having to cycle into Blandford every day, but at least she's got a job, even if it's only cleaning for the family who own the brewery.'

Maurice waited outside while Kate bought a stamp and posted her letter, then they retraced their steps to the bridge, which they crossed. It seemed natural to take a leisurely stroll through the churchyard and out along the towpath.

'I can walk back to Sherbrook House this way,' Kate said, and Maurice asked about her work with the Maitland family.

The first signs of the late-arriving spring were everywhere. Along the bank primroses were in bud, and lamb's tails hung from trees alongside pussy willow. Birds displayed, mated, and called to one another in the sunlight while the smell of fresh growth rose from the earth. It wasn't long before Kate was talking amicably to Maurice with little hint of antagonism. The path wound through meadows and fields belonging to the Sherbrook estate, and finally they came to the lake.

'I'll have to go in now,' Kate said. 'You're on private property and no one must see us.'

'We aren't doing anything wrong, and I've asked Sam's permission to walk out with you.'

'Hmph! Cheek!' Kate exclaimed. 'How d'you know I want to walk out with you?'

Maurice smiled, a knowing, cheeky smile. ''Cos I says you do,' he said, with winning confidence. 'When can we meet again, Katie?'

'I . . . I don't know,' she said.

Maurice looked all round at the scenery, then he nodded. 'Is that a boat-house over there?'

''Course.'

'Then we'll meet there tonight at nine o'clock.'

Kate shook her head. 'No, I can't,' she said.

'Yes, you can.'

Kate couldn't explain why she didn't argue, and that evening was the first of many spent in the small wooden boat-house. They chatted about their respective families, and Maurice told her all about his life at college where he was studying to become an architect and surveyor. On the last day Maurice was at home before returning to college they spent Sunday afternoon together and Kate was invited to his home to tea. At first she felt uneasy, there were so many memories of her grandparents here, but Mr and Mrs Lambert understood. They were a happy family, doing everything to put Kate at her ease, and she was soon experiencing the loving warmth of her new friends. When Maurice walked her back to the big house after the evening service at St Stephen's Church, he pulled Kate back into the rhododendron bushes and held her tightly. One kiss led to another until she felt his passion igniting flames of desire in her.

His mouth sucked hers until it was submerged in the heat of his violent wanting. He urged her close to him until she felt something hard and throbbing pulsating against her body. With large, compelling hands he smoothed her back and caressed her young tender breasts. Then one hand groped beneath her clothes, clumsily seeking out the tops of her stockings until in fury he was tugging at her knickers.

'No! *No*!' Kate whispered frantically. 'What d'you think you're doin', Maurice Lambert? You aren't any better than your friend.' She tried to pull free, but with great gasps of breath he clung to her.

'Katie . . . Katie . . . I want to do it. I . . . *must* . . . oh, my God!'

Somehow his fingers found her bare flesh. Control was lost as he anguished inside the tightness of his trousers. Kate slapped his cheek in innocent confusion.

Maurice groaned. 'Katie, hasn't anyone told you how it is with a man?' he said after a few seconds.

'Man?' she questioned indignantly. 'What makes you think you're anything more than a boy? Just because you go to college doesn't mean you can take liberties.'

'I do have feelings just like any other man or boy of my age. Doesn't matter what you call me, Kate. Now I'm in a mess – it had to come, Kate. The feel of your skin – 'twas like velvet. Let me touch you again – please?' he begged.

In the fading light of the spring evening Kate's cheeks were scarlet as she said: 'No!' but with less protest than before. ''Tis wrong, Maurice. My mum would be furious.'

'She doesn't have to know. For goodness sakes, Katie, you've got to learn somewhere. I know you like me and I like you – more'n a bit. There'll be no harm – I can't do it again for a while – and I promise I won't take advantage. I'd never force you. I stopped Felix, didn't I? There were two of us that night. 'Twould have been easy enough – you must see that – but I like to treat a girl tenderly. I want her to want me. You've never complained when I've tickled you, or run my fingers up and down your bare arms.'

'That was different,' Kate snapped.

'So you only want the fun without getting serious? If you think anything of me, Kate, you'd want me to get some pleasure too. Let's go down to the boathouse – 'tis my last night.'

'No!' Kate paused, and the thought of not seeing Maurice for several weeks made her sad. She did like him a great deal. She wanted him to do all the things her imagination could dream up, but she had considered that they were her very private desires not experienced by anyone else in the whole wide world. 'We-ell,' she began, 'if you promise not to –'

'I won't do anything you don't want me to,' Maurice said, and with hands held tightly they found the narrow path which skirted all round the huge garden. A wooden seat spanned the back wall of the boat-house, and as they sat side by side and kissed in the darkness, the only other sound was the gentle lapping of the water against the sides of a rowing boat housed here.

'We could lie in the boat, Kate,' Maurice suggested.

Kate giggled at the suggestion and while Maurice steadied the boat Kate clambered into it.

'Take your knickers off for me now, Katie,' Maurice urged, but Kate shook her head coyly. She didn't object when he gently did it for her. As his slender fingers caressed the lower part of her abdomen she gasped with pleasure at the strange fluttering feeling inside her. Something far away was telling her that this was wrong but she had no inclination to ask Maurice to stop. It was as if something very precious of Maurice's was being passed on to her. No one had ever touched her intimately before, though she had seen one of the estate men with his hand up a girl's skirt. Now she understood why the girl had writhed about on the barn floor, why the laughter had changed into heavy breathing and why the man had started to undo his breeches. In embarrassment she had left the barn then and tried to forget the incident, believing it was just the way men and women frolicked about the way her parents had done in the past.

As Maurice explored, Kate's breath ebbed away. She stretched her legs, then drew one up as the boat rocked precariously. Maurice forced her legs apart, placing one of his knees over hers. She quickly pulled her other leg in to collide with his, but he as urgently knocked it back and pushed it to balance on the edge of the boat.

'You won't feel anything with your legs together,' he whispered.

She couldn't believe anything could bring about such a warm glow to that part of her body. His actions were gentle, giving her a tingling sensation both inside and out, and then his fingers delved further ... She arched her body to gain the full ecstasy of his caressing and suddenly she was wanting too – desperately, frantically – but she didn't know what, until she felt as if she were climbing a mountain where at the summit she panted, ached, enjoyed ... and found herself losing control as she reached the pinnacle of excited frenzy. She moaned as if in a mystic trance as Maurice kissed her, still pleasuring her with the gentle rhythm of his fingers which had penetrated deep into her unknown depths. For several minutes they lay together in complete harmony.

'Can I do it now, Katie? I need to be inside you – let me have a memory to take back to college,' Maurice pleaded.

Kate struggled to sit up. 'A memory is one thing, Maurice, but you aren't going to leave me with more! You'll have to be patient – there's such as thing as marriage, you know.'

'I can't wait that long – and neither can you.'

'I'm not that kind of girl, Maurice. 'Twould be wrong – a terrible sin –'

'Not if we love each other.'

'It's too soon to say that.'

Maurice sighed. 'I respect you, Kate, and I'm sure I love you.'

'Only my body,' she said haughtily, suddenly realising just how far the petting had gone on this, their last evening together. 'We must be patient,' she said again.

He pulled her into his arms and she gave in to his cuddles. Passionate kisses were exchanged, but when the exploring began again Kate put a stop to it. 'No,' she said. 'I shall bleed and then there'll be some explaining to do.

'Promise me that we will when I come home again? I'll bring a French letter with me, then you'll be safe.'

'Whatever's that?'

Maurice chuckled gently. 'A thing men wear to prevent a girl falling for a baby. It's a good thing I came along, Kate Sheldon, or you might have got yourself into real trouble with the first man who tried it on.'

'Like Felix?' she taunted.

'Felix won't ever touch you again. You're my Katie – *my* girl – agreed?'

They sealed their pact with a loving kiss. Kate put her knickers back on and Maurice escorted her as near to the house as he dared, then Kate ran under cover of shrubs to the servants' door at the back of the house. With a last wave to the void in the dark she let herself in, took her shoes off and crept up the stairs to the attic. She climbed on to the small wooden chair and peered through the lattice window towards the towpath where she knew Maurice would be walking home. She spotted his jaunty figure and when he turned and looked back towards the house Kate waved her white handkerchief. They went on waving until he was forced to carry on out of sight.

With mixed feelings of guilt, excitement, and disappointment that she wouldn't see Maurice now until the summer, she vigorously washed herself before getting into the narrow bed. She couldn't sleep as she relived the events of the evening. She thought of her mother's words about men taking advantage of her, but that was what Felix had wanted to do. Maurice was too kind to treat her brutally. He had saved her from Felix. What she and Maurice had done was natural if you felt anything for one another, so Maurice had said, so it couldn't be wrong. She could hardly believe that he had given her such ecstatic feelings, feelings that quickly rose to the surface even now when she thought of his hands caressing her. Feelings that were indescribably beautiful ...

Kate drifted into a happy sleep, and from then on watched and waited for the postman to bring her a letter from Maurice.

It was over a week later that Mrs Sturmey came downstairs at breakfast-time and handed Kate two letters.

'Your ma's from Brimdene, and – this one.' The housekeeper eyed Kate suspiciously. 'Hope you haven't been up to no good with that young Lambert boy?' she said, watching Kate's reaction.

Kate's cheeks burned uncomfortably as all eyes rested on her expression. 'I've only just met him,' she said nonchalantly.

'You behave yourself, my girl. Remember you're in my charge. Any trouble you get into is a reflection on us, especially Mrs Maitland. Think of your dear departed father, Kate. Don't do anything that would vex him or your ma.'

'There's no harm in just writing to a boy, is there?' Kate demanded.

'If a boy writes to a girl it usually follows previous assignations. Oh, I saw you skulking down to the boat-house with him a time or two.' Mrs Sturmey sniffed. 'Still,' she went on, 'it'll be light evenings when he comes home again so you won't get the chance to canoodle in the dark.'

She turned to leave the kitchen and Kate made a face behind her back. She wished that Mrs Sturmey hadn't mentioned her father, though. Somehow it took all the gilt off the happiness she had felt since getting to know Maurice better. She supposed she had better tell her mother that she was walking out with Maurice. It would be easier to explain in a letter, and suddenly the idea of being found a job in Brimdene lost its attraction.

Fran decided to take the girls to Sherbrook for the Whitsun Bank Holiday. She was eager to see Kate again as guilt heaped upon guilt each time she saw her. The desperate unvoiced plea of 'When am I coming to Brimdene to live?' was so evident in her expression. Fran felt the pain for her as her daughter's lovely brown eyes filled with unshed tears when goodbyes had to be said. She was fearful that Kate would harbour a grudge at having to stay in Sherbrook, away from the rest of the family. Now she had an ideal opportunity to go off for a days outing because Ma had gone to stay with Eric, Fran's brother, his wife Annie and their daughter May, who lived in Stockclere, on the Hampshire-Berkshire border.

The girls danced with joy to be back again so soon in their old village, and Prue hugged Fran, nearly suffocating her.

'I'm so glad you could come,' she enthused. 'There's so much news to catch up on.'

'Really? It's only six weeks since we were here before,' Fran said wide-eyed. 'Nothing ever happens in Sherbrook, so we always said.' Her face clouded briefly, remembering that something terrible had happened in Sherbrook, then she hastened to add: 'Is Kate all right?'

'Kate's in love,' Prue told Fran. They were sitting at the kitchen table enjoying coffee before going up to the barrow for a picnic.

Fran laughed. 'That all? Suppose it had to happen eventually. As long as she's not serious.'

'Your Katie is seventeen, eighteen come Christmas, Fran. Most of us were walking out steady by then, you know.'

'But not my Kate. She's keen to come to Brimdene to live. She'll meet lots of nice young men there. Who is this boy?' she demanded to know. 'I can't think of anyone local who would be suitable.'

'They're a very nice family, Fran. Come on, the girls are ready now so we'll talk as we walk.'

Each one was given something to carry and they went down the long garden, across the stile and along the narrow bridle path that led up to the barrow. Prue had reckoned that Fran wouldn't want to face going past the old mill house and the shepherd's cottage today.

'Come on then,' Fran pursued. 'Who is this boy?'

'The shepherd's son, Maurice Lambert. Poor Kate, when you were here last time she had a puncture coming back from the station. This young lad walked with her as it was getting dark, and then he mended it for her. It seems they hit it off right from the start and he came to speak to Sam about it before he invited Kate to their home for tea.'

'She didn't go, of course?' Fran retorted.

'Well, we didn't think you'd mind, Fran. It seemed better to agree than to have them meeting secretly. The Lamberts really are a very good family. Maurice is at college, he's very clever. Anyway, you'll be able to decide for yourself later on. He's home for a few days and he's coming up to the barrow with Kate so that you can meet him.'

Fran sighed. 'Goodness knows how I'm going to cope with all this on my own, Prue.' She tried not to think too much about her own courting days, and the unfortunate meeting with Luke Hammond just before she married Henry. Suddenly she felt afraid for Kate, but she knew she had to guard against being overprotective.

An old mackintosh of Sam's was spread out on the grass and then a rug. Prue began to unload the basket of food, and when Ruby shouted that she could see Kate coming up the hill Fran stood up to get a glimpse of this boy called Maurice. She felt wary of anyone new, and instantly began to wonder how Henry would have reacted at the news. 'No boyfriends for my girls until they're seventeen,' she remembered him telling a neighbour once. Kate was seventeen. A pretty seventeen at that, far too pretty for the stocky young man who presented himself to be introduced.

He offered his hand politely. 'Pleased to meet you, Mrs Sheldon,' he said in a quiet voice.

'This is Maurice, Mum,' Kate said breathlessly. 'They live in Gran's cottage. He mended my bike for me.'

Fran smiled, hugged and kissed her daughter. She was growing up and no mistake. There was a new bloom about her even since Easter. Whatever reprimands Fran had conjured up to try to end this friendship before it went too far, slipped unvoiced out of her mind. It was enough to see Kate happy, without the pain of rejection in her eyes. And even when the brilliant sunshine began to fade and Sam came up the hill as far as he could with a horse and old wagon to take them back to the station, there was no sign of tears or disappointment. The all climbed in and sang happily as they bumped over the gravel track down to the bridge. There they paused while Fran went alone to the gravesides of her departed family. No florist's bouquets again this time, reminding her that Luke Hammond must still be away at sea. Salty tears overflowed as she placed flowers in the vases. Some late tulips and lily-of-the-valley from her own garden in Brimdene. 'Not a very good show yet,' she whispered to Henry. 'The soil needs attention before we can get good crops. Never been cultivated before, you see, but I'll grow lots of flowers and vegetables. Be near me, my darling. I can't go on without you . . .' Birdsong drowned out her sobs as she beat at the bare earth with her fists.

Kate wished the summer would last for ever. Maurice had come home to Sherbrook for six long weeks. He helped his father with the sheep, or Sam at the forge, and in the evenings he and Kate went for long walks by the river. They sometimes cycled far away from Sherbrook where prying eyes didn't see them lying together on the coarse dry grass. Kate learned to respond to his youthful kisses. She was frightened to let Maurice become too intimate even though her inner self longed for something more to happen. She didn't know what it was. She only knew that she was blissfully happy in Maurice's company, and grew close to him in spirit. When she wrote to her mother every week she mentioned Maurice in passing, but didn't enlarge on their growing friendship. Whereas once Kate had begged to be allowed to join the rest of the family in Brimdene, now Maurice had provided her with a very good reason for being content to remain working at the big house.

At the beginning of August Kate went to Brimdene to spend the bank holiday with the family on the beach. Maurice accompanied her and enjoyed the day's outing, but Kate stayed on for her week's holiday, and as the days passed she became impatient to return to Sherbrook.

Kate realised that there was something to be said for keeping her independence by staying in Sherbrook. Her mother made it quite plain that she considered Kate too young to be thinking seriously of Maurice Lambert.

'What do you think you know of young men?' Fran said derisively. 'You'll need to meet a few more chaps before you can make a choice – and you're far too young anyway. Your father certainly wouldn't approve.'

Kate had lapsed into silence. By Christmas she would be eighteen. Lots of girls were married at that age. She and Maurice talked earnestly about the future, but mainly in the light of Maurice's career. He had a few more years at college yet so marriage was out of the question. There was no rush except that they longed to be together for always. Aunt Prue said that it was a good thing that they couldn't be together all the time, that they must prove their maturity by controlling their feelings. She had even suggested that to go to work in a hotel in Brimdene might be just the thing for Kate, as with tips she could earn a better living with some to spare to save for the future.

'Your dad would be proud of you then,' Prue Belmont had said, and Kate could see the logic of that. Unfortunately, Aunt Sissy seemed to be a long while finding her a job, so meanwhile Kate had to be satisfied with things the way they were. She was content to return to Sherbrook after her holiday and not only because of Maurice.

'Mum's always going on about something,' she grumbled to Maurice. 'If she isn't nagging Gran, then she's on at Ruby or Babs. I know how hard life is for her, but Gran and Ruby do all they can to help.'

'It can't be easy for her, Katie,' Maurice said. 'I'll hate it if you go to live in Brimdene, but it won't be the end of the world.'

'Mum doesn't really approve of us walking out, you know. She'll always be watching us. I want to work in the town to earn more money, but at least we can do what we like here.'

'Not quite, my Katie,' Maurice said. 'We must think of our families. We're lucky in having good parents. Not like poor old Felix.'

'*Poor* Felix?' Kate echoed. 'I didn't like him much. Can't understand why you chose him as a friend, Maurice.'

'You don't understand, Kate. He's had a really rough time. It's made me appreciate my parents more than I did. His parents have split up, but no one likes to mention divorce. It leaked out at college, and some of the chaps have given him a hard time, which makes him aggressive. He's on the defensive all the time. He naturally feels let down. On the other hand he blames himself, thinking that it's something he's done that has caused the rift between his parents.'

'If he treats everyone badly he shouldn't expect sympathy.'

'He's not too bright, and finds college work difficult. His father expects too much, putting the pressure on all the time. I feel really sorry for him so I've done my best to be a good friend to him. I've tried to understand, but it's not easy with someone who picks a fight at the least provocation. He's taken to drinking too much and he can't hold his drink. One drink too many and there's always trouble.'

'As long as you don't get like him,' Kate whispered, and they indulged in meaningful kisses and petting until they were forced to go home.

The summer was over, yielding to autumn with strong winds and rain-filled skies, and Kate was left with nothing but happy memories. She exchanged letters with Maurice, bringing contentment which had to last until Christmas.

One day she was given an unexpected day off to go to Brimdene. Mrs Maitland, the lady of Sherbrook House, was too unwell to make the trip herself to fetch a new dress she'd had made at an exclusive dressmakers in the town.

'Mrs Maitland says you may visit your mother, Kate,' the housekeeper, Mrs Sturmey, said. 'You're a good girl and we all know how much you must miss your family. Take great care of the parcel, though, and don't leave it too late getting back as you'll have to walk from the station.'

Kate set off in high spirits. Mrs Maitland had given her a warm tweed cape which she had finished with, mainly because it was out of fashion. The neck edge was trimmed with fur and Kate found the matching fur hat at the church jumble sale.

Mrs Maitland got up from her sickbed to give instructions to Kate and was agreeably surprised at the young housemaid's appearance.

'My word, Kate, you do look smart,' she said. 'It's important to look nice as you're to visit my dressmakers, and I'm sure your mother will be pleased to see how grown-up you look. I've got just the thing to brighten up the outfit. You're only young, perhaps tweed is a trifle too mature for you.' She went away, to return a few moments later with a colourful square scarf.

'I want you to have this, and the brooch for your birthday, Kate dear. I know you won't be eighteen until nearly Christmas but you may as well have it to wear today.'

Kate could hardly believe how lucky she was. The brooch was gold, circular in shape, inset with brightly coloured stones.

The carter from the estate, on another errand for Mr Maitland, took Kate as far as the station in a horse-drawn wagon. Kate sat up beside him, fingering the beautiful brooch and feeling quite grand. If only Maurice could see me now, she thought.

It was one of the happiest days of her life. Fran was so surprised and delighted to see her that she gave up all her attention to her, making her feel really special. The girls were at school until teatime, by which time Gran had made a light sponge cake as a treat for them all. Ruby was envious of Kate's new clothes and such was the excitement that Kate almost forgot she had a train to catch. Hasty goodbyes were said as she hurried off to catch the tram, carefully guarding her precious parcel for Mrs Maitland.

Dusk was descending and the evening air was chill and damp by the time Kate reached Sherbrook. A fault in a signal box somewhere along the line had delayed the train by nearly an hour. She didn't relish the walk back to the big house, and wondered how angry Mrs Sturmey was going to be. She had promised that she would be home well before dark. She wished now that she had used her bicycle and left it at Mr Cutler's garage so that she could ride home from the station, but Mrs Maitland had said she looked too well-dressed to ride her bicycle. The real reason, Kate knew, was that Mrs Maitland thought her expensive new dress might get damaged if it fell from the handlebars. Kate thought she might have enough money for a taxi, but somehow that seemed wasteful, or she was sure her mother would consider it so.

By the time Kate crossed the bridge over the river in Blandford it was really dark. She looked down into its murky depths and felt a quiver of fear as she thought about the lane along which she must walk until she reached the gates of Sherbrook House. She wouldn't glimpse the river again until she was safely back in her attic room. It wasn't really late, she consoled herself as she stepped out bravely. She had anticipated that other people would be walking the lane too, and hoped that someone might offer her a lift in a cart or taxi, but tonight she was the only person going in the direction of Sherbrook.

She hurried along without meeting anyone. Then she thought she saw a dark figure ahead darting in and out of the hedge. It could be one of the farmer's lads out looking for a lost sheep or dog, but when she reached the place all was quiet and there was no one about at all. She breathed a sigh of relief when she came to the five-barred gate that led into the estate's home farm. Soon she would reach the wrought-iron gates to the main entrance, then she would be safe. A swift movement behind her as someone jumped the five-barred gate made her reel round anxiously.

A hand grabbed her arm in a vicelike grip. 'Hullo, Katie. It's me, Felix. Maurice's friend.'

A cold sweat broke out over Kate. Shock at the sudden appearance of anyone, fear when she realised who it was. Maurice didn't think so badly of Felix, she remembered, as long as he hadn't been drinking.

'W – what are you doing here?' she stammered, wishing he would release his grip from her arm.

'Just, um, paying a visit – to see you actually.' He was close enough to Kate for her to smell his breath, which confirmed that he had been drinking.

She had a horrible premonition that history was repeating itself, only this time there was no Maurice to protect her.

'I'll have to go in, Felix. Mrs Sturmey will be very angry as I'm so late.'

'But it isn't that late, Katie.'

Kate prickled at the use of her familiarised name. It sounded provocative coming from him, quite different from the way Maurice said it.

'It's late, and it's dark, and I'm tired so I'm going in.' She tried to assert herself, but instantly knew she hadn't a hope with Felix. He tightened his grip on her arm, and no matter how frantically she tried to free herself, she was ensnared. His strong arms encircled her until she could hardly breathe, and then he guided her across the lane to where a narrow bridle path led into an overgrown copse. 'Felix!' Kate yelled. 'For goodness sake don't be such an idiot!' Her cape hatched on a bramble bush, but he pulled her along, regardless of the ripping sound, until they were enveloped by tall trees and bushes. Her hat tumbled away on the damp grass as she fought in vain for freedom. The whites of his cold, venomous eyes showed clear in the night gloom as he flung her to the ground, falling on top of her heavily, winding her.

'This time I'm going to get what I want, so it's no use you fightin' and screamin', my darlin'. If Maurice can have it, then so can I.'

'Felix, you're hurting me. *Ple – ease*,' she begged, panting for breath, 'let me get up. Maurice hasn't – we haven't . . .'

His reply was a fierce, wet kiss on her trembling mouth. She was pinned down, her arms useless under the weight of his knees. He pushed her cape upwards until it was a crushed heap across her chest, then, as his mouth ravaged hers, his hands groped and tore at her clothes. She was helpless, and gave a frightened scream as he pulled off her knickers. It was as if the lower part of her body had been severed from the rest of her, yet the pain was real enough.

Feeling Maurice's hardness through his trousers was exciting, she had learned, but the hairy, throbbing organ that invaded her filled her with terror. His pumping action seemed as if it would never end and the animal cry that accompanied the final thrust pierced the still, dark night.

Kate wept with humiliation as he flopped down on her exhausted. Her body, reviled with the warm, sticky substance of his lust, fought back, and in a new effort to rid herself of this violation she pulled the brooch from her cape and tore wildly at Felix's face with the long, sharp pin. His fearful cry as he rolled away from her remained with her all the way back along the bridle path. She raced across the road and up the drive to the big house, convinced he was chasing after her. Her first impulse was to bang on the front door, but some sort of sanity was returning in a hazy kind of way. She ran on again to the servants' entrance, then stopped short by the coal cellars and outside lavatory. No one must ever know what Felix had done to her.

Irrational thoughts twisted and turned until her brain felt weary and she slipped into the lavatory and bolted the door. Never could anyone have been so grateful for this new amenity as Kate was in that moment. It was one of the old wood stores converted for the use of the men who worked outside. Kate sat down on the wooden seat with an urgency to flush away all the contents of her inside, especially that which Felix had so cruelly bestowed on her.

She was so cold that her body shook uncontrollably, and then she held her breath as tiptoeing footsteps stealthily reached her keen hearing. Dear God, she thought, now I shall have to stay here all night. It had to be Felix. Prowlers were unlikely to creep about this early on a damp, miserable night, and the staff would be walking more briskly than this person. She waited, holding her breath in the total darkness, thankful that there was no light in the lavatory to give her presence away. From inside the house the sound of one of the dogs barking could be heard. The latch on the lavatory door was tried in agitation, and when Kate heard the back door being opened the footsteps rushed away.

'Anyone there?' Kate heard Mrs Sturmey's shrill voice distantly. A loud slam followed, and she breathed a sigh of relief that the dog had not been sent out to investigate. Mrs Sturmey would be expecting Kate, of course. Now what should she do? She called up all her reserves of courage, and decided that she must excuse her state of dishevelment by saying that she had fallen down. The precious parcel and her hat were left behind somewhere on the bridle path or in the copse. Mrs Sturmey would want to send someone to find them. What explanation could there possibly be for them to be on the bridle path? Kate knew that Mrs Sturmey was much too astute to be fobbed off with lies – and Kate had never told a lie before so she knew she wouldn't be very convincing.

The minutes ticked by. Kate became accustomed to the dim light seeping through the notched top of the door. There was even a wash basin here, so with a wad of toilet paper she managed to rid herself of the smell of Felix before she faced Mrs Sturmey. She couldn't bring herself to venture outside, but at length she knew she must.

With her ears tuned to even the slightest sound, she waited after drawing back the bolt. All was quiet, the loudest noise her own breathing, and she was sure her heartbeats must echo right out to the road. She closed the lavatory door behind her as quietly as she could, still trying to solve the puzzle of what to tell the housekeeper. Then, as she took a step surreptitiously along the wall of the house towards the back door, she fell over something. She went down clumsily on the gravel path, uttering a cry of fright, tearing her stockings and grazing her knees. One calamity after another, she thought, despondently.

As she pulled herself up she was amazed to discover that what she had fallen over was the parcel with her hat as well. She offered up a silent prayer of thanks. No lie was necessary now – she really had fallen over! But what of Felix? Had he known that she was in the lavatory or was he looking for somewhere to hide? The college term hadn't ended, so what was he doing here in Sherbrook? Kate was baffled, and terrified that he would seek her out again. Suddenly the back door burst open, spilling light out on to the path.

'That you, Kate? Where on earth have you been until this hour, child?' Mrs Sturmey's voice was high-pitched with annoyance. 'And what are you doing kneeling down there, for goodness sake?'

Kate struggled to her feet. She hadn't realised that she had only got as far as her knees. 'I . . . I fell down, Mrs Sturmey,' she stammered. In spite of herself, Kate burst into tears.

'There, there, child. You aren't a baby now. Come on in and let's see what damage you've done to yourself.'

The housekeeper wrapped her shawl closer round her shoulders and came outside to help Kate.

'I . . . I've had a dreadful journey, Mrs Sturmey, that's why I'm so late.'

'Oh, only your knees grazed,' Mrs Sturmey said unsympathetically. 'I expect you're chilled, and tired. I certainly am, waiting up for you. Just look at the state of you. How on earth did you manage to rip this lovely cape the missus gave you?'

'I . . . I . . . walked too near the hedge. It was a bit eerie down the lane tonight. There was no one about.' Kate felt guilty that lying came so easily after all.

'Then no reason for you to be so scared, Kate.' She walked over to a tall kitchen cupboard and took out a bottle. 'Here, child. Put a couple of drops of this in the water and bathe your knees well. Better have an aspirin, too. Not like you to be so scared.' Now in the kitchen light Mrs Sturmey took closer stock of Kate, and made no secret of her concern by the fear in the young girl's eyes. 'You sure you're all right? No one made advances on the train, I hope?'

Kate shook her head. 'No, the guard kept his eye on me. I got worried when the train was so late starting off. I . . . I thought about having a taxi home but Mum would have thought that extravagant.'

Mrs Sturmey sniffed haughtily. 'Should think so indeed! You know the lane is safe enough. You've walked it plenty of times. Now get off to bed so that I can do the same. Take your things up and then come down again and I'll have your cocoa ready. You can carry it up to the attic tonight for a treat. I'll have your hot-water bottle ready too. That'll warm you up a bit.'

Kate's knees felt stiff as she climbed the narrow attic stairs for the second time. She couldn't believe her luck in being given a hot-water bottle. Now at least she would be able to wash herself properly. She unscrewed the knob on the stone bottle and poured the water out into her china basin. She started with her face, neck and arms and worked her way down, horrified at the dried blood stuck to the tops of her stockings. She scrubbed every inch of herself with two lots of soap, and even then she didn't feel really clean. She put the empty bottle between her sheets to glean the last ounce of warmth from it, and, when she had taken the aspirin and drunk her cocoa, she blew out the candle and snuggled up in bed. But not to sleep for a further hour as she relived each horrible minute of Felix's rape of her virginity. What was Maurice going to say? He often talked affectionately of her youthful innocence, and how he longed to be the one to claim her as his very own, by breaking the last barrier of her maidenhood. Now she wasn't pure any more, and through no fault of her own. If her mother should ever find out . . . Kate turned over, closed her eyes, covered her face with her hands and prayed God that she never would.

Chapter Six

Kate woke with a monstrous headache next morning. But still she got up at six o'clock and went downstairs for a jug of hot water. In the privacy of her attic room she scrubbed herself all over yet again before putting on clean underwear and the coarse dress and white cap and apron ready for the day's work. She had found her knickers tucked inside her bag. Her first instinct was to throw them away, but someone might discover them and questions would be asked. She thought of tossing them into the river but that idea was no better. Clothes were too expensive just to cast aside when they were perfectly wearable, so she put them in the bottom of a drawer until she could bring herself to wash them. She couldn't bear to look at them. They were a symbol of her lost virginity, a reminder of the hateful Felix. How on earth had Maurice, who was decent and kind, have ever got mixed up with such a fellow?

Kate went about her work in a daydream. Unexpressed anger added to her distress. She was afraid to leave the house or even go out to fill the coal scuttle lest Felix should be lying in wait somewhere. Then she remembered the brooch and the savage way she had scored his face. Revenge, such as it was, was sweet, even though a scratched face didn't make up in any degree for what he had done to her. She would never wear the brooch again, she vowed.

Her letter to her mother was short and strained that week, and she couldn't bring herself to write to Maurice. Even though she had received a letter from him the day before she went to Brimdene, when he failed to receive her usual reply he wrote again, hoping that she was all right. He added a postscript saying that Felix had been in trouble at college and had run away. No one knew of his whereabouts and the police had been informed. Maurice indicated that they were fearful that he might attempt suicide.

Oh, if only he were successful, Kate thought, and then in guilty desperation she knelt beside her bed and begged God's forgiveness. Maurice was concerned for his friend, and, after all, there must be some good in Felix since he had returned her belongings. Her only grain of hope was that he had taken himself as far away as possible from Sherbrook. In the kitchen she heard talk that the police had visited Maurice's parents in their search for Felix. Outhouses, barns and stables were all searched, and everyone in the village was advised to keep a lookout for anything suspicious.

Kate even found herself worrying about Felix. He knew about the bridle path and copse. Was it possible that he had made himself a hideout there? But if he had, what would he eat? There would soon be signs of pilfering from people's kitchens, she supposed. The concern for him seemed to overshadow what he had done to her. She would never, ever forget – how could she? – but as time went by the humiliation at least lessened, until, one morning early in December, she got out of bed and was suddenly sick. She gazed at herself in the mirror, waking up to the fact that what she saw was a mother-to-be!

In her wretchedness Kate contemplated suicide herself. How could she tell her mother? And, dear God, if ever she needed her mother it was now. She went alone to the graveside of her father and wept. How vexed he would be, but somehow she felt that he would understand. Her mother wouldn't. Kate could envisage her anger. She would be embittered at the disgrace Kate had brought upon the family. Kate's story would never be believed. All her mother would worry about was what the neighbours would say. Rain beat down on her head as she remained kneeling on the wet ground. Perhaps she could run away – but where could she go? And who would employ her carrying an illegitimate child? What was she going to do after it was born? The questions went round and round in her tired brain, but there were no answers.

'Katie?' At first Kate didn't hear the voice, then her name was called a second time and she looked up into Mrs Maitland's face. 'Kate, whatever d'you think you're doing kneeling on the damp grass, my dear?' Kate allowed herself to be helped up. Her hot, unhappy tears flowed thick and fast. 'You're shivering with the cold and you're soaked to the skin. Come along, let's get you back and into a hot bath.'

'It ... it's all right, Mrs Maitland, really. I meant to call on Aunt Prue ... b – but I stopped at D – Dad's g – grave ...'

'You can't go anywhere in this state.' Mrs Maitland placed protective arms round Kate's shoulders and hurried her through the churchyard back to the house. Mrs Sturmey rushed to greet them with motherly concern.

'Oh, my dear child, whatever 'as happened to you? Have you fallen again?' Kate was persuaded to sit on a whitewood kitchen chair near the range while Mrs Sturmey pulled off her shoes and stockings. 'These are wringing wet through, child,' she scolded.

Kate felt so utterly despondent that she wept and wailed as only her sister Ruby usually did.

'It's all right, dear. Best have a bath to prevent you catching a chill,' Mrs Maitland said kindly. Then, after an uncomfortable pause, she added: 'Is something wrong, Katie? Mrs Sturmey has already told me how worried she's been about you lately. You've been tired and listless, and unusually pale. It's more than grief for your father now, isn't it?'

With eyes and nose running profusely Kate looked up at her employer with a frightened expression.

'I . . . I'm all right,' she said in a timid whisper.

Mrs Maitland sat herself down in the rocking chair opposite Kate, and Mrs Sturmey perched on the edge of the kitchen table.

'Come now, Kate, you aren't all right. You've been vomiting in the mornings. And I have reason to suspect that you haven't seen anything for well over a month. You haven't have you, Kate?' Mrs Sturmey pursued her questioning accusingly.

Their positive diagnosis, without Kate mentioning a single word to anyone, came as a shock to her. It was no use trying to hide the truth now.

'I – I don't want my mother to find out,' she said tearfully.

'Has that young Maurice Lambert taken advantage of you, Kate?' Mrs Maitland asked gently.

Kate shook her head vigorously. 'No! *No*! He hasn't been home. It doesn't matter who . . . It was – an accident.'

Mrs Sturmey sniffed indignantly. 'Accident indeed!' she scoffed. 'Takes two, young Kate, and I must say I'm surprised at you. No wonder you don't want your mother to find out. She'll be that vexed, just as your dear departed father would have been.'

'You've betrayed my trust in you, Kate,' Mrs Maitland said with slow deliberation, and Kate looked up into the older woman's reproachful expression, knowing that she was being condemned for something that was not her fault. 'Your mother will blame us and so will Mr and Mrs Belmont. It's a bad business. You'd better tell me exactly how it did happen.'

Kate hung her head in shame. She had blamed Felix, but maybe she was the one who did wrong after all. She was confused, and now that the attitude of those she thought were trying to help her had changed, she felt as if she were on trial.

'I . . . I can't say . . .' she faltered.

'Why won't you name the young man? Why are you shielding him? You may be equally to blame, Kate, but he must share the responsibility. There'll be a baby to provide for in a few months' time. You won't be able to work, child,' Mrs Sturmey warned. 'How are you going to manage, I'd like to know?'

Kate continued to weep great tears of misery, which softened the hearts of both employer and housekeeper.

'I knew it,' Mrs Sturmey said, getting off the table suddenly. 'It was that night you came home late, wasn't it? What did you get up to, young Katie?'

'I – I was . . . I – I . . . was raped!' The words finally came out, and she cried uncontrollably.

'There, there, Kate dear.' Mrs Maitland tried to console her. 'We'll do all we can to help you – but you must tell us what happened.'

Kate shook her head. It was bad enough that she had been so ill-used – she couldn't bring herself to tell the story to anyone, let alone her employer. 'I can't tell you anything,' she sobbed. 'Please help me – *please*, Mrs Maitland – how can I get rid of it?'

Through her tearful gaze Kate saw Mrs Maitland look questioningly at Mrs Sturmey. They seemed to be communicating without uttering a sound.

'You go off to the bathroom, Kate, and have a good soak to get the chill out of your bones while Mrs Sturmey and I try to think of . . .' Her voice trailed away almost guiltily. She ushered Kate to the door, and as Kate climbed the back stairs she heard the door close decisively behind her. They would have to send her home to her mother, of course. Instead of feeling relieved that the truth had spilled out about her condition, she felt in a worse dilemma than before. Never could she face her mother – never!

In a daze she went up to the attic room and fetched clean clothes, then she crept back to the lower landing where one of the bathrooms was situated. Hot water flooded out of the huge taps, creating a room full of steam. She took off all her clothes and paused while running cold water on top of the hot. She held her belly gently, then squeezed and with an anguished cry told her unborn child, 'I hate you, I hate *you* . . .' and without thinking she stepped into the bath of hot water. The pain of scalding toes caught her breath, but she fought back any further cries as she endeavoured to sit down in as hot water as she could bear. Maybe, just maybe this would do the trick. She had heard some of the girls talking once about how to get rid of an unwanted baby. It was all too common an occurrence in service and hot baths were usually tried – but in vain, if the dismissal of Dottie and Mavis was anything to go by. Mrs Sturmey had given them all a good lecture after that. Instant dismissal, she had warned, and here was Kate in the same predicament.

The brass bell jingled noisily in her attic room while she was dressing and brushing her hair. She made haste to return to the kitchen to learn her fate, but there was quite a commotion going on between Mr Withers and Mrs Sturmey when she entered.

'Ah, Kate, be a good girl and lay up in the dining room quickly. Mr Nicholas has returned with Captain Hammond and some other friends. There's to be a dinner party. We're cooking dinner earlier so there's plenty to be done and not a moment to be wasted.'

Kate's condition evidently meant nothing now. Well, at least she wasn't being turned out on the streets immediately. There was little time to feel sorry for herself during the next couple of hours. Mrs Sturmey kept everyone running hither and thither while Cook became red-faced and harassed, her cap askew and flour settling like fine snow all around her. Kate was detailed to help Tilly in the dining room and for the first time was to help wait at table.

'Here, child,' Mrs Sturmey commanded, pushing a black dress in Kate's arms, 'try this dress on for size. Here's the apron and cap, then let me look at you.'

A few minutes later Kate reported to the housekeeper.

'Oh, very good,' Mrs Sturmey complimented. 'Very nice indeed.' Then she looked directly into Kate's deep-brown eyes. 'Oh, Katie, why have you let us all down so? You had a good position here – still, all is not lost. When you have your cocoa tonight I'll give you some herbal medicine. If that doesn't work, nothing will.' She waved a warning finger at Kate. 'I'm only doing this for your poor mother's sake, but, like the missus says, she'll most likely blame us for letting you go astray. How could you do it? You're nearly eighteen, old enough to know better, my girl. Now, be off with you and watch your manners, mind. If you get flummoxed, ask Tilly.'

This was the day Kate had dreamed of. A neat black dress with a white frilly apron and small cap to adorn her auburn hair, and the most grown-up thing of all were the black stockings. She kept asking Tilly to check that the seams were straight, and just before the gong sounded Tilly went over all that she thought Kate should know about serving at table.

They stood straight and still in front of the long oak sideboard as the family and guests came in for dinner. Captain Hammond accompanied Mrs Maitland, with Mr Maitland and a young lady walking behind. Mr Nicholas Maitland, the eldest son, was laughing amiably with a tall, very elegant young lady, and Gordon Maitland, the youngest of the family, followed with his sister Virginia. Dr Gibbs came last with another young woman on his arm, whom Kate hadn't seen before. Kate wondered if Mr Nicholas was about to announce his engagement or something since they all seemed in high spirits and were dressed up for the occasion. But nothing in the conversation indicated such a celebration. Mr Nicholas and Captain Hammond were simply pleased to be back in England in time for Christmas, and it appeared there was going to be quite a house party during the festive season.

Course followed course so that Kate and Tilly were kept busy. Their feet ached and Kate longed to kick off her shoes, but she knew she dared not, though no one would have noticed, she felt sure, because they were too busy laughing and chattering.

At last the men retired to their port wine. As Dr Gibbs passed Kate, he paused to light his pipe. Shaking the match to extinguish it, he looked at Kate and smiled. 'Well, young Katie, you seem to be doing very well, and how's the family? Your mother well?'

Kate bobbed a curtsey. 'They're all well, thank you, sir,' she said politely.

Dr Gibbs walked on towards the drawing room and Captain Hammond came up to Kate. 'I believe you must be one of the Sheldon girls,' he said. Kate noticed a twinkle in his eye, but not for her; it was just the effect of the many glasses of wine he had drunk with the meal.

'Yes, sir, I'm Kate Sheldon,' she answered demurely. Surely he must know that it wasn't ethical to address one of the servants? But there was something about this man's manner that suggested he was a law unto himself.

'You don't live with the family?' he asked.

'No, sir, not yet. I wanted to go to Brimdene with them, but work there is scarce.'

'Your mother has been through a very rough patch, Kate. Please give her my kind regards when you go home next time.' He sauntered on to catch up with the others. Kate heard Mr Nicholas make some remark about hobnobbing with the staff, after which there was loud laughter and then the door was closed, so Kate heard nothing more.

The clearing-up took the rest of the evening. She longed to go to bed. Hearing the family discussing Christmas arrangements had made her realise that she would soon be going home and her mother would notice that something was wrong. Her thoughts wafted to

Brimdene and her own family as they prepared for Christmas. Ruby, Hilda and even Babs would all be helping to prepare the fruit for the cake and puddings. Gran would seed the raisins, and her mother would wash and then push the small silver charms into the big family-sized Christmas pudding. There would be the usual rush to write cards, buy and wrap presents secretly, and decorate the house with holly and paper chains. And all the time the festivities would be marred by the fact that Kate Sheldon, eldest daughter of Fran Sheldon, was pregnant.

Kate thought she had never felt so weary in all her life, and in three days' time she would reach the age of eighteen. There was no anticipation, though, of a happy birthday this year. Her desperate longing to join the family in Brimdene to live had been overtaken by her friendship with Maurice, but now she was consumed with guilt and fear. She would open her cards and presents and have to pretend that she was happy, but no one, not even Mrs Sturmey, could know the heartache that was ripping her apart. Instead of looking forward to going home, she dreaded it.

At last all signs of the dinner party had been cleared away and the staff sat down to their own supper. Game pie had been on the menu and there was a good portion left, which was to be divided among the staff, but the mere smell of it made Kate feel nauseated.

'I'll keep a bit back for you, Kate. I'm afraid you caught a chill when you went out in all that rain today,' Mrs Sturmey said, covering up for her. 'Before you go up tonight I'll give you some medicine.'

'Can't miss an opportunity like this,' Tilly said enthusiastically. 'Never had no more than a morsel of game pie before.'

'And that you pinched,' Mr Withers said dryly.

Kate was too tired to eat much, but she pushed some food down to save any embarrassment. Later, when the rest of the staff had retired to their quarters, Mrs Sturmey gave Kate some revolting-smelling liquid to drink.

'Now you'll have to be on your guard, Katie,' she whispered. 'It may take a day or two to work and when you come on you'll have a flood, so be prepared, dearie.'

Kate closed her eyes and swallowed the potion in one go. She retched and had to swallow hard to prevent it from coming up again, but Mrs Sturmey had a piece of dry bread at the ready. 'Eat this quickly and the unpleasant taste will soon go off.'

'It won't do me any harm, will it, Mrs Sturmey?'

'Gracious, no, child. 'Tis only herbs. I can't promise that it'll do any good though. Depends how far on you are. If it happened that night you were so late home 'tis only about six weeks so you should be safe enough.' Mrs Sturmey sniffed and placed a restraining hand on Kate's arm. 'Whoever did it to you, Katie, don't you think it's wrong to let him get away with it? He'll try it on with some other innocent young girl. And if he's some wicked blackguard preying on young girls he'll stop at nothing, and 'twill end in murder.'

'He'd been drinking,' Kate said, then she turned quickly and made for the back stairs.

When she said her prayers that night she begged forgiveness for all the wrong she had ever done, and then asked God to make the potion work.

Kate enjoyed her birthday, feeling brighter and more hopeful than she had done for some weeks, but after three days there was still no sign of the medicine having done any good. Cook baked her a birthday cake with eighteen candles. She blew them out in one almighty puff, wishing that soon she would be relieved of the worry of an unwanted pregnancy. If only it would happen before she went home for the weekend ... The staff sang 'Happy Birthday', there were cards to look at and presents to open, and Mr Withers gave them all a drink of port wine to celebrate the occasion. Kate felt slightly light-headed by the time she climbed the attic stairs and she was soon drifting towards dreamland, trying to imagine the real birthday party she expected to have when she went home to Brimdene, and forgetting her condition and how she would find the courage to break the news eventually to her mother.

She woke suddenly, in intense pain. She felt cold, yet her body was wet with perspiration and she knew she was bleeding profusely. She sat up and with trembling fingers lit her candle. Blood was everywhere, far more than she had ever seen before, and she was terribly frightened. It felt as if her very lifeblood was being pumped out of her body. She must seek the housekeeper's help. Somehow she managed to totter down from the attic to the half-landing where Mrs Sturmey's room overlooked the side of the house.

'Mrs Sturmey, Mrs Sturmey! Help me, please,' she cried as she banged on the door.

Mrs Sturmey came out in her nightgown and switched on the electric light. It was a new innovation at the big house, which had not been extended to the attic rooms. The housekeeper appeared less sleepy than Kate had expected. She took one look at Kate and put her hands to her mouth. 'Dear God, Kate! I told you to be prepared. It looks as if someone's tried to murder you.'

She fetched a large bath towel and wrapped it round and between

Kate's legs, but still the blood poured down, staining everything in its wake. The last thing Kate remembered was thanking God for answering her prayer, and then Mrs Sturmey got smaller and smaller. As she receded into the background, Kate tried to find her voice to beg her not to leave her, but she could make no sound, and then there was nothing . . .

From time to time she rallied enough to know that Dr Gibbs gave her an injection and Aunt Prue was with her – dear Aunt Prue, everything would be all right now. Voices, faces subdued in the half-light, Mrs Maitland's and Captain Hammond's coming out of the confusion.

'There's no time to wait for the ambulance,' he said. 'I'll take her in my car – maybe I'll meet them halfway, ring them and tell them to watch for me.'

'Aunt Prue,' Kate said weakly. 'Don't leave me, please don't leave me.'

'I won't, Katie dear. I'll go to Brimdene with you, never fear.'

Kate felt awful, but at least everything was going to be all right now. She drifted into unconsciousness again until voices began to haunt her. She felt herself being lifted and tried to protest.

'It's all right,' Aunt Prue assured her. 'You're being transferred to the ambulance. It won't be long now until we reach the hospital.'

'Kate, dear, can you hear me?' It was Captain Hammond's voice. Kate nodded, but she couldn't seem to open her eyes. 'I'll fetch your mother. Can you tell me her address?'

'It's all right, it's all right, I know it,' Prue said. 'I'm going with Kate anyway.'

'I want to fetch Mrs Sheldon immediately. She'll want to be with Kate, won't she?'

Prue had to agree with the captain, though why he was being so concerned she couldn't imagine. As she soothed Kate's brow and watched over the frightened, pale young girl, Prue could only wonder how much more Fran could take. She was a strong woman, no one could deny that, but the dreadful things that seemed to happen one after another were enough to put her into a mental institution. And this situation to a woman of Fran's integrity was the last straw. Girls of eighteen didn't haemorrhage to this extent unless a miscarriage was the cause – and Prue's midwifery experience told her that Kate was in a serious condition. She was losing her lifeblood – pray God they would reach the hospital in time.

Fran rubbed her fingers until the blood circulated faster. It was a cold, bleak December morning. When she let the blind up she saw that Jack Frost had been busy turning cobwebs into picturesque lace hanging from the roof and windows. Babs was still asleep, and it being Saturday morning she left her there while she went downstairs to clean the grate and light the fire.

'Can I help, Mum?' Fran was surprised when Ruby appeared behind her.

'My goodness, what's got you up so early this morning, and without being called even?'

'Brrr ... it's so cold, and there's a lot to do to get ready for Kate's party. I'm so excited, Mum. It seems ages since she came home.'

'I'll empty the ash-can, you lay the paper and sticks and get the fire going.' Fran managed to give Ruby a warm smile at her enthusiasm for her older sister. 'At least there's no black-leading to do,' she said meaningfully.

Fran put on an old overcoat of Henry's and went out into the back yard to the galvanised dustbin, where she emptied the ashes into a large, round sieve. She was shaking it vigorously when she thought she heard a car stop outside. Someone for Mr Blake, she supposed. Then came the unmistakable click of the front gate. This was followed by loud, urgent knocking. Kate? So early? No, couldn't possibly be, she thought, so she went on with what she was doing, leaving Ruby to answer the door. A vague suggestion came into her head that it might be the gypsies who often called on a Saturday morning, selling lavender, pegs or flowers, but it was far too early even for them.

The back door opened. 'Mum, there's a gentleman to see you,' Ruby whispered frantically. 'Says it's very urgent. I've shown him into the front sitting room.'

'Good Lord!' exclaimed Fran. 'Who on earth would want to see me at this hour? Even the landlord wouldn't be this anxious.'

'No, Fran, I'm not the landlord.' The voice, usually so smooth and cultured in Fran's memory, though satiny soft now, held a more compelling appeal. 'I'm sorry to come at such an inconvenient time, but I happened to be at Sherbrook House when your daughter Kate was taken ill.'

'Kate? Ill?' Panic urged Fran to leave the ashes and rush inside the house, shutting the door firmly and standing with her back to it. She must be dreaming. Luke Hammond was here, tall and good-looking as ever, standing in front of her and telling her some unlikely story about Kate being ill. 'She can't be!'

'Fran – I'm sorry. Make haste and I'll take you to the hospital. Mrs Belmont is with Kate. She's had a bad haemorrhage, lost a great deal of blood. I just happened to be there ... She's your daughter so I wanted to help.'

'Ruby, go tell your gran and the others. See to the breakfast. I ... I'll ...'

'Fran, dear, you look as if you don't believe me. It's true – there isn't a kinder way of telling you. Kate needs you. Hurry, please.'

Fran found it difficult to get her thoughts in some semblance of order of importance. The shock of Luke arriving was enough on its own without the added worry of news about Kate. She pushed past him. Upstairs she quickly changed her clothes to something more suitable for hospital visiting, and then, picking up her bag, she hurried along to her mother's room.

'They've come for me, Ma. Our Katie's in hospital. I must go at once. Ruby's seeing to breakfast.'

She didn't wait for any reaction but joined Luke at the front door.

'I'm so sorry to be the bearer of bad news, Fran, but I want to be with you to support you. I'm sure she's going to be all right.' He ushered her out to his car, and, as they drove along the streets, deserted except for the milk cart and a coal cart starting on his round, Luke explained briefly what had happened. Fran barely spoke, except to give him directions. Shock had brought about some kind of stupor, while inwardly she was willing the car to go more speedily to the hospital.

'It's lucky you were at Sherbrook House,' she managed to say at last as the hospital came into view.

'My dear Fran, we invariably find ourselves in the right place when we're most needed. The Maitlands would, of course, have done everything possible for Kate, but I was there, and as I've told you before, sleep doesn't come easy after months away at sea. I like to think I would have acted the same way whoever was in trouble. Fortunately I heard the commotion and went to investigate. Dr Gibbs was already awake – no time was wasted.'

He pulled into the forecourt of the old Victorian hospital and a porter appeared at once to open the door. With a hand at Fran's elbow Luke guided her through the long corridor, following the porter's instructions to the ward where Kate had been taken.

A nursing sister met them at the door. 'Mrs Sheldon?' She was a petite young woman whose smile transformed an otherwise colourless face to warm radiance. 'You're just in time to see your daughter before she goes to theatre.'

'Theatre?' Fran echoed, her stomach muscles knotting painfully. 'What for?'

'Plenty of time for questions later, Mrs Sheldon. Just pop in and have a quick word. Kate is very weak as she's lost a great deal of blood, but she'll be pleased to see you if she's still conscious. She's had her pre-med, you see. Would Mr Sheldon like to come in too?'

Fran felt herself go suddenly cold, then her cheeks turned pink. 'Not my husband,' she said quickly. 'A very kind friend.'

'It's all right, Fran, I'll stay outside and wait for you.'

Fran turned back to face Luke. 'There's no need,' she said quietly. 'I'm so grateful, Captain Hammond, but I'll be all right now.'

He half raised a hand. 'I'll wait,' he answered positively. The sister led Fran into the long clinical ward to some screens just inside the double doors on the left-hand side.

'Katie? Oh, my poor Katie! Are you all right, darling?' Fran had the utmost difficulty in keeping her voice steady. The sight of Kate with cheeks drained of colour, contrasting against her chestnut-red hair framing the still, girlish face, gave her a dreadful shock. Kate's eyelids flickered, opened briefly and then closed again. But as Fran looked down at her daughter she noticed tears oozing from beneath her dark lashes. That was what made her girls so special, she thought in a moment of maternal admiration. Kate and Babs both had rich auburn hair like her own, but eyes and lashes as sable-black as Henry's. Fran placed her hand over Kate's and squeezed. 'I don't know what's wrong yet, Kate, but I'm sure everything can be put right,' she whispered in a trembling voice. The sister urged Fran away but Kate was grasping Fran's hand desperately. 'God be with you,' she added as her own strength surpassed Kate's.

'We're going to take her down now, Mrs Sheldon, so perhaps you'd like to come to my office.'

Fran followed meekly, her thoughts at last beginning to grasp the situation. Kate had suffered a massive haemorrhage, and the awful truth was dawning: her Kate – a miscarriage? It seemed the only explanation and yet she dared not, could not, would *not* believe it of her.

Outside in the corridor Luke was sitting on a bench beside Prue. Her friends were there to support her, that was a comfort – even if Luke Hammond was the last person she had expected to see. He raised his eyebrows in sympathy before she disappeared into the office.

'Sit down, Mrs Sheldon. Obviously this has been an enormous shock for you so a nurse is bringing a cup of tea – and one for your friend as well.'

'Is Kate going to be all right, Sister?'

'The surgeon will investigate her condition and do all that's necessary. I . . . take it that you probably didn't know that Kate was pregnant?'

Fran shook her head solemnly as tears threatened. She wished the truth could have been delayed. She needed to hear it from Kate's own lips – and yet she knew that these medical people were hardly likely to make a mistake. 'I – I didn't know,' she sobbed, and the sister placed an arm around Fran's shoulders and patiently waited while the shock flushed out with hot, emotional tears.

'She could have lost her life,' the sister went on gently. 'But, thanks to prompt attention and a speedy journey here, she will be all right. As yet we don't have all the details. Kate is too weak to be questioned except for the relevant details, and we'll know more when the surgeon has completed his investigation.'

'I just can't believe it,' Fran said at last, and in faltering sentences explained her situation to the sister, who was deeply moved by the tragedy that had necessitated Kate's staying in Sherbrook.

'You mustn't blame yourself, Mrs Sheldon. Kate is eighteen, after all, and it does happen frequently.'

'Not in my family!' Fran exclaimed vehemently. 'What will my in-laws say and think? And my friends and neighbours?'

The sister was silent for a few moments, then she said: 'In cases like this we have to record the truth of course, but for the sake of propriety you are at liberty so say that Kate required an emergency appendicectomy.' The sister smiled. 'I'm sure that's the best idea.'

'I hate lies and deceit,' Fran mumbled. 'My husband wouldn't tolerate it.'

'But it's for Kate's good in the long run. She's the one who has to live with it.'

'She should be ashamed,' Fran spat out. 'I hope she'll have the grace to feel guilty.'

'Right now, Mrs Sheldon, she's lucky to be alive. I'm sure your late husband would be thankful that Kate's life has been spared.'

Fran's chin trembled. She felt sick inside. Of course she was thankful that Kate was alive – and Henry would have been philosophical in such a situation. There were things she needed to know, but that could wait until later. 'When can I see the doctor?' she asked humbly.

'Right now, Mrs Sheldon, I think it would be better if you went home with your friends. Give yourself time to get over the shock, and perhaps tomorrow when you visit Kate you'll be able to have a word with Mr Radcliffe, the consultant. Don't worry, Mrs Sheldon, Kate is in good hands. Now, do you feel up to giving me a few particulars? Kate's full name, your address, her date of birth and where we can contact you, should we need to?'

Fran's mind was not at all clear, but she gave the sister the necessary details. Then Luke and Prue helped her along the corridors and out into the forecourt, where the cold northeasterly wind chilled her cheeks and brought fresh tears to her eyes. She sat in the back seat with Prue but hardly spoke a word until Luke drew up in front of the house. Ruby ran to meet her mother at the gate.

'Is Kate all right, Mum?' she asked anxiously.

Fran reasserted herself. She wanted to rest her head against a masculine chest and weep for ever, but she was the head of this household and needed to show strong courage.

'We'll have to pray that she will be, dear,' she said with a calmness she didn't feel. 'An emergency appendix – she's in the operating theatre now.' She turned to Prue and glanced at Luke. 'You'll come in for a bite and something warm, won't you?'

They followed her in. She showed them into the back kitchen, where coals glowed red in the grate and a log hissed and spat.

'I'll put the kettle on,' she said. 'Please make yourselves comfortable. The front room is too cold to sit in.'

Ma was peeling potatoes, and Ruby set out the best china cups and saucers on an oak tray, while Hilda and Babs went to greet Aunt Prue and survey, not without some suspicion, the stranger.

Fran's energies would have been better spent, she felt, on swearing vengeance on that Maurice Lambert, who she felt certain was responsible for Kate's condition, but with the younger girls around she played the role of hostess to the best of her ability. An Irish stew prepared the previous day was simmering on the stove and Fran invited her guests to eat with the family.

'It isn't much,' she said. 'At least it will keep out the cold before you start back for Sherbrook. We were preparing a birthday tea for Kate, but we shan't be needing that now.'

'I'd like to wait to hear news of Kate to take back to the Maitlands,' Luke said. 'I'll be happy to take you back with me, Mrs Belmont.'

'I feel Fran needs someone,' Prue said. 'I could stay overnight if you need company, Fran. Sam and Marion can manage without me, same as they have to when I get a difficult delivery.'

Fran sighed. She knew they meant well, but what she really wanted was to be by herself to think and try to come to terms with what had happened. 'If only Henry were here,' she murmured disconsolately.

Ruby went to her mother's side and put her hand in Fran's. 'Kate'll be all right, Mum. I'll be good and do all I can to help. We'll be able to visit Kate in hospital, won't we?'

'Oh yes, please, Mummy,' Babs cried eagerly, not realising the seriousness of the situation.

'Fran's eyes filled yet again. 'Kate is very ill,' she said softly. 'But as soon as the doctor thinks it's all right, we'll all go to see her. Meanwhile you can write to her, of course, and draw her some pictures.'

Fran went out into the scullery where Ma had brewed the tea. She carried the tray into the kitchen. 'Come on, Ma, have a cup of tea with us.'

Gran Brown was pleased to see Prue, but doubtful about Luke Hammond's presence. There was something in his dark, bewitching eyes that was just that bit too mysterious, yet he had offered his services gallantly and helped to get Kate to hospital quickly. She felt an atmosphere in the kitchen as they sipped their tea in silence. Fran was hiding something, she could tell, and was bursting with it. Maybe she should be grateful for the visitors' presence in preventing an outburst.

'You have to ring the hospital at two o'clock, I believe you said,' Luke commented. 'Can I take you to the telephone box? You don't have the telephone yourself?'

Fran grunted. 'Heavens, no! And I can't use a telephone. I'll have to see if my neighbour will help me out. He's a policeman and has been very good to me since we came here.'

'I'll phone for you, of course, Mrs Sheldon. There's no need to bother your neighbours. There must be a telephone kiosk nearby.'

'Yes, in the next street. I don't like imposing on you though, Captain Hammond. I'm sure you must be wanting to get back to Sherbrook.'

She endeavoured to sound officious but in truth was grateful for Luke Hammond's help.

'I want to know how Kate fares first, and if there's any way in which I can help further you have only to say.'

'You've been most kind as it is, but you intended to spend your leave with the Maitlands.'

'It's only a short leave now as I'm hoping to return to Sherbrook for Christmas, then it's a three-month trip to the Mediterranean.'

'I meant what I said about staying overnight, Fran,' Prue said. 'Or I could take the two little ones back to Sherbrook with me until things have settled down here?'

Fran answered without hesitation. 'No, you've both been very kind but I can't impose any more. It was nice of you to accompany

Kate to the hospital, Prue, and it's lovely to have you here for a bit, but your family needs you. I'm over the shock now. I've got to prepare myself for when Kate comes home. She'll have to convalesce for quite a while. I must write to Mrs Maitland later on.' She sighed, and looked directly at Luke. 'Perhaps you'd be good enough to thank her from me, for seeing to Kate, and tell her I'll be in touch as soon as we know that Kate is well on the road to recovery.'

'I'm sure she'll want to visit you herself, perhaps when Kate comes out of hospital, but that won't be for at least two weeks, I should think.'

'Mrs Maitland will be busy preparing for Christmas. This couldn't have happened at a worse time.'

Fran busied herself in the scullery, and with Gran's and Prue's help made the meagre Irish stew stretch to feed the visitors and themselves, with plenty of fresh, home-grown vegetables. They had hardly finished eating when Luke reminded Fran that it was almost two o'clock. She felt less strained now after eating the hot food, and there was more colour in her cheeks, but she was in no hurry to contact the hospital. Or was she feeling inadequate because she had been forced to admit that she couldn't use a telephone? Back in the village of Sherbrook there had been no need of such things, and since coming to live in Brimdene she had come to rely on kind neighbours.

'I'd really like to freshen myself up before I go anywhere,' she said. In the bathroom she locked herself in, and while she washed she fought back more tears as she considered the disgrace Kate had brought upon them all. Whether family, friends or neighbours ever found out or not, she would know that Kate had cheapened herself, given her body to the first young man who made demands. Luke's presence here reminded her all too clearly of a certain Christmas party when she had not behaved with as much decorum as she should. She had been disloyal to Henry – and paid a high price. First Lennie, then Henry and Pa, and now Kate in trouble – was there no end to the burdens she must bear? And alone, that was the worst part.

Chapter Seven

The news, when Luke was put through to the hospital ward, was that Kate was back from the operating theatre and was comfortable. She was not allowed to have visitors until the following day. Luke insisted on Ruby accompanying them to the telephone kiosk, and he did his best to show both Fran and Ruby how to use a public call box. Fran was still too on edge to take in what he said, but Ruby quickly picked it up and was able to follow the written directions.

'Just make sure you come with plenty of pennies,' Luke warned, 'as sometimes the phone is out of order. If the operator can't get a reply, she'll tell you to press button B to get your money back before she asks to you try again later. It's quite simple really, and when you've done it once or twice you won't be afraid of it. Then you can teach your mother and sisters.'

Fran was grateful for the trouble Luke was taking to help them, but she was glad when they took their leave. Ruby was sent hotfoot to tell her other grandparents and Aunt Sissy, but Sissy was at work until the next day.

Fran couldn't settle to doing anything, even though there was so much to prepare for Christmas. She knew she had to carry on for the sake of the girls but the burden in her heart was heavy. Everyone was sympathetic and help came from many quarters but Fran was obliged to keep her secret to herself. There was no one she could turn to or confide in.

Kate was frail-looking when Fran visited her the following afternoon. It was Sunday so she went alone while the girls were at Sunday school. The buses had all been full so Fran felt tensed up even before she arrived at Ward 14. Luke had thoughtfully gone out to buy flowers for Fran to take to Kate before he left, but Kate hardly opened her eyes.

'How d'you feel dear?' Fran asked gently, stroking the slim, limp hand.

Kate's eyes flickered and she opened them briefly, but it was as if she couldn't bring herself to look at her mother. 'I'm sorry, Mum,' she whispered huskily, and tears trickled down her cheeks.

'We've weathered a few storms, Katie dear, and we'll get through this one, I dare say. All we want is for you to get well quickly, and come home to us.'

After that there didn't seem much to say. Fran explained that she had brought a clean nightie and some toilet things, but Kate continued to lie still and silent as if she were waiting to die. After a while the sister came on duty and asked Fran to go to the office.

'Your daughter has had a blood transfusion to replace some of what she lost. She might well have died but for the prompt action in getting her here, Mrs Sheldon. You have a lot to thank them for, whoever it was, but Kate is not out of the wood yet.' The sister turned her head to gaze unseeing at papers on her desk and Fran knew that there was more to come. 'Mr Radcliffe will see you himself on Tuesday, but he asked me to tell you that she may never be able to conceive again. She had been quite violently used, Mrs Sheldon. He suspects that internal damage was incurred before the bleeding commenced. She's too ill at the present time to be questioned, so he particularly asked that she be allowed to remain undisturbed for the next few days. She's feeling lonely and hurt. The anaesthetic causes sickness to add to her troubles – but we'll do all in our power to get her well again.'

Fran went home feeling cold and dejected. She knew that Kate's life had hung in the balance, but to hear it from the sister – fear engulfed her. It was her fault, of course; she ought to have brought Kate with the rest of the family to Brimdene. It was too much to expect that Mrs Maitland would keep her eye on Kate, and why should Prue and Sam be made to feel responsible? They had all promised to look after her but she couldn't be watched all the time. Dear Henry, he had done his best to teach the girls honesty and how to behave well. Fran had continued to instruct them in the rights and wrongs of society and she really had thought Kate was old enough to know better. How could she ever hold her head up again?

And to think that Luke Hammond had been the one to give his time to help in matters which, she was sure, were of no consequence to him. He had been kind, Fran had to admit, but once back at sea he would quickly forget her and her troubles in spite of all that he had said in the past. He wouldn't want anything to do with her now that her reputation was scarred. Anger and vexation tore her to pieces, and being obliged to keep the truth to herself did nothing to ease her guilty conscience. She realised she had been a trifle offhand with Prue yesterday, but today she longed for someone in whom she could confide. Instead she returned home. Tea was set out, and the other grandparents had come with Nathan and his family, all eager to hear news of Kate and to sympathise with Fran.

The next week passed uneventfully. Mr Radcliffe saw Fran at last, explaining that Kate would remain weak for some time and must not be upset.

'I have gently tried to persuade her to tell me what happened,' he said, 'for the sake of treating her. But she only says that someone took advantage of her. She will name no names – so I'm afraid there's nothing we can do to bring the young man to justice. I'm presuming it was a *young* man.'

'She was walking out with a boy who is away at college. He could have gone home for a weekend, I suppose. I can only pray that Kate will tell me the truth eventually,' Fran said.

'She's on the mend,' Mr Radcliffe reassured. 'I am confident of that, but only time will tell if permanent damage has been done. It will be some months before she can return to work, though.'

'She won't be returning to her previous employment,' Fran said hastily. 'That's one thing I have decided. She must live with us here in Brimdene.'

'That seems a sensible idea, but that won't be for some considerable time yet.'

Fran didn't feel too happy about her sudden decision. It was as if the words had been put into her mouth, for she hadn't planned to say any such thing. It must be the right decision, though – and she felt it was Henry's influence that had compelled her to make it.

When she told Kate, she remained totally unmoved, showing no sign of pleasure or regret. Although they said she was making progress, she refused to talk to her mother and seemed afraid to look directly at her. Fran took this as a sign of guilt. It created a rift between them and made the situation much more difficult for Fran to handle. Every step she took through the long corridor seemed to be a stamp of disapproval on her own hitherto good character. She was weary of the daily journeys to hospital, and lethargic about the so-called festive season – what did she have to be festive about? She faced the driving rain to go to the bus stop. In seconds she would be soaked to the skin, and shoppers would push and shove to get on the infrequent buses as the late afternoon became dark and dismal.

Suddenly a hand clasped hers round the unbrella handle and raised it higher.

'Here, let me share – the car is just across the road.' Luke's voice was welcome in her moment of self-pity.

'Luke!' she gasped in surprise, her eyes brightening as she gazed up at him. 'I thought you'd gone away?'

'Not yet, tomorrow actually, but I wanted to see you before I left. I would have come in to see Kate but I wasn't sure of what reception I'd get.' He smiled a warm, hopeful smile.

'You should have done. She knows you and you might have been able to cheer her up. They say she's improving, but she won't say much to me.'

They waited to cross the road as an ambulance came rushing round the corner, its bell clanging discordantly.

'How I hate that sound! It makes me feel quite sick,' Fran said.

'Then let's get away from here for a while. I'm sure you know somewhere where we can get a cup of tea?'

'No, Luke, really, I must get home to the children.'

'Your mother is there, and we needn't be long. You look as if you're the one who needs cheering up – and I won't take no for an answer.'

Fran didn't need to direct him to a teashop, he had already seen one on the main street of the suburb where the hospital was situated. It was an 'olde worlde' quaint place with willow-patterned plates, cups and saucers, and the waitress was a middle-aged woman with wrinkled stockings. Her dress, cap and apron had seen better days.

'This isn't quite what you're used to,' Fran said apologetically.

'We can be alone and undisturbed here. I want you to know how pleased I am that Kate is all right. Mrs Maitland would have visited herself, but –' he shrugged – 'you know how it is, Fran. Christmas and all that.'

Fran smiled. 'Yes, Luke, I know how it is. If she won't come to me, then I shall have to visit her. Kate is my daughter, but being employed by the Maitlands she was in their charge. Surely I have some rights? Don't you think they owe it to me to tell me as much as they know?' Fran clenched her fists across the table as her tone became more aggressive.

Luke covered her hands with his and gently unknotted them.

'They want to give you time. I want to try to give you peace of mind. Forget the Maitlands, forget Kate even – just for half an hour. I want to look at you and hypnotise your worries away. I want to see you smile – just for me . . .'

Fran pulled her hands away angrily. 'For goodness sake, Luke,' she hissed. 'That's the last thing *I* want. For the past eighteen months I've had nothing but trouble to cope with on my own – I don't know that I can take any more – and now Kate brings this disgrace on me.' She fumbled for a handkerchief. She didn't mean to let herself go but the tears fell unbidden for several seconds. When the waitress brought the tea and toasted teacakes that Luke had ordered, Fran turned her head towards the curtained window and composed herself.

'I . . . I'm sorry, Luke. You see, you shouldn't have come here. This isn't your problem.'

'Oh, but it is, and you must let me share it with you, Fran dear. I may not have any family of my own, but no one can ever know just how much I'd like to have someone to share things with. I've thought about you so often, wondered just how you were coping since you were forced to move, but I realised I had to be discreet. I had no address to write to, and it wouldn't have been prudent to send via the Maitlands. That doesn't mean that every waking thought hasn't been tortured with visions of you.'

Fran sniffed and dabbed again at her eyes. 'That's no way to talk. I don't want to hear such things. You're a young man with a different girl in every port,' she said, trying to make light of this embarrassing conversation.

'Oh yes, I admit to being a few years younger than you, and to having a girl in every port – but not a different one.'

Fran looked across at him quizzically, then saw the mischievous twinkle in his eyes. 'You're there in a mist of loveliness on every quayside waiting for me, Fran. It's no use denying it. I'm serious – deadly serious – and now that I've found you I shan't let you go.'

Fran poured the tea solemnly. Luke's presence gave her peace. He was right, he offered her peace of mind. He was outside the family and only he knew the truth of Kate's condition. In-laws, her own brother and his family were all sympathetic, but she couldn't open her heart to any of them, not even dear Sissy. At times she felt like a castaway when Kate wouldn't speak to her.

'Cheer up, Fran,' he urged. 'I can imagine just how desolate you've been feeling over these past few days. Express your fears, and your hopes – I want to be part of them.'

'I have plenty of friends and family,' she said quietly. For a brief moment she had allowed herself to be lured by his persuasive charm, but Luke Hammond had seduced her once before and she wasn't likely to make the same mistake again. She changed her expression to one of cold disdain and sniffed haughtily. 'I've made my life in Brimdene now and live solely for the girls. You've been kind. I don't wish to offend you, Luke, but please, forget me – go away and forget we ever met.'

'How can I when my son, the only thing that is really mine, my flesh and blood, lies in a grave in Sherbrook? One day, when my days in the Navy are over, I want to return there to live – and with you, Lennie's mother, the only woman I have ever loved,' he declared.

'Don't insult my intelligence, Luke,' she snapped impatiently. 'You've travelled across the breadth and length of Great Britain, visited countries all over the world, and haven't given me so much as a mite's consideration. I'm not a fool.'

'If I didn't love you, would I continue to visit the Maitlands for the sole purpose of placing flowers on my son's grave? With an obsession to get a glimpse of you? And in the past torture myself with what might be going on behind the curtains at the old mill house? We were destined for each other, Fran,' he said, leaning towards her.

There was a long pause while Fran fought for control of a situation she seemed in danger of losing.

'I must hurry home to the family. I'll catch the bus, Luke. It would be better. That doesn't mean, though, that I'm not grateful for your support. You might have saved Kate's life – I couldn't have borne another . . .'

'Calm down. The last thing I want is to upset or hurry you into anything. But I shan't let go easily, I promise you.'

Fran drank the tea, her mind in utter confusion. As if she didn't have enough on her plate without this man wooing her! She was past all that, and surely there were many women in the world far more sophisticated and attractive than she?

'Perhaps it would be better to wait until after Christmas to see Mrs Maitland,' she said after a while. 'I've decided to keep Kate here in Brimdene, but when she's ready for a job, goodness knows what she'll do. I want to write to these people, the Lamberts, in my parents' old cottage, but until I can get some kind of sense out of Kate I can't go accusing anyone.'

'Give yourself time to think things out, Fran. I know it's a well-worn cliché, but it takes two, you know.'

'Does it? Then perhaps I should refresh your memory, which seems to be equally well worn, Luke Hammond.' She refused to be patronised. 'You took advantage of me all those many years ago. I don't recall that I had much say in the matter, and any disgrace I felt I had to bear alone as well as live with the shame of deceiving the man I married. There was no sharing the experience. The one takes what he wants, the other has to accept the consquences. I was more fortunate than Kate, my wedding was all prepared so my shame was veiled – and luckily I married a kind, thoughtful, good man. You went on your merry way and never gave the matter another thought.'

'Fran, I did – I never ceased to think about you! But what could I do once you were married to Henry? I loved you too much – and still do – to hurt you.' He pushed his empty plate away. 'Besides, my dear,' he added, 'I was not the first.'

Fran's cheeks glowed a dark crimson as she faced him with resentment.

'And *that*,' she said pointedly, 'is not hurting me? How could you be so cruel?'

Luke looked suitably chastened. 'I . . . I'm sorry, Fran. That was unforgivable of me.'

'I agree, it was, but for your information and to put the record straight, Henry and I had been engaged for a long time. My employer would not release me and it was only by putting up the banns that we finally made her agree. We were forced to wait – wait beyond human endurance. We saw one another so seldom, and when we did . . . As if it's any concern of yours!' Then, with bitter passion, she said: 'You'll never be half the man Henry was.'

During the ensuing silence Fran regretted her condemnation. Her cruel tongue had matched his thoughtlessness.

'I think we had better go,' he said softly but firmly. 'It seems we are both capable of hurting one another. I can only excuse myself by admitting to a feverish jealousy, and I don't intend to apologise for that.'

He clicked his fingers impatiently for the bill, and a few moments later they were walking back towards the hospital. He insisted that he drive her home. She thanked him shortly and ran into the house without inviting him in.

The girls had broken up from school and were excited, so full of chatter and laughter that Fran was obliged to enter into the Christmas spirit, albeit with an aching heart.

Kate improved slowly. She begged to be allowed home in time for Christmas but the surgeon advised against it.

'Another haemorrhage could be fatal,' he warned Fran. 'And,' he added, inclining his head with a sympathetic expression, 'Kate is unhappy. I appreciate that at home with her sisters she might come out of her depression, but it doesn't seem fair to them. I don't want to hurry things, and I must remind you that she will take a long while to recuperate from the fright alone. I'd like to keep her here until the New Year. Perhaps you could come and spend a whole day with her. An unusual request, I know, but I believe there are bridges to be built and I'd like the foundation laid before she leaves here.'

'Naturally I want to know how all this happened, Mr Radcliffe, but I'm not going to reprimand her if that's what you think.'

The senior surgeon was a portly man, every inch the gentleman, with soft grey-blue eyes and an unhurried manner. He laid a convincing hand on Fran's arm. 'I've become very fond of young Katie,' he said. 'There's pain in her eyes. By now, most young girls would have accepted the inevitable – the kind of girl who finds herself in Kate's predicament, that is.'

'Is there a "kind of girl"?' Fran asked.

'Yes, indeed, Mrs Sheldon. But in Kate's case it has become very obvious that this situation arose through no fault of hers, and that the worst hurt is because she believes she has vexed you. I might be quite wrong, of course. Night Sister reports that she cries a lot and when she does sleep she has very disturbing dreams. Now, all I'm suggesting is that after Christmas, when all the revelry is over, you try to find time to spend with Kate to get across your . . . well, your forgiveness, perhaps?'

'I'm sorry, Mr Radcliffe,' Fran said in a small voice. 'I wasn't aware that my feelings were so obvious. I'm old-fashioned, and without a father now the girls have to depend on me for their upbringing. I do blame myself for what's happened. If I had paid more heed to the fact that Kate was desperate to come to Brimdene to live, this might have been avoided. I'll do all I can to help Kate, of course.'

The surgeon walked away from the petite, auburn-haired woman, feeling desperately sorry for her. The local GP had given him all the relevant details of the family, and he realised that Mrs Sheldon had borne her crosses stoically. He suspected, though, that she was so determined to bring the girls up the way their father had wished that she was both overprotective and dominant. He didn't tell her that Kate had confided in him and told him everything except the culprit's name. Gently he had explained to Kate that when she was feeling better she must sit down with her mother and tell her the story just as she had told him. But Kate had wept, admitting that she was terrified of what her mother would say and do.

'She can't eat you, child,' he had comforted. 'And when she knows the truth she'll be as sorry for you as we all are. But it's over now, my Katie, and you're going to put the past behind you. Let's hope no one wants to see your appendix scar,' he added conspiratorially, and with a friendly pat he passed on to the next patient.

It was a strange Christmas. To all outward appearances the usual festivities took place. Plenty of good food, mince pies and Christmas pudding, the girls all excited when they found the small silver charms in their portion. Oohs, and aahs at the goodies they found in their stockings and presents, and real excitement that they were going to spend the afternoon and evening with Uncle Nathan and his family. Even Gran Brown was going too, as well as the other grandparents, while Fran walked the three miles to the hospital to spend part of the day with Kate.

Thankfully it was a dry day, and not too cold. Fran set off laden with Kate's gifts and an enormous bunch of flowers. They had arrived by special delivery on Christmas Eve from Luke to Fran with a gold-edged card sending his greetings and begging her forgiveness. She put the card on the fire, once read, then explained the bouquet away by saying they were intended for Kate. Luke need never know.

During that long walk Fran had plenty of time to think. The timing of Luke's reappearance into her life was fortuitous. But for his prompt action Kate might well have bled to death in the ambulance, no matter how efficient the ambulance crew were. He was kind and considerate, handsome, well-mannered – she should be flattered that he paid court to her, a mere humble widow from a different class and background. In a way, deep down she supposed she was flattered by his attention. She had to admit that it was good to have someone to talk to about Kate's problem, but the idea struck her that perhaps he was interested in Kate, not her! The notion grew – was he the man who had taken advantage of Kate, just as he had taken her years before? His concern might be a way of appeasing his conscience, and of course he would have sworn Kate to secrecy. Yes, it would have been so easy for him, visiting the Maitland household with the son of the family – gentry sons made it their sport to seduce young servants. But then her idea was squashed. As she neared the hospital she remembered that Luke had been away at sea for the past eighteen months. She refused to relent, though, and shrugged off the notion that she was quite relieved that Kate's seducer could not have been Luke Hammond – if he had told her the truth.

With so many thoughts swirling round in her brain, Fran reached the hospital sooner than she anticipated. In spite of the parcels she carried, her step had quickened in tune to her ideas. Now she had to convince Kate that she was not an ogre. She accused Kate of not communicating but she guessed that in her turmoil she was equally to blame, so she lifted her head high, put on a happy smile and entered the ward.

Her spirits tumbled. Kate's bed was made up and empty. The blood coursed through her veins and Fran felt dizzy. Then someone touched her arm.

'Hullo, Mrs Sheldon, merry Christmas,' Sister said cheerfully. 'We've moved Kate out on the balcony. We've another patient here a year or so older than Kate. She's made an excellent recovery after her operation and we thought Kate might respond to someone of her own age.' Sister pointed to the double doors where, to Fran's surprise, Kate was coming to greet her.

'Oh, Kate, how lovely to see you walking about! Happy Christmas, darling.' They fell on each other and wept, the barrier of mistrust suddenly crushed. 'Oh, this is silly, isn't it?' Fran mopped up her tears. 'We missed you so much this morning. The girls and Gran all send their love and say, "hurry home".'

'It's been quite exciting here, Mum,' Kate enthused. 'We all had a present, even old Mrs Court who'll be ninety-three on New Year's Day. Come and see. I had a little embroidered picture, which says "The best teacher is Life, the best friend is God", isn't that lovely? I shall keep it for always.'

Kate opened her presents excitedly, while Fran read the picture verse several times over. Such a wise saying. Was this responsible for Kate's change in attitude? What she, Kate's mother, should have been able to achieve, this little picture had done?

'What gorgeous flowers, Mum!' Kate said as she pulled the wrapping off one of the gifts. 'Who sent those? I hope you didn't – ?'

'No, dear.' Fran sighed. 'I'm afraid my pension won't stretch to buying flowers at this time of the year. Captain Hammond sent these. Wasn't that kind? I don't know how you'll thank him, though, as he'll be back at sea by now.'

'He is a very kind man, Mum,' Kate said slowly, and there was some hidden meaning in her words and look which made Fran feel embarrassed. She urged Kate on to open the rest of the presents and cards to hide the faint flush that had coloured her cheeks, and shortly afterwards the nurses brought tea, sandwiches and small fancy cakes as well as slices of rich Christmas cake for visitors and patients to enjoy on this special day.

'The nurses and doctors came round with lanterns singing carols last evening, Mum,' Kate said. 'And tomorrow they're putting on a pantomime. Sister said you could bring the others if you like. There'll be buses, won't there? It's at three o'clock, in the main hall downstairs.'

'The girls will like that. I should think you'll soon be able to come home now. You're looking so much better, Kate.'

Kate's eyes misted over and she dropped her head. 'I want to come home, Mum, of course I do, but I'll think everyone knows – you know?'

'You've had your appendix out so you won't be able to do any heavy work for a while.' Fran made a rare gesture and held Kate's hand firmly in her own. 'I'm your mother, Kate, so naturally I want to know exactly what happened, and I think you'll feel better if you tell me the truth. After all, I shall hve to go and see the Maitlands and the Lamberts . . .'

'No! No! It wasn't Maurice, Mum, really, truly it wasn't. I haven't seen him since the summer, he's been away at college.'

'If you don't tell me who it was dear, how can I believe you?'

'It was dark, late, the night I got held up going back to Sherbrook from here.'

'Kate dear, look at me. We'll talk about it when you come home, calmly, rationally, but just set my mind at rest on one thing, please.'

'What's that, Mum?'

'Was it someone at Sherbrook House? Or – um – someone who visits there, maybe?'

'You can't think Captain Hammond would do such a thing! Oh no, Mum, he's so gentle and kind. He acted so quickly, he knew what to do – but he's old enough to be my father. Oh, Mum, whatever would Dad say to all this? I would never bring such shame on you or Dad, you know that, don't you? Please, Mum, *please* . . . say you do?' Kate's weeping was heartbreaking. A nurse brought a screen and left Fran and Kate alone in their sorrow – a sorrow at last shared. In hushed tones they talked until the hurt was bearable between them. Fran was horrified at the thought of her Kate being molested and raped almost on the doorstep of Sherbrook House. She chided Kate gently for not telling Mrs Sturmey the truth at once.

'You must have known he might have put you in the family way.'

'I did tell Mrs Maitland eventually. When I realised, I wanted to die, Mum. I thought you'd blame me and honestly there was nothing I could do, nothing.' As she sobbed she remembered scratching

Felix's face with the brooch pin, but she decided against telling anyone that. 'I tried my best to fight him off, but he was too big, too heavy.'

'What made you tell Mrs Maitland then?' Fran asked.

'I went to Dad's grave. I just w – wanted to be n – near him ... She found me and I was soaked through so she took me home. Mrs Sturmey had already guessed what was wrong with me. I'd been vomiting in the mornings, you see. They gave me some herbal medicine to take to get rid of it, and – well, you know the rest. They all thought it was Maurice, but he's not like that, Mum, honestly he isn't.'

'All men are like that, Kate,' Fran said dispassionately. 'From now on you'll be wary of the types of men around. Give them a hint of opportunity and they'll take what they want, so be on your guard.' Fran sniffed her contempt. 'Still, after this you won't want anything more to do with young men for a while. I don't blame you, Kate. The doctor says you were ill-used, so now you know what men are capable of. You'll have to resign yourself to being a spinster. No man wants a wife who can't give him sons – and it's unlikely you'll be able to bear children.'

'B – but I could still get married, Mum. Maurice and I – '

'I don't want to know, Kate. And don't think Maurice Lambert will have noble ideas of still wanting you. When he knows what's happened – and you'd have to tell him – he'll want nothing more to do with you. No, Kate, you'd best forget him. You'll be staying at home from now on until work can be found for you. But first we want to see you fit and well again. When I go to Sherbrook I'll explain that you've been very ill – they'll understand.'

During the long walk home Fran felt pangs of guilt. Had she been too hard on her daughter? Had she taken advantage of Kate's honesty? Had Kate been truly honest? This college lad, nice though he appeared, wasn't Kate's type. No, all the things she had said had to be said sooner or later. She could not allow Kate to continue the friendship with Maurice Lambert. Henry wouldn't have allowed it and Fran was determined to keep up the standards set by him.

As the January cold, snowy weather came in, and Kate was at last home, she became sick and tired of hearing her mother's words, 'Your father wouldn't approve and that's final.'

One Monday morning when Fran was busy at the wash tub, Kate dusted the kitchen and then sat down by the fire to read the *News Chronicle*. She tired easily and was still seeing the doctor for anaemia but did all she could to help around the house. She took over some of the cooking, which she loved to do, but when her mother and grandmother were doing the family wash she knew better than to intrude into their argy-bargy. It was always over some trivial disagreement, usually involving Uncle Eric, Auntie Annie and May, and Kate was old enough to realise that it was because her mother was tired from overwork and worry.

Kate was eager to be allowed out so that she could post the long letter she was secretly writing to Maurice. Her mother had forbidden her to correspond with him, so she kept silent about the several letters that had been exchanged during her stay in hospital. The young probationer nurse on duty at night had willingly posted patients' mail first thing in the morning when she went off duty. But by now Maurice must be wondering why the letters had stopped, and Kate couldn't understand why she had received nothing at home. Her thoughts were frequently with Maurice. She longed to meet him and explain all that had happened because she knew he would understand.

She turned the paper over and there on the back page the name Felix leapt out at her. She read on to learn that the body of a young man had been found hanging from a branch of a tree in Hyde Park, London. At first they had been unable to identify him except to publish his description, which included a deep, savage scar on his cheek. His friend at college, Maurice Lambert, had then come forward to identify him, saying that the young man had been in trouble at college, as well as with the police for drunken behaviour. His family had disowned him. Unwanted, penniless, a disturbed vagrant, he had finally reached the end of his tether and been driven to commit suicide.

Kate just stared at the printed words in the column. As she read and reread every single word she realised that Maurice must have seen him after the rape incident, as he evidently knew about the scar. How had Felix explained that away? she wondered. Did Maurice know what happened that night or did he have a distorted version from Felix and blame her? It was imperative for Kate to send a letter to Maurice, if only to say how sorry she was for his friend. What Felix had done to her seemed to pale into insignificance now as she visualised him hanging lifeless from a tree. She could never forget what he had done, but he didn't deserve such an end as that.

Later in the afternoon Kate feigned a headache and went upstairs to lie down in the little boxroom, which Fran had lovingly prepared for when Kate came out of hospital. The wallpaper was pale pink with dainty rosebuds all over it, and now Kate sat on the side of her bed and stared blankly at it. She couldn't tell Maurice the true story in a letter lest it got into the wrong hands. She did tell him that she had been forbidden to correspond with him, but that when her mother visited Sherbrook, weather permitting in a week's time, she could meet him mid-morning on the station at Brimdene. In order to post the letter surreptitiously she asked if she might go to meet the younger girls from school to try to get rid of her headache, and Fran agreed. Kate begged Maurice to reply and waited anxiously, but every morning when she asked her mother if there were any letters for her, the answer was always the same: 'Who on earth are you expecting a letter from?'

When a letter had arrived bearing a Sherbrook postmark, Fran knew that somehow Kate had disobeyed her. She was as determined to put a stop to the friendship as Kate was to continue it, so she used it to light the fire in the kitchen grate. Fran watched it blacken and curl, then disintegrate. Only when it was completely destroyed did she feel remorse for her hasty action. She should have confronted Kate with the evidence, but hadn't she had enough to contend with?

Even though there was still no word from Maurice, Kate decided to go to town while her mother was at Sherbrook.

'I'll come with you to the station to see you off,' she told Fran.

'But your interview with Mrs Neale at the hotel isn't until two o'clock,' Fran said.

'I might go to the Labour Exchange and find out if any other jobs are going.'

'But Aunt Sissy has gone to a lot of trouble to fix this interview up, Kate.'

'I shall still go to the hotel, Mum. I'm determined to find a job if I can't go back to the Maitlands. It's pretty obvious they don't want me anyway as they've taken on Maurice's sister – so Aunt Prue said in her Christmas letter.'

'They would know I wouldn't let you return there after what's happened. Mrs Maitland did write quite a nice letter at Christmas. Better to be polite and friendly, I suppose, but I shall speak my mind when I go up to the big house to fetch your wages today.'

'Mum, it wasn't their fault, was it? How were they to know that the train would be delayed that night?'

Fran grunted. 'I wish I could find out whose fault it was,' she said huffily.

'No one knows but me, and I'm not telling you any more than I've told you already,' Kate replied firmly. 'It's over and done with, Mum. It's me that's got to live with the memory, but I want to try to forget.' She buttoned up her warm coat and pulled on her woollen gloves. 'I've realised since I've been home that I quite like cooking, so I might try to find a job in a kitchen somewhere. Come on, Mum, or you'll miss the train.'

At the station Kate bought a platform ticket and waited to see her mother safely in a compartment where it was warm. Soon the whistle blew and the train eased away from the platform. She watched it get smaller and smaller until it turned the bend and disappeared out of sight. She stood still for a moment. It occurred to her that Maurice might already be on the platform. Not having received any reply to her letter, she didn't know whether he had returned to college, but she knew he would make every effort to get here if he could. She had indicated that the reason she needed to see him was most urgent and couldn't be discussed in letters.

There were few people about since it was not yet ten o'clock, so she idled the time away by looking at things on the newsagent's stall. She enquired about the next trains due in. Another half an hour to wait for the Sherbrook one, and from the other direction the London train was not expected for over an hour. As the minutes ticked by she began to feel cold and empty. She hadn't eaten much breakfast so she went into the buffet and bought a large bun and a pot of tea. If Maurice arrived he could share it with her. She longed to see him again. There was so much to talk about, but she couldn't imagine what his reaction would be to her accusations against Felix. And now he was dead and unable to confess to what he had done. Whenever she thought about him she felt sick inside. He had caused her a great deal of pain and distress, but it hadn't warranted killing himself and she managed to feel some compassion for him. She wondered if he had left a letter giving a reason for taking his own life. There had been nothing more about it in the papers, and she was glad that her mother had made no comment about the story.

Kate sat in the buffet for as long as she dared. The Sherbrook train came in but there was no sign of Maurice, so she waited on the platform for the London train. She became very tired of pacing up and down. Eventually she went to the ladies' waiting room where a good fire burned in the hearth. The London train came and went, a later one from Sherbrook, but still no sign of Maurice. By now Kate's spirits had ebbed low. She went to buy a paper and returned to the waiting room to read it, but she couldn't settle. A woman came in to make up the fire for the third time. She looked suspiciously at Kate and grunted 'Ain't you got no place to go, young woman?'

'It isn't any business of yours,' Kate said shortly and with that stood up and went outside. Just one more train – he must be on the next one. But the midday trains arrived without Maurice.

With a heavy heart, aching legs and cold feet, Kate dragged herself away from the station. She mustn't be late for her appointment with Aunt Sissy's employer. Maurice wasn't coming. She must accept the fact that he couldn't make it. The new term must have started, she told herself, but that didn't explain why he hadn't written. A nasty chill crept over her as the thought occurred to her that he might have heard the truth about her illness when he was home at Christmas. While she had been in hospital his letters had been warm, loving and full of concern, especially at the length of time she had to remain there. Usually, Maurice said, after an operation for the removal of one's appendix the patient was allowed home after two weeks. Had there been complications? he wanted to know. In reply she tried to make light of her condition, only assuring him of her love.

Now Kate was forced to admit that her mother could be right. If Maurice had heard a rumour that she may never be able to have children, he might have lost interest. She needed his friendship. There was time enough to divulge the truth, she had thought, but now that Felix had committed suicide, and Maurice had been home to Sherbrook, had she left it too late?

In spite of her dismay Kate's interview went well, but the fact that at last she had secured a job in Brimdene did little to cheer her up. She knew it would please her mother, though, and she was thankful that she arrived home well before Fran. She was preparing the tea by the time she heard her mother's footsteps coming round the path at the side of the house. Hilda and Babs were squabbling as usual, and Ruby was helping Gran butter the bread.

'Whatever's all this commotion?' Fran exclaimed as she closed the back door behind her. She pulled out the hat pin, took off her hat and tossed it onto the sofa wearily. Kate was almost afraid to ask how she got on at the big house.

'Well, Katie, how did your interview go?' Fran asked.

'I can start as soon as the doctor gives me a certificate to say I'm fit. Oh, Mum, he will, won't he? Mrs Neale is so nice and wants to train me for hotel work. I told her I like cooking and she seemed pleased about that.'

Fran smiled. Kate had a job here at Brimdene. She experienced some disappointment when she heard that Kate had to live in. She had looked forward to having the family complete for a while but appreciated that it wasn't safe for young girls to be about at odd hours.

Kate didn't seem over-enthusiastic at her good fortune though. Fran supposed it was not hearing from Maurice that was making her downcast and she wished with all her heart she could rescind her hasty action. She knew she ought to own up to what she had done, but she didn't have the courage. If only Kate had been open and honest with her it need never have happened. Kate and Maurice would still be friends. Why was it that mothers and daughters couldn't seem to win one another's confidence? Fran had gone to Sherbrook unaware of the truth. She had been shocked to learn from Prue and Sam the story about Maurice's friend, Felix. By all accounts he had been in the village at the time Kate was raped. Maurice had told his parents all he knew and rumours soon spread so that Prue put two and two together.

The Maitlands had been kind but distant, and Fran was glad that all connections with them had now been severed. They had been reluctant to discuss all that had happened except to offer their sympathy.

Now Fran resolved to put the incident behind her, though she doubted that Kate would ever be able to forget. Kate needed her love and understanding. They must make a new start and at least she had the satisfaction of knowing that Kate had not let her down.

Chapter Eight

As the winter winds and snows were superseded by the bursting of spring, the Sheldons enjoyed happy times as a united family. The second anniversary of Henry's death and that of Fran's father came round and, though the pain strengthened, it became more bearable with the passage of time.

At Easter Gran Brown went to stay with Eric and his family. Fran decided to make the most of this opportunity to repaper her mother's room while the girls visited Sherbrook with Prue, Sam and Marion. The invitation was extended to Fran as well but she was in an industrious frame of mind. It was good to have time and space for herself for a change.

The weather was better than she could have hoped for. With a scarf tied round her head to keep her hair dust-free, and an old worn dress beneath her pinafore, Fran emptied all Ma's drawers and cupboards of their contents. She placed the clothes and linen in tidy piles in the girls' bedroom; then she began the task of tearing off the old wallpaper. It wasn't that dirty, but it wasn't Ma's dirt anyway, she thought, as she scraped and ripped. The previous tenants had chosen dull colours in most of the rooms, but Fran had not redecorated any room except Kate's until now. The room was south-facing, and before long she was flushed from the warmth of the sun and the exertion. Full of enthusiasm, she even began to sing as she worked.

It was strange to have the house all to herself. She was quite alone with her memories, reliving the happy days when she and Henry had first taken over the old mill house. There had been so much work to do to make it habitable, but they shared the renovations and put as much love as hard work into their home. Henry, usually acting the fool, would come home after the day's work smelling of horses, but he still caught her in a bearlike hug, kissing her face and neck in spite of varnish or paste, according to what job she was in the middle of. No amount of protest thwarted his affectionate advances, and tea was forgotten as they made love wherever they happened to find it convenient.

Fran paused and gazed out of the window. In the pit of her stomach she felt an ache, the kind of longing that could not be satiated. Her body throbbed, she felt the sap of desire, and was quite shocked at herself for having such feelings. What was the use of having feelings when there was no man to satisfy her? And, she told herself severely, there was no point in wishing. Henry was gone. Her cheeks bright crimson, Fran put twice as much energy as before into what she was doing, and when she went to bed she fell asleep exhausted.

Each day, loneliness tempted her with sensuous thoughts and desires, but she fought against such dreams as she scrubbed and revarnished the woodwork. Towards the end of the week she was ready to hang the wallpaper. She studied it carefully for the length of the pattern and to make sure she had it the right way up. She managed to find a moment's gratitude to Eric for supplying Ma with some decent wallpaper. It was a soft honeysuckle colour which wouldn't fade too easily, with tiny sprays of flowers all over it. This was the part she liked. It was akin to dressmaking, matching, cutting, placing, and she felt a sense of pride when the first piece was pasted and smoothed into position. By dinnertime she had completed one wall. She was hoping to get it all finished by Friday. Kate had a day off on Saturday and had promised to come home to help her mother. Fran stopped work briefly at midday for a light snack of bread, cheese and pickle. She couldn't spare the time to prepare meals because she was determined to finish everything before Sunday when Eric was bringing Ma home. She looked forward to the girls' returning a few days later. Prue was so generous in having them, but Fran knew it was no hardship to her since she loved children.

She left her plate on the draining board and took her second cup of tea up to Ma's room with her. Yes, she was quite impressed with her handiwork. The paper was going on like a dream. She sipped her tea. She should finish well before –

A loud knock on the front door startled her. Now who on earth could that be? she wondered. The past few weeks, with Kate settled down in her job and at last looking healthier and more content, had brought about a feeling of complacency. Uncertainty now returned. Knowing her luck, Fran thought, it had to be bad news of some kind and she delayed going to the door. Canvassers, someone selling something, she supposed. There wasn't much point in bothering to answer the door – but as she went down the stairs she could see that a man in uniform was standing in the porch. Must be Mr Blake, the policeman who lived next door, who had kindly offered to help during his off-duty period. But he was in uniform so he hadn't come for that. Fran went down the last two stairs as the knocking came again, and this time she realised that it wasn't Mr Blake. The silhouette was familiar, and a strange feeling of excitement leapt inside her. She had to stand for a few seconds before opening the door. Irrational thoughts like dashing to change into some decent clothes spun round in her head – but if she didn't hurry, Luke would go away . . .

'I thought you must be out, Fran,' he said, removing his naval cap.

Fran laughed lamely. 'I . . . I'm busy papering Ma's room,' she said quickly.

'Does that mean you aren't going to let me in?' In the dim light of the porch his eyes sparkled more than usual.

'Of course you can come in,' she said, a trifle hesitantly, 'but look at the state of me? And the house.'

'I came to see you, Fran, and you look wonderful.' He placed two hands round her waist and gazed at her. 'I like the image of a working woman. My life is full of pomp and ceremony, everyone and everything neat and tidy. The women I'm obliged to meet socially seldom have a hair out of place, with their marcel waves and perms. I like you just the way you are, a hard-working wife and mother.'

'You should have let me know you were coming. The girls are in Sherbrook with the Belmonts.'

His mouth relaxed into a sensuous smile and he inclined his head. He knew! He had plotted . . . Fran went very red and became flustered, pushing his hands away and hurrying for no particular reason into the kitchen.

'I thought you'd gone back to sea,' she said, trying to impress him with a hint of indifference.

'The refit isn't finished yet, so I've got a bit longer, and I'm beginning to like Brimdene. I've booked in at Cliff Edge Manor Hotel.'

'Oh, that's nice,' Fran said. 'That happens to be one of the hotels owned by the Neale family. They own most of Brimdene, if it comes to that. Kate's got a job at the Sand Dune Hotel, one of theirs.'

'I'm familiar with the Neale family. The youngest son was a junior officer in the Navy and has served under me. He had a bad accident abroad, so I believe he's involved in the family business now. But

I didn't come here to talk about them I came to invite you to the theatre with supper afterwards.'

'Oh, but I couldn't, Luke,' Fran said. 'It's very kind of you, but Ma will be returning soon, and I have to get everything straight before the girls come home. There's a lot still to be done.'

'Nothing that can't wait, and I insist. You're looking better than the last time we met. I trust I've been forgiven at last?'

'You presume too much then,' she said. 'I thought you'd come to enquire after Kate.'

'Well, all right, how's Kate?' He was gently mocking her and she found the wicked twinkle in his dark eyes irresistible.

'She's very well,' she said, unable to prevent herself from smiling. 'She's enjoying her work very much. On her day off tomorrow she's coming home to help me finish the room.'

'The past put firmly behind her?'

'As much as it can ever be,' Fran replied with a sigh. 'The future doesn't look too rosy for her personal life.'

Luke surveyed Fran critically. 'You've had a hard time these past two years, Fran. One accident seems to have sparked off a whole string of unfortunate incidents. Have you heard – did you know – that a certain young man committed suicide?'

'I have heard the rumour, but we've no proof that he was connected with Kate's condition. Kate still refuses to discuss the matter and there seemed no point in pursuing it. I'm just thankful that's she's alive.'

'A sensible attitude. I have a nasty feeling that you might have suspected me?'

Fran shrugged this off. 'Of course not,' she said. 'Kate's just a child.'

'I respect women too much to treat them that badly,' he said in a low voice. 'I want to take you out to show you that I respect you, Fran. Please, please say you'll come. I have the tickets here in my pocket. It's one of Ivor Novello's musicals. I know you'll enjoy it, Fran. It's time you got out and about, and I shan't be here for long.'

'But . . . but . . .' she began.

'There isn't one good reason why you shouldn't come, is there?'

She shook her head. 'You make it sound so easy,' she said simply.

'It is. Just be ready tomorrow evening at seven. I'm so looking forward to it, and I'm sure Kate will understand.'

He strode to the front door purposefully and in the porch turned as he replaced his hat. He touched it politely, his eyes magical as he smiled his farewell.

Fran could hardly breathe. She went into the front room and over the privet hedge watched his sleek saloon car drive away. He had made no attempt to touch her, not even said goodbye, just a smile, a look – yes, it was that expression that rendered her helpless – and she hadn't protested . . .

At first she didn't think she could carry on working. Her mind was awash with questions and suppositions. What were the neighbours thinking now? How many had noticed the handsome naval officer arrive? How many had timed his visit? She smoothed down the front of her pinafore as she went back to Ma's room. She had lost some weight. No wonder, with all the worry and work, and over this past week she had not eaten really enough. The thought of supper out in some posh restaurant filled her with both dread and excitement. What could she wear? Gradually, as the minutes slipped by, she managed to return to a level keel and carried on with the papering. Mr Blake came round during the evening and gave her a hand to complete the third wall.

'You've done very well, Mrs Sheldon,' he remarked, admiring the room. 'Hope you've stopped to eat, though?'

'I can get by on very little,' she said with a laugh. 'This job was more important than eating. Captain Hammond is on leave. He called to enquire after Kate, but he has some theatre tickets and wants me to accompany him. D'you think I should go?'

Mr Blake looked down at Fran with a warm smile 'Why ever not? It's time you had some outings, my dear. You work too hard. Now, you've got the chance to get out while Ma and the girls are away, you take it. Go off and enjoy yourself.'

'But whatever will people think?'

'It's your life. Never mind about the gossips.'

Fran felt better for talking to Mr Blake. It was better to be honest. It was sensible for the neighbours to know when she was out and the house left empty, anyway.

Kate arrived next morning soon after nine o'clock. It was another lovely day and she was delighted to see Gran's room nearly finished.

'You've worked hard, Mum,' Kate said. 'It looks lovely. Gran will be pleased. I'm sorry I won't be able to stay as long as I'd planned, though. One of the kitchen girls has gone sick and Mrs Neale wondered if I'd like to help out, so I jumped at the chance. Hope you don't mind Mum?' she asked apologetically.

'Actually I'm going out this evening, Kate. Let's hurry up and see if we can finish this last wall by dinnertime.'

As they worked, Fran told Kate about her evening's outing. Kate appeared surprised but pleased, and together they decided on Fran's outfit.

'It really is time you stopped wearing black, Mum,' Kate said. 'It makes you look so old.'

'Thank you very much,' Fran said. After some thought, she went on: 'I don't know, though, perhaps I ought to've said no. I shan't feel comfortable with someone so . . . so . . . you know.'

'Captain Hammond is very nice. But wear that pretty dress you made last summer. It's got long sleeves and looks elegant. Navy blue is smart, Mum, and it isn't too dowdy with the sprigs of white flowers on it. You've got that good navy-blue coat that Mrs Maitland passed on.'

Fran was glad of Kate's advice. Working in the centre of town in the hotel, she had become quite knowledgeable about the latest fashions. With Fran's expertise with her needle, they all benefited by having clothes that were exclusive to them and up to date.

They completed the papering in good time, then Kate shared the job of scrubbing the lino.

'I'll leave the window wide open to let it dry while we have dinner, and to let the smell of the paste go off. I must say it looks better than I thought it would.'

'You worry too much, Mum,' Kate scolded good-naturedly. 'I'll help you with the drawers and cupboards, but I can't stay longer than half past three. But after I've gone you're not to do any more – promise?'

'Why ever not?' asked Fran. 'I can carry on for another couple of hours at least.'

'No, Mum. You must have a bath, then a cup of tea while you cool down, then get dressed. You don't want to have to rush and end up looking hot and bothered.'

'I shall be that anyway,' Fran laughed.

'Not if you give yourself plenty of time.'

'Kate, I'm not a young girl going out on a date,' Fran protested.

'Maybe not, but you are going out to the theatre – and that's reason enough to dress up. All our guests wear glittery things and carry evening bags, and wear high heels.'

'Oh, Kate, you are funny. I can't change the way I look, dear. I've had five children, for goodness sake.'

'But you can look stunning, Mum. You've got a lovely face and such blue eyes – and you're *my* mum.' She gave Fran a sudden cuddle and kissed her cheek affectionately. The unexpected gesture brought a lump to Fran's throat, and she was conscious again of the wrong she had done Kate.

'I wish it were you going to the theatre, Kate, ' she said.

'What – with Captain Hammond?'

'No dear, someone nice of your own age, of course.'

Kate sighed and pursed her lips. 'Who'd want *me*?'

'Plenty of young men would love to have a good-looking girl like you on their arm, my dear. Not every man wants to have babies about the place. You might meet someone who's more interested in a career, and as long as they love you for yourself – because you're *you* – that's all that matters.'

Kate went off to the lavatory, leaving Fran a little despondent about her eldest daughter. Maurice Lambert was a hard-working chap with good prospects when he left college. She couldn't have asked for anyone more suitable, and she had come between them. Guilt nagged away at her, and yet Kate didn't seem as upset now. Maybe it hadn't been right – maybe already she had found some new interest . . .

On the dot of seven-thirty a light knock sounded on the front door. Fran had carried out Kate's instructions to the letter and had been patiently waiting for the past twenty minutes. Her shoes tapped out a rhythm on the hall lino as she went to let Luke in.

'Ah! I see you're ready, and very smart you look too, if I may be so personal. I must confess I half-expected to be jilted,' he said with a grin.

'That wouldn't have been very fair, would it? I had second and third thoughts, Luke. It's the first time I've been anywhere without at least one of the girls.

'Then it's time you started to live your own life, Fran. At least have time off from your family occasionally to enjoy yourself.'

'The girls are my life, Luke, and provide me with all the enjoyment I need.'

He leaned forward and dropped a teasing kiss just short of her lips.

'The kind of enjoyment I mean has to be shared between a man and a woman,' he said. 'Do you realise that this will be our very first date?' He cupped her chin in his hand as he whispered: 'Let's make it a night to remember.'

Dusk was falling, and some sea mist was hanging low in the town square as Luke parked the car in the forecourt of the theatre. Fran experienced a mixture of excitement and apprehension when she saw so many fashionable people going up the marble stairs leading into the foyer. Luke was not dressed in uniform. His light-brown suit was well cut and styled perfectly over his slim hips and trim waist. He had a confident walk, straight-backed with a military bearing, and Fran felt proud to be his companion. She had dressed up, as Kate called it, as much as she dared. Her dress fitted her neat figure without unnecessary creases; she felt self-conscious about her well-developed bust, but she knew many a woman might envy her. Beneath the navy-blue felt hat, trimmed in the modern style with white ribbon and small wispy feathers, her auburn hair was freshly washed, soft and springy. She didn't like having to wear a hat immediately after washing it, but this gadabout evening had come like a bolt out of the blue. It beat hanging wallpaper and scrubbing floors, she thought as she sat beside her handsome escort and listened to the overture, played by Brimdene's own orchestra.

The show was colourful, the music easy to listen to and the romance of the story enough to touch the hardest of hearts. Fran was quite overwhelmed by it. During the interval Luke excused himself, only to return with a large, beribboned box of chocolates. He smiled down at her protests, and helped her eat some of the sweets until the curtain rose again.

After they had stood to acknowledge the national anthem, they went out into the evening air, which had turned somewhat chill. The mist had rolled away and there was a pleasant, springlike atmosphere in the town in spite of the coolness. Fran wondered where they would be going for supper. Luke ushered her back into the car and drove off towards the cliff. With a screech of brakes he stopped in the car park of his hotel. Fran felt her stomach muscles tighten. She ought to have insisted that he took her straight home afterwards but she was, she realised, entirely at his mercy.

'It's quite late,' she said in a small voice. 'I ought to go straight home.'

He turned to look at her. 'There's no one at home to report to, Fran. This is your night, let's make the most of it.'

'B – but I'm not used to eating in places like this,' she pleaded.

'Then now is the time to start.' He got out of the car and came round to her side to help her out. With his hand supporting her elbow, he took her inside. A huge palm in the centre of the floor was surrounded by plush leatherette seats.

'Just take a seat,' he said. 'I have to go to the reception desk.'

Fran watched as the gentleman behind the counter treated Luke with the utmost respect and then handed over a key. Her nervousness increased. She wasn't sure she could cope with this situation, but Luke smiled reassuringly as he strode back to where she was sitting.

'I expect you'd like to freshen up,' he suggested, and seconds later they were in the lift with other guests going up to the top floor.

The corridors were wide and thickly carpeted so that their shoes made no sound as they walked along. Luke unlocked a door marked 217 and showed Fran inside.

'I believe in home comforts where possible,' he said. 'Not that hotels are in the least like a real home, but this is an improvement on my cabin, where I seldom get any peace.'

'Where is your real home?' Fran asked curiously.

'Mm . . . haven't got one.' Fran thought he seemed less exuberant briefly, then with a smile he said: 'I like to take a suite when I'm in a nice town like Brimdene, especially when I can get one overlooking the sea.' He took off his jacket in the warmth of the room and then walked over to the huge window. 'I can't live too far away from the sea, and this hotel is ideal. The bathroom is through that door if you'd like to freshen up before our supper arrives.'

'We're going to eat up here?'

'Don't look so surprised, Fran. Why not? I've ordered some of their specialities so I hope you have a good appetite. I don't need to enquire whether or not you enjoyed the show, I know you did. Whenever I glanced across at you, your eyes were sparkling and you were engrossed in everything. I'm glad I've been able to give you some pleasure, Fran.'

'The show was splendid,' she said huskily. 'I've never had the time or money for such extravagances. Not since I've been married, anyway. I thought it was a bit late for supper.'

'Not when I can treat you to a real supper. I bet you haven't eaten properly while your family have all been away. You seem to thrive on hard work.'

'There are times when I feel like running away,' she confessed. 'Without a man it's difficult, having to make the decisions – and I don't always make the right ones.' She hurried away into the bathroom. She had nearly dropped her guard and told him about burning Kate's letter. She needed someone to talk to and Luke was evoking her confidence. She recalled how gullible she was in his company, how easily she had succumbed to his charm twenty years ago. She mustn't fall under his spell now. But, as the evening progressed, without her being aware of it, any restraint she had erected between them as a safety barrier was soon broken down.

The topic of conversation was varied. Luke gave her graphic

accounts of the countries he had visited from Ceylon to South America, India, Rhodesia and Australia. Fran was soon laughing at the stories he could amuse her with. After a spell of small talk while they ate the fish dish he had ordered, she asked him again about his family. He kept his gaze on his food. She noticed the long, elegant fingers which held the cutlery so delicately. Only small portions went into his mouth, and she found herself comparing him with the men she had been associated with all her life. Working men with rough hands, too hungry after a day in the fields to bother about genteel table manners.

'My family are of little consequence, Fran. They're all in the North Riding of Yorkshire. My father planned to take me into the family iron-ore business, but the sea became my obsession. I'm afraid I broke my parents' hearts by running away to sea at sixteen, leaving the very expensive boarding school that they had thought would tame me.'

'Do you regret it now?'

'No, most definitely not.' His eyes seemed to cloud over for a moment. 'I was the only son, you see. I have three sisters, who aren't much good in the iron-ore trade. I've been disinherited.'

'Oh, Luke, that's terrible!' Fran exclaimed.

'Why? What use is money if your heart is rebelling against family ties and expectations?'

'Isn't that a bit hard on your parents?'

'They wouldn't meet me halfway, so I went ahead and did what I wanted to do – what's in my blood, Fran. Was in my grandfather's blood before me. I didn't mean to hurt them. I believed in my innocent youth that when they saw how keen a sailor I was they would understand, but they disowned me completely. Good friends are often more valuable than family, even though blood is supposed to be thicker than water.'

Fran remained silent, feeling some sympathy for Luke's family.

'Being a mother yourself, I expect your compassion is for them. If I had made a mess of my life I could understand it, but I've reached the height of my career without blemish. If my son did half as well I would be proud of him.'

'But the older generation doesn't think like us, Luke. I feel sorry for them, but I also feel sorry for you. Surely you've missed out on a happy family life? They could have given you so much when you're home from long voyages.'

At the concern in Fran's voice, Luke looked up. His dark, hooded eyes softened with tenderness. This close to him she could see the deep furrows in his brow, the creases that showed white against an otherwise swarthy skin. Each furrow, every crease depicted the kind of life he led away from Yorkshire in hot, passionate countries, and she knew now why he had taken advantage of her all those years ago. He needed a woman's love. He hadn't ever known a mother's care. She felt the atmosphere thicken with emotion. As if on a magic carpet she was flown back to the Hinckleys' household. She recalled the party where several bottles of wine had been consumed. She couldn't remember how Luke Hammond had become involved in a staff party when he was a guest of the family, but she did remember his strong arms which had carried her to her room next to the children's nursery.

'Life has given me compensations,' he said in a low voice. 'The Maitlands, the Hinckleys and others. Families of fellow officers have all made me welcome – but it's not like having a family of one's own.'

Fran drank her coffee slowly. She thought how sad it was that he had nowhere to call his own.

He stood up, pushing the chair back with his legs. He came to her side and as she rose he removed her chair.

'There's more coffee,' he offered, being the perfect host. 'Let's sit on the couch by the window.'

It was totally dark outside now. Luke dimmed the room lights and they sat looking out to sea, sipping their coffee without speaking. A pale crescent moon hung like a lantern in the sky, and the waves lapped gently on the shore below. He took the cups back to the trolley and rang for a waiter to come and remove it. While they waited, Fran went to the bathroom. She looked at herself in the mirror. Flushed, expectant, enjoying these few moments of freedom ...

Luke was standing close to the huge window when she returned.

'It's been lovely,' she said in a soft voice, 'but I ought to be going now.'

Luke turned slowly – so very slowly. Fran's heart began jumping nervously. You're not a young girl, she reminded herself. But she was a woman. A lonely one – with love to spare only for her children?

Luke took her in his arms gently. She melted in his embrace in spite of some warning which she didn't intend to heed. He stooped to place his mouth over hers and she didn't resist. No longer was he the handsome naval officer for whom she felt sorry. Like the hands of a clock spinning backwards at a fantastic speed, he became the hungry, masculine lover of twenty years ago.

'I love you,' he murmured. 'I really love you, Fran. The only woman I have ever truly loved. My woman, my family, this is what

I've longed for and there's no going back. There's no reason at all to feel guilty, Fran. No one can expect you to remain on your own forever. You had a good marriage to Henry – I hope he realised what a lucky man he was to have a woman so utterly capable of making a man happy – but that's in the past now. We must build a future together for ourselves and our children.'

'Luke, I've already got four daughters,' she reminded him.

'And now they'll be my daughters, just as Lennie was my son.'

She knew she ought to argue that point just as she had in the past, but if it pleased Luke to fantasise about her first-born what harm could it do?

'You will marry me, won't you?' he whispered.

Fran turned from him. All the frustration of the past two years had been wiped out this evening. Her feelings of desire made her feel like a whole woman again, but she could not forget the many times she had rejected Henry when fatigue prevented her from being a good wife to him. He had been the capable one, she thought. Virile, untiring, patient in persuasion – he had been the perfect teacher, the perfect partner.

'You're going too fast,' she pleaded quietly. 'Marriage is a big step to take.'

'If you're feeling unfaithful to Henry's memory, then don't. He wouldn't like you to have to share so many burdens alone, Fran. He made you happy, he would be pleased that you found someone else who could look after you and help to keep you young – and I will, I swear before God I'll do everything I can to make life easier for you.'

What a dilemma! How could she refuse? Instead of her having to make important decisions, Luke would be there to advise and give her courage. She should count herself lucky that a man in such a good position wanted her and her family. Most widows of a similar age didn't get a second chance of happiness.

'I can't make that kind of decision without giving the matter a great deal of thought,' she said. 'Whatever will the girls say? And Ma, and my in-laws? Somehow I don't think they'll like it. I can't promise that they'll all accept you without reservations.'

'Then I shall have to persuade them.' He held her shoulders firmly.

'Just as I must persuade you to say what I want to hear.' He kissed her gently, wooing her, until she was returning his kisses with ardour.

Chapter Nine

'Luke and I are going to be married, Ma,' Fran said, doubtful about the timing of such a statement. Would there ever be a right time to tell her mother? She was languishing under a cloud of uncertainty, elevated by a measure of excitement. She wasn't sure of her own reactions, let alone those of her family.

Had she given in because she loved Luke or because it was an easy way out of her troubles? Was her decision made on the rebound?

'I hope you'll give us your blessing, Mrs Brown?' Luke said, standing tall in his naval uniform. 'I'm not taking Fran away from you for ever.'

Ma gazed as if mesmerised from Fran to Luke. Luke placed an arm about her.

'Come and sit down,' he said kindly. 'I'm sorry if this has come as a shock to you. We thought you might have guessed.'

'I knew you were keen on her,' Ma said, disparagingly. 'I'm not blind, but I didn't realise it had gone this far so quickly.'

'It isn't as if we're young, Ma,' Fran excused. Her voice cracked with more uncertainty as she realised the implication of what Luke had just said. Caught up in a whirlwind of romantic adventure, being courted with such flair, she had given little consideration to the future. It wasn't just a decision to become Luke's wife. There was more to it than that. He had talked of appointments abroad. How was that going to affect the girls and Ma? His words 'I'm not taking Fran away from you for ever' brought home the full realisation of what marriage to Luke entailed. She felt her stomach muscles tighten into a knot. To a younger woman there might be some attraction in the lifestyle of a naval officer. Fran felt she was getting out of her depth. They needed to discuss forthcoming plans which involved all the family. Luke had revived sensuous desires in Fran which had lain dormant for too long, desires she thought were dead for ever.

'Fran wanted you to be the first to know,' Luke said. 'Before she tells the girls when they get back from Sherbrook – my girls now,' he added, evidently trying to impress his future mother-in-law.

'I'm sure I don't know what to think, let alone say,' Ma said. 'I hope you know what you're doing, Fran, that's all.' She turned and left the room, leaving Luke and Fran staring after her blankly.

Luke placed an arm round Fran's waist. 'She'll come round, darling,' he consoled. 'It's been a shock to her.'

Fran pulled away. 'I'll get the tea. The girls will be here soon.'

Luke knew better than to press Fran. Her mother's opinion would naturally be important to her. He just hoped she didn't have too much influence over her daughter but already he sensed a stiffness in Fran.

Ma fetched the best china cups and saucers from the cabinet in the front sitting room. She and Fran worked silently together to prepare afternoon tea for all the family except Kate, but including Prue and Marion, who were bringing the girls back on the train.

'I could have gone to fetch them from the station,' Luke said as he watched the procedure with slight misgivings.

'There wouldn't be room for all of us. I told Prue to take a taxi. Ah! Sounds like them now. I'll go and help with the luggage.'

'Want me to come too?' he offered.

'No, it's all right, we'll manage.'

Luke caught Fran before she left the room. 'What's up? You've suddenly changed. Is it your mother's attitude?'

'No!' Fran pushed his hands away and looked up into his eyes. The warmth had vanished from her own, changing them from cornflower blue to the sharpness of steel. 'Your attitude, Luke. I never said I would travel with you and leave the children. You made it sound as if I would.'

'But you'll have to. I have a house in Portsmouth. You surely don't imagine that I'm going to live there and leave you here? No, Fran, it isn't going to be that kind of marriage. I shall probably be given a shore-based job for a couple of years – it'll most likely be in Scotland and you'll be going there with me.'

'I – well, I thought I'd stay here and you'd come home to us when you have leave,' she said. 'I simply cannot part with my girls, Luke.'

'And I simply cannot embark on married life with a ready-made family. The girls have your mother.'

'She's too old to take the responsibility.' Fran turned and went to open the front door. In seconds the house was full of women talking together, until Babs came face to face with a vaguely familiar person.

'Hullo, Copperknob,' Luke said, holding out his hand to her. 'Have you had a lovely holiday back in Sherbrook? That's where we first met – d'you remember? In your garden at the old mill house?'

Babs went all shy and ran to her mother, clutching her tightly.

'It's all right, darling,' Fran said. 'Captain Hammond was very kind when Kate was ill in hospital, wasn't he?' Fran ushered Hilda and Ruby in and they shook hands politely. 'And this is Prue's daughter, Marion; I'm not sure whether you've met or not.'

When the greetings were over, Gran made the tea, and Fran seated everyone round the extended kitchen table.

'Are you going back to Sherbrook tonight?' Luke asked Prue.

'No, they're staying here,' Fran put in sharply. The girls all whooped with delight.

Luke was well aware that this arrangement was a surprise to everyone. He didn't intend to be outdone, and as the children were finishing their meal he looked across at Fran with a smile. 'I think now is as good a time as any, darling,' he said softly but with the hint of a command.

Fran went slightly pink as she stood up. 'I . . . I know it'll be a bit of a shock to you, girls,' she began hesitantly.

'Your mother and I are going to be married,' Luke said, taking over the situation.

There was a deathly hush. The girls seemed to shrink in their seats. Babs left her chair and ran to Fran, who had sat down quickly.

'That's marvellous,' Prue said. 'So, congratulations are in order, then?' She reached across and shook Luke by the hand, then went to Fran and kissed her warmly.

'I hope everyone else will be as pleased as you are, Prue,' Luke said. 'Unfortunately I have to return to my ship tomorrow, so it means that I shall have to leave the arrangements to Fran, but I'm sure I can count on you as her closest friend to give her all the help and support she'll need.'

'Of course,' Prue said, but she saw that Fran's eyes were moist.

'I'm sure no one will mind if I take Fran away for this evening,' Luke went on. 'Being my last night we'd like to be together.'

'I must see the girls to bed tonight,' Fran insisted. 'They've been away for over a week.'

'I can see to them,' Prue offered eagerly. 'But first I'll help Gran with the washing-up – or, better still, Marion and Ruby can help me, while Fran sees to the two little ones.'

'We'd better get the case upstairs first,' Fran said pointedly, and Prue took the bait.

Upstairs in the main bedroom Fran collapsed in tears. 'What have I done, Prue? I didn't say I'd leave the girls with Ma to go off wherever he wanted.'

'Now start at the beginning and tell me how all this came about.'

Fran had to tell her story briefly and Prue listened patiently, doing her best to calm her friend down.

'You obviously fell overboard for him, Fran dear. I admire your choice – he's a very nice man – but it sounds to me as if you've rushed into it all without spending enough time thrashing things out.'

'He talked about the girls being his – I naturally thought we would carry on living here and he'd come home when he gets leave.'

Prue raised her eyebrows. 'You've certainly been bitten by the love-bug, Fran dear. A naval captain living here? He'll expect you to join him in naval quarters.'

'He's got a house in Portsmouth which I didn't know about. Now he says he'll be posted to Scotland, and expects me to accompany him. I simply can't leave the girls with Ma. It would be too much for her.'

Prue opened the girls' case and started unpacking. 'I can see why you suddenly decided that we were staying. You'd better have all this out with him before he goes away. Were you really serious about us staying?'

'Please do, Prue,' Fran begged. 'I need someone to talk to – and there's Ma, she hasn't taken too kindly to the news.'

'When you've gone out I'll go and telephone the Maitlands, ask Withers if he'll give Sam a message to say we're staying over. But we'll have to do a bit of borrowing, I'm afraid.'

'The beds have all been remade with clean sheets. My three girls can manage in one bed, you and Marion can have my bed, and I'll go in Kate's room.' Fran wept again. 'Prue, you can't know what it's been like without Henry. So much responsibility, so much worry. When Luke was there when Kate was ill I was grateful for his comfort, and then to turn up out of the blue while I was here alone . . . I'm afraid I just got carried away.'

'I saw him about with the Maitlands, and presumed he'd gone back to sea. There's talk that Mr Nicholas is walking out with a young lady and is likely to be married soon.'

'It must be in the air. I suppose they're getting older and think it's time they settled down. Obviously Luke knew that everyone was away – there aren't any secrets in Sherbrook – so he took the opportunity.'

'I think you're right to remarry, Fran. You aren't old and it isn't right to let the girls dominate your life. After all, they'll all marry one day and you'll be left on your own.'

'That's a long way ahead in the future. I vowed I'd live for them and not let them down for Henry's sake.'

'Remembering Henry as I do, Fran,' Prue said, 'he'd be the last person to stand in your way. Your happiness would have to come first.'

'It all seemed so right before today,' she said miserably.

'You go and get ready and I'll see to everything here. Have a good talk and let Luke know how you feel. It'll be all right, you'll see,' Prue assured her.

Fran kissed the two little girls good night and left the family in Prue's charge. Luke drove to the hotel and immediately ordered dinner to be sent up to his room.

'We may as well make the most of our last evening together,' he said as they went up in the lift.

In the privacy of his suite he gathered Fran in his arms, but she gave him a cold kiss and pushed him away.

'I hope you're not regretting your decision already, Fran?' he asked. 'I'm astounded at your naivety. A serviceman can hardly take a large family around everywhere with him. You must see that, my dear. It wouldn't be good for their education. Schools vary so much from county to county.'

'We should have discussed things more, Luke. It was silly of me to think you'd want my girls.'

'Darling,' he implored, 'I do want your girls – I want what's best for them, and it isn't with us. If your mother can't manage alone, we'll get someone in to help her. Or there's Kate – she could stay at home to look after them all, and I'll pay her the equivalent of wages.'

'No, no, that wouldn't be fair on Kate. She's only eighteen and look what happened when I left her behind at Sherbrook.'

'She met Maurice Lambert and if it hadn't been for that rotten friend of his I dare say he and Kate would be engaged by now. The girls won't consider you when they want to leave the nest.'

They were interrupted by their dinner trolley arriving. Fran wasn't hungry and only toyed with her food.

'Fran, I'm sorry if I've spoilt things between us, but you are rather making a mountain out of a molehill, you know.'

'My girls are my life, Luke. I've devoted my days and nights to those children for Henry's sake, and now you're asking me to desert them.'

Luke dabbed at his mouth with his table napkin. 'Not *asking* you to, Fran, I'm afraid I must insist that you make arrangements for their wellbeing. When the time comes for me to go away to sea for a long stretch, you can return to Brimdene then.'

'I understood you to say that you liked Brimdene?'

'You misconstrued my meaning. I do like Brimdene – because you were here – but I cannot overlook the fact that I'm committed to the Royal Navy.'

'I can't see why we can't all live here together,' Fran said, trying to keep her temper.

'Because we can't,' Luke said adamantly. '*I* can't live without you for weeks on end – until I am obliged to,' he added, 'but maybe this has all been fun and frolic to you. I didn't think you were capable of shallow intentions.'

'That's not fair, Luke,' she cried hotly. 'There was nothing shallow in my thoughts or actions, but I did think you'd have more consideration for my feelings where my children are concerned. Perhaps this has all been a terrible mistake. If you think I was just husband-hunting then I'd better leave.' She stood up abruptly. 'Don't bother coming down with me, I'll call a taxi.'

Luke was on his feet in a flash, and the tension between them was electric.

Later, as Fran lay in Luke's arms relishing the warmth of his affections, her mind was confused about the future. Luke kissed her forehead tenderly.

'Let's talk about this sensibly. Perhaps we could have little Copperknob with us eventually,' he whispered into her hair, diffusing the situation.

'I can't give up my Hilda, Luke, not for you or anyone else – ever. She's not strong, she's like Lennie, she'll always need me. I expect Ruby would be all right with Ma, but Babs – she's so young – and she was Henry's baby . . .'

'What about Prue? She's had the girls over Easter – she seems to love children and at least you'd be certain she would look after them well. When she travelled with me the night Kate was taken ill she told me that they adopted Marion.'

Fran murmured in reply. She hated herself for what was happening, angry that she could seem to do nothing to prevent it.

'I'm sure she'd love to have Babs,' Luke continued. 'Children adapt more easily that one would expect. Like animals, as long as they're fed regularly, they're happy.'

'I can't believe my girls will be happy without me,' she sobbed.

'Prue wanted to adopt Babs when Henry died, so she said.'

This was all like a beautiful dream changing dramatically into a nightmare. 'I must go home, Luke,' Fran said. 'They'll be wondering where I am.'

'I'll take you, of course. It's only ten-thirty – quite a respectable hour, but I do have to be up early tomorrow.'

As Fran put on her hat in front of the mirror, Luke pulled out his wallet.

'Here's fifty pounds, Fran.' She looked aghast, as if he might be paying her off. 'There'll be clothes to buy for our honeymoon, extras for things the girls will need and for the wedding – where is it to be?'

'Goodness, I hadn't even thought about *that*,' she said crossly.

He held her fast and looked directly into her eyes. 'Nothing's changed, my sweet. I refuse to let you go now. I'm not a particularly religious man so we can have a quiet civil ceremony if you prefer – but somehow I think you'd like a church wedding. The girls should be there, and as many of your family as you like. Nick Maitland will be my best man and my only other guest will be my sister Elizabeth. We've always kept in touch and I know you'll like each other.'

'What other secrets have you kept from me?' she demanded icily. 'You said you had no home, no family, yet now I learn that you have a house in Portsmouth, parents and sisters.'

'I said that I had no family and home as such. That's what I want more than anything, darling. To know that you're there waiting for me just as I've always dreamed.'

Fran shook her head sadly. 'Oh, what a mess! I never meant to get involved again,' she cried passionately.

'It's happened rather suddenly, I grant you. Time is never on my side, but our dream can be reality if we want it to be. The children won't suffer nearly as much as you imagine and as they grow up they'll be glad to have a step father to turn to sometimes. They'll be concerned for your happiness, Fran.' He went to a small briefcase and took something from it. 'Please wear my ring, darling.' Fran gasped as he opened the small box, revealing a sparkling diamond set in a cluster of sapphires. 'To match your eyes – well, nearly. And now there's no going back,' he said, as he slipped Henry's rings on to the third finger of her right hand, and slipped his engagement ring on the left.

He pressed her fingers to his mouth. 'No longer than three months until we seal this with a wedding ring,' he promised. 'I'll write each week, but you may receive several letters together. Please write to me as often as you can. I'll be as helpful as is humanly possible with any problems you may come up against.'

Fran hadn't the heart to put a stop to this charade. It couldn't, it mustn't happen for the sake of the girls, but neither could she deny herself Luke's love.

Fran thought things might look better next morning, but everyone got up with a gloomy expression.

'You can't marry him, Mum!' Ruby burst out the moment she saw her mother. 'Daddy would hate it – you know he would. It's horrible – I hate him, and I hate you too.' As always Ruby let forth great wails of dissent, and Babs clung to Fran wherever she went. It was as if she knew what her fate was to be.

After breakfast Fran insisted that the girls went out into the garden to play while she and Prue sat down to talk.

'Well, what have you decided?' Prue asked.

'*He's* decided,' Fran said slowly, 'that I can take Hilda with me and you can have Babs, but I can't do it, Prue.'

'And what about your mother and Ruby?'

'They've always been quite close. Ruby's twelve now and it isn't as if Kate's far away. There's Sissy, too – though how I'm going to tell Henry's family, I just don't know.'

'You've just said you can't do it, but you seem to have made all the arrangements' Prue perceived.

'Oh, Prue, I hardly slept a wink. My mind was in such a turmoil.'

'Answer me one thing, Fran dear – do you love Luke Hammond, enough to marry him?'

'Oh yes! I don't have any doubts on that score. But it isn't fair to make me choose between him and my children.'

Prue sighed, and placed a comforting hand over Fran's. 'This is one time when I agree with him. It's your life. It was your life that was ruined by the accident. You've been a good mother to the girls, and no one dare say otherwise. Surely now you can grab some happiness while you've got the chance. He might not be ashore for as long as he thinks, and then you can come home again. It won't be the end of the world, Fran. And you know you don't need an answer to whether Sam and I will give Babs a good home or not. We'll love to have her.'

Fran looked at Prue through bloodshot eyes. Yes, she thought, but what would Babs think about it? Her baby! How could she bear to part with any one of them?

Prue and Marion went home later that day. The girls had all quarrelled a great deal, and Fran was glad to see the back of her visitors even though she valued Prue's opinion. But wasn't Prue biased? She had always coveted Babs, so it was to her own advantage to be on Luke's side. Kate was all right at the hotel, doing well in fact, and Fran was proud of her for picking herself up and getting on with her work. But Ma was already seventy-three. Was it fair to give her the responsibility of Ruby? Ruby was the one who was never going to forgive her.

'Stop worrying, Fran,' Ma said as they prepared dinner together. 'I admit it all seems a bit hasty, but Luke appears to be a kind man and I reckon he thinks it's time he settled down. He won't always be in the Navy, will he? I dare say he never intended to fall for a woman with four daughters. You're the one who has to make the choice. 'Tis your life, and if he can offer you the kind of life you want then you must follow your heart.'

Fran couldn't bear to see the uncertainty in her mother's eyes even though she was the one who, having recovered from the initial shock, was now accepting the inevitable. Fran felt guilty. Surely her mother of all people should be attributing blame? It wasn't fair to leave her in this house, which was still strange even after two years. If she had been able to leave her in the shepherd's cottage in Sherbrook it would have been a different matter. Fran was confused, sure that behind the pleasant accord her mother must be feeling aggrieved at what was taking place.

When the meal was over and her mother went upstairs for her afternoon nap, Fran stood on the landing feeling claustrophobic.

'I must get out for a bit, Ma,' she said suddenly. 'I've got a headache coming on and a breath of sea air might blow it away.'

Ma's brow puckered in a frown, but her warm smile reassured her daughter that she understood, and Fran set off to catch the bus into town.

The day was overcast, but still people crowded on to the bus, and when she reached the gardens leading down to the sea there was no shortage of folk admiring the beautiful tulips and late daffodils and narcissi in decorative beds and borders. Nothing looked beautiful to Fran. Her footsteps took her out to the promenade and she walked along, the bracing air fanning her cheeks, while she argued with herself as she fought against the fateful choice she had to make.

She walked briskly until she was midway between the two piers, and there were fewer people. She went to sit in one of the shelters, and took out her brother Eric's letter to read again. He was very good at accusing, she thought defiantly, but his life had been an easy one.

The blue-eyed boy, he usually managed to sway anyone to his way of thinking if he tried hard enough, but he hadn't succeeded in getting Ma on his side this time. Dear Ma! Fran knew she didn't deserve her blessing. She hadn't always been as thoughtful and patient as she should have been, and now she was casting her responsibilities on old shoulders. She tried to picture Ruby and Ma together. Ruby was wilful and stubborn, but she was also kind and caring and if anyone would look after her gran it was Ruby.

Fran realised why Luke didn't want the children, of course. Their presence would affect their marriage, and since they were not his offspring it was understandable he might feel they were in the way. Just thinking about the controlled passion that existed between them brought a glow to her cheeks and a pain in the pit of her stomach. She had thought of no one but the children since Henry's death, resulting in emotional frustration as well as physical. Surely no one had the right to deny her this new-found happiness? She ought to be feeling deliriously happy. Most women would envy her, especially widows who, like her, had found it difficult to make ends meet, not to mention coping with the loneliness. It was as if fortune was smiling on her for once. It wasn't as if Luke was a complete stranger either – far from it. Time and distance seemed to have strengthened his affection for her. If she was truly honest, she had never quite put him out of her thoughts even in nearly twenty years. It was like a daydream come true. An age-old fantasy of the kitchen maid falling in love with the elegant master of the house, only in this case it was the nanny and here she was realising the idle fancy. She ought to be counting her blessings.

But it was the price she had to pay for her new way of life that troubled her conscience. The loss of her children, splitting the family, each of the girls somewhere different. Hilda would be with her, but she would miss Babs just as Babs was going to pine for Hilda. How was Babs going to like being taken over by Prue and Sam? They'd be good to her, she didn't doubt that, but Babs was hers, hers and Henry's. A funny little thing who showed her affection in a variety of ways. She was demonstrative, needing to be cuddled and kissed. She had accepted Luke and was ever ready to sit on his knee and allow him to fondle her. No wonder he wanted to take her as part of the deal. Part of the deal? What was she thinking about? This was marriage – for better or worse, richer or poorer, in sickness and in health, to love, honour and obey.

The sea stretched out to the far horizon. Waves rolling into the shore with an occasional white horse, before they lapped at the water's edge and disappeared. Luke loved the sea, just as much as Henry had loved his horses. The sea brought a calm to Fran's troubled breast, and she listened for some distant voice to advise her, but there was no answer to her agonised plea. Was it so wrong to want to change her life style? To want more than working, keeping house, thinking for so many people, sewing to make ends meet, and no one to share the burdens of everyday complications?

Destiny had offered her an escape route, a means to freedom. Chances like this came but once in a lifetime, and Luke had made the decision for her. Who was she to disobey?

Chapter Ten

Fran had cause to be proud of her girls. Once they got over the shock of her decision to marry Luke Hammond, they viewed the event with mounting excitement. During the weeks leading up to the June wedding day Fran was fraught with changing emotions, but she worked all her doubts into the dresses she made for the girls. Long, lonely hours of toil while with every stitch she tried to qualify her decision. Ma, bless her, uttered not one word of reproach, yet Eric made loud noises of disapproval. As an act of protest he decided not to accept the invitation to come to the wedding. Fran was sure that Annie and May were disappointed to miss such an occasion.

The morning started with an overcast sky, but by midday, when the bridal party stood ready and waiting in the front sitting room, the sun broke through with the promise of a warm day.

Ruby, Hilda and Babs looked enchanting in dainty voile dresses decorated with satin ribbons and bows. They travelled to the church in one car with Gran Brown and Kate, who acted as Fran's bridesmaid. She wore an ankle-length dress. Her hair was hidden by a large-brimmed straw hat and she appeared three inches taller in her high-heeled patent-leather shoes.

Fran, looking elegant in a midnight-blue silk dress and jacket with grey accessories, tightened her grip on the ivory-covered prayer book she carried. A white ribbon bookmark with a spray of pink rosebuds hung from it. Nathan, who was giving her away, noticed that she was trembling. He took her gloved hand in his and squeezed affectionately.

'I know you're having doubts, Fran dear,' he said gently. 'Don't. Henry would give you his blessing, be sure of that.'

'Not to the price I'm paying for my selfishness,' she said softly. 'I've done everything to try to make Luke change his mind about taking the girls to Scotland with us, but he'll only agree to taking Hilda. The others will never forgive me, will they?'

'You're feeling guilty, but I dare say that Luke's decision is best for the girls. It won't be for ever, Fran. You deserve a holiday, a break from the past. You know we'll be here for Ruby and Ma, should they need us. Kate will be on hand, too, as well as Sissy. Babs will be fine with your friends in Sherbrook. For her it will be like going home again and she'll meet up with her old friends. You worry too much. None of us are indispensable.' Nathan lifted Fran's quivering chin and wiped away a stray tear with his finger. 'Come on now. Head up, walk tall with a big smile to greet Luke, who's a very lucky man.'

The parish church in Brimdene was only a five-minute drive away. Soon Fran was walking down the aisle on Nathan's arm. All her fears and doubt vanished as Luke turned to admire his bride – the woman of his dreams.

Fran's expression lifted as Luke smiled lovingly at her. Two handsome naval officers were standing side by side below the altar, one of whom was to be her husband. How could she have doubts when happiness beckoned invitingly? Happiness because she knew how fortunate she was to have a second chance in life. The chance to make Luke happy, and in return have someone with whom to share the responsibility of her family.

In a soft, barely audible whisper Fran made her vows solemnly before God, promising to love, honour and obey her husband. Luke responded with his vows in a clear, polished and confident voice. The ceremony lasted only half an hour and after signing the register they emerged in the sunshine to pose for the photographer.

The rest of the day passed so swiftly that Fran had to search her mind afterwards to recall certain incidents. The girls throwing confetti, everyone's amusement when Babs asked for another piece of wedding cake, and after the small reception the worst part of saying goodbye. Not just goodbye for the three-day honeymoon but – for how long? Her darling Babs was going home to Sherbrook without her. Fran felt a tightness in her chest when the moment of parting came.

The sea crossing to the Isle of Wight was calm, and it was growing dusk as a taxi took the newlyweds to their hotel. Luke had made most of the arrangements and Fran could find no fault with anything.

'Would you like a meal sent up?' Luke asked her as the porter delivered the suitcases to their room.

'No thanks, I couldn't eat a thing.'

The porter left hurriedly and Luke gave his wife a wicked kind of smile. 'And all I want to eat is you, my darling.' With no more than a couple of long strides he spanned the distance between them and gathered her in his arms. 'How I've managed to restrain myself all day I can't imagine,' he said, laughing down at her. 'Was everything the way you wanted it, Fran?' he asked, suddenly serious.

'It was a very happy day, Luke,' she said. 'Thank you for everything. I hope it all came up to your expectations too?'

'All I've ever wanted was you, and now you're mine – really mine. I'm a very lucky man.' His mouth touched hers with the briefest of kisses. 'Let's unpack in the morning.'

Fran went to the bathroom, where she looked at herself in the mirror. Flushed, expectant, she knew the moment of reckoning had come. For over twenty years she had kept a memory locked inside her heart, never exposing it to anyone lest it should fade. Was it all a young girl's dream? Had almost twenty years of marital bliss with Henry devalued that night of passionate embraces?

Fran didn't hear the bathroom door open without so much as a creak, but suddenly she was looking at two faces in the mirror. Luke rested his cheek against hers, then his moist lips found the sensitive spot in her neck and the memory quickly changed to reality.

'You've kept me waiting too long, Mrs Hammond,' he said playfully. 'You cruelly denied me before I went to sea, now you'll have to forgive my impatience.'

In spite of all the thoughts that were taunting her, Fran melted in Luke's arms. His body was firm and strong, protective too. Luke demanded, Fran gave. He turned her round to face him.

'My dream fulfilled at last,' he whispered breathlessly, then he picked her up and carried her to the large bed. His lips forced hers apart, his tongue curling around hers, hot and passionate with a thirst as yet unsatiated.

Every pulse in Fran's body was racing as he helped her to undress. Her new shimmering nightgown was unnecessary. She could hardly wait while he took off his clothes and then he was teasing, exploring, exciting her to breathtaking heights. The past drifted into oblivion, everyone else forgotten as she felt a sweet breeze waft over the lower half of her body. He was astride her, eager yet holding himself in check as he took his fill of the beauty of her cornflower-blue eyes. 'We shall always be good together, my darling,' he whispered.

Fran was conscious of the rise and fall of her breasts, fuller now than they had been twenty years ago. Luke's lips travelled down from her throat, briefly caressing each breast in turn, causing her the wildest sensations. There was satisfaction for him in just gazing at her beautiful white skin and he moaned with delight as he buried his face in the soft valley of her bosom. Fran wrapped her arms around his bronzed torso, drawing him ever closer. They were both in their prime, eager for each other ...

Clouds scudding across the sky passed unnoticed as Luke and Fran explored quaint villages and old churches and admired Osborne House and Carisbrooke Castle. They were staying in Shanklin, one of the island's most popular resorts, and after dinner in the evening of the second day they strolled through the lovely Chine where a cascade of water flowed beneath an ivy-clad stone bridge to the sea. Life here was unhurried, uncomplicated. With their common love of the sea they could bask in the summer sun by day and allow their feelings for each other full rein during the hours of darkness.

Last-minute shopping brought their three-day idyll to a close. As they stood on the deck of the ferry returning to the mainland, Fran shivered with the cold realisation of the heartache she had brought upon herself. No matter how much she loved her husband and wanted to please him, she couldn't rid herself of the heavy burden of guilt at splitting up her girls.

But Luke saw to it that she didn't have time for recriminations. No sooner were they back in Brimdene than the family were waving them off on the train to London, where they boarded the night train to Edinburgh.

Nine-year-old Hilda showed no signs of dismay at having left her sisters behind, The majestic *Flying Scotsman* standing at the platform at King's Cross station hissed impatiently as passengers climbed aboard, and Hilda ran along the corridor enthusiastically to find their compartment. Fran did her best to appear light-hearted but she was coming down to earth with a bump. Once they were on their way it seemed to Fran as if the metal chattering on metal was sending out a message for her ears alone. 'You're left them behind, you've left them behind ... clackety-clack ... clackety-clack ...' Fran's head began to ache and she felt she wanted to run, to place her hands over her ears to shut out the condemnation. She thought she was a strong woman, had grown stronger since being left a widow, and yet she had fallen under Luke's spell almost gratefully. Had she only considered the plus side? Was having a handsome husband to pay all the bills more important than having the girls under her wing?

The night journey seemed never ending even though the bunks were relatively comfortable. Hilda was quickly asleep and Fran could tell by Luke's even breathing that he was too. But sleep only came in fits and starts for Fran, and as dawn came up she went to the washroom at the end of the corridor. On the way back to their compartment she paused, the pretty sky attracting her attention. An orange glow on the eastern horizon touched the fluffy balls of white cloud, turning them into pale pink snowflakes floating in a turquoise-coloured heaven. She clung to the handrail as she stood at the window looking out. Looking out to a new future, which appeared bright at this moment. The scenery that sped past was unfamiliar to her, yet it was green countryside similar to her native Dorset. For Luke's sake she must be happy. They wouldn't live in Scotland for ever. Eventually Luke would return to the sea for a long period, and then she would go home to Brimdene and her house full of women.

Smoke-blackened buildings, tall church spires and a distant castle on a hill were their first sight of Edinburgh.

'How's your head now?' Luke asked Fran with concern.

'Still throbs a bit, but the Aspro helped.'

'Getting out in the crisp morning air will make you feel more human. You're not used to travelling such long distances. We'll have a break now for breakfast – a proper one, not just tea and toast.'

'I couldn't have eaten anything else on the journey,' Fran said. 'And Hilda looks rather pale.'

'We'll find a nice restaurant and have scrambled eggs and some coffee.'

'What's the matter with the station buffet?' Fran asked.

'Too crowded, and it'll be nice to get away from the smell of engines. Our connecting train to Dunfermline doesn't leave Edinburgh until mid-morning so we've plenty of time.'

'When are we going to get to our new house?' Hilda whined.

'Not much longer, Hilda,' Luke said. 'It's a cottage, similar to the old mill house at Sherbrook. There's a lake nearby – well, the Scots call lakes lochs – and we'll be sheltered from the winds by the Cleish Hills.'

'I wish we were going to a town like Brimdene.' Although Hilda had slept for most of the long journey north it was evident that she was travel-weary.

'Your mother prefers the country, Hilda,' Luke said shortly. 'Dunfermline is only about five miles away and there's a school bus every day.'

Hilda didn't appear to be impressed by the mention of school, but after they had walked to the restaurant in Princes Street, and enjoyed their breakfast, she perked up considerably.

Luke left Fran and Hilda window-shopping while he went to a telephone kiosk and made a call.

'The car is waiting at Dunfermline station,' he said, as he rejoined them. 'I had it transported earlier in the week so I needed to check that it had arrived safely. Hope it hasn't got too battered about.'

Fran loved everything about Princes Street, the different tartans colourful in the shops, and the friendly atmosphere.

'We'll be able to come here sometimes, darling,' Luke assured her. 'We can drive in for dinner or go to a show.'

Fran shot Luke a doubtful glance. He replied by giving her an affectionate squeeze. 'I know,' he murmured softly, 'we have to think about Hilda. I have thought, and arranged that the woman who will be our housekeeper will also act as Hilda's minder. She lives in the same village of Craiglee, but as she's a widow she'll be free to stay overnight any time we need her to.'

'But I couldn't leave Hilda with a complete stranger.'

Luke laughed. 'I didn't say we were going to paint the town every night, or even tomorrow or the next day. I shall be more than content to be at the cottage with you. When you get to know Mrs Logan you'll find she's most trustworthy.'

'But how d'you know?' Fran asked. 'You haven't seen the cottage yet, have you?'

'No. But I know my sister Elizabeth wouldn't have employed anyone she wasn't completely confident about. The Royal Navy made most of the arrangements. They have certain properties on their list for naval personnel, and Elizabeth came up one weekend about a month ago to check everything out. Mrs Logan comes highly recommended, so I'm sure you've no need to worry.'

'That was kind of your sister,' Fran said. 'I wish I'd had time to get to know her better, Luke, but it was nice that she could attend the wedding. It's a shame you don't even correspond with your parents, though.'

'Elizabeth and I are very close, even though we may not see one another for months or even years. There's only ten months' difference in our ages. We were more like twins in many ways. My other sisters are younger.'

'Tell me about them, Luke?'

'Oh,' he sighed, 'not much to tell really. Cecilia comes next, she's about thirty now, I suppose, and Dorinda is the youngest, she's twenty-eight. They're both married with families. Boys mostly, who'll go into the family business.'

'And you were the only boy?'

'There were two more after Elizabeth, but both died in infancy.

That's why there's a large gap between Elizabeth and Cecilia.'

'It does seem a shame that as the eldest of the family, and only son, you've distanced yourself from them all.'

Luke shrugged. 'The sea is my life and always will be until I'm forced to retire. Being the eldest and only boy my parents gave me the best education, sending me away to boarding school, so it wasn't surprising that I grew away from them all and made my own decision about my career. I didn't feel the foundry was the place for me. I do realise how disappointed my father must have been, and if I hadn't run away to sea he would have compelled me to go into the business.'

He sounded bitter, Fran thought.

'I think we'd better go back to the station,' he said, indicating that he didn't wish to discuss his family any further. Fran had heard enough to understand what it must have been like for him, an only boy with three younger sisters. She didn't blame him for the decision he had made. He was something of a rebel, and he had obviously wounded his parents deeply. Being a parent herself she could sympathise with them. On the other hand, after all these years she felt that they should have forgiven him. He had proved himself and they ought to be proud of him.

The steam train puffed its way out of the station and was soon passing over the magnificent cantilever bridge that spanned the Firth of Forth.

'The Forth Bridge is one of the great wonders of the world,' Luke explained as he took Fran and Hilda to the window to look out. 'A great engineering achievement. Here's a penny each for you to throw out for luck, as it's your first time across.'

'This will be something to write and tell your sisters about,' Fran said, and immediately became engulfed in remorse that the others were not able to share these new experiences.

They returned to their seats and very quickly reached their destination on the other side of the water, the neat little town of Dunfermline. Then came the task of collecting their many trunks and cases, which a porter took to Luke's car. The five-mile journey was the climax now to so many hours of travelling. Hills rose from green pastures where sheep and cattle grazed undisturbed, and nestling in the valley was the Craiglee Loch, blue from the reflection of an azure sky. The village consisted of a few isolated whitewashed cottages dotted among rocky hillocks.

'This is the main street, if you can call it that,' Luke said. 'There's a post office and general stores where you can get most of the supplies you'll need. The local kirk – '

'What's *that*?' Hilda demanded.

'Church, and attached to it is a local infant's school, but you're past that, aren't you? So you'll go by bus into Dunfermline every day. I expect you'll soon get used to it and make friends with the other children.'

Hilda remained thoughtful after that, and Fran too, as Luke drove beyond the so-called main street, past the cluster of cottages, and down a steep hill where he turned left and up an incline until a handsome stone house came into view. Fran gasped with pleasure. It was larger than she had imagined. Several windows on the upper floor were curtained with dainty lace, and on the lower floor the front door was reached by a flight of steps running down the side of the house. Even before Luke had switched off the car engine, the front door opened and a thin little woman ran down the steps.

'Hullo there,' she called cheerily. 'You'll be Captain and Mrs Hammond. I'm Jenny Logan. I'm pleased to meet you.'

Luke got out of the car and went to shake hands with the housekeeper, and then he introduced Fran and Hilda. Jenny Logan was well past sixty, Fran thought, but the warmth and friendliness of her welcome made her seem much younger.

First Fran just had to inspect her new home, and it was the view from each window that took precedence. Below street level was the basement floor housing the kitchen and living rooms, which at the back of the house looked out over green pastures and a stream that led into the loch half a mile away. It was past noon and the sun was high, its reflection glistening on the distant water. Fran was enchanted.

'This house was owned by a wealthy landowner many years ago,' Jenny said. 'Not many houses here run to three floors and two bathrooms. By town standards it's regarded as a cottage, but most in the area are very tiny compared with this. You have other children, I understand, so there's plenty of room for them to come to stay for their holidays. It's been well modernised, but they had to conform to keeping the original character of the house. I hope you like it, Mrs Hammond, and I hope you'll be happy here in our little community.'

'It's quite lovely,' Fran said. 'I'm sure we'll be very happy here.' She looked at Luke, wondering whether he was responsible for telling Jenny Logan about the other girls. She felt her spirits lift at once at the suggestion that they might come for their school holidays.

'I'll serve dinner as soon as you're ready,' Jenny said. 'And then I'll start the unpacking while you're eating.'

They freshened up in the basement cloakroom, and then sat at the long oak refectory table in front of the dining-room window. Luke placed a hand over Fran's. 'Happy, darling?' he whispered.

'Couldn't be happier,' she answered, her blue eyes shining contentedly. 'It's all so fresh and the air so bracing. The house is much larger than you led me to believe.'

'I wanted to surprise you. From the information passed on to me it seemed ideal. On the next floor there's a large sitting room where we can entertain. The smaller one can connect up to it by opening the folding doors, but we can enjoy long winter evenings cosily there together. Then there's a smaller room at the front next to my study which you could use for your sewing room. It can double up as a spare bedroom since it has a sofa bed in it. On the top floor we have four good-sized bedrooms and a bathroom. I know you can't wait to investigate everywhere properly when Jenny Logan has gone home.' He mouthed a kiss. 'I'll get rid of her as quickly as I can,' he whispered.

'How do you know so much detail about the house if you haven't seen it before?'

'I told you; Elizabeth. She came to inspect it, made a plan of the house, the rooms and everything in the rooms. I didn't want you to get here and not have everything you might need. Elizabeth did a good job – and in finding Jenny Logan. How often she comes and the hours she works will be our joint decision.' He leaned across and held her chin gently. 'Just make sure you're never too tired for me when I come home.'

'By what you've told me about your work I'll never know when to expect you.'

His dark eyes smouldered as he gazed into hers. 'That's the whole idea, darling. The element of surprise. Never let me come home to find you wallpapering, as you were in Brimdene. That life style is over for you now. I want you to have time to enjoy our married life.'

The light went out of Fran's eyes. Could she possibly cope with this new life of grandeur? Without Ma and the girls to work for, how ever was she going to occupy her time? She was grateful that at that moment Jenny's footsteps could be heard coming from the stone-floored kitchen with Hilda assisting her.

'Now you sit yourself down with your mummy and daddy. I haven't prepared anything heavy, Mrs Hammond,' Jenny said, half apologetically. 'But in my experience travelling lessens the appetite, so I've cooked some potatoes to go with a cold platter and a green salad.'

'It looks delicious, Jenny,' Luke said. 'Kind of you to take so much trouble. So many hours' travelling has made us all tired. I think you can leave whenever you're ready.'

Jenny looked surprised. 'But the clearing, and washing-up?'

'Um, well, yes . . . after you've done that, of course.' Luke smiled at the housekeeper in his own charming way. 'We can help ourselves to anything else we might need. It'll be an early night, I think. Time to explore tomorrow.'

'I'll leave you to eat in peace then,' Jenny said. 'I'll start on the unpacking.'

When she had left the room, Fran said: 'I could have done that, Luke. And the washing-up. I hope I won't be banned from my own kitchen.'

'Not at all. Jenny will want at least one day off a week, and part of Sundays, but you must arrange all that with her. Just put yourself in Mrs Maitland's shoes now. You're the lady of the house.'

'Are you really my daddy?' Hilda chipped in.

'I'm officially your step father,' Luke said. 'It is a kind of adopted Daddy. I would consider it a great honour if you would call me daddy, even though I can't hope to take the place of your own father. It'll sound nice and homely, don't you think?'

Hilda looked at Fran, and Fran averted her gaze. It was small details like this that she felt she couldn't handle. Luke was very good at answering Hilda's awkward questions, so she decided it was best left to him.

'My real daddy's been gone a long time, so I don't expect he'd mind if you take his place.'

'Eat your dinner and stop chattering, Hilda,' Fran said. 'We'll have a rest afterwards and then explore the garden.'

Hilda ate quite well for her, but Fran's appetite had vanished.

'You'll have to do better than that, Mrs Hammond,' Luke said, after Hilda had left the room to go and find Jenny Logan.

'I'm just not hungry, Luke,' Fran excused. 'We've had so little exercise, and the long, tiring journey is beginning to catch up with me. I shall feel better after a good night's sleep.'

'Sounds as if you're warning me off.'

'Don't be silly. But we do have to come down to earth sometime.'

'You wouldn't let me make love to you at Brimdene because you were embarrassed with your mother and the girls under the same roof. I can't promise that I can always be so accommodating. This is still our honeymoon, you know.'

'Give me time, Luke – please?'

Luke stood up and helped Fran to her feet. He held her in the circle of his arms, placing his mouth over hers until she relaxed and he knew that he was drawing the doubts away from the forefront of her mind. When her body became supple he relaxed his hold. Just the hint of arousing a response in her satisfied him for the moment. Didn't he have a lifetime to indulge himself with his lovely wife? He must be the happiest sailor in the world, he thought. At last the woman of his dreams was really his, to make him happy for the rest of his days.

Chapter Eleven

There were just about six weeks left of the school term, and Fran felt it was of little value to send Hilda to school for that short period of time, but Luke insisted that it would help Hilda to adjust. Each morning they got up early so that Hilda was in the village to catch the eight-thirty school bus into Dunfermline. Fran went with her the first day, but after that Hilda went with the other children from Craiglee and the surrounding villages.

Luke was on leave for a further three weeks, and the weather was fine and warm for most of that time. Once Hilda had left for school and Jenny Logan had arrived to look after the house, Fran and Luke were free to explore their new habitat. At first there was a slight tension between them. Luke wanted to make the most of every minute they were alone together, while Fran worried about Hilda and needed constant reassurance that she was all right. She worried, too, about the family back in Brimdene. Her mother's letters, instead of helping her to settle, had the opposite effect and made her homesick, even though Ma assured her that they were all fine.

Luke drove them into Edinburgh so that Fran could see the castle and visit the shops. He did everything he could to keep her mind occupied. On the way home they picked Hilda up from school as they passed through Dunfermline.

Instead of sitting in the car to wait near the gate, Luke got out and helped Fran from the passenger seat.

'We can't go in,' she said hesitantly. 'We'd best wait here.'

'We're going in to see the head teacher,' Luke said. 'Just to put our minds at rest that Hilda is quite happy here.'

Fran looked up at her husband with a new understanding. What a kind man, she thought. He was doing this for her, recognising her concern for Hilda. It was so good to have a strong man, a masterful man to take her arm and guide her along, demanding attention.

They were shown into the head mistress's study almost at once, and invited to sit and take tea, which Luke politely refused.

'It's a big step to bring our daughter from the south to the north,' Luke said. 'She's quite a delicate child and we felt we needed to know, without her knowledge, of course, how she has settled in.'

Fran listened with nothing but admiration. The middle-aged head mistress took off her glasses and looked at her visitors with favourable esteem.

'How sensible of you to come to see me, Captain Hammond – Mrs Hammond. Hilda seems a bright child, and is enjoying her school work. I'd say that mebbe she's a wee bit behind the other girls of her age, but it's early days yet. I'm sure it's nothing serious, and if necessary when we make an end-of-term assessment we'll give her special coaching in order that she catches up before it's time for her to take the scholarship. Naturally she was a wee bit cautious to begin with, but already she's making friends with her classmates.'

'We'll help in any way we can, Miss McGregor. I shall be away at sea periodically so my wife will be able to give her extra tuition if you can advise her.'

'I've tried to help her as much as I can in the past,' Fran put in. 'She's lost quite a lot of schooling due to illness, especially in the winter, so I shall be very grateful if you can allow her to bring work home.'

'That shouldn't be necessary for the rest of this term, Mrs Hammond. We'll take time to make a proper valuation of her capabilities and tell you our findings on the end-of-term report.'

Luke carried the interview to its conclusion in his usual charming manner, and then they went to sit in the car to wait until the school bell rang and the children, aged between eight and eleven, poured out. When Hilda appeared she was surrounded by other girls of her own age and seemed reluctant to make for the school bus.

'She looks contented enough to me,' Luke observed. 'This change could be the making of her. She's evidently the sociable type and has quickly made friends.'

'It depends on the Scottish winter,' Fran said. 'It just might be too much for her.'

Fran caught the impatient sigh Luke gave as he got out of the car and called Hilda. She guessed that like everyone else he considered she pampered Hilda too much, but he didn't know – no one knew – the worry she'd had in bringing Hilda up. Like Lennie she was frail, fell victim easily to coughs, colds and winter chills, and no one was going to tell Fran how to rear her own children.

On the drive home Hilda sang them a new song she had learned at school, and was full of all the activities she was enjoying with her new friends, so that any tension between Fran and Luke quickly vanished.

At the weekend, Hilda's first week at school over, they drove to Loch Lomond for a picnic and then travelled farther north to stay overnight in a small crofter's cottage on the shore of the loch in Glen Dochart. They enjoyed a leisurely two days, driving in a circular route to return to Craiglee by late Sunday afternoon. Luke saw the colour back in Fran's cheeks, and he thought Hilda had never looked better. The Scottish air was suiting them, and they appeared to be enjoying the new adventure. Fran was more at peace with herself, he thought, though he knew she watched eagerly for the postman to come each weekday.

As soon as Hilda had left for school the following morning, and Jenny had begun her work, Luke suggested a long walk over the hills. At first Fran seemed reluctant. There had been no word from Prue, and she was worried that Babs might be pining for her. She knew it was no use talking to Luke about it. He was being considerate about Hilda but she couldn't expect him to worry over the other girls the way she did. When the postman had passed by, Luke managed to persuade her.

'It's going to be a very hot day according to the paper so we shan't need coats or anything,' he said.

They walked across hillsides where sheep grazed in the morning sunshine, rested on boulders before going on while Luke related amusing stories of his life in the Navy to lift Fran's spirits. At midday they found an isolated spot among some rocks to sit and eat the sandwiches Jenny had prepared, and afterwards they spread out the day's papers to read together.

'I don't like the look of the news from Germany,' Luke said with a worried frown.

'You don't think there's going to be trouble, do you?' Fran asked.

'Who can say? This Adolf Hitler sounds like a maniac, bent on persecuting the Jewish people. Hundreds are being taken from their homes and put in concentration camps. I don't care for the sound of it, Fran.'

'There isn't going to be another war, is there? Oh, Luke, I couldn't bear it! The last one was bad enough.'

'We mustn't look on the black side, darling – but, just in case there is, we mustn't waste a minute, must we?'

He snatched the pages of newspaper she was holding and pulled her into his arms.

'Not here, Luke!' she protested.

'I can't wait any longer, and why not out here? Not a soul about except for the sheep, and I'm sure they'll be discreet and leave us alone.'

They had left the beaten track to rest on a lonely hillside overlooking a small loch.

'These huge boulders of rock will protect us from the breeze, and keep us out of sight of stray walkers,' Luke said, as his mouth explored hers, silencing her protests. The grass was dry and soft beneath them as he gently undressed her, fear of war forgotten in such peaceful surroundings. Her porcelain-white skin was sensitive to his touch, her breasts cool beneath his lips. Tender hands smoothed her rounded belly, and long fingers teased in the silky hair between her thighs. She moaned with ecstasy, arched herself in an urgent need to mate with him. Their heavy sighs and measured heartbeats melded together as the rhythm increased until an explosive climax united them as one.

'My God!' Luke panted. 'You devastate me – how can I go away and leave you even for a day?'

Fran coiled her arms round Luke's neck and drew him down again so that their cheeks rested gently against one another.

'Don't speak of leaving – not yet,' she said. 'I'm sorry if I've rejected you, but I'm not completely here, if you know what I mean.'

'I do understand, and the parting will get easier as time passes. Just remember that I shall be back, wanting you just the way you are today. Say you love me, Fran. I want to hear the words as well as enjoy the action.'

'You know I love you, Luke. What woman in her right mind would even consider . . . doing . . . what I've done . . .' She sat up suddenly, sobs of anguish escaping unchecked.

Luke wrapped her in his arms, lovingly protective. 'Darling, forgive me,' he begged. 'Have I been utterly selfish? Your girls are the one thing that comes between us – they make me feel inadequate. However perfect our union is, I don't feel that I can compete with them.'

'Luke,' Fran said. 'There's no question of competition. I'm the mother of four girls and nothing can change that. I can't help my feelings for them and I can't rid myself of the terrible guilt. They shouldn't, they mustn't come between us. But why – oh, why can't they come here to live with us? We could be happy all together. They'd be company for me when you're away at sea, and you'd learn to love them. It would give them a chance to learn to love you.

At least during their schooldays. They'll leave home soon enough. Please, Luke, I can't bear the pain of rejecting them.'

'So now you know the pain I had to endure when you rejected me,' he said savagely. 'You've never tried to understand what hell my life was. First I was rejected by my own parents, spurned and made to feel like an outcast. You were the one good thing that ever happened to me, Fran. But you went off with another man.'

'Luke, I was practically married. If only you'd never invited yourself to that wretched party. The pain you experienced you brought on yourself. You knew the situation – but no, you became obsessed with the notion that you wanted me. I wasn't even aware of it. We shouldn't be compatible – we're from different backgrounds. How am I ever going to feel at ease with the other officers' wives?'

She had tried to sit up but he kept her securely on her back, his body almost covering her nakedness.

'But we are compatible, Fran darling. You know that, and whatever differences we have, our love will prove to be strong enough to surmount them. Let not the sun go down upon thy wrath – rather let the sun go down every night on our union.' He kissed her again, ingeniously inducing her lips to respond to his desire. 'It's inhibiting enough having Hilda with us, let alone four of them.'

'There would only be three. Babs should be here for company for Hilda, and Ruby would keep her eye out for both of them. Kate wouldn't want to leave her job now, and she could watch out for Ma. It would be all right, Luke, really it would.'

'No, Fran. Don't build up a dream that can never be reality. You'll only torture yourself. They're better off as things are. Too much change in children's lives can ruin them. It's much wiser to let them remain in familiar surroundings and school. They've already had one major change in moving to Brimdene.' He kissed her again with passionate aggression. 'This is my dream, and I'm going to hold on to it. As to fitting in with my life style, of course you will. I shall always be at your side to carry you through any awkward moments, but the other women will love you – just as I do. Just take care, though, that you don't let any other officer fall in love with you. I'd kill to keep what I own.'

'Now you're being ridiculous, Luke. Don't talk such utter nonsense. You sound so possessive.'

He growled, and caught a fold of her neck in his teeth, biting playfully as his hands roamed over her pliable body. Fran lay replete, with her eyes closed against the glare of the sun, while Luke caressed, knowing that he would always be the winner of this contest. But he was also clever enough to know that in order to retain Fran's love he must share her concern for her girls. He sighed, knowing he must forgo any further pleasures to make sure they were back in the village in time to meet Hilda off the school bus.

They sat on the stone wall that fronted the shop and post office, Luke with his arm casually round Fran's shoulder. Neighbours passed the time of day as they went in and out of the shop.

'I'm sure people will think it strange for a couple of our age to be behaving like this,' she said, feeling that they were drawing attention to themselves.

'Behaving like what?' Luke asked. 'They know that I've most likely been away at sea for weeks or even months. Some chaps think separation keeps the sparkle in a marriage. The waiting, wanting – and then the satisfaction.'

'We may have only just got married but we're not in our twenties, for goodness sake.'

'No one knows that we've only just got married. That's our secret, my darling. People will look at us and see how we feel about each other, and envy us.'

Fran stood up as the bus came chugging round the bend in the narrow road. She supposed Luke was right. What did it matter to anyone in this vicinity that she had been a widow until recently?

As always the boys were first off the bus, and then some little girls who lived nearby; then a pause – where was Hilda? Fran went closer to the open door and saw a young teacher who came from the next village helping Hilda along.

'What's the matter?' Fran asked with considerable concern. 'What's happened?'

Miss Murray helped Hilda down the steps until Luke stepped forward and lifted her the rest of the way. Her leg was stiff with white bandages, and at once she began to cry and reached out for Fran.

'It isn't very serious, Mrs Sheldon,' Miss Murray began.

'Hammond,' Luke put in shortly.

What an unnecessary interruption, Fran thought, glancing back to Miss Murray with impatience.

'Oh, I do beg your pardon,' the embarrassed young woman said, flushing as her gaze met Luke's. 'I didn't realise – '

'Please, Miss Murray, what's happened to Hilda?'

'She fell in the playground. She's grazed her knee rather badly. We cleaned her up and as it happened the school nurse was in the building so she attended to Hilda. She put some healing cream on it and bandaged it up.' Miss Murray smiled at Hilda. 'Now, come along, Hilda, you've been so brave all day. You'll be all right, and we don't let a little thing like a fall interfere with our school work, do we?'

Hilda, with dirty wet streaks running down her cheeks, opened her large brown eyes and stared at the teacher. 'No, Miss Murray,' she replied softly, but with a hint of defiance.

'Perhaps we should let the doctor look at it,' Fran said, her blue eyes ice-cold. 'She may have got dirt, glass or anything in it.'

Luke placed a hand on Fran's shoulder. 'Thank you very much for looking after Hilda, Miss Murray,' he said. 'We'll see how it is in the morning. Better not to disturb the dressing for today.'

Miss Murray's face was still scarlet, and her eyes burned with obvious admiration for the handsome man. 'That's what the nurse advised,' she said breathlessly. As the bus driver revved his engine, she added: 'I'm sure you'll be all right, Hilda. See you tomorrow, dear.'

'Not if I have anything to do with it,' Fran muttered crossly as the bus drew away.

'Fran dear,' Luke said quietly, 'don't jump to conclusions so easily. It's probably nothing. I don't always have a ship's doctor on board so as captain I have to deal with quite a few minor ailments. Let's wait and see how things are in the morning.'

'You may be used to tough sailors, but you don't know anything about children,' Fran snapped.

'No,' he responded softly, after a lengthy pause. 'I never got the chance, did I? I was denied caring for my own son.'

'He wasn't *your* son,' Fran hissed. She reached out and took Hilda's hand, but the child made a great display of her stiff leg. Luke swung her up in his arms and hurried along the narrow road to the track which led to their home. No one spoke, but there was a tight spring of tension between them.

'Oh, deary me,' Jenny said when they got in. 'What have you been up to, lassie?'

'Fallen in the school yard,' Fran said shortly. 'That's the trouble with a mixed school. Boys are always so rough. At home the girls went to a proper girls' school.'

Fran helped Hilda to sit on the couch in the sitting room and Jenny went away to prepare afternoon tea.

'It wasn't the boys who pushed me, Mummy,' Hilda explained, now less tearful. 'We were playing a game and I just fell. It wasn't anyone's fault.'

'Well, you just rest there, dear,' Fran said. 'What would you like for your tea?'

'She'll have the same as the rest of us, and she'll sit at the table,' Luke said. 'It will only get stiffer by keeping it immobile. I doubt very much that such a large bandage is really necessary.'

Fran shot him an angry frown, which was met by a look of exasperation.

'Let's do a puzzle, Hilda, to help us forget,' Luke said brightly, and he went away to fetch some of Hilda's things. Fran followed him up to Hilda's bedroom.

'You're deliberately undermining my authority,' Fran said, her cheeks glowing red with impatience.

'You look delightful when you're angry, darling, but we're not going to embark on a slanging match after such a perfect day. You know as well as I do that you're making a mountain out of a molehill just as you usually do where Hilda's concerned. Children fall and hurt themselves all the time. The average mother would do nothing except tend her children if they all pampered their offspring like you do Hilda.'

'I do not pamper her!' Fran shouted. 'You just don't care.'

'I care a great deal more than you realise. I want to see Hilda grow up to be independent of you, Fran. You won't always be able to run to her aid. She can stand on her own feet much better than you give her credit for and she's a devious little madam, she knows she can use you for her own ends.'

'Just as you use me for your own ends.'

Luke grabbed Fran's wrist tightly. 'And what is that supposed to mean?'

'Let go,' she pleaded in a softer tone. 'You're hurting me.'

'And you're hurting me by your insinuations. How do I use you, for goodness sake?'

'Didn't you use me for your own pleasure that first time we met?' She inclined her head as she was forced to look upwards into his demanding glare. 'Haven't you used me ever since to satisfy your own guilt? Lennie was not your son, so stop saying that he was. And don't you use me just to go to bed with?'

Luke flung her hand away from him and Fran burst into tears. Hot, angry, frustrated tears. Tears that no man could understand, let alone Luke Hammond.

Luke picked up the few items he wanted for Hilda, started for the door and then turned back. 'If you're not in a warm bath in five minutes I shall come and dump you in one. You're over- reacting, Fran. A bath will soothe away your troubles. I can appreciate that you're homesick, but you made the sacrifice – don't plead martyrdom as well.' He stalked off with determined footsteps, and Fran threw herself down on Hilda's bed and wept.

She felt angry with herself for allowing such a minor incident to blow up out of all proportion, but the truth was she felt guilty on so many counts. Guilty that she had allowed Luke to come between her and the family. Guilty that she had split the girls up. Guilty that she had not insisted that they have the girls with them wherever they went. And, most of all, today – guilty at allowing Luke to make love to her out there on the hills. In fact, she had to admit, if only to herself, that she felt guilty at the way she responded so readily to Luke's demands. She wished she could say that in times of passion she thought only of Henry, but she loved Luke with a different kind of love. The physical side of marriage had become less important to her after bearing five children. She and Henry had enjoyed intimate times but left to her those occasions would have become even less frequent. There was always work and worry, and she had been too tired really to enjoy the mating times. Now Luke saw to it that she had little of importance to do except keep him happy. And, to her chagrin, making him happy made her happy too.

The fact that Hilda was hurt at school while she and Luke were indulging their new marital status pricked her conscience with a degree of shame and remorse. Luke was right, she did coddle Hilda, perhaps over-zealously. She couldn't excuse it as salving her conscience in the present circumstances, for even Henry had gently chided her over the same thing. She felt the need to cherish Hilda more than the others. Fran didn't care what other people said, Hilda was more delicate, and so much like Lennie.

A tender touch on her arm interrupted the bout of self-criticism.

'I've run the bath, darling,' Luke said. 'Have a good long soak. I've asked Jenny to delay tea for an hour to give you time.' He pulled her to her feet and held her close. 'Forgive me, darling, I know it's time you need. We'll make up later.' Luke kissed her cheek lightly and guided her to the bathroom. 'I'll keep Hilda company.'

As Fran removed her clothes and stepped into the cloud of steam she thought of the moments of sheer bliss enjoyed earlier. This, after all, was still their honeymoon, and Luke on leave for just another ten days. She felt herself shiver with apprehension. With Hilda away at school, and Luke absent from home, how on earth was she going to fill her time? She must raise the subject with Luke before he returned to duty. Maybe she could dispense with Jenny Logan's services? She could run the house by herself.

Soothed and much calmer, Fran went downstairs to the sitting room, where Luke was beside Hilda on the couch fitting pieces of a jigsaw puzzle to make a picture of a farmyard scene. Their dark heads were almost touching, and at the sound of her footsteps they both looked up simultaneously. Fran stared, shocked by the similarity in their looks. Dark eyes, dark hair, and an expression of – she couldn't put it into words – a mixture of self-satisfaction, triumph or curiosity? Hilda was exactly like Lennie in looks, which was why Fran adored her so much – and for the first time a flash of real doubt entered her mind.

'Feeling better, dear?' Luke asked softly. 'Less tense, I'm sure. A nice cup of tea and all will be well.' He stood up, and smiled right into her blue eyes as if he could read her troubled thoughts. 'I'll go and have a wash and shave while you keep Hilda company for fifteen minutes.'

Everything organised for her – isn't that just what she had longed for?

'Daddy's so good at finding the right pieces,' Hilda said.

Fran experienced a stab of pain at the easy way Hilda referred to Luke as Daddy, but she knew she should be getting used to it. Luke hadn't forced the issue, she remembered. Hilda herself had suggested it.

'We've nearly finished this puzzle,' Hilda continued. 'Daddy said that he's taking you into Edinburgh tomorrow to do some shopping and he'll buy me another one to do. A bigger, more difficult one to last me while he's away.'

'I don't know about that,' Fran said quickly. 'We'll have to see how your leg is, won't we?'

'It's nothing, really. Daddy says I'm too grown up to stay home just because I fell over. I cried only a little bit at school, otherwise the boys would have called me cry-baby. And if I don't go to school tomorrow they'll laugh at me. Besides, I want Daddy to buy me that new puzzle.'

Jenny came to announce that tea was ready so they went downstairs to the dining room. Fran noticed that Hilda's leg wasn't so stiff that she couldn't manage the stairs quite easily now.

Across the table Luke's gaze met Fran's. A moment of indecision, a warm smile from Luke – and any animosity vanished.

They were up a little earlier next morning after a good night's sleep. Undisturbed sleep, after a time of apologies, followed by cuddles and gentle kisses, but no further demands made by Luke. Fran almost wished he had been aggressively passionate; instead he had cradled her in his arms and lulled her to sleep.

By the time Fran emerged from the bathroom, Hilda was lying on her bed while Luke removed the bandages on her leg.

'Come and inspect this, Fran,' Luke called. 'It's very clean-looking, and with a new dry dressing each day it shouldn't fester.'

'Mm,' Fran agreed, 'it doesn't look too angry. Will you rebandage it or shall I?'

'Hilda? Your choice,' Luke said.

'Daddy can do it while you see to breakfast. Are my sandwiches done?'

'I'll see to it now,' Fran said. She went downstairs to the kitchen, where Jenny had just arrived.

'Morning, Mrs Hammond. Another good day by the feel of it. Quite a haze over the hills – heat haze, I shouldn't wonder. How's the lassie this morning?'

'Oh, she's fine, Jenny, thanks. My husband is rebandaging her leg. She seems keen to go to school, so we're going to Edinburgh. Must make the most of the time my husband is home on leave. It goes all too quickly.'

'Ah. Morning, Jenny.' Luke came striding into the kitchen. 'Mrs Hammond has told you we're going into Edinburgh today? I'd really like to take her out to dinner there – how are you fixed today?'

'Nothing so important that I can't be free when Hilda comes home from school, sir,' Jenny said, with an understanding smile.

After breakfast, Fran paused in their bedroom to look out over the landscape. The meadows were white with sheep this morning, and the sun glistened on the ribbon of water as the stream chortled its way through the valley. So much like Sherbrook, Fran thought, yet vastly different with craggy hillocks and boulders, an altogether more rugged scene. She remembered the rising river back home. Here the house was situated on high ground so that there was no fear of flooding. So much had happened in the past two years that the bad memories were less frightening, but she could still call them to mind and a chill ran through her.

She heard a car engine running so she hurried to complete her toilet, and within the hour she was sitting beside Luke, starting out on the day's adventure. The road was quietly pleasant to Dunfermline and then they were on the ferry, crossing the wide stretch of water to enter the capital city.

Luke was a good companion and an expert guide. They visited places of interest, had coffee in a plush restaurant, and then shopped in the elegant stores, Luke insisting that they buy presents for the girls and Ma. They sat in the gardens while Fran wrote on picture postcards to include in the parcel. She hadn't had much opportunity to write long letters yet, but she knew that a surprise parcel would please them, especially Babs. Her heart ached with longing for them all, and writing to them brought a lump to her throat as she penned several kisses to each one.

After the parcel had been posted they reclined on the grass in the gardens and listened to the band of the Scots Guards. Fran took off her shoes and sat up, hugging her knees. The music was too nosiy to allow any conversation and she was grateful for a time during which she could allow her thoughts free rein. Tomorrow she could expect to receive her weekly letter from her mother. She wished one would come every day, but she knew Ma didn't have the time. Here, life went at a slower pace, and with no washing, cooking, or cleaning to do, she had all the time in the world to express her feelings on paper, even if her long screeds usually ended up in the kitchen fire. She had to rethink each and every sentence. To Ruby and Ma she compiled a long list of do's and don'ts, hoping that they were remembering to turn the gas off at night and change the bed linen and their clothes regularly. To Kate, her instructions were to visit Ma and Ruby at every opportunity. And to Babs she wrote saying how much she loved her, and how sorry she was that she couldn't have her in Scotland with them. That letter always went into the fire, usually several attempts, before she could compose what she considered was a happy, lively letter that wouldn't make her baby unhappy.

Fran prayed that her second marriage would strengthen, so that she could influence Luke in bringing them all together again. The thought of returning to Brimdene for the long summer holidays kept her going, yet at the back of her mind lurked a dreadful feeling that it wasn't going to happen. How could it, when Luke was going to be working from the Rosyth dockyard? The ship of which he was now captain was undergoing major repairs and refurbishment, so his hours would initially be similar to those of a bank clerk. As the weeks and months went by, the ship would be taken out for trials, and instead of preparing to return south, Fran knew she was expected to remain in Craiglee like a dutiful wife, ready to greet her husband with open arms on his return, just like other naval women. She hesitantly suggested that perhaps Ruby and Babs could visit them in Scotland with Kate, while Ma was having a holiday with Eric and Annie, but Luke quickly reminded her that Kate, being in the hotel trade, would not be able to take her holiday during the season. He considered it unwise to allow Ruby and Babs to make such a long journey on their own.

'There'll be other times, darling,' he consoled. 'I may be away for a longer period, and then if it coincides with school holidays you and Hilda can go down to Brimdene.' It didn't take Fran long to realise that either Luke wasn't telling, or he really didn't know how long he was likely to be at sea at any given time and her hopes of going home diminished rapidly.

Chapter Twelve

Hilda had begun to make friends with girls of her own age. Fran was left on her own. At first the other naval wives invited her for afternoon tea, or coffee, or to help with some project for the needy. Luke had cleverly used that last visit to Edinburgh to attend a dinner for officers and their wives. Fran had protested that she wasn't suitably dressed for such an occasion but it had turned out to be a casual affair and she had enjoyed meeting the other women, while Luke had become acquainted with some of the men he would be working with. Various invitations had followed, and before Luke's leave was over he gave a small cocktail party for some of his colleagues and their wives. Fran had blossomed, organising the affair with Jenny Logan, whose niece helped with the preparations as well as being waitress for the evening. Hilda proudly wore the dress she had worn at her mother's wedding and was quite the sophisticated daughter of Captain and Mrs Luke Hammond.

By the time the long school holidays had arrived, though, Fran noticed that no further invitations were forthcoming. Luke had assured her that naval wives always stuck together while their husbands were away at sea, but it was Hilda who enjoyed the most exciting social life.

When Fran came out of the post office one morning, she collided with a woman she had met on several occasions. Hilda frequently visited their house for tea with the daughter, Alice.

'Not a very nice morning, is it?' Fran greeted, after they had apologised for literally bumping into each other.

The woman looked sternly into Fran's face, shrugging indifferently as she said: 'Can't expect anything else up here in Scotland.' Then Alice's mother turned and hurried into the post office.

Fran felt the rebuff keenly. She couldn't believe that she had offended the woman in any way and they had always seemed on the best of terms. Maybe Luke was her husband's superior officer. There was, she knew, some professional ranking jealousy, more among the wives than the men. Fran walked home perplexed, then decided that maybe the woman wasn't feeling too good that day and dismissed the incident from her mind.

On another occasion, when Fran and Hilda were approaching the bus stop on their way in to Dunfermline, Alice and her mother, who were already waiting there, suddenly turned back towards their house.

'Oh, can we wait for Alice?' Hilda begged. The bus could already be heard in the distance, rumbling along the lonely country road.

'Better not, dear, there isn't another one for ages. If Alice and her mother don't get a move on they'll miss it. They either changed their minds or had forgotten something.'

Fran and Hilda boarded the bus and it started off with no sign of Alice and her mother. Fran experienced a feeling of unease. No, she thought, she was imagining things. Alice's mother couldn't possibly have missed the bus on purpose because she and Hilda approached. All the same, it did look as if they had turned back as soon as they saw them.

Walking along the narrow streets of Dunfermline they met one or two other officers' wives and their children. Not many of them lived as far out as Craiglee. Some lived in Dunfermline, but most as near to the dockyard as possible. The girls exchanged greetings, but the women all seemed in a mighty hurry today. Fran felt as if she were being sent to Coventry – but why? What had she done? Did they know, could they tell that she had come from a less affluent background than most of them?

That evening, when the rain had begun to pour down in torrents, and Hilda was in her room playing with her dolls, Fran went down to the kitchen to help Jenny pot the jam she was making.

'I can manage, Mrs Hammond. It's a messy old job.'

'Oh no, not you as well, Jenny. I made plenty of jam at home in the country. I can't get used to having nothing to do except sew, and I don't feel like that this evening. I get the feeling that everyone's sending me to Coventry. Perhaps you can tell me why?'

Jenny turned the gas up until the jam in the large preserving pan boiled and spat angrily. She went on stirring briskly, not wanting to face Fran.

'There is something,' Fran said, now indignant. 'Jenny, please, for goodness sake, what have I done?'

'Well, ma'am,' Jenny said hesitantly, 'it's a story that's going about, but I dare say there's little truth in it.' She sniffed haughtily as if she didn't intend to reveal anything further.

'Go on, Jenny. It's better that I know what people are saying about me.'

Jenny turned the gas lower, balanced the long-handled wooden spoon across the top of the pan, and looked straight at Fran. 'I don't really like to say . . .' she began.

'Please, go on, Jenny,' Fran said.

'There's always gossip in a small village, ma'am, and especially among servicemen's wives. Some of the women have been asking me about you . . . and your other children, ma'am.'

'My other children? I'm sure by now everyone knows that we have three other daughters back home.'

'But they aren't – Hilda isn't – the captain's children?'

'No.' Fran paused. So, in spite of Luke's reticence, it hadn't taken long for the truth somehow to come out. 'I'm a widow. Was a widow, until I married Captain Hammond. I would have thought that was fairly obvious as Hilda's name is Sheldon.'

'It's just that the women feel it was wrong of you to leave the others behind when you came north. If you could bring Hilda, couldn't her sisters have come too?'

Fran felt her lips stiffen and her cheeks pale as she bit into the side of her mouth.

'It wasn't up to me,' she managed to say in a low voice, and then she fled to the seclusion of her bedroom.

Fran's guilt exploded into hurt, angry tears. Now Luke must let the girls come to them. Surely he wouldn't want himself and his wife criticised for the neglect of their children, even if they weren't actually his? But they were his, Fran thought angrily. They were his stepdaughters, and when he married her he became responsible for them too. How was she ever going to hold her head up again? Shame was something she had seldom felt before. People had admired her and Henry for the way they lived and conducted themselves. And more recently they respected Fran for being able to manage on her pension, the girls always looking well turned out and their home kept clean and comfortable. Whatever would Henry have said? Brother Eric too, and Henry's parents? They would all share her shame and feel so vexed – thank goodness she was many miles away from them.

It was no use indulging in self-pitying tears, though. She splashed her face with cold water and went back to the kitchen.

'I'm so sorry, Ma'am, I didn't mean to upset you,' Jenny said kindly. 'Folk are quick to condemn without knowing all the facts. I can see now that it has been a terrible wrench for you to leave your family.' She placed a hand on Fran's arm and led her into the dining room. 'Look,' she said softly, 'I've taken the liberty of making a pot of tea. I'm sure it will help. I've finished potting the jam and it looks good. Setting just right.'

Fran sat down heavily in the chair Jenny pulled out for her. 'This is the price one has to pay for marrying a man in the Royal Navy,' she said dismally.

'I don't know all the facts, Mrs Hammond, but I do know you care about your girls. You've spent hours making new dresses for them, and you write regularly.'

'I hoped Hilda and I would be going home for the long school holidays, but my husband is uncertain about his movements, and it's only right that I should be here when he comes home.'

Jenny sniffed disapprovingly as she poured the tea. Fran couldn't help wondering how Mrs Maitland would have handled this situation, but no one in her employ would have dared to question or criticise anything she did.

'Of course,' Jenny said, 'especially as you haven't been married that long.'

'Sit down and have a cup of tea with me, Jenny,' Fran said. 'My husband doesn't like our affairs discussed publicly, which is only natural, but I need to talk to someone as I miss the girls so much – so very much . . .' Her voice broke as sobs persisted.

'Tell me more about them,' Jenny said. 'It might help – and bring them closer to you. I was hoping they'd be coming to stay with you for a holiday. That's what servicemen's children usually do for the longest holidays.'

'Katie, my eldest girl, works in a hotel in Brimdene. She has to live in as she wants to make a career of the hotel trade. She's good at her job, loves cooking and in her last letter she says that her employer is going to pay for her to go to night school in the autumn to learn hotel management and book-keeping. And on another evening she's going to cookery classes.'

'My word, she must be keen! Most young girls are off out with boys at the first opportunity,' Jenny said.

'Not my Katie,' Fran said, remembering and hating herself for not responding to Kate's needs much earlier than she had done. 'I suppose everything happened so quickly really.'

It was a relief to talk to someone, even though Fran knew Luke would be angry at how much she had divulged. That night she lay awake for several hours, her heart aching, her body burning up with an anguish that seemed to tear limb from limb. Not because she had talked to Jenny Logan – Fran knew that she could trust her to be discreet – but her guilt was out in the open now. Her unshared guilt had been bad enough, but to think that women had been discussing the situation behind her back, learning as much as they could, it seemed, from Hilda, an innocent child. Fran was at a loss to know how to react. Luke would insist that she carry on as if nothing had happened, but Fran was capable of sending everyone else to Coventry just as they had her.

By the time Hilda returned to school for the autumn term, Fran had succeeded in building a barrier around herself. She noticed that the attitude of her neighbours changed. The women wanted to acknowledge her, but Fran merely nodded and passed by. She suspected that Jenny Logan had loyally defended her and endeavoured to put down the rumours, but, as always, Fran had her pride.

Early September, and Luke miraculously reappeared. He had been away for almost the whole of August, and Fran felt annoyed that she had been obliged to remain in Scotland when there had been no earthly reason that she couldn't have gone home to Brimdene – except that she didn't have sufficient money to make the decision herself. Luke was generous up to a point, insisting on certain standards in their comfortable life style to keep up appearances with fellow officers and their families. He saw to all the domestic financial arrangements, allowing Fran an ample allowance so that she could keep herself well dressed, but Fran quickly realised that he kept her on a tight purse string when he was away.

As always Luke's charm and sensuality swept her off her feet when he returned. She quickly forgot the unpleasantness she had encountered during his absence as he demonstrated his need for her. For several days he drew her firmly into his aura so that they loved and laughed in complete harmony. Then came the anticlimax as Luke tried to adapt to being on dry land again. He relived his month away by relating stories of some of his adventures, but he was restless, and was soon eager to attend social functions.

'We'll go to the dinner dance at the officers' mess at the weekend,' he suggested one evening as they sat in the small cosy sitting room.

Fran was thoughtful. She sat sewing the hem on a dress for Babs. 'Do we have to?' she asked.

'We do have to mix, darling. It's important to be seen to socialise. I thought you'd got over any shyness.'

'It's not that, Luke.' She stitched on, then looked up at her husband. 'I know you don't like people knowing that we've only recently got married, but Hilda has been talking to her friends.'

Luke's expression became serious. 'What's she been saying?'

'I don't know, but enough so that the women showed their dislike of me. It was almost as if they were sending me to Coventry.'

'You must be imagining things, Fran.'

'I don't think so. I mentioned it to Jenny and she was aware of the rumour which was circulating, that I had chosen to bring Hilda here with me but left the other girls behind.'

Luke stood up and paced the room. 'I knew I should have stuck to my guns and insisted that we start our married life on our own like any normal couple.'

'But we aren't a normal couple, Luke. I was a widow, with daughters who are my responsibility – and yours, if you wanted me to give up my independence to marry you.'

'You didn't need much persuading, as I recall.'

'You didn't give me much time to think about all that getting married again entailed.'

'So now you regret it?' His dark eyes flashed angrily.

'Luke,' Fran pleaded softly. 'You know I don't regret it. I don't like being parted from the girls. What woman – what mother – would? But I still can't see the reasoning behind leaving them down south when we've got room for them here. It isn't as if they'd get in your way. You aren't at home that much.'

'But when I am I want you to myself. I considered we had resolved such matters amicably and sensibly. Ruby is a capable girl and is company for your mother. I would have preferred that Babs had come with us. She's younger and would have adapted better than Hilda.'

'Hilda has settled down extremely well, though how she'll fare during a bad winter I don't know.'

'Hilda is old enough to be able to talk too much. You must make her understand that what goes on in this house is our business and must not be discussed outside.'

'She has always understood that. All my children know better than to talk too much outside the home, but children will be children. You can't expect her to forget that she's got other sisters.' She inclined her head with a wry smile. 'Even if you would prefer to dismiss them as if they don't exist.'

'You won't let me forget. For heaven's sake, I'm only home for a few days.' He ran his fingers through his hair in agitation. It sprang back into the mass of waves that helped to make him so attractive.

'We'll definitely go to the dinner dance,' he said. 'We have nothing to reproach ourselves with, so we can go with a clear conscience. We've done what we consider to be best for the girls, and it's no one else's business.'

'Wouldn't it be more sensible to reconsider and let the girls come here?'

'No! Definitely not, Fran, and don't get ideas about returning to Brimdene. Your home is with me.'

'But you aren't here all the time. I'm not used to having so much time on my hands. It's all such a – waste.'

'Waste!' Luke repeated with contempt. 'Is that how you see our marriage – a waste?'

Fran put aside her sewing and stood up to face him. 'You know I didn't mean it like that, Luke,' she said softly. 'I appreciate that you consider my happiness, but you can't know the unhappiness I've had to endure when you're away and I have time to think. Whatever would Henry say to the girls being separated like they are? It's so unjust, so unfair of me to have put my happiness before theirs.' Her chin quivered slightly but she fought off the emotion, which Luke would see as weakness. 'I find it very hard to live with myself,' she said.

She made for the door, but Luke was quick to grasp her arm and encircle her with a fierce embrace. 'You've been very brave. I do understand what it must be like. More so than you realise. Haven't I been separated from my family for far too many years?'

'But you made that choice. And you were sixteen when you ran away to sea.'

'Only a couple or so years older than Ruby. I hated the Navy at first. I hated the sea for luring me away from the security of a loving family. Maybe I'd have returned, with enough persuasion, but being totally rejected there was little choice but to stick it out. There was the matter of pride too, which became more important as the years went by.'

'We all suffer from too much pride,' Fran said. 'Maybe your parents would accept you willingly now. It often only takes one person to make the first move.'

'They rejected me, they must make that first move,' Luke said defiantly. 'The sea is my life now.'

'Does Elizabeth talk about you at home? Do they know you and she have always corresponded?'

'As far as I know my name is never mentioned. My being the only son, you'd have thought they'd have forgiven me and tried to understand, but it's too late now.' He sighed deeply, and Fran saw that he cared about the situation much more than he let on. 'Twenty-four years, to be exact. The longer the separation, the harder it is to be reconciled.' He bent and kissed her with some aggression. 'That's all in the past. It's our future that matters now, and we will go to the weekend event.'

'I don't want to go, Luke,' Fran said. 'I can't pretend that everything's all right when it's far from that.'

'You'll have me there to protect you. Just be your lovely smiling self. No other woman holds a candle to you – they're only jealous, after all.'

With his usual expertise Luke managed to quell all Fran's fears.

Blizzards, snow and ice heralded the beginning of a winter unlike anything Fran had ever experienced in the south of the country. Luke came home at intervals but for only short periods and when Hilda went down with a cold, Fran was glad to keep her home from school for company. Together they prepared for Christmas. Fran was ever hopeful that Luke would relent and please her by suggesting they all went to spend Christmas in Brimdene. Hilda painted pictures of the snowy scene on cards for all her sisters and grandparents, while her mother sewed and embroidered to make pretty garments for Kate, Ruby and Babs.

Luke arrived home on the day before Christmas Eve and Fran had to hide her disappointment. Ma had written to say that Kate would have to work over the Christmas holiday. Ruby's letter was full of the plans for her and Gran to spend the time with Gran and Grandad Sheldon, Uncle Nathan and his family. Babs, in her childish writing, expressed her excitement and hopes of all the presents that Father Christmas was expected to bring. Fran felt as if her heart had frozen solid. Wasn't it *her* duty to fill stockings and make the festive season as jolly for them all as possible? She sat in the kirk beside Luke and Hilda on Christmas Eve, which was a Sunday, and felt numb. Nothing could punish her more than not being part of a complete family at Christmastime. But they never could be a complete family again. Sometimes she visualised returning to Sherbrook, imagining that Henry and her father would be there, but with their deaths everything had changed. She found no enjoyment or solace in her devotions. Singing carols and watching the children act out the nativity play gave her no pleasure. She felt sick and empty inside.

Fran was almost relieved when Luke returned to his naval duties after she had experienced her first Scottish New Year. There was much to look back on with some measure of enjoyment. The pipe band, tartan skirts twirling in precision folk dancing, and the ceremonial serving of the haggis. She had to admit that Luke had done everything he could to make her happy, and Hilda had enjoyed a succession of parties before the new school term began. But the weather worsened. Snowdrifts reached window ledges, and the depth of it on the roads made going out an impossibility so that Hilda had to be coached at home by Fran. The postman was unable to deliver mail, and Fran knew it was hopeless to expect her letters to get any further than the post office, so she wrote to Ma and the girls in diary form, saving the pages for several weeks until at last the thaw came.

She was overjoyed when a batch of mail eventually reached Craiglee from all the family. It brought them all together during the time she spent reading and re-reading the news from home.

Kate had begun night school courses in catering and hotel management. She assured her mother that she was well, and so were the rest of the family, apart from the usual coughs and colds. Uncle Sam and Aunt Prue had brought Marion and Babs to Brimdene for the day before the younger girls returned to school. Gran was looking after the house very well with Ruby's help. Aunt Sissy visited them often and supervised things. Ruby was doing well at school and was nearly always top of the class in every subject. Fran felt the hint of guilt as she remembered how she had persistently grumbled at Ruby. As she stood, letter in hand, gazing out of the back windows at the distant, snow-capped hills, she could see Ruby clearly, kneeling in front of the old mill-house range, her small fingers black as she black-leaded the stove doors. Henry's voice came clear and gently reproaching, 'She's only ten, love.' Now Ruby was heading for her teens. A difficult time for most girls, and Fran wasn't there to see her through it. But she had to admit, as she read Kate's letter again, they seemed to be managing very well without her at the helm. She couldn't help wondering, though, whether they were conspiring together to make sure that Fran had nothing to worry about. Was everything really as serene as they made out? Another year had to pass before she could look forward to returning south again. Luke had made it clear that during his two-year service in Scotland she was to remain in Craiglee.

Before Luke came home again, Hilda caught a cold. Fran kept her home from school for much longer than was necessary, so that at the end of the next term her report was far from satisfactory. Luke's homecoming after several weeks at sea coincided with the arrival of the report, accompanied by a letter to Fran from the headmistress. Fran hurriedly folded the letter and tried to stuff it back into the envelope.

'Something I should see?' Luke asked. They were in the bedroom, still in night attire.

'Only a letter with Hilda's report,' Fran mumbled, as she sat on the side of the bed, pulling her knickers on. Luke had just come from the bathroom. Now he came to Fran's side of the bed and took her knickers away from her.

'I've only just got home after being starved for weeks,' he said softly.

They played tug of war with Fran's underwear for a few seconds.

'Jenny will be back in a minute,' Fran protested.

'She's gone shopping and won't be back for the next couple of hours.'

'Oh, Luke, how could you? It's not nice her knowing what we're doing.'

Luke smiled knowingly. 'So you know what to expect then?' He bent and kissed Fran's forehead. 'Jenny will be discreet. You should know that by now. She's worked for naval people before, you know.' He pushed Fran back across the bed, lifting her nightgown above her head while he teased, forcing her to roll in a ball. Luke was naked, having removed the loose-fitting robe he had been wearing, and just the feel of his virility next to her body roused Fran's womanly instincts. He looked almost out of place in the chilly climes of Scotland after spending some weeks in the Mediterranean. His body was healthily tanned from head to toe, an exciting image of masculine perfection.

Fran entwined her arms around his neck, momentarily forgetting the school report. Following the period of separation she was receptive to his kisses, and his intimate caresses stirred her to an impatient longing for the ladder of ecstasy they soared together. She surprised herself at the desperation she experienced in wanting to feel his power thrusting inside her. She was conscious of how much Luke adored her as he controlled his passion, pleasing her with gentle words while she begged to be satisfied.

'Now, Luke, now – I can't wait,' she implored.

He drew away, just enough to make her gasp and clutch at his buttocks with her hands, urging him to match her rhythm. She knew that she had the power to make him lose control as she wrapped her legs around him. He was sweating as he endeavoured to reach far into her secret lair. They climaxed together, holding the union, wanting it to last for ever . . .

*

After a few days of such passionate activity they came back to earth, and Fran was obliged to share her concern with Luke over Hilda's report.

'Maybe it's the teacher's fault,' Fran said, hardly able to bear to look at the low marks for most subjects. 'She's much more capable than this report says.'

Luke took the sheet of paper from Fran and paced the room as he studied it. He went to sit in the window seat of the small sitting room in the morning sun and re-read it. Then Fran realised that he was surveying her with a troubled expression.

'I'm afraid, Fran darling,' he said slowly, 'you have no one but yourself to blame for this. I don't wish to be cruel or hurt your feelings, but by the look of Hilda's attendances you've been keeping her away from school far too often. Last term she was hardly at school at all, so what else can you expect?'

'Of course she went to school,' Fran replied tersely. 'Except when there was no school bus on account of the weather. And she did have a bad cold and cough through January and February.'

'Here in the north people can cope with bad weather. The roads are always cleared, the school bus is rarely cancelled, so don't make excuses. You know perfectly well, my dear, that you keep Hilda home to satisfy your whims.'

'I do not!' Fran snapped angrily. 'She's a delicate child and I do have to protect her.'

'From what? Attending school is subject to law, thank goodness. She won't thank you in years to come when she can't get a job because she's not had the education. She's a bright child, but she needs both the company of other children and the tuition of qualified teachers.'

'We've always managed before. I know enough to help her when they let me have the proper books, but the ones Miss Murray sent were for a younger child.'

'Nonsense, Fran. I'm afraid you leave me no alternative but to send her to a boarding school. That way she'll be on the spot, and the weather can't be an excuse to be absent so frequently.'

Fran stared at Luke in horror. The shock of his suggestion was such that she was stunned to silence.

Luke observed that he had dealt his wife a cruel blow. He had been considering this move for some weeks now. Not because he didn't want Hilda living with them, although he had to admit it did curtail their life style somewhat, but he recognised that she was capable of better things if she wasn't so strongly influenced by Fran. Smothered would be more apt, he thought as he recalled, with wounded pride, some of the snide remarks overheard from colleagues since their arrival in Scotland. It was evidence of how the other women gossiped, and there was the danger of Hilda talking too much to the other children. He hadn't been able to hide the fact that he had only recently married a widow with a daughter, but no one need have known that Fran had three other daughters if it hadn't been for Hilda's chatter. He quite liked the child and found her a challenge, though he was sure he would have preferred having the youngest one, Babs.

'I hope you're not serious,' Fran said in a low, hurt tone.

'I'm afraid I am, darling,' Luke said, lifting his voice slightly to ease the tension. 'I've been thinking about it for some time. Most of the senior officers send their children to a very good school in Aberdeen.'

'If Hilda goes to Aberdeen, then I go too,' Fran said.

'Don't be ridiculous, Fran. Aberdeen is a charming town, rather like Brimdene in many ways. Sea air like Hilda is used to, and an all-girls school, which I think you'd prefer.'

'Hilda stays here with me, or we'll go home to Brimdene.'

Luke noted that Fran's cheeks were quite pink. He had expected a confrontation of sorts but he wasn't prepared for that statement.

He stood up, deciding that the battle may as well commence now as later. It was Jenny Logan's day off and the day was young.

'And how will you do that, my dear? The train fare is rather expensive, which is why you've had to remain here. It costs too much to travel back and forth often.'

'I haven't said I wanted to go often,' Fran argued. 'But we could have gone for the summer holiday. It isn't being fair to the girls. I haven't seen them for nearly a year now. It's no wonder Hilda can't settle in her new school.'

'You won't let her settle,' Luke said, raising his voice. 'And there's always a chance that my next appointment will be abroad. India is on the cards, and then you'll be expected to join me there.'

'Never!' Five hundred miles was distance enough; Fran couldn't begin to comprehend three thousand and more. She felt her muscles tighten throughout her body. Luke was planning a strategy she didn't like, hadn't even considered, and one that she was adamantly going to refuse to accept. 'I don't ever intend to go overseas,' she said.

Luke spanned the distance between them. He towered over her, tall, masterly, humiliating her.

'I think you'll have to do whatever I think is best,' he said.

'You can go wherever you like,' Fran said, 'but I know what's best for me.'

'I'm your husband. I vowed to love, honour and keep you, and you vowed to obey me. I won't ever let you forget that. Too many years have been wasted. You made your own happiness while I had nothing except exile.'

'Don't be so melodramatic, Luke,' Fran shouted at the top of her voice. 'You chose your way of life, and you enjoyed all the travelling, so don't try to tell me otherwise. You just saw middle age looming, and you took advantage of me when I was in a vulnerable state. I was just beginning to get on top of things when Kate got into trouble.'

'You were glad of me then,' he reminded her. 'Glad of my support and glad to have some of the responsibility taken from your shoulders. Well, now I'm taking more of the responsibility still. I agreed to bring Hilda north but you're making a fool of the girl. You must let her go, Fran. She's ten years old, and it's time she pulled her socks up at school. She'll be better away from you where she can concentrate on her studies. I've already got the prospectus and when you're calmer you can see it. In fact I shall show Hilda before I let you see it. Her reaction can decide whether she goes to Aberdeen or not.'

'No, Luke, please – *please* – don't do this to me, Luke.' Fran buried her face in her hands and wept bitterly.

'Don't think you can soften me up with tears,' Luke said savagely. 'I'm doing it for Hilda's sake. You're far too emotional about her, so you may as well get used to the idea.'

'I . . . I'll leave you, Luke. As soon as you go back to your ship I shall fetch Hilda, and we'll walk, if need be, back to Brimdene.'

Luke tossed his head back defiantly. 'Don't talk such utter rubbish,' he said. 'You don't know how well off you are with me. Do I keep you short of anything? Do you go hungry or have to wear worn-out clothing – you, or any of your girls? Aren't you well provided for? And your mother – who pays the rent on that house? If you leave me, my dear, who's going to pay it then? You can't live off your mother's old-age pension and you aren't a widow any longer.'

Fran was reduced to silent penitence for a second, then she ground her teeth. 'I think I hate you,' she said. 'I've always hated you.'

Her crimson, tear-stained cheeks did not evoke any pity from Luke. He inclined his head, a slow smile widening his sensuous mouth, his eyes alight with desire. 'Oh, yes?' He stepped forward just as she raised her fists to beat on his chest. He caught her wrists and twisted her round so that she fell away from him. He held her up awkwardly, laughing down at her, taunting her. 'You don't hate this, though, do you?' He lowered her to the floor and sat astride her, still holding her wrists tightly.

'No, Luke, for God's sake. This issue is too important to make fun of.'

'I'm not making fun, darling. I'm deadly serious. I married you to have this to look forward to. At every opportunity. What do you think fills my thoughts when I'm away? I told you once and now I'll remind you – a quayside with the vision of you waiting for me. Now you're my wife that vision has changed slightly. I carry a vivid picture in my mind of the most beautiful woman lying beneath me, panting, begging for more, her bosom heaving with anticipation, just as it is now.' He let go of her wrists and placed both hands over her breasts, squeezing gently. Fran gulped, shutting her eyes tightly, trying to turn over, hitting him for all she was worth. They fought, they rolled across the sitting-room carpet, pushing a chair out of the way as they struggled frantically. Fran quickly ran out of breath as Luke stretched beside her, his hands firmly holding hers above her shoulders. His fingers entwined in hers, and one long powerful leg lay over one of hers.

'This is silly, Luke,' she managed to say. 'Let me get up, please?'

She could hardly bear to look up into his eyes, but no response from him forced her to. His dark, satanic eyes glinted in the sunlight – and Fran knew she would have to submit. But she didn't give in easily; she fought against him as she tried to escape his clutches, while at the same time she voiced all her malice.

'You're the most despicable man I've ever met,' she said as he tore away her underwear. Her dress was pushed up over her face. 'And forcing yourself on me doesn't change anything – I shall still leave you,' she yelled. She tried to bring one knee up to make contact with his groin but this only seemed to increase his feverish enthusiasm, and he laughed as he bent his head and kissed her intimately. Her struggling diminished. God, she thought, he knows every weak, sensitive spot. Even though she tore at his hair, her body reacted spontaneously, arching up to derive the maximum amount of pleasure from his exploring mouth. But still she refused to give in completely. Even when their bodies were as one she drew her knees up and pounded on the floor with her feet in protest. And as she pounded, the force of her actions lifted her bottom off the floor, tightening their coition until wanton craving had to be satiated. Violent in nature, the climax of their lust resulted in Fran sobbing as if her heart had been broken.

Luke was unable to pacify her. When he did finally release her she got up and rushed upstairs to the bathroom. She wanted to soak away all contact with this demon of a man she had married. She had known he was his own man, that he took rather than persuaded, but there was a better side when he was considerate and loving. Love or lust? That was a question she simply couldn't answer.

Chapter Thirteen

To Fran's surprise, when Hilda was told about the boarding school she was delighted. Her ready acceptance of going away for weeks at a stretch wounded Fran deeply. Hilda was the one she had felt would always stand by her whatever happened. Now she had to admit that Luke had come between them. Hilda idolised her stepfather as much, it seemed to Fran, as Ruby had adored Henry. But Fran could not forgive Luke for what he had done, and she made this quite clear to him by her belligerent attitude.

As the weather got better, Luke took Hilda on long hillside walks while Fran chose to remain at home sewing. She put all her aggression into the tacking stitches along seams of a dress for Babs. Somehow this year she would get home to see the other girls, she vowed. Her heart ached with longing for the family to be reunited, even though her mother assured her that everything was all right. Prue's letters confirmed much the same, but Babs's own letters became less frequent. 'She's only young,' Prue wrote, 'and although very good at her school work, placed in the top ten after the examinations, she finds writing letters take up too much playing time. Everywhere Sam goes, Babs follows.' When Kate wrote, she was full of all her activities at work and in her night school studies. She sounded happy, and that should have pleased Fran, but doubts lingered as to what any of them were keeping from her.

Ruby wrote more than any of the others: neatly written pages of news, always ending with a declaration of her love for her mother and Hilda. This brought pain and only added to Fran's guilt. Ruby had felt the parting more acutely than the others. In spite of her waywardness she was the most sensitive of them all. She mourned the loss of her father and grandfather, and was not ashamed to show that grief. Nor was she ashamed to show her contempt of the man who had taken her mother away. Her letters always began the same: 'Dearest Mummy and Hilda'. Fran knew that Luke must notice that he was not included, but he never commented. Dear Ruby, for all the impatience Fran had shown her at home, was now the one who brought the most love through her letters in return. Fran regretted her resentment of her middle daughter now. She wished she could turn the clock back. Wished with all her heart she had taken heed of Ruby's outburst when she had announced her intention of marrying Luke. 'Mummy, you can't marry him. Daddy would hate it!' But Fran had married Luke Hammond – in haste – and was reaping her reward. Was Henry looking down on her and frowning, wreaking his revenge? And well he might, Fran thought. Their children, who had meant everything to Henry, were all living apart. Fran disliked herself intensely, and Luke even more for being the reason she had acted so hastily.

The rift between them grew wider as the weeks passed, and after Easter, when Luke drove them to Aberdeen to leave Hilda at her new school, Fran felt nothing but cold antagonism towards him.

Aberdeen was everything Luke had said it would be. A pleasant seaside town with bracing air, surrounded by beautiful countryside. Apparently ignoring Fran's resentment, Luke had booked them in at a hotel near the school for a week.

'We can visit Hilda at Melville House at the weekend, and you'll see for yourself how well she's settled in,' he told Fran.

Fran knew that Luke expected her to weep and wail as the time for parting drew near. Maybe he wanted another battle. Surely he didn't imagine that her frosty silences meant that she had given in? She hardly spoke to him and gave little response to any suggestions he made. To the school authorities she appeared the submissive little wife, letting Luke do all the talking. But inside she was desperately unhappy, and angry too. She might have won Luke round if Hilda had resisted. Fran could hardly believe that her favourite had actually become wild with excitement at going away to school. While Luke was signing documents and paying what Fran considered were exorbitant fees, she helped Hilda unpack her clothes and personal belongings in a small dormitory.

'Now you will write each week, won't you, darling?' she said.

'Of course, Mummy. It's one of the rules. Didn't you read the prospectus properly? Our letters have to be read by the matron before we can post them.' She ran to look out of the window. 'Isn't it beautiful here? Aren't I lucky? I shall make lots of new friends, too. It would have been nice if Babs could have come as well, but she'd only keep crying for you, I expect.'

Fran and Luke were invited to stay to tea before having to say goodbye to Hilda. She wrapped her arms round Fran's neck as she kissed her, but with excitement rather than any other emotion. Then Hilda threw herself into Luke's arms.

'Thank you so much for letting me come here, Daddy,' she said, planting a big kiss on his cheek. 'You will come to see me and take me out to tea if your ship comes to Aberdeen, won't you?'

Luke assured her that he would. He laughed with her, patted her bottom and then shook hands with the headmistress before accompanying Fran outside.

'I'm sure you have nothing at all to worry about, darling,' he said, placing his arm round Fran's shoulder. Fran didn't answer. She was biting her lip to control her anguish, while at the same time she felt too angry for words. Why did she allow this man to rule her life? To possess her the way he did? Why hadn't she stood up to him and refused to allow Hilda to be separated from her? Why on earth had she married him in the first place? Bitter contempt ate away inside her. She longed to lash out at Luke but she had learned that he revelled in that kind of action, and it was likely to end in the way he chose to resolve any differences. So she remained cool outwardly and seemingly indifferent.

At the small hotel, overlooking a sandy bay where white-edged waves washed in from the North Sea, they changed for dinner, hardly exchanging a word. During the meal Fran listened impassively as Luke tried to discuss world events – events that were gloomy with rumour that Germany was re-arming. Troubles in Austria, Greece, Italy and Spain all contributed to the dark clouds that were accumulating in Europe. Fran couldn't be bothered with such matters, which did not appear to concern her or her family. It was all happening somewhere else, too far away to be of any interest to her. Luke, having travelled abroad extensively, obviously was deeply disturbed by the news and soon became engrossed in conversation with a middle-aged couple seated at the next table. When Fran had finished eating she put aside the crisp white table napkin and excused herself.

'It's been a tiring day,' she said. 'I hope you'll excuse me.'

Luke stood up briefly, but was evidently keen to resume his conversation, for which Fran was profoundly grateful. She went to their room. After taking deep breaths of sea air she closed the window and prepared for bed, thinking and worrying about Hilda. Her head ached, so she took two Aspros, and once she lay down in the darkened room, her hair unpinned and plaited, she was soon fast asleep.

The chill of early morning made Fran shiver as she woke. She was surprised that she had slept so soundly all night, and had not heard Luke come to bed. Immediately he responded to her movement by placing his arm across her waist. Fran wriggled farther away out of his reach in the outsized bed. She pushed her feet free of the sheets on the other side, and slid noiselessly to the floor. With slippers and dressing gown on she went along to the bathroom at the end of the passageway. Her headache had gone. Before returning to the bedroom she stood at the landing window and looked out on the peaceful scene. A promenade empty of people. Blue skies as far as the eye could see, and the sun rising in the east to greet a new spring day. Fran knew that she ought to be content, and feel privileged to be seeing sea and landscapes that until now had been but pictures in books and magazines. She felt less fractious, but she was determined to remain aloof towards Luke.

She tiptoed back to the bedroom and stood against the closed door as she surveyed her husband. He looked so devilishly appealing in sleep. She wondered whether he was feigning sleep and would jump to catch her at any moment, but his breathing was even. His eyes were hidden by smooth lids fringed with long black lashes. An elegantly straight nose and a jawline set firm, with the hint of self-satisfaction in his expression. Why had he chosen her of all the women in the world? During this first year of marriage she had enjoyed the delights of conjugal bliss. Learned that Luke Hammond was determined and masterful. Thoughtful, kind and lovingly considerate too when it suited him. She could appreciate that he wanted them to share a private existence when he was home on leave, but he was away more than he was home. What was she supposed to do with herself when he returned to his ship? She couldn't bear to imagine life without Hilda now. It was all right for him. He lived with a group of men who sailed the seas to exotic places. He said that he thought of no one but Fran while he was away, but she doubted the truth in that. In Far Eastern countries she knew there were brothels where a man's lust could be indulged. It filled her with disgust. To choose a life in the services seemed an unnatural way of life to her. She couldn't believe that Luke could remain celibate for long. He was too virile, too intensely potent. He might be in his prime but he hadn't survived all these years without using women. He certainly did not lack experience.

Luke stirred, and opened his eyes lazily. Fran moved away from the door.

'Come back to bed.'

'I'd rather get up,' she replied.

As she sat at the dressing-table mirror, she kept a watchful eye on her husband, hoping he would go to sleep again. She unplaited her long hair and began to brush it vigorously. Luke yawned and stretched, then pulled himself higher in the bed. He wore only pyjama trousers in bed and Fran felt a twinge of admiration at the glimpse of his bronzed torso. She knew he was watching her so she avoided eye contact through the mirror.

'How long do you propose to keep up this cold war?' His voice was low, and gravelly seductive.

'I don't know what you mean,' Fran said after a few seconds.

'Oh yes you do, and you're making a martyr of yourself again. Fran, I do understand how you feel. After all you've been through, this must seem like the last straw, but you didn't realise just how you were suffocating Hilda.'

'You're suffocating me!' Fran retorted crossly.

'With love perhaps – to make up for all the years I longed for you and couldn't have you. I didn't expect to find life easy being married to you. You've had one married life which was happy, or so you say. I realise that it is hard for you to adapt, but I consider we've have a good first year. You evidently like being married but you want all your own way, and married to me that's not the way it'll be. A serviceman's life is difficult enough and what he needs most of all is an understanding wife.'

'And you tell me that it's me who likes my own way? You're the selfish one. You've given no consideration at all to my feelings. Just get Hilda out of the way so that you can indulge yourself in my bed.'

'I have no wish to go to bed with a woman who is so obviously hostile.' Luke got out of bed and walked slowly towards the dressing table, his hands on his hips. 'I could force myself on you. I daresay you'd like me to do just that so that you could show your righteous indignation and hurl abuse at me. No, Fran. I'll show you the respect a wife deserves. You are, after all, only hurting yourself. I know that it's hard for you to admit that Hilda was actually excited about coming to Aberdeen, but she needs her freedom.'

'She's only just ten years old.' Fran felt a shiver go through her, like a ghost walking over her grave. Henry's words so often haunted her. He had pleaded on Ruby's behalf, now she was doing the same over Hilda. Only the situation was much, much worse, she thought with despair.

'And by the time I get a new commission she'll have taken the scholarship. Who knows what results a different environment and new methods may bring forth? Above all she needs lots of encouragement, as well as discipline, and she'll get that at Melville House. I would have done the same for Babs, had it been she who came north with us.'

Fran paused, her cheeks tight with unspent passion. Realisation hit hard. Luke Hammond had planned this from the moment he agreed to bring Hilda to Scotland.

'You may as well get used to the idea, Fran. I've paid advance fees for her to stay at Melville House until they break up for the summer holiday in 1935. That will be the time for you to return south. That can be your goal, so you may as well get used to the idea.'

'And if Hilda is ill? Or begs to leave Melville House?' Fran tried to retain her scorn, but her voice betrayed her pain.

'We'll cross that bridge if we come to it. According to the matron and headmistress, you can expect Hilda to show signs of homesickness during the first couple of weeks. It'll be up to you to reassure her. I shall be back at sea.'

Luke picked up his towel and toilet bag and went along to the bathroom. Fran could hardly believe his cruelty. No hope of seeing the girls until next year? Now she had been parted from each one of them. How could she bear it? What was she going to do with her time? One thing was certain – she would not be waiting like a dutiful wife to indulge her unfeeling husband the moment he returned home.

Pride helped Fran through. She knew that Jenny Logan was watching her every move, so she kept herself busy at her sewing machine and started knitting as well. But nothing would entice her to join the officers' wives' club. She wrote frequently to her mother and the girls, trying to sound cheerful, but there seemed hardly any news now that Hilda was not in Craiglee. Inwardly she hoped that Hilda would become homesick, and perhaps make such a fuss that the school would be glad to have her removed, but Hilda hardly had time to write a weekly letter. When a batch of letters arrived from Luke saying that he was well, but busy and unable to tell her his whereabouts, he commented on the delightful letters he had received from Hilda.

Fran felt desolate. She was torn between taking a train to Aberdeen one weekend, or taking out some of her own meagre savings to travel south, but she knew that once she set foot back on Dorset soil she would never return to Scotland again. She began to make plans for the Whitsun holiday, short though it would be. Then Hilda wrote saying that she had been invited to spend the bank-holiday weekend with one of her school chums. She hoped Fran wouldn't mind if she didn't come home after all.

Fran couldn't believe it. She roamed the house, alternately weeping and declaring to the walls her contempt for Luke. Jenny Logan was away visiting relatives on the Isle of Skye for a week. Fran experienced the worst loneliness of her life. She managed to rid herself of some of the despondency by scrubbing floors that were already clean. She turned out cupboards and drawers. Luke was meticulous in his personal habits, his belongings always kept in neat and tidy order. She found a bundle of letters under a pile of civilian shirts. After cleaning out the empty drawer, Fran was overcome by curiosity. The postmark was foreign, from some remote part of Asia, she thought. Prying wasn't something she was in the habit of but she untied the bundle and looked at the date on the first envelope. It was 1921. She peeped inside, then drew out the single sheet of paper. The writing was small and in a foreign language, but the signature was clear enough: Sarita.

Fran became even more curious. Here were hidden secrets of Luke's past. She felt mildly jealous of the woman who had written regularly to Luke from the other side of the world and whom he thought so highly of that he had kept her letters for thirteen years. She looked at each letter in turn. Half-way through the bundle she came across a thicker package which contained photographs. The image of the young, virile Luke Hammond leapt out at her. He was standing, naked except for a pair of swimming trunks, at the water's edge of a palm-fringed, sandy beach, and encircled in his right arm was a petite and very beautiful girl. Fran could tell that the girl was probably a native of Asia. Fran's mind whirled round with all kinds of notions, not least the vision of Luke making love to this gorgeous creature. She wished she could read the messages, but then decided that it was probably best that she couldn't, for the language of love was clearly evident from the poses isn the photographs. Luke sitting on the sand with the girl lying across his thighs, laughing up into his face. The two of them kneeling in the shallow water, facing each other, their lips just touching in a light kiss. A wooden fishing boat with Luke and the girl lying intimately together. Fran could almost feel the kiss of the breeze, the heat of the sun and the magnetism of Luke's desire. Was this then the reason that he had never married previously? Was Sarita his mistress whom he visited when calling at some foreign port? Where was she now? Why did he never receive letters from abroad? The last envelope was dated 1930, the year before he had returned to Sherbrook.

Fran felt a tightness growing in her chest. Had he used this poor girl for his physical needs and, when he had discovered that Fran had become widowed, rejected her? Or was Sarita still his mistress? Did he keep her in reserve for when he was away from home, but forbade her to correspond with him any more? Fran felt numb with inquisitiveness. She couldn't identify her emotions. Was she jealous? A little bit, yes, she had to admit. Hurt, too, that Luke had not mentioned Sarita, whoever she was.

After a long time Fran tied up the letters just as she had found them and returned them to the bottom of the drawer. If she was experiencing the pain of rejection, wasn't that her own stupid fault? When she calmed a little she realised that she should be thankful that such letters were not delivered through their letterbox regularly.

Fran was very glad to see Jenny back, she was good company.

'So you've been here by yourself all week?' Jenny asked in astonishment.

'Yes, but it was only a week, thank goodness.'

'Ooh, deary me,' Jenny sympathised. 'I would'na gone if I'd known.'

'Then it's as well you didn't know, Jenny,' Fran said. 'You look after us so well, you deserved your holiday and I'm glad you enjoyed it.'

'I wouldn't have if I'd known that neither Captain Hammond nor young Hilda weren't coming home.'

'I didn't really expect my husband to come home yet. It does get lonely when he's away.' Fran sighed. 'A man can't really understand what it's like to not have your children round you.'

'This past year has gone by quickly though, and the second year won't be as difficult as the first. The time will rush by, you'll see.'

'It would if Hilda were still here, but counting days with nothing much to do is quite foreign to me, Jenny.'

'Have you no' thought about doing some charity work, Mrs Hammond? There are some wives who either don't have children, or their children are away at school like Hilda, and there's plenty needs doing for the poor folk in Glasgow. You'd be a real boon to some wi' your ability with your needle.'

'Glasgow?' Fran echoed in surprise. 'That's too far away, surely?'

'We-ell, yes, mebbe it is, but a few of the wives do give up some of their spare time to help with charitable organisations. You could ask the vicar. He'd know where help is most needed, I'm sure.'

Fran wondered afterwards whether Jenny had spoken to the vicar on her behalf, for a few days later the Reverend Jimmy Kyle called to see her about teatime.

Jenny fussed about, serving tea in the sitting room upstairs promptly at four o'clock, while the rather shabbily dressed, elderly vicar enquired abut the health of Fran and her family.

'It must be quiet for you around these parts with your man away at sea, and your young wee girlie up in Aberdeen, especially after moving from the south of England,' he said.

'I'm used to living in the country, but I've always had so many family members with me,' Fran said. She was wary of giving too much away about her private affairs. 'The days are long, though,' she admitted.

'My dear wife is crippled with arthritis now and finds it most frustrating that she can't do the parish work she once did. There's an orphanage just outside Dunfermline where she goes to help three days a week. She used to play the piano and help teach the talented children, but she can't do that any longer.'

'And I'm afraid I can't offer my services there, vicar, as I can't play or read music.'

'But you have other talents, my dear Mrs Hammond. The little garments you made for the Christmas bazaar were quite unique.'

'I do like sewing, but that wouldn't be much help to orphan children.'

'On the contrary, dear lady, there's always a great need for clothes for the poor unfortunate children who have been abandoned. We get plenty of cloth given to us from the mills but it isn't easy to find someone willing to give up their time, or indeed with the necessary competence to use it wisely.'

Fran laughed nervously, remembering Jenny's suggestion. 'I'm not a professional seamstress,' she said, 'and I'm not sure that my husband would approve.'

'I think the men understand that time hangs heavily while they're at sea. Of course we wouldn't hold you to any commitment when he returns home. Your assistance would please my wife enormously and be greatly valued. Perhaps you would care to come to the Manse for tea tomorrow afternoon to discuss the matter?'

Fran didn't have a valid excuse for refusing the invitation, and the longer she stayed in the company of Mrs Kyle the following day, the better she liked her. Fran was overwhelmed with pity at the sight of the poor woman's disability. Her hands were crooked and difficult to use, yet she had baked a cake and managed to pour tea without spilling it. Fran felt that such a painful condition should be etched in her face, yet Mrs Kyle had a radiance about her that was breathtaking. Her features were almost flawless. She had soft, blue, sparkling eyes set wide above high cheekbones, and skin of a delicate peach colour. Her lower lip was full and sensuous, but she didn't need to part her lips to smile, because her generous zest for life shone from her face. They were soon chatting like old friends, and Fran found consolation from the experiences of the older woman.

'We have children in the orphanage of a wide age range,' Mrs Kyle explained. 'From babies through to twelve years old. At twelve they go to a hostel to prepare them for work. Mostly the girls go into service, though it's getting more and more difficult to place them these days. If you want to, and we know you love children, you can assist in looking after the children in a general way, but sewing would be a marvellous help, and at the same time you could have a group of the older girls to teach.'

'I'd like that,' Fran said eagerly. 'Before I went into service as a nanny I helped in our village school. That was a long time ago, though. As I said, I'm not a professional needlewoman, Mrs Kyle, but Lady Hinckley paid for me to have a course of lessons which gave me a good start. Since then, with four daughters, I've had plenty of practice.'

Fran's spirits lifted from her very first week at the orphanage. Life was worth living again, her days full, and her letters to her own family were hastily composed ones filled with news of the children who had been rejected for one reason or another, usually because they were illegitimate. At first she went three mornings a week, but soon she was so engrossed in the work of caring for the tiny mites who had been separated from their mothers at birth that she decided to stay in the afternoons to sew and help the older girls to learn to make clothes for themselves. In some of the children she saw reflections of her own girls, and in the dark-haired boys of about ten years her vision of Lennie was refreshed. Her somewhat saintly memory of Lennie gradually faded, and in its place she remembered him as the teasing, mischievous boy he sometimes was. The boys endeared themselves to Fran and she to them, but she was also good at controlling the girls. Her methods of strict discipline earned her their respect, and on occasion a wayward girl or boy who appeared to be unmanageable reacted favourably to Fran's persuasion. There were times when she felt guilty at harsh words spoken in the heat of the moment to Ruby or Kate in the past. Now she could couple her experience with the compassion she knew these children needed. And she had all the time required to give of herself to them.

She wrote to Luke, telling him what she was doing to keep herself occupied, but after several weeks, when a batch of letters arrived from him, it was apparent that her news had not yet caught up with him. At the sight of his handwriting she felt a pang of jealousy. Did he still write to the Asian girl, Sarita? Were they letters of love as hers were in spite of the rift? What if he was spending time with this girl during his long absence? There was no means of checking his whereabouts. She might never know whether he was living a Jekyll and Hyde existence.

The weather grew warmer, the days long and bright, which matched Fran's cheerfulness. Her thoughts were always with her family, and she longed to see both Hilda and Luke again. The weeks had passed quickly, just as Jenny had said they would, and she was quite surprised when she turned the calendar over to the first of June. She was working so hard now that she looked forward to the quiet peacefulness of Sundays, and on the first Sunday in June, after going to morning service at the kirk, she set off alone to walk over the hills to the lock.

The sky was azure blue with smudges of white cloud. Sheep grazed contentedly, and birds sang as they rested on trees and boulders after flying on the currents of warm air high in the sky. Fran's mind drifted back over the year. It was time for stock-taking. Three years now since Henry and her father had perished in the flash tide. The pain was easing but the memories vivid as if it had happened yesterday. Would Henry think she had been disloyal to his memory? Her brief courtship and marriage to Luke had been another flash tide. She had been swept away on a current of emotion, and yes, there had been many moments of regret, but now, oh, how she longed to lie in his arms again to be comforted.

The yearning to see Luke again, to be made to feel a desirable woman, was marred by the thought that another whole year had to pass before she could be reunited with her family. She glanced at the gold fob-watch pinned to the front of her dress, which Luke had given her as a wedding gift. It was nearly four o'clock. She decided it was time to walk back, have a cup of tea, and then write to the girls. She stood up and stretched. Voices from far away floated across the loch. Some children were playing near the water's edge and she could see one or two fishermen trying their luck. It was almost too lovely a scene to leave. There was such peace here, but it was a peace impaired by the painful guilt that tormented her.

Already in her mind she was penning the words she was about to write to Kate as she picked her way across the craggy hillside. The sun was at its highest now, and bore through the clothes on her back as she skirted the burn in the valley. She met one or two families out for their Sunday afternoon walk, and as she drew near to home she felt she was being watched. She stopped to look up, and saw a tall figure standing in their garden. Her heart leapt, pulsating hard against the wall of her chest. It couldn't be – was it? Yes, there was no mistaking Luke's upright stance. She waved excitedly and began to run, all past differences forgotten, as well as the Asian girl, Sarita. Luke vaulted the low stone wall and hurried towards Fran. The distance between them was greater than either of them imagined. They were impatient to bridge the gap, and at last Fran fell into Luke's embrace, unable to speak from lack of breath.

Luke held her close to him, his hand caressing her back, his lips nuzzling in the folds of her neck. She regained some breath and pulled away to gaze up at him. 'It's so good to see you, Luke,' she whispered.

'My darling, you can't know how I've longed for this moment. You look as perfect as ever – more radiant than I dared hope.' With arms entwined about each other they walked along the length of the stone wall to the track at the side of the house. They went in through the front gate and round to the back door, which Fran found unlocked. 'How long have you been here?' she asked, her blue eyes alight with affection. Dear God, she thought, would he ever know just how much she loved him in spite of everything?

'About half an hour, and from the bedroom window I saw you out there on the hill.'

Over tea they chatted amicably, yet Fran felt that this time it was Luke who was in a reticent mood. He asked about the girls and Fran's mother. She begged to know where he had been and how long he expected to be at home. He didn't reply at once but kept stirring his tea. Then she noticed some sign of strain in his furrowed brow.

'I'm home on compassionate leave, Fran,' he said.

'Compassionate leave?' she questioned, all kinds of ridiculous thoughts crowding into her brain. Her mother – or Ruby? Kate? Babs? No, he had enquired about them all.

'My father has had an accident at the foundry. It's bad. You won't have heard from Elizabeth because she's helping Mother look after him. She contacted me and I was able to transfer ship in the Indian Ocean to get home quickly. I'm afraid we have to pack up and drive to Middlesbrough tomorrow as my parents have requested that I visit.'

'Oh, Luke, I'm so sorry,' Fran said. 'To think it takes something like this to get you all together again.'

'It's my mother who wants to see me. I doubt very much that my father will acknowledge or ever forgive me, Fran.'

Fran did everything to support Luke, and by midnight their cases were packed, ready for the long journey the next day.

If Fran expected a passionate reunion she was disappointed. But, in spite of the anxiety she knew Luke felt, once they were lying together in the big bed he could not resist showing his feelings with tender caresses. His kisses were long and ardent, demonstrating his love until his desperate need of Fran took precedence over concern for his father. Their coming together was a unique experience of gentle satisfaction, healing the wound that had remained festering for too long.

Chapter Fourteen

'How long will the journey take?' Fran asked, as she spread butter lavishly on a crusty roll. They had stopped for mid-morning refreshment in the delightful town of Berwick-on-Tweed. They had spoken very little thus far, but now she could tell that Luke was readjusting to land and his features looked less strained.

'Something between five and six hours. It's well over a hundred and fifty miles, I reckon. We'll have a proper meal when we reach Newcastle. We can freshen up, too, before we make the last lap to Middlesbrough. We'll find a hotel not too far away from the family home.'

'Won't they expect you to stay with them?'

Luke grunted. 'I doubt it. I can't imagine what kind of reception we'll get. I expect it'll be best if you leave most of the talking to me, darling. I wouldn't have put you through this ordeal, but it's important to me that my parents meet my wife at last.'

'How long is it since you saw them?'

'Many years. During my earliest days in the Navy I did go home to spend my leaves there. Stupidly I thought they needed to see that I was all right, but my father made it quite clear that I was an embarrassment to him.'

'But surely your mother didn't reject you, Luke?'

Luke's chin trembled slightly. 'I think I broke her heart,' he said at length.

'You know I'll be with you and support you, whatever happens,' Fran declared loyally. 'Did Elizabeth tell you just what your father's injuries are?'

'It sounded as if he may have damaged his spine. As soon as I docked I telephoned Elizabeth. She's the businesswoman of the family. She manages the firm's accounts department, but she lives in a delightful cottage of her own away from the foundry. I know she would want us to stay with her, but after so long I feel I can't impose. I need to tread warily. There were faults on both sides, I dare say, but if I'm to – well – to become on better terms with my parents and sisters, I must be discreet.'

'I can't imagine why you should need to be discreet, Luke,' Fran said, finishing her coffee as she gazed across at Luke affectionately. 'I'm sure your parents, especially your mother, and your sisters will welcome you with open arms.'

Luke's dark eyes glinted in the sunlight, which streamed through the curtained window where they were sitting. A smile fleetingly passed across his face, the kind of smile Fran had never seen before, and she was suspicious of it. The foreign letters came back to torment her. The girl called Sarita. Was it the Navy that had come betwen Luke and his parents? Or was it the Asian girl? A shiver of mistrust swept over Fran as she stood up. She wished there wasn't this feeling of secrecy about Luke Hammond. But that enigmatic smile confirmed that there was an area in his life which she knew nothing about.

As the day became warmer, the temperature inside the car rose to unbearable heights even with the windows down. Fran didn't care for the smell of engine fumes which blew in on them, and she was relieved when at last they reached the cathedral city of Newcastle-upon-Tyne, 'capital' of Tyneside. Luke seemed to know exactly where he was heading, and they parked on the forecourt of the Railway Inn. They had an excellent meal, before continuing towards Middlesbrough.

Pleasant countryside seemed to open up the coal-mining city's dark sky, but, after a further hour's travelling, as they came to the border between Durham and North Yorkshire, the heavily industrialised Teesside became even more of a reality to Fran. There was evidence of blast furnaces, foundries and mills. Tall chimneys emitted thick, dirty smoke which clung round the high, blackened brick buildings.

'The foundry is just south of the river. My father has the ideal site close to transportation, but Hammond House is nearer the east coast. Elizabeth lives just outside Skelton in a tiny village.'

Fran felt that she was growing nearer to Luke's past, but she also felt tension increasing.

She wasn't prepared for the narrow country lane or the ornate iron gates that led to Hammond House. A low iron fence bordered grassy meadows in the grounds, where sheep grazed and a horse cantered excitedly at the sound of the car's engine. The wheels crunched on the gravel drive as Luke brought the car to a standstill below a flight of stone steps. The huge oak door appeared forbidding. Fran gasped.

'This is your home? Where you spent your childhood?' she asked, with a hint of disbelief.

Luke managed to laugh. 'I suppose it does seem rather grand, even to me now, after all these years. It's old, probably some might say ugly, large, cold and unfriendly – so be warned.'

'You sound bitter, Luke.' Fran placed a hand on his arm and he covered it with his own. 'Maybe the years have brought warmth to the house,' she said. 'I'm sure you'll find it more welcoming than you imagine. Think of the pleasure you're going to give your parents.'

Luke leaned across and kissed her lips. 'What would I do without you?' he said.

Voices distracted Fran from replying, and they saw a woman coming down the steps to greet them. She pushed her head in the window.

'You must be Fran,' she said. Then, with a wry twist to her mouth, she glanced across at Luke. 'Well, well, brother dear, who ever thought you'd grace us with your presence after all these years?'

'How did you know I was coming?' Luke asked.

'Elizabeth didn't want Mother having a heart attack with shock. She'd had shock enough with Father's accident.'

'How is he? Oh, by the way, darling, this is Dorinda, my youngest sister.'

Fran smiled at Dorinda, but received only a frosty look in return.

'He's just about holding his own. You might not have got here in time, but I suppose that wouldn't have mattered to the old man. He hasn't changed his mind, if that's what you're hoping for. He gets more crotchety with each year. Still, Mother will be delighted to see her darling son.'

Another figure appeared at the front door.

'For goodness sake, don't stay out there. Dorrie, we all want to share him,' the woman called.

Luke opened his door and got out. Before he could get round to Fran's side, Dorinda had opened the door and was helping Fran to her feet.

'Stiff, I expect, if you've travelled from Scotland,' Dorinda said. 'Golly, aren't you tiny?'

Fran smiled. 'You all seem to be taller than average. I'm very pleased to meet you, but I wish it were in happier circumstances.'

'Can't imagine why Luke hasn't brought you home long before this.'

Fran just caught the exchange of vindictive looks between brother and sister, and she feared that this visit might not be as pleasant as she hoped.

With an arm around Fran, Luke guided her up the steps after Dorinda. The woman waiting at the top was more attractive than Dorinda, maybe because she seemed less hostile. She held her arms out to her brother and they kissed with some measure of affection.

'Cecilia, this is my wife, Fran.'

'It's really good to meet you at last. We never ever thought Luke would marry and now we hear that he's been hiding you away for all these years.'

Fran began to repudiate this statement, but was suddenly aware of Luke's fingers jerking a warning against hers.

'I'm sorry to hear . . . about your father,' she said falteringly. She went quite hot, and was glad that at that moment a frail, elderly woman came through the hall.

'Let me see you both.' There was no doubting that this was Luke's mother. She came with arms outstretched and tears running down her narrow face. She fell on Luke, sobbing unashamedly. 'He wouldn't let me ever send for you, my dear, dear boy,' she said. 'I can hardly take it in that so many years have gone by. And now our days are numbered. We're both growing old, and it looks as if Father may be taken from us. I'm glad Elizabeth could contact you in time, Luke. It wouldn't be right not to see his only son before he dies.'

'I came as soon as I could, Mother, but I was in the Indian Ocean. Have you told Father that I was coming? I wouldn't want to upset him.'

'Oh, you'll do that all right,' Dorinda said sharply. 'He's still the supreme head of the family, in spite of anything Liz may have told you, and don't expect him to rush to change his will.'

'That will do, Dorinda.' Mrs Hammond turned quickly to her youngest daughter. 'We're all a little overwrought with worry.' She smiled gently at Fran. 'So you're the woman who has brought happiness into my son's life? I might have known you'd be pretty – and a redhead. He always did have an eye for something special.'

'Fran is very special to me, Mother,' Luke said, drawing Fran close to him. Then he raised his eyebrows at his mother. 'And we have come a long way. We're tired and dying for a cup of tea.'

'I'm so sorry – of course. Why on earth are we standing out

here? Well, it's probably warmer out than in. This old house keeps out the sun, you see, my dear.' She took Fran's hand and tucked it through her arm as she led the way into the dim, musty smelling hallway.

After the glare of the June sun, Fran found it difficult to see inside, but she welcomed the coolness. Taken into the drawing room, she fell in love with the comfort of the house.

Luke did not follow at once and Fran suspected that he was having a confrontation with his younger sister.

The Adam fireplace looked well used and the grate was laid ready with paper and sticks. A tall Chinese vase containing branches of mauve and white lilac stood by the side of the hearth, and a bowl of sweet-smelling roses in a variety of shades stood in the centre of an occasional table. The room was cold, yet warm in atmosphere. Mrs Hammond sat in her chair between hearth and table as Luke joined them.

'I can't do much these days,' she said, half apologetically, 'but the girls will make sure you're comfortable.'

'We're going to stay in the Founder's Arms, Mother,' Luke said gently. 'We don't want to put anyone out – and it happens to be our wedding anniversary next weekend, so I thought it was about time Fran had a special celebration break.'

The door opened softly and Cecilia came in carrying a tray. Fran glanced to the doorway and saw that Dorinda was hovering uncertainly.

'And how many years is that?' Mrs Hammond asked.

'More than we care to admit to – eh, darling?' Luke's expression was one of daring as he glanced at Fran. They were sitting side by side on a long sofa and he took Fran's hand in his and squeezed.

'Elizabeth tells me that you have four daughters. What ages are they?'

Fran felt her muscles tighten in her cheeks as Luke answered quickly. 'From seven to nineteen, Mother.'

'So you've been married this past twenty years or more and we never knew.'

Fran couldn't believe what she was hearing. Luke was playing a game of charades, which was evidently why he had said he would do all the talking. It seemed as if he anticipated his mother's questions and had the answers ready on the tip of his lying tongue. For what reason? The girl Sarita laughed up at Fran from her memory of the photos. Just what had Luke been up to? Then Fran recalled Dorinda's sarcasm about their father and his will. Was that the real reason for this sudden decision to visit? Could Luke really be capable of such scheming? The conversation drifted on above her head as suppositions and accusations muddled her weary brain. She was glad of a good strong cup of tea, but declined to eat anything.

'Perhaps you're being sensible,' her mother-in-law said kindly. 'We shouldn't spoil our appetites before supper.'

Supper! How on earth could they keep up this pretence? Was Luke planning to stay here for the rest of the day? Fran felt sure she would forget herself and tell the truth. She simply wasn't used to deceiving anyone. What reason could Luke have for deceiving his family? Could it be that he had been disinherited because of Sarita? As she sat quietly observing the Hammond family, she came to the conclusion that this must be the answer. Luke Hammond had certainly not been celibate during the past twenty years and now Fran began to wonder if in fact he had been married while overseas? Bigamy, a family of dark-skinned children, all began to agitate in Fran's mind and she longed to get away.

When the tea tray had been removed, Cecilia suggested that Luke and Fran should go upstairs to see James Hammond.

'Perhaps you'd prefer to go on your own as you haven't seen him for so long,' Fran said to Luke as he stood up. 'It might not be good to have too much excitement in his condition.'

'No, we don't want him killed off just yet, do we, Luke?' Dorinda said. She had been sitting on the wide window seat as if she didn't want to be a part of this family reunion. 'He doesn't say very much, but it's my opinion that he's quite capable of knowing what's going on, and hearing everything.' She went to the door. 'My boys will be in from school shortly, so I must prepare their tea.' She left the room, and in her wake Fran sensed a venomous sting in the air.

'That's one sister who isn't pleased to see me,' Luke said, trying to laugh it off.

'Well, you can't blame her, Luke,' Cecilia said as she led the way upstairs. 'You know Dorrie. She has the foundry earmarked for her two boys.'

'You have sons as well,' Luke said.

'Dorrie was married before me, even if I am two years older than she. Her boys are the eldest so she thinks they're entitled to the family business as you have no sons.'

They had reached the large square landing. There was a faint smell of disinfectant, and Fran guessed which the sickroom was by the heavy brocade curtain that hung across one door. She felt nauseous. She didn't want to be part of this at all, and by the anguish in Luke's face she guessed he was dreading this meeting with his father.

Cecilia drew back the curtain and opened the door softly. Luke followed her in. As Fran hesitated, a nurse in starched blue and white came forward and ushered her in quickly.

'I shall be just outside, should you need me,' she said.

For a brief moment Fran thought she could smell death in the room. An involuntary shiver swept over her body. She tried to avoid looking at the bed, but suddenly Luke was drawing her forward to greet his father.

'A surprise for you, Father,' Cecilia said. 'Luke's come home, with his wife.'

'Hullo, Father,' Luke said. 'We were so sorry to hear about your accident.'

'Bet you were,' came the mumbled reply from the bed.

Fran looked at the white-faced figure lying flat in the bed. She had prepared herself to meet a man near to his end but James Hammond's eyes were bright and alert. He stared hard at his son and Fran saw that a moistness came into his eyes. Eyes that had faded with time, she suspected, but they had once been as magnetic as his son's. He still had a shock of dark-brown hair and a wiry moustache. As devilishly handsome once as Luke is now, Fran thought. Luke went closer to the bedside and took the hand lying outside the covers. The word 'foundry' had presented a picture of heavy metal, black dust and gnarled hands, but, to Fran's amazement, James Hammond's hands were like a gentleman's hands. Long, tapering fingers with well-manicured nails, as if they had never wielded the tools of a rough, tough, working life.

'Let me see the woman,' a shaky voice demanded.

Luke urged Fran nearer, and all her anger subsided. The old man's eyes were seeping tears, but she doubted that he even realised. There was strength in the features even if his condition caused a general weakness.

'I'm so sorry to have to meet you when you're not feeling well,' Fran said, gently clasping his hand.

'You can kiss me,' the old man said. 'I shan't bite.'

Fran placed her lips against his cheek and kept them there for a moment. She felt her warmth transfer to his cold face, and he tightened his grip on her hand.

'Why has it taken you so long to come?' he asked, in a quivering voice.

'Luke has to travel about,' Fran answered.

'And where are the children?'

'Because of my job, Father, we feel it's best that they remain at school in the south while I'm away at sea.'

James looked at his son with pitying scrutiny. Then he closed his eyes, and his face screwed up as if he was in pain.

'Shouldn't he have something for the pain?' Luke asked Ceclia.

'Yes, I expect it's time for his medicine. It might be best if we leave him now.'

They walked downstairs in solemn procession. Dorinda was nowhere to be seen, and Luke's mother was dozing in her chair.

'You haven't asked about his injuries,' Fran whispered to Luke.

'I told you, it's a spinal injury.'

'What was he doing, then? How did the accident happen?'

'Poking his nose in the most dangerous part of the foundry, by all accounts.'

'You heard that from Elizabeth?'

'Why the inquisition?' Luke hissed impatiently.

Footsteps in the hall echoed loudly, and in a few moments two young boys of about seven and eight entered the room.

Mrs Hammond came to life again. 'Ah, my grandsons. Come along, Howard and Jamie. Come and meet your Uncle Luke and Auntie Fran.'

The boys were very much alike, with mousy hair and hazel eyes. They were still wearing school uniform and making an effort to be on their best behaviour. Fran was certain that boyish giggles were being suppressed.

'Hullo,' she greeted brightly. 'How was school today? What was it – football, games or boring old geography?'

The younger boy, Jamie took a step closer and smiled. 'History today, but I enjoy it. English isn't bad, but I hate arithmetic.'

'Not too good at sums?' Luke said with a smile.

'No, sir. Well, I'm not bad, I supposed. At least I'm not at the bottom of the class.'

'Not quite,' his elder brother put in.

'And how was your school day, Howard dear?' his grandmother enquired.

'Quite good, Gran. I came top in last week's tests so now I can join the science group.'

Fran was quick to hear the distant screech of car brakes outside in the drive, and a few moments later the door was flung open and Elizabeth rushed in.

'Oh,' she said, breathlessly, 'you got here before me. I'm sorry Luke, I got held up at the bank.' Elizabeth kissed her brother and then hugged Fran warmly as she kissed her too. 'How are you both? Looking very well, I see.'

'We seem to have managed without you very well,' Luke said in a low voice as Mrs Hammond took the two boys outside.

'I'm sorry, Luke,' Elizabeth said again. 'I'm afraid I couldn't help it. How did it go?'

'Cecilia and Mother were pleased to see me, but Dorinda is ready to fight me all the way.'

'More important, how did Father react? How does he seem to you?'

'Better, I think, than you led me to believe. He managed to say a few words, and he didn't order me out of the house, but it's obvious that he's in considerable pain.'

'By tomorrow we shall know the results of the X-rays. They kept him in hospital for the first, critical week, and I really doubted whether you could possibly arrive here in time, but then he rallied. He's made every effort to survive.'

Luke and Elizabeth were talking in subdued tones. Fran felt as if they had forgotten that she was there, so she moved away to the window. The two boys, now wearing clothes suitable for playing in, were kicking a ball out in the meadow. The whole scene appeared somewhat bizarre to Fran. She had never expected to meet Luke's family, and it seemed odd to her that out of the blue his mother had requested a visit. Not so unlikely, she told herself, when the head of the household had been involved in an accident that could have resulted in his death. Fran was glad that he was recovering, and pleased that Luke had made the effort to see him, but she was suspicious of an ulterior motive.

This was confirmed at supper. Fran was tired after the long tedious journey, and would much have preferred to go to the hotel and return the next day when they were fresher. Now she struggled to eat the roast beef on her plate. She was pressed to take larger helpings of home-grown vegetables than she wanted and found it difficult to push them down.

Cecilia's husband, Alex, was a pleasant-mannered man who said little and seemed subservient to his wife. Their three small children were introduced briefly before supper: Edna, aged six, Teddy, four, and an eighteen-month-old baby boy, Derek. A young nanny whisked them away to the nursery before the supper gong sounded.

Dorinda's husband, Giles, was late arriving. He was shorter than Alex, stocky and round-faced with plump red cheeks, and something of an exhibitionist, Fran decided, as he took his place at the table next to her. He constantly nudged her elbow and made silly remarks while slurping his soup, and ate the main course as if he were afraid someone might remove it if he didn't hurry. Fran learned that he was a wages clerk at one of the many coal mines in the area. Alex worked in the ship-building industry. Fran silently thought how uncharacteristic of their jobs they were. She could well have imagined the burly Giles with blackened face and miner's lamp, heaving a truckload of coal along a tunnel down a mine, while Alex was a much more likely candidate for a white-collar office job.

The women contributed little to the conversation during the lengthy meal, but the men all appeared to converse easily, and Luke was in his element, recounting sea stories. They adjourned to the drawing room for coffee. Luke's mother was eager to hear about the girls while Luke and Elizabeth chatted secretly in a corner.

'Suppose when you heard father was about to snuff it you thought Luke ought to reinstate himself in the family circle?'

Fran had been enjoying a quiet conversation with Mrs Hammond and was surprised at the animosity in Dorinda's voice. She had long legs, long face, long everything, Fran thought, as she glanced up at her sister-in-law.

'Why should you think this visit has anything to do with me?' Fran said shortly. 'I was most surprised when Luke came home unexpectedly and announced that we were to come to Middlesbrough.'

'I bet,' Dorinda said. 'We expected him to return like the prodigal son when retirement from the Navy was approaching, but we didn't think he'd make his reappearance so obvious just when Dad was critically ill.'

'That's enough, Dorrie,' Elizabeth said. 'It has nothing to do with Fran. I felt it was right that Luke should know the situation. Besides, Mother wanted to see Luke. He is her only son, after all.'

'Yes, a disinherited one, remember. He hasn't cared one jot for Mother all these years. Don't you think it strange that he should come home now? We aren't stupid, Liz. Pity you couldn't conjure up a son yourself, Luke. That way you might be successful in wheedling your way into Father's affections.'

Luke dug his hands into his pockets. Fran saw a frown crease his brow and to her surprise he said: 'Actually, we had a son soon after we were married. Sadly he died of consumption at the age of ten.'

Fran opened her mouth in surprise. She wasn't aware of gasping, but she heard an intake of breath from the rest of the company. There was a thick silence.

'Fran has never quite got over it, although she is devoted to the four girls.' He put a tight grip on Fran's arm. 'Now I think we'll go to our hotel. Good night, Mother. Will it be all right if we call again tomorrow?'

Mrs Hammond, clearly shocked, stood up. She clung to Fran, kissing her and offering her sympathy, which brought fresh tears to Fran's eyes. Tears of anger as well as sorrow. Then Luke's mother wept on her son's shoulder as Elizabeth accosted Dorinda.

'I hope you're satisfied. You always were a vindictive little horror. Luke and Fran have as much right as you in this house, and don't you forget it.'

'I'm sorry, Fran. I ... I didn't know ...' Dorinda tossed her head then in defiance. 'It still doesn't alter the fact, though, that Father disinherited Luke when he ran away to sea.'

Fran thought that Luke was about to strike his youngest sister, but he resisted the temptation. He tugged at Fran's arm, and they went outside to the car.

He opened the door for Fran, but she paused before sitting inside.

'You've got some explaining to do,' she said, tight-lipped.

'Not now, for heaven's sake, Fran,' he said between his teeth.

Elizabeth had come after them. ''Bye for now, Fran. It's just a question of time. They'll come round to accepting Luke again, you'll see.'

'I'm not sure I know what's going on,' Fran said, 'but I don't think I approve.'

'Hammond House is where Luke belongs. He's the only son and when he retires from the Navy he should come into the business. It's what I've always wanted and what I shall go on working towards, regardless of what the others may think or say. Mother naturally wants Luke to have his inheritance in due course.'

'I don't wish to be party to any scheming, Elizabeth.'

Luke drew his sister away from the car and they stood aside talking in low voices so that Fran could not hear. Fran watched, noticing how alike they were. Elizabeth was almost as tall as Luke, and both were bright and alert like their father. Luke kissed Elizabeth and she waved again to Fran as they drove away.

Fran decided to let the tension ease before saying anything. The hotel seemed quite a distance away from Hammond House, but at last they left behind the riverside traffic and came to the coast. The air was clear and sweeter-smelling.

'It's not a large place, just a small family-run hotel. It's comfortable and serves excellent food,' Luke said.

'And how long are we to stay here? Until you're sure of your birthright?'

'Don't be sarcastic, Fran. You don't understand.'

'I understand that you've tricked me as well as your parents. I can see a lot more clearly now, and I do believe you've used me from the very beginning to get back in their favour.'

'Come along, I don't intend to sit here and argue things out. We must sign in.'

He fetched the cases from the boot of the car and Fran reluctantly followed him into the reception. She stood aloof from him. She could hardly believe that she was in this situation. She had vowed she hated him when he took Hilda away from her, but now to discover that he had planned to use her from the start was shocking. A young pageboy took them up in the lift to the first floor, where they were shown into a room overlooking the sea. It reminded Fran of the hotel Luke had stayed in when he visited her in Brimdene. What a fool she had been to fall for his scheming plans! Luke tipped the young boy and then closed the door firmly.

'All right,' he said angrily. 'So you think you've found me out in some dastardly plot. Is it wrong of me to want to get to know my family again?'

'For the wrong reasons, yes, Luke, it is. I thought you were genuine in wanting to make it up with your parents, but not for one moment did I believe it was to make monetary gain. Have you no pride? Creeping and crawling to your father so that he'll put you back in his will? It's the most despicable thing I've ever heard of, and then to use me – and my dead son – for your own ends. To pretend that the girls are yours? What else have you stooped to for your selfish greed? Yours and Elizabeth's, I suppose.'

'Leave Liz out of this. At least she gave me hope and love during my early days at sea.'

'And then Sarita came into your life,' Fran flung at him. 'Now where does *she* fit in? Is she your other wife? Mother of your children, perhaps? Is that why your father disowned you – because you married a foreign girl?'

Luke was stunned. He turned quite pale and his cheeks looked drawn. It was as if his tongue had cramp. He just stood and stared at Fran, unnerving her. Then he slowly walked towards her, clenching his fists into a tight ball as he did so.

'You've been prying,' he accused. 'How else would you know anything about Sarita?'

'You took my Hilda away, so I was left in Craiglee alone when Jenny had her holiday. I couldn't bear it without Hilda – and you. But you wouldn't know what it's like for a woman to be separated from the children she bore. I had to occupy my time as best I could so I cleared out drawers and cupboards. Husbands and wives shouldn't have secrets, Luke. Henry and I never had any – and I thought we didn't either. Yes, I found the bundle of letters by accident, and I had to satisfy my curiosity. Snapshots of you and a beautiful girl – and you maintain that it was the image of me you carried everywhere with you.'

'I never claimed to be celibate.'

Fran was sick of hearing those words. 'But you never told me you had loved another woman that much before?'

'How can you know how much I loved Sarita?' He glared at Fran with contempt, then covered his face with his hands as if he couldn't bear the truth.

'Are we within the law, Luke?' Fran asked, almost afraid of what she might hear. 'For goodness sake, you've used me enough, I must know everything now.'

Luke went to look out of the window. He turned and stared at Fran unseeing. He paced the room in agitation. Fran felt afraid of him, yet she knew she mustn't show it.

'If we're not legally married, Luke, then I want to go to Aberdeen, fetch Hilda, pack up everything in Craiglee and go home to my family.'

Luke came out of his trance. 'What are you saying? Darling – do you think so badly of me that you think I'd coerce you into a bigamous marriage? For what purpose?'

'To gain your inheritance, of course. You're a liar and a cheat!' Fran shouted.

Luke shook his head solemnly. 'No, not that, Fran. I admit to this little scheme to regain my position in the family, but nothing more.'

'Then you might have had the decency to tell me. I could have repudiated everything you were saying. I've always been honest and straight. If this is how the wealthy live, then I'm glad I came from a poor, working-class background. I hope they turn you away and I pray that I may never have to face your parents again.'

'Please don't desert me now, Fran. My parents are getting on, Dad already into his seventies. It isn't so much the money as that I'm getting older too and I don't want the rift to go to the grave with them. I know the other girls see me as a fortune hunter. But there's room in the foundry for all the male heirs, for goodness sake, and I can't stay in the navy for ever.' He arched his back and flexed his muscles.

He'd never seem old, Fran thought. Right now he was tired, and possible a little relieved that the awkward moment of meeting his family again was over.

He turned to her after more pacing, and placed his hands on her shoulders. 'I should have told you about Sarita.' He ran his hand through his tousled hair. He looked so unhappy. 'We met when I was in my early twenties. She adored me, waited at the dockside for me whenever we returned to Asia. In her I saw you. Oh, I know you're nothing like each other in looks, but she loved me passionately, gave herself to me just as you did that Christmas at Lady Hinckley's. She said she was expecting our baby. I thought it was a trick to get money from me. When I went away I did give her some money and then gave little further thought to her, much to my chagrin. My thoughts were truly only of you and Lennie.'

'And you expect me to believe that?' Fran said in a high-pitched voice.

Luke shrugged. 'It is the truth,' he said. 'Then one day when I went back to Asia she wasn't there. I made enquiries, only to be told by the barman on the quay that she died giving birth to my baby. Only then did I realise that I had loved her quite deeply. It was you that prevented me from recognising that love. Then, when I returned to Sherbrook one day, I heard that Lennie had died, and I felt I had lost everything. I needed you desperately then, Fran, but you had a husband.'

'It sounds to me as if you're making it up as you go along, Luke,' Fran said bitterly. 'Sailors aren't renowned for acknowledging their foreign mistresses once they've left them behind on the quayside, and I don't imagine for one minute that you're any different. It was only your own guilty conscience that made you believe Sarita was any more special than the others.'

Luke bit his lip emotionally and turned away from her. 'I suppose I can't expect you to see any good in me. I'm fond of children, Fran, and I would love to have had a family similar to yours. But, as time went by, the Royal Navy and my commitment to king and country became all-important. It was my way of life, and women and children couldn't really have a place in it.'

'Other men marry, have children and remain loyal to them, even when they're away at sea for long stretches.'

'That's what the women think, my dear. Few men can do without a woman for long, which is why there are established brothels in dockside areas.'

'Don't be so disgusting,' Fran spat out.

'I'm afraid you've lived a sheltered life, Fran. Probably the most daring thing you've ever done in your life was to go to bed with me when you were under the influence of too much wine.'

'And haven't I lived to regret *that* incident? We all have to pay for our mistakes, Luke, especially when they're made with evil intent, just as you and Elizabeth are doing now.'

'You're a hard woman, Fran.' He glared at her. The words were spoken as if he really meant them, and yet was hurt by having uttered them.

She turned away and wept. Henry had seldom needed to say such words; just one look from him had been enough to subdue her.

Luke took his time before taking her in his arms to console her. 'You really are and have been the only woman I've ever wanted, darling,' he whispered. 'I do love you, and I want us both to be a part of the Hammond family.'

'I wish I could believe you, Luke,' she said. 'But everything you do seems to have an ulterior motive. Why on earth couldn't you have told your parents the truth? That we weren't married until a year ago. How can I pretend that the accident never happened to Henry and my father? I'm not used to being secretive over such important matters. I just hate deception.'

'But you deceived Henry,' Luke reminded her. 'Why didn't you tell him that you slept with another man before you made your vows in church?'

'It . . . it would have upset everything,' she said miserably. 'Don't you think I've suffered torment over that? And haven't I been punished enough for my sins? Losing my son, and then Henry – all the people I loved most in the world.'

'And what of our love, Fran?'

'I believed we had made a new beginning. I really tried to love and obey you, Luke,' she said tearfully. 'Your deception is deliberate. In just one year you've taken me from my children, sent Hilda away to school, and now you've lied about us to your parents. How can I love a man who has no conscience? You can't really love me or you wouldn't use me so shamefully. I . . . I wish I never had to lay eyes on you again!'

'But we made vows in a church, and there's no way out. I need you more than ever now. You promised to be my wife, and I vowed to be as good a father to your children as I know how. Don't I pay for the rented house in Brimdene? Who sends money to Prue and Sam for Babs, and who's paying for Hilda's education?'

'We were happy as we were in Brimdene. It was a struggle, there's no denying, but at least we had each other. My in-laws were good to us then; now they can barely bring themselves to acknowledge me.'

'Don't you think you owed yourself a little happiness?'

'Where's the happiness?' she questioned.

'Come on, Fran. You know you've enjoyed the marital relationship.'

'And that's the answer to everything? Well, not any more, Luke. I'll sleep in the chair.'

'And I say you will not,' he said decisively.

Fran was afraid to carry her rejection any further. She went to the bathroom at the end of the corridor and then undressed in silence, hoping against hope that Luke would be the one to sleep in the large armchair.

He slid into bed beside her, turned his back on her and soon his even breathing told her that he was asleep.

Fran did her best to lie still even though she was unable to sleep. Dawn was poking its nose in the opening between the curtains before, from heartache and weariness, she too fell asleep.

Chapter Fifteen

A light knock on the door roused Fran, although she had been coming out of a deep slumber gradually for some time. Before she could answer, the door opened and a young girl came in carrying a tray.

'Morning, ma'am. I'm sorry you weren't feeling too well after your journey from Scotland. Captain Hammond requested that we bring you a breakfast tray for eleven o'clock.'

Fran sat up and looked at the girl through bleary vision.

'Thank you, that's very kind,' she said softly.

'Your husband said not to hurry, he'll be back midday.'

The tray was set down close to the bed and the girl left. Fran looked around her at the emptiness of the hotel bedroom. She felt desolate, and lonely for Luke. She despised him for the way he behaved, for the way he had used her so calculatingly. And yet . . . and yet . . . she knew she couldn't do without him.

She took the breakfast tray to the small table near the window. A cool breeze wafted through the open window and she was glad of the clean, fresh air. Far away on the horizon, where sea met sky, a mist hung. It promised to be another warm, sunny day, she thought. She sipped the hot tea slowly, letting it warm her right through. Feeling revived, she ate the scrambled eggs that had been kept hot underneath a cover on the tray. She was glad of the chance to be alone to think things out. Her conscience told her that she ought to go to Luke's family and explain exactly how they had first met – but what did that matter after all these years? At least she felt she owed them an explanation of how she had been widowed and then married Luke a year ago. She couldn't really believe that it would make any difference to the way they thought of Luke. His mother was just so happy to see him again that Fran was convinced she would never turn him away, whatever he had done. Perhaps it didn't really matter what his sisters thought, but it did matter what his father made of the prodigal son's return. At present, though, James Hammond wasn't in a stable condition, and it was best not to add to his worries. Fran had steeled herself for the shock of seeing a sick, dying man, but he was far from that, she considered. She had felt that she could trust Elizabeth, but now she wondered if this whole episode had been magnified in order to get Luke back into family favour.

It was a disturbing thought that Luke, now over forty years old, had to confront his upcoming retirement from the Royal Navy. Fran had never thought to enquire how many more years he had to serve. What he would do when that event occurred had certainly never entered her head. Now she could see more clearly his reason for wanting to be married. He would need a wife to satisfy his needs as well as run his home. He had a house in Portsmouth, rented out to other officers and their families when he had no use for it, so why then did he seek to reinstate himself within his family circle in the north?

The more Fran thoughts about the situation, the more she realised that, being the eldest, and the only son, he must feel piqued that he had been disinherited. She had to admit that as far as she knew he had not done anything that bad to discredit the family name or honour. Most parents would be proud of a son who had fought for his country during the Great War, and risen by his own merits in the ranks of the senior service. She supposed it all came down to money in the end. Did money matter so much to him? He was reasonably generous in every respect to her and her family, as he had reminded her. When he came out of the Navy he would need to find a job. Was he hankering after going into the family business as Elizabeth had suggested? Deep down, Fran knew that she could never be mean enough to divulge the details of her past to Luke's parents. She just wished there was no need for the deception. Something at some time was sure to leak out. She only hoped it wouldn't come from her.

After she had eaten she took a long warm bath and felt refreshed. She put on a pale-blue silk dress with slim-fitting sleeves. The V neck had a deep cleavage and was elegantly finished with a wide picot-edged frill of the same material, exactly meeting the shoulder seams. From the dropped waist, unpressed pleats hung gracefully down to the mid-calf hemline. For the first time in her married life Fran was able to spend time and money on her own clothes. She had enjoyed making this dress in readiness for when Luke came home on leave. But she had packed mostly dark clothes in view of the reason for the hasty visit to Middlesbrough. Now, believing that James Hammond was not in a critical condition any longer, she felt she could wear a lighter-coloured dress. Surveying herself in the mirror, she knew she looked elegant with navy-blue accessories, including high-heeled T-bar shoes, and that her appearance would impress Luke.

When she had finished brushing and styling her hair, she tidied the room and went to look out of the window. The sun was high and glaring down. She longed to go out and walk by the sea, but it was well past noon, and the maid had said that Luke would be back before midday.

Soon she saw him coming along the sea road at the top of the cliffs. He was wearing grey flannels, white shirt and a sports jacket in dog-tooth check. His dark hair was blown free by the wind. Her heart seemed to skip in time to his brisk tread as he hurried towards the hotel. He glanced up as he crossed the road towards the entrance to the hotel. Even from this distance she could see his solemn expression change to one of pleasure as he spotted her, lifted his hand and waved. How could they be at odds on such a lovely day, and in such a pleasant seaside resort as Saltburn-by-the-Sea?

Fran remained at the window until the door opened and Luke came in. He came straight towards her, hands outstretched.

'Darling, you look lovely,' he said, holding her at arm's length. 'A new dress – especially for me?'

Fran felt herself colouring slightly. 'I've had plenty of time to sew,' she said softly.

'You made it? It's splendid – I thought you were going to tell me it had set me back several guineas.' He laughed as he pulled her towards him and planted his mouth very firmly over hers.

If she had wanted to continue feeling angry towards him, it would have been useless. His dark eyes melted her heart, and before she knew it she was returning his passionate kisses.

'I wish I'd got back before you'd dressed,' he whispered. 'But we have a luncheon appointment with Elizabeth. I hope you don't mind?'

'Why should I?' She looked up at him, unable to disguise her admiration. 'I wish you had woken me earlier. I'd have loved a walk by the sea to chase away – well – you know.'

'I'm sorry I gave you cause to be angry, Fran dear. I realise how things must look to you, but to be reunited with my family is important to me. You may think I should be content with my lovely wife and family of girls, and believe me, I am. But if anything happened to either of my parents, and I hadn't made the effort to be reconciled, I should find it hard to live with myself.'

'But is deceit really necessary, Luke? Do we have to tell lies? Surely they'll understand about us meeting after I was widowed?'

'Father never cared about me as a son – only that I would marry and produce a son and heir for him. Fate has been unkind to me in that Lennie died. But it might make all the difference to Father if he knows I had a son, once.'

'But you didn't, Luke. Lennie was Henry's son and you'll never persuade me otherwise.'

'There's no way of knowing. I feel it in my gut that he was mine, and I shall go on believing that. All I beg of you is that you won't tell Father that you've been married before. What harm can it do to allow those years to fade out of our lives? If we really love one another it shouldn't be difficult to imagine that we've been together for a lifetime.'

'You asking me to forget Henry? That's impossible, Luke.'

'Of course not, but for the sake of my parents and sisters, let them think that there hasn't been anyone else in our lives. No Henry, no Sarita.'

Fran sighed. 'You are asking a great deal of me, Luke,' she said.

'I know, darling, and I'm truly sorry. Please do it for me? Elizabeth knows everything and understands. She wants us to do it this way and she'll always be supportive.'

'You must do what you feel is necessary but I shall prefer to remain silent. I'm not a good liar and no good will come of making up stories for gain.'

'I can't agree that it is for gain, Fran,' Luke said solemnly. 'It's to make my elderly parents happy. Merely a white lie to save any further hurt.'

'Put like that you make me appear selfish, but I've always been honest, so I shall leave the talking to you. Now, what time do we have to meet Elizabeth, and where?'

'At her cottage at one o'clock.' Luke looked at his pocket watch. 'It's time we left – are you ready?'

Fran was relieved that they were on better terms. She hated deception and lies, but she hated animosity between them even more.

They took the road south, and then turned inland to travel through rural countryside. The scenery was more like Dorset, Fran thought. Fresh fields, cows and sheep grazing, picturesque villages and hamlets. Luke stopped outside an ivy-covered cottage beside the village green. Elizabeth appeared at the door immediately and came to open the neat garden gate.

'Welcome to Purbeck Cottage,' she said, kissing Fran warmly.

'Purback Cottage?' Fran repeated in surprise at the familiar name.

'Yes, I fell in love with your part of the world, Fran. The family think I just wanted to get as far south as possible for some clean air. Naturally I enthused about Dorset and the Purbecks when I returned home, so I decided to name my cottage as a constant reminder of that area.'

'It's certainly very much like a Dorset cottage,' Fran agreed. 'I'm glad you enjoyed your visit south.'

'It was a real pleasure, especially as at last Luke took the plunge and got married. Come along in – we have a lot to discuss.'

Elizabeth talked non-stop until they were seated at the table in the living room. A vase of sweet peas of varying shades of pink and mauve, with some white ones, placed in the centre of the table, gave off a gentle perfume, reminding Fran of the splendid flowers Henry had grown and been so proud of at the old mill house. Here, in a country cottage again, much smaller than the house in Craiglee, she couldn't help feeling nostalgic for Sherbrook.

'Father seemed much brighter this morning,' Elizabeth said. 'I always go to visit before I go into work.' She put an extra slice of boiled ham on Fran's plate. 'Do have plenty,' she said, 'and we must eat up the cauliflower cheese. It isn't nice kept, is it?'

'Your father seems to have turned the danger point,' Fran said.

'I expect you're thinking that I sent for Luke needlessly, but honestly, Fran, Father was in a very poor condition after the fall. Some machinery failed to function and Father being Father had to go to investigate, probably cursing the men because they couldn't get it to work. The doctors believe he may have had some kind of blackout going up so high at his age. A metal bucket swung round, hitting him in the back, which caused him to fall several feet on to a concrete floor. Fortunately there was a pile of sacking on the floor, and this broke his fall. We were afraid he'd broken his back, and at his age that would have been the end of him, but you know Father, Luke. He'll never give up as long as he can draw breath.'

'Any news from the hospital about the X-rays?' Luke asked.

'I telephoned Dr Ackroyd and he was going to chase things up before he visited Father this morning. You're going to see him, aren't you? Mother is expecting you to dine with us tonight at Hammond House.'

'I think Fran finds such a large family altogether something of a strain, don't you, darling?'

'If your mother is expecting us we'd best not disappoint her,' Fran said. 'I am quite used to large family gatherings, Luke.'

'Take no notice of the girls and their sniping,' Elizabeth said. 'They're only jealous that Luke has returned to the fold, but why shouldn't he? It's a shame you don't have any sons – that would really have pleased Father. Dorinda has got her boys' future all mapped out to take over the business. Maybe they won't want to after they've completed their posh education. Foundry work is heavy and dirty and I can't see any of them really wanting to actually work there. Times are changing, and there's so much opportunity for youngsters these days in much more exciting careers.'

Fran didn't feel that it was quite fair of Luke, wanting to return to the business when he had chosen to go to sea against his parents' wishes. She could see both sides of the argument. She appreciated how his sisters felt. She just hoped that once Luke was reconciled with his father they could return north to Craiglee and get on with their lives.

After the very nice meal Elizabeth had prepared, they sat and talked for over an hour. Then Elizabeth said she must return to the works. Luke drove on a circular route to Hammond House. Everywhere seemed quiet. The boys were are school, the younger ones and Cecilia were out walking in the park, and Mrs Hammond was resting.

A maid showed them in to the sitting room and shortly afterwards Dorinda joined them.

'I'm sure you'll be pleased to know that father shows signs of improvement.' Her voice was cold, and she eyed Fran contemptuously. 'Can't think why he should be so pleased to see you after all these years. Mother too, though heaven knows the shock is enough to kill the pair of them. Still, I suppose that's your intention.'

'Dorinda, dear,' Luke said patiently, 'I haven't come here to antagonise you, or upset our parents. I'm glad that Elizabeth sent for me, and as we're living in Scotland at present, the journey here was much shorter than if I'd had to travel up from Portsmouth. We shall only be here for the rest of this week. Surely you can make an effort to be amicable for that short time – at least to my wife.'

'Suppose it was her idea to come home, cap in hand? Trying out your charm on Father to see what you can get out of him, eh?'

'Fran had no say in coming here. By the way you're behaving I imagine that she'll be jolly pleased to leave and never return.'

'My place is beside Luke,' Fran said in a strong voice. 'I can understand why he needed to see his parents again, but I do assure you, Dorinda, that neither he nor I have any ulterior motive. Luke has a good rank, and is well provided for when he retires from the

Navy. Not everyone sees things from a mercenary point of view as you seem to do.'

Fran was quite surprised at her own eloquent speech, and she knew Luke was impressed when she felt his hand smooth across her back.

'It's time to let bygones be bygones, Dorinda,' Luke said. 'I've never had anything from Father and I don't expect anything. But I am his eldest child, his only son.'

'And it's rotten luck for you that you don't have a son of your own,' Dorinda flung at him.

Fran felt Luke flinch. By the venom in Dorinda's eyes, Fran was afraid that somehow this younger sister of Luke's had learned the truth.

'We came to see Father. I think the less said the better,' Luke said in a quiet tone.

'Go on up,' Dorinda said haughtily. 'He can't leave a business or money to a ghost.'

She flounced away, her head held high in defiance.

'Take no notice,' Luke said softly in Fran's ear. 'I never thought she'd behave so badly or I wouldn't have brought you with me.'

'We must put up a united front – although I'm still not happy about deceiving your parents, Luke. If you're not bothered about an inheritance, why can't we tell them the truth?'

'It's too late now, Fran. We must stick to the same story. Father will certainly never want to see me again if he discovers we've misled him.'

'If only you had discussed this with me on the way here, Luke,' Fran said heatedly. 'There was no need for any animosity at all.'

'You wouldn't have understood, darling. You don't fully understand now.'

'I understand that you're using my Lennie to gain favour with your father – and that's unforgiveable.'

'But you can't deny me – can you?'

'Your charm won't always get you out of trouble, Luke. I'll stand by you this time, but don't ever try to deceive me again.'

'So you're back?' James Hammond greeted his son.

'Yes, Father. I only have a week's leave,' Luke said.

'Stupid woman, insisting that I should sleep all day and all night too,'

'Probably for your own good, Father,' Luke said. 'Sleep is the best healer.'

'What would you know, boy? You're a sea captain, not a doctor.'

'I have to have a certain kowledge about a number of things. Anyway, how are you today?'

'No better for staying in this confounded bed,' James Hammond complained. He looked directly at Fran. 'Well, lass, and what d'you make of your husband's family?'

Fran smiled and went to take the old man's hand. 'I've hardly had time to get to know everyone yet,' she said. 'We're here to visit you. It must be irksome having to remain on your back, but it'll be worth it if it means you can resume your life again in due course.'

'And what would a pretty young woman like you know about such things, I wonder?' He screwed his eyes up and surveyed Fran as if he could see into her very soul. She was sure that reflected in his haunting eyes she could see a mischievous twinkle.

'Life teaches us what we need to know,' she replied gently.

'And it's taught you a thing or two, I can tell,' he said with a wicked grin. Like father, like son, Fran thought. There was no mistaking whose son Luke was. James Hammond must have been a bit of a devil in his younger days, she reckoned.

'Well, now that you're here, sit down and make yourselves comfortable. Have you had dinner?'

'With Elizabeth, Father.'

'Ah, yes, my Lizzie. Good girl. Wish she'd married and given me a grandson – but it wouldn't bear the name of Hammond, any more'n any of the other scheming wenches' offspring do.' He turned his head to one side and looked at Luke. The mischief was gone and in its place Fran saw a moistness in the old man's eyes. 'Pity you didn't have a son, Luke.' He looked across at Fran. 'You can't be too old to bear your husband another child, surely?'

Fran nearly chocked. 'I – I – my youngest is seven now, and I've borne five children. Isn't that enough for any woman?'

'My Emma had seven altogether, my dear.' James Hammond's voice was softer now as he recalled his youthful years. 'Beautiful, she was, and blossomed when the first boys were born. Twins, you see – died within the week. Poor Emma never got over that.' He sighed deeply. 'Then Luke came along, and another boy within the year, but he died too – of convulsion at a year old.' There was a deep sigh and Luke's father caught his breath in what was almost a sob. 'Nothing but damned girls after that,' he added aggressively to hide his emotion. 'Every man should have a son to carry on the family name. When Luke's gone the name will die out.' He glanced at Luke, but Fran could see no love there and she felt for her husband. 'Tell me about your son, me dear, if you will.'

Fran had to turn away. Her heart was full with compassion for her father-in-law and renewed sorrow for her own first-born. Guilt pressed painfully side by side with pity.

'Lennie had consumption and died when he was ten years old,' she said. Then, as if she could not bear to speak of him, she got up and went to the window.

'Fran has never been able to come to terms with our son's death,' Luke said.

Fran glared at Luke, and saw fear in his expression. She burst into tears and rushed from the room.

Back at the hotel that evening, after a meal eaten with the Hammond family under obvious restraint, Luke took Fran in his arms.

'I'm sorry that today was so difficult for you.'

'Sorry? Oh, Luke, no good can ever come of this cheating. For God's sake tell your father the truth. I can't go on with this charade. Lennie belonged to Henry and me, and you know that. You're not only deceiving your father but yourself as well. You haven't worried about your family all these years – why now?'

Luke ground his teeth in bitter agitation. 'Because this is where I belong. Don't they owe me something for turning their backs on me? Father goes on about wanting sons, but he disowned me for joining the Navy. It isn't too late, surely, to put my experience and knowledge of foreign countries into the business, and be the son he always wanted?'

'But you chose your way of life, and you can't expect them to understand why, Luke,' Fran said.

Luke paced the floor. 'We'll try for a baby,' he suddenly said. 'That would really please Father.'

'Luke!' Fran laughed him to scorn. 'You can't be serious. At my age? I don't want all that work again.'

'Father will make it worth your while, Fran. A baby of our own would draw us closer together, darling.'

'No, Luke! For goodness sake, think what you're saying. I'm forty-five years old. A child would look on us as old parents by the time it was ten or twelve. Whatever would people think? It was you who made me split up my girls and desert them – what else will you demand of me? No, Luke! I'm definitely not having any more children. I probably can't anyway.'

He came towards her with a glint in his eye. Fran backed away.

'There's no harm in trying,' he said. A struggle ensued. Fran kept her shrieks of protest in check lest other guests or the proprietors heard what was going on. Her lovely new dress was almost ripped off her back and thrown to the floor. Luke pushed her back across the bed as he pulled off her stockings, and although she fought desperately her underwear was quickly discarded. He was like a savage – wild, relentless in his passion. There were no caresses, no tender words of love, not even a kiss, only a cruel bite into her shoulder as she tried to get up. She slapped his face, but this only served to strengthen his intent. He was inside her easily as he forced her legs apart, and the weight of him seemed unbearable. She wanted to reason with him. Had they kept themselves in check during this year of marriage? For the most part no, and yet she had not conceived. Why did he think that this brutal attack could result in conception just because he wanted it to? He was selfish – a greedy, selfish animal. After his lusting he collapsed on top of Fran, crying with relief.

'Oh, my darling, I know it's going to work, I just know it.'

Fran turned her head away, bit into her handkerchief and wept bitterly.

'Fran, darling, can you ever forgive me? I hate myself for what I've done to you.' He was stalking the floor, still naked, while Fran sneaked in between the sheets and pulled them tightly round her. 'I know you think I'm cruel, but you don't know how hard it is for me when I come home. I just want to make love to you all the time. You mean everything to me, Fran, *everything*,' he pleaded desperately. 'I promise that if you do conceive, I'll do all in my power to make it easy for you. It could happen, Fran. Some of the men go on giving their wives babies until well into their fifties. Being abstemious while we're away at sea makes our sperm grow strong, darling.'

'Then why hasn't it happened during this past year?' Fran flung over her shoulder. 'Why don't you wake up to reality, Luke? I'm almost past child-bearing age. A woman's body is not an object to be used just any way a man wants to satisfy his lust. Babies should be conceived in love and with tenderness, not in that barbaric way.'

Luke sat on the side of the bed and caressed her cheek with his hand.

'Darling, I do love you, and it wasn't lust – not in that sense. Desperation perhaps. Life at sea has never compensated me for not having a loving family to return to. Maybe I'm growing older and wiser now. I feel the need of my parents. You've been put to the test throughout your marriage to Henry. You've had to undergo the most dreadful tragedies. But you had your mother to lean on, and your in-laws.'

'And thanks to you I now have no one. Now, when my mother and I need each other most of all, I'm at one end of the country and she at the other. I must have been crazy to allow you to talk me into this situation.'

'It was love, Fran dear. Despite your contempt for me at this moment, you know you love me – have always loved me – and our son was proof of it.'

'*No*! You took advantage of me then and you've done so ever since we met again. Why couldn't you have kept out of my life?'

'I offered you security and affection. Alone with your problems in Brimdene you'd have grown old before your time, darling. Now you've become even more beautiful to me. You're fulfilled again and with another baby of our own you could blossom into a new phase of motherhood.'

'Oh, you and your clever words,' she shouted, as she beat her fists into her pillow. 'I want to go home to my own people.'

'Thy people shall be my people, and my people shall be thine,' Luke quoted quietly.

Luke seemed well pleased with the outcome of his visit. His parents made him promise to write when he could and visit again at the earliest opportunity. But when he rejoined his ship it was to make a voyage to the Americas which was to last six months, perhaps longer. He went away in good spirits, telling Fran to take good care of herself in readiness for the new life that he felt sure was growing inside her.

Fran was amused at his boyish enthusiasm. She managed to put aside the memory of his brutal attack on her, excusing his behaviour as eagerness to please his father. She busied herself at the orphanage, and the summer passed pleasantly enough for her. Hilda came home for the whole of August. Fran could hardly believe the change in her daughter, who seemed far too sophisticated for a Sheldon girl. It was heartening to read her school report, and Fran was forced to admit that Luke had been right in giving Hilda the chance of better schooling. She had caught up with her classmates and was placed fourth in the exam results.

Fran's heart ached with longing, though, when she read letters from the other girls and Ma. Kate wrote that she had been given her week's holiday immediately after Whitsun, and Uncle Eric had come to take Gran Brown back to Stockclere for a week, so that Kate and Ruby could go to stay with Aunt Prue, Uncle Sam, Marion and Babs. Fran looked out over the mists of time, and wished she was back with them all. When she replied to their letters she hid her heartache, even though tears flowed freely, but said how much she and Hilda were looking forward to their return south when Luke was reappointed in a year's time.

Hilda went with her mother to the orphanage three times a week during her summer holidays. She showed an ability to care for the younger children, especially babies of under a year old. Fran was quite surprised, as Hilda's place in the family was the second youngest. She and Babs had been the two little ones, sometimes protected, sometimes bullied, often tormented by Ruby and even by Kate before she had gone into service.

When they weren't at the orphanage they visited Edinburgh and Glasgow and enjoyed bus rides up into the mountains on hot sunny days, but all too soon they were checking school uniform and packing Hilda's case ready for her return to Aberdeen. Luke had given strict instructions that when Fran took Hilda back to school she was to remain in Aberdeen, in the same hotel they had stayed in before, for as long as she needed before making the return trip to Craiglee. But Fran was fortunate in obtaining a lift by car back to Dunfermline with the parents of another girl. They assured her that she need not make the journey again: they would bring Hilda back and forth while Luke was away at sea.

A batch of letters arrived from Luke after several weeks. Only in the first two did he mention the hope that Fran was expecting his baby. The rest of his letters contained little but details of his visit to the Americas, and it was evident to Fran that he was thoroughly enjoying himself. Dear Luke, she thought wistfully. A man of his time. Totally devoted to whatever took his fancy at any given moment. He was much too fascinated by foreign countries to worry any further about his wife's condition. Fran doubted that he would really want to have the extra responsibility of a child of his own. The thought intrigued him, and when he was with the family it seemed important, but once he sailed the high seas, domestic matters were quickly forgotten.

Perhaps not as easily as Fran thought. When the first shades of autumn appeared, followed by early snowfalls on the surrounding hills and mountains, she received a letter from Luke, telling her that they were making their way back to Britain, and he was looking forward to being with her for Christmas. Secretly, Fran had hoped he might not return until some time in the new year. She had been syphoning off a small amount of cash each week from the allowance Luke made her, saving it up for a surreptitious visit down south for the festive season. Her hopes were dashed. Instead, Luke informed her that they had been invited to spend Christmas and New Year with his family at Hammond House. Her hard-saved money had to be spent on presents for his sisters' children. Luke was bringing gifts from exotic South American countries for the senior members of the family, but he thought she would know best what to buy for the children.

Fran dreaded the visit. She hated having to be on her guard. More pretence, more lies, renewed hope that she would produce more offspring. Just this one last time, she told herself, and by next year she could revert to being her old self, back among her own kith and kin. Once they were settled back in Portsmouth, the journey would be too long for them to visit Hammond House again.

Luke arrived in Craiglee three days before Christmas. To Fran's surprise all the plans had been made, and because of the icy weather they were to travel by train to Middlesbrough on Christmas Eve.

Any disappointment Fran had experienced was quickly forgotten once she was cradled in Luke's arms. He was full of energy, warmth and love. Apologetic, too, for the way he had behaved previously.

'Of course it would please me if you were to have my baby,' he said, 'but we must be patient. Above all, I want it to be conceived in love.'

Fran responded as she usually did so that Luke's homecoming was a memorable one, and as dawn broke with him sleeping contentedly beside her, she smiled to herself, satisfied with the knowledge that she would not, could not conceive, however much he willed it to happen.

Chapter Sixteen

Hilda was excited to be going to Hammond House. Luke drove as far as Edinburgh, where he left the car at a garage for servicing. Although it was bitterly cold, the train journey was pleasant enough and when they arrived at Middlesbrough they took a taxi to Hammond House.

It was late afternoon, the daylight fading, but the large, old house looked inviting with coloured lights strung out in the entrance hall. A tall Christmas tree, festooned with gaudy baubles and plenty of sparkling tinsel, could be seen standing majestically in the huge bay window of the sitting room. Hilda skipped up to the heavy oak front door in happy anticipation.

'Come along in, my dears,' Emma Hammond greeted them, kissing Fran's cold cheeks. Then she lifted her thin, bony hands to frame Luke's face. 'There's log fires in all the bedrooms, and it's lovely to think we're going to be a complete family at last.' She turned to look with admiration at Hilda, who was wearing a mid-blue coat and hat which Fran had made herself. 'So this is Hilda – how d'you do, my dear child.'

Hilda seemed a little in awe of both the size of the hall and the graciousness of Luke's mother. Coats were taken off and a servant took the cases up to their room. In the dim light of the back of the hall, Fran noticed a solitary figure leaning heavily on a stick. She knew that James Hammond was now up and about but she hadn't realised what a tall man he was. She went up to him and he hugged her to him, his rough tweed jacket smelling of tobacco. 'How are you?' she asked.

James refused to let Fran go. She had said like father, like son, before, but now that he was standing tall and looking a better colour, she could only remain in his embrace and observe him with deep admiration. Now this man, she thought, I could really fall in love with. What was she thinking of? Admitting that her marriage to Luke was a failure? Not in the marital bed, that was for sure. But in some ways she felt that she and Luke were miles apart. Luke had returned home full of energy, warmth and love, so what made this older edition so much more attractive? There was strength in his grasp and warmth emanated from his body. And in his dark, brooding eyes she saw every emotion she longed for. A certain wickedness, a definite twinkle, and a fondness for the feel of a woman.

She placed her hands on his arms. 'It's lovely to see you up and about, Mr Hammond,' she said in a low, husky voice. 'I didn't realise that you're as tall as your son.'

James gave her an affectionate cuddle. 'But much better looking, Fran, my dear, and I'd rather you called me James, if you will.' He placed his lips gently over hers. 'I just know we're going to be friends.' Fran began to feel uneasy at being held so long in his grip, so she asked again, 'How do you feel, Mr Hammond?'

'Not as agile as I'd like to be,' he said slowly. 'Not quite back to my old self, but getting there, and all the better for seeing you again.' His hand slid down her back and he gave her a light tap on her bottom. 'Don't forget, it's James. It's also Christmas, a time for behaving a little less formally.' He glanced up, indicating that she should follow his gaze. She laughed aloud when she saw the huge bunch of mistletoe hanging immediately above them.

'I wondered what you were up to,' she said.

James held her head steady with one hand as he planted his mouth over hers. 'Getting old I may be,' he said mischievously, 'but never too old to kiss a pretty woman.'

Luke hurried forward and claimed his wife then, to kiss her in his own special, intimate way. All Fran's fears melted away. This was how she remembered Christmases in the past. A family – a large, happy family – and even if the faces of those around her were somewhat different on this occasion, she knew she was being accepted into the Hammond tribe.

They went up to their bedroom, a large, airy room overlooking the gardens at the back of the house, with Hilda in a smaller room next door. They even had their own bathroom along the corridor, and when they had freshened up they went downstairs for afternoon tea.

With the rest of the family they sat round the magnificient sitting room in cosy armchairs, with small occasional tables beside each person. Hilda was being carefully assessed by Dorinda's two young boys, who had been allowed to join them, but Cecilia's two youngest children were having tea in the nursery with their nanny. Edna, Cecilia's daughter of six, had already made a friend of Hilda. Fran thought Edna probably reminded Hilda of Babs, being roughly the same age.

The room glowed with warmth and festive goodwill. A pile of presents lay stacked beneath the Christmas tree and the children eyed them hopefully. Luke had brought their contributions downstairs to add to the rest.

Before they had finished their tea, the door opened and Elizabeth joined them. There were greetings all round.

'This is Hilda,' Luke's mother said. 'Isn't it nice that at least one of Luke's children has been able to join us?'

'Hullo, Aunt Elizabeth.'

The familiarity in the child's voice brought the room to an embarrassed hush.

'Oh, I supposed you've met before when Elizabeth visited Dorset?' Emma Hammond asked innocently.

'Yes, of course,' Hilda replied pertly. 'When Mummy and Daddy got married in Brimdene.'

A deathly silence, a few embarrassed smiles, a cough from Luke as if he hoped he could erase what Hilda had just said.

'I . . . I don't think I quite understand,' Emma Hammond said shakily.

Dorinda stood up. 'I think I do,' she said, tossing her head defiantly.

'No, you don't,' Elizabeth interrupted, 'so sit down and get on with your tea.'

Dorinda's cheeks turned crimson. 'Don't speak to me like that, Liz. I'm not a child. Indeed I'm *not*! You've been covering up for Luke this past couple of years, trying to get him back on good terms with Dad.'

She stared hard at Fran, who suddenly felt as if every drop of blood had drained from her cheeks. A few minutes ago she had been enjoying herself. Now her beloved Hilda had ruined everything. She and Luke had been so convinced that everything was going to be all right that they had overlooked the fact of Hilda's knowledge. Out of the mouth of babes, she thought.

'So you're the sly, scheming one,' Dorinda accused. 'Let's have the truth. How long have you known Luke? How many children has he got, I wonder? All you're after is his inheritance, I suppose!'

'No! *No*, that isn't so,' Luke said. 'None of this is Fran's doing.' He laughed lamely. 'Can't see what you're making a fuss about, Dorrie. Fran and I met years ago – 1912, to be exact – but circumstances prevented us from getting married then. We did have a son, and he died when he was ten. Fran married someone else. The girls aren't mine. Fran's husband was killed in a dreadful accident in 1931. I waited until a respectable amount of time had passed and then I asked her to marry me. The rest you know.'

'Take the children to the nursery,' a voice thundered from the largest armchair near the fireplace.

Cecilia seemed relieved to get up and leave the room, hustling the children before her, Hilda included.

James Hammond stood up and faced Luke, who by now was also on his feet.

'I ought to turn you out this instant,' he said. 'You're a liar and a cheat!'

'Oh no, James, don't say such things!' Emma whined.

'And as for you, Lizzie,' James said, 'I find it hard to believe such scheming of you. I know you've always kept in touch with Luke, and I was glad that you did. It was right that Luke had one member of the family to turn to. But he made his own destiny. He chose to leave his family and join the Royal Navy – nothing changes that.' James's gaze fell on Fran and she stared him out. She had nothing to be ashamed of, but she did intend to remain loyal to Luke, even though she didn't agree with what he had done.

'You are a guest in my house,' James said to Fran. 'I find it hard to believe that you knew you were marrying a cheat. Perhaps we ought to hear the truth about your past from you?'

'It's as Luke said. We did meet in 1912 when I was in service as nanny to Lady Hinckley's children. There's no need to go into the sordid details. There is one detail on which Luke and I disagree and that is who the father of my son was. Luke is obsessed with the idea that it was he, but I'm sure it was my husband, Henry Sheldon, who fathered all my children. I'm afraid, Mr Hammond, Luke has not sired any grandsons for you, and I'm sure I'm past the age of child-bearing.'

'There you are, father,' Dorinda said. 'I told you they were a scheming pair. I could tell it the minute I laid eyes on her.'

'Then you aren't a very good judge of character, my dear,' James yelled angrily at his younger daughter. 'If you aren't very careful, there's not one of you will benefit from my death.'

Dorinda burst into a flood of tears and hurried from the room.

'Well, that's got rid of her,' James said without pity.

'Poor Dorrie,' Emma Hammond said. 'I'd best go to her. Oh, what a dreadful start to Christmas, and I was so looking forward to being a family again.'

'Go to her if you must,' James shouted.

As the door closed behind his wife, James sat down again and motioned that the others should do so too.

'I'm sorry, Father,' Luke said humbly. 'I didn't mean to spoil Christmas for everyone.'

'It isn't going to spoil anything. And what's the point of being sorry, I'd like to know? Once you've lied and cheated, no amount of being sorry will retract your mistake, my boy.' The sparkle had gone out of his eyes now as he gazed into the fire. The only sound came from a spitting log. 'I'm disappointed in you, Luke, and you, Elizabeth. So, Luke, you married a widow woman with daughters. How many?'

'Four,' Fran said quietly.

'Are you wealthy? Is that why my son married you?'

'I had nothing but the widow's pension when Luke asked me to marry him'

'So he cheated you too, eh?'

'No, I'm sure he didn't. What could he possibly gain by marrying a penniless widow?' Fran asked.

'He's very good at scheming, Fran, my dear. I dare say he and Elizabeth thought that once he got you to Scotland he'd somehow manage to worm his way into his home. Yes, Luke, this is your home and nothing can change that. I can't deny a mother her son, but don't expect any medals from me for what you've done. You thought you'd get the best life out of being in the Navy and still be able to claim an inheritance when I'm dead and gone. You cheated the girls out of their pocket money many a time and I know you for what you are. I hoped the service had knocked some sense of fair play into you. Your mother spoilt you and now she can see what a fool she made of you.'

'Doesn't the fact that I've reached the rank of captain in the Navy mean anything to you?' Luke said heatedly.

His father eyed him suspiciously. 'If you earned your rank, Luke Hammond, then yes, I am proud of my son. But you and I know there are things about you which I'd rather not know.'

'What happened in the past is over and done with.'

Fran noticed that Luke's face was stained dark red with guilt down the sides. She wondered what else there was in the family cupboard that ought to be aired.

'You thought to use Fran's son to get your birthright,' James went on. 'You thought that you could use the boy's death to gain our sympathy. And to think you aided and abetted him, Elizabeth. I'm thoroughly ashamed of you both.'

'It wasn't like that, Father,' Elizabeth said. 'Mother wanted to see Luke again, and surely, when you had your accident, it was right to send for him?'

'Oh yes, Liz, you've done well in bringing us all together again.' James got to his feet and lit his pipe thoughtfully. 'You've done me a good service, for in Fran here I see the daughter I could have been proud of. I'm sorry she had to marry a scoundrel like our Luke, but I reckon she's a match for him any day. One day, my dear,' he said to Fran, 'I'd like to know a great deal more about your past life, but it's Christmas Eve. We must consider the children and bury our differences for the next few days. I can't say I'm not shocked. A man never thinks his own children will practise deceit on him, but I did think there was something not quite above board by Fran's attitude. Remember this, Luke. Fran's eyes tell all.' He drew on his pipe, keeping his gaze fixed firmly on his son until Luke was obliged to turn away. 'Now, let's get the children in for a song before they go to bed, and then we'll get ready for supper.'

'Father, please let me explain,' Luke pleaded. 'There is one thing I want you to know before you judge me too harshly. I admit I hated the Royal Navy within three weeks of joining. I would have come home then, but you told Liz you never wanted to see me again. I also had my pride, so I was obliged to go through the hell that all boys go through in the services, bullied, tormented, abused. But my time at boarding school stood me in good stead, and for that I thank you. If I don't sign on again for further service in the navy I shall need to work, and I'd like to put something back into your firm, perhaps in an administrative capacity. I've travelled the world, can speak a smattering of a few languages besides French and German fluently, which should be helpful in trading abroad. I could even help Liz.'

'I see, you've got it all worked out so that you and she can bleed me of my profits. Why should I trust you now? Either of you? Don't blame me for having to live a hellish kind of life.' He screwed his eyes up cannily as he scrutinised his son. 'All you had to do, my boy, was come home and tell me then what you've told me now. Was I such an ogre that you couldn't talk to me?'

'Yes, Father, you were – and you haven't changed that much either.' The contemptuous tone in Luke's voice indicated that he assumed he had lost everything now, so there was no point in hiding his feelings.

Fran felt some compassion for him. How would Henry have reacted if Lennie had wanted to go to sea? For a brief moment Fran felt glad that Lennie had died before he had to face the forces of evil in the world. Probably Luke had been forced to live by his wits, and that was an ugly thought for a boy of sixteen.

'If you'd stayed at home you'd have ended up a wimp, I dare say, in a house full of women,' James said. 'At least you learned one of life's hardest lessons, Luke: how to be a man. And yes, I am proud of you for standing on your own two feet and getting to the top in your career. Don't tell me, though, that you didn't come to love the service in the end. Being the shrewd man you are you'd have got out long before this if you'd hated it that much.'

'I said I'd have got out during the first few weeks, Father. But I stuck it out, and yes, the sea is my life now. But there comes a time in a man's life when he looks back and acknowledges his mistakes. I realise what pain I caused both you and Mother. I needed to see you all again. Most of all I wanted you to meet Fran.'

'So you finally got the woman you wanted?'

Luke placed his arm round Fran's shoulder as he sat on the arm of her chair. 'She's made me very happy. She was worth waiting for.'

Fran watched the old man's expression. She knew that if he had voiced his thoughts he might ironically have called it 'a moving story', but was he convinced that Luke was truly contrite?

'Why the need for secrecy that Fran has been married before, and that the children are hers, not yours?' James asked quietly.

'I . . . I suppose it was silly, but –' Luke shrugged – 'I felt embarrassed that I've only just got around to getting married at my age.'

'You mean you thought I'd look on you more kindly if you'd had a son. I might at that, Luke Hammond, but deceit is something I will not tolerate. You and Elizabeth have conspired to hoodwink me. Don't blame the young lassie for being truthful – remember the truth will out eventually. Now, the air is cleared, let's get on with Christmas. It's a time for children, games and presents and I want my grandchildren round me – who knows for maybe the last time?'

He suddenly looked rather older than when he had kissed Fran underneath the mistletoe. Fran wanted to go after him as he left the room, planting his stick on the carpet very purposefully with each tread. But she was the outsider.

Immediately the door had closed behind him, Luke and Elizabeth accosted each other irritably.

'We weren't very clever, were we, Luke?' Elizabeth said.

'That's all Dorrie needed to get what she wants.' Luke turned to Fran. 'Couldn't you have warned Hilda not to let on she had met Elizabeth?'

'I had no reason to keep secrets, Luke. It's no use blaming Hilda. It might have been better if you'd let me go home to my family and you'd spent Christmas with yours. I refuse to collaborate in anything underhand. You knew I was against it from the start. What could you possibly hope to gain? What have you got to lose by telling the truth?'

'More than you think, Fran dear, more than you think,' Luke said.

'Money? Is that what this is all about? A family business? I imagine you've lost all hope of that now. For goodness sake hold your head high and earn what you get in life. I don't want anyone else's money or pity.'

'You've had a better life since you married me,' Luke said.

'If you think money is more important than people. All the money and high living in the world can't make up for being separated from my girls. This kind of Christmas is all a farce as far as I'm concerned. Where d'you think my heart really is, Luke Hammond?' The stressful situation was too much for Fran. She burst into tears and hurried from the room, straight into the arms of James Hammond who was hovering outside the door.

She wasn't aware of how she got into the small, cosy room her father-in-law used as his study, but she was grateful for his comforting support.

'Come now, my dear,' he crooned. 'We don't want a pretty face spoilt with tears, especially at Christmas.' He allowed Fran to weep as he patted her head gently.

'I'm so very sorry,' she said at length.

'Why? What have you got to be sorry about?' James laughed mockingly. 'I know my family. Any family, if it comes to that, where there's a bit o' brass to gain. Have no fear, Fran. I haven't lost my senses yet. I know, too, that you had no part in this deception. I saw that much in your eyes when we spoke of your son way back when you visited me after the accident. Your tears then puzzled me. I can understand any mother weeping for her lost children even after ten years, but I saw some other hurt in your eyes, my dear. Maybe Luke hasn't come up to your expectations in this marriage?'

'Oh, it isn't that,' Fran said. 'Luke has been kind and helpful in the past, but the children aren't his, so how can he understand how much I miss them?'

'He insisted that you came to Scotland with him, I believe?'

'Well, yes.' Admitting that was admitting to her own weakness. 'He did rather sweep me off my feet just when I was beginning to come to terms with all that had happened. I should have thought things through more thoroughly. I can see that now, but Luke has a way with him, and it was good to have a man to lean on after such a struggle. I never should have agreed to leave my girls.'

The sound of children running through the hall interrupted her train of thought.

'I can understand the private grief you experience every time you hear the sound of these children,' James said softly. 'I want to get to know my new daughter-in-law much better.' He leaned across from his leather armchair and took both her hands in his. 'Not now, not here, but later, when the weather improves, we'll meet again. Just the two of us, and we'll learn about each other – through honesty.'

'But I . . . I'm an outsider – James.'

'That's the first hurdle bridged. Now we can be friends.' He had a warm, understanding smile which won her heart just as Luke's charm had in the past. 'I want to try to understand my son,' he said. 'No, I don't mean pry, but I reckon that if he's loved one woman for over twenty years and tried to trick his own father in order to gain wealth for her – then there must be things his pretty wife can tell me about him.'

Fran could have told her father-in-law about Luke's bitterness at being disinherited. She doubted, though, that such a disclosure would help Luke now. And wasn't James Hammond the type of man who would know of his son's bitterness? Luke didn't exactly hide it. She could also have said that Luke didn't want wealth for her, only for himself and his future.

'I've only lived with Luke for eighteen months,' she said. 'And for much of that time he's been away at sea so I'm still learning about him myself. It's a big step to take to marry a woman with four daughters.'

'A cruel step to take her from them,' James put in. 'How often do you see them?'

Tears spilled from Fran's eyes again as she shook her head solemnly.

'I haven't seen them since we married. Luke would have allowed me to bring the youngest one, Babs, to Scotland with us, but I insisted on keeping Hilda with me. She was born just before I lost my Lennie, so she's very dear to me, and delicate too. I refused to be parted from her. Kate is the eldest, now twenty years old. She's working in a hotel. My mother lives in Brimdene with Ruby, who's thirteen, and my baby lives with some very dear friends in Sherbrook, she's seven now. Luke has been very generous. He pays the rent on the house in Brimdene as well as sending Hilda to a good private school.'

'But he makes sure you don't have enough ready cash to go hurrying back south?' James shook his head sadly. 'I'm truly sorry, Fran. Luke is a selfish bastard. I'm ashamed to own him as my son.'

Fran looked at James with a shocked expression. She had hated Luke in the past for the misery he had caused her. But wasn't forgiveness easy lying close to him between sheets of marital bliss? Now, for the first time she realised just how all this looked to an outsider. She couldn't understand why James Hammond was speaking so confidentially to her, or being so understanding. She just knew that here was a man who was just, and possessed qualities lacking in his son.

'It won't be for much longer,' she said, as if excusing Luke's mean behaviour. 'Luke will get a new appointment next summer, and then we'll move back to Portsmouth. Naturally I can't wait to see the girls again, and Ma.' Fran sighed. 'I must confess I'd been saving hard in case Luke didn't get home for Christmas. I was determined to go down to Brimdene if he didn't.'

'Luke is very clever at managing his own destiny, my dear. He didn't visit me out of sympathy, or loyalty, or trying to make amends. He wants what he thinks is his right. Selfishness never earns respect or wealth.'

There was a knock on the door and Dorinda put her head inside.

'Come along, Dad. You wanted the children to sing some carols before they go to bed.'

James stood up and took Fran's hand. 'We're coming,' he said. 'And remember, Dorrie, no more back-biting. I'm still quite capable of managing my own business and signing my own will. At least let's show Fran here that we can be a happy family and behave with some dignity. She's missing her own children, so let's try to make up for that.'

With his hand at Fran's waist reassuringly, James led her back into the sitting room, where Cecilia was already seated at the piano. Fran placed her hands on Hilda's shoulders as they stood round the piano with the Hammond family, but her thoughts were elsewhere. It was a scene she had participated in for as long as she could remember, and now James Hammond's strong bass voice reminded her of Henry's. She didn't try to check the tears that streamed down her cheeks as she did her best to join in the singing of favourite carols.

There were emotional goodbyes when James Hammond drove Luke, Fran and Hilda to the station on 2 January 1935.

James kissed Hilda affectionately, offering a few words of advice about her school work. Then he shook hands with Luke.

'This will be a Christmas to remember, Luke,' he said. 'I wish I could say it's brought me pleasure, but I can't pretend to be anything but vexed at your secret plotting to get back in my good books. But I'm growing tired of schemes and deals, and it's time we buried the hatchet. The one good thing is that for once you've made a sensible choice in marrying Fran. I hope her honesty will influence you for the better. It's time you realised that a man gets the best out of life by treating other people well. Be good to Fran and her family. They're our family too now, and I shall be watching developments.' His ageing eyes were still keen, and could, Fran observed, cause a reaction in Luke.

'All I want is for us to be a united family again, Father,' Luke said. 'I shall go away much happier knowing that Fran has you to turn to in an emergency. I wish Dorrie and Cecilia would accept her more kindly, though.'

'You can't blame them for the way they feel. I did hope that I'd have the joy of seeing a Hammond boy come into the family, but it seems it's not to be.'

Luke glanced at Fran and there was the immediate glow of intimacy as he said: 'There's still time, isn't there, darling?'

Fran responded with a wistful smile. How could she disillusion him? She had tried to explain that it could no longer be, but he refused to accept it. He looked young, and so hopeful for the future. She knew that the bond created during that first union over twenty years ago could never be broken entirely. Their relationship would hang precariously by many a fraying thread, but the deep-rooted need of each other would always weave a cord of reparation. Was it really love?

James turned to take Fran in his embrace.

'And you, my dear, take care.' Fran felt the rustle of paper rather than heard it as something was pressed into her gloved hand. 'Use it to go south, Fran dear, at the first opportunity. And let me know if your mother or girls need anything,' James whispered.

Fran broke away as tears threatened. She opened her bag to find her handkerchief, and managed to hastily conceal the paper money inside, out of Luke's sight, which she knew was what James intended.

'Keep in touch, my dear,' James said. 'I hope you don't think too badly of me and my family?

'You've been most kind,' Fran said. 'Now it's back to work in the orphanage and preparing Hilda for school. And Luke – who knows where he's going next?'

'To the China seas most likely, for several months. Trouble is brewing in various areas of the world. I could be sent anywhere.'

It seemed a sombre note to leave on, but news worldwide was causing concern, and Fran felt a renewed drawing towards Luke as the ugly thought of war crossed her mind.

At the earliest opportunity Fran investigated her bag and found that Luke's father had given her two white, crisp five-pound notes. She was amazed at his generosity, having hardly ever had in her possession so much wealth. She wished he hadn't tempted her with it, though. It would be so easy to take herself off, away from Scotland, to visit the family. But after the reunion would come another parting, and she knew that she wouldn't be able to tear herself away ever again. So she decided to put it in her Post Office account when Luke had gone away, and then send a handsome sum of money by postal order to Ma to use in any way she chose.

In the privacy of their bedroom back at Craiglee, Fran waited, expectantly for the accusations to come. She was certain that Luke would blame her for Hilda's indiscretion. She was ready to defend both herself and Hilda. She would not be party to any more deceit. Luke had to understand that children were normally open and honest. But the matter was not mentioned. Luke had only one thing on his mind and that was to give her a baby before he returned to his ship. Fran tried to tell him that he must not be too optimistic, but he was about to go away for a long time so she did all she could to satisfy his desires, which gave her a measure of enjoyment too. She was genuinely sad when he left, and even more sorrowful when Hilda returned to school in Aberdeen.

Work at the orphanage was her saviour. Here were children who needed a mother's love, and she was able to give them that as well as using her talents as a needlewoman, and teaching it to some of the older girls. They made clothes and began a patchwork quilt, involving helpers and girls alike.

For a few weeks into the new year there was no communication from either Luke or his family. Fran began to think that the money had been the final pay-off, that James and Emma Hammond were heartily glad to see the back of them.

Then a registered letter arrived, which contained letters from each of Luke's parents, and tucked inside James's was another five-pound note.

'I want you to use this to come and visit us one weekend, Fran dear,' James wrote. 'I've booked a room for you at a small private hotel called the Hawthorne, as I think it best if my wife and daughters don't know of your visit. I'd like to show you over the foundry, so that you can see the family business for yourself.'

Fran read and re-read the letter. It was true that the weekends dragged. She went to the kirk, talked briefly with her neighbours, and occasionally went to tea with Jenny or the vicar and his wife, but on the whole she spent the time writing letters to the family. Right until the last moment she couldn't decide whether to go to Middlesbrough or not, but it seemed churlish not to accept the invitation when James had gone to the trouble of booking a room for her.

As the train steamed out of Edinburgh's Waverley station she experienced some misgivings. Supposing Hilda had an accident or came home unexpectedly? But as the train chugged its way over frosted lines and icy points, she felt in her bones that she was doing the right thing. If James wanted to see her, then for Luke's sake she should honour his request. She just hoped that he wouldn't harp on about having a Hammond heir. She was certain that she was in the 'change'. It was almost a disappointment to know that she was not capable of conceiving again. It meant that she was no longer young, and seeing the tiny abandoned babies at the orphanage made her broody and secretly wish she could please Luke by having his child.

On arrival at Middlesbrough, Fran had to take a taxi to the hotel because she was unfamiliar with the town. The Hawthorne was a small but clean and tidy hotel. After settling in she went down to the lounge for afternoon tea. To her surprise James Hammond was already there waiting for her.

'How did you know I'd come?' she asked, responding to the intimate smile with which he greeted her.

'Ah, I know women,' he said, as he pulled her towards him and kissed her. 'If it was any other woman, Fran, my dear, I'd say you came to see what I had to offer, but not you. You came for Luke's sake, and that I both admire and respect.'

Fran felt indignant. She opened her purse. 'I came,' she said, 'to return this, James. I don't want your money.'

James bent her hand, containing a five-pound note, in his. 'I didn't mean that. I was teasing you, Fran. If I was a few years younger I'd give young Luke a challenge. Don't look so shocked. I'm no saint, any more than my son is.' He chuckled as he indicated one of the wicker armchairs to Fran. She noticed that he sat heavily, putting most of his weight on his stick. 'I dare say I could even find a Hammond heir if I wanted to renew old acquaintances. But that's a young man's foolish dreams. I don't get such urges any longer.' He leaned across and patted Fran's knee. 'I'm sorry, my dear, I don't wish to embarrass you, but I am very envious of Luke. He's a lucky man and he doesn't deserve you.'

'You flatter me,' Fran said. 'But I'm sure you didn't want me to come all this way just to tell me that. Why the secrecy?'

At that moment a waitress brought a tray of freshly brewed tea, warm teacakes hidden beneath a domed silver cover, and a variety of home-made preserves. Fran was desperately in need of refreshment, and felt revived even after the first sip of tea.

'Women gossip too much for my liking. Besides, away from the rest of the family we can talk honestly, I hope. I want you to tell me all about your background and family, Fran. I want to know why a nice woman like you should fall in love with a scoundrel like my son.'

'You know you don't really believe that of Luke,' Fran said. 'We all have our faults. Lack of family life has contributed to Luke's, I'm sure you'll agree.'

'So you're blaming me?' James pursed his lips and shook his head sadly. 'There are things you don't know about us, and that's what I want to put straight, Fran. Maybe it was being the only boy, the apple of his mother's eye, but Luke was always something of a rebel. We thought a boarding school where he could be with lads of his own age would help him to mature. It did that all right. He got involved in several petty pranks. Now I reckon he won't have told you that?'

'No,' Fran said, 'he hasn't. But it was all so long ago. Why should he?'

'Perhaps the last one wasn't so petty, certainly not for the unfortunate young woman he got into trouble. It cost me a lot of money to get him out of that one. Well, like I said, I'm no saint, but I had to reprimand him, and to hurt him over money was the only way he understood. I stopped his allowance. I hoped that would make him toe the line – settle down to hard work and study. Instead he ran off and joined the crew of a cargo vessel.'

'He was always eager to go to sea, though, wasn't he?'

'Oh yes. He didn't get that from the Hammond side, mind you. Emma's father and grandfather were all seafaring men, so I suppose to a certain extent it was in his blood. He was brought up on sea stories.' James sighed. 'Emma was heartbroken when she heard the news, as you can guess. When Luke came home after several weeks at sea, I offered to pay for further education, but the cheeky bastard gave me an ultimatum, if you please. A place in the running of the foundry – of which he knew nothing – or he'd join the Royal Navy.' James drank his tea thoughtfully. 'What would you have done, Fran? I had to call his bluff. He had to be brought down off his high horse, and I reckoned the Navy were the best people to do it.'

'It must have been a hard decision to make. And a cruel one for your wife.'

'She never forgave me – which is why now, after all these years, I'm glad he's wormed his way back into the family home.' James leaned towards Fran. 'Can he be trusted, though? Or is the selfish greed still there?'

'That,' Fran said softly, 'you'll have to judge for yourself, James.'

'He wants to run the business himself. He wants to be cock of the walk. He's still a young man, strong and virile, and he doesn't see why my grandsons should inherit the position in Hammond's he thinks is his. He'll need something to do when he retires from the Navy. Trouble is with Luke he wants everything his own way.'

'But surely his knowledge and capabilities would be advantageous in the business?'

'I may not have many more years left, Fran dear. The accident shook me up. I'm lucky to be alive, lucky to be able to get to the foundry at all.'

'I thought you'd made a good recovery.'

'Ye-es, as far as we can tell, but I worry as to who will succeed me when I do pass on. The name of Hammond has been well thought of among tradesmen hereabouts for over a century. Emma's no good at business. A woman's place is in the home.' He chuckled. 'Except where Liz is concerned. She's good, much to everyone's surprise, but the men won't take a woman boss. If I let her succeed me, she'll take Luke on board, and my grandsons will lose out.'

'Surely that depends on how you leave everything in your will. But really, James, this is a ridiculous conversation. You're good for a few years yet. If you want the young boys to be taken into the business, then it's up to you, and there's plenty of time to have them trained for it.'

'But they won't be Hammonds, will they? Elizabeth and Luke both are, but they have no offspring.'

Fran smiled. 'You could persuade your married daughters to include the name Hammond with their surnames, couldn't you?'

James screwed his eyes up as he surveyed his daughter-in-law. 'Would that any of my children had your canny perceptions, my dear. What did you say you did before you got married – a nanny? You were capable of something more mind-stretching than that.'

'You know as well as I that girls have always been the domestics in life. A nanny was considered quite something, you know.'

'Don't I just know it? They've cost me a pretty penny over the years. Some were made for the job, others were too soft, while many were the opposite. You fit into the first category. You obviously love children, so why can't I dream an old man's dream of having a grandson on the Hammond side?'

Fran sighed. 'Because, James, as I told you, I'm past the age of child-bearing. I'll be forty-six this year. It wouldn't be fair to the child even if I could suddenly become fertile again. But you can't alter nature. I've tried to tell Luke, but he refuses to accept it. I felt certain that you would understand. What's so special anyway in having a grandson who bears the name Hammond? Your grandsons are your grandsons whatever their name.'

'And I felt sure that you would understand how important it is to me to have the name carry on after me.'

'Perhaps you should have taken Luke back when he wanted to come into the business?' Fran suggested hesitantly. 'Maybe he should have married the girl he got into trouble. Did she have a boy?'

'No.' James laughed. 'Twin girls, would you believe? Family moved to Ireland to live down their shame at my expense. Luke had to be made to pay for that, Fran. A man must be master in his own household.'

Fran listened patiently as James unburdened himself. It seemed as if everything had been said by the time they had finished their tea, but James was eager to see Fran again that evening after dinner.

'I suppose I'm being thoroughly selfish,' he said, as he again joined Fran in the seclusion of the hotel's lounge. There were few visitors at this time of year, just one or two commercial travellers, who went to their room immediately after their evening meal. James ordered a whisky for himself and a Maderia for Fran. It warmed her, and she experienced a cosiness in the atmosphere. They chatted about many things and soon she found herself telling her father-in-law how she and Luke had first met.

'Go on,' he urged. 'These are the things I want to know – not out of idle curiosity, Fran, but to help me understand and know about Luke's life in the years we lost track of him.'

'He had a charm that few women could resist, James,' Fran explained. 'I suppose you could call our first meeting an illicit night of love. It would never have happened if I hadn't been given such a rousing send-off by the Hinckleys. It was Christmas, and everyone was pretty merry even before we started celebrating my departure. Luke had no right to go below stairs, let alone take me to the nursery and – '

'He forced himself on you? He raped you?'

Fran shook her head. 'Goodness, no! I can't accuse him of that. It . . . well, it just happened, as these things do. We were young, only human, after all – and I was about to get married. Henry and I had been through a frustrating time as Lady Hinckley refused to allow me to leave. Luke wasn't the first, you see. Henry and I resorted to hoping that I would get pregnant, that way I would have to be released. But I wasn't aware of being in the family way when we got married that Boxing Day, and I'm almost positive that Lennie was Henry's son, not Luke's. Luke just turned up out of the blue after Lennie died, with this obsession that Lennie was his son.'

'Did he try blackmail? Did he threaten to tell your husband about your liaison?'

'No, he never did that, nor did I ever think he would, strange though it may seem. He went back to sea, of course, and I seldom thought about him. The memory quickly faded once I was a busy housewife and mother. I didn't even know that he knew the Maitland family in Sherbrook, until he appeared in the churchyard after Lennie died.'

'I suspect he did genuinely love you then as he does now, Fran. There was another woman, though, who seems to have been important to him.'

'Yes, I know. An Asian girl called Sarita?'

'He told you about her?'

'No. I only found out quite recently when I tidied some cupboards and drawers. I accidentally found a bundle of letters and a picture. A very beautiful girl. She was expecting his baby, I understand, and died in childbirth.'

'He was genuinely fond of this girl, according to Liz. In fact he tried to get me to arrange for her to come to England and have her baby here. Perhaps I should have done, but we would have found it difficult to accept a foreigner. I suppose life has been unkind to Luke in some ways.' James grasped Fran's arm. 'I do love my son, Fran,' he said earnestly. 'I only wish I could trust him, but I don't entirely, especially now, having discovered his plotting with Liz to get back in my favour. They're jealous of the two younger girls being married and with children. I know their little game. They mean to get the business for themselves before the grandsons are old enough to be taken into it.'

'Is it really so important, James? Human life is more important than money and goods. Henry and I never had much. He worked hard for small wages, but we had a good family life. It all ended so suddenly.' Her chin quivered as the memory of that horrific freak tide came into her thoughts. 'That nightmare still haunts me,' she said.

Gently, and without causing too many tears, James extracted the full story from Fran, of Henry's death by drowning, and her father's too. She doubted that he could possibly understand the trauma of uprooting to move away to a town, living simply to make the pennies stretch for the necessities of life, or the added worry of leaving Kate behind with the Maitlands, and the reason for her leaving Sherbrook in disgrace.

So much of the past had been bottled up in Fran's thoughts with no one to share it with. It was a relief to pour it all out to James, who appeared to be sympathetic to the reasons she had for marrying Luke. In some ways, too, it helped to hear that James was doubtful of Luke's intentions.

'I'm sure he loves you,' he said. 'But he also may have used you, and your son, Lennie, to try to win favour with me. So far, nothing he's done convinces me that he is truly repentant for the past. I doubt that he'll be competent enough to take over the foundry from me. He may work towards its success while I'm alive, but then what? A business in ruins while he squanders the profits?'

During Sunday morning, while the family were at church, James fetched Fran from the hotel and took her to the foundry, where machinery lay silent as if it too was resting on the Sabbath.

The name HAMMOND was blazoned on the front of the building across a huge brick archway over the main gates. It was all much larger and more prominent than Fran had envisaged, and as she toured the works, with James pointing out blast furnaces and moulds as they went along, she was much impressed by all that she saw. She learned how the castings were made in the foundry where pig iron was melted down with coke in something called a cupola. It was similar to a small blast furnace where hot gas was allowed to escape from the top.

'Cast iron is stronger than pig iron, you see,' James explained. 'The castings are brittle, though, compared with steel, so it's mostly used for lamp-posts, domestic boilers and cookers, and cylinder blocks for motor cars. It's useful for gas mains and sewage and water pipes, too. It's a thriving industry, as you can see.'

'I can now understand your concern for the future of the business,' Fran said to James as they went into his office. 'You must be proud of your achievements in supplying work for such a large number of men. They and their families depend on Hammond's for their livelihood.'

'Indeed they do and it would be a shame if it were allowed to run down or be sold off for monetary gain. I hope the name Hammond will long be seen as visitors enter the approaches to Middlesbrough.'

'I'm sure it will, James, and I feel equally sure that Luke must be proud of the family business. All your children will be. They'll never let it be sold, or run down, for the sake of their children. I'm sorry I can't oblige you with a grandson, James, but you already have four. Whether you allow Luke to enter the foundry is your decision and yours alone. I'm sure your wife would love to see him take your place eventually.'

'With you at his side, Fran?'

Fran looked at James quizzically. 'I'll support him as his wife, of course,' she answered.

'When he's got what he wants he might not want you,' James warned.

'I thought you were of the opinion that he truly loves me?'

'I am, my dear. But whether his love of worldly goods and money exceeds his love of you, I cannot say. His love for you has not prevented him from hurting you in most painful ways. Taking you from your children, for instance, sending Hilda to boarding school, almost as if he were paying you back for being sent away to school himself.'

'I suspect he knew that if Hilda went to Aberdeen I was not so likely to up and return south while he was away. I know Luke now. I know he schemes for his own ends. He's different in every way from Henry, and I have to admit that if I could have afforded to I probably would have left him. The trouble is,' she added with a gentle smile, 'he has a hold over me. There's something magnetic about him. I want and need my children – I feel the same way about Luke.'

Chapter Seventeen

On the train journey returning to Craiglee, Fran had plenty of time to reflect on her visit to Middlesbrough. She had talked far more intimately to James Hammond than to anyone over the past two years. They were like kindred spirits with similar attitudes and standards. They both loved Luke, yet neither could be sure of his intentions.

Fran cared nothing for the foundry. The thought of living permanently this far north depressed her, but, as James had said, Luke wasn't due for retirement from the Royal Navy yet, and when he was, her girls would probably be grown up and making their own lives. That thought depressed her too. She couldn't forgive herself for deserting them. She wished that she could turn the clock back and carry on with their upbringing as Henry would have wanted. But there was no going back. Her destiny now was with Luke. As Ma would say, she had made her bed so she must lie on it. She wondered what life would be like if Luke was at home all the time. His homecomings were an adventure that kept the freshness in their marriage.

She caught sight of her own image in the carriage window, dirty and sooted though it was. A middle-aged woman. Back in Brimdene she knew that she had begun to look old before her time. Now she was able to dress fashionably. Her hands were white, her fingers long and slender. No more the roughened, chapped skin from her years of washing and cleaning for the family. She supposed people thought she had married Luke to make good her escape from the life of drudgery. Well, hadn't she? No! Nothing, not all the clothes from the best shops in Edinburgh, nor the freedom from scrubbing floors, could make up for being parted from Ma and the girls. Still, it wouldn't be too long now before she could begin to pack up her belongings in Craiglee. In fact, spring was only just around the corner even if there was still snow on the mountains. Down south it would already be warming up. Lambing time was about to start, with Easter only a few weeks away. It wasn't too soon to start thinking about preparing to go home.

Fran experienced mixed feelings. She was a woman of the world now. A few years ago, when Henry and her father had been alive, she had never given travel a single thought. She smiled a secret little smile. Going to Brimdene on the train from Sherbrook was the big adventure then.

Her thoughts raced ahead of time, to hot, sunny days sitting on the beach while Hilda, Babs and Ruby played on the sand. How exciting the reunion would be! She felt love and longing swelling in her breast. But her home wouldn't be in Brimdene, it was to be in Portsmouth with Luke. Brochures were already arriving from grammar schools in that area. Luke was determined to be Hilda's mentor. He organised everything, even when he was miles away.

When Fran reached Edinburgh she went into a café for a meal, and then did some shopping. Everywhere was fairly quiet, it being Monday morning, so she was able to browse and take her time.

It was quite late in the afternoon when she let herself into the house in Craiglee. She was desperate for a cup of tea so she put the kettle on even before she took her hat and coat off. She had enjoyed her long weekend away. Without Luke and Hilda the weekends were the worst and she hoped James might invite her again. She wondered how he explained away his absence from home, and why he was so keen not to let the family know of their meeting. She didn't mind. In a ridiculously childish way she felt that it made her special to him. She thought he was genuinely fond of her but, knowing his son as she did, now that she was home with time to consider the matter she wondered if James had some ulterior motive in seeking her company. What could he possibly want from her, though? Then she smiled. A grandson, a male heir to carry on the name after Luke, and she wished with all her heart that she could oblige him.

After the first sip of tea, Fran went into the sitting room and found the mail lying on the side table where Jenny always left letters if Fran was out. There were two from Luke, but she didn't open them immediately. Instead she noticed a telegram propped up against the vase of daffodils Jenny had picked. Fran's heart jumped. Was it to say that Luke was coming home unexpectedly? Was he ill or injured? Or could it be Ma or one of the girls? With unsteady fingers she tore open the yellow envelope, and drew out the single sheet of off-white paper. The printed message read: 'Epidemic of scarlet fever. Hilda only mildly ill. School in quarantine.'

Fran put her fingers to her lips. Her Hilda – scarlet fever! She read and re-read the message, her first motherly instinct to go to Aberdeen at once, no matter what the consequences. Hilda was ill and needed her. Surely quarantine didn't affect Fran? She heard the back door open and close. Jenny hurried in with a worried expression.

'Mrs Hammond, I've been so anxious. I didn't know what to do when the telegram came. I do hope it isn't bad news? I thought I'd best come to you in case there's anything I can do.'

'Hilda has scarlet fever, Jenny. Oh, dear, what am I going to do? The school is in quarantine. How long for, do you suppose?'

'Mm . . . we-ell, I dare say it'll be a month at the least, but more likely to be six weeks.'

'Will she have to go in hospital?'

'Not if the school has a good sanatorium. They may keep the girls there to contain the disease. Don't worry, Mrs Hammond. She'll be well looked after.'

'If only I'd been here,' Fran said.

'It wouldn'a made any difference, Mrs Hammond,' Jenny consoled her. 'There's nothing anyone can do. Let's hope and pray that she doesn'a have it badly. Have you eaten today? Is there anything I can get you?'

'No, Jenny. I'm being silly. It was a shock seeing that telegram. I thought it might have been my mother or one of the other girls who was ill. You're right. If I'd been here there was nothing I could do. I'll write, of course, to Hilda and the school. I must think of things to make up a parcel for her. She'll need something to occupy her time when she begins to feel better.'

'Scarlet fever isn't considered to be so serious these days. If she was fit and healthy to begin with she'll likely have it mildly.'

'That's what the telegram says, but Hilda's never been strong.'

Jenny stayed until she felt that Fran had recovered from the shock, then she left. Fran sat down to write to Hilda, and by the time she went to bed she had written several letters, including one to James Hammond and her new in-laws. She wished they lived closer and that one day her sisters-in-law would accept her as a friend – that was what she needed in times of stress.

Fran kept herself busy during the next few days, writing to Hilda and buying books and puzzles to send so that she would have plenty to keep her amused as she convalesced. When she wrote to the family in Brimdene and her friends in Sherbrook, she begged them all to write to Hilda so that links with home and family were sustained.

Fran watched for a letter from Luke's parents, but each day she was disappointed. She was so thankful to be able to go to the orphanage, where she could forget her worries over Hilda and her loneliness.

When she reached the house late one afternoon, as she put her key into the front-door lock she heard footsteps coming from the side of the house. Luke? Always her first thought. Next she wondered if they had sent Hilda home to complete her convalescence. Instead the slow tapping of a stick on the path made her hold her breath, and then with relief she smiled a welcome to James Hammond.

'James!' she exclaimed. 'You're the last person I expected to see.'

'Fran, my dear, dear girl.' James held her close for some seconds before he allowed her to open the door.

They went inside, and Fran's questions followed quickly with some curiosity.

'How did you travel? Why didn't you let me know you were coming?'

'Because, my dear, you don't have the telephone, and I've come by cargo vessel. Happened to be one owned by an old friend, and as he was coming to Leith, I begged a lift.'

Fran busied herself making tea and warming some scones she had made the day before.

'I don't have too much in the larder, James,' she said. 'Living almost entirely alone means that I only buy small quantities.'

'I had a meal near the station before catching the train here. We were sorry to hear about young Hilda. How is she now, getting better?'

'Yes, she wrote saying that they're all doing lessons in the mornings now. She won't be able to travel home for Easter, but she's looking forward to a long weekend at Whitsun maybe. I'm counting the days, of course, and that'll be the last holiday before we can pack up and start for the south again.'

'You know, Fran, I've been thinking, and wondering why Luke hasn't had the telephone connected for you. It's mighty thoughtless of him to leave you here on your own with no contact with your folks. So I'll be staying a few days, if that's all right with you, and I'll see that it's installed as soon as possible.'

'That isn't really necessary, James,' Fran said with a smile. 'For just a few months it would hardly be worth it.'

'Well, I think it would, so I'm going to do it anyway. At least I can ring you up to see that you're well, and if there's an emergency you'll be able to get in touch with me immediately.'

'But I can't use the telephone, James.' She laughed weakly. 'To tell the truth, I'm a bit scared of such contraptions.'

'Then all the more reason to have it in your own home so that you can get acquainted with it. A mixed blessing, I'll grant you that, but I'm surprised Luke didn't think of it when you first came here.'

'He'd be thinking of the enormous bills he'd have to pay, I expect,' Fran said with a smile. 'If I'd had it when we first came here I'd have been ringing Brimdene or Sherbrook every day.' Her expression changed to one of sombre reasoning. 'It's a kind thought, James, but to be able to talk to my girls now at this late stage would only make the time seem longer until I actually see them. No, I think it's best to let things remain as they are.'

'I'm going to get it fixed, my dear. I want to know that you can call on me any time, and I can get in touch with you. If you'd had the telephone, you see, I'd have been able to ring you early this morning and tell you that I was on my way.' He went closer to the window and looked out over the valley. 'This is a lovely spot. I'd no idea Luke had such good taste when it came to setting up house. Ideal for a newly married couple, but not so good for a wife being left on her own for weeks and months at a stretch.'

'I haven't minded for most of the time. When Hilda first went to Aberdeen it was lonely. I have to admit that if I could have afforded to I would have left Luke then, but I love the country, and since I went to work at the orphanage I've managed to fill my days satisfactorily.'

'But you can't wait for summer to come.' James looked at his daughter-in-law with admiration. 'I wish Luke had brought you to see us when you first came here. Such silly nonsense, trying to make me believe you and he had been married for twenty years or so. As if he would have been able to keep a secret that long. I had ways of knowing where he went during his leaves from duty.'

Fran set the table, and they sat opposite one another, going back once again over the past. Here, where they were on neutral ground, it was easy for them to be honest, even more so than when Fran had visited Middlesbrough by herself.

'I want to see as much of you as I can before you return to Brimdene,' James said.

'Why don't you bring Mrs Hammond to stay for a few days' holiday?' Fran suggested.

James was thoughtful. 'Emma doesn't take kindly to travelling, Fran. With the girls living at Hammond House, and their husbands and children, she's much more tied up with them than with me. Oh, I know I have the works to supervise.' He laughed with an edge of scorn. 'If I hadn't, I reckon I'd have spent many hours looking for a mistress.'

'James! You mustn't say things like that.'

'She never got over losing Luke to the sea. Nor forgiven me for disinheriting him. We've grown apart, Fran – sadly. We should be able to spend time together enjoying our old age.'

'But you're not old yet.'

'Emma will be seventy next birthday, and I was seventy-two just before my accident.'

'But you wouldn't like to give up working at the foundry – or at least managing it, would you?'

'No. I'd like to rest up more than I can, but there's only a few of the old workers left who I can trust to put in a good day's work. Now, if Luke had come into the business, by now he would be taking over completely from me.' James shook his head. 'It's too late now. He'd be all right to organise things, but the men wouldn't take kindly to a boss who hadn't worked his way up the same as they. What am I going to do, Fran?'

'What about Dorinda's husband, or Cecilia's?'

James threw back his head and laughed. 'Don't you let my girls hear you say that. They'd fight then over who should be the boss, and to tell you the truth, although they're nice enough fellows, neither of them has the guts to take over from me – and the men wouldn't wear that either.'

'I don't know what else to suggest, then, James. You'll just have to keep going until your grandsons are old enough to learn the business thoroughly.'

'But that'll be years yet, and I doubt that I have that much time left, Fran.'

'Let's see, Howard is eight, and Jamie seven. Howard needs another eight years at school – but what are you worrying about, James? Aren't you forgetting Elizabeth?'

'No, my dear, I'm not forgetting my Lizzie. She's keen and she's an expert with the book-keeping, the wages and the like.'

'There you are then. Make sure that she can take over from you when the time comes.'

'I know you mean well, Fran. I respect your advice – you've a great deal of commonsense, and few in business have that. A good head for business usually means a love of money. Small matters get overlooked in the quest for profits. In my foundry I know each and every one of my workers, their families, what kind of homes they live in – and if they suddenly have money to burn, I ask the question, Where did it come from?'

'But surely Elizabeth has the workers' welfare at heart, too?'

'She does – but in a womanly manner. The men need a strong man at the top.'

'James, there must be someone you can trust enough to be manager, under Elizabeth?'

'Yes, my present manager is reliable and trustworthy, but he's like me – getting on in years. That fall made me realise – and too late – that I should have persuaded Luke to come into the business many years ago. Don't tell him that, though. Seeing him again – and his lovely wife – helped me to recover, as well as seeing things differently. I was pompous enough to believe that I would go on for ever.'

'Maybe Luke would come out of the Navy now if he realises that you feel like this.'

James shook his head vigorously. '*No*! Oh, no! He and Lizzie between them tried to deceive me – did deceive me, in fact. But for young Hilda I'd have gone on believing that your son was Luke's too. And I was prepared to overlook Luke's past, and would have given him shares in the foundry because of the tragedy of losing his only son. But he has no son, which brings us back to the same old question – who is going to take over after me?'

'Oh, James, I wish I could help you, but I can't, I'm afraid.'

James sat opposite Fran and stared directly at her. 'Forgive me, my dear. I shouldn't be asking such personal questions, but is it really impossible for you to have more children?'

Fran laughed. 'Yes, James, I'm afraid I think it is. And if I could conceive again, how would that help you?'

'I'd have a real Hammond to leave the works to. I'd make certain that suitable men were put in charge for the next twenty years under Lizzie's supervision. I'd die a happy man knowing that there was a Hammond boy to follow in my footsteps.'

Fran didn't know how to tell an old man that he was dreaming impossible dreams. Luke was the genuine Hammond heir. Fran could understand now how much his running away to sea had grieved his father.

As the days went by she came to understand a greal deal more about James Hammond, the man. His fiery temper when things didn't go his way. The Post Office came in for some flak when they didn't come as arranged to install the telephone, and Fran reckoned all Craiglee heard about it. But he was also good company. He talked at length about the old days and the Hammond ancestors. He also listened with interest to all that Fran would divulge about her family, and when the time came for him to depart she felt genuinely sad. She went with him to Leith docks to see him off with the promise that they would meet again as soon as was convenient.

'I shall be telephoning you quite often, Fran, my dear. I understand what you mean about not getting in touch with your family in the south, though.'

'If I give Ruby and Kate the number,' she said happily, 'they'll be ringing up every few minutes. I'm really grateful to you, James, for being so thoughtful, though, and I promise I'll use it.'

'You take care now, d'you hear?' James said as he kissed her goodbye. 'And you just ring me when I'm at the works. You can talk to Lizzie if I'm not there. She'll like that.' He pressed crisp notes into Fran's hand. 'Buy yourself something pretty for when Luke comes home. It isn't to be for quite a while, though, did you say?'

Fran sighed. 'Several months. China is a great way off and the news everywhere, especially from Europe, isn't good, is it?'

'It's this damned man Hitler and his Nazis. Germany is increasing armaments all the time. Churchill has been warning since last year that we're not up to full strength in our defences. War might be good for business, but that's all. Luke has fought in one war, I wouldn't like to see him involved in another one. Maybe it's just as well I don't have adult grandsons after all.'

Fran watched the cargo vessel chug its way out into the Firth of Forth until it was a black dot in the distance. It was a nice morning so she walked into Edinburgh, had coffee and then sat in the gardens on Princes Street to listen to a military band. Then she went to the post office. She put one of the five-pound notes in a registered envelope which she addressed to Kate, asking her to buy Easter eggs and something special for each member of the family for next weekend.

Fran didn't mind that she would be alone for Easter. Extra help was needed at the orphanage, there were flowers to arrange in the kirk, and she had plenty of sewing to do in readiness for the summer.

During the month of May the country celebrated the king's silver jubilee. Fran cut out all the photographs from the daily papers so that Hilda could add them to her scrapbook. She bought several newspapers so that she had extra pictures to send to Ruby and Babs. London enjoyed a day of pageantry. Everyone was interested in the two young princesses, Elizabeth and Margaret Rose, granddaughters of King George V and Queen Mary, but it was a small dog trotting in front of the royal carriage that became the centre of attraction. It eventually hid beneath the carriage. Soldiers tried to corner it with their swords, and policemen made a brave effort with their truncheons. It became known among the crowds as the Jubilee Dog.

When Hilda came home for the Whitsun weekend Fran was amazed to see her looking so well. Her cheeks were quite rosy. She had filled out as well as grown, and her hair shone black and glossy.

Fran hadn't made any plans to do anything special. Instead they began to pack cases and trunks ready to go home to Brimdene in August.

Hilda returned to school in Aberdeen for the last term. If Fran was excited about going home it seemed that Hilda was reluctant to say goodbye to her friends. She even hesitantly suggested that she might be allowed to go to a grammar school in Scotland, where some of her chums would be going.

'It would be much too far away to keep journeying to and fro,' Fran said in horror. 'Besides, surely you want to see Kate, Babs and Ruby?'

'Ye-es,' Hilda replied indifferently. 'But they aren't the same as my friends.'

'No,' Fran said sternly. 'They're your sisters, and if you aren't anxious to go home, then I most certainly am.'

In her own private thoughts Fran decided that if there was going to be another war she must be with the rest of her family. But she did her best to forget thoughts of war as the summer arrived, and she was able to tick off the days on the calendar. Luke seemed happy to give Fran instructions on getting to Portsmouth and taking up residence in his house at Southsea.

James frequently telephoned, usually admonishing Fran for not ringing him.

'If you won't come to see us, then I'm coming to see you,' he said one day. 'Or I can see you'll be going off to your own people and we shan't get to say goodbye even.'

He arrived by car one evening. Fran had made up the spare bed and was genuinely delighted to see him.

'I've decided to take more holidays,' James said as he greeted her. 'So you'd best keep a bed aired for me when you get to Portsmouth. The LNER now has a steam train which travels at 108 miles per hour on the journey from London to Newcastle.'

'You know you'll be welcome any time, James. I hope, though, you won't mind if this week I carry on with my work at the orphanage. We're short-staffed at present and soon I shan't be here to care for the babies.'

'You're going to miss them all – and they'll miss you, I fancy,' James said.

'We see such sad cases: children whose mothers have died and the fathers can't cope. Lots of unwanted babies – I'd just love to give them all a home,' she said earnestly.

'You can always start up a home down south. I suppose there's as many unwanted babies there as anywhere else.'

'Don't.' Fran laughed. 'You're giving me ideas.'

'Your love of children is very obvious, my dear. I'd help you. Now, that's a good idea – why not the Hammond Orphanage?'

'If you have money you don't know what to do with, James, we need every penny we can get at our orphanage.'

'Mm. Who owns and finances it now?'

'The actual house, which is old, large, cold and always in need of repair, was donated to the Church of Scotland for use as an orphanage. We have to rely on voluntary helpers to run it, and money from the kirk and any charitable organisations that will contribute.' Fran looked at her father-in-law and smiled. 'Now I'm feeling guilty, James,' she said. 'All those notes you've been giving me I've been sending to my family, but I realise that there's a greater need here.'

'But you give of your time, Fran. Money can't supply love – and I believe that's what you're giving to these poor unfortunate children.' He stroked his chin thoughtfully. 'I want to come in to the orphanage tomorrow with you. Will anyone object?'

'I shouldn't think so. We only get the dignitaries occasionally when their consciences prick. Since it's Jubilee Year we've had extra money, parcels of clothing and an abundance of goodies. It's all very nice, but we don't want everything at once. We need a steady income, genuine helpers who will be permanent, and enough food to feed them all.'

Fran was surprised that James appeared to be so interested the next day when they reached the orphanage. Fran was able to get on with her work feeding the babies, bathing and changing them, while Mrs Muir, a war widow from the Great War, escorted James round the large mansion house, explaining in great detail the history of the orphanage.

Fran was feeding her special charge when Mrs Muir brought James to find her.

'I never need look long for Fran,' Mrs Muir said in her strong Scottish accent. 'She loves the wee ones. She's many a talent, has our Fran. Beautiful needlework she does, and the older girls listen and learn from her, but if there's a wee, newborn baby in, then no one but Fran is allowed to care for him.'

'Meet young Gordon,' Fran said, lifting the top of the shawl to reveal a shock of black, curly hair. 'Only four days old. Isn't he gorgeous?'

'He is indeed, if you like tiny babies,' James said with a mischievous twinkle. 'Not really my department.'

'Such a sad case,' Mrs Muir put in. 'Young wee lassie not really old enough to be wed. No' illegitimate is young Gordon here. Ach, no! They came from Herefordshire originally. The father was a young stable boy who took the lassie of the big house off to Gretna Green to marry. Family were against it, d'you ken. He managed to get a job here in Glasgow, but the wages weren't enough to feed both of them properly and she died giving birth. The young man was so heartbroken he hanged himsel' from the nearest tree. If ever a child was born of love it was this one. Poor wee laddie. And to think the girl's family don't want anything to do wi' him.'

'Will you be able to place him in a good home?' James asked.

'Mebbe, in time, but Fran won't let him go easily.'

'He's so much like my Lennie,' Fran said wistfully. 'I just wish I was young enough to adopt him. I suppose I'll be gone before a home can be found, but I sincerely hope it'll be a good one. My heart bleeds for all these children.'

'You can't take on the worries of the world, Fran, my dear.' James sounded genuinely sorry. He stayed a while longer, but Fran got the impression that he wasn't happy in such surroundings. 'I'll take a walk now and then go back to the house for a rest.'

'Don't overdo it, James,' Fran warned, and turned her attention back to the sleepy babe in her arms.

Before she left that evening she went to look at Gordon in his crib. Memories tumbled painfully, and happily too, in her brain as she relived the early days of her marriage to Henry. The excitement they had shared when Lennie was born, a tiny wee mite with similar black hair and pale skin. What was Gordon's destiny? Lennie may have lived to be only ten years old, but he had been born of loving, caring parents who had done their best for him. Fran was filled with despair for the parents of this orphan. They had defied their family code of honour. Run away to the notorious blacksmith's shop in Gretna Green to get married as honourably as they knew how. How could fate be so cruel? To take a young mother's life?

Fran wept tears of anguish for them both as she laid her finger on the child's cheek. She felt the same way over all the babes who were brought in unwanted and unloved. But at least Gordon had been wanted, and had been conceived in love. Fran placed her fingers to her lips and then on the baby's delicate rosebud mouth before she tore herself away.

It had taken her nearly two years to become accustomed to a new way of life. Now she was finding it difficult to imagine herself anywhere else, and yet her heart yearned to see her own daughters and Ma again. She was glad of the walk home, which gave her time to recover.

Jenny had prepared supper, which was all set out and ready when she got in. James was sitting outside on the garden wall, gazing out over the valley of meadows where the sheep with their young grazed in peaceful contentment. The hills and mountains were green now, and somewhere up there roamed the local red deer, only seen occasionally.

Fran washed and changed. Then she went to the dining room and called James from the window. He came in slowly and Fran was afraid that he felt unwell.

'Are you all right, James?' she asked with concern.

James nodded and sat down in the huge carver chair heavily. He ate slowly, hardly speaking at all. Fran gabbled on about nothing in particular until, receiving no response, she too fell into an awkward silence. What had she done, she wondered? Suddenly she felt nervous in James's company, whereas before she had always felt so much at ease. When she offered him some hot blackcurrant-and-apple pie, he raised his hand and dabbed at his mouth with the crisp, white table napkin.

'You don't seem hungry tonight,' Fran ventured. 'Was it not to your liking?'

'The food was fine, my dear. I've something on my mind, that's all.'

'Can you share it? Or is it to do with business?'

'Business – in a way. I expect you'll tell me that I'm a foolish old man, and I dare say you'd be right.'

Fran leaned on the table, looking expectantly at her father-in-law. 'It must be something serious, James, or is it that you're tired? Maybe coming all this way by car was too much for you.'

'Now you sound like Emma and the girls.' He sat back in the chair and toyed with his elegant silver watch chain. 'Seeing you with that babe today, knowing the circumstances, and something that you said, gave me strange stirrings – and an idea, Fran.'

'Whatever d'you mean?' Fran sighed. 'Oh, dear, James, I do hope you aren't expecting too much of me. I have explained that I can no longer conceive. I'm simply too old and that's the end of it.' She hadn't realised just how obsessed James had become about a grandson. The mere mention of a baby and he embarked on his favourite subject.

'I appreciate what you're telling me, Fran. I understand, really, and I'm not being totally unbalanced about it. You lost your son and it must have been a great tragedy for you. I know how it was when we lost our boys. It may seem like an old man's whim to worry about the future of the family name, but my life has been spent making the Hammond foundry well respected. It's not the immediate future that bothers me. If I'm spared to continue for a few more years I'll see that Lizzie is accepted as the new boss with an under-manager. But what will happen in twenty years' time? There'll be no more Hammonds to take over. Oh, I know what you're going to say – I do have grandsons, and yes, I could insist that they add the name Hammond to theirs, but it just wouldn't be the same.'

'What's in a name, James? The foundry will still be Hammond's, no matter who runs it.'

'I've been conjuring up a – scheme. Just between you and me, my dear. You obviously love that small boy. You said you'd like to adopt him – so how about it? Take him back south as your own son?'

'*James*!' Fran shrieked. 'You must be out of your mind! I ... I ...'

James laughed. Fran was relieved to see the laughter lines back at the corners of his eyes. What a joke! What a silly notion to come up with! But he was looking solemn again, and by his expression she realised that he didn't intend it as a joke.

'Money will buy almost anything, Fran,' he went on. 'I know it can't be the same as having your own son. Even I can't make him a genuine Hammond, but under your care he'll grow up just the way a Hammond boy should. He's not illegitimate, remember, and it almost seems to me he came as an answer to a prayer.'

Fran dropped her head in her hands. How could she tell this dear old man that he was being ridiculous?

'James, you're just letting this obsession of yours get out of hand. They wouldn't let me adopt a baby at my age. Think of the child's future. By the time he's fourteen I shall be sixty. It wouldn't be fair.'

'There's little that's fair in life, Fran, as you well know. No one would ever need to know – not even Luke. He was home at Christmas. We're nearly into August. Babies often come a month early. The birth certificate can be a brief one. I'll deal with all the formalities. All you have to do is to bring the boy up to be a Hammond. Yours and Luke's son – my grandson.'

'James, I can't . . . I *won't*. It wouldn't be right.'

'Luke tried to deceive me, so did Lizzie, and the other girls will always quarrel over who has what. This way I shall have settled the matter to my liking. And you won't have to say goodbye to that baby. Just seeing you sitting there feeding him, loving him – Fran dear, he can be yours. In twenty years' time he can be well trained in the foundry.'

'But supposing he doesn't want to do that kind of work? You can't impose your will on others, James. You should know that from losing Luke.' Fran knew that she was being unkind, but someone had to make James see that his idea was preposterous.

'That's hurtful, Fran. I thought you were more sensitive to my feelings than that – but I'll put it down to the shock of my suggestion. The idea was there at the back of *your* mind or you wouldn't have mentioned adoption. You're so honest and straight. You'd never think of plotting and planning your destiny. Sometimes an opportunity comes along that enables us to steer our lives along a certain course. I believe this is one of those opportunities. Now, aren't I going to get a cup of tea?'

Fran got up and hurried away to the kitchen. She looked out over the country scene in soulful dismay while she waited for the kettle to boil. When it did, she scalded her hand and tipped tea over the stove with her unsteady fingers.

'He wouldn't be mine, and he wouldn't be Luke's,' she said irritably as she placed the teapot on the iron stand. 'Moreover, he wouldn't be your grandson, James.'

'Let's sleep on it, my dear. Don't be angry, please. Think of the good you'd be doing, apart from pleasing me. Giving a home to a poor wee orphan child. You said yourself he was like Lennie to look at.'

'And he might grow up to be quite different.'

'I know you'll bring him up to be God-fearing and trustworthy. Luke tried to cheat me, remember, so where's the harm in beating him at his own game? He need never know the truth, but I shall honour your decision about that. Adoptions are legalised under the strictest conditions of confidence, as you must know, but money will always talk, my dear. I shall pay for absolute secrecy, and the orphanage will benefit greatly.'

'James Hammond, you're doing your best to bribe me, I do believe,' Fran said.

'I can't force you to make a decision one way or the other. There isn't much time. You travel south in less than two weeks' time.'

Fran ran her hands over her cheeks, pausing, feeling the blood hot beneath her fingers.

'But what could I tell Luke?' she asked in despair. 'I'd have told him if I'd been expecting his baby. It's what he wanted more than anything else in the world.'

'Gets better and better, Fran. You thought you were at that certain age when you couldn't conceive again. You won't be the first woman to confuse pregnancy with the change. It does happen. Might easily to you as you aren't yet fifty.'

'You're too knowledgeable for your own good,' Fran flung at her father-in-law crossly. This was getting out of hand. She must put a stop to it at once before he actually persuaded her to go through with his devious little scheme. Not such a little scheme. It was a mighty big one, and not impossible at that.

Chapter Eighteen

Two weeks later Fran and Hilda waved goodbye to James Hammond from the London-bound train as it puffed and complained its way out of Waverley station in Edinburgh.

Fran looked down on the plush seat of the first-class compartment which James had insisted upon. It held a brand-new wicker basket covered with a snow-white shawl. The baby bonnet revealed nothing of the infant's jet-black hair.

Hilda sat beside the basket proudly. 'Oh, Mummy, isn't it lovely to have a new baby? He's so beautiful – and to think you didn't even tell me.'

'Your step-grandfather thought it was best that you concentrate on your school work, especially as these last examinations were so important.'

'I wish we didn't have to go to Portsmouth first. I do want to show him off to the others.'

'Mr Hammond thought it was foolish to take all our luggage to Brimdene and then have to move it all again when we go to Portsmouth. I'm just as anxious as you to see the family after all this time. Two whole years – it's been a lifetime.'

Fran sat back and closed her eyes. Gordon James Hammond slept on, blissfully unaware of life's new adventure, and Fran herself was hardly aware of the enormity of what James had convinced her was a grand gesture towards protecting the helpless baby.

If Luke was a schemer, his father was even more adept at secret intrigue. He had put the plan in operation, demanding that no one knew except those in authority. The babe would take the name Hammond and that was all anyone needed to know. A sizeable amount of money changed hands. Legal papers were rushed through the local magistrates' court to satisfy the Adoption of Children Act 1926, though no one questioned the rights of James

Hammond. The child's future and wellbeing were assured, and Gordon might as easily have been physically borne by Fran as by his unfortunate young parents, neither of whom could return to claim the child at a later date. Fran signed the legal agreement. James Hammond put himself in loco parentis, which meant that he undertook to pay for the education of Gordon, agreeing to accept all duties and liabilities of the child, since his son, Luke Hammond was mostly away at sea.

Fran had been swept along on James's tide of enthusiasm. Like father, like son, she thought, and not for the first time.

She felt quite weary now. There had been hasty letters to write to her family. She informed them that she had thought the symptoms she had been experiencing were due to her age, so it had come as something of a revelation to herself that she was about to produce another child. But the arrival of Gordon James made her feel young again.

James had remained at Craiglee with her. Advising her, telling her how to break the news to family and friends, even to Luke, while he passed on the joyous tidings to his own family. Elizabeth had telephoned and wanted to visit but he had put his daughter off. Better, he told Fran, that this was just between the two of them. He had thought of everything, seeing that Jenny was handsomely rewarded for her diligent care of Fran during her time in Scotland, and supervising the removal of their personal belongings, which he had arranged to have picked up and delivered by a carrier within the week to the house in Portsmouth. Fran had the barest of necessities to carry herself. James had done everything to make it easy for her, yet she still worried that someone would find out.

'So what?' James had said with a raucous laugh. 'The adoption is legal enough. I shall be generous in acknowledging you for giving me a grandson, Fran, my dear. A Hammond boy at last.'

'But he isn't, James. Not truthfully. We're deceiving everyone. I never thought myself capable of deceiving my own husband.'

'Luke will be so overjoyed at the prospects for himself and his son that he won't question anything. The legal documents as to my claim on Gordon will be in the hands of my solicitor. A clause will be inserted in my will for the boy's future – education and so on – which any grandfather is likely to make.'

'Don't be too generous, James,' Fran had said. 'Or Luke and the rest of the family will be suspicious. At least let Luke and me bring Gordon up as our own, or I can't be party to the deception.'

James had reassured Fran on all counts, but now that she was actually on her way home at last she had grave misgivings as to what she had done.

The baby quirked. It was almost time for his feed, which she had brought in a flask. After two years of so-called luxury living she was back to changing nappies and feeding. Above all, she had a baby boy to love and cherish. James was right – it was of no consequence to anyone else.

The taxi pulled up outside a terraced house in Southsea, a suburb of Portsmouth. The street was long and straight, tree-lined, with a wide pavement. Fran, cradling the tiny babe in her arms, sat still for a few moments as she viewed her new abode with mixed feelings. The iron railings and tall gate were newly painted, shiny black, as was the guttering and pipe-work, but the sash window frames were sparkling white, giving the house a distinctive appearance in an otherwise somewhat dreary residential area. Dreary-looking perhaps to Fran, but prestigious.

Luke had informed her a month ago that the last tenants had vacated the property in good time, so that repairs and redecoration could be carried out before she and Hilda arrived. He hoped he would be joining them by the end of August or the beginning of September. Fran took a deep breath. By now, she hoped, he would have received her letter informing him that he was the father of a son.

The taxi driver carried the suitcases and bags to the front door. He rang the bell, and almost immediately it was opened by a young woman in maid's uniform. She bobbed a curtsey as Fran walked up the steps to the front door.

'Evening, Ma'am. You must be very tired aftera long day's travelling down from Scotland.'

'Yes, we are rather weary,' Fran said, and held the bundle out to the girl. 'Take the baby for a moment while I pay the driver.'

'I can have him, I can have him,' Hilda cried, but Fran had already passed the baby to the maid.

A few minutes later Fran stood in a large square hall with deep red carpeting. She took off her hat and gloves and placed them on the oak hall stand, looking at herself in the mirror. She looked like Fran Hammond, but she didn't feel at all like herself. Another house, a new home, different surroundings – if only she could have gone home to Brimdene, better still to Sherbrook, where memories of her past still beckoned. The third move in four years. How many more times? She'd had enough of adventure, she just wanted to go home. But this is your home, her conscience said loud and clear, and Fran felt a lump come into her throat as the dull ache of longing returned to punish her.

Movement behind her made her turn quickly, and to her astonishment she came face to face with strange people.

Now she knew why she didn't feel like herself. These, she supposed, were her appointed servants, but hadn't she been raised to be one of them?

A middle-aged man stepped forward and politely lowered his balding head in acknowledgement. 'Rudgwick, Ma'am, and this is my wife, Edie. We've always managed for Captain Hammond, and we're very pleased to welcome his wife and the new baby.'

Fran shook hands with them both, and then with the young woman who had answered the door. 'This is Betty, the housemaid, and –' Rudgwick paused where a young girl in a blue uniform dress with starched white apron stood, holding the baby – 'this is Nanny, Miss Norma Marlow.'

Fran was hesitant as she said: 'This is my daughter Hilda. It's getting rather late, but it's nice of you to be here to meet us. I expect you're anxious to get to bed, and we certainly are. A warm milky drink would be nice to help us settle for the night.'

'I've taken the liberty of laying up trays, Ma'am, which you may care to have brought up to your rooms,' Edie Rudgwick said. 'But first, I think you should come into the drawing room.'

Fran looked nonplussed. Not trouble already, she hoped. She really was too tired for confrontations of any sort.

Edie opened the varnished door. There was a distinct smell of fresh varnish, paint and wallpaper paste pervading the whole house, Fran thought, but then a lovely sweet scent wafted out of the large drawing room to greet her. The huge bay window was a blaze of colour with flowers of every shade and variety.

'We managed to find enough vases,' Edie said hesitantly. 'Your husband arranged by cable to have them specially delivered on the day of your expected arrival.'

Tears filled Fran's eyes. Until she married Luke she had never been used to lavish presents and flowers. It was all done for show, of course, but the thought touched her deeply.

'And this letter arrived for you yesterday, Ma'am.'

Fran felt her heart jump with anticipation, even a little fear. She knew that Luke would be delighted about the baby, but he might be put out that he hadn't been told earlier.

'These are quite beautiful,' Fran managed to say for the benefit of the staff. 'Thank you for arranging them so well.' She ran a hand across her weary brow. 'Now I think we all ought to get to bed. Nanny, perhaps you'd carry the baby upstairs. I'll come to see to him at once. And Hilda, you can bring up your own small case and get ready for bed too.'

'Oh, can't I see over the house, Mummy, please?' Hilda begged.

'Tomorrow, after a good night's sleep. We'll explore it together.'

The suitcases and bags were taken upstairs to the bedrooms that Edie had prepared.

'The nursery is at the back of the house, with Nanny's room adjoining,' she explained. 'I thought Miss Hilda would perhaps like the middle room. And the master bedroom en suite occupies the front of the house. If anything is not to your liking, Ma'am, we shall be pleased to change things tomorrow.'

Fran assured the housekeeper that everything was in order. She was amazed at the way things had been organised. Luke could not have known about the baby in time to employ a nanny. Fran wasn't sure that she required the services of a nanny. She was quite capable of looking after Gordon herself. It would give her something to do when Hilda went to the grammar school in the autumn term.

Hilda had followed Nanny to the nursery and Fran was guided there by their voices.

'I'll see to the baby,' Fran said. 'Top and tail will do tonight, a bath in the morning.'

'I was just undressing him, Ma'am. That is why I'm here. I'm sure you must be travel sick.' Fran's expression evidently showed the doubt at the back of her mind. 'I can be putting the baby down while you have your supper,' Nanny suggested. 'My references came back from Middlesbrough today. I have them in my room if you wish to see them, but I am properly trained, Ma'am.'

'Of course, Nanny.' Fran smiled. 'I didn't mean to imply that your ability is in question.'

Middlesbrough! So all this was James's doing. The old rascal hadn't said a word.

Edie was coming up the stairs carrying a large tray. 'I've put the young lady's in her room,' she said. 'Just a few sandwiches in case you feel like something to eat.'

Fran was glad to kick her shoes off and sit down in the easy chair in the huge bay window. She decided she couldn't put off opening Luke's letter any longer. It was warm and loving. Didn't he know she could give him a son? He was full of gratitude and effusive in his praise of her, making her feel thoroughly guilty. He hoped she would like the Rudgwicks, who were to engage any additional staff they considered necessary for number 10 Kingswood Grove, but he thought the employment of a nanny was best left to her. But employ one she must, he insisted, as he didn't want her to be overworked. What he really meant, she knew, was that he didn't want the baby or anyone else to intrude into their private lives when he came home on leave. He seemed to be very clever in arranging his homecomings to coincide with term times, she had noticed. Fran didn't mind one bit. It meant that she was free to visit the family in Brimdene at the earliest opportunity.

When the telephone rang early next morning, Fran picked up the extension on her bedside table.

'Are you feeling tired after your long journey?' James asked.

'It seemed a long day, James,' Fran said. 'But I've had a good night's sleep. Haven't heard a thing – thanks to the nanny you engaged.'

James laughed. 'The least I could do in the circumstances.'

'You could have told me,' Fran said.

'Not in front of the lassie, my dear. I dealt through a well-known agency. The girls are very well trained and this one has worked for Royal Navy officers before, so she should be all right, according to her references.'

Fran told her father-in-law about Luke's letter and the flowers. 'He's thrilled to bits about Gordon,' she said happily.

'And so he should be. If you need anything or run into problems before Luke gets home, don't hesitate to get in touch, Fran.'

She still doubted the wisdom of what she had agreed to, but she knew that she had made James very happy, and Luke too. From the tone of his letter she questioned whether she would ever be able to tell her husband the truth, but she knew that he had a right to know.

It was a sunny summer morning. After breakfast the housekeeper showed her all over the house, which was both appealing and impressive.

The Rudgwicks lived in the basement flat, which they insisted Fran should view so that she could see for herself that they were clean and respectable people. Betty had a gabled attic room right at the top of the house. It reminded Fran of the Hinckleys' house, and the Maitlands' in Sherbrook, where Kate's bedroom had been right up in the roof. Fran wished with all her heart that she could have Kate, Ruby and Babs join her here in Southsea. Now that she had provided her father-in-law with a Hammond heir, and her husband with the son he longed for, maybe she could use her powers of persuasion in getting Luke to let the family live all together again. There was plenty of room here for everyone, even a room for Ma. But did she really have any persuasive influence? She was the one whom others influenced! She had fallen victim all too easily to Luke's charm, and once she had agreed to become his wife she had been carried along with whatever he chose to do. And now, submitting to James's crazy plan of adopting young Gordon. Luke and James both seemed able to sway her to their way of thinking without undue pressure.

When she looked in on the sleeping babe, though, she had few doubts that she had done the right thing. He was adorable; his dark-blue eyes, which she felt certain would soon change to brown, seemed to look right into her very soul. He had a lusty cry and strong limbs, as well as a healthy appetite. Nanny Marlow was already quite possessive about her new charge.

Although Fran was anxious to visit Brimdene at the first opportunity, she remained in Southsea for the rest of that week in order to unpack and generally settle down. Then she gave Nanny a week off, with the excuse that there was not sufficient accommodation for her to go with them to Brimdene.

'I'll have enough nursemaids in my other daughters when I get there,' she explained. 'We'll be going to Sherbrook, too, to visit old friends from when I lived there.'

'Are you sure you can manage on the trains, Ma'am?' Nanny said. 'I could travel with you and stay with an aunt in the New Forest. Then meet you again at Brimdene station to come home.'

'Home'! Would this ever seem like home? Fran wondered. In time, when she was used to the streets, the shops and parks, and when Luke returned, she supposed she would fall into her new life style with few problems. She recalled with some pain her arrival in Craiglee. It was inevitable that those first few months were fraught with misery and guilt. At least here she was within easy reach of her family again.

Fran agreed to Nanny's proposal readily. James Hammond had been crafty in choosing a nanny who had relations living not too far away from Brimdene. Fran had no doubts as to the depth of his inquiry into the girl's qualifications and background, which made her ideal for the post.

The station at Brimdene was packed with holiday visitors so that Fran had to strain in her search for familiar faces. Then a tall girl rushed into her arms and hugged her, nearly knocking her off her feet.

'Mummy! Oh, Mummy, how lovely to see you,' Ruby cried. She refused to let go as she kissed her mother not once but several times. She didn't seem to care about Hilda or the new baby, she just clung to Fran as if she never intended to let her go ever again. Tears ran down their faces as mother and daughter, who had so often been at odds before, tried to make up for the lost two years. 'Let me help with the luggage,' Ruby said, brushing away the wetness from her cheeks. 'Gran can't wait to see you again. Oh, Mummy, it's been *such* a long, long time,' she said with passionate emotion.

'Look,' Hilda interrupted excitedly as she put her arms round Ruby and kissed her sister, 'we've got a new brother. His name is Gordon James. And this is Nanny.'

Ruby glanced at Nanny, who smiled reassuringly, and then went to peep inside the shawl.

'Kate couldn't get off, I suppose,' Fran said.

'No, but she's cycling up from town this afternoon, just for her two hours off.'

'My, you've grown, Ruby. Had your hair cut, I see,' Fran said.

Ruby looked quickly at her mother, apprehension in her eyes, as she recognised the voice of authority she had almost forgotten.

'Gran thought it was best because she couldn't do it the way you always did. Aunt Sissy tried, but it looked awful and the plaits came undone.'

Fran laughed, and Ruby's expression relaxed again.

'How is Gran? She's all right? And the other grandparents, Uncle Nathan and his family? Has Uncle Eric been down lately?' Suddenly Fran wanted to know everything, and the platform was empty by the time she remembered that they must go in search of a taxi.

Nanny held on to the baby until they were all settled inside the large, shiny, black car; then she passed him to Fran, and in minutes they were on their way. Fran was at last reunited with two of her girls, her stomach cold with the ache of strangeness, warm with longing.

While she paid the taxi driver the two girls rushed into the house, Hilda carrying the baby, to show off the new arrival, and then Fran saw Ma. She looked pale and small, as if she had shrunk. Her pale-blue eyes quickly filled with moisture as they fell on each other's necks and wept unashamedly. What have I done to her? Fran rebuked herself. Leaving an old lady of seventy-five to manage a house as well as a young, wayward girl like Ruby.

'And to think you've had another baby,' Ma wept. 'At your age!'

She turned away from Fran and went to look at the crying infant lying on the couch where Hilda had lain him.

'And if I know anything about babies,' Fran said brusquely, 'he wants changing and feeding.'

It helped to diffuse the situation as everyone gathered round, admiring Gordon James Hammond.

'I'll see to the dinner, Ma,' Fran said, when the bottle was heated up. 'You sit quietly to give him his bottle, and get to know your new grandson.'

Fran went from room to room, reacquainting herself with everything that had once been the centre of her life. A great gnawing in the pit of her stomach made her feel quite sick, and she was glad to have a few moments alone in her bedroom, where she had spent lonely nights weeping for Henry and Lennie. Tossing, turning, trying to rid herself of the anger aimed at God for His injustice. Now she could hear angry words from God accusing her of deserting her family. She had run away from her responsibilities with a man who said he loved her, but who had not treated her with the love and respect she had known from Henry. But Luke and Henry were two vastly different people.

She looked about the room, recognising her belongings which she had not been able to take with her: the dressing-table set comprising an engraved glass tray with matching trinkets; the ring stand that Henry had given her when they had married on Boxing Day in 1912 – twenty-three years ago come Christmas. Suddenly there was a great roar in her ears and she was back in Sherbrook running for dear life, shouting at Ruby to get in the house before the wall of water swallowed them up. Little knowing that her father, his sheep, and her husband were being carried away downriver to their deaths. Fran placed her head in her hands, and wept as if her heart was breaking all over again. She was seated on the edge of the bed when Ruby found her.

'Don't cry, Mum,' she said softly, placing her arms round Fran's shoulders. 'You're home now. We're all together again.'

Fran wiped her eyes, sniffed, and stood up abruptly. 'It's been such a long time, dear,' she said. 'Seeing you and Ma, being back in my own bedroom – where did you get the cot, for heaven's sake?'

'Gran and Grandad Sheldon's got new neighbours. Their youngest little boy is nearly four, so he's ready to go into a proper bed. Uncle Nathan said the least he could do was to buy a cot for your new baby, and we're all to go to tea on Thursday when Kate's off for the day.'

'D'you mean to Uncle Nathan's, or to Gran and Grandad Sheldon's house?'

'Gran and Grandad Sheldon's for a big family party. They're all excited about the new baby.'

'And are you pleased, Ruby?'

Ruby looked away to avoid her mother's gaze. 'Yes, 'course. But I didn't think you'd ever want another baby. I thought you'd had enough of all of us.'

Fran sat down again, and it was a few moments before she could compose herself. She drew Ruby close, both hands round her waist affectionately. 'Things are different now,' she said solemnly. 'We don't understand why things have to change – but sometimes they do even when we don't want them to. It was a very sad day for us when that nasty storm took Grandad Brown and your father away from us all. But we just had to make the best of things. It was hard for me to manage on just the pension, dear. I didn't plan to marry again, but Luke has been very kind. You've had lots of things you wouldn't have been able to have otherwise. And although I went away for a while, I still thought about you every day. I still love you just the same. I didn't go away because I'd had enough of you. You must never ever think that, Ruby. Once I'd decided to marry Luke I was committed, as his wife, to go wherever the Royal Navy sent him. Now, tell me how Babs is. Have you seen her lately?'

'They're coming tomorrow. We see them once a month. Auntie Prue thought you'd want to go to Sherbrook, too?'

'Of course I do. We'll be seeing a lot of each other from now on. Portsmouth isn't nearly as far away as Scotland. You must let Hilda tell you all about her school, and about Luke's family in Middlesbrough.'

'I don't really want to know. I'm just glad you're back. I wish you could stay here all the time.'

Fran pushed Ruby aside gently, and they went downstairs. Fran found that Ruby had everything ready for dinner. Young, new potatoes from the garden, peas and carrots which Nathan had planted, and a lovely piece of boiled ham, with a treacle sponge pudding to follow.

It didn't take Fran long to realise that the family had managed very well without her. Although she looked for signs of neglect around the home, she could find no evidence of it. The pantry was spotless, the chimney had been swept, curtains and paintwork washed and carpets beaten. On enquiring who did what, she learned that Ma and Ruby did most of it. When they knew Fran was returning, Aunt Sissy organised a working party, and with Kate's help they had spring-cleaned the whole house from top to bottom during the Whitsun holiday. Now they refused to let Fran do anything. Didn't she have a new baby to care for? She mustn't spoil her lovely hands now that she no longer had to slave away to keep house.

They ate their meal in comparative silence. Ruby and Hilda, having argued over some trivial matter, had nothing more to say to each other. Although Fran asked lots of questions, wanting to know how Ruby was doing at school and how all the neighbours were, as well as the family, the conversation seemed strained. Fran watched the minutes ticking by, longing for Kate to arrive. When she did, she came into the house breathless and quite flustered.

'Oh, Mum, how lovely that you're home at last!' She kissed and hugged her mother. 'I couldn't make my pedals go round fast enough. It was such hard work cycling up that hill.'

'Let me look at you, our Katie.' Fran said, holding her at arm's length. 'You look different, older – oh, dear, you're all growing up so fast. Ah, it's the hair, you've got it in a bun.'

'D'you like it? It's nice and neat for work.'

'And how is work, dear?'

'We're busy this month, of course. I help in the kitchen when anyone's away.'

'And what about your studies? D'you still enjoy cooking?'

'I love it. I love everything about hotel work, Mum. One day I'm going to have a hotel of my very own.'

'Such grand ideas, Kate. You just be careful you're not heading for a fall, my girl. Anyway, at twenty you'll be thinking about getting married soon, I expect.'

Kate's eyes misted with memories. Then she laughed. 'Not me, Mum. I don't want to tie myself down for a long time yet.'

Fran knew by the look in Kate's eyes that she had briefly thought of Maurice. She felt a knot in her stomach at the reminder of her guilt in confiscating Maurice's letter. She didn't like to ask whether Kate ever saw him when she went to Sherbrook to Aunt Prue's to see Babs. It was an episode in their lives that Fran preferred to try to forget, but her shame would go with her through the rest of her life. She had confided in James Hammond about the whole horrid affair, and he had shown sympathy, saying that it was a parent's lot to have to contend with such events within the family circle.

'You did what you thought was right at the time,' he said. 'Best to put the matter out of your mind, as young people soon get on with the business of living.' But Fran knew that Kate would never forget how ill-used she had been by Maurice's friend Felix. She wasn't likely to forgive Maurice either for deserting her just when she needed a true friend, and no one was to blame for that but Fran herself.

Kate's two hours off was quickly spent, and by the end of the day Fran felt weary. Emotionally weary – perhaps a little hurt that they didn't really seem to be at ease with her. There was tomorrow to look forward to, she thought. At least Babs would be overjoyed to see her.

Gordon James was fretful, and Fran was up several times during the night. She had just managed to get off to sleep when Ruby brought her a cup of tea in bed.

'Oh, Ruby, and I'd only just dropped off again.' Ruby left the room hurriedly.

Later Fran heard Ruby and Hilda arguing about who should feed Gordon, and it was as if she had never been away, except that no matter how hard she tried to fit in she felt like a stranger. They waited on her, fetched and carried when she was seeing to Gordon, and even Ma appeared to be reluctant to chat about things the way they had always done before. Fran watched the clock eagerly, and was at the window when the bus passed the end of the road. She ran out of the front door and waited by the gate until Prue appeared hand in hand with the little girl with bright copper curls. Fran waved. Prue waved back, but Babs sidled closer to Prue's skirt. No, that was only in Fran's imagination. Babs had never been the shy one. Marion was coming behind, carrying the bag. Babs's belongings, Fran supposed. From now on things would be like the old days – a house full of women, she thought wryly.

Fran opened the gate and walked the remaining few paces to meet her youngest daughter.

'Darling,' she breathed with emotion, as she clasped the child to her bosom. 'Oh, my baby, my Babs!'

Fran could not believe it. Babs fought to get out of her embrace.

'You can't have forgotten me,' Fran said, trying to make light of it.

'Hullo, Fran dear,' Prue said, as the two women kissed a warm greeting. 'Give her time, Fran,' she whispered. 'Two years is a long time to a child.'

When Fran tried to take Bab's hand she pulled away and hung on more tightly to Prue's.

'Shall we go in and see our new baby?' Fran tried, but two large brown eyes surveyed her with disdain. 'You've got a new brother, called Gordon. Have you missed me, darling? I've missed you dreadfully. But now I'm home and we'll all be together again. Won't that be nice?'

But Babs didn't think anything was nice. And very soon Fran began to feel even more wretched. When the time came for Prue to catch the train in the late afternoon, Babs refused to be left behind.

'I'm coming home on the train with you,' she shouted to Prue. 'I want to go to Uncle Sam. I want to sleep in my own bed.'

'Let Marion stay as well?' Fran suggested. Ruby and Marion had spent most of the day pushing Gordon about in the pram, largely disregarding Fran and Hilda. Babs had hardly moved from Prue's side and looked at her sister Hilda as if she couldn't understand her at all.

'No, no!' Babs screamed. 'We'll all go home together.'

Prue looked at Fran apologetically, but Fran's expression was one of anger. Prue and Sam had deliberately set out to help Babs forget her. Prue had always wanted Babs, and now she had brainwashed her into not knowing her own family.

'Aren't you pleased that Hilda and I have come home from Scotland? I've written to you all every week,' Fran said, on the verge of frustrated tears. 'You knew I was coming home again, dear.' She knew she had said the wrong thing as soon as she had spoken.

'You went away,' Babs accused. 'Auntie Prue is my mummy now, and Uncle Sam is my dad.' She looked up at Prue with pleading. 'Let's go home now.'

Ruby and Hilda tried to reason with her but she yelled and became hysterical.

'I'm sorry, Fran, really I am,' Prue said. 'Perhaps we'd better take things step by step. It isn't any good to upset her any more for today. When are you coming to Sherbrook?'

'I think I'd better come tomorrow,' Fran said shortly. If Prue and Sam thought they'd got Babs for good, they had another think coming.

But when the house was quiet again, Fran realised that she couldn't retrace her steps.

'You must be thankful that Prue and Sam have been so good to Babs,' Ma said softly, feeling helpless in the situation and knowing how deeply wounded Fran felt. 'We can't go back, Fran dear. In the circumstances it was best that she went with them. Sherbrook was familiar, after all, and I couldn't have managed Babs. Not at my age.'

'Have you had any trouble with Ruby, Ma? Be honest now, don't try to hide things from me.'

'Bless you, no. She's been a good girl. She's settled down. She missed her father most of all of them, you know. And you and she never got on because you're both alike, Fran. She's done well at school – well, you've seen her reports.'

'I wish I could go to the school to see the teachers myself. Maybe I can come again in school termtime.'

'You don't need to fret about Ruby. Miss Baker came along to see me. They knew I couldn't get to the school, and although Sissy offered to go, Miss Baker sent me a letter to say she was coming here. She's very nice, and they're so pleased with Ruby that they want her to stay on until next summer. She'll be all right when it comes to getting work, Fran. Henry would be proud of her.'

Fran dabbed at her eyes. 'He wouldn't be proud of me, though, would he, for leaving them, splitting them all up? Babs looked at me as if she hated me.'

'Well, two years is a long time to a child. She was a mite of six when you went away and she's only eight now. Give them all time, Fran.'

'What difference will time make, Ma? We can never be back all together again. We can't bring Pa and Henry back any more than I can pretend I didn't marry Luke. Everything has changed,' she said dismally.

'That's right enough, Fran, but you can plan for the future, and you've got this young son of yours now, to take Lennie's place.'

'No one can ever do that, Ma.'

Fran's mind and heart were in turmoil, and when she visited Sherbrook the following day her spirits drooped still lower. It was no use thinking that she should never have left Sherbrook four years ago; there had been no choice. The only choice she'd had was in marrying Luke. Now she doubted that she had made the right decision. Her family had grown away from her – or was it she who had grown away from them?

She stood at the graveside of lost loved ones and wept bitterly. This wasn't how she had imagined her homecoming. She had been greeted cordially, no one could deny that, but things were not the way she wanted them to be. Sam and Prue looked at her pityingly, and she knew she couldn't blame them for Babs's rejection of her. A child of that age needed constant love and security, and Babs had found that with the Belmonts. At least Henry would have been pleased for his Babe. But Fran knew that he wouldn't condone what she had done in splitting up the family. The other girls were old enough to fend for themselves under supervision. Kate was a young woman now, and had proved herself to be capable in her work and in watching out for Ma and Ruby.

After visiting Henry's family later in the week, Fran found herself wanting to run way. It wasn't anything they said, but she felt that they found her new baby an embarrassment. They looked upon him as an affront to Henry's memory, she supposed. She was relieved when the visit was over and she could leave.

During the journey back to Southsea, Hilda chatted to Nanny, who had met them at the station, while Fran tucked herself into a corner of the compartment, trying to sort out her emotions as the train carried her along the track. A new track. A new beginning, for now she must come to terms with the fact that she, having deserted her family, her house full of women, was no longer important to them. She wasn't really needed. Their lives had continued much the same as before, whereas hers had changed dramatically. She thought of the hours of longing and weeping into the night during the past two years of separation. She had no way of knowing how they had coped emotionally in her absence. Even Ruby, who had written so lovingly while Fran and Hilda were in Scotland, appeared to be relieved to see the back of them. Fran had begun to feel as if she were in the way.

It was a bitter pill to swallow, after yearning to be home for so long.

Chapter Nineteen

In spite of several visits throughout the month of August, during which the family bond was restored to some degree, Fran realised that things could never be the same again.

Gordon grew, and gained weight. Smiled his first smile, which pleased the girls when they visited Southsea with Aunt Sissy. They loved the house and gardens, and admired Hilda's new school uniform, ready for her first term at a girls' grammar school. And even Babs seemed happier and more approachable when she visited with Sam and Prue during Sam's holiday from work.

'It's all a question of time, Fran, my dear,' Sam said wisely. 'It isn't that we haven't talked about you coming home, because we have, but if Luke doesn't intend that you should all live together again, then it was unkind to build up Babs's hopes, wasn't it?'

'The old times are past,' Fran said, with trembling chin. 'I must look to the future, and do the best I can to make it up to them all.'

''Tis a worry – what kind of future will this maniac Hitler let them have, I wonder?'

'You sound as worried as Luke sounds in his letters,' Fran said. 'There won't be a war, will there, Sam? The last one was bad enough. Didn't we learn anything from that?'

'There'll always be wars and rumours of wars – and when you get a man who is obsessed with ridding his country of Jewish people by such violent means, there's bound to be trouble. I'm trying to think rationally, Fran, but the news doesn't give us much hope.'

Fran tried not to dwell on the rumours. Luke would be in the thick of things if there should be a war, and she would have to protect her girls as well as Ma and the new little life entrusted to her care.

When Luke arrived home at the end of September he was so overjoyed with Gordon that he refused to be drawn into any war-mongering.

'Don't spoil my leave, darling,' Luke breathed impatiently as he gathered Fran in his arms. 'I hear enough about Hitler and Germany while I'm at sea. All I want to do now is to love you, my dearest, dearest Fran.'

He had arrived mid-morning, and after he had been introduced to his new son, Nanny had taken Gordon to be walked in the park, leaving Fran and Luke free to do the first thing that was always on Luke's mind. At the sight of her handsome husband, elegant in naval uniform, Fran never failed to feel the tiniest bit shy, but in his own inimitable way Luke swept her off her feet, literally.

The bedroom door was locked, and with an almost indecent haste to rid themselves of clothes, Fran lay in Luke's bronzed arms where she felt that nothing in the world mattered. This moment was sacred, intimacies shared as they explored each other as if they were young lovers all over again.

'Was it an easy birth?' Luke whispered into her hair. 'Is it all right to carry on as before? Will I hurt you? My darling, to think you went through all that pain and discomfort for me, and without letting me share it with you, even in thought.'

'Luke ...' Fran panicked. She must tell him the truth now, rather then let him go on thinking that Gordon was their own child. But his tender, loving, warm, sensuous mouth, drawing every emotion from within her, soon made her forget about the adoption. They were crazy with desire. Hearts beating in complete harmony, their bodies eager to ride the crest of the wave, waves that eventually exploded in unison ...

The need to express their love seemed insatiable. After a bath together, drying each other with loving caresses, it seemed the most natural thing in the world to begin all over again.

Luke's only interruption came when Nanny went off duty and Fran had to look after Gordon. Luke remained at Fran's side no matter how menial the task, and even offered to give the baby his bottle. The more Fran saw Luke tending to his son, the harder it was even to consider telling him the truth. She couldn't bear to hurt him, and she knew it would.

As the days and weeks passed, Luke, working from Portsmouth docks, was at home much more frequently than ever before. A new contentment drew them together as a family. Although she was estranged from her girls, even from Hilda, who had made new friends at her school now and was hardly at home, Fran at last felt that her life had taken a turn for the better. Any previous animosity or mistrust between her and Luke vanished as Gordon James became the idol of their lives.

One night as they settled down together between the sheets, Luke asked Fran how the girls had reacted to her homecoming and the new baby.

'I've been so wrapped up in my son,' he said, 'but I don't want you to think I haven't thought about them.'

'Babs had forgotten me, Luke,' she said softly. 'Can you imagine that? She actually rejected me.'

'I'm sure it's only temporary, and it's probably just your imagination, Fran,' Luke said gently, kissing her forehead. 'You've never been able to forgive me for taking you away from them, and you're haunted by your own guilt.'

'I don't blame *you*, Luke,' she said. 'I didn't *have* to marry you. I could have made a stand and refused to leave Brimdene.' She sobbed while she entwined her slender fingers in the tangle of hair on his chest. 'I think you take after your father. You both have an irresistible charm. I should have been stronger – I thought I was – but not where you're concerned.'

'What's my father got to do with anything?'

'I've become very fond of him, Luke. He came up to Craiglee – would you believe on a cargo vessel?'

'And he disinherited me because I went away to sea?' Luke laughed. 'Maybe we aren't so unalike after all. I'm glad you've been getting on so well. It was something to look forward to – letters from my parents, and the very last one from Mother was full of the new baby. They really are pleased, Fran. It might make all the difference to my place within the family.'

Fran remained quiet for several minutes. She had her opportunity now to be totally honest, but somehow the right words just refused to come. Instead she murmured: 'Money isn't everything. Position and status don't count for much. It's human relationships that matter. Caring for each other, being kind and understanding is what makes for a happy life.'

'And you've made me happier than I could ever describe, my darling. Remember that I told you the girls would all grow up and leave home, make their own lives? Now, when that happens it won't be so hard for you. You'll have Gordon – we'll have Gordon. I know he can't ever take Lennie's place, but he's so dark, so good, so perfect in every way that he must keep your memories of Lennie very much alive.' He lifted her chin, forcing her to look at him. 'You don't regret marrying me, do you, Fran?'

She shook her head. 'Of course not. It's just taken me a while to adjust. I wasn't bred for your kind of life, for one thing.'

It was because Lennie was so frequently in Fran's thoughts that at times her guilt cast a great shadow over her happiness. But as time passed she delighted in the baby boy, and her love for both husband and son grew stronger.

Preparations were made for Christmas and New Year. The house at Southsea was large enough to have Ma and the girls to stay for several days, but Babs refused to leave Prue, Sam and Marion.

'Don't fret about it,' Luke consoled. 'When she's older, just try keeping her away. She'll see things very differently as she matures.'

Apart from that one disappointment, the festive season was thoroughly enjoyed by everyone. After Ma and the girls had returned to Brimdene, Luke, Fran, Nanny and Gordon set off for Middlesbrough to celebrate the New Year at Hammond House. It was only a four-day visit because Luke was due to take up his duties aboard ship, but it was long enough for James Hammond to see for himself that his adopted grandson was well and established within his son's household.

'My worries are over, thanks to you, Fran, my dear,' he said as they walked alone in the frost-covered garden after breakfast one morning. 'I can never tell you how truly grateful I am that you agreed to our little deception.' He chuckled mischievously. 'And Luke doesn't know?' He shook his head as if he could hardly believe his luck. 'There's no point in spoiling the fun now, is there?'

'I should have told him at once, James,' Fran said. 'I wanted to, but he was so pleased about Gordon that I just didn't have the heart. The longer I've left it, the harder it has become.'

'Having the boy has helped your relationship with Luke?'

'We're extremely happy,' Fran said with a beaming smile. 'The girls are coming round slowly, all except Babs, and Luke assures me she will, given time. It was so hard to feel the barrier between us all. I hated it, but most of all I hated myself.'

'And that was punishment enough.' James Hammond tucked his arm reassuringly through his daughter-in-law's arm. 'Let it go now, Fran. The girls have had their own space to develop, which they'd do anyway in their own good time. Now be a good and trusty friend to them whenever they need you. Be a real mother to young Gordon. Bear in mind what his young parents had to sacrifice to have him – he'll always be very special to you and me, because we know the truth of it. This is a new phase in your life, and you're still young enough to make the most of all the opportunities that come your way. Officers in the services have a good life. Enjoy every damned minute of it. You deserve some good times.' He squeezed her hand affectionately.

There was a sombre beginning to 1938 when the government announced that all schoolchildren must be fitted with gas masks. Trouble in Europe was increasing all the time and Luke feared that at any moment he might be sent out on the high seas. But he had had two good years spent mostly at home. During their annual visit to Middlesbrough for New Year, Fran, Luke and little Gordon, now a bonny toddler, entered into the party spirit at Hammond House, and tried not to think too much about what might or might not happen in the near future. They were all together as a big happy family, too busy enjoying themselves to notice that James was not his usual masterful self.

When Elizabeth Hammond telephoned Luke at the end of January to tell him that their father had been rushed into hospital in a critical condition, Fran suggested to Luke that perhaps James had been under the weather.

'I didn't notice it at the time,' she said thoughtfully. 'But on reflection, James was quieter than he normally is. He didn't suggest our early-morning walks, and he took a longer rest during the afternoons.'

'But, darling, it was freezing cold, and he is an old man.'

'All the more reason to notice changes. And now that I come to think of it, his complexion was quite grey, and sometimes he was irritable with the children.'

'I think we hardly see him often enough to compare.'

'That's the trouble, Luke. When you're with someone constantly, as Elizabeth and the rest of the family are, you aren't aware of anyone gradually changing, but *we* should have been more observant. D'you think we should go to Middlesbrough – or me at any rate?'

'You're panicking, Fran,' Luke said. 'I know you and father seem to have a special relationship, but it may be nothing more than some kind of spasm. Maybe the excitement of Christmas and New Year, seeing young Gordon, which obviously gave him so much pleasure, was a bit too much for him. Let's just wait and see. I'll telephone tomorrow evening when I get in and we'll see how he is then.'

But time ran out for James. At 6.30 the following morning the telephone rang while Luke was in the bathroom. Fran answered it and at first thought no one was there. Then a tearful Elizabeth spoke.

'Oh, Fra-an . . . It – it's Dad. He's gone.'

'Gone?' Fran replied.

'Ye-es, he died at four o'clock this morning. An embolism, the doctor said, probably relating back to when he had that fall at the foundry.'

'Elizabeth!' Fran gasped. 'I'm so sorry – oh, my dear, so *very* sorry. Luke's in the bathroom. Shall I get him to ring you back? It sounds as if he and Gordon are having a high old time. Just give him five or ten minutes.'

Fran dashed upstairs to the bathroom and banged on the door. Shrieks of laughter were coming from inside. Fran guessed that Gordon was probably by now pasted with shaving soap, and it would be all over everywhere as Luke and his young son enjoyed their usual early-morning frivolity.

Fran banged again. 'Luke! *Luke*! Open the door.'

He did and promptly dabbed his shaving brush on Fran's nose.

'What's the rush? I'm not late,' he said.

'Oh, Luke,' Fran said with a trembling voice. 'Elizabeth has just telephoned. It's bad news, I'm afraid.' Fran wiped the soap from her nose. 'Your – your father. He's . . . dead.'

They stood facing each other as if the world had suddenly stopped turning. It was Luke's complexion that was ashen now, and Fran burst into tears as the full realisation hit her. Gordon was still eager to continue his game, but Fran ushered him away, calling to Nanny to take her charge down to breakfast.

'We'll see you in a moment, darling,' Fran said. 'Be a good boy and eat up your breakfast.'

'Father's dead?' Luke echoed. 'Are you sure? Is that what Lizzie actually said? Poor Mother. I shall have to go to her now. But first, I must speak to Liz.'

'I told her you'd telephone back in five minutes. I did call, but you were making such a racket with Gordon.'

Luke was sombre as he dried his face on the towel. 'Wouldn't have made any difference, Fran,' he said as if in a trance. 'If he's dead, he's dead.'

'Hurry up, darling,' Fran said. 'Elizabeth was in such a state. It's you she wants to speak to.'

Later, when Luke put the receiver back in its cradle and turned from the phone, Fran saw a steely look in his eyes. She couldn't identify her husband's reaction to the news, except that it had come as a shock to both of them.

'We must go, of course,' he said solemnly, and the expression changed to one of concern for his mother and sisters.

It was a cold February morning when they boarded the northbound train. Luke, smartly dressed in his heavy naval greatcoat, and Fran, dressed warmly in a thick, black, woollen coat with astrakhan collar and cuffs, both looked strained. They left Gordon behind with Nanny.

'I hate leaving Gordon,' Fran said with moist eyes. 'But it's much too cold, and such a long journey for a small child.'

'It's too sad an occasion for him,' Luke said. They were sitting opposite one another in a first-class compartment. 'He'll be fine with Nanny.'

'James did want to see him grow up. It's such a tragedy that he has passed away so suddenly, and without warning.'

'As you said, my dear, the warnings were probably there, but we didn't see them. Perhaps it's as well. At least he had his family round him for the New Year, which he always enjoyed.'

'And thankfully you were reconciled with them all.'

'Thanks largely to you, I'm sure.' Luke smiled warmly. 'It's good of you to come with me, Fran.'

'Why wouldn't I? I'm your wife.'

'You've been through so much of this kind of thing. It hardly seems fair, darling.'

'I suppose that's the penalty for growing older. We do have to face these unpleasant tasks. No one likes funerals – they're so depressing.'

'That's why we couldn't possibly bring Gordon. It was hard enough for your girls. Being in the same village they couldn't escape – but even you must agree, Fran, they don't seem to have been affected by it too much.'

Fran watched the bleak countryside weaving past as the train clacketty-clacked over the rails.

'Only time will tell whether or not my deserting them has affected them,' she said with a great sigh. 'With the worrying news from Germany, and Europe in general, I feel anxious for all the family. For Ma, in particular. At nearly seventy-eight she shouldn't have to keep house. If there is another war – oh, God forbid . . .'

'We'll cross that bridge when we come to it, Fran. You worry too much. For all your concern over the girls, they haven't come to any harm during these past few years. Kate's working in the kitchen of the hotel, which is what she wanted to do. She's a fine young woman.'

'Yes, she looks well and happy, but never speaks of boyfriends. I'm concerned that her experience with Felix has put her off men for good.'

'I doubt that. She probably wouldn't tell you even if she did have boyfriends. And Ruby seems all right even if she still doesn't like me. You must be proud of the way she's turned out.'

'It doesn't seem possible that she'll be seventeen this year. Henry would be pleased that she did so well at school. It's a relief that she was able to train as a telephonist at the Brimdene telephone exchange. She's the fashion-conscious one. I don't think Henry would be pleased about her cutting her long hair short, though.' Fran had to admit, although only to herself, that Ruby's fair hair, waved and curled, suited her, and probably contributed to the number of boyfriends she obviously attracted.

Hilda had learned self-confidence at the private schools she had attended. She wasn't top academically, but she conversed like a much older girl, and she liked to show off in front of Ruby, which usually ended in conflict when they were together.

Whenever Fran looked at her youngest daughter, though, she was filled with remorse. The fact that Babs felt secure with the Belmonts was small comfort. She had grown into a pretty girl of eleven, who was bright at school and evidently happy in Sherbrook with Sam and Prue. As Luke said, the changes did not seem to have done the girls any real harm. But now uncertain times loomed ahead.

Of late, Fran and Luke had not had time for serious discussion about the family. Gordon was a sturdy little boy. The experience and competence of Norma Marlow enabled Luke and Fran to enjoy a happy social life in the company of other officers and their wives. Fran, like Hilda, had become much more sophisticated and self-confident. She had never dreamed that her marriage to Luke would have become so satisfactory in every way.

He leaned across and placed his hand over hers. 'Didn't I tell you that your girls would grow up and leave the nest eventually? I may have been wrong to force the issue. Perhaps it would have been kinder to wait until they were past school age – I was selfish – but that's all in the past now. You're your own woman, Fran. You've changed so much – you're quite a hit with everyone at social events. And Father adored you.'

Fran dropped her gaze into her lap. She hated the sound of the past tense. She had grown to love James Hammond – why else would she have done what she did? She felt the knot in her stomach tighten. Here, where they were alone, was an opportunity to tell her husband the truth. Life had gone rushing past, giving her time to push the secret into the dark crevices of her brain.

'I owe you so much, Fran, dear,' Luke was saying gently. 'You helped to bind the Hammonds together as a family again. And you've given me the most precious thing I've ever possessed. I really had given up all hope of having a son of my own. And by the woman I love most in the world.'

There was a long silence before Fran said softly: 'You did give Sarita a baby, though. You must have loved her very much.'

'I – I'm afraid I have to admit that I used Sarita. When we were together I imagined that she was you. She merely filled a physical need, Fran.'

'But what became of the child?'

'Her family refused to let me have access to it.'

'Was it a boy or a girl?'

'They wouldn't even tell me that.' Luke gazed out of the window. 'I can hardly believe that at last I have the things most dear to me.'

Fran was surprised to see an almost excited anticipation about Luke's expression. Was it because of Gordon? Or was there an even stronger motive for his eagerness to reach Middlesbrough?

He drew his long, elegant hands round his carefully shaved chin in a gesture of impatience. Then he looked directly at Fran again, his mood warm and brown.

'I lost Sarita and my child in Asia. I came home to discover that I'd lost Lennie too. I felt at times as if I were useless as a man. How could life be so cruel? I had position and financial security, but no family of my own.'

Fran smiled in a meaningless fashion. How could she ever tell Luke the truth about Gordon? She thought that, like his father, he needed a son to carry on the Hammond name, but there was a disturbing thought in the back of her mind that all Luke needed a son for was to inherit some of his father's wealth. Had James been astute enough to realise that fact fully? Fran turned things over and over in her mind, wanting the train journey to end, yet afraid of what was about to be revealed. Suppose James mentioned their little plot in his will? That would surely upset the apple-cart, and Dorinda and Cecilia would have every right to contest any future James had earmarked for Gordon. If Luke found out the truth he would have every right to dissolve his marriage to her and refuse to have anything more to do with Gordon James. It was a sobering thought, which troubled her for the rest of the journey.

All Middlesbrough turned out to bid a last farewell to James Hammond, founder and owner of the vast ironworks, which provided work for many men in the area. In solemn procession they walked behind the funeral cortege, caps in hand, despite the inclement weather. After the church service, followed by interment in the cheerless churchyard, the men returned to the foundry, where they were given refreshment and drink before going to their homes. Work would be resumed the following day.

The family, cold and emotionally numb, were thankful when at last they were behind the closed doors of Hammond House to eat and drink while they talked affectionately of James Hammond, husband and father. Fran sat in the background watching and wondering why, once people fortified themselves with food and wine, they became a different species. Dorinda and her husband flitted from one person to the next, while Cecilia and her husband cosseted Emma Hammond. Elizabeth and Luke were in earnest conversation until different members of the far-reaching Hammond family interrupted. Fran felt the tension grow. No one in her family had either possessions or money to be divided between would-be beneficiaries, so this was yet another new experience for her.

The tension grew until a thick silence fell, and then a middle-aged man entered the room and bowed slightly.

'Good afternoon, everyone. I wonder if I might ask the immediate members of the family to join me in the small sitting room? Mrs Hammond senior – Mrs Emma Hammond, that is.' He offered his arm to Luke's mother, who looked rather dazed as if she wasn't really aware of what was happening. 'Mr and Mrs Luke Hammond,' the solicitor intoned, 'also Miss Elizabeth Hammond, and daughters Dorinda and Cecilia and their respective husbands.'

'Not me,' Fran whispered frantically to Luke. 'I'm not family. I'll stay here.'

'You will be required, Mrs Hammond,' Mr Hindle said, glancing over his shoulder.

Fran had viewed the tension as coming from the others; now she felt it within herself. She took Luke's arm and they followed the solicitor and Luke's mother to the back of the house. The room had a dark atmosphere and looked horribly formal with a long oak table placed in the centre, covered with papers and legal-looking documents. Fran pressed her lips together. James was a wily old devil. What tricks was he going to play on them all? Without realising, she tightened her fingers on Luke's arm. He reacted by placing his other hand over hers, and looked down at her with concern.

A few moments later they were seated in various armchairs spread round the room. A huge fire burned in the grate, yet a chill cut across Fran's back and she shivered involuntarily. Luke let go of her hands and sat forward in his chair almost eagerly. Fran noticed Dorinda watching him and she felt a renewed urgency to escape. She wasn't a Hammond. She had no right to be here.

With solemn expression Mr Hindle untied the bundle of legal documents on the table and opened it out flat. He coughed, and Fran thought it was like watching a film at the cinema.

'This is the last will and testament of James Montague Hammond . . .'

The solicitor's voice droned on monotonously as to James's state of mind when he signed the will, but at last he began the bequests.

'To Emma, my dear wife, I leave Hammond House and an annuity of one hundred and fifty pounds for the rest of her life, as well as 10 per cent of the profits from the foundry.'

Luke leaned forward even more prominently. Fran was somewhat bewildered by the legal jargon, but she understood that Elizabeth now owned a row of cottages in Middlesbrough and would inherit Hammond House after her mother's death. It would then pass to the youngest grandson, Gordon James Hammond. A stifled gasp rippled round the room. All eyes turned towards Fran, and Luke sat back in his chair as if he might be trying to hide from embarrassment.

Subsidiary companies that James owned were left between Dorinda, Cecilia and his only granddaughter, Edna. A small percentage of shares in the foundry were left in trust for the four other grandsons with the proviso that at twenty-one they had served their apprenticeship and continued to work in the foundry.

Seventy-five per cent of the shares in the foundry were left in for Gordon James Hammond if he too worked his way up in the foundry and showed capabilities towards running the ironworks. It took several seconds for this to sink in. Fran dared not look round the company, for she guessed there would be tight lips and long faces.

'Lastly, to Mrs Frances Hammond, a very dear and special friend and daughter-in-law, who has given me the Hammond heir, I leave . . .'

The sum of money was incomprehensible to Fran. She buried her face in her hands as she silently cried, Oh no, James, how could you? How could you do this to me?

Fran sensed the fidgety movements of everyone present. But the eminent solicitor had not yet finished.

'This last bequest is to be passed down to her four daughters in the event of her death. She has suffered greatly at the hands of my son, Luke Hammond, who needlessly lured her away from her girls at a time when they needed her. He also tried to trick me into believing that Fran's children were his offspring in order to gain favour with me. But for young Hilda I might never have learned the truth. Luke chose to desert the family home. I choose to leave all that I have worked a lifetime for to those who have proved themselves to be honest and loyal to me. In order that Luke never again forgets his heritage, I leave a token from the foundry. A brass plate, the last moulding I have cast myself of the family name, HAMMOND, which he may care to display on his front door.'

The air was thick, and then suddenly Dorinda burst out laughing. Her hysterical screams filled the room and no one seemed to know how to react, until Luke stood up. With one long stride he crossed to where Dorinda was seated, lifted his hand and struck her across her left cheek. Giles, Dorinda's husband, counter-reacted by punching Luke straight in the face. Blood gushed from Luke's nose. Elizabeth placed herself between the two men, and Cecilia's husband, Alex, remonstrated, while the stunned Mr Hindle cried in astonishment: 'Gentlemen, *please*!'

Fran caught Luke's sleeve. 'Come to the cloakroom, Luke,' she said. 'Don't make a mess on the carpet.'

'Never mind the carpet,' Mr Hindle said impatiently. 'This is disgusting behaviour from a naval officer. An apology must be made.'

'Do stop it! All of you!' Emma Hammond shrieked in a quivering voice.

Elizabeth rushed to her mother's side and tried to comfort her while the others heatedly disputed the contents of the will.

Fran led Luke away, and in the downstairs cloakroom blotted the blood up with anything she could lay her hands on.

'Get me a brandy,' Luke growled angrily. 'Stop fussing, Fran. It isn't the first time I've had a bloody nose and I don't suppose it'll be the last.'

'I sincerely hope it is,' Fran said. 'You're a grown man, for heaven's sake, not a schoolboy. You're much too old to get involved in brawls.'

'I am not that old!' Luke replied savagely.

'Darling, calm down, you'll give yourself a heart attack,' Fran said.

'It's all right for you.' Luke turned on her aggressively. 'You seem to have come out of this better than anyone. All that money – '

'But it's ours – yours as well as mine, Luke.'

'Didn't hear you properly? I get nothing but a blasted brass plate. As if I should be grateful for being a Hammond.'

'Isn't that why you wanted a son so badly?'

Luke didn't answer but tipped his head back, keeping the wet towel over the bridge of his nose.

Elizabeth came to see how they were getting on. 'It'll soon stop bleeding, Luke,' she said. 'Come on back and sit down. We all need a drink.'

'I suppose you were in on all this?' Luke demanded of his sister.

'Luke, you know Father. He was a law unto himself. Mr Hindle has just told us that he tried to dissuade Father from leaving you out – from playing that mean trick on you – but he was adamant that Gordon was the main beneficiary. It's for his future, Luke, for the future of Hammond's.'

'And to hell with the rest of us except Fran?'

Elizabeth took her brother's arm and led him back to the room where the family were in earnest conversation.

The solicitor called them to order, asking them to be patient while he concluded the business by reading details of certain clauses as to where money and property went in the case of the grandsons not fulfilling their obligations, or predeceasing their parents.

Emma Hammond needed smelling-salts and was escorted to her bedroom by Cecilia, while the others argued passionately.

'Those are the wishes of your father,' Mr Hindle said dryly. 'Of course, there are avenues open to any of you who wish to contest, but it would be a costly business, and I strongly advise against it.'

Luke paced the floor angrily, not defending Fran when the others issued spiteful accusations against her. Even Elizabeth had turned sour.

'I knew father was besotted with you, Fran, but I never thought you'd wangle so much out of him,' she said.

'I did not *wangle* anything out of anyone,' Fran said. 'I didn't – I don't want the money, so go ahead and contest the will.'

'We all know that would be a waste of money,' Alex said. 'The old man did what he wanted to do – set you all against one another – and you're showing yourselves in your true colours.'

'And what have you got to be so damned patronising about?' Luke demanded. 'What did you manage to wheedle out of the old man while he was alive?'

'Nothing!' Cecilia came to her husband's rescue. Alex was a mild-mannered man, seldom ruffled, always pleasant. The furore had sickened him and now, finding himself the butt of Luke's anger, he left the room, pulling his wife behind him.

'I hope you're satisfied.' Dorinda accosted Fran. 'You certainly knew how to play up to a man – just like you did to Luke, I suppose. All this nonsense about deserting your girls – you didn't need much persuading, did you? Well – did you?'

'When I agreed to marry Luke,' Fran said calmly, 'I didn't realise that he meant me to leave the girls to accompany him to Scotland. I know now that I should have stuck to my guns. I should have remained in Brimdene. Then I would not have met any of you, or your father. I don't want anyone else's wealth. I've been hard-working all my life and earned my bread and butter. If this is how wealthy people quarrel among themselves, then I want no part of it – and you're welcome to James's money. When I get it I'll divide it between you – have the lot for all I care.'

'Oh no you don't!' Luke said. 'Father wanted you to have it – and I can see that he wanted an heir so badly that he was besotted with you because you gave him one.'

'You've been away, Luke,' Dorinda said. 'How can you be sure that Gordon is your son?'

Fran felt the colour drain from her cheeks, then flush dark red. Luke stared at her, but eventually said: 'That's a pretty low thing to insinuate, Dorrie. Of course Gordon is our son, and it pleased father that at last he had a Hammond heir.'

Mr Hindle packed up his briefcase. 'Mrs Hammond, I wonder if I might have a word with you before I leave?'

'Can't it be said in front of all of us?' Luke said.

'Um, er – it is just a small private matter. Something that concerns only Mrs Hammond and her legacy.'

'Come on,' Dorinda snapped. 'Let's go and leave them to it. It becomes more obvious by the minute that Fran wormed her way into Father's affections to get what she could – not for Luke but for herself. Funny when you think about it. Luke marries her to help him reinstate himself within the family – to get money, of course. Instead, his wife and son get it all. Rough justice, if you ask me.'

She laughed sardonically and led the way to the large front sitting room, leaving Fran feeling very vulnerable alone with Mr Hindle. He smiled and indicated that she should sit down while he made sure that the door was firmly closed and locked.

'I'm sure it's nothing that my husband shouldn't hear –' Fran began.

'On the contrary, my dear, this must be for your ears alone.

Perhaps you hadn't realised that I had some dealing with the legal matter of the adoption of your son, Gordon James?'

'No. I left it all to James. It was done in rather a rush, which I regretted afterwards.'

'I'm sure you don't now, Mrs Hammond.' Mr Hindle inclined his head with a rare smile. 'James assured me that it was exactly the right thing to do. He was very proud of his grandson, and he knew that Gordon made up in part for much of your unhappy past.'

'He is growing into a fine boy,' Fran said. 'But inheriting into this family is going to make life hard for him in the future. I should have told Luke at the outset, but he's become so passionately fond of Gordon that I haven't had the heart.'

'It'll probably be best if you never tell him. This is why I had to see you alone. James Hammond asked me to keep the adoption papers in my safe, which I have done, but at his death he wanted you to have them. Keep them in a safe place or, better still, deposit them at the bank wherever you live.'

'That's something I hadn't given any thought to. Gordon has a brief birth certificate and we assumed that would be sufficient.'

'It will be for most legal purposes, but someone should have the rights of the case for – shall we say – posterity?'

'I hope Gordon never finds out his true identity. It would be a dreadful shock to him.'

'There's no reason why he should, Mrs Hammond. His parents came from a different part of the country, and you live down south. In years to come, when Gordon comes north to work in the foundry, there should never be any query as to his parentage. I've prepared a copy of the will for each member of the family, and a copy for you separately as there is just one other matter James asked me to divulge in private to you.' He watched the expression on Fran's face. 'James had the notion that you may at some time in the future wish to leave your husband.'

'Leave Luke?' Fran exclaimed. 'Why should he have that idea?'

'Maybe there was a conversation between you – some hint that you were not happy, perhaps?'

Fran lowered her gaze and tried to recall some of the many intimate conversations she'd had with her father-in-law. She was weary of the day's events. The day which should have been solemn, leaving happy memories of James Hammond; instead it had ended in disharmony. She wished James had consulted her about his intentions. He could easily have done during their walks and quiet moments together. Then she remembered. She had told him once that she would have left Luke if she could have afforded to. That was all so long ago.

'There was a time when we first went to Scotland,' she admitted. 'I don't suppose I was really serious, though. Evidently James thought I was.'

'He knew the extent of family discord his will would evoke. He probably guessed that Luke might turn against you, so he thought, if he left a substantial sum to you, it would leave you in a position to live independently of your husband, should you wish to – and you'll have sufficient to keep yourself, Gordon and your girls in reasonable comfort for the rest of your life.'

'It's most generous of James. But,' Fran sighed, 'I do wish he hadn't left any money to me. It should, by right, be Luke's, and I'm pleased to say that since Luke came home we have lived most harmoniously. Gordon has made all the difference to us. My own girls – well, they don't need me now in quite the way I assumed they would.'

Mr Hindle smiled again, this time with a hint of sympathy. 'A lesson perhaps that we are all dispensable.'

'I suppose a mother does not like having to admit that,' Fran said. She put the papers the solicitor handed her away in her bag. 'I'm quite overwhelmed by what has happened today. I must contact you in the near future when the shock of James's death has lessened a little, and perhaps you would draw up some kind of agreement that half of the money is to be transferred to Luke, or at least put into a joint account.'

Mr Hindle shook his head. 'I'm not at liberty to do that. The money is yours and yours alone – to secure a financial future for yourself and your girls, mainly. Mr Hammond senior foresaw your generous intentions, and made a clause to the effect that it must remain under the jurisdiction of the trustee.'

'But if it's my money, why can't I use it any way I want?'

'Because much of it is in securities, only to be released by agreement with the trustee – who happens to be me and, in the event of my death, my partner and his son. You can draw substantial amounts at any time which, of course, you may share with your husband. But Mr James Hammond was well aware of his son's – I don't like to use the word greed, but . . . Believe me, Mrs Hammond, your father-in-law was most particular in every detail of his wishes, and there is no way round it.'

Fran bade the solicitor goodbye and went in search of Luke. The sitting room was empty. Upstairs in their room she found him lying on his back on the bed, hands clasped behind his head.

'Well,' he said sarcastically, 'what was all that about?'

'Just to explain how I can withdraw money. It seems to be very much tied up. I wanted him to transfer it to a joint account, but it's mostly securities or something, and held in trust.'

'In other words, if you wanted to share it with me you can't?'

'Something like that. Oh, Luke, it's all so horrible! So mercenary,' Fran said, flinging her bag on the chair. 'I don't want your father's money.'

'Then why did he think you did?'

'I suppose it was his way of saying thank you for Gordon.'

'But he's left him better off than anyone else. Why you as well?'

Fran sat down heavily in the chair on top of her bag. She retrieved it and put it away at the bottom of the wardrobe, remembering the secret that was hidden inside.

'When are we going home?' she asked.

'Got what you came for so now we can leave the others to it, I suppose,' Luke said unkindly.

'That's not fair, Luke. I never knew about the money or how your father was going to share his wealth. I liked him as a man. We understood each other and we got on well together.'

Suddenly Luke got off the bed and gripped Fran's arm. 'They tell me he was always going off to Craiglee to stay with you. They also say that you came to Middlesbrough and stayed in a hotel with him? Now, tell me that isn't true? Tell me who Gordon's father really is?' His eyes narrowed, his grip tightened and he looked at Fran as if he despised her.

'What on earth are you suggesting?' she said. 'Luke! You're as bad as the rest of the family – cold, calculating, scheming –'

'And some might well think those things of you, Fran. My father was not renowned for his generosity or liberality towards others – women in particular.'

'Then you didn't know him very well. He saw you all for what you were. He was kind, very kind to those in need. He was caring, too, in his own way. We had things in common: the loss of our children. He understood my grief, my concern for my girls. He was far more understanding than you've ever been. I thought you were changing, Luke – had changed – since Gordon was born.'

'So you went to my father's bed in order to satisfy an old man's lust? To satisfy an old man's whim of having a Hammond heir? Strange that he should be successful where I failed.'

Luke twisted Fran's arm behind her back and forced her body against his. She could feel his strength – a strength of rage in his belief that she had committed adultery, and that his father had tricked him. She gave no thought to the consequences as fear made her shriek: 'All right – so I'll tell you the truth. You failed because my time for child-bearing has long been over. I have been faithful to you, Luke Hammond, but you bring out the very worst in everyone. You can believe what you like of me and your father. We were friends – real friends – with trust in one another, which is more than can be said for the rest of your family. James didn't trust any of you except your mother. But there was never any question of us having an affair, or of me knowing what he had left to anyone. I didn't even know that he had property and money, and I certainly didn't want any of it. But you won't believe that because you were so desperate to get what you considered was your birthright.'

'So why the secrecy in meeting in a hotel? And if you couldn't have children, where did Gordon come from? Answer me, damn you, answer me!'

'Stop it, Luke. stop it! I'm trying to tell you the truth.'

'That Father went off with some whore to have a child for us to bring up as his grandson and heir? God, Fran – have you stooped that low?'

'Your father visited me at Craiglee. He became interested in the orphanage and just before Hilda and I were due to go to Southsea this baby came to us. I got very attached to him, knowing the facts of his parentage and the tragedy surrounding his birth, but it was James who suggested that we adopt him.'

'We?'

'James dealt with all the legal matters, but the actual adoption is in my name. Gordon is my legal son. Our son, and I meant to tell you, but you were so overboard, so obsessed with the fact that he was our baby. He made you so happy, how could I refute it, Luke?'

Luke's face was dark with disbelief. Ugly with thoughts of revenge. Fran went to get her bag to show him proof, but Luke wasn't interested.

'The wicked old devil,' he said. 'He was far more cunning than me. And you deceived me. Between you, you connived and schemed against *me* – your own husband!'

'It wasn't like that, Luke. If you'll just calm down we can talk about this sensibly. James didn't want anyone else to know. There still isn't any reason for your family to know.'

Luke ran his hand over his head in fierce frustration. He beat one fist into the other palm and then he turned on Fran once more.

'And you hadn't better ever tell anyone. What a fool this makes me! What a complete idiot – to think I actually believed that you had borne me a son. God! I could . . . I could . . .'

'Kill me? Oh, Luke, sometimes you behave worse than any of my girls. If anything should ever happen to me, everyone will know the truth then.'

Luke sat down in the nearest chair and sobbed.

Fran looked on helplessly, realising that he had lost face, that his pride was hurt. That once more Luke Hammond had not got one over on his father. And what hurt most of all was that his wife had reaped the rewards of his furtive efforts.

The atmosphere at Hammond House was too explosive for them to remain. After a visit to Mr Hindle's office, where Luke received confirmation of the adoption and was satisfied that all had been executed legally, they travelled down to York and then caught the night train to King's Cross.

When they reached Southsea the following day, Luke packed his belongings and went back to his ship. He refused to see Gordon and said no more than was important to Fran.

Fran took to her bed, exhausted from all the recent events and lack of sleep, and with a monstrous headache.

She had lost face with her girls, Luke had lost face by his father's cunning, and now they had lost faith in each other.

Chapter Twenty

Fran found it difficult to believe that James's family had behaved so badly after his sudden death. She wished with all her heart that he had not left her such a vast sum of money. Just when the family appeared united he had created a bigger rift than ever before, and she felt responsible. She couldn't imagine what the outcome might be, but she disliked the idea of Luke being away at sea, especially in the shadow of impending war, and not on speaking terms with her. She tried to write to him, but after several unsuccessful attempts gave up the idea. James had every right to share his wealth any way he wanted to, but with her help he had cheated his family. It made the blood rush to her cheeks even to think of it. She experienced a measure of guilt that he had found in her a willing ally to his scheming. What was it about the Hammond men that they could persuade her so easily to do their bidding? She spent many unhappy hours sitting miserably in the armchair in her bedroom thinking by bygone days. Tears were ever ready to fall steadily down her cheeks. She was unable to share her burden with anyone, and yet she desperately needed to talk to someone.

'What would you do, Henry? Pa?' Instead of looking ahead at all that her fortune could provide, Fran found herself looking back at the mistakes she had made. She couldn't seem to find answers to her problems, and although there were times when she wished she had never set eyes on Luke Hammond and his wretched family, she still loved and missed him. Even more so since they had enjoyed an especially happy relationship over the past two years, both together and with Luke's family. She supposed she had enjoyed a sense of false security once Luke had accepted Gordon as his own, never anticipating James's death. How stupid she had been! Her own commonsense should have warned her that James would not live for ever.

Fran found it incredible that James obviously did not want Luke in the foundry after his death. No one could question that it was Luke's birthright, but for some reason James could not forgive his son for running away to sea. She despised herself now for being party to a mean conspiracy. She wished there was some way she could make it up to Luke, but he knew that his father would have done everything to protect Fran's interest. It was all so hateful! Her only problem with money had been the lack of it, until she married Luke. Now, thanks to James, she had enough to live comfortably and see that her girls were well provided for. That was what James had wanted for her.

Fran stood up suddenly and gazed down the deserted street, seeing four happy young girls in her mind's eye. Yes, that was what James had intended: that she should go back to Brimdene to take her rightful place as mother. She could make her own decisions now. Hadn't the solicitor said that James had indicated that at some time in the future she might wish to leave her husband? 'Oh, dear God!' she cried. 'But I don't, I *don't*!'

Fran paced the floor for what seemed like hours. She ate little, slept even less, her mind in total confusion, and this continued for several days.

Nanny brought Gordon to her every evening at five o'clock and that was the only time she managed to come back into the real world.

Even Hilda gave up trying to discuss anything with her mother. She finally yelled one day that she wanted to spend the Easter holidays with one of her school friends.

'You don't seem to hear anything I say, Mum,' she said as patiently as she could. 'I know you're upset about Daddy being away at sea, and old Mr Hammond gone, but any other time you'd be getting ready to go to Brimdene, and I'd rather not go with you this time.'

Fran blinked at her daughter. 'Well, you're coming with me. We're going back to Brimdene – for good.'

Hilda stared in shocked disbelief.

'W-we – we can't to that, Mum,' Hilda said. 'There's school. Daddy went to great lengths to get me into this grammar school. It would be letting him down.'

'What's the difference between one school and another, Hilda?' Fran braced herself, feeling much more confident. 'James Hammond left me some money, which he wanted me to use wisely. Not only for myself, but to help make up to all of you for – well – losing your own father. Being separated, leaving Gran to take care of things in

Brimdene.' Weakness prevented her from continuing and she rushed away to her bedroom, where she lay on the huge double bed and cried away her guilt and regret. She couldn't turn the clock back, but she could endeavour to make amends. Wasn't Easter a time of passion and sorrow, to be followed by great rejoicing at the resurrection?

The Rudgwicks and Nanny Marlow weren't able to hide their relief that Fran was emerging from what they thought was a period of deep mourning for her father-in-law. If they noticed an absence of letters from abroad, they chose not to comment upon it – after all, the country was expecting a war, and yet people seemed hell-bent on having as good a time as they could before their lives were turned upside down. Perhaps their mistress was going to make the best of the way things were.

'I don't know when I'll be back – *if* I'll be back,' Fran said. 'Nanny, you can return here with Hilda after the holiday, but I shall try to place her in a school in Brimdene in readiness for the new September term. My mother is seventy-eight and I should be there to look after her now. I want us to be all together if there's going to be a war.'

'Will Captain Hammond return here, Ma'am, or to Brimdene?' Edie Rudgwick asked hesitantly.

'I dare say he'll come here when his ship docks,' Fran said. 'If he wants to see us he'll have to come to Brimdene – but I'm sure he'll agree that Brimdene is likely to be a safer place than here. I expect you'll want to discuss your future with him, but if he doesn't come home for some time, then I suggest you think of going to the country, too.'

Their expressions registered surprise. They had never known any discord within the family. Mrs Hammond had been easy to work for and mild in manner, but now she was showing unusual decisiveness. They put it down to the worry of her husband being on the high seas, and made allowances for the obvious anxiety caused by the daily news of gloom on the continent and elsewhere.

They felt somewhat sad as they helped with the packing of cases and trunks, and there was much speculation about their own future employment. By the time Hilda broke up from school, Betty, the housemaid, had been given a month's notice, and Nanny Marlow informed Fran that she would probably try to join the WRENS if she was no longer required to look after Gordon by the autumn.

'Everything is uncertain at present,' Fran said. 'I'd like to have you stay with us in Brimdene, Nanny, but there just isn't enough room. Besides, I shan't be short of helpers when I get settled in at home.' She sighed. 'I've been away too long. I've neglected my girls and now I must work towards getting the family reunited.'

The Rudgwicks were sorry to say goodbye, especially to little Gordon, who was a happy child and fresh as a summer breeze. They admitted to having been in something of a rut before the new Mrs Hammond had come to Southsea. For the past two years, though, there had been laughter and life in the house. Where young Hilda was concerned you never knew what to expect, and when Mrs Hammond's mother and other daughters came to stay there had been plenty of extra work, but an abundance of fun as well. They waved the family off and watched the taxi until it turned the corner out of sight. Sidney Rudgwick placed his arm round his wife's shoulder as she dabbed at her eyes with her handkerchief.

'There's something not quite right, if you ask me,' he said slowly. 'Can't put me finger on it, but there's changes afoot.'

'Change all right,' Edie retorted. 'A blinkin' war. Goodness knows where we'll all end up – dead, I shouldn't wonder.'

Sidney tried to comfort his wife. He just wished the master would turn up, and jolly quick too. He had a nasty feeling in his bones that the mistress had left Southsea without her husband's knowledge, and Captain Hammond didn't like folk doing things on the sly. Still, there was nothing he could do. Mrs Hammond seemed in a very determined frame of mind.

Ma and Ruby stood and looked at the huge amount of luggage that was plonked in the hall by the taxi driver. He touched his cap politely at Fran's generous tip, then she closed the door after him.

'Well,' she said at last, 'it's nice to be home – and for good.'

'For good?' Ma echoed.

'You mean you aren't going back to Southsea? Ever?' Ruby said.

'I don't know about never, dear, but for the foreseeable future we're home to stay.'

The announcement was received with polite silence. Gordon ran off to find the toys that the girls always kept at hand for him to play with, and Hilda picked up her bag and carried it into the living room.

'Just when I'd really got used to the school,' she grumbled to Ruby, who seemed to be looking to her for an explanation.

'Why? What's happened?' Ruby asked wide-eyed.

'We've just come home,' Fran said, as if they should have known it had only been a matter of time. 'If there is going to be a war, we should all be together.' She burst into a flood of tears as she hugged Ma closer to her.

Gran Brown seemed perplexed by the news, and Ruby felt as if the war had already begun. Fran was too tired to explain the whys and wherefores of her decision. There was time enough to give account of her actions when they were all together. And this time she meant *all* together. She had contacted Prue and Sam, requesting that Babs come to Brimdene to spend some of the holiday with the family. Now it was with trepidation that she opened the envelope propped up in front of the clock on the mantelpiece. She recognised Prue's handwriting. Inside were two Easter cards, one from Prue, Sam and Marion, and the other a hand-drawn one from Babs.

Prue's note was short but to the point, saying that Babs had reluctantly agreed to visit for a couple of days during Easter week, but she was adamant that she should remain in Sherbrook to take part in the Easter pageant which was to take place in the church there. Fran pursed her lips. More than anything she wanted to go to Sherbrook herself. Her mind was set on finding out if there was a vacant cottage anywhere in the area. In her heart she knew she was being optimistic, for there was never enough accommodation for farmworkers as it was. If trying to return to the life she had known before Luke was a means to getting the girls back, then she must do it. She was desperate to make everything right again. If Babs wouldn't come to Brimdene to settle then she – they – must all go back to Sherbrook.

When Fran laid her head on the pillow in the familiar bed in the front bedroom, she knew she was searching for an impossible redemption. She lay awake for hours listening to noises which were strange to her now after five years away. The groaning chains on the grandfather clock, the whirring mechanism and the constant chimes every quarter of an hour. She could hardly believe the way life had changed. Inevitably they had all changed too, so what was the point of trying to regain favour within her family unit? But try she must, and she hoped that James's legacy might tip the balance.

Over the bank holiday period the girls accepted Fran just as if it were any other holiday. They went to church on Easter Sunday, and afterwards visited the other grandparents and Aunt Sissy. Nathan, Laura and the cousins all came to tea on another occasion, but Fran made light of the fact that she had come home for good. They all gawped at her in astonishment, and she suspected that they thought she and Luke had quarrelled. No doubt they assumed that when the rift was patched up she would be off again with her husband. Fran was genuinely disappointed that they didn't trust her. She realised that not only had she lost face with her girls, but that they too were now suspicious of anything she might do or say.

It was a cold, wet and windy day when Prue and Sam arrived with Babs. They stayed for a meal before returning to Sherbrook.

'It'll be quiet without Marion and Babs,' Prue said with an awkward laugh. 'Marion doesn't need us now. She likes to go places by herself, or at least with friends of her own age.'

'She's settled and happy in her job?' Fran asked.

'We didn't like her having to cycle into Blandford every day, Fran, as you'll appreciate,' Prue said. 'But she's eighteen now and you have to let them learn their independence some time.'

Fran knew they were reminding her of the trouble Kate had got into, cycling along the lonely road from Blandford station to Sherbrook when she was eighteen.

'We must be satisfied that she's got a good job in the offices of the Town Hall,' Sam said. 'And you must be very proud of your Ruby doing so well at the telephone exchange.'

'I still feel guilty at leaving them,' Fran said. 'But maybe it gave them the chance to grow up and prove themselves.'

'It isn't going to be quite so simple with Babs,' Prue said. 'She says she wants to stay in Sherbrook with her friends.'

'I shan't pressurise her at all, Prue,' Fran said. 'I just want to talk to them – if only to try to make them understand why I did what I did.'

Sam laid a gentle, understanding hand on Fran's arm. 'You did what you thought was best at the time,' he said. 'Everything is all right between you and Luke?'

Fran sighed. 'Things are a little strained since Luke's father died. He's worried about the war, too – like everyone else – and at present I don't even know where he is. With things in the world the way they are, I just made my own decision, and that's to be where my girls are.'

Prue and Sam nodded their assent and very soon went on their way, leaving Fran to reacquaint herself with her youngest daughter, now eleven years old. Gordon was besotted with Babs, and it seemed to Fran that when Hilda was in the company of younger children, she lost some of her pretentiousness, and all three were soon playing lively games.

After dinner, Ma went to her room to rest, and Gordon had his nap too. Fran watched the clock. Kate was due home at about four o'clock, and Ruby finished work at six. The hour of reckoning was drawing closer, and she began to feel nervous. Nervous! she thought. Of her own girls? She tried in vain to put her thoughts into words but her head started to ache with the mental struggle. She would have to play it by ear.

It was gone five o'clock when Kate walked in. She hugged her mother affectionately and was soon making tea. Fran marvelled at her efficiency. Her lovely hair had grown darker and was almost chestnut colour now. It was plaited and wound round her head in a very neat style, suitable for the work she did in the hotel catering trade. She had brought some scones with her and some leftover steak-and-kidney pie. 'Are you allowed to do that, Kate?' Fran asked.

'I didn't pinch it, if that's what you're thinking, Mum,' Kate said indignantly. 'It's been kept in the big fridge at work, but it can't be served to the guests. I made the scones myself specially to bring home. My boss knows I like to cook for the family sometimes, and it's quite all right. They're very good to us, aren't they, Gran?'

Kate had matured and was quite the businesswoman. As well as doing her catering and book-keeping studies at night school and working in the hot kitchens by day, it appeared that she also managed the home. Fran's guilt magnified. She felt as if she were an outsider, but she vowed she would make it up to them. From the kitchen window she could see Kate's old 'sit and up and beg' type of bicycle propped up against the wall outside. She would use some of James's money to buy her a new one. A nice modern one with three gears and a dynamo light. Never again would she have to walk lonely lanes because her lights had failed.

Ruby arrived home from work soon after Kate had made the tea. They were all sitting round the table enjoying the pie when Kate said: 'How long are you staying, Mum?'

'Mummy and Gordon are staying for good,' Hilda announced. 'I'm going back to Southsea with Nanny. I jolly well hope you can't get me into a school here. I like living in Southsea.'

Kate's fork was poised halfway to her mouth. She stared across at her mother. 'You've come home for good?'

'Yes, dear. You always knew it was only a temporary separation because of Luke's work in the Royal Navy.'

'Where is he now, then?' Ruby asked.

'At sea, of course, and goodness knows when he'll get home if this wretched war starts.'

'Well, I don't want to come back here to live,' Hilda said.

'I'm afraid you'll have to do whatever's best. The grammar school here is very good, and there's talk of evacuation anyway.'

'Too posh for us now, I suppose?' Ruby taunted her sister. 'I don't know that we want you here.'

'That's enough, you two. We'll have a talk after tea.' Fran decided she had better call a halt to the conversation for the present, and as soon as tea was over she prepared Gordon for bed. Usually the girls were all eager to assist her, but tonight they seemed to prefer to help Gran with the washing-up.

There was tension in the room when she returned downstairs. Ruby was sitting at the dining table in front of a mirror, painting her lips with red lipstick.

'I don't think your father would like to see you doing that, Ruby,' Fran admonished. 'And it looks to me as if you've been bleaching your hair. It always looked so pretty before. Daddy would be vexed.'

'He'd be more vexed at the way you left us all,' Ruby snapped. Her eyes burned with defiance. 'And if you think you can bring your husband here to live, then I shall leave home for good.'

'That's no way to speak of Luke,' Fran said. 'He's been good to us all, providing you with a home.'

'And taking you away – as far away as possible, it seemed to us.'

Fran paused, pain in her expression as she looked at her rebellious daughter.

'I – I wanted to talk . . . I need to explain that I didn't intend to leave you all in the lurch. It was the hardest thing I've ever done in my life, but I doubt that any of you can understand how difficult things were getting here. It was a real job to make the money go round.'

'We've managed, Mum,' Kate said. 'That's all over and done with now.'

'But I shouldn't have left you at Sherbrook, Kate. I'm sorry about that – it must have been awful for you.'

'Not as awful as it was for Gran and me here, having to do everything,' Ruby snapped. 'And when other parents went to things at school I had no one. You might as well have been dead – the same as Dad!'

'That's a hateful thing to say,' Hilda yelled at Ruby.

'It's all right for you – she made sure you weren't left behind. You've had the best of everything,' Ruby said.

'No, I haven't. Luke made me feel special to begin with, and I liked him, but they soon got fed up with me around so I had to go away to school. Miles away to Aberdeen where I didn't know anyone at all. At least you and Kate had Gran, and Babs was happy enough with Aunt Prue and Uncle Sam.'

'No, I wasn't,' Babs said in a soft tone. 'I hated it at first. I cried myself to sleep every night, and Auntie Prue got cross because I wanted to sleep in their bed all the time.'

'Then you'll be pleased to be back with me and your sisters, darling?' Fran said.

Babs sat on the edge of her chair, her two palms together as she rubbed her hands slowly back and forth in the crease of her warm dress, between her knees.

'It . . . it isn't that I don't love you all, Mummy, and Auntie Prue and Uncle Sam.' She glanced up at Fran, liquid fear in her big brown eyes. Fran remembered that Luke would have been happy to have Copperknob accompany them to Scotland, but she had chosen Hilda at the expense of Henry's Babe. Fran's heartbeat thumped against the wall of her chest. She felt that at any moment she might stop breathing, but Babs went on falteringly: 'But – but my home is in Sherbrook, and I don't want to live anywhere else.'

'Prue tells me that you want to be a nurse like her when you're old enough. You've got to have had a good education for that, Babs. I thought that maybe you'd like to go to the grammar school here with Hilda?'

'I might not pass the scholarship,' Babs said.

'That doesn't matter. Luke's father left me some money when he died and I can afford to pay for your education now.' Fran hesitated. 'That's if you'd like to. Maybe you can think about it. If you like you could live here during school termtime and go to stay with Prue and Sam in the holidays?'

Babs glanced at her mother, tears threatening. 'But you might go away again and – and I couldn't bear that.' She burst out crying.

'Now see what you've done,' Ruby accused. 'We were all right as we were. We had to be, because you didn't care – and Daddy would have hated you for what you did. Money won't make up for it either. You can't just walk out on us one minute and come back the next as if nothing has happened.'

'How dare you speak to Mummy like that?' Hilda shouted. 'You don't know what she's had to put up with. It wasn't easy for her – and there have been times when she's been unhappy too.'

'Serves her right for going off with that man,' Ruby shouted. 'He was much more important than us. She never liked *me* anyway.'

'Then we'd best go on back to Southsea, Mum,' Hilda said triumphantly. 'They don't want us here – Ruby said so.'

'Ruby! Oh, dear Ruby, it wasn't that I didn't like you, darling,' Fran pleaded. 'You and me – well, I suppose we're alike in some ways. I know I was too hard on you, but you were always the obstinate one, and I had to correct you. I'm sorry if I ever gave you the impression that I didn't like you. I love you. I love all of you very much. You're Henry's girls as well as mine.'

'Then you know how angry Daddy would have been at you getting married again to that – that *sailor*! I don't want you and Hilda coming back here and ruining my life.'

Gran Brown had listened to the rumpus without interfering. Now she stood up, slightly tottering, and said clearly: ' "Honour thy father and thy mother that thy days may be long upon the land which the Lord thy God giveth thee." That's what the Bible says, and you girls had better just think about that. I'm ashamed of you, Ruby. Your mother had a difficult decision to make five years ago. She did what she thought was best for all of you and a lot of thanks she's getting. You'll know when you get married and have babies of your own how hard life can be – cruel too. Bad enough to lose Lennie, then to lose her father and husband on one day – you may feel hurt, what d'you think your poor mother felt?'

'Oh, Ma!' Fran cried, burying her face in her hands on the table. 'I know I did wrong. I shouldn't have married again so soon. I should have kept us all together however poor we were. I was weak where Luke was concerned. I let him persuade me. I didn't want to split up my family – I never meant to treat you all so shamefully.' She wept uncontrollably, unaware that Ma had made her way out of the room.

'I'm sorry – all of you. I'm dreadfully sorry,' Fran wailed. 'Please at least try to forgive me. I'm sure Daddy would have done. Wherever he is, I feel that he understands. You can't know how I've hated myself. The anguish of knowing how I deserted you . . .'

Ruby rushed to her mother. 'I didn't mean all those nasty things, Mum. Really I didn't. It would be lovely to be all together again. But Luke will come and take you away – I just know he will – and I hate him!' She buried her face in her mother's neck and cried loudly as only Ruby could.

'No, no!' Fran said. 'I promise you that I'll never go away again unless you want me to. The money Luke's father left me has given me independence, freedom if I want it.'

'You mean you've left Luke?' Ruby asked.

'No, but I'm in a position now where I can choose where I want to be, and that's here with my girls. You're so special to me – more now than ever before. We've all got such happy memories of Daddy, we must never do anything that he wouldn't approve of. We can't be sure what the future holds but we must all stick together. Gran's getting old, and it's my job to care for her now.'

'And we'll all help with Gordon,' Babs said. She had been crying quietly. Now she went to Fran and put two arms tightly round her mother's neck. 'I love you best of all, Mum,' she whispered.

'And I really won't mind too much if I have to go to school here,' Hilda said condescendingly.

Fran dried her eyes. 'Put the kettle on, Hilda,' she said.

No one had noticed that Kate was missing until she collided with Hilda at the door.

'Here's a cup of tea, Mum. I've taken one up to Gran – she's pretty upset too.'

'I'll go to her. I just want you all to know that I'll always want to be a part of your life, wherever you go. You're all growing up and you'll go your own ways, but I hope you'll want to come home sometimes, and look upon me as your friend.' Fran stood up quickly. Drying the deluge of tears away as she went, she hurried to her mother's room.

Ma was standing by the window. There was no light in the room save for the moonlight, which made a pale beam across the uncurtained window.

Fran placed her arm round her mother's shoulders. 'Ma? You've never condemned me for what I did – and I must have hurt you most of all.'

'I'm an old woman, my dear. When Henry was taken you were in the prime of life. You deserved better than a life of mean drudgery, and that's all I wanted for you – happiness. The girls may feel insecure now. They're frightened, and you can't blame them for worrying that you might up and leave them again. But they're old enough now to understand a bit of what you went through.'

'But you've suffered too – it was so thoughtless of me, Ma. How can I ever expect you to forgive me?'

'There's nothing to forgive, Fran dear. But I fancy there might be some forgiveness needed where you and Luke are concerned. You said in your letters that he was upset because his father left you a legacy and not him?'

Fran briefly explained the details of the will to her mother.

'James knew that I had seriously considered leaving Luke when he insisted that Hilda be sent away to boarding school, but I had no money of my own. I don't mean that Luke kept me short exactly, but I reckon he knew what was in my mind. It was a risk he couldn't take by being over-generous. My loyalties were divided, but I stuck it out, and everything changed when James had his accident. James left me the money so that if I wanted my freedom I could have it.'

'And do you, Fran? Want your freedom? Or is Luke coming here to live?'

'He'll come here. He'll have to if he wants to share his father's money. He can only get any through me.' She sighed and gave Ma a squeeze. 'No, Ma, I don't want to be free of Luke. He's got his faults the same as the next man, the same as me, but I do love him. Like father, like son – they're both lovable rogues. But,' she added solemnly, 'I'll be stronger from now on. Heaven knows I thought I was fairly strong-minded before, but now, if – *when* Luke turns up again he'll come to me on my terms. I know where my duty lies, and firstly it's to you and the girls. I know I've got to earn their love and respect. I must try to persuade them to at least listen to my point of view. It was awful hearing their accusations against me, and they were all true. I know I've been utterly ruthless and selfish. I can understand why Ruby hates Luke – because she loved Henry so much. Tomorrow we'll begin again. And I must begin by making a confession to Kate.'

'A confession, Mum – to me – why?'

Fran turned in surprise. She thought she was alone with Ma. She kissed her mother's cheek. 'Night, Ma, sleep well.' With her arm round Kate's waist she ushered her out of the room and they went along to Kate's small bedroom, where they sat side by side on the bed.

'When you were so ill, dear, Maurice did write to you. I did a terrible thing, my Katie, and burnt his letter. You see, I really thought it was he who had raped you, and I could never forgive him for that. If only I had waited! It was all a misunderstanding, Kate – I did it because I couldn't bear your hurt.'

'That's all in the past, Mum, and anyway, I've seen Maurice when I visited Sherbrook to see Babs. We had a long talk. He said he'd written. I told him that I'd waited ages on the station for him to come to Brimdene. We soon realised that something had gone wrong and I guessed that you might have intercepted his letter.' Kate laughed. 'It was our first love, Mum. We've both changed and our feelings have cooled. Men only seem to want one thing so I'm concentrating on my work. I'm glad you're back – I just want us all to be happy.'

They hugged each other warmly. 'We will be, Kate. We'll go back to being a house full of women,' Fran said.

'We'll never be that again, Mum. Don't leave Gordon out – and when Luke comes home we'll give him the best welcome he's ever had.'

Three weeks went by while Fran settled down with the family in Brimdene, but no word came from Luke. She wished she could visit him, but his ship was on the high seas somewhere. Military establishments, airfields and dockyards were all under strict security. Everyone was issued with gas masks – war was becoming more than a threat, it was imminent. Fran couldn't bear the thought that something might happen to Luke without a reconciliation between them. She decided it was time to act.

When everyone else had gone to bed one evening she sat at the kitchen table and began to pen the words that had been going round in her head for the past few weeks.

> 'My dearest Luke, she began.
> I am writing from Brimdene, which is where I want to be with my girls and Ma. It is my duty to be here now in these troubled times, and safer for Gordon too. I can hardly believe you went away without so much as a goodbye, especially to Gordon, and no word since. I miss you terribly, darling, and need you. Please forgive me for my part in the deception. I meant to tell you about Gordon's adoption, I tried to, but you made it so difficult. James was very persuasive, and I only agreed because of your obsession that Lennie was yours. I know you think I cheated you, and I'm sorry. Surely it was worth it to have a lovely little boy like Gordon to bear your name? He misses you and asks every day when you are coming home. I nursed him from the tiniest mite and he has always seemed like ours. You thought of him as ours too.

Fran paused to wipe away a tear of regret. Not regret at having adopted Gordon, but regret that such a letter as this was necessary. She went on:

> We've both made mistakes, Luke! You can't deny that you deceived and used me. Isn't it time to forgive and forget? Surely we can come together with mutual contrition now? I want you to try to understand how important it is for me to atone for deserting the girls and Ma. I left them for you, darling, as well as for my own selfish reasons, after those two dreadful years following Henry's death. Your father realised how necessary it was for me to return to Brimdene, and, bless him, he made it possible, though I swear I had no idea prior to his death.
>
> But I want our marriage to continue as it was in the best of times. Can't you see how much I need your help to rear Gordon and prepare him for a future in the foundry? It's so long since Lennie died, but the pain never quite goes away. Never in my wildest dreams did I ever expect to be given a second chance, not only to have the support of a loving husband but to bring

up a son just as I would have brought up Lennie. But I can't do it alone, darling.

Please write to us if you are able. The girls are ready to accept you now. They send their love and pray for your safety just as I do. Hilda's school is being evacuated to Brimdene so it seems sensible to remain here all together, a house full of women again, except for Gordon. We hope that it won't be too long before the empty chair at the head of the table is occupied by you.

The next day Fran posted her letter with renewed hope.

The waiting seemed interminable. Still no news as the gloomy clouds of war darkened the summer sky.

Fran was standing at the kitchen window one afternoon watching Gordon playing with a box cart on wheels which Nathan had made for him. Ma was having her rest, and Fran decided it would be pleasant to take Gordon to the nearby park before meeting Babs from school.

The sound of the doorbell echoed through the hall and she wondered who it could be. The postman? Rather late for him, but maybe a telegram? She found herself clutching at the front of her dress as she willed herself to go to the door. She couldn't see anyone through the glass panel. Cautiously she opened the door a crack, then wider when the porch appeared to be empty. Was it Babs home early from school, playing one of her tricks?

But it was Luke who bobbed into view. As ever his dark eyes were mischievous, and then warm with love and longing as he dropped his suitcase and gathered her into his outstretched arms.

'Luke, Luke! You're suffocating me,' Fran protested, even though she was loath to break free.

Luke drew back an inch or so, looking down at her with an intensity that made her gasp.

'Darling,' he breathed. 'I've been a fool! Such foolish pride – which only caused both of us needless pain.' He hugged her close to him. 'I love you so much . . .' He kissed her passionately, and they clung together with wild abandonment right there in the porch for the world to witness. 'Out there with nothing but miles of ocean to look at gave me time to think,' he said huskily. 'Time to come to my senses and realise what I had left behind – what I might lose if this war can't be avoided.'

Fran felt choked. Stunned by this unforgettable moment of reunion.

'Come inside, for goodness sake,' she said after several seconds.

As they closed the front door, Gordon came running through the hall.

'Daddy! Daddy! You're back, you're back!' With a whoop Luke swung the excited boy up into his arms, kissing him and hugging him. At the sound of a slight movement he let him slither to the floor as he saw Babs shyly watching the reunion. Luke didn't wait for her reaction but hurried to embrace her too.

Fran felt a moment's jealousy at the attention Luke showed the girls as each one arrived home for tea, and when she went to the kitchen to help Ma prepare the meal she was sure she saw tears trickling down her mother's cheeks. Luke joined them and stood with an arm round each of them.

'It's great to be home,' he said with an emotional sigh.

'If only there wasn't going to be a war,' Ma said despondently.

'But it hasn't started yet, Ma, and we aren't going to even think about that for the next few days,' Luke said, giving her an affectionate squeeze.

He took his place at the head of the table. Already Gordon had his two small hands together in readiness for grace to be said, which was usually Ruby's prerogative. Ruby glanced towards her mother, and Fran felt her stomach muscles tighten briefly. Ruby smiled and looked directly at Luke.

'Whoever's at the head of the table says grace,' she said, with the kind of impish grin Henry was renowned for when he was making peace.

Luke stood up and looked at each one of them in turn before closing his eyes. Then in a clear, strong voice he said: 'Dear Lord, I thank thee for bringing me safely into port, into the harbour of my beloved family to whom I owe so much. Grant us all pardon for those deeds which have displeased thee, give us grace to be humble before thee and to love and honour one another. Oh, and a special plea from Gordon and myself, Lord, that the sun may always shine on our house full of women.'

All the family joined together in the loud 'Amen'.

THE STRAWBERRY GIRL

For Grace and Phil
with love and many thanks for
your help and inspiration

PROLOGUE
1899

Agnes Mead straightened herself from the back-breaking work of picking strawberries. She looked towards the west where the sun was hanging low in the June sky. Only another half hour or so and she could go home. As she savoured the balmy evening air, taking deep breaths to fill her tired lungs, she ran her hands gently over her belly. Home was a small brick house she shared with her husband, Dick, and their brood of five children. As if she didn't have enough to do caring for them all as well as thinking for them without the added burden of working until sunset. She was of medium height but much too thin. Never enough food to satisfy her own stomach after giving the others their fill, and never enough rest or sleep to prepare her body for the next day's toil. What had she done to deserve such a punishing life? she wondered.

A couple of crows chasing one another cawed excitedly as they made for the rookery in distant tall trees. The thickly wooded Forest of Bere, situated in the north-west and east of Hampshire, sheltered vast acres of fertile fields where strawberry growing had brought prosperity to the local community. The warm southern aspect created an ideal climate in and around Hundred Acres in Wickham where long, tidy rows of rich green foliage hid the ripened plump fruit growing in abundance.

More crows circled and swooped above Nessie's head. Spring and summer – a time for mating, time for rearing young. The blackness of the huge birds reminded her of Dick and she smiled to herself. When sober he was a bit of a lad, fond of horseplay, seldom serious. With his gypsy dark hair and fiery black eyes not unlike the rook who noisily chased after his mate. Nessie wasn't sure whether the rook had another side to his nature but Dick certainly did when he'd had too much to drink. He wasn't too clever at holding his liquor, and the after effects caused nothing but disruption in an otherwise happy homestead. If he wasn't such a slave to the drink he'd be able to hold down a job, and if only he'd do an honest day's work to keep his wife and family there'd be no need for Nessie to be picking strawberries. No rent, no home. Dick had little pride.

It piqued Nessie that Jake Taylor, her one time suitor and Dick's rival, was the new rent collector. He was as embarrassed as she when she'd had to admit that she couldn't pay the rent but had quickly come up with the suggestion that she work in the estate fields in lieu. Nessie knew that Dick would be furious. She'd toyed with the idea of telling him in the hope that he would turn over a new leaf, but with his quick temper to consider she knew it would mean a beating instead. It was easier this way. As soon as he'd left for the inn in Wickham each weekday evening, Nessie could leave the children in the care of her younger sister, Beth, while she came out into the fields to work. Although she was weary she did find a small measure of peace here in God's sweet-scented air.

A wave of nausea swept over her. She passed a hand across her brow against the setting sun and gulped for air. The moment passed. Down on her haunches again. She must get on, payment was according to baskets filled. No time to feel hungry. If she earned enough and to spare Benjie needed new shoes. In solitude she could romance about all the things money might buy . . .

A shadow blotted out the sun momentarily and Nessie came back to reality. Not another fainting fit – the hand on her shoulder made her start, and she looked up to find Jake Taylor standing over her.

''Evening, Nessie,' he said in a voice which was just a mite too friendly.

'Hullo, Jake.' She found it difficult to meet his gaze. He was taller than Dick, his intense dark eyes revealing the strain of gypsy blood which most of the local families had inherited, being descendants of squatters who had lived, worked and moved about in the forest region for the past century.

'Working late again, I see.'

Nessie daren't glance up as she said with irritation: 'Got to earn the rent, as well you know.'

'There's another way you could earn it – a way we'd both enjoy much better.'

Nessie moved along the row of strawberry plants trying to put more distance between herself and Jake. He was as aware as she of how his handsome good looks could charm any woman. In their younger days she had almost fallen victim to his fatal charm, but Dick Mead had seen the danger signs and made sure he put his girl in the family way so that a shot-gun wedding was necessary. Jake had never forgiven

Dick for taking Nessie, and she could never look him in the eye for fear of seeing his blatant desire. He could still stir some feeling in her breast. She was, after all, only twenty-five, for all she had borne Dick five children over the past seven years.

Jake followed Nessie along the row. He bent down inches behind her.

'You know you always fancied me better 'n Dick Mead,' he said in a low voice. 'That scruff was too old for you, too vulgar and coarse with his rough habits. What sort of life can he ever give you when he spends every penny on drink? By the time you're thirty he'll have worn you out having babies.'

'Dick's only five years older than me, and I'm happy with my children,' Nessie replied defiantly.

'But I'm nearer your age and you would have been mine if that swine hadn't . . .'

'Don't dare speak ill of my Dick!' Nessie spat out at him over her shoulder. Just one glimpse of his narrowing covetous eyes gave her a warning which came too late. He was atop her with more savagery than Dick ever showed.

'Get off me, Jack Taylor,' she shouted, but her cries were lost amidst the screeches of the flock of rooks homeward bound in the pale pink sky.

She tried to fight him off but her wasting muscles were no match for his prime strength. In seconds her skirt was pulled off along with patched underwear and he entered her with no preliminary wooing. Her body was no stranger to abuse but this sudden, vicious attack made her retch before she fainted and went limp beneath Jake's bulk.

The faint was genuine, though if by orchestrating it she had hoped to put Jake off she was mistaken. As she revived it was to realise that the attack was far from over. He was demented, slapping her back to life, urging her frail body to respond to his demands, and when she didn't he pulled back only to plunge into her with renewed force, again and again, until with a hideous cry he lost control. Groans of lust changed to moans of pleasurable satisfaction which filled Nessie with total disgust. She turned her head to spew away the contents of her heaving stomach.

'That's how I want the rent paid, Nessie, my dear – but don't let's make such hard work of it next time. Be ready for me. Clean sheets in the bed when Dick goes off on his drinking binges,' he whispered in her ear. 'Your young sister will be glad of a copper or two to take the kids off your hands.'

'Dick'll kill you when he hears . . .'

Jake laughed. 'You know you'll never have the courage to tell him – he'd kill you first and ask questions afterwards.' He got up and turned from her, making towards the edge of the field to keep out of sight although thankfully there was no one else around. Laughter from other pickers in the next field had long since died away as dusk cloistered Hundred Acres.

Nessie didn't know how long she remained motionless on the ground. She moaned and wept from humiliation, hardly aware that her cries made an eerie sound across the fields. She tried to put the memory of Jake's laughter out of her mind. He had succeeded at last and now there would be no stopping him. There was a way, of course. She only had to tell Dick. But the force of his anger would be felt by her first. Nessie was so distraught that she didn't hear the soft thud of a horse's hooves approaching. Then a figure bent over her with concern.

'Why, Nessie, it's you – whatever's the matter?'

With great relief she recognised the voice of Doctor Grant. She struggled to get up, desperate to disguise the evidence, but swayed crazily and would have fallen if he hadn't caught her.

'Are you ill? Did you faint? Cyril Grant glanced down at her dishevelled state. 'Your clothes!' The truth dawned. 'My God!' he exclaimed. 'Jake Taylor? Was it Jake? I've just seen him going home. He was looking dishevelled. I . . .'

Nessie tried to pull away from the doctor with embarrassment but he steadied her. 'Nessie – was it Jake Taylor? Did he attack you?'

She shook her head, trying to pretend that it hadn't happened. She turned from the doctor, scooped up a handful of straw, and keeping her back to him, tried to clean herself down with it.

'Come along, my dear. That's no way to get clean. You need soap and water. On my horse and back to my house.'

'No! No, thanks. I must get home before Dick.'

'And you know you can't let him see you like this. Besides, he'll be at the inn for a couple more hours yet, and when he does leave it'll take him half the night to totter his way home. You shouldn't be working, let alone until this late, Nessie.'

'Someone has to pay the rent.'

'Ah! So that's what this is all about. Jake's suggestion?'

Nessie nodded. 'But Dick mustn't know.'

'He won't hear anything from me – now, up on Benedict. No!' He raised his hand against her protests. 'I know you're a proud woman, Nessie, but for once you'll do as you're told.'

They met no one until they reached Wickham Square and then Nessie slid to the ground and shot up an alleyway to wait by the side door to the doctor's surgery.

Cyril Grant unlocked the side door from inside and led Nessie into the consulting room. His mind was racing ahead in leaps and bounds.

He doubted that this poor young woman would survive many more pregnancies. Nessie was the eldest of eight children herself, but they had all been conceived with love. He supposed Dick loved her in his own simple way, but there had been plenty of evidence in the past that Nessie, and each of their five children, suffered from his drunken abuse.

'I'll go through and have a word with Doctor Serle to let him know how old Mr Andrews is. While I'm gone you have a good wash at the basin here. Then we'll talk about what's to be done.'

Nice scented soap, soft warm water . . . never did Nessie have such luxury to bathe herself in at home. She sighed, wondering how she was going to explain the bruises away. Dick wouldn't notice anyway, and if he did he'd think he was responsible. He regarded bruises as a measure of his prowess.

With trembling fingers she straightened her skirt and was rebuttoning her blouse when Cyril Grant knocked lightly before entering.

'Oh, you're dressed,' he said. 'Don't you think I ought to examine you? Make sure no damage has been done – I could give you something. You've enough of Dick's offspring.'

'It . . . it's all right, Doctor Grant, really.' Cyril Grant knew that Nessie was about ripe to conceive again, her youngest girl being just over a year old. 'Maybe it'll be all right – I don't want anything done – it wouldn't be natural – if it's meant to be –'

'But if it was a case of violent rape, Nessie. You may be injured. This is a special situation. You should try to rest for the next few days.'

'I'll try, Doctor, and thank you for helping me, though I'm sorry you had to come along just when you did.'

'It's a good thing I did. I ought to inform the authorities, you know. Rape is a punishable offence. Men like Jake Taylor shouldn't be allowed to get away with it.'

Nessie shook her head. 'You know my Dick, Doctor. If he ever finds out, he'll do his own punishing. Least said, soonest mended, I reckon. I'd best get off home now. Beth will be wondering where I am.'

Cyril wanted to drive her home in the pony and trap but she wouldn't hear of it. People might notice and gossip, she said. Dick would demand to know the reason.

After she'd crept away into the night the doctor paced up and down in the carpeted surgery, concerned for Nessie Mead and angry with Jake Taylor.

Nessie implored the God she'd been taught to believe in as a child to make her infertile. With each passing day the thought of having to carry Jake's child filled her with dread. She couldn't understand why she conceived so easily when it was obvious she was not the healthiest woman in the world. Took after her mother she supposed, who'd reared eight children and grieved over two miscarriages. Nessie had enough on her plate without another mouth to feed, let alone the trying months of carrying an unwanted babe. It mustn't happen, it couldn't happen . . .

When Jake Taylor called each week for the rent Nessie did her best to keep him at bay. She'd give him the rent book and he'd sign it. Then: 'Did you say you wanted me to look at that sink?' Or: 'Nasty thunderstorm we had last night, Nessie. Your bedroom ceiling leaking again? Perhaps I ought to take a look.'

Nessie's younger sister Beth didn't care much for school so to be offered a few coppers to take the children off for an hour or two was enticement enough to stay away from lessons. She was a trouble-maker in class anyway so the teachers were glad when she didn't show up, and no one bothered to find out why she was absent so frequently.

'Take the children down to the bridge, Beth,' Jake said. 'Give your sister a break.' With a bewitching smile he handed the eleven-year-old girl some coins, and followed Nessie into the house.

'You'll have to stop this, Jake,' she said as soon as he'd locked the door. 'If Dick ever finds out he'll kill us both. Think what the scandal would do to your Lily and young Adam, for goodness sake,' she begged.

'No one's going to know. Let's have a look at that ceiling – from the comfort of your feather mattress.'

'No, Jake, I won't do it. Besides, you can't – I . . .'

'Can't? he interrupted. 'What's that supposed to mean? I'll soon show you that I can and will.' He laughed and caught at Nessie's slender waist, drawing her close and planting his mouth firmly over hers. She struggled against his clawing hands at her buttocks but he held her so tightly she couldn't escape, and already his loins were rubbing frantically against her stomach.

'D . . . don't think I can make it . . . up the stairs, Nessie,' he panted.

'No, you won't and you can't – because I'm pregnant.'

He gulped. Her words stunned him, then when he'd had time to digest them he grinned fiendishly.

'That's the best news I've had all day,' he said. 'No need to worry any more, Nessie my love. What's done is done. Now we can really enjoy ourselves. You realise what this means? I knew it wasn't me who couldn't father any more children. Now I know 'tis Lily's fault.'

'You don't understand,' Nessie protested. 'This baby is Dick's. I was already pregnant when you . . .'

He held her at arm's length, studying her expression. Then between gritted teeth he said: 'You lying bitch. Don't expect me to fall for that old trick. You can't cheat me that easily.' He grabbed her arm and pulled her behind him up the stairs.

'No, Jake, please,' she pleaded. 'I don't *want* to.'

'Since when did a woman have any right to choose? I'll make damned sure this child carries my mark, Nessie Mead. You should have been Nessie Taylor and well you know it. For years you've taunted me with your sweet smile, goading me on, asking, begging for it. Well, now you now how it is – and I'm going to have my fill.' He threw her on the bed and added with a leer. 'Or rather fill you to the brim.'

Jake was incensed with aggressive passion. Nessie regretted having voiced her wish that any infant she carried must be Dick's. She knew it wasn't true, indeed she wasn't even sure yet that she was with child except for a nagging feeling from past experience.

Of late when Dick came home from the inn, singing and shouting, waking everyone up with his: 'Where's me little woman? Come 'ere, me darlin, I needs you more an more,' eager to keep him quiet she helped him up the narrow stairs and into the front bedroom. He would flop heavily on to the feather mattress and allow Nessie to remove his boots and socks. Whereas once the drink had added to his virility, nowadays he was so sodden with it he was unable to reach his goal. By the next day his hangover was so bad that he no longer had the desire.

As she suffered Jake's torment she prayed again that she might escape becoming pregnant – but in her heart she knew it was too late.

When the strawberry season ended Nessie hoped Jake's visits would cease, but as the evenings drew in he took to calling as soon as Dick had left for the inn, when the children were in bed.

The period of morning sickness passed, and for a few brief weeks Nessie felt and looked better. She tried appealing to Jake.

'I reckon I've more 'n paid the rent,' she said. 'There's no need for you to come any more. You must understand that this baby isn't yours, it's Dick's. He isn't drinking as much now he knows we'll soon have another little one, so he'll like as not walk in and then there'll be trouble.'

Jake pushed his way inside and closed the door behind him.

'Rent's gone up, Nessie. You can't deny me now. You enjoy it as much as I do. It's even better when you put up a fight. That's always been the trouble with my Lily. Just lies there waiting for it all to end. What pleasure is there in that for a man?' He gathered her in his arms and kissed her almost tenderly. 'Don't worry about that drunken swine of a husband of yours. I can handle him – he's drinking himself to an early grave, and you know it.'

'I told you, he's not drinking so much these days. He's not as bad as you think and he's doing everything to help me.'

'And it's *my* baby – don't you forget that, Nessie. Keep me happy and I'll give you all the help you need.'

As she lay beneath him, her body responding in spite of her guilt and distaste, she couldn't help thinking how much easier her life might have been if she had married Jake Taylor.

By Christmas, though, Jake no longer found her appealing as she became bigger and much less energetic. His visits became infrequent as wintry weather turned Nessie's bedroom into an ice-box. He called only occasionally to collect his dues. She found her burden cumbersome, gaining strength at her expense. It kicked her viciously, sapping every ounce of nourishment from her so that she was obliged to remain in bed for the last few weeks.

As winter progressed the doctor was kept busy with the usual coughs and colds. Times had changed over the past fifty years in these parts from what he'd heard. The frost-bitten earth crunched beneath the horse's hoofs as he made his way from village to hamlet visiting the sick. It wasn't difficult to conjure up a picture of the hard-working forest inhabitants living in roughly made houses in the woods, making hoops and faggots, spars and hurdles. They'd lived and loved much to their own rules, hardy against the elements until the area had been enclosed by the Squire who wanted his park to look nice. After having a selected area of some sixty acres on another part of his estate cleared, two dozen houses in pairs were erected which he offered to the squatters with the added enticement of an acre of land with each at an incredibly cheap rent. This was the birth of Hundred Acres. Cyril wished he'd known it in the old days which many of his elderly patients loved to tell him about. They were the ones who hadn't welcomed change, but the younger generation reckoned they had come up in the world. They had benefited from their parents and grandparents hard toil to make the land as profitable as it was today. Not that there was much doing in the winter months when the ground was covered with frost or snow, usually after a blustery autumn when fallen leaves made their colourful carpet and trees fell as easily as matchsticks during a gale.

As he wound his way through the woods, avoiding branches of the broad oaks which had broken off, he recalled his senior partner telling him how things used to be in this area. He could almost smell the smoke which would have hung among the trees from the makeshift houses occupied by the squatters. Matt Serle had learned to keep a few scraps of food in his pocket to keep at bay the flea-bitten dogs which bared their teeth and barked furiously at his approach. In the summer the air was pungent with the smell of rotten vegetables mixed with sewage odours, and when the local women gave birth it was a miracle any of them survived in such squalid conditions.

Cyril smiled to himself as he thought of all the births he'd attended since his arrival here five years ago. Not so many though, since Minnie Fletcher considered confinements her responsibility and there was no one better. He only attended when things got difficult, as when Charlie Mead was born. Poor Nessie, just a slip of a girl at twenty-three, lying on a bed of linen smelling of windblown country fragrance in a room freshly whitewashed in spite of next to no income. Nessie's widowed mother assisted Minnie as Nessie continued to emit loud animal cries while the ten pound baby inside her struggled for delivery. After several hours, while he and Minnie sweated almost as much as Nessie, the screaming infant was safely delivered, his nose squashed, his large head covered with a mass of dark brown curly hair. Even his hands and feet seemed to belong to a child a year old, but at least he was a healthy boy even if it turned out he didn't have his full quota of intelligence. Nessie's fifth child, and third girl, had come easily enough, being barely seven pounds. She had a larger family than she could cope with, he thought now, while other women had trouble enough to conceive even one.

He was concerned for Nessie's health. At first she'd blossomed, but latterly she'd become rundown and listless. She didn't consult him often but if he was that way he sometimes called to make sure she was getting enough food and rest. They never mentioned that June evening. As far as anyone else knew, the child she was carrying was her husband's and Dick did appear to be more considerate towards her. But Cyril was disturbed by the rumours which had circulated back in the autumn that Jake Taylor was a frequent visitor to the Meads' house, and not only to collect rent. Nessie had seemed distressed at the time but could he have been wrong about violent rape? She had refused his offer of help and had recovered sufficiently to walk home. Was it possible that she had been a willing participant?

It was a dark, chill March night when someone banged noisily on the back door of the doctor's surgery. Cyril excused himself from his patient and knew at once something was wrong by the state of the midwife. Minnie's face was purple from over-exertion and she was puffing badly.

'You must come, Doctor, you must!' she said in a frightened whisper.

'Go round to the kitchen door, Minnie. I'll see you there.'

Cyril Grant endeavoured to keep calm as he completed his consultation, then instead of opening the waiting-room door to call in the next patient, went through to the back of the house and let Minnie into the kitchen.

''Tis Nessie Mead, Doctor,' she said urgently. 'Dick sent Benjie over for me at dawn. All last night and throughout today she's been screaming and wailing. But it's delivered, and it's all right. Small for Nessie – only about six pounds, I reckon. Remember her two boys were nearly ten each but they were easier to deliver than this one was. It was as if it didn't want to come into this world – and I'm not surprised!'

'Why?'

'It's got the strawberry mark on it,' Minnie said in a hushed voice. 'A great red patch on its forehead, real ugly, and a girl at that.'

Doctor and midwife stared at each other.

'I'll get over there as soon as surgery is finished,' Cyril said. 'Doctor Serle is unwell today so I'm on my own.'

Minnie hesitated. 'I'm worried, Doctor. Dick's going mad, threatening to kill it, but first he's off to the inn to drown his sorrows.'

'Leave him to me, Minnie.'

Cyril could hardly concentrate on the rest of his patients but he did his best then saddled Benedict and set off at a trot for the Meads' homestead. Benedict was no stranger to hurried trips across the landscape, and tonight, though bleak with a heavy frost, there was a good high moon to light the way across the fields. A short cut here and there and he made the journey in less than half the usual time. Benjie the eldest boy, aged seven, took the reins and secured the doctor's horse to a nearby tree.

'Time you were in bed, Benjie,' Cyril said kindly. 'No need to fret, your ma will be all right.' He lowered his head to climb the narrow staircase where Dick's voice could be heard cursing and swearing as he stomped around from bedroom to landing.

'Come on now, Dick,' Cyril said, 'you're not helping Nessie or the younger children.'

'And who's helping me, I'd like to know? Dear god in heaven have you ever seen such a freak? It must be a bastard – it can't be mine.' He threw his arms in the air, waving his large meaty hands in utter despair. 'Get rid of it, Doctor, or I'll put it out of its misery even if I need an extra drink or two to do it.'

'You'll have the extra drink or two in any case. Now calm yourself, Dick, until I've had a chance to look at the child. Birthmarks aren't that rare. Plenty of people have them even if they can't be seen.'

'But no child of mine has one,' Dick roared unreasonably. 'It isn't mine, I tell you, and it hadn't better be here when I get back.'

'Then don't bother coming back until you're sober,' Cyril answered angrily. He didn't often lose his temper but he didn't like the situation he found himself in. Dick Mead was quite capable of committing murder if driven – both mother and child could well be victims, and if he, the doctor, dared to tell the truth of the matter, Jake Taylor might also be added to the list.

Dick brushed past him as he tore off down the stairs and out into the night. Cyril went softly into the front bedroom where the first thing he saw by candlelight was Nessie's rich chestnut-coloured hair spread out over the pillow. Poor though they were, Nessie's housekeeping and cleanliness were a credit to her. Minnie Fletcher had done her job well and now the mother of the new infant was resting comfortably between clean white sheets and soft feather pillows covered in starched white pillowcases. Cyril knew that she was crying. He laid a gentle hand on the turned back sheet.

'Nessie, my dear, it's all right. The mark will most likely fade in time.'

'Have you seen it?' She half-turned. 'I can't bear to look at it. Dick's right – it mustn't live. I can't take any more.'

'But you must give it love and nourishment, or it'll die.'

'Then let it – I want nothing to do with it! Dick says it's hideous. It's a curse – a curse, I tell you. Take it away. Do whatever you must before Dick does. And he'll not do it humanely.'

'Nessie, there's no need for anyone to ever know what happened. It's our secret. It's your babe – you've given birth to it – it has the right to live and be brought up with the rest of your family.'

A floorboard creaked and Cyril turned in time to see someone move away from the door.

'Who's there? Benjie, is that you?' he called.

'It's my sister, I expect,' Nessie said in a tired voice. 'Beth, I thought you were making tea. Doctor Grant must have something warm before he goes home.'

It was several minutes before footsteps sounded outside and Nessie's younger sister entered carrying a small round tin tray. She avoided looking directly at Cyril. Had she heard any of their conversation? he wondered. For eleven years old she was tall and well-developed, her young breasts pushing forward against her jumper. Although the Waterstone family was such a large one they were highly respectable, but Beth had the hallmarks of a flighty piece.

'You're here to help your sister then?' he asked now.

'Ma's leg is too bad for her to come,' Beth said. 'I can look after Nessie and the children.'

'Good girl. I'm sure you'll do a good job, Beth.'

Cyril drank his tea before taking a look in the crib. Even he started at the sight of the small round head covered with the thick black hair so typical of the inhabitants of Hundred Acres. The left side of the face looked dark too – dark and ugly. Cyril lifted the small bundle from the crib and turned back the white knitted shawl, hardly able to believe what he saw. For once Dick Mead was right. The birthmark made the infant look grotesque.

'I'm sure the mark will fade in time. Probably by the time she's ten, if not sooner. It's the type that does disappear without trace eventually. Once you've started to feed her you'll love her like the others,' he hastened to assure his patient.

'No, Doctor, and you know why. That strawberry mark will always be a reminder, and if Dick ever finds out . . .'

'Who's going to tell him? Certainly not me – and I'm the only one who knows. Get some rest now, Nessie. Nurse Fletcher will be here first thing in the morning and I'll look in too. You'll feel better after a good night's sleep. That's what you need most now.'

But Nessie had no will to live, no love or instinct to feed her new baby or even look at it. She went into a deep depression, lying back against her pillow with her eyes closed, pleading with Nurse Fletcher not to draw back the faded and worn curtains. She refused visitors – she just wanted to die. Guilt was uppermost in her thoughts. Not that she could have prevented Jake Taylor from raping her, but she was filled with remorse because she had tried all manner of things to terminate the pregnancy – one she'd never intended to carry full term. This ugly child was her punishment and it was more than she could bear. The child didn't deserve to be marked and have to face a life of shame. The shame was hers, Nessie's. Dying would have been too good for her.

For the next day and night Dick Mead was missing. Some said he was too drunk to leave The King's Head, others said he was with another woman, but some time after midnight on the second day he turned up at the doctors' house, ranting and raving like a lunatic.

Cyril Grant went down to the door in his dressing-gown.

'For goodness' sake, Dick, do you want to get arrested? Get off home and look after Nessie and the children. She's gone into depression and needs you.'

'Depression, d'you say?' Dick roared. 'How the hell d'you think I feel helping to produce that . . . that . . . imbecile? It's got no right in my family so I'll not go home 'till it's been put down.'

'You can't know what you're saying, Dick. You know I can't take a life. It would be a criminal act.'

'You can do it painlessly – but I'll do it if I have to.'

Cyril Grant watched Dick shuffle away in the direction of Fareham. It was cruel to see a man so wretched with himself, and if the doctor hadn't known so much about him he'd have felt sorry for Dick Mead. His sympathy now wasn't so much for Nessie even but the poor child who hadn't asked to be conceived. He couldn't take its life. He knew of doctors and midwives who would, in pity for the child. What kind of future did it have? Dick would surely ill-treat it even if he could be persuaded to spare its life, and Nessie – what a mess? She believed this was a curse put on her for having a relationship with Jake Taylor.

Cyril didn't sleep well and was up early the next morning before any of the local people went to work. Out for a morning canter to all intents and purposes – a canter which took him to the midwife's cottage, Beech Cottage, set in a copse of the trees which in summer helped to keep the cottage cool. Cyril loved this spot and recalled reading about the famous sixteenth-century herbalist Gerard who had warned people against taking beech leaves into their houses in case they brought death. He remembered too that Joan of Arc had seen visions under a beech tree. Yet he knew that no forest tree had richer foliage than the beech, in autumn providing a pageant of colour in rich bronze-browns. He shrugged off his superstitions though admitted that at this moment he could well do with a vision of what to do. He should, of course, be sharing his dilemma with his senior partner but Matt Serle was going downhill rapidly. Cyril knew that very soon he would be holding the fort alone, but he would accept the challenge readily.

Minnie was already up and had seen him coming so the door was flung open. Ice-cold in temperature the cottage might be, even in summer, but it was a haven of warm friendliness like nowhere else in the whole district.

'What brings you here so early?' she asked, stoking up the fire she'd kept going all night. 'You're worried about Nessie Mead, I daresay?'

Cyril made himself comfortable by Minnie's hearth, and over an early morning cup of tea told her all he knew.

'I can't do what Dick says,' he said wearily. 'I'm just not made that way. There's no reason to put the child out of its misery when it's perfectly healthy in all other respects, and as far as I can tell will look as normal as any other child in a few years. But at the same time neither can I leave it to Dick's not-so-tender mercies, or even Nessie's come to that. The child is unwanted on more than one count.'

'She still refuses to look at it. I even held it to her breast but it wouldn't feed. I believe Dick may be right – it is a freak. We've both seen unsightly children before but we don't have the right to decide their fate, do we?'

'Life can be hard and cruel for such children but what can *we* do?'

'Not much – except . . .'

'Except what, Minnie? If you've any ideas please speak up. I'm at my wit's end.'

'We-ell – I was in the New Forest visiting my sister last Sunday. As you know she's a midwife too and was rejoicing with a couple who've just had their first baby after waiting and wanting for several years. Phoebe Hunter is thirty-five and this would probably have been her last chance after being barren for so long. Now they've got a baby girl and are mighty grateful that she's arrived safely. Small but healthy.'

'What are you suggesting, Minnie? What's this couple in the New Forest got to do with my problem – or rather Nessie's?'

'I was just thinking, there's the Hunter couple rejoicing in the birth of their babe – a much wanted babe – and we've got one in the village that's unwanted.'

'Minnie, I can't imagine what you're suggesting but it sounds – interesting.'

'More'n interesting, Doctor. Who's to know that the Hunters didn't have twins? I met Phoebe only hours after Belinda was born. They were so happy. They're good Christian folk who would give Nessie's infant a much better chance in life than ever Dick and Nessie can. They live in an isolated cottage in the Forest, miles from anyone else. He's a master carpenter, and they're the kind of people who keep themselves to themselves. Ideal to take Nessie's babe.'

'Only they won't want it either when they see it,' Cyril said.

'You could be wrong there. They believe in fate and I think they'd see it as a special request from God, in thanks for at last having one of their own. Besides, they're the kind of intelligent couple who will understand that the mark will fade in time. What could be better than going to a family miles from gawping neighbours? The locals here won't ever get to see her, so what they don't know about they won't fret over.'

There was a long pause while Cyril thanked the beech trees for her timely vision. A vision which scared him as much as it did Minnie Fletcher.

'What could we tell Nessie and Dick though?' he mused. Then, with a click of his fingers, 'I know – the baby died naturally, of course.' He rushed round the small oak table and placed his hands excitedly on Minnie's shoulders. 'Is it feasible, Min? Dare we? Think of the child, and the good home it would be brought up in.'

'There'll be a few white lies to tell and a few forged papers to sign,' she reminded him.

'To save a child's life? Anything is worth that!' he declared. 'No one must ever find out – but then, by the time she grows up we shall be long gone. Retired or moved on. All we have to do now is to think of a way to get the baby to its new home before Dick Mead commits a crime.'

While Minnie hastened to visit her sister in her pony and trap, Doctor Grant paid a visit to the Meads' house. He felt duty bound to make one last effort to persuade Nessie to take her baby.

'What are you going to call her?' he asked.

There was no reply. Nessie remained facing the wall and refused to look at the doctor or the baby.

'Are you being fair, Nessie? Doesn't she have a right to your love, the same as the others?'

'No – I wanted no part of it. I'm weary of bringing up children, tired of being tired.'

'I'll do all I can to help you get on your feet again.'

'I don't feel as if I shall ever walk again. God is punishing me for what I've done.'

'But it wasn't your fault, my dear. You should have let me help you then – at least have Jake Taylor brought to justice.'

'I felt sorry for his wife and child, and I knew if Dick ever found out there'd be a murder. That would have been both our families having to live with disgrace of one kind or another. None of the children deserves that, and this one, even though I hate it, doesn't deserve the taunts of unkind people in the world. Better that it should die.'

Cyril Grant bent over the crib. 'Her breathing's not good,' he said, and it was true. It was in a poor state and if something wasn't done soon the baby surely would die of starvation.

'I'll be back later today to have another look but get Beth to see if she can get the child to feed from the bottle.'

He went away and had great difficulty in channelling his thoughts towards other people's ills. He was glad when it was dark and he could ride over to Beech Cottage where he found Minnie having a meal with her sister.

''Tis all arranged if the situation is the same, Doctor.'

'Worse, I'm afraid. The infant's breathing is shallow and if it doesn't get love and care in the next forty-eight hours, it really will die.'

'Then that's settled. The Hunters are overjoyed at having a twin sister for Belinda. They know nothing of the circumstances though and there's no need for them to. I'll visit Nessie as soon as I think Beth has gone home but before Dick gets back from the inn. A spot of ether will ensure that the babe doesn't suddenly cry out.'

Cyril Grant looked at the two middle-aged women with a worried frown.

'Is it going to work?'

'Like you said, to save a child's life it must work, and God help us.'

The small house was eerily quiet when Minnie drove up to the gate. It was after ten o'clock when most people were already in their beds. The front door was unlocked so she crept in and went up the stairs.

''Tis only me, Nessie dear.' She knew Nessie would know her voice and would trust her whatever she told her.

'Doctor Grant was worried about the babe. 'I'm sorry I haven't been in today but I had to visit my sister as she's not been well. Not easy when you live alone. Now, dearie, let's have a look – oh dear! Oh, my goodness, poor wee mite.'

She took out her handkerchief to feign distress but quickly placed the faintly-smelling ether pad over the babe's nose. There was no sound except for the faint rustling of sheets as Nessie turned over in the big bed.

'What's the matter?'

'I . . . I'm afraid 'tis gone, Nessie. And without being baptised or anything. I'm so sorry, my dear, but I have to tell you that even if I'd come before there was nothing I could have done for it.'

'See to it all, Nurse Fletcher. And before Dick gets home – if he ever does come home, that is.'

'Well, the doctor must attend, or perhaps I could take it straight to him now, to ease your heartbreak?'

'There's no heartbreak, Nurse. 'Tis better for it. May the Lord rest its tiny soul.' Her voice cracked and Minnie knew that Nessie was quietly weeping.

'I'll bring back its clothes after –'

'No need for any funeral, just do whatever they do with stillborn babies, and do it with its clothes on. I'm not going to want baby clothes any more.'

'Shall I ride over and fetch your ma or Beth?'

'No, they'll be in bed. There's no need for grieving for this one. 'Tis better off wherever it's gone.' Nessie snuggled down under the bedclothes. 'At least Dick will be satisfied now.'

Minnie Fletcher let herself out of the house after wrapping the infant up in two blankets. She laid it on the floor of the trap and set off for Doctor Grant's house. Together they finalised the conspiracy by forging a death certificate and then Minnie urged her pony at a good trot for Beech Cottage.

The deed was done. The cold night air brought the baby round and Minnie sat by the fire contentedly as the perfect rosebud mouth sucked eagerly from the bottle. At least the little one had a future with good parents, and Minnie would be able to follow her progress through her sister who was going to take her to her new home as soon as it was light.

Chapter One

'Strawberry girl . . . strawberry girl . . . strawberry girl . . .'

Seven-year-old Rachel Hunter covered her ears with her hands against the unkind taunts. Hot and on the verge of tears she ran for dear life. The boys quickly gained on her and the leader of the gang, Charlie Mead, grabbed and caught his prey with a shout of triumph.

'Pull 'er 'air back – 'ave a look,' he ordered his mates. 'She's a witch – she's got the mark of the strawberry on 'er.' They pulled and tugged at Rachel's hair, laughing and peering at the raised red patch which tainted her otherwise pretty white skin. 'Did yer ma 'ave a craving for strawberries when you was comin', Rachel Hunter?' Charlie squealed with glee. 'Reckon as 'ow she ate too many an' they came out on you.'

The other boys cheered him on but Rachel kicked backwards with her foot causing Charlie to loosen his hold. She managed to escape and ran and ran, on through the wood, the boys screaming and yelling after her. Her throat burned horribly and she began to cough as tears fell from hot, hurting eyes. She didn't see the tree root and suddenly went sprawling. The boys descended on her like a pack of hungry wolves.

She banged her head on the ground and both knees felt as if they were rubbed raw. The boys were pounding her back as they shrieked obscenities. She was sure they were going to strip her of every last item of clothing.

'Get off, you mongrels!' an angry voice bellowed through the giant oaks. A horse snorted, footsteps scuffled on the dry, parched earth, and when Rachel managed to scramble to her feet she saw most of the boys running away in all directions while Dr Grant held Charlie Mead fast in a stranglehold.

'What the devil d'you think you're up to?' Doctor Cyril Grant growled angrily.

'We . . . we was jest lookin' at 'er mark,' Charlie snivelled.

'And you'll be lucky if I don't put a mark on you, my lad.'

'I'll tell . . . my dad of you,' Charlie choked, his cheeks getting redder by the minute. Rachel began to feel a bit sorry for him as the doctor did seem to be exerting more pressure than was necessary. 'He's . . . bigger 'an you.'

'And when he's had a drink or two he's only fit for battering defenceless women,' Doctor Grant muttered. 'Be off home to Hundred Acres where you belong, boy. Don't let me see you molesting Rachel again.' He threw the boy to the ground with disgust.

Rachel was weeping desperately. Her throat was really painful, but she could bear that. The humiliation she had suffered from the boys making sport of her disfigurement was much worse. It was the school nurse's fault for remarking about the strawberry birthmark and bringing it to Charlie Mead's attention. It just wasn't fair, and on a day when her twin sister Belinda had to stay at home because she had measles.

'You all right, Rachel my dear?' Doctor Grant asked kindly.

Blood and tears mingled together as Rachel lifted her face for the doctor's scrutiny. He opened his bag and took out a piece of bandage to clean her. 'There, that's better. Can't have you going home to your mother looking as if you've quarrelled with the ground, now can we?'

He closed his bag, hitched it over his shoulder on its long leather strap, and then lifted Rachel up on the saddle before hoisting himself up behind her.

Rachel wasn't normally a cry baby but she had been very afraid of the boys and alarmed at the amount of blood which poured from her forehead.

'Good thing I came along at just the right time,' Doctor Grant said. 'I'm sorry Nurse Cull commented on your birthmark today. It was thoughtless of her. She won't mention it again, but as you get older, my dear, I'm afraid you'll come across people who might be unkind about it. You're a very brave girl, and I can assure you that it will fade in time. Don't worry about the bleeding, Rachel, it will soon stop.'

The horse, unused to carrying anyone other than its master, trotted along the bridlepath dutifully, occasionally tossing its head with a protesting snort and flick of its mane.

'Now that's enough of that, Benedict,' the doctor said. 'You're highly honoured to have a pretty young maiden riding on your back.'

Rachel thought she was the one who was highly honoured, and was very thankful that the doctor had intervened on her behalf and saved her from an unthinkable fate.

Rachel's mother, Phoebe Hunter, was standing at the garden gate, her hand shielding her eyes from the sun's glare as she stared in disbelief at the approaching horse and rider.

'Why, Doctor Grant,' she exclaimed, 'whatever are you doing with our Rachel?'

'It's all right, Mrs Hunter, no cause for alarm.' He pulled the horse in by the fence and hung the reins over the post before jumping down, Rachel in his arms. 'There we are, Rachel, safe and sound.'

She looked up at her mother, expecting a scolding for a dirty dress and grazed face and knees.

'Whatever happened to you, darling?' Phoebe asked with concern.

'She had a little altercation with some naughty boys.'

'But you haven't come all this way just to bring her home, Doctor?' Phoebe asked.

'No, I'm on my way to see Nurse Fletcher. She had a nasty fall last week, cutting her leg quite badly. The wound was ulcerated so I need to keep an eye on it. It's such a lovely day I decided to ride over there after my annual school visit.'

'Will you stop by for a glass of something, Doctor? A cup of tea, perhaps?'

'A cool drink would be most appreciated, Mrs Hunter.' He followed the small, wiry woman into the thatched cottage, lowering his head to avoid knocking himself out on the oak rafters. The rooms were small but cool, with an aromatic smell of freshly carved wood to titillate his nostrils. Wally Hunter, Phoebe's husband, was a master carpenter who had turned Calder Cottage into a showplace for his craftsmanship in just the few short months since they had come to live in Kingsmere. A round mahogany table stood in front of the latticed window, so highly polished you could almost see your face in it. Cyril Grant was surprised that Wally allowed his wife to put a bowl of roses on it though. He sat down in the dark oak rocker while Phoebe filled a tall tumbler with fizzy lemonade. She had sent Rachel outside into the garden to drink hers.

'So what's this all about then, Doctor Grant?'

Cyril sighed. 'I've been half expecting something like this to happen ever since Rachel started at Wickham School, Mrs Hunter,' he said sadly. 'Our nurse is not the most tactful of people and when she spotted the birthmark she remarked about it, and unfortunately Charlie Mead saw it too. He and his gang followed Rachel into the woods and were setting about her when I happened along. By the look of her throat when I examined her today she's in for measles any minute so I should keep her at home tomorrow. I s'pose I ought to have suggested it when Belinda went down with it, but I don't hold with children missing their education unless absolutely necessary.'

'Poor Rachel,' Phoebe said in a low voice. 'Life isn't going to be easy for her, is it?'

'We must guard against being over-protective. The birthmark will fade, God willing. Many I've seen have gone by the time the child reaches the age of five or six. Rachel seems to be one of the unlucky ones so we must do our best for her and be especially understanding. Meanwhile she has to face the world, I'm afraid.' Cyril Grant stood up, thanked Phoebe for the drink and returned outside to where Rachel was holding a bucket of water for Benedict to take a drink.

'There's a good girl, Rachel,' he said patting her head before he rode off to the other side of the wood to take the Waltham Chase road.

There was a cool, restful breeze through the trees and Cyril let his horse set a slow pace, glad of the peacefulness of the wood and the time to wonder if he had done right to allow Minnie Fletcher to find a new home for the unwanted, ugly baby seven years ago. His conscience had taken a knock today, seeing that young thug with Rachel beneath him on the ground, especially as he knew they were half-brother and sister, but he refused to allow his memory to torment him with what had happened on that fateful day nearly eight years ago in the strawberry field.

When he reached the cottage where the retired midwife lived, he tied Benedict to the beech tree.

'Hullo there, Minnie?' he called as he knocked on the back door.

'Come in, Doctor,' the seventy-three-year-old spinster invited. Any visitor knew by the tone of her voice that they were assured of a warm welcome. Minnie Fletcher was round as she was high with rosy red cheeks and a genuine sparkle in her soft blue-grey eyes. She was sitting on a sofa by the window.

'Glad to see you're keeping that leg up.'

''Tis good of you to come over all this way, Doctor. I'm sure there's no real need though. I can manage well enough.'

'I know that, Minnie. But to tell you the truth I needed to be out in the fresh air for a bit and there's nothing better than a ride through the woods. Made my school visit today. Lot of measles about – wonder the whole school isn't down with it.'

They chatted easily in the manner of old chums while Cyril examined the wound on Minnie's leg and as he redressed it he told her how unkind the school nurse had been to Rachel Hunter.

'Tactless woman,' he said. 'Too bossy, totally unsuitable to deal with children, and of all the children to pick on, it had to be little Rachel. Today of all days when Belinda's home from school with the measles. Charlie mead and his gang took full advantage of Rachel having to go through the woods by herself.'

'Did they hurt her?' Minnie asked, with concern.

'I think she was more scared than anything else. A few cuts and bruises. Bumped her head and grazed her birthmark which bled profusely. That frightened her. Now Charlie Mead and his gang know, everyone for miles around will know too but they'll soon forget. Mrs Hunter has made an excellent job of styling Rachel's hair so that the mark is barely noticeable in the normal way.' He sighed. 'Someone sooner or later would have noticed it, I suppose. Never did we imagine that the Hunters would up and move in this direction did we? Has fate cheated us, Minnie?'

''Tis only you and me knows what happened that night, and after all this time any rumours about Nessie Mead and Jake Taylor will have long been forgotten, let alone a baby that died.'

'I can hardly believe Rachel's the same child. She's bonny enough now and will grow up to be a fine-looking young woman. It's going to be hard on her though till the mark fades.

'Looks aren't everything. Rachel may well have the stronger character. Only time will tell who she really takes after.'

'I ask myself time and time again, Minnie – did we do right to let her live? Wouldn't it have been kinder to do as Dick Mead asked?'

'Kinder? For Rachel? Either way we have to live with our consciences. Nessie and Dick believe their infant died of natural causes, and heaven alone knows she was sickly enough and caused enough trouble for poor Agnes a'growing and a 'coming. But you took the Hippocratic Oath, and it wouldn't have been right to deny the infant the right to live. No, Doctor, I reckon we did what was right in the sight of God. She'll have a better life and upbringing with Phoebe and Wally than she ever would fightin' for survival with Nessie and Dick's brood.'

'I feel responsible, Minnie, and weighed down with guilt all over again since the Hunters moved to Kingsmere.'

'Reckon we're both responsible. I aided and abetted you, Doctor – but I'm getting old and past worrying. Have no fear, no one will ever hear a word from me,' Minnie assured him. 'Wally Hunter's made a name for himself so when Squire offered him regular work and a cottage as well, who could blame him for moving? There's four of them in the family, two of them growing girls to clothe and educate. Takes some doing these days, and they weren't to know they were bringing Rachel back to her roots.'

After Cyril had enjoyed a cup of tea with Minnie, he set off on the homeward route deep in thought. He just prayed that Dick Mead never found out that Jake had taken his wife or there'd be trouble. Everyone knew that Dick Mead was capable of murder, and Jake

Taylor probably deserved it. But the Meads and Taylors of this world didn't warrant much consideration. It was little Rachel Hunter he worried about. His conscience was always going to trouble him over this one, whatever comfort Minnie tried to give him. He'd never believed in superstitions yet here it was before his very eyes. Conceived by rape in a strawberry field. Born with a hideous strawberry mark. The mark of the devil if ever he'd seen it. Maybe it was time he moved on to a different district, but he doubted that he ever would as that would be a coward's way out. He felt responsible for all the people in the Meon Valley who depended on him and whom he had come to love over the years. They in turn showed him affection and respect which he valued. Now that Rachel was back in the area he felt he owed her his protection if nothing else. How she turned out and what she made of her life would convince him whether or not he'd done the right thing seven years ago.

Phoebe Hunter squeezed the cold water out of the piece of soft flannel and wiped it round Rachel's face.

'There,' she said gently, 'I do believe the fever has gone at last. Let's change your nightie and the sheets. You can lie in Mummy's bed, darling, while I make up a nice clean bed for you. Then I reckon you'll sleep 'till the cows come home.'

She lifted the little girl into her own place in the high double bed and set about stripping the truckle bed of the damp, smelly bed-linen.

'Must be all nice and clean when Doctor Grant comes to see you. He'll be pleased that your temperature's down, and I expect your cough will soon get better now.' Phoebe bundled the nightie, sheets and pillow case into a ball. 'You just lie there quietly while I get your dad's breakfast, then, when I've got these things into boil I'll come up and get you back in your own bed.'

Phoebe went down the narrow twisted staircase carefully, hurried to the outhouse where the brick copper stood empty, and had begun to fill it with buckets of water when a strong hand took one from her.

'I'll do that, Phoebe love,' Wally said. 'You've had no rest, hardly a wink of sleep for too many nights. I've put the kettle on and started my breakfast. I'll fill up with water and get the fire started.'

Phoebe grated slivers of household soap off a new bar and left her husband to set light to the cardboard and sticks under the copper. Soon, from the kitchen window she could see a thin streak of smoke coming from the small brick chimney. It was a dry, sunny morning and there was the promise of a long hot summer in the air.

It was still only six-thirty. She sat beside Wally as he ate his bacon and eggs, sipping her much needed cup of tea thoughtfully.

'Don't reckon Rachel will go back to school now 'til after the summer holidays,' she said. There was a tone of relief in her voice.

'No use being too protective, Phoebe. It's something she's going to have to get used to – people are bound to notice her mark and there's nothing we can do about it.'

'Thank God for measles, I say,' Phoebe said. 'Won't be so bad for her though if the two girls can stick together.'

'I never knew measles could be so bad,' Wally said. 'But then no two young'uns are ever the same. You can't expect the girls to be side by side all their lives, Phoebe. Belinda mustn't be made to feel she's Rachel's protector.'

Phoebe looked at Wally. They were divided over their loyalties. Wally favoured Belinda, Phoebe knew. Not that he ever showed favouritism where presents and such were concerned, but sometimes his expression revealed the love he felt for his own daughter, whereas for Rachel Phoebe suspected it was nothing but pity. So, she knew it was up to her.

'The girls are devoted to one another,' she said. 'They'll always look out for each other whatever happens, Charlie Mead or no Charlie Mead.'

'If it isn't Charlie, it may well be someone else. Children can be cruel.'

'Cruel one minute, loving the next. At least they'll go through school together, and Doctor Grant says that the mark will fade as time passes.'

Wally grunted. 'Reckon he doesn't know too much about it. No sign of any change as far as I can see.'

'But you don't see, Wally,' Phoebe said. 'I have to look at it every day when I wash her and brush her hair. It breaks my heart. It might have been Belinda, remember.'

Wally pushed back his chair and with a non-committal grunt went out of the back door and along the path to the privy. Phoebe had touched a raw nerve but he needed to be reminded occasionally of the need for consideration. After about ten minutes Wally came back, stood at the sink and washed his hands, then turned to Phoebe who was buttering bread for Belinda's breakfast and lunch box.

He pecked her cheek, and with his hand round her upper arm gently squeezed reassuringly.

'We won't let Rachel down,' he said softly. 'She's our responsibility and the girls will be treated the same. We knew it wouldn't be easy for her. I hadn't reckoned on trouble the minute she started at the new school, though.'

'It need not have happened but for that stupid school nurse. I've worked hard to train Rachel's hair to cover up the blemish, and it's been all right until now. I suppose the children she grew up with in the New Forest didn't pay any attention to it. She's too young to take this on her own shoulders, Wally. We've got to help her all we can. You know, watching her while she's been ill I've noticed how pretty she's getting. As long as that mark is covered up she'll be as bonny as any other child of her age. She's as dark as Belinda is fair, and yet Rachel has whiter, more delicate skin. Her eyes are so big and black too – shouldn't wonder if she isn't a real beauty when she gets to be a young woman,'

'Maybe you're right. Now I must be off. I'll be at the big house all day. Squire wants some work doing there. Cook'll give me dinner, I dare say, save me coming all the way home when it's so hot.'

Phoebe went to the garden gate and watched him walk off down the lane towards the river. The air was sultry, and she wasn't sorry to get back inside the cottage where it was cooler. She went quietly up the stairs to look in on Rachel. A mass of dark hair was spread out over the pillow – Phoebe's pillow – as if the child gained comfort from lying where her mother had lain a short while ago. Her small thin face was pale but her expression was more restful now in sleep. This was what she needed, rest and good food to build her up until she was strong and healthy again. Phoebe tiptoed to the bedside and smoothed the damp tendrils of hair away. Rachel was lying on her left side so that the strawberry mark wasn't visible. Yes, Phoebe thought, she has the makings of a fine young woman with good looks. Different in every way from Belinda who was the spitting image of herself at a similar age. It didn't seem likely that anyone would really be fooled into thinking the girls were twins. But then again, Wally was dark-haired with warm brown eyes. Folk would think Rachel took after him. Phoebe bent and kissed the soft cheek, then went across the small landing to the other bedroom.

'Belinda?' Phoebe shook the child gently. 'Time to get up, dear.'

Belinda rolled over, moaned, and then sat up abruptly.

'Is Rachel all right, Mummy?'

'Yes. She's asleep now, so don't make a noise when you come down. I think the fever has left her at last.'

'Will she soon be able to come back to school?'

'Not until after the summer holidays, I expect. She'll be weak for a while but she's on the mend. Doctor Grant's coming to see her today.'

Belinda pushed the single sheet away. The night had been too hot for any more bedding. She drew her knees up to her chin and looked at her mother with shining eyes. 'I'm *so* glad she's better,' she said with genuine earnestness. 'I couldn't bear not to have Rachel. We'll stay together always, Mummy. I wish I had a mark like her, then she wouldn't feel so bad, would she?'

'None of us is exactly alike, dear,' Phoebe said. 'Rachel's mark will fade in time. And mostly I think she forgets it's there.'

'It was horrid of that school nurse to remark about it,' Belinda said as she swung her legs over the side of the bed. 'And it would have to be Charlie Mead who saw it. He's such a hateful boy.'

'He hasn't been bothering you at school, has he?'

Belinda didn't answer at once. She sat on the floor to put her white socks on. 'No-oo, not much,' she said. 'I told his sisters, Susan and June, that he'd better not say another word to Rachel about it or I'd get my dad on to him.'

Phoebe helped Belinda with her bodice, petticoat and dress.

'Best not to take any notice of them, then Charlie and his friends will soon forget.'

Phoebe wasn't convinced but prayed that Rachel would soon be delivered from the scourge.

Charlie Mead sat at the breakfast table in the overcrowded kitchen of the little house in Hundred Acres and chewed noisily on his crust of bread. For once his father was sitting at the head of the long whitewood table. Dick Mead, a rough and ready labourer, was often sleeping off a night's drinking at this time and scarcely saw any of his five children.

'Shut your mouth when you're eating, Charlie,' Dick growled over his enamel mug full of strong black tea.

'How can I get the food in me mouth if it's shut?' the boy retorted.

'Don't answer your father back,' his mother scolded.

'Why shouldn't he? You do it often enough?' Dick said, looking up at his wife with a cheeky grin.

'You're not my father,' Nessie answered shortly.

Dick roared with coarse laughter. 'You can say that again. Else I'd be in clink for incest, eh?'

Nessie shot him an indignant glance and got on with serving the girl's their breakfast. It was a never-ending task, feeding the family, preparing lunch boxes, washing, ironing and mending, as well as cleaning for two hours a day at St Nicholas Church School.

Dick was in convivial mood. No money for drink so he'd spent the evening annoying his wife and eventually demanding his conjugal rights when the kids had gone to bed. He'd had her knickers off even before Charlie had left the room – just to make the boy see red. Nessie had managed to ward Dick off until she'd shut the door behind their son.

'You've no right, Dick. Behaving like that in front of the children. All the village must know what you're like.'

He had only laughed. 'Reckon they do. Come 'ere – let's have a feel . . .'

Nessie had long since lost any feelings of real desire. Yet in spite of the hardships of the past few years she still managed to retain a gentle prettiness about her which made many a man look twice in her direction.

'Got time for a quick frolic after the kids have left for school?' Dick said now, pinching her bottom as she refilled his mug.

'I've got to get to school to do my cleaning and I should think it's time you were off. If you're late again they'll be giving you the sack. 'Tis a busy time during the strawberry season.'

'Stop your nagging, woman. 'Tis only just seven. Plenty of time.'

Charlie suddenly started giggling in his babyish way.

'And what's so funny to you?' Dick shouted, waving his hand in a mock clout.

Charlie's expression changed instantly. He was never quite sure how to take his father. He glanced across at his mother.

'Rachel Hunter's got the mark of strawberries on her face,' he said. 'I saw it the day Nitty Norah came to school.'

Nessie cuffed him round the ear. 'Don't let me hear you speak like that about the nurse, Charlie. We may be poor but we don't have to be common.'

Dick looked at his great oaf of a son. Simple and yet not so simple.

'Hunter?' The name was unfamiliar. 'Is that the new people over at Kingsmere who've got two girls?' he asked.

Nessie turned to the old stone sink and began to stack the dishes.

'Got the strawberry mark, d'you say?' Dick asked Charlie.

'Yeah – she's ugly and I told her so. Told her, her ma must have eaten too many strawberries when she was coming. Told her she had the witches' mark on her.' Charlie nearly fell off the chair with laughter.

'And if you go on at her again, Belinda's going to get their dad on to you, so there,' his younger sister June said, sticking her tongue out rudely.

'I ain't afraid of 'im,' Charlie said.

'That's right, son. Don't you let no one boss you about.' Suddenly Dick stood up and lashed out at Charlie. 'But don't you mock someone with an affliction either or I'll have your hide.'

Charlie began to bawl. Nessie gripped the side of the sink. She hadn't heard about anyone in the district having a strawberry birthmark. Memories came rushing back. After seven years she had begun to forget – forget that Jake Taylor had offered her a job in the strawberry fields to help pay the rent and then taken a mean advantage of her. One peep at the baby who came nine months later had been enough to remind her how it had been conceived. She could only look at it with undisguised hatred because its ugly stigma reminded her of Jake Taylor. She'd been brought up in a Christian home to defy superstitions. Yet there was no doubt that the innocent baby carried the brand of its father's sin. She felt a measure of guilt for hadn't she always felt an attraction to Jake Taylor? But she would never be unfaithful to Dick. It had been a stormy marriage because of his drinking problem, but five healthy children, who brought pleasure as well as a mountain of work, were compensation enough.

As she worked at the scullery sink the memory of that time eight years ago was torture. Her body had become a tool – for the child to sap her strength, for Jake and Dick to use at will. When the last weeks wearied her beyond endurance, Jake had grown impatient with her so left her alone to face the consequences. The confinement was long and more painful than all five previous births put together. Her health was poor afterwards and it was weeks before she was on her feet again.

Jake never bothered her after hearing that she had lost her baby. The following year, though, he made sure she got a job in the strawberry fields again to earn extra money, but she never ate another one.

Nessie sighed. Things were better these days. Since the strawberry growing had continued to prosper there was full-time work for Dick, when she could persuade him to take advantage of it, and as Nessie had no more unwanted pregnancies to contend with she became much healthier.

For two years now she had worked at the school, making sure that she kept her own wages to help feed and clothe all of them.

She still felt a degree of desolation at losing her baby, guilt too because she had felt no love or compassion for it – until it was gone. But, in the circumstances, she was just so thankful that the baby had died soon after birth.

Chapter Two

By the time Rachel and Belinda Hunter reached the age of eleven years, Rachel's birthmark was receding, but very slowly. Much too slowly for a lively, high-spirited young girl who asked for nothing more than to be as pretty as her twin sister.

Rachel stood by the window peering into a speckled old mirror, trying to assess the size of her mark.

'It won't go away by keeping on looking at it,' Belinda said. 'You're for ever looking at yourself, Rachel – as Daddy says, one day you'll see the devil.'

Rachel made a gruesome face. 'I *am* the devil,' she said in a low, menacing voice. The girls laughed as they curled up on the end of their bed to share secrets. 'Belinda, you just don't know how lucky you are,' Rachel said. 'Your hair is fair and wavy, and your eyes are the prettiest blue, like Mummy's.'

'And I wish I had dark curly hair and big brown eyes like you and Daddy,' Belinda said wistfully.

Rachel guessed that her sister only said these things to try to make her feel better. When they were out with their parents people always spoke first to Belinda as if Rachel wasn't even there. No one actually remarked on her blemish. Rachel almost wished they would, at least she would get some attention instead of being made to feel unworthy of notice.

At school it was different. Most of the children at the Church School in Wickham had got used to it by now, and it was only the older boys like Charlie Mead and his gang who took every opportunity to taunt her about it. But they were coming up to fourteen years old and would soon be leaving to start work.

Just before Easter when there was an air of excitement in anticipation of a few days' holiday, and Easter Eggs too, Rachel had to stay behind in class to finish a composition before she could go out to play.

It hadn't been a good day because Miss Davis was in a bad mood, and Rachel had been unable to concentrate. But now the teacher wanted to get to the staff room for her cup of tea so she took Rachel's exercise book away from her with a sigh.

'You'll have to do better than this, Rachel,' she scolded. 'You can do as well as your sister, you know you can, but you seem to waste so much time daydreaming. This work is poor. Untidy and dirty. You'd better wash your hands before you go outside for what's left of playtime.'

Rachel did as she was told and as she came out of the cloakroom she saw a group of boys in the hall. Needless to say it was Charlie Mead at the centre, standing on a stool and straining to reach a picture hanging on the wall. With a bright red crayon he was colouring in the side of the girl's face.

'Charlie Mead, you'll be for it now,' Rachel said in a loud voice.

The boys giggled. ''Tis you, Rachel Hunter,' Charlie mocked. 'See, the mark of a witch – the only one in Wickham School, I reckon.'

'I'm going to tell,' she said and ran off through the door.

Rachel wasn't a tell-tale but she did want to distance herself from such wanton vandalism as quickly as possible, knowing that the picture was quite valuable. The girl wasn't a bit like herself, she thought crossly. She was fair haired, red-lipped, standing beneath a tree in a poppy field, carrying a straw hat with blue ribbon round it. But now everyone would see the girl in the picture as Rachel, and Mr Stanley would be sure to think she had something to do with its mutilation.

To avoid suspicion she joined in with some other girls who were skipping but didn't have a chance to have a go before the bell went. They lined up and to everyone's surprise were led into the hall. Rachel wanted to die. The girl in the picture looked hideous, seemingly glaring down on the whole school accusingly. Rachel felt as if all eyes must be on her but when she glanced round no one appeared to have even noticed.

Mr Stanley the headmaster quickly changed all that, though. With a long cane in his hand he pointed to the picture and proceeded to lecture the whole school of one hundred and fifty children.

'No doubt the artist of this evil deed won't have the courage to stand up and admit to his crime, but I'll find him and when I do he will be made to suffer his punishment in front of you all.'

There was an ominous silence. Now, all heads turned from the picture to where Rachel was standing.

Mr Stanley rapped on his reading desk sharply to command attention.

'We should all have learnt during Scripture lessons that we do not mock the afflicted. If we do we are guilty of sin and will be punished.' He was a tall man with a mean-looking long thin nose with nostrils that were almost closed. His mouth appeared like a narrow stripe across his bony face, but when he parted his lips his voice echoed deep and hollow from a great cavern.

'Now, I want you all to hold out your hands in front of you, palms uppermost.' His tone was menacing and some of the younger children who thought they were about to be smacked unjustly started whimpering.

With long strides Mr Stanley walked briskly through the first two or three rows of children, hardly glancing at their small trembling hands.

'Lead these off to their classroom, Miss Davis,' he said in a softer tone. Then with more diligence, he went through each row examining every hand carefully.

There was some kind of skirmish in the back row before he reached it. Mr Stanley pushed his way through the frightened scholars and grabbed Charlie Mead by the collar of his well-worn jacket.

'I thought as much,' he growled.

Charlie was frantically wiping his hands down the side of his size-too-small trousers but the headmaster saw the evidence he needed. He pushed him to the front of the hall.

'You are a menace to this school, Mead,' he roared. 'Who are you to ridicule anyone else? You haven't got an inch of brain between your ears, lad. This picture, the Poppy Girl, was very valuable, given to the school by the members of Wickham Council many years ago on the accession to the throne of Queen Victoria.' Mr Stanley's face was becoming rather red as anger increased. He began tapping his palm with the cane as if impatient to mete out punishment. Charlie stood looking up at him with his usual stupid grin. He was no stranger to beatings everyone knew. Nothing the head master could do to him would match the abuse he had already suffered. Rachel was tall enough to look over the heads of the children in front of her. She could see Charlie's sister June, two years older than Rachel but several inches shorter, already weeping.

'Prepare yourself, boy, to be the laughing stock of Wickham. Remove your trousers.'

A gasp went up. Spankings were a common enough occurrence but never in a state of undress, and in front of the entire school. Charlie's expression changed only slightly as he paused then started to undo his buttons. Rachel could hardly bear to look. Time seemed suspended as Charlie shrugged his braces over his shoulders. Rachel couldn't stand any more. Some unbidden force urged her forward and on to the platform where she stood defiantly between Mr Stanley and Charlie.

'Don't do it, sir,' she begged. 'I know he did it because of my mark, but he doesn't understand. I . . . I can't help having a birthmark and Charlie can't help being soft in the head. He didn't know the picture was worth anything. He's always in trouble and it isn't fair.'

Mr Stanley looked down at Rachel in disbelief. He could scarcely believe what was happening. This poor girl with an unfortunate brand on her face was actually standing up for Charlie Mead who had caused her nothing but misery ever since the Hunter twins came to Wickham School.

'Rachel, child, don't you think he should be punished?'

'We-ell, yes, for damaging a good painting, sir. But beatings don't mean much to Charlie. I reckon he's had the sense knocked out of him already. Couldn't we just wash it off, Mr Stanley – sir?'

The headmaster's expression softened but he was obliged to ask: 'Did you have some part in this, Rachel Hunter?'

'No! Would I make fun of myself? Charlie's always made fun of me – but he can't help it, sir. The other boys egg him on.'

No child had ever seen Mr Stanley at a loss for words but he didn't seem to know what to do next.

'Apart from the aspect of Charlie's ridicule of you, Rachel, to have this crayon removed will cost a great deal of money and I doubt whether you or Charlie Mead has the wherewithal to pay for it.'

'Perhaps we could have a collection?' she suggested hesitantly.

Now Mr Stanley thought she was being facetious and pulled himself up to his full height. 'The punishment must fit the crime, Rachel Hunter, but since you plead so eloquently on behalf of Charlie Mead I will spare the feelings of the other children.' He glanced across at Miss Davis and the rest of the school was led away.

Rachel supposed she was in for a caning as well, but at least she had bought time for Charlie Mead. She walked sedately by Charlie's side as Mr Stanley urged them towards his study.

'Now, Charlie Mead, bend over.'

'No! No, please Mr Stanley – don't,' Rachel pleaded.

But the cane whizzed through the air and came to rest on Charlie's backside with a dull thud. Once, twice, three times . . .

Rachel had placed her hands over her ears, but suddenly she rushed between master and boy and took the force of the cane descending for the fourth time on the right side of her face.

Charlie waited, gritting his teeth to prevent himself crying out, and realised that the caning had been halted. He stood up and turned to see Rachel holding her cheek.

'You *never*!' he shouted at the headmaster.

'It . . . was an accident. Rachel, I'm sorry, my dear. I didn't mean to hit you – you of all people.' There was a tremor in his voice.

'Why? Because I'm already marked? Now I've got another one to match!' she shouted in order to stem the flow of tears. Her eyes smarted uncomfortable as Mr Stanley threw the cane down in disgust.

'Get out of here, Mead, before I do something I shall regret even more,' Mr Stanley ordered.

Charlie started for the door then stopped and looked at Rachel. 'You all right?'

She nodded.

'T'was your own fault for meddlin' – and don't you ever say I'm soft in the 'ead again or it'll be the worse for you. I 'aint no crybaby. I can take a beating better 'n you, soppy girl! Now look what you got for not minding your own business. All over some silly picture too.' He shuffled away, rubbing the seat of his pants.

'Oh dear, poor Rachel. I know you meant well, my dear, but I'm afraid Charlie doesn't have the sense to realise.'

'Caning's one thing, Mr Stanley, but not in front of the whole school.'

He sat down on his chair behind the large oak desk strewn with official-looking papers. For a second or two he closed his eyes then rubbed his hands over his face in agitation.

'Since when has your opinion been of importance in this school, may I ask?'

'I was only being what Vicar said we should be to those less fortunate than ourselves – compassionate.'

'And why do you think Charlie Mead deserves your compassion, Rachel?'

''Cos, whatever he says, we all know he's twopenneth short of a shilling, sir.' Rachel looked down at the handkerchief she was twisting between her fingers. 'I don't really know why I did it. I just did, sir.'

Mr Stanley pressed his fingertips together. 'You'd better let Miss Davis look at your cheek,' he said quietly and with deep regret.

'It'll be all right. I'll just go and wash it. I know you didn't mean to hit me, Mr Stanley.' Rachel walked towards the door then turned back. 'Will the picture be all right, sir? I mean, can it be cleaned? T'was only crayon.'

'Only crayon, Rachel,' he repeated patiently, 'but an oil painting shouldn't be defaced, and it can only be cleaned by an expert.'

'I don't think Charlie Mead will be able to pay for the damage – nor his dad.'

'There you may well be right, Rachel. Please return to your class. I must write a letter of explanation to your parents.'

At hometime when all the children gathered round Rachel, most in admiration of her courage, shocked too at her scored cheek, she began to worry what her parents were going to say, and once she and Belinda were alone to walk the last mile to Kingsmead she voiced her fear.

'They'll be cross, won't they?' she said.

'Whatever made you do it, Rachel?' Belinda asked wide-eyed.

'Don't know – that devil that's in me, I s'pose.'

'And for Charlie Mead of all people.'

'He won't be at school much longer, thank goodness.'

Phoebe Hunter's first words when the girls reached Calder Cottage were: 'What on earth have you done now, Rachel?'

'It's nothing,' she said, but dutifully handed over the letter Mr Stanley had entrusted her to deliver to her parents. It wasn't that she hadn't considered throwing it in the river on the way home, but Mr Stanley would see her parents at Church on Sunday and there was a risk he would mention it.

Belinda stood by her sister as the questioning continued until bedtime, and Phoebe did her best to explain that a girl of eleven was in no position to take matters into her own hands, let alone question the actions of the headmaster. Wally took himself out to his shed. Planing a nice piece of oak until it had a satin finish helped to take his mind off the cost of cleaning the picture in the school hall. He wasn't sure that he agreed with his wife that it was their duty to contribute but Phoebe was anxious to do the right thing.

After morning service on Easter Sunday, as the congregation assembled outside to meet and chat with friends from outlying villages, Nessie Mead, with June hanging on her arm, joined the small group where Phoebe and Wally were in conversation with George Cropper, the local lumberjack and his wife.

'Excuse me,' Nessie said, 'but I believe you're Mr and Mrs Hunter? I just want to say I'm sorry for what our Charlie did. It was unforgivable of him to poke fun at your daughter.' Nessie turned her attention to Rachel and Belinda and after a few seconds said with a smile: 'You aren't much like twins but at least with different coloured hair your mum can't get you mixed up.' She placed her hand on Rachel's arm in a friendly gesture. 'It was brave to stand up for him like you did, dear. He didn't deserve it. I hope your face is better now?'

'Children have high spirits,' Phoebe said. 'Especially after a long winter when they're kept in. They're all growing up so fast –'

'And it's time our Charlie was put to work, I reckon. I understand you've kindly offered to pay for the picture to be cleaned, but there'll be no need. I've asked Mr Stanley to deduct so much a week from my wages and as soon as Charlie begins to earn he'll have to pay me back. After all, it wasn't your fault – or Rachel's.' She stopped short of saying more. Didn't she know what a shock it was to have a child born with a disfigurement? She found herself staring intently at Rachel Hunter. The child's mark was hardly noticeable with her hair styled to cover the left-hand side of her forehead, and June had said that it was fading gradually. Belinda was such a pretty, delicate child in contrast to her sister who was taller with rich dark hair and eyes which had a fierce intensity about them.

Nessie's duties at the school were to clean before the children got there and after they'd gone home, so she wasn't familiar with many of them except the locals who came from Hundred Acres like herself. She knew the Hunter family hadn't been in Kingsmere more than a few years. Rumour had it that Wally Hunter thought he was a cut above the rest, having a good trade and Squire giving him work. That didn't mean that Nessie was going to allow him to pay their debts. She was far too proud for that. Nessie saw the Hunters out together in Wickham sometimes, or at Church on the rare occasions that she went. The fair girl, Belinda, was more like a fairy doll, Nessie considered, usually holding her father's hand as if they were particularly close. She might almost envy them their happy family image, reminiscent of her upbringing but far removed from the life she led with Dick and their children.

Out of the corner of her eye Nessie saw the Taylor family walking in her direction so bade the Hunters good morning and hurried away from the Church. Jake Taylor wasn't above giving her the glad eye when he got the chance, whether accompanied by his wife Lily and son Adam or not, but mostly his affections were directed at any young girl who took his fancy. Nessie had further cause to feel aggrieved because sixteen-year-old Adam had been taken on as apprentice carpenter at the Manor House. How she wished there was a place somewhere for Charlie, but he wasn't the brightest lad and with his father's reputation well-known in the district no one was willing to give the boy a chance. At least her eldest, Benjie, now nineteen, had a regular job with the blacksmith, and both of the older girls, Kittie and Susan, seventeen and fifteen, were in reliable domestic service. Life was a good deal easier for Nessie with them living in, but she was always glad when they managed to get home together and the house was full again. She supposed even Charlie would be useful weeding and hoeing when the strawberry season started in earnest. June, her baby, was Nessie's closest companion. After losing the strawberry marked infant she had devoted her time and love to June, then a year and nine months old. Now she was growing into a young woman, at thirteen older than the Hunter twins but still shorter than Rachel. June took after Nessie in colouring with her chestnut-coloured hair and pale green eyes. She was timid, sensitive, always ready to rush to her mother's defence when Dick was in one of his difficult moods, eager to defend Charlie too when the world seemed against him. When the time came for her to go away in service Nessie knew she would be lost. But that was a whole year away.

The summer came and went, a summer during which the harvest of fruit was as plentiful as ever and Charlie Mead's physical strength was appreciated by several of the local smallholders. By the end of September Nessie's debt was paid and she could enjoy her sister Beth's wedding with a clear conscience.

Beth had surprised everyone by remaining single until she reached the age of twenty-three. From an early age she had shown herself to be flirtatious and showy, much too generous with powder and rouge. She liked to paint her full sensuous lips bright red in order to attract attention. Somehow she managed to dress in the latest fashions which showed off her well-developed figure to the best advantage. No one ever went as far as calling her a fallen woman but few doubted that she was well paid for her services which provided her with the necessary pounds, shillings and pence to spend on herself.

But she made a beautiful bride dressed in white satin with lace inserts. She was a clever needlewoman, following in her mother's footsteps, and together they had made the dress and those for the three bridesmaids, her nieces Kittie, Susan and June Mead, all dressed in pretty blue taffeta. Even Dick, who gave her away in the absence of her deceased father, managed to stay sober until after the ceremony and for once looked quite presentable in a dark suit borrowed for the occasion.

Relatives, friends and neighbours filled the Church of St Nicholas in Wickham as the bells peeled out across the Meon valley, though the main interest was whether or not Beth was already pregnant. In that she disappointed everyone. People gossiped and twittered. Had Beth Waterstone really turned over a new leaf? Was it possible that she hadn't seduced the handsome Harry Cropper, son of the lumberjack? Could this be a real love-match? By the expressions of adoration exchanged during the photographic session it would seem it was.

Nessie helped her elderly mother over the rough gravel pathway leading to the lych gate.

'That's the last of us to fly the coop, Ma,' she said.

'Never thought our Beth would be that,' Mrs Waterstone said. 'Even let our Esther get to the altar ahead of her by two years, and she the youngest.'

'Maybe Beth wanted to sow her wild oats first before settling down. She made a lovely bride – and fooled everyone into the bargain, but I guess it won't be long before we'll have to start knitting.'

'She's done well for herself, Nessie. Harry is hardworking and it's done young Charlie some good too if George is going to take him on for the winter months. Lumbering's no light work but I reckon your Charlie was built for the job. Let's hope he makes some'at of his self now.'

Things were looking up, Nessie thought, even if she did have to listen to Dick's coarse jokes about the newlyweds.

Autumn brought dark evenings and a spiky chill in the air but on Bonfire Night everyone for miles around joined in the celebrations on the green. For the past few weeks even the children had been collecting anything and everything to help build the mammoth-sized bonfire according to custom.

The Hunters walked in from Kingsmere, the girls dressed in warm coats, woolly hats, scarves and mitts.

'Now don't get too close,' Phoebe warned, 'and stay near us. Don't go wandering off by yourselves.'

But Rachel had a mind of her own. She saw a group of youngsters, among them some of her friends. Since the affair of the damaged picture she had become the most popular girl in the school. They danced round the bonfire enjoying the warmth from the crackling faggots, mostly stolen from people's back yards, running wildly when sparks flew in the air.

One of the older girls who had recently left school had a bottle of cider which she passed round to everyone who wanted to take a swig.

'Isn't this the Strawberry Girl?' she taunted, picking out Rachel. 'Ain't she the one who got a whack for sticking up for Charlie Mead?'

Rachel, in her innocence, didn't realise that the girl was under the influence of drink.

'What if I did?' she challenged with a toss of her head. 'Charlie Mead gets all the blame and it isn't fair.'

'Cm'on then, let's have a look at your mark? S'pose you think it makes you more important than the rest of us?'

'No!' Rachel decided it was time to return to the safety of her parents but the girls gathered round her excitedly, reminding her of a scene four years earlier. But she was older now and wiser. She wouldn't let them see that she was scared.

'Take 'er hat off. Hold back 'er hair,' Dottie Coombes said. Rachel backed away and there was a bit of a struggle. 'Reckon I'm as good a witch as you. I bet I could magic that away. Cm'on let's go to our secret hiding place.'

Rachel began to feel afraid. She was held fast by one girl on each side of her and the others brought up the rear. With some degree of panic she realised that most of these girls were the elder sisters of her own particular school friends.

'No need to be scared, Rachel,' Dottie assured her. 'You don't want to live for the rest of your life with that mark, do you?'

'It's getting fainter,' Rachel said in a small voice. 'The doctor said so. I'll have to get back to my parents or they'll be worried.'

'Not until we've put a charm on you. It'll work, you'll see.'

With the raucous noise at the bonfire no one noticed the small group of girls heading in the direction of the Manor House. When they reached a door in the high brick wall it opened easily and Dottie led the way across the grounds to a tall ominous-looking building known as the folly. They pushed open a rickety door. It was very dark inside and Rachel was frightened.

'I don't like it here,' she said. 'My mum will be looking for me.'

'Then she won't find you, will she, so shut up. And don't you dare tell anyone where you've been. This is our secret. This is where we come and talk. We make up stories and things, and cast spells on people.'

One of the girls had some matches and lit a candle. It was a cold, eerie place with no windows on the ground floor. A narrow spiral staircase stretched up in the centre – to where? Rachel wondered, but she didn't ask.

'Sit down, Rachel, and we'll all sit round you.'

'No!' she said indignantly. 'This place is dirty and I shall spoil my coat.'

'Then your dad will have to buy you a new one, won't he?' Dottie pushed Rachel to the ground and she found herself sitting in the middle of the group holding the candle.

'We need something to rub on your mark. What can we use?' Dottie began walking round. 'I know – we'll make a powder out of some leaves. There's plenty of 'em 'ere.'

Rachel was surprised at the amount of light the candle gave. She could see rubbish lying everywhere – leaves and paper, a few tufts of sheep's wool which had blown in from the meadows on the estate.

Dottie and her friend called Rose gathered handfuls of leaves and screwed them up between their hands. They held it over Rachel's forehead but it wouldn't stick so they threw it over her head. Then they all held hands and danced round her, singing a lot of words she had never heard before. Dottie kept stopping to drink some more cider and soon could hardly stand up. They all fell about laughing hysterically. Rachel thought she'd get up and run but they made sure she didn't get away.

'That's the first bit,' Dottie said. 'Now we've got to blindfold you and then chant until the mark has vanished.'

Rachel found that it was no use remonstrating, she was quite powerless against so many of them fussing round her. They used her own scarf to tie round her eyes and then wheeled her round and round until she was giddy, all the while chanting gobbledygook.

'Oh, stop, do stop – *please* . . . ,' she implored, but no one took any heed of what she said.

'It'll take at least five minutes,' Rose whispered in her ear, and after that it went horribly quiet.

Rachel was so giddy she lost her bearings and when she came up against the wall slid down it on to the floor again. Dottie had tied the scarf so tightly round her head that it was several minutes before Rachel could free herself and then to her horror she found herself in total darkness. She rubbed her eyes but that only made things worse. Where were the others? Where was the door? She began to panic and rushed frantically this way and that but to no avail.

'Now take hold of yourself, Rachel Hunter,' she said to herself. 'You're not a baby and it stands to reason those girls were just making fun of you. You know they couldn't magic the strawberry mark away. Haven't you tried enough times yourself? Let your eyes get accustomed to the dark gradually.' She stood with her back against the wall and closed her eyes gently, then she opened them and waited. Out of the gloom she was able to see a pale strand of light – it must be the doorway, so she rushed at it and breathed a sigh of relief when it opened. There was no sign of anyone. She knew that she was trespassing on private land and would get into trouble if caught. She began to feel frightened again and very angry at Dottie, Rose and the others for leaving her stranded.

Far away on the night air came a shout, probably the men going home from the bonfire or pub. From another direction came the sound of cats fighting and a dog barked too. Rachel had only ever visited the big house with Belinda for the annual Christmas party and then accompanied by their father. Somehow she had to get out of the grounds without being seen but although she walked for what seemed like hours she couldn't find the high brick wall which surrounded the Squire's estate. In desperation she just kept walking not realising that she had left the park and was entering the woods.

The Manor House parkland was vast in itself and now Rachel found herself obliged to walk through a part of the woods she was unfamiliar with. But, somehow, she had to get to Kingsmere. She was tired and worried, aware of how anxious her parents must be. If only she could find a pathway which would indicate where she was but everywhere was deserted and there were only night sounds to scare her. Well, she thought with renewed hope, everywhere must lead to somewhere, she must keep going.

She walked for a further half an hour, then in the distance she could hear a baby crying. Life – there was life somewhere ahead, and she quickened her pace. A loud barking made her stop in her tracks. There in front of her baring its teeth was a vicious-looking animal. She stood frozen to the spot. Her father had taught the girls never to run from any animal but to brazen it out as if prepared for a full frontal attack.

'It . . . it's all right. I'm your . . . friend,' she managed to stammer in a frightened whisper.

The large alsatian dog responded with a low suspicious growl.

'Quiet, Jip!' a voice commanded, but the dog wouldn't be pacified that easily.

'Who's there? What you making that row for, Jipper?' A man stepped out of the trees and was astounded to see his dog holding Rachel at bay.

'God Almighty!' he exclaimed. 'And who are you, and what d'you think you're a doing of, frightening Jipper like that?'

'I . . . I'm ever so sorry, sir,' Rachel said. She hoped that politeness would be her passport from whatever peril she had walked into. 'I'm lost, you see.'

'Lost!' the man echoed. 'Should think you be, my dear. Out here in the forest all alone. Wherefore you goin' then, may I ask?'

'Who you talking to, Josh?' Now a woman appeared as if from nowhere. She peered ahead of her. 'A maid! A maid, all alone in the forest? You run away from 'ome, young miss?' she asked. Her voice was harsh and Rachel began to tremble with fear. Should she stay or take to her heels and run? But where could she go? Which way? Already she was lost and the prospect of being chased through the woods in the dark was worse than trying to talk herself out of difficulty.

'I've been to the bonfire on the green,' she explained in a meek voice. 'I went with some girls to the folly and then – well – I just got left behind.'

'Up to mischief, I dare say,' the woman snapped.

'Come now, Merle, don't be hard on the maid.'

There were more voices, and people emerged from the darkness until Rachel was confronted with quite a gathering. She could smell wood smoke and cooking – she had walked into a gypsy camp. All she knew about these people was that they made clothes pegs and faggots, and knocked on people's doors selling their wares. Sometimes they offered white heather or good luck charms as long as you crossed their palm with silver.

'I live at Kingsmere,' she said in a timid voice. 'I thought I was still in the Manor House grounds but, truth to tell, I don't really know where I am.' She ended the sentence on a high note as the situation became too much for her and she broke down and sobbed.

An arm went about her shoulders. 'Come now, Missie, don't you fret. We'll have you 'ome in no time. Your folks will be worried sick, I shouldn't wonder.' The woman called Merle urged her forward. Rachel was fearful that they might be going to kidnap her so she pulled back.

'Come along, my dear. Just you have a hot drink before we gets you 'ome. You'm cold and afeared, but never you mind, us travelling folk never turns a body away without refreshment.'

A clearing among the trees revealed several painted waggons, and by the light of one of the lanterns hanging on the front Rachel could see horses tethered to a tree in the distance. There was a comforting smell of food and warmth which helped dispel her fear.

She had never been inside a gypsy caravan before and was surprised at the cleanliness as well as the space it provided. The bed in the back looked mightily inviting but she knew she must get home.

'Please,' she begged, 'I ought to get home if you'll just tell me the way to go.'

Merle poured her a cup of tea from the iron pot on the stove. It was good to wrap her cold hands round the earthenware mug and sip. At first she wasn't sure she liked the tea, it wasn't the same as she had at home.

'Herbal, my dearie,' Merle said as if reading her thoughts. 'Do you good, though you look healthy enough to me.' The woman took one of Rachel's hands in hers and opened the palm. 'Mmm,' she murmured. 'A long life ahead of you, me dear,' she said. 'But a troubled one. You've had trouble already, I see. Let's see – a brand – is it a name?' Her voice drifted into a softer tone as she peered more closely at Rachel's hand. 'Poor child – a mark, a birthmark.'

'Yes, yes,' Rachel said eagerly. 'The girls were trying to magic it away in the folly.'

Merle shook her head. 'That's no good. They were trying to trick you and it's wicked to make fun of others.' She studied Rachel's hand in detail. 'Ever had owt to do with our kind?' she asked bluntly.

'No . . . no.'

'Mmm, must be my mistake, but take my word for it, Missie, your mark will go.'

'But everyone says that,' Rachel said indignantly. 'Even the doctor said it would fade by the time I was ten. I'm eleven now and I've still got it.'

'Have faith in what I tell you, Missie. It will go in its own good time if you stop fretting. Then you'll be prettier than your . . . er . . . sister, is it?'

'How could you tell I've got a sister?' Rachel asked in surprise. 'But I could never be prettier than Belinda.'

'Like a fairy doll, I do declare,' Merle said slowly, thoughtfully.

'Yes, she's smaller than me and very fair.'

Merle turned Rachel's palm this way and that, caressing gently until Rachel could feel a soothing element passing through her body. Instead of being frightened now she experienced a tremendous feeling of security.

'Yes, your mark will go but you'll have to be patient. You aren't fully grown yet, me dear, so I can't tell your destiny, but there'll be happy times and then . . . and then some unhappiness. But you'll find your own way . . .' Merle's voice became so soft that Rachel could hardly hear what she was saying, and then it petered out as if Merle was in some kind of trance.

Seconds later she dropped Rachel's hand abruptly. 'Drink your tea, child.' And to no one in particular outside the caravan: 'Fetch Kasan here at once.'

'What time is it?' Rachel dared to ask. She thought it must be midnight after such unimagined events.

'We don't have a need for clocks – but I'd say it's near to nine-thirty. Kingsmere's only a mile away through the woods, but Kas will take you there.'

'What's up, Merle?' a masculine voice called from the doorway.

'Come inside and meet – what's your name, child?'

'Rachel. Rachel Hunter.'

'Then see that Miss Rachel gets home to Kingsmere safely, Kas.' Merle took Rachel's hand in hers and clasped it closely against her chest. 'Godspeed, child – have a happy life.'

'You've been ever so kind,' Rachel began but Merle waved her away.

At the foot of the steps a young man waited. He smiled and took Rachel's hand as she descended the steps.

'We'll take the short cut through the woods. I think I know the cottage where you live,' he said with a warm smile.

Rachel thought she had never seen such a handsome young man before. He was very tall, with a mop of curly, jet black hair which reached down to his shoulders. In the gloom of the night if she hadn't known by his voice that he was a man she would have thought he was a girl. He was wearing a jerkin over dark trousers and had a knotted scarf at his throat.

'No need to be afraid, Rachel. There'll be no one but us in the woods at this time of night, not even the poachers.' His voice was strong yet strangely calm and Rachel had no qualms about walking along with him.

'I've never heard that name before – Kasan.' she said.

'Don't suppose you have. I was born in Ireland – suppose it comes from there. You can call me Kas, everyone does. How did you come to get lost then?'

Rachel poured out her story to him. It seemed to help to talk about her birthmark. She felt that here was someone who wouldn't make fun of her.

'Merle says it will fade if I'm patient but people have been telling me that ever since I can remember.'

'If Merle says so then you must believe it.'

'Is she your mother?' Rachel asked.

'Good gracious no! I haven't got any folks. Merle and Josh took me in when my parents died of a fever. I was only a baby, and they were travelling through Ireland at the time.'

'Do you like being a – gypsy?'

'It's a free life and a happy one. We don't poach and rob like some folks think we do. We try to live peaceably and take good care of each other and anyone else who crosses our path. Sometimes we're rich and sometimes – well, mostly, I s'pose – we're poor.'

'Does Merle tell fortunes?'

'She has the gift of seeing into the future and can tell a bit of the past too.'

'Is that a bit like magic?'

'No, nothing like magic. That's illusion – a kind of trickery.'

They walked in silence for a while and then through the veil of trees as the smokiness of the November night began to clear Rachel could see a lighter patch.

'There, see?' Kasan said. 'Kingsmere. And your cottage is down the road a bit on the right.'

'Oh, thank goodness,' Rachel said with relief. 'Would you like to come in and meet my parents? That's if they're home yet. I'll be in terrible trouble if they've been looking all over the place for me.'

Kasan laughed. 'I think I'll leave you to face the music. I reckon you can take care of yourself, but it was nice meeting you. And here – have this, Rachel.' He pressed something cold into her palm and when she looked she saw it was a round, smooth stone with a hole in the middle. 'For good luck – it's been my lucky charm for years. Perhaps it'll charm your birthmark away quicker.'

'Thank you but I couldn't take it,' Rachel said. But still she kept holding on to it tightly.

'I want you to keep it, to remember me by.'

'Will you be staying in the woods for long?' she asked hesitantly.

'No, I reckon we'll be moving on any day now, but one day maybe I shall knock on your door selling faggots or pegs or asking for work. By then you'll have forgotten you ever had a birthmark.'

'Oh, I do hope so, but I s'pose they'll still go on calling me Strawberry Girl.'

'That's a nice name. Strawberries are sweet. Everyone likes strawberries.'

A light spilled out on to the garden of Calder Cottage.

'Rachel, is that you? Where on earth did you get to,' Phoebe called with some degree of annoyance.

She turned to ask Kasán to go with her but he had vanished. Without so much as a rustle he had disappeared back into the woods. Rachel ran into the house and was about to explain about her visit to the folly when something prevented her.

'I got talking to some girls,' she said. 'They went off and left me and I got lost trying to find my way back to you. I . . . I met some . . . people and they brought me home through the woods. They were very kind.'

'Well, you're a very naughty girl for going off in the first place. Don't you ever do that again. You've had us worried out of our minds. Now get ready for bed and hurry up about it,' Phoebe said crossly. 'You never know who people are and there's gypsies in the forest. You should have stayed with Belinda.'

Rachel was quite glad to go to bed. She considered telling Belinda about her adventure but decided against it. This was her secret, her very own and the first ever from her sister. She stood at the window and looked out into the eerie night. Kasan would be about eighteen years old, she thought.

Long after she had blown out the candle and snuggled under the cosy sheets she lay awake thinking about her gypsy boy.

She supposed she had fallen in love with him at first sight. His soft friendly voice lingered in her head. She'd never ever lose her precious stone, his now her lucky charm. That made it *theirs*. She turned it over in her hand, held it close to her heart and wished with all her might that it would help to make her beautiful. And also that one day she would meet Kasan again, although she knew that was most unlikely.

Chapter Three

By the time the girls reached their thirteenth birthday Rachel could proudly push back her hair to show off her blemish-free forehead. All that remained was a pinkish stain, a pale thin outline which appeared more prominently when he was upset, angry or worried. Rachel was convinced that it was all due to Kas's lucky stone. She knew she must never lose it whatever happened and neither must she ever share her secret with anyone.

Her cross to bear as she entered her teens was that her nickname Strawberry Girl had stuck. Charlie Mead had started it and during the last couple of years others had picked it up, but hadn't Kas told her that it was a nice name? Strawberries were sweet, he had said, so it didn't bother her nearly as much as it once had.

Wickham's Spring Fair, held annually on May 20, was an exciting event. It was an important occasion when farmers met tradesmen at the huge market to pay their yearly accounts. Tents were erected where business could be transacted over a glass of beer or spirits and orders were placed for the forthcoming year. While the men completed deals their wives went shopping in Wickham Square, or the more adventurous crept surreptitiously into the travelling gypsy's tent to have their fortune told.

There was every sideshow imaginable to tempt young and old alike to part with their hard-saved pennies. Stalls of trinkets to attract keen buyers, and balloons and streamers giving an air of festivity to the market town. Loud music bellowed continuously and young men drank far more than was good for them as they gathered round the shooting galleries and boxing booths.

Wally and Phoebe Hunter allowed the girls to wander off and amuse themselves while they went to watch the sale of horses, sheep, cattle and pigs which totalled some several hundred in all and covered a large area. Business was brisk, sometimes carried out in a good-humoured way but frequently a fight between competitors would break out and Wally and Phoebe temporarily forgot about their growing daughters.

The girls were fascinated by the enthusiasm of everyone as money flowed freely. Not that they had much to spend themselves as they were only allowed a shilling or two out of their birthday money to fritter away on what Phoebe declared was rubbish. Rachel's spirits lifted when they came to the fortune teller's tent. Was it possible that Merle was inside? she wondered. Dressed in colourful skirt and shawl, gazing knowingly into a crystal ball.

'Let's go in here,' she suggested eagerly, but Belinda was horrified.

'How can you think of such a thing. You know Mummy would be cross, Rachel.' She hurried on saying brightly: 'Let's have a go on the swings and roundabouts.'

After they had tired of being spun round and swung high into the air they went to find the toffee stall where they purchased large humbugs for a farthing. They were ambling along watching with amazement everything that was going on around them when a voice suddenly boomed out: 'Why, if it isn't the Strawberry Girl.'

Rachel turned quickly, readily on the defensive at the sound of Charlie Mead's voice.

'Don't call me that,' she said crossly. 'I haven't got a mark any more, so there.'

Belinda, white with apprehension, tried to pull Rachel away but she stood her ground, forgetting that Kas considered it a nice name. She was anxious to settle the matter once and for all. She pulled her hair back to show off her flawless white forehead as she stepped nearer to Charlie and his gang of yobs. Too late she realised that these young men had consumed more than their fill of beer. Charlie's breath reeked of it. He grabbed Rachel roughly, and although she tried to fight him off he was too strong and began to wrestle with her. To Rachel's surprise a young man came out of the crowd to her assistance.

'Leave her alone, you great bully. Don't you know that's not the way to treat girls?'

'Aw, who 'ave we got 'ere then? Cor, 'tis Adam Taylor! And what would you know, fancy boy?' Charlie sneered. 'Still clutching at your ma's apron, you are. If I want to tease the girls, I will.'

'Leave Rachel and Belinda alone,' Adam said.

'Want to make some'at of it then?' Charlie challenged, releasing Rachel and putting up his fists.

'No, I don't want to fight,' Adam said, 'but I will if it keeps you away from the girls.' He squared up to the bulky Charlie who by comparison made Adam appear quite puny although he was only an inch short of six feet but very slim. Adam Taylor was a good-looking young man with dark curly hair and black eyes. He'd been above average with his school work so was not particularly popular with other young men in the village. At eighteen he kept himself to himself, keeping his mother company rather than going off gallivanting.

'Now, now, now, boys, that's not the way to go about things.' The boxing booth owner saw a golden opportunity to draw an audience. Already several people were showing interest in the situation which threatened to grow ugly. 'Come on inside, boys, and let the best man win.'

Charlie's friends roared their approval and before Adam knew it he was being hoisted to the back of the booth and urged to change into some large boxing shorts.

'Trade not going too well, me lads, so I'll give you a pound each for a good fair fight,' the man whispered. 'Got to get the people in though so I'll advertise two pounds for the winner.' He went to the front of the booth. 'Roll up, roll up!' he shouted, and had little difficulty in rallying a large number of people. 'Come and support these gallant young men in a most exciting three-round contest. Two pounds for the winner,' he yelled.

Belinda clutched at Rachel's arm. 'Oh, poor Adam,' she said. 'Rachel, we can't let him do it. Charlie will murder him.'

Rachel laughed. 'Nothing we can do about it – he didn't have to interfere, did he?'

'That's not very nice. He did it for you – and *I'm* very grateful even if you're not.'

'He got us out of an awkward spot,' Rachel giggled. 'He's all right – a bit of a Mummy's boy. He's quite nice-looking though.'

Belinda would have extricated herself from the situation, but by now onlookers were packed in closely behind them making escape impossible.

'I daren't look, Rachel,' Belinda said. 'I wish we could get away.'

'Somehow I don't think Adam will survive three rounds,' Rachel said, suddenly feeling remorseful, but they had to stick it out.

The fight began, the crowd urging it on, mostly yelling on Adam's behalf because he looked such an unlikely candidate. Blood was soon flowing from a cut on his lip. Both eyes were swollen up so that he could hardly see his opponent but still miraculously he kept on his feet. Rachel cheered with the rest of them but Belinda only peeped from between trembling fingers when the response from the crowd suggested that Adam might be down. Charlie was like a great lumbering bear after his prey but Adam managed to get in a few hard blows to his challenger's body which hurt. The final bell sounded. At last the three gruelling rounds were over and the boxing booth owner held up Charlie's hands as the winner, Adam's as a game loser. There were boos and jibes as Charlie received the two pounds, but the crowd quickly lost interest and dispersed. Rachel and Belinda remained, thinking that at least they owed Adam their sympathy. They stood at the side of the booth where they saw an argument in progress.

'You said a pound each,' Adam said snatching one of the pound notes the boxing booth owner had demanded back from Charlie.

'That was only to draw the crowd, lad. You surely didn't think I meant it? You two had a score to settle so I let you do it in my ring.'

'You're a liar and a cheat,' Adam said, blinking the blood from his eyes. 'Two pounds for the winner you said publicly, and that's Charlie fair and square.' The man grabbed the money from Adam's hand, he tried to take it back but it was securely held, and while Charlie beat a hasty retreat Adam threw a vicious punch which sent the owner of the boxing booth reeling on his own canvas.

Adam took to his heels. 'Get away from here,' he said to the girls before quickly merging with the throng of people milling around.

Few took any notice of the bloodied youth who fled from the fair meadow with two girls chasing after him.

'Rachel – we can't – we mustn't! Supposing Mum and Dad see us,' Belinda panted, finding it difficult to keep up with her long-legged sister. 'Let Adam go. He'll be all right when he goes home to his mother.'

'He won't want his mother seeing him like that. Wasn't he brave? I think we should make sure he's all right.'

Belinda had little option but to follow her sister who, being tall, managed to keep Adam in her sights as he ran towards the river.

Rachel guessed where he was making for and at the end of the fence by the mill she found him at the bottom of the steps at Dip Hole. He was frantically splashing water over his face, washing away the blood to make himself respectable.

'Can we help, Adam?' she asked.

'I'm all right. Don't worry about me. You get on back to your folks, and don't dare tell anyone what happened.'

'But it wasn't your fault. I mean – well – it was mine, I s'pose. I shouldn't have taken any notice of Charlie Mead. I didn't mean you to get into a fight on my account, Adam.'

He came slowly up the steps, drying his face on his neck tie.

'I hope I'd have done the same for any girl who was being molested by Charlie Mead. I may look feeble but he didn't get things all his own way '

'You knocked that horrible booth man flat!' Belinda said with undisguised admiration. 'That was very brave.'

Rachel saw Adam gaze at her sister with more than passing interest, but then – didn't everyone look at pretty Belinda with a sense of enchantment.

'Fair's fair,' he replied softly. 'I may not like Charlie Mead but he won the fight even if we weren't very well matched. That rotter didn't want to pay up at all – it was all a farce for *him* to make money. I hate cheats. He made me mad so I just lashed out. I reckon if I could have gone a few more rounds with Charlie I might have winded him and all.' Suddenly he laughed then said: 'Ouch!'

'Your poor mouth – you won't be able to eat, will you?' Rachel said.

'Right now I could do with a strong drink so I'd best get home to Ma and keep my head down. No doubt the boxing owner will tell the police he was assaulted and I won't be too hard to find, will I? You leave me and don't worry. Your father won't be very pleased at you getting involved in a brawl. I'll make my way home through all the side tracks.'

'Thank you for rescuing me from Charlie,' Rachel said shyly. 'I'm sorry you got hurt though. I think you should each have had your pound.'

'Charlie won the fight – I did try to get him his winnings. Maybe he'll buy me a drink one of these days.'

'Not if I know Charlie Mead,' Rachel said. 'We'll see you up at the big house perhaps when we visit our Dad one day.'

'I'll look out for you. I like working with your father, he's a good man.'

Adam glanced from Belinda to Rachel, and back at Belinda again. Then he hurried away. The two girls walked sedately back to the fair. No, thought Rachel, he fought for me. Belinda's not going to have him. Kasan was forgotten. Adam was her new hero. He was learning a trade, was attractive and well liked. She knew she must be the one to make advances though. Wasn't she still tarnished with the strawberry mark, even if it had completely vanished? She was convinced people still thought of her as the witch of Wickham so she had to make Adam notice her. Belinda would have the pick of young men, not just any eligible young man but probably a wealthy one. Their parents would see to that. Nothing but the best for Belinda.

On Saturdays when there was no school Rachel and Belinda usually went into Wickham to do some shopping for Phoebe, and as the days grew warmer they would stop by the river to feed the ducks. Occasionally they would have to go to the big house to find their father to take his lunch.

Phoebe noticed the sudden eagerness to run any errand which took the girls to the big house.

'They're growing up, Wally,' she said one balmy evening when they had strolled to the bottom of their large garden to feed the hens. 'I reckon there's a lad they fancy somewhere about.'

Wally looked fondly at his wife and smiled. 'And I can tell you who he is – young Adam Taylor.' He threw a handful of corn to the cackling chickens who came strutting after them. 'I've been wondering which of them 'tis he's after.'

'They're both nice-looking girls. I just hope they make good matches when the time comes. Somehow I don't think Belinda's that interested in boys though.'

'Rachel's the one with high spirits,' Wally said dryly. 'Have to watch her.' He did watch and with interest as Adam seemed friendly with both the girls.

As summer progressed the girls knew where to find Adam fishing and would spend long happy hours chatting to him. It was an enlightening time when they broadened their outlook and felt the first flush of young love. Belinda kept her feelings and thoughts close to her heart but Rachel had no such inhibitions.

One day when Belinda was in bed with summer 'flu Rachel had to take a basket of eggs to Beech Cottage. Everyone loved Minnie Fletcher and Rachel was pleased to sit awhile and chat to the old lady now in her eightieth year. She prepared tea and enjoyed a piece of fruit cake with Minnie before starting the long walk home through the woods. It was cool under the shade of the trees. Rachel hummed a tune as she went along swinging her empty basket. Her thoughts were all happy ones and she recalled meeting the travelling gypsies here almost two years ago. Where were they now? she wondered. What was Kasan doing? Did he ever think of her? She felt in her pocket and turned the lucky stone over in her palm. She didn't really need it any more, it had done the trick and taken away her birthmark, yet she knew she would never part with it, that would be courting disaster. Most of all she wanted Adam to like her more than he did Belinda so she held on tightly to the stone and wished with all her might.

The following day Rachel had to take her father's tea up to the big house. He was very busy and wanted to remain working for another couple of hours. Rachel sat with him in his workshop while he emptied the flask and ate the sandwiches Phoebe had prepared. Adam came in with some new wood from the store. He smiled politely at Rachel and nodded, not daring to say too much in front of Wally.

'You can get off home now, Adam,' Wally said. 'You've put in a good day's work so be on your way and get your tea.'

'I can stay, Mr Hunter, if there's anything I can do to help,' Adam offered. 'I know Squire wants to get that panel put in the drawing room.'

Wally surveyed the two youngsters and observed their covert glances.

'No, lad, your ma might worry if you aren't home by six.' He liked Adam well enough but maybe it was time to take precautions. He wasn't blind to what was going on so purposely kept Rachel talking until he'd finished eating so that she could take the empty flask home. Rachel knew she mustn't appear to be in a hurry but as soon as she was out of sight of the big house she took the tow path by the river and found to her delight that Adam was waiting for her by the old River Inn.

'I guessed you'd come this way,' he said. 'Where's Belinda today then?'

Rachel felt a flicker of jealousy. 'In bed with summer 'flu. She's a bit delicate and Mum's afraid she'll get pneumonia. I hadn't better be long as Mum will wonder where I am.'

'She'll think you're with your dad.'

'And I expect your mum will be expecting you for tea.'

'She'll only miss me when she wants me to do something.'

'Don't you wish you had brothers and sisters, Adam?'

''Course I do. You're lucky having Belinda.'

They walked along for a while then sat down on a grassy bank watching the water hurrying past. There was no embarrassment between them and as Rachel lay back looking up at the clear blue sky she said bluntly: 'You'll have to choose, Adam Taylor. I don't intend to play second fiddle while you wait your opportunity to get Belinda on her own.'

He pulled a blade of grass and chewed on it, then he turned to gaze down at Rachel. 'Who says I want to get Belinda on her own?'

Adam knew that what had first started out as youthful friendship with the Hunter twins was developing into something different. Now he knew his feelings were demanding more. He liked them both. Perhaps the dainty Belinda did have the edge but she was often sickly and more serious than her sister. He had always felt sorry for Rachel having that nasty birthmark which caused her to be the butt of remarks by the likes of Charlie Mead. When her wayward curls blew away from her forehead he could see for himself that the mark was no longer there, and he had to admit he found her dark bewitching eyes hard to resist. She had the stronger character. She was forceful, carrying her twin along with a zest for life.

'Belinda's the prettiest,' Rachel breathed almost inaudibly as if afraid he might agree with her.

'She's pretty, yes,' Adam said. 'But you're – well – different.'

Rachel thought he was blushing slightly so gave him a playful shove. 'You're only saying that not to offend either of us,' she taunted wickedly.

'I like you both – but I'm older than you. Your parents . . .'

'What about our parents? They can't choose for you – if they could it would be Belinda.'

'No! You mustn't say things like that, Rachel. I'll choose for myself and if . . . if you let me kiss you, then it'll have to be you.'

'I don't want you to feel obliged,' she answered back pertly and got up and ran along the river bank.

Adam was soon on his feet chasing after her and when he caught her as she fully intended him to they fell together on the grass.

His hands spanned her waist and he slowly bent his head until his mouth touched hers.

'Now, does that convince you?' he asked. 'But we can't – well – be serious until you're older.'

'I'm nearly fourteen,' Rachel informed him proudly.

'When?' Adam asked.

'Next year – March.'

'That's months away yet.'

'Only seven months.' She sighed. 'S'pose you'll meet someone else and get married and forget all about me?'

'No question of me getting married yet awhile, Rachel. What have I got to offer a girl? I've only just finished by apprenticeship.'

'But I heard my dad tell Mum that Squire thinks very highly of you and would like to keep you on.'

'But how long for? Work's getting short. I love working with wood but there are other things I'd like to do more.'

'Nothing much you can do around here. There's the basket factory of course, but I can't see you working there, especially as Charlie Mead and his father have both got jobs there.'

Adam laughed. 'It's a good proposition. The factory has brought more work for local people and Dad reckons that at last Dick Mead might stay off the booze now that he's got a regular job as carter. Charlie's just right for storeman with his strength. What are you going to do when you leave school, Rachel?'

'They talk about me going into service.'

'And Belinda?'

'No, she's much too delicate to work – although she has thought about being a nanny but Mum said she'd better wait until she's sixteen or seventeen. They don't want her to go away from home but I expect I'll have to.'

'Perhaps you could go into the factory – I hope you don't have to go away, Rachel.'

It was the first sign of real interest and she was flattered. She smiled up at him seductively, smoothed his ruffled eyebrows and ran her finger over his cheek. Adam got up quickly, sensing that things could get out of hand if he wasn't careful. He respected Rachel and her family too much to let that happen.

During their clandestine meetings, though, they declared that they were sweethearts, that as soon as Rachel was old enough they would make known their intentions.

Belinda soon realised that things had progressed between her sister and Adam. When they met all together she began to feel in the way, an odd one out.

'Did you see Adam while I was ill, Rachel?' she challenged one night as they prepared to go to bed.

'Only once or twice,' Rachel said, hiding her guilt-stained cheeks behind the cascade of rich ebony-coloured hair which she brushed frantically. 'I saw him up at the big house when I took Dad's tea and we walked home together.'

'But he doesn't live this way.'

'No, but he wanted to ask after you.'

Belinda felt better but only temporarily as when they next went to church she saw Adam and Rachel eyeing each other with familiarity. Belinda felt cheated, not so much because of the new intimacy between her sister and Adam but because Rachel hadn't confided in her. She was well aware that Adam preferred the outgoing Rachel more than her so had to be content to stand aside and watch the boy she was attracted to fall in love with her twin sister.

October gales were followed by autumn mists and damp dark nights. Winter in the countryside meant that few folk ventured far after dark. Rachel didn't see Adam very often except when she went into the woods to gather firewood, or visited her father at the big house on some errand for her mother, but she thought about him all the time. Occasionally after morning service at the church of St Nicholas she and Belinda managed to have Adam to themselves for a chat, but it was all too brief. Rachel was convinced that she loved Adam and he her even if he did show friendship to both of them. Her parents would think she was too young so she knew they must be discreet.

In the spring of 1914 the girls celebrated their fourteenth birthday and Rachel announced that she was going to support the suffragette movement which was constantly in the news. Wally and Phoebe listened to her pontificating on her views with a measure of amusement. After all, living in the country didn't allow their daughter much freedom to express those views. Rachel wrote letters in support of Mrs Pankhurst and her followers, talked of going to London, but then at the end of June the suffragettes were forgotten as world news dominated the headlines.

A wave of indignation swept over Europe when a nineteen-year-old student killed the heir to the Austro-Hungarian throne. The *Daily Chronicle* reported the incident as a 'clap of thunder', while *The Times* said that the atrocity in Sarajevo 'shakes the conscience of the world'. Events unfolded with extraordinary speed, completely overtaken when the Kaiser took offence at what he saw as British insolence by proposing mediation to avert the catastrophe of war.

But war was inevitable and by August of that year young men cheered as they made their way to recruiting offices to join Kitchener's Army, among them the local lads who had gone through school with Rachel and Belinda, Adam Taylor, Charlie Mead and Benjie Mead included. A special service was held in the church in Wickham with refreshments afterwards to bid the men Godspeed. Phoebe Hunter thanked God that at forty-nine Wally was too old, but several of the women wept as they said farewell to husband and sons.

Adam managed to persuade Rachel to go outside the school hall into a small copse nearby.

'I'll miss you, Rachel,' he said in a husky voice. 'I'm not going to pretend that I want to go and fight but neither am I a coward. Take care of yourself and when I came home we'll start walking out properly.'

'Oh, Adam, it's you who must take care. I shall look out of the window every night and pray for you wherever you are. Hold me tightly and promise you'll write.'

Adam hugged and kissed her. 'I don't know about writing, Rachel. The trenches don't sound the ideal place to use pencil and paper but I'll try.'

Rachel rummaged in her small bag. 'Here, this brought me luck and took away my birthmark. Keep it on you and it'll bring you luck as well.' She handed over the precious stone Kasan had given her. Adam needed it more than she did now.

At first there was something quite exciting about the local boys going off to do their bit in fighting spirit and the belief that hostilities would last a few months at most. It was an adventure offering escape from hard work on the land or jobs they didn't much care for. But Rachel soon realised that there were more sinister connotations to war than handsome young men in uniform. News came from across the Channel of fierce and bloody battles and everyone dreaded the arrival of military telegrams bringing notice of wounded relatives or worse still death at the front line.

At home everything had to carry on as near normally as possible. Hospitals were set up all along the south coast in readiness for ships bringing home wounded men. Women and girls left their regular jobs in service or on the land to train as nurses which left opportunities for young school leavers.

Belinda went daily with her father to the big house to help look after the family's children while Rachel went to work at the basket factory which was badly affected by the war as timber bought from Russia ceased to arrive. Much of the machinery was German-made so spare parts were unobtainable, but somehow the basket factory managed to survive.

Beth Cropper, still childless, was one of the many married women who stepped into the men's shoes though sadly she was one of the earliest war widows as Harry was fatally wounded during the early days at Mon. Beth quickly reverted to being flighty, and flirtatious with the men at the factory. most of all with her own brother-in-law, Dick Mead, so earning herself the nickname of Merry Widow while insisting on calling Rachel Strawberry Girl.

Rachel had to learn to stick up for herself which she did easily. She didn't enjoy the type of work much so was grateful that it didn't take the manager, Jimmy Cole, long to realise that she was capable of more exacting tasks. She was moved from the basket-packing benches to despatch where her arithmetical abilities and neat handwriting were an advantage, but unfortunately this didn't make her very popular with the other workers, many of whom had been employed at the factory ever since it started.

Nessie and Dick Mead continued to live together as man and wife but there was little love lost. Nessie worked hard keeping a clean and orderly home as well as working at the school. She wrote weekly letters to Benjie and Charlie, fearful that she might lose either or both of her sons. She had neither the will nor the desire to please Dick any longer so he responded to Beth's womanly wiles. Nessie felt that Beth had no shame and after Dick had gone off to the inn one evening rebuked her sister.

'Just widowed, Beth,' Nessie said as she folded the washing just brought in from the line. 'Whatever will people say?'

'Who cares what anyone says? With this war on we've got to make the best of things. It's not my fault that Harry got himself killed.'

'That's an outrageous thing to say. Haven't you got any consideration for what these men are going through? If you don't feel any grief for Harry just remember how his parents feel. It's made poor George an old man before his time.'

Beth took the ends of the sheet to fold. 'Poor old Harry, wasn't his fault that we didn't have a kid, I s'pose,' she said with momentary regret. 'His mum and dad blame me, naturally. Keep on about having an heir. It's obvious they don't want me around so I'm thinking of coming here to live. You won't mind, will you?'

'*Mind*!' Nessie said in high-pitched voice. 'Of course I mind. You should stay with the Croppers and help them through this sad time.'

'I just told you, they don't want me.'

'Well, is that surprising? You're an embarrassment to them I shouldn't wonder. And, no, you can't come here, there isn't enough room.'

Beth laughed lightly. 'No room, she says,' she mocked. 'With Benjie and Charlie away, Kittie and Susan living in, you've only got June here.'

'I intend to keep the boys' room just as it is ready for when they come back.'

'You mean you're using one of their beds for yourself rather than sleep with Dick? Don't think he hasn't told me how things are with you, Nessie, so you can't blame him if he looks elsewhere for his enjoyment.'

'And we all know where he gets it, young madam. Goodness knows where you get your sinful ways from, Beth Cropper. You didn't learn any of it from our family.'

'No, I learned all and more than I should have by coming here helping you when the kids were small. Dick always did have a roving eye, especially for me. You haven't got any passion in you – except, that is, for Jake Taylor.'

'How dare you! Don't mention that man's name in this house. You know nothing about him, nor me either for that matter, and if you had to sleep night after night with a man that reeks of drink and snores disgustingly you'd be glad of a bed to yourself, I can tell you.' Nessie knew her cheeks were aflame at the audacity of her younger sister. Memories came flooding back of a time she'd much rather forget.

'If you won't be a proper wife to Dick then you must expect him to find someone else. And if you don't shut up and let me come here to live with you then I shall tell him about your affair with Jake Taylor.' Beth stood over Nessie gloating. 'Dick might not realise that the marked baby you had wasn't his, but you and I both knew that it was Jake Taylor's bastard.'

Shock paralysed Nessie, albeit briefly, and then she smacked Beth's face with the full force of her anger behind it.

'Jake was never more to me than a nuisance,' she yelled in self-defence. 'There was never anything between us even if he and Dick have always been rivals, and as to my baby being his . . .' She covered her face with her hands.

Beth nursed her smarting cheek as she warned angrily, 'Now you'd better watch out, Agnes Mead. I'll get my revenge for that, see if I don't. In my own way and in my own time – but one thing is sure, I shan't ever forget what I owe you.'

With a haughty toss of her head she rushed away from the silent brick house leaving Nessie ashamed for having lashed out at her sister but alarmed at what Beth might do. Everyone thought marriage had changed Beth, but she had been clever to wheedle her way into the Cropper household for her own ends. A good hard-working family which provided plenty and to spare for their only son and his wife. Since the death of Harry, Beth had reverted to her old ways. She was free again to seduce any man she chose and for the moment that was Dick. Nessie stood looking out of the window, remembering. Was it possible that Beth knew too much? Enough to harm her? For if she decided to tell Dick what she thought she knew of the situation all those years ago, he was still capable of murder. Beth had shown signs of being a devious schemer from her earliest years. Nessie recalled her mother voicing her fears for the black sheep of her family. Yet Nessie had cause to be grateful to her sister for the help she'd been to her when the children were small. She'd been well paid though. Jake Taylor had rewarded her for her services, and Nessie had been naive enough to believe that her young sister was too innocent to suspect anything. Now she realised that Beth was quite capable of causing trouble.

Weren't there enough men around without her making a play for Dick? No, Nessie thought, the eligible ones were fighting for their country. Of the men left in the area, apart from the middle-aged and elderly, there were a few who hadn't passed their medical and one or two who had returned from Flanders with war wounds. Dick might be rough and ready but he wasn't unattractive, and if a woman was of easy virtue with loose morals as Beth was, the two of them might well make satisfactory bed-fellows. Nessie couldn't help it if she felt nothing for her husband now. Dick had been the recipient of Nessie's youth. Degraded and abused, weighed down with sheer hard work and responsibility, she had at last reasserted herself to be independent of him. Since he had obtained regular work at the basket factory their daily lives had taken an upward turn. Was Beth, in her frivolous, capricious way, about to destroy everything that Nessie had worked for?

Chapter Four

'Love letter, Strawberry Girl?' Beth Cropper teased.

'What's it to you?' Rachel retorted with some embarrassment.

'Let's have a look. From – now who could it be from, I wonder? – oh, Adam Taylor, I bet.'

'It isn't anything to do with you. It's my private letter,' Rachel said heatedly.

Beth took a deceptive step backwards and then pounced, snatching the letter and dancing away with it across the yard. By the time Rachel caught up with her, Beth was reading it aloud.

'Oh, "love as always",' she taunted. 'Walking out together and you hardly out of school yet.' She tut-tutted as she re-read the letter before tossing it away on the breeze. Fortunately it fluttered straight into Rachel's hands. She quickly folded it and returned it to her pocket.

'Adam and I have been friends for a long time,' she said with a toss of her rich black hair. 'I'm sixteen anyway.'

Adam had been gone for nearly two years now and letters were few and far between so this last one was precious even though she was disappointed at the length of it. On one single side he explained that since completing his course in stretcher-bearer duties he spent all his time transporting casualties from the forward position back to the Regimental Aid Post, and from there on to the main dressing station.

Conditions were unpleasant, he wrote, but the job has to be done.

'I think often of the happy times we spent together, Rachel, and look forward to being back in Wickham again. My regards to your parents and Belinda. Please keep writing, it brings you closer to me even when I get several letters together. Your lucky stone is safe and proving its worth so far. Love you always, Adam.'

Rachel read and re-read the letter but guarded it jealously from inquisitive eyes, especially Beth Cropper's who from then gave her no peace. Every morning she greeted Rachel with 'Heard from lover-boy today?' and soon all the other girls and some of the men too tormented her about Adam. At first it hurt that her feelings weren't sacred any more, but she was used to being scoffed at so she was able to disregard much of Beth's taunting and concentrate on her work, boring though it was. Checking baskets going out, keeping neat accounting of all despatch work, was better than being on the packing benches, though she hadn't minded helping actually to make the baskets. The spring was a busy time when they were preparing for the strawberry season and one late afternoon Jimmy Cole asked Rachel to go along to the store shed to check on the stock there. She climbed up the tall ladder to get to the top stacking shelves and after counting carefully wrote down the number on a piece of paper. The shelves reached high into the sloping roof and Rachel was hidden while she was at the top. Beth Cropper evidently thought the store was empty when she came running in, chased by her brother-in-law, Dick Mead.

Beth was laughing in her usual coarse way. Everyone knew that grief for her late husband had been short-lived and an intimate friendship with Dick had developed speedily. Rumours were rife, most of them started by Beth herself who boasted her success in seducing any man who took her fancy.

'Come 'ere, wench,' Dick growled playfully as he caught her and threw her down on some sacks in a corner of the store shed. 'Can't get enough of you, my girl.'

Rachel descended a few rungs of the ladder as softly as she could, and then more swiftly as she became aware that what they were planning to do was not for her eyes. But when she reached the bottom she knew she had to creep past them and simply didn't have the courage. Dick pushed Beth's skirts up to squeals of her obvious delight. Rachel could only watch open-mouthed as in desperation she tried to squeeze in between some wooden crates. The horse-play went on for several minutes and then Dick, breathing heavily, sat back to undo his trousers. Rachel didn't think she had made any sound but he half-turned and in that instant saw her. As he shouted some obscenity she took to her heels and fled toward the door. He made a grab for her leg as she passed but she was fleet-footed and escaped out into the yard, Dick's voice echoing after her.

'You just wait until one dark night, Strawberry Girl. I'll have your drawers off you, see if I don't!'

Strong arms caught Rachel as she ran up against a brawny figure.

'You all right?' a deep voice asked.

Rachel didn't recognise the soldier who had stopped her in her tracks before she could emerge into the sunlight. She struggled to get away then realised that the voice was vaguely familiar.

'Charlie Mead!' Rachel managed to gasp. She wasn't sure whether or not she was pleased to see her old adversary. But then she laughed, her brain racing ahead in leaps and bounds. If Charlie was here then Adam might be as well. 'What are you doing here? When did you get home?'

'I got a blighty in me leg. T'weren't much, just enough to get me sent back to hospital. It went septic after they got the shrapnel out, but it's better now. At least I got the chance to come home for a couple of days.'

'No one told me that you'd been injured. I bet your mum's glad to see you, Charlie.'

'Yep. Reckon she is. Trouble is, I got to go back next week.'

'I don't suppose you've seen or heard anything of Adam Taylor?'

'Not lately. We did our training together then got separated.'

'He wrote saying that he's a stretcher bearer now. Is that dangerous, Charlie?'

''Tis all dangerous, Strawberry Girl. Shells flying about everywhere, and when you go over the top its either Fritz or you.'

'Oh, you poor thing. It must be dreadful.'

Charlie actually looked embarrassed at her sympathetic interest. Then he suddenly asked with genuine concern, 'Are you all right?'

The shock of seeing Charlie so unexpectedly had taken Rachel's fright clean away. He looked so handsome in his uniform; taller – could he possibly have grown? – he certainly didn't look as bulky as she remembered. Cleanshaven now where once much of his face had been hidden beneath coarse stubble, and the untidy matted hair of schooldays was cut very short and neatly combed. He looked every inch the proud soldier with a ramrod straight back.

'Yes, 'course I am,' she replied with a friendly smile.

'My Dad and Aunt Beth – did he molest you?'

'No, they were only teasing like they always do.'

'No need to lie for them, Rachel.' Charlie leaned forward a little to speak in confidence and she recognised a strange quiver in his voice at his use of her real name. This wasn't the big bullying Charlie Mead who had scared her when she was younger. 'I do know about them,' he went on in a low voice, 'and I bet they're up to no good in there right now. I heard what he shouted after you but he hadn't better touch you – or else.'

'Look, Charlie. I'll have to go. Mr Cole is waiting for these figures. I'm sorry you got wounded but I know how pleased your mum and the girls must be to see you.'

'T'won't be long before you knock off, will it? Can I wait for you and walk home with you?'

Rachel hesitated. Different though he seemed old memories weren't that easily erased. But he had been fighting in the front line – for her as much as for anyone else.

'Yes, 'course you can. There's the hooter now. Sometimes I work on a bit but there's no need tonight.'

Rachel hurried back to the despatch department and from the window saw everyone making a great fuss of Charlie in the yard. He only had a little 'blighty' according to him but it was enough to make him one of Wickham's heroes. Rachel finished up a few things on her desk and then went out into the evening sunshine.

'Are you sure you didn't ought to be getting home to your family, Charlie?' she said. 'You aren't here for long and I'm sure your mum wants to see as much of you as she can.'

To Rachel's surprise Charlie sighed, and his expression was one of despondency. 'I've had lots of time to talk to Ma,' he said. 'I don't particularly want to be at home when Dad's around, especially if Aunt Beth's there too. Been a bit of trouble at home, Rachel, since Benjie and me left for the war.'

Rachel walked along beside him in silence. There was gossip about the Meads – hadn't there always been? – which was why she supposed she couldn't help feeling pity for Charlie.

'I'm sorry,' she said softly. ''Specially for your mum. There's no love lost between Beth Cropper and me, though.'

'She's evil,' Charlie said vehemently, 'and so's me dad.' They had come to the bridlepath through the woods where the birds' evensong was the only accompaniment. 'Ma says Beth wanted to move into our house. Can you believe it? Carrying on right under Ma's nose? 'T'ain't decent. Ma ain't never had an easy life. Me dad ought to be the one out there in France fighting. Do 'im good, teach 'im a thing or two, I can tell you. No one would mind if he got done in.'

'Oh, Charlie, you mustn't say things like that.'

'You don't know what he's like, Rachel. Reckon you couldn't begin to understand what a rotter he's been to Ma.'

'I've heard rumours, Charlie, but it's drink, I expect.'

'Yeah, well, that's the excuse. But I've made me mind up. When this war's over and I come 'ome, he's got to behave 'imself or out he goes.'

Rachel admired Charlie's protectiveness towards his mother.

'Do you think the war is going to last much longer?' she asked.

Charlie grunted. 'Can't say – but we'll win in the end.'

'I wouldn't have thought you'd have to go back after being wounded.'

'I told you, t'weren't much. I'm glad it was bad enough to get 'ome to see me ma. I'm ready to go back to the trenches now, though I daresay I'll be put on light duties somewhere behind the lines for a while. Got to report back on Monday. No point in being back 'ome with all me mates out there. I hear even old Doc Grant's been called up.'

'Yes, but he hasn't gone abroad. We heard that he's on the Kent coast working in a hospital for the wounded. I wouldn't have minded being a nurse or joining the Red Cross, but I'm not quite old enough. By the time I am, I suppose the war will be over.'

'Won't be yet awhile, Rachel. You might get your chance.'

They had reached Kingsmere, but still Charlie continued to walk with her to the gate of Calder Cottage.

'I . . . I s'pose you wouldn't . . . look, Rachel, the person I most wanted to see at the factory was you.' She looked across at him in surprise. 'I won't ever forget that you saved me from a beating in front of the whole school.' He smiled. Rachel thought she had never seen him smile this way before, and was touched by his words.

'I'll never know why I did that,' she said. 'Most unladylike, my parents thought.'

'You shocked us all, even old Stanley, and I felt bad about you getting hurt . . .'

'Best forgotten, Charlie,' she interrupted. 'We're grown up now. Our schooldays are over and done with.'

'Well, I'm sorry for the way I teased you at school. Reckon I had my fair share of the same once, but things are different now. Being in the Army is hard, especially at first being away from home, but some of the chaps helped me through me training. I soon learnt that we all had to help each other, and I've met some good mates. But most of 'em have girlfriends. They carry pictures of them to look at when there's a lull in the fighting, but I've never had a girlfriend and I ain't likely to meet one in the trenches. I know you're keen on Adam Taylor, but, well, I was wondering if you'd write to me? I'd write back,' he hurried on. 'Not a very good scholar but me Sarge has been helping me.'

'Charlie . . . I'm very flattered that you should ask me but Adam and I do have an understanding.'

He shifted from one foot to the other. She couldn't help noticing how shiny his Army boots were, but then she'd never seen Charlie Mead so smartly dressed before.

'Yes, I understand that, Rachel. But – y'see – we don't know what's going to happen to us, do we? I don't know any other girls. Please, Rachel, say you'll write to me – just once?'

She didn't know why she agreed, to write to Charlie Mead of all people, but as they parted company she promised that she would.

The sun was sinking low behind the trees and Rachel's thoughts turned as they often did at the end of the day to Adam. Most evenings she wrote to him in the form of a journal, posting it off on Monday mornings, but tonight she just wanted to sit and think. Her mother had sounded quite disapproving of her agreeing to write to Charlie. What would Adam think? But he could never be jealous of Charlie Mead surely? She found it hard to imagine what it could be like for the men on the battlefields and the danger sailors faced at sea. Every Sunday at Church she sat with her family and listened, almost holding her breath, as names of those killed and wounded, some reported missing, were read out and special prayers offered for them and their families. Now she offered her own silent prayer for Adam – and Kas too. She hadn't thought about him for ages but somewhere he might also be fighting for his country. When she'd kept the lucky stone in her pocket she often wondered about him, but time was weakening the memory of the dark-haired gypsy boy. Her parents, being deeply religious, said there was no such thing as luck, good or bad, but Rachel had every faith in Kas's lucky stone. It had taken away her birthmark; she was sure it would help to keep Adam safe.

The summer days became shorter, light faded early and autumn gales wreaked savage destruction on the countryside, and still there was no let up in the war. The Germans suffered defeat at the Somme, several divisions having their numbers greatly reduced which weakened morale. Winter brought active operations to a temporary halt while the Germans retreated to a shorter front to prepare for the next battle.

Christmas 1916 was the bleakest for the troops. Two years earlier they had gone to war confident that they would soon be home but now there was no such optimism. The great breakthrough they had envisaged during 1916 had not materialised, and the cost in lives was huge, many thousands of British and Allied soldiers lost along with a comparable number of Germans.

Rachel spent the long winter months writing to Adam and Charlie, knitting gloves and socks for both of them. Adam's letters became more frequent and loving, while Charlie struggled to pen his thoughts in a childlike way. He was pleased to receive Rachel's regular letters and the snapshot she had sent him, but then the mail ceased to arrive. News came of the new Allied offensive on the Hindenberg Line, fighting had begun again in earnest and old fears were renewed.

During the summer of 1917 when the third battle of Ypres was unfolding, bombardments were timed with relentless accuracy and soldiers feared the mud of Flanders as much as the enemy. Ground was lost and retaken and stretcher bearer Corporal Adam Taylor, along with his comrades, found it almost impossible to struggle through the quagmire with the wounded. It was a relief to reach the Regimental Aid Post. As he wandered among the lines of men waiting to be treated he heard his name being called.

'Taylor – Adam Taylor? Adam picked his way carefully through the rows of makeshift beds in a large crowded hut behind enemy lines. At first he didn't recognise the lower half of a bloodied face which was all that was visible below the bandage and above the blanket. He bent lower to look more closely.

'Charlie Mead?' He reached down and grasped the hand which was held out to him. 'It's good to see you.' This was a rare treat – someone from home, someone from Wickham. 'How are you, Charlie? Not too badly hurt, I hope?'

Charlie's grin was instantly recognisable. 'Reckon being that this is me third blighty, I've had me share. Shrapnel in me leg first time. They sent me home then, that was last year. Only for a few days but I saw Rachel Hunter at the basket factory. I know she's your girl, Adam, but I didn't have anyone else except me ma to send me letters so I asked if she'd write to me.'

'I know, Charlie, Rachel told me.'

'And you didn't mind, did you? 'T'weren't nothing serious. I know'd she wouldn't want to walk out with me but I wanted to have a girl's picture to show off. 'Tis in me top pocket, Adam, if you want it.'

He patted Charlie's shoulder gently. 'You keep it, I expect it's the same as the one in my top pocket.' He patted the place next to his heart where he carried Rachels' last letter and photo. 'Lucky you, getting home, and if this is your third injury you'll probably go home again soon before me – p'raps for good.'

'Got it in me gut this time so reckon you may be right. Second time t'was in me backside so they soon got that splinter out. Anything's better 'an being taken by Fritz. I'd rather die than surrender to 'im.'

'That's the spirit, Charlie. If you do go back to blighty, give Rachel my love and tell them all we're doing our best to get it over and done with.'

Even as he spoke he could see Charlie's breathing becoming spasmodic, and he was desperately trying not to let Adam see the effects of the pain he was in.

'A doctor will soon be round to you and I expect they'll inject morphia before you go on to a field hospital. Want a cigarette, Charlie?'

His eyes had taken on a glazed look as he did his best to nod. Adam lit the cigarette for him and placed it between his dry lips. The medical officer was moving along the row getting closer to Charlie so

Adam stayed as long as he dared, offering what consolation he could, and then it was back to the trenches to remove more of the casualties. He wished he could have stayed longer to find out how Charlie got on. Things didn't look too good for him. Poor old Charlie Mead, a third blighty. Well, third time lucky, Adam thought hopefully. Maybe he'd get home for good when they'd patched him up enough to stand the journey across the Channel.

Another summer passed. Adam was weary beyond belief with the constant shelling and moving from place to place, camp to camp. Letters took some time to reach him but at last several arrived together at a time when he was back behind the lines in a small village sheltered by woods, his unit having been ordered a much deserved rest. He recognised his mother's small, even handwriting, the long loops penned a little shakily, he thought. He decided to read the two from her before opening Rachel's. Lily Taylor's letters contained many complaints about the effects the war was having on their food supply, and her fear of enemy bomb attacks was obvious. She should be out here, Adam thought before he opened the second letter. The news it contained shocked him. 'Charlie Mead was killed when the ship he was returning home on was torpedoed,' his mother wrote.

Adam searched for more detailed information but her letters were always short, never more than one single sheet, and the lone sentence telling of Charlie's death seemed to indicate just how cold and insensitive she was. She had no particular reason to feel any more sad than anyone else at the news, but war drew people together in shared compassion. Adam didn't know why his mother's attitude made him feel cross but he tossed her letters aside to rip open Rachel's hurriedly. In the first letter she said she had received a short letter from Charlie from a field hospital somewhere in Belgium where he was recovering well from his stomach wound. He had fallen in love with a beautiful Dutch nurse called Else.

'He is quite besotted with her,' Rachel wrote, 'and tells me that she is as fair as I am dark. I half expected to find my photo returned but at least he spared me that embarrassment.' It was obvious to Adam that she was much amused and probably relieved that Charlie had found a girl of his own. Mention of the dissimilarity between Rachel and the Dutch nurse reminded him of her twin sister, Belinda, who bore no resemblance at all. He tore open the second letter which confirmed what his mother had told him.

'Oh, dear Adam, such shocking news, made even worse because when you wrote you said that you had seen Charlie Mead. You sounded so concerned for him and hoped that by now he had reached

Wickham safe and well. Dearest Adam, how can I be the one to tell you – the ship bringing him home was torpedoed with all hands lost. His mother has taken the news so badly, they say she is inconsolable. Even Mr Mead seems a broken man.'

During the past two years Adam had been forced to come into close contact with dead and wounded soldiers. At first it had affected him emotionally just as it did his comrades, but eventually he had become hardened to the scars of the battlefield. Somehow, though, Charlie's death seemed more cruel than all the others. Now his thoughts searched out all the events of his past at home in Wickham. Memories went deep. He knew all the Mead family, Charlie especially – didn't he have cause to remember the notable puddinghead of Hundred Acres? But even Charlie hadn't been such a dunce that he couldn't fight for his country! Given his life for it. The stress of recent weeks and months suddenly took its toll. Bitterness, anger, hatred – all these emotions fought against the integrity of the real Adam Taylor. He couldn't stand the company of the other men a moment longer so went for a walk through the woods that reminded him of home and felt an uncontrollable desire to throw himself on the ground and weep.

In the Church of St Nicholas in Wickham, local people and villagers from miles around outnumbered the gentry who came to mourn the dead. Not for the first time a special family – on this occasion, the Meads – was singled out for prayer and sympathetic understanding.

The church was packed for Sunday morning worship and Rachel wasn't able to sit beside either her parents or Belinda. Instead she squeezed in at the end of a pew, then realised with some consternation that she was sitting beside Charlie Mead's mother, her face hardly visible through the black veil which covered head and shoulders over a black winter coat. Rachel felt embarrassed. Had she taken Mr Mead's place or that of another member of the Mead family? Nessie Mead lifted her head slightly so Rachel took the opportunity to whisper, 'Is this someone's seat? Shall I move?'

Nessie shook her head. Rachel thought she made a brave effort to smile but there was no mistaking the great burden of sorrow which engulfed the poor woman. The service commenced and during the singing of the first hymn, Rachel being taller than average, could see the rest of the Mead family occupying the pew at the front of the church. Even Mr Mead, who never ever crossed the threshold of any place of worship except for weddings, funerals and baptisms, was sitting beside his three daughters.

As the service continued with mention of the recent death of Charlie, Rachel could feel Nessie shaking with sobs beside her.

Charlie had vowed to take care of his mother. Why wasn't one of the girls here to comfort her? she wondered. The mother's grief transferred itself to those around her. On an impulse Rachel tucked her arm through Nessie's and held her hand. To her surprise, far from rejecting her Nessie leaned against Rachel as if gaining much needed support, and drew strength from the girl.

When the last hymn had been sung and after the final blessing Nessie turned to Rachel. 'Thank you for writing to my Charlie,' she said, her voice husky with emotion. 'He didn't have many friends and I know he wasn't very nice to you once, but he really appreciated your kindness.' Nessie squeezed Rachel's hand affectionately. 'Thank you too for helping me through his morning,' she said. 'I could see there wasn't going to be room for us all in that pew so I sat down where I could.'

She didn't know what to say, but very quickly local people began to gather round Nessie to offer their condolences so Rachel slipped away. Each little group of people, every family, was in sombre mood as they walked to their homes.

Dick was stunned by his son's death. After the shock, remorse set in for the way he'd treated the boy, and for a few weeks he tried to make it up to Nessie by staying at home in the evenings. But she remained uncommunicative and he realised that he had left it too late to make amends. Mrs Waterstone was ailing and Nessie was having to spend all her spare time at her mother's cottage. Beth should have been the one to care for their mother but having been refused a place at the Meads' home she remained with her in-laws. She was always one to watch out for herself and reckoned if she kept in with them she would come in for whatever there was going when the time came.

Dick was soon drawn back to The King's Head where a few drinks helped to take his mind off his troubles. Afterwards Beth would be waiting for him. She had the knack of twisting him round her little finger. Never lacking the ability to seduce her fifty-year-old brother-in-law, her unbridled passion was beginning to be too much for Dick. Yet he simply could not deny her. He tried to keep her at bay by saying that his place was at home with Nessie.

'She's still grievin' for our Charlie. I feel it too, I ought to be with her.'

In an old barn at the Croppers' homestead Beth knew she only had to lift her skirts to make him weaken, and later they lay huddled together among the dry hay as she did her best to console him.

'I shouldn't be here,' he said with remorse. 'Nessie's been a good wife to me, Beth. Many a woman would have upped and left me long ago after all I've put her through. I know she don't want me any more – reckon she didn't really want me ever, if the truth be told – but we've had twenty-five years together. Heading to be Darby and Joan now. Reckon it's time you found yourself a younger man. Someone needin' a wife.'

'There's no decent men around, and who says I want another husband? First time was bad enough. I like things the way they are, Dick. You and me are good together, only one thing on our minds. You can't say that with Nessie, now can you? Cold hard bitch if you ask me.'

'I ain't asking you – and I reckon I knows Nessie better'n you if you think that. We've had our good times. She's still pretty too, and not many women can say that after having six kids. I haven't done right by her and it's time I made it up. Not – well, not where this kind of thing's concerned, but if you want to chase around after someone younger I'll understand, Beth. I'm grateful for all you've given me.'

'And so you should be, Dick Mead,' Beth flung at him angrily. 'You take the best years of my life and then want to cast me off like an old coat.' She got to her feet and stood looking down at him with contempt. No, he wasn't much of a catch, she decided, but where was she going to find another man as easy to persuade as Dick? 'I've not had another man while we've been seeing each other.' She suddenly laughed, remembering the hold she had over Nessie. Now was the time to deliver her blow to this old fool. 'You were glad enough of me when Nessie didn't want anything to do with you – and you were always too drunk to know why she didn't want to sleep with you.'

Dick struggled to his feet to face Beth. 'What's that supposed to mean? Don't tar everyone with the same brush as yourself.'

She laughed in his face. 'That's just it, Dick, Nessie and me, we are out of the same mould. She's had her flings, same as me.'

Dick grabbed the giggling Beth and held her against him roughly. His bloodshot eyes bored right through hers as he gritted his teeth angrily.

'Tell me, you whore! Tell me what you mean – damn you!'

Suddenly his hands were round her throat, squeezing as his cheeks grew red with anger.

'Dick, stop! Let me go – you're hurting me.'

'Then you just tell me exactly what you meant about my Nessie.'

'*Your* Nessie, indeed. She was probably Jake Taylor's long before she was ever yours.'

'What stupid nonsense is this you're talking? I know well enough that Jake Taylor had his eye on her but I made sure of her by getting her in the family way – and I can tell you this, young miss, she were a virgin then all right. Not something I'm ever likely to forget – bloody hard work t'was. So what d'you think you know that I don't?' He forced her chin upwards until she thought her neck would snap.

'You aren't as clever as you think,' Beth said. 'How d'you think the rent ever got paid when you spent every penny on drink when the kids were small? I got paid a shilling to take the kids out when Jake came to collect his dues, and it wasn't paid in money!'

'You lying little cheat.' His grip tightened round Beth's throat until her eyes were bulging. 'Tell me you're lying – tell me.'

Beth gasped for breath. She hadn't expected him to take it out on her. Wasn't she the one who had given him what he wanted and needed? She hadn't thought he had this much strength left in him either.

'Let me – go – please, Dick. *Please*?' she begged.

He released her slowly yet never quite letting her free.

'Now, my girl, let's be having the truth,' he snarled viciously.

'You won't like it, Dick, and when I accused Nessie she smacked my face so I reckon it's true. But . . . but I don't want to spoil what we've got, Dick. She isn't worth it,' Beth pleaded.

'Let me be the judge of that. Tell me, I say, tell me.'

'It's just as I said. Jake Taylor always had a soft spot for Nessie. He used to visit her a lot until she had that last baby. He gave her the job of picking strawberries in the season. She used to go out after you'd gone to The King's Head.'

'You say he gave you money to take the kids off while he . . .?'

'Yes, and that's the truth, but it's all a long time ago now, Dick. What does it matter?'

'It matters because my wife deceived me – and no man will stand for that. So Jake Taylor got her after all – the *swine*!'

'The last baby she had – she wouldn't look at it – and I reckon it was because it was Jake's.'

'What makes you think that?'

'It was obvious. That hideous mark – the strawberry mark – the kid was tainted with sin. Even you said it couldn't be yours.'

Dick's eyes narrowed as he started to remember lots of little details – if only he hadn't been too drunk to notice at the time. He'd thought Nessie had rejected him because of the baby. She'd looked so ill – the infant so horribly disfigured – that for him there was only drink to take away the awful memory.

'You'd better be telling the truth, Beth Cropper, or I'll find you and kill you. Telling tales on your own sister, for your own ends. You're a wicked one and no mistake. If it's true I'll kill her, and you'll marry me and take her place just as you've always wanted to do. But it won't be the easy life you're a'hankering after. I'll make you pay for this as well as Nessie.' He pushed her up against the bales of hay, shaking with anger. 'You're a devious bitch, but I'll get to the bottom of this once and for all.'

Beth watched him shuffle away. She put her trembling fingers round her sore throat. He was capable of committing murder. She'd felt the strength of his rage in his hands. His victim was going to be her own sister Nessie, and after that . . .

'God Almighty!' she cried. 'What have I done?'

She seemed too paralysed to move, but move she must before a terrible crime was committed.

Chapter Five

Shortly after hearing of the death of Charlie Mead, Adam wrote to Rachel asking her to marry him.

'As soon as you can,' he said, 'visit my parents and mother will give you the ring. I do so want you to be friends. Mother doesn't go out much so you'll have to make the first move, Rachel, but I have written and told them about our plans.'

Our plans! Adam seemed to have changed so much lately, she could tell, from his letters in which he wrote of his need of her and she read all kinds of hidden meanings. She felt nervous yet excited as she prepared to go to meet his parents. She brushed her thick dark hair, black and silky as a raven's wing, and then stood still just looking at herself. The gilt-edged triple mirror had been her seventeenth birthday present from her parents. Rachel knew it had come from the big house via the auction rooms. Hadn't she changed too beyond all recognition? How many times had she stood on tip-toe to peer at the ugly raised mark on her forehead, mostly hidden by her hair, in that old speckled mirror she used to have. But now there was so sign at all of any blemish. Perhaps when she was officially engaged the unkind people like Beth Cropper would stop calling her Strawberry Girl. Her dark eyes twinkled mischievously as she recalled with a slight flutter the black-haired gypsy boy, Kas. 'Strawberries are sweet,' he'd said, meaning that he thought she was sweet too. Then he'd given her his lucky stone, and now Adam had it. It had worked magic for her, it could for Adam too. It must keep him safe – it *must*!

Rachel put on her best hat and coat and went downstairs. Belinda was standing at the window staring into space.

'Come with me, Belinda, please?' she urged. 'It's a nice day and I won't feel so nervous if you're with me.'

'I think you should go alone,' her sister said softly.

'I want you to come. I don't see you that often now, we can have a good gossip on the way.

'Yes, dear,' Phoebe said. 'You'll be company for Rachel.'

Belinda went upstairs to get her coat and hat. She was almost too obedient and whatever Phoebe or Wally suggested she agreed instantly.

Phoebe went to the gate to watch her two girls walk down the lane towards Hundred Acres about two miles away.

'The evenings are drawing in now so don't leave it too late starting back,' she called after them. She felt so proud of their appearance. Two smart young women and Rachel about to be engaged. She was secretly glad it was Rachel and not Belinda, and knew Wally felt the same. Not that they didn't want Belinda to marry, they did, but for her someone special, someone who would understand her delicacy.

Once Rachel was married their responsibility for her would be over. They loved her dearly and believed they had done their duty, but it had been no easy task bringing her up. They couldn't have chosen better for her than Adam Taylor, though, as they considered him a respectable lad. They hadn't been able to fault his letter to them. Phoebe and Wally were pleased to give their consent to the marriage but with one proviso: that they waited until Rachel reached the age of eighteen. Phoebe smiled as she watched the two girls link arms happily.

Lily Taylor looked pinched with cold when she opened the door to the two Hunter girls.

'Good afternoon,' she said politely but in a shaky voice. 'Come along in. After receiving Adam's letter I guessed you might visit me today.'

She showed them into the front parlour where a small round oak table was covered with a white lace cloth and set for afternoon tea with the daintiest of china.

'Now, let me look at you. The pretty one – you must be Belinda.' Lily Taylor was quite short and very thin underneath the woollen dress with its matching shawl. The girls thought she was rather old-fashioned with her small mobcap made of velvet. She had a grey pallor which seemed less prominent because of the blueness of her eyes, and in spite of her reputation of being unsociable, even a misery, she did have a warm smile. 'So you're my future daughter-in-law, Rachel?' she said turning to look up at the taller of the two girls.

Rachel gave a swift short curtsey more from fear than from politeness. 'Adam asked me to call to pay my respects,' she said in what was quite a small voice for her.

Heavy footsteps sounded through the hallway and a loud voice said: 'And we're delighted that you did, my dear.'

Jake Taylor was almost as formidable a character to the girls as Dick Mead but in quite a different way. Dick was usually too drunk to know whether he was insulting people or not so no one took any notice of him. But there was something about the toothy leer of Jake Taylor which made Rachel suspicious. He was handsome, there was no denying that, she thought, but something in those dark searching eyes suggested an unhealthy interest. Adam's parents were obviously younger than her own yet Lily Taylor appeared to be much older than Phoebe.

'Sit yourselves down and I'll fetch the tea,' Jake said, and when it was brought Lily uncovered a side table on which were plates of appetising sandwiches and cakes.

'So we're to have a wedding in the family?' Jake said with a wide grin. 'Let's hope the war doesn't go on for too much longer.' He gave Rachel a nudge. 'And I bet you do too.' His nearness made her shudder.

'My parents are happy about our engagement but have asked that we wait a while before setting the date to be married,' Rachel said as positively as she could.

'The war will obviously decide this ' Lily said. 'Let's pray that dear Adam comes home to us safely.' She glanced up at her husband. 'Give the child the ring,' she said, 'and then you can be off. I shall be glad of a little company.'

Jake took a small red box down from the high mantelshelf, opened it and displayed its contents to the girls.

'It's quite magnificent,' Rachel breathed with sparkling eyes.

'Then it's yours, my dear,' Lily said. 'As long as you promise to be good to my Adam and above all be faithful, like the good book says, unto death.'

'Oh, I will, I will,' Rachel said enthusiastically.

Rachel was so enamoured of the ring she didn't notice the fierce meaningful glance Lily gave Jake.

'Then let me do the honours,' Jake said, as he took the diamond cluster ring from its case and held Rachel's trembling hand.

'Oh dear,' he said as he tried to push the ring over her knuckle, 'I'm afraid you seem to have slightly larger fingers than Adam's grandmother.'

'My mother was petite, I take after her.' Lily took a closer look and then relieved Jake of the ring and put it on her own finger. 'Now, my dear, at least you can see how it looks. I'm afraid it would seem that you will have to be patient until Adam comes home. He'll have to have it made larger for you.'

Rachel felt the disappointment keenly but tried not to show it as Lily proceeded to pour out some tea.

'It's not a disaster,' Jake said. 'Nothing that can't be remedied. Now, if you delightful young ladies will excuse me, I prefer a beverage of the stronger kind.' He shook hands with each of the girls, kissed his wife lightly on the cheek and left the house.

Lily appeared to be more relaxed afterwards as she passed round the delicacies. 'If I could get out and about more I'd take it myself and have it altered,' she said. 'You could do it yourself, of course.'

'Thank you, but I'll write and explain to Adam first,' Rachel said. 'Our parents send their regards and asked if you would care to come to Calder Cottage one Sunday afternoon for tea?'

'Very kind, very kind, but I don't go out much these days. Perhaps we can all get better acquainted when Adam comes home.'

It became clear to Rachel that Lily Taylor did not enjoy entertaining very much. She feigned tiredness so Rachel and Belinda departed when it seemed polite to do so. There was a chill breeze blowing as the first colourful leaves fell from the trees. The girls had to hang on to their hats for fear of them blowing away.

'Are you very disappointed about the ring?' Belinda asked. 'It's a very beautiful one, Rachel.'

At that moment the wind whipped up into quite a frenzy and Rachel was unable to speak as she turned her head to one side holding her hat on to her wilful curls. At the same time a figure came rushing headlong into the girls from around the corner of the lane. It was Beth Cropper, clearly in a state of distress.

'Have you seen Jake Taylor?' she demanded breathlessly. I must find him . . . Dick's gone for Nessie . . .'

'Mr Taylor went out a short while ago,' Rachel said. 'Probably to The King's Head.'

'Can we do anything to help?' Belinda asked.

'Mmm . . . yes . . . no . . . perhaps . . . come with me.' It was unlike Beth Cropper to be so indecisive but she grabbed Rachel's arm and pulled her along with Belinda trying to keep up behind. 'Dick's going to kill my sister – I need help – Jake ought to . . .' her voice trailed away.

Rachel thought it all sounded melodramatic but Beth was an excitable girl so she allowed herself to be propelled along to the Meads' house. The back door was open. A flat iron lay on the floor along with other items strewn about as if the place had been ransacked. Then a moan led Beth into the living room where the girls found Nessie lying semi-conscious with blood pouring from a head wound.

'Nessie! *Nessie*!' Beth cried, bending down to her sister. I'm sorry, I didn't mean it to come to this.'

Nessie lifted a hand and pointed towards the door. 'He's gone after Jake,' she said in a weak voice. 'There'll be a fight. Find the constable to stop them. Go quickly, before someone gets killed.'

'I must tend to you . . . Oh, Nessie!'

'Go – quickly,' Nessie repeated in a stronger voice.

Beth looked apologetically at the two girls who were surveying the chaotic scene before them in wide-eyed astonishment.

'I'll go to find Jake Taylor,' Beth said. 'Could you help Nessie, please? Looks as if she needs a doctor – oh, dear God, I never meant this to happen.'

'I could go for the doctor,' Rachel offered.

'And I'll help Mrs Mead – at least find some towels to clean up the blood,' Belinda said helpfully as she started to take her coat off.

Beth tore off down the lane with Rachel in hot pursuit until they came to the Square in Wickham. Rachel made for the doctor's house while Beth ran on towards The King's Head.

Doctor Barber, a middle-aged, balding man who was Doctor Cyril Grant's substitute during his absence, was none too pleased at being disturbed on a Saturday evening.

'It's Mrs Mead, Doctor,' Rachel explained. 'She's been . . .'

'Well, spit it out, girl,' he said impatiently.

'She's been hurt – quite badly. There's a lot of blood and . . .'

'Where is she?'

'At her home. She lives at Hundred Acres.'

'I know where she lives,' Dr Barber grunted, turning inside to fetch his bag. 'I'll go in the trap.' He closed the door with a slam and Rachel turned to walk away. He could have offered to take her back with him, she thought, but he wasn't that kind of man. Not the friendly sort like Doctor Grant who had once rescued her from Charlie Mead and his gang in the woods. He'd lifted her up on to the saddle of his horse and taken her home. There'd never be another doctor as popular as he had been. Rachel heard voices, loud voices, shouting and hollering, and it was coming from the bridge over the river. She wanted to get back to help Belinda but curiosity got the better of her and she ran out of the Square towards the Mill.

Where on earth had all the people come from? she wondered. It seemed as if all of Wickham had turned out to witness the fight which was going on in earnest on the bridge. Rachel was thankful that Belinda was not here to see this, while she felt an urge to cheer Jake Taylor on. Dick Mead wasn't at all a likeable man and if he was responsible for leaving his wife in such a pitiful state Rachel could only hope he was going to come off the worse. Jake Taylor was several years younger than Dick Mead and although he enjoyed a drink he wasn't a renowned drunkard like Dick was. Both men were looking bloodied, Dick swearing as he punched, vowing to kill his old rival. Then Jake seemed to be getting the better of Dick who looked as if he were crumbling and losing his balance. Jake, realising he had the advantage, fought with renewed strength hitting Dick in the eyes until he could hardly see and in consequence Dick staggered backwards. One final push into the mill stream to cool him off hailed Jake Taylor the winner, and then to a gasp from the crowd he gave a loud groan and collapsed to the ground. Rachel pressed forward in time to see a last shudder as Jake Taylor breathed his very last breath.

The urgent ringing of a bicycle bell heralded the arrival of the village constable. Suddenly everyone felt compelled to return to their homes as quickly as possible and Rachel slowly made her way back to the Meads' house. Her lasting vision was of Dick Mead being hauled out of the stream by his mates, the constable waiting with handcuffs at the ready, while the landlord of the King's Head covered Jake's body with a blanket.

Rachel felt numb with shock. She didn't want to hurry and yet she needed to get back to her sister. Her boots felt heavy on her feet as if they were dragging her back. At the same time she was breathless by the time she reached the unhappy homestead still mourning Charlie's loss. She pushed open the back door, walked over the obstacles scattered in angry abandon and entered the small living room where Nessie was lying on the couch. Belinda, sleeves rolled up, was doing her best to restore the room to some semblance of order. Nessie opened her good eye, the one not blackened and covered by the same bandage which was protecting the wound on her head.

'Thank you for fetching the doctor, he's just left.' She tried to peer closer at Rachel, sensing the strain in the younger girl's expression. 'What . . . what's happened? Something terrible, I can see it in your face.' She eased herself up into a sitting position.' Belinda paused in her task and went to Rachel's side. 'What is it, Rachel?' she asked softly.

'Adam's father collapsed and died.'

'My Dick's killed Jake Taylor?' Nessie said in a frightened voice.

'They had a dreadful fight on the bridge. Mr Taylor pushed Mr Mead into the stream – and then Mr Taylor just groaned and fell to the ground.'

'Didn't anyone try to stop them? Surely Beth could have . . .'

'People seemed to be egging them on, Mrs Mead. The constable came too late to stop them – and I think Mr Mead's been arrested.'

'For murder?' Oh *no*!' She struggled to get up from the couch but pain forced her to lie back again. 'Doctor says my ribs are broken – what can I do? Dick needs me now. Where's Beth?'

'I'm afraid I didn't see her again. Is there anyone we can fetch? Where's June?' Rachel asked.

'She'll be here presently,' Nessie said. 'She went to visit my mother. You've both been so kind but I mustn't detain you any longer. Your mother will wonder where you are. It's quite dark now – you'd best get off home – but thank you for all you've done.'

'I don't think we should leave you, Mrs Mead,' Belinda said with kind concern. 'Rachel, you could go home and tell Mum and Dad where I am. I think someone ought to stay, don't you?'

Running footsteps could be heard then before the door burst open and Beth came in looking white with alarm.

'What's happening here?' she asked.

'What's happened to my Dick?' Nessie said shortly.

'They've arrested him and kept him in custody.'

'Thanks to you he really has committed murder now,' Nessie said.

'No, it wasn't murder – I waited to find out – and they think Jake had a heart attack. It may have been as a result of the fight but Dick didn't kill him.'

'As good as – the intent was there,' Nessie said with bitterness in her croaky voice.

'I think they're both guilty of those intentions, but the doctor has reported your condition to the constable and now Dick is being accused of assaulting you with intent to kill.'

Nessie's eyes filled with tears then she said, 'They'll never make that stick. I'll see to that.'

'But for goodness' sake, he tried to kill you – and me as well for that matter,' Beth said heatedly.

'Oh? Why? Rejected him, did you?'

Beth blinked and noticed the two younger girls still present.

'You can get off home,' she said in an accusing voice. 'Nothing for you to do here.'

Rachel glanced at Belinda and then enquiringly at Nessie. 'Yes, my dears,' she assured them, 'I'll be all right now and thank you again, Belinda, you were a wonderful help, you'd make a good nurse. Tell your parents I'm sorry you got involved in all this. Best not to say anything to anyone else though.'

Belinda hesitated, not wanting to leave the poor injured woman in Beth's hands, but Rachel took her arm and they left the house.

'I don't trust Beth Cropper,' Belinda said in a whisper. 'Should we have left, d'you think?'

'I don't know. I don't like her either, but they are sisters.'

'So different though, aren't they? Whatever makes Beth like she is? She quite frightens me,' Belinda said.

'She does seem to be an evil person. What an afternoon!' Rachel said. 'Poor Adam – who will tell him? Who's going to tell Mrs Taylor? To think we only left her a short while before her husband was killed.'

'Died, Rachel,' Belinda corrected. 'If what Beth says is true, Mr Taylor died of a heart attack, he wasn't killed.'

'But it was as good as. If he hadn't been fighting it would probably never have happened, and I doubt if he started it,' Rachel said.

'Wonder what it's all about?' Belinda said thoughtfully as she tucked her arm through Rachel's.

They hurried along the road to Kingsmere as Rachel told her sister some of the rumours she'd heard at the basket factory.

'They say Mr Mead and Mr Taylor are old rivals, going back as far as their school days. Beth is always saying that Mr Taylor waited until Mr Mead went to The King's Head and then he – you know?'

'P'raps that's only jealous gossip, Rachel,' Belinda said. 'Mrs Mead is such a sweet person. She was very loyal to her husband too, especially when the doctor asked her so many questions about their married life. It was rather embarrassing so I went into the kitchen and cleared up there as best I could. Mrs Mead would only say that she was as much to blame as Mr Mead – she said it was no one else's business and that Mr Taylor should be left out of it.'

'The trouble is when Mr Mead is drunk he'll probably beat her again,' Rachel said. 'Charlie told me how he intended to look after his mother when he got home after the war. He didn't have an easy life, Belinda. His father has been a very wicked man, I think.'

'We shouldn't judge,' Belinda said. 'We don't really know and we must honour what Mrs Mead requested, that we don't spread stories around.'

'Oh, you, Miss Goody-Two-Shoes,' Rachel laughed. You've lived too sheltered a life. If you worked at the factory you'd have to be more broad-minded or they'd make your life a misery. Still,' she added happily, 'I like you the way you are.' Rachel squeezed her sister's arm as they battered against the wind which cut across the river.

When they reached home Rachel ran up to her room on the pretext of putting her coat and hat away. She threw them down on the bed and then went to the window where she looked out into the cloudy night sky. Adam might soon be home. Then they could be officially engaged, she hoped. Would that be right? Or would it be what her mother referred to as 'unethical'? she wondered. Her heart was full to bursting with suppressed excitement. She felt sorry for Mrs Taylor, of course she did and especially for Adam, whose homecoming was all that mattered to her now. She prayed desperately that if they allowed him to return to England his journey would be safe and not a repetition of Charlie Mead's fate. Thinking of Charlie brought back all too vivid memories of the afternoon. How could any man treat his wife with such violence as to break her ribs? She couldn't comprehend such vicious actions and realised how lucky she was that her parents were so loving to each other and to herself and Belinda. She knew her father loved Belinda best. In his own quiet way his fondness for her was evident to Rachel if no one else. When she was younger she had thought her horrid birthmark had disgusted him, but that had disappeared and she knew she was, if not daintily pretty like Belinda, not altogether unattractive. She tried to please him, endeavoured to show as much affection to him as to her mother, but she sensed there was a barrier between them. It was as if he were subconsciously trying to push her away. She wished with all her heart that she could be more like Belinda.

Still, Adam had chosen *her*, and she dreamed of the day when they could be married and start a family of their own.

The people of Meon Valley, especially residents of the village of Hundred Acres and nearby hamlets were shocked at the news of Jake Taylor's sudden death. Being rent collector for the manor he was well known though not altogether loved. There were rumours and counter rumours about the feud between the dead man and Dick Mead and when Beth Cropper gave in her notice at the basket factory everyone assumed she was the cause of the dispute. She was renowned for brazening things out, but now refused to enlighten anyone and unable to face the world deserted her in-laws and went home to care for her mother, Mrs Waterstone, grateful for the privacy of the isolated railway cottage.

Rachel and Belinda accompanied their parents to pay their respects to Mrs Taylor on Sunday afternoon.

'If there's anything we can do to help,' Wally said, 'you have only to ask. It's such a tragedy, and to happen when young Adam is away at the war makes it all the more difficult for you.'

'Squire is doing all he can to get him home,' Lily Taylor said. 'But it won't be until after the funeral.' She sniffed into a handkerchief but Rachel was quick to observe there were no real tears.

'You'll need help with preparing the tea, Mrs Taylor,' Phoebe ventured. 'I understand the funeral is in three days' time?'

Lily Taylor surveyed her visitors and decided that it was not unpleasant to be the centre of attention for once. The Hunters were a well respected family in the area even if they were not natives of the immediate locality.

She looked directly at Rachel. Such a tall girl compared with her sister. Amazing how the ugly birthmark had disappeared without trace, Lily thought. Sign of the devil all the same. Belinda was more like an angel. Strange for twins – one to be like the devil, the other an angel.

'Since you're going to be my daughter-in-law, Rachel,' she said pointedly, 'perhaps you'd like to help me?'

'Yes, of course, Mrs Taylor,' Rachel agreed readily.

'The girls usually do things together, Mrs Taylor,' Phoebe said. 'They're good girls. Well trained in the kitchen, I've made sure of that. It's a most distressing time for you so if you just tell them the way you want things done, they'll be happy to do the work.'

Lily sighed. 'You're very kind and I'm pleased that Adam has found himself a good wife, even if Rachel is a bit young. But they won't be getting married yet awhile, and when they do they'll make their home here, of course. I shall need my Adam now.' The handkerchief was delicately dabbed against her closed eyes briefly. Then she sat forward with defiance in her expression. 'I hope Dick Mead gets his punishment for what he did. How's a woman to manage without a man's wage coming in?'

'T'was a terrible business,' Wally said. 'But we mustn't forget that your husband died of natural causes.'

'More's the pity,' Lily said in a loud voice. 'Saved Dick Mead's neck – that's all! Grown men fighting – over what, I'd like to know? What was it to my Jacob that Dick Mead battered his wife? The woman's put up with it for years – everyone knows that. Filthy *swine*! *Drunkard*!' She was becoming quite heated, her normally white cheeks pink with anger, and then she glanced at Belinda's shocked look and sank back against her large feather cushion, exhausted.

'I'm afraid it's drink which has caused most of Dick's problems,' Phoebe said. 'Mrs Mead is a hardworking little woman and devoted her life to her children.'

'She should have left that mongrel years ago,' Lily retorted. 'If I'd known that Jacob was still hankering after Nessie Waterstone, I'd never have married him. Persuaded me on the rebound – well, now he hasn't got either of us. Good thing I come from a better class than he did and can keep myself, young Adam as well if it comes to that. But if my son weds your girl then he's got to work to keep her.'

'Adam is a fine, capable young man, Mrs Taylor,' Wally said. 'I've taught him a trade that he'll never forget and he isn't the kind of lad that would want his mother to keep him. I'm sure our Rachel will do her best to look after him the way you've done and keep up standards likewise.'

There was an awkward silence until Phoebe changed the subject by saying, 'I understand that Mr Mead is to be kept in custody for seven days, then he'll come up before the magistrate.'

'And I've already heard that Nessie Mead won't bring charges against him,' Lily said. 'I'm the one who should do that. He's responsible for picking the fight in the first place though heaven knows what it was all about. He's robbed my Adam of his father. He's a wicked no-good scoundrel and the police should prosecute – causing an affray, being drunk and disorderly – anything that would put him away for a bit.'

'Perhaps we should try to be charitable, Mrs Taylor,' Phoebe said. 'The Meads have had their troubles and I daresay Mr Mead drank more than usual to drown his grief over losing Charlie. Just when the boy was on his way home. Injured three times – you can't help but pity the Meads.'

Lily eyed the sanctimonious Phoebe Hunter suspiciously. What did she know about anything? She hadn't just lost her husband. 'S'pose you're thinking it might have been my Adam – he's still out there in danger. I've got enough to worry about without concerning myself over the Meads of this world. They've brought their damnation upon themselves.'

'We can but pray that Adam will be kept safe, Mrs Taylor, and that this wretched war will soon be over.'

Lily Taylor offered the Hunters afternoon tea before they went to the evening service in Wickham where there was much speculation and gossip among the parishioners. Phoebe and Wally kept their own counsel until they returned to Calder Cottage and the curtains were pulled against the darkened sky and howling winds which were persistent.

'They say there was never much love lost between Lily and Jacob Taylor,' Phoebe said, looking across the hearth at her husband.

Wally was deep in thought as he drew on his pipe.

'Who's to say what's between a man and his wife?' he said slowly. 'She's lucky that she's got means of her own and will be all right financially. It's Mrs Mead I feel sorry for. Bad enough to be ill-used by Dick but if he goes to prison how will she cope alone? Benjie's still in France and the girls are all away in service. She comes from a good family, except for that flighty sister, Beth. Mrs Mead didn't deserve what she's had to put up with.'

'If what Lily Taylor says is true and Nessie won't prosecute, what happens now?'

'We shall have to wait and see,' Wally replied wisely.

Rachel and Belinda were sitting at the table playing draughts, but Rachel's thoughts were not on the game. She had one ear tuned in to her parent's conversation and wondered how long it would be before Dick Mead was back at the basket factory. Or would he be dismissed? She felt a bit afraid of him but on the other hand she knew that whatever his destiny was it would have unpleasant repercussions for his wife. Seeing Mrs Mead lying on the floor in such a dreadful state was etched indelibly on Rachel's mind. She felt a desire to help her for Charlie's sake and for the girls'. The Meads were the kind of family that were avoided whenever possible, yet they had all made good, even dear Charlie, and Rachel for some inexplicable reason felt she had an affinity with them.

Chapter Six

Dick Mead pushed open the back door of the house and went in sheepishly. He wasn't sure what kind of reception he'd get. He knew he deserved to find the doors locked against him. Seven days in prison for causing a disturbance with a fine of five pounds to find as well wasn't going to afford him a welcome home. They'd let him out at eight o'clock on this wintry first day of November, still in the clothes he'd been wearing ten days earlier. Dirty and smelling of dried blood, he hardly knew how to face his family. They would be expecting him and probably the girls would all be here to protect Nessie.

It was bleak and gloomy outside but through the scullery door he could see the faint reflection of light from the oil lamp. He forced himself to move further in to the half open doorway. Nessie was sitting at the table, her elbows propped up as she sipped from a cup.

'Can I come in?' he asked hesitantly.

'Why shouldn't you? 'Tis your home as well as mine. The tea's just brewed. I'll pour you a cup. Get out of that stinking coat, for heaven's sake.'

Dick obeyed meekly and without question, probably for the first time in his life.

The two of them . . . there was no one else in the house and it felt ominous. Nessie placed the cup of tea in front of him and she thought she had never seen him look so humiliated before. A wave of pity swept over her but that was quickly replaced by contempt.

'The copper's on ready for you to have a bath,' she said. 'I daresay you're lousy so there's some Keating's powder for you to use. I'll burn those clothes. Mum found out some old stuff of Dad's you can wear. Goodness knows why she's kept it all these years. Just couldn't bring herself to part with his things, I s'pose, but Beth's been having a clear out.'

'Nessie . . .' Dick glanced up but found facing his wife was the hardest thing he had ever had to do.

'Yes? Get everything off your chest, Dick. We'll talk now while we're alone and you're sober.'

'I'll always be sober from now on, I swear to God I will.'

'Save your breath – I'll believe that when I see it. Now, what was it you wanted to say?'

'I . . . I'm sorry . . . really sorry. God, I never want to go to prison again – it's *hell*!' Dick buried his head in his hands and sobbed.

Nessie's heart swelled with a variety of emotions. How many tears had *she* shed over the past twenty-five years? But if Dick really felt remorse then maybe her bruises were worth it.

'Nothing to the hell I've got to suffer with these broken ribs, not to mention the bruises for all the world to see – and the humiliation. Not just humiliation now, Dick Mead, but twenty-five years' worth. Don't you dare sit there and feel sorry for yourself.'

''Tis the drink. Don't let me have another drop, Nessie.'

'How can I stop you? If you can lay you hands on a tanner you'll go to The King's Head. No, you can't go there any more, the landlord has banned you. Not that there's much point in you stopping drinking as you've probably poisoned yourself with the stuff already. Might as well go on and finish the job.'

Dick looked up ready to abuse his wife verbally but the sight of the large wound on her forehead where she'd bashed her head as she fell a week earlier subdued his quick temper.

'I s'pose I can't blame you for being hard on me,' he said. 'You'd be better off without me, but Jake Taylor's gone now. Nessie, I've got to know – how long were you carrying on with him?'

'Pity you didn't listen the other day before beating me to silence and you'd have heard the truth then. No point in going over the past but you're going to listen all the same. When the children were small I often couldn't find enough money to pay the rent. Mum helped me out a few times and she a widow. I could have died when Jake Taylor got the job of rent collector. I'd always managed to steer clear of him. He offered me the job of strawberry picking to pay our debts. It seemed a good idea but then when everyone else had left the fields one evening he turned up and – well, he forced himself on me.'

'You could have run, screamed or something.'

'How could I have known what was in his mind? It all happened so suddenly and I didn't have the strength to fight him off. After that what chance did I have? By always being out you played right into his hands. If I'd told you, you'd have killed him and me. But,' Nessie sighed, the memories painful, 'then at least I'd have been spared the agony of having that last baby with that awful disfigurement, I s'pose. All this has come to a head twenty years too late, Dick.'

'Was Beth right? Are you sure it was Jake's child?'

'Well, of course it was! What have I just been telling you? You never listen – you haven't got the sense our Charlie had. At least *he* loved me and wanted to protect me. He was coming home from the war to take care of me – and you'd have been *out*.' She pointed to the door fearlessly but tears began to trickle down her cheeks. Dick stretched out a hand and placed it over Nessie's.'

'I am sorry, Nessie love,' he said in a croaky whisper. 'I do love you, more'n anything else in the world.'

'And what about Beth? My own sister . . . God, how pathetic you are, Dick Mead. Have you no shame?' She pulled her hand away quickly.

'You shunned me. That's why – well, you know her, tart that she is.'

'And I know you for what you are – weak and selfish. It was lucky for us that that baby died. Its life would have been a living hell with that mark. I prayed that it would die and thank God my prayers were answered. But a lot you cared – even if the child had been yours, and you didn't know any different at the time.'

'But you still carried on with Jake, so Beth says.'

Nessie took out her handkerchief and wiped her eyes. She looked away from her husband now and remembered things she had spent years trying to forget.

'I didn't want to – I tried to make him leave me alone,' she said with desperation echoing from the past. 'He paid Beth to take the children out while you were at The King's Head. In the end,' she said slowly, 'when I got big, weary and ill, he tired of me.'

'So . . . so you don't wish you'd married him instead of me?'

Nessie didn't answer straight away. She had no love for Jake Taylor. There had been times in her youth when he'd seemed attractive, but never after that fateful June night. When her baby had died she'd been consumed with guilt, and after that all feelings for men faded.

'I might have had an easier life with Jake,' she said. 'At least he wasn't afraid of work and he'd have provided for his family.'

'That's easy to say knowing that he only had one son, and his wife having money of her own. It might have been a different story if he'd had to manage the same way we had to.'

'I married you and gave you five healthy children and a lot you cared about them or how we managed! If you'd been a good caring father you could be proud of them all. The fact that they've grown up respectable is no credit to you. They saw you for what you are – a lazy boozer and womaniser – and they were determined to make good themselves.'

'Oh, so now you're taking all the credit, I s'pose,' Dick sneered.

'I only did my best with what I had. I've had to work to keep the home together – and I did it for them. It's no use you having second thoughts now that you've nearly killed a man and lost one of your sons in the war. You're waking up too late, Dick Mead.'

'I'll change. Believe me I will. Give me another chance, Nessie? I've been without the booze while I've been inside so I'll prove to you that I can do without it for good.'

'How many times have I heard that before? I could cope with you getting drunk, Dick. I don't like it but at least I'm used to it. But not other women, and my own sister at that. I've had enough humiliation to last me a lifetime.'

Dick looked directly at his wife in an attempt to be honest.

'Have you any notion what it's like in prison?' he asked softly.

'No, and I don't want to know. You put yourself in there. Getting yourself in this kind of trouble not only lets you down but your family as well.'

Dick remained silent for several minutes while he drank tea which would have tasted good if he hadn't been compelled to have this conversation with his wife. They'd had some good times, he remembered. She hadn't seemed to mind that he was a bit of a lad in his youth. The children coming had changed everything, and that's when he'd turned to drink – no, that was no excuse, he'd always over indulged. Nessie was right. He was a rotter and she deserved better, but he'd made damned sure Jake Taylor wasn't going to get to her first. And to think he'd got her in the end, and Dick too sozzled to realise what was going on. He wished he could remember the baby. It all seemed a haze, something in the back of his mind that wouldn't quite go away. Yet in a strange way he was glad the faint memory was there. Of one thing he was sure, and that was that if he had known it was Jake Taylor's bastard he'd have killed it there and then. Yes, Nessie knew him so well, he'd have killed her too.

'It was just as well the infant died, Nessie. The world is a cruel place for disfigured children. I don't recall much about it – was it a boy or girl?'

'A little girl – and it was hideous. The mark of Jake Taylor was on her all right. I thought I'd never take to it.' Nessie suddenly gave way to anguished sobs. 'But I would – I *would*!' she cried, banging her fist down on the table. 'I was too weak and ill and angry to help it survive. Doctor Grant said the mark would fade in time. I didn't believe him but he was right. The Hunter girl's birthmark has gone completely and look at her now? She's a fine-looking girl. I was so wicked not to care for that baby, God forgive me.'

‘’Tis all in the past now, Nessie. We can start again.’

Nessie shook her head. ‘Oh no, Dick Mead. Not after all you’ve put me through. We’ve got the girls to think about so the home stays the same. It’s you who must change. Whether you stay or go is your decision. I’ll cook and clean for you the same as I’ve always done, but you won’t have a job. I don’t want you round my feet all day and there’ll be no money for drink. No doubt Beth will keep you satisfied, but not in my mother’s house or here. If you want her then get out of Hundred Acres and don’t come back.’

‘You’re turning me out?’ Dick looked shocked.

Nessie shook her head again. ‘I made my marriage vows, hard though it’s been to keep them. The love’s gone, Dick. I’ve had too much grief to bear. It’s up to you.’

‘I will make amends. I’ll get a job even if it means walking miles to work every morning. While the war’s still on they need men at the mill, the brewery, anywhere – I promise.’

‘Don’t make promises, Dick. I’ve heard them so many times before.’ She stood up with the teapot in her hand. ‘I must get on, the girls will be home presently.’

She cleared the breakfast things and then went upstairs while Dick filled the hip bath with hot water from the copper. She couldn’t go down. She knew she’d end up scrubbing his back and before she knew it the old ways would be forced on her. This time it had to be different.

For a few weeks Dick gave a plausible impression of having turned over a new leaf, then while he was helping Beth’s father-in-law, George Cropper the lumber-jack, clear fallen trees after the fierce autumn gales, his and Beth’s paths crossed yet again. By late November both had disappeared.

Rachel watched eagerly for letters from Adam which never came. At weekends she and Belinda would go to the railway station and watch every train in the hope that Adam would return home.

‘A watched pot never boils,’ Phoebe said, trying to be light-hearted about it, but even she felt on edge lest something should happen to Adam before he could reach Hampshire.

Rachel was quite happy now at the basket factory. The two people she most feared, Dick Mead and Beth Cropper, had left and since the rumour had spread that they had gone off together she secretly felt greatly relieved. She felt awkward though whenever she met Mrs Mead or one of the girls.

‘I don’t know what to say to them,’ she told her mother when they came out of Sunday morning service ten days before Christmas. ‘Poor Mrs Mead has had such a terrible time, losing Charlie and all.’

'Just behave as if nothing has happened, dear, the way Nessie Mead does. She's a brave little woman and the girls are good to her. She works very hard and Squire's letting her stay on in the house. They have every reason to hold their heads up with pride. There's no need for folks round here to shun them. None of us is perfect.'

Phoebe tucked her arm through Wally's and urged him away from Wickham village. Usually people gathered around chatting. It was the one day of the week when folk had time and opportunity to exchange news and views with neighbours they might not see much of during the week.

'Why are we in such a hurry?' Belinda asked.

'It's too cold for your father to stand about,' Phoebe answered shortly.

Rachel raised her eyebrows in response to Belinda's glance. They were both aware that Phoebe didn't always practice what she preached. Not quite a snob yet not willing to be seen talking to any of the Meads they guessed. With their parents hurrying along the towpath by the river, the girls slowed their pace as they chatted. Rachel turned round suddenly when a bird made a curious whistle.

'That's a strange bird,' she said. 'I don't recognise the sound.'

'Could be a migratory bird, one that's lost its way,' Belinda said with concern. She was passionately fond of all birds and animals.

They walked on in silence until the sound came again, this time in close proximity.

Rachel stopped in her tracks. 'It's not a bird,' she said in a whisper, 'it's human. Someone playing tricks. Made me think of dear old Charlie Mead for a minute.'

She pulled Belinda on then stopped suddenly and turned – and there was Adam stealthily creeping up behind them.

'Adam!' Rachel exclaimed, lifting her skirts and running back to greet him.

He caught her in his arms and their lips met with fierce passion. When he released her Rachel found herself blushing. All their feelings so lovingly expressed in correspondence seemed exposed, but there was only Belinda to witness the scene.

'Come on,' Adam said with a laugh. 'You're going to be my sister-in-law so a kiss is permissible.' Belinda went shyly forward and lifted her face to his.

With a girl on each arm Adam walked proudly on to Calder Cottage, unaffected by the biting north-easterly wind which promised ice and snow.

'I'm only home for ten days,' he explained as they warmed themselves by the huge fire Wally stoked up. 'Mother isn't too pleased.

She had the notion that Squire could get me released from further duties.' He sighed. 'I know this is a dreadful time for her, but I was in at the beginning and I want to see it through to the end.'

'Is the end in sight, Adam?' Rachel asked.

'Who knows? The battle still rages on. It's all a game of advance and retreat then advance again.'

'How close to the front line are you?' Wally asked.

'We've been on the move a great deal this past few weeks which was why the news of my father's death took a while to reach me. The weather has been awful, up to our necks in mud and recently bitterly cold. There's devastation everywhere, villages and towns in ruins. Just when you think it's all gone quiet the shelling starts gain and then us stretcher bearers are called for.'

'I'm sure you're doing a very worthwhile job,' Phoebe said quietly. She didn't consider first-hand stories from the battlefield suitable for her two girls. 'We're very sorry indeed about your father's death. Will you stay for dinner, Adam?'

'No thanks, Mrs Hunter. I'd best get back to Mother, but she asked if Rachel might like to come to afternoon tea? I'll walk over to fetch you when mother has her rest if that's all right, Rachel.'

She went to the gate with Adam to see him off. He kissed her cheek lightly and whispered: 'We've got a lot of catching up to do, Rachel, and lots of preparations to make for the future.'

'If only this wretched war would end soon,' she said desperately.

'You'll have plenty to keep you busy – that way the time will pass much more quickly. Next year some time should see Fritz on the run. It seems strange to be back in Hampshire. Everything's so peaceful and quiet.'

'You must have been shocked by the news about your father, Adam? It was such a tragedy.'

He seemed reluctant to speak of the affair. 'We'll talk about that later,' he whispered as he squeezed Rachel's shoulder and strode away towards his own home. She watched him until he was out of sight despite the fact that her mother opened the front door and called to her.

'Don't stand about in the cold, Rachel. You'll catch your death with no coat on.'

But Rachel was warm with contented happiness. She knew it wouldn't last for long, how could it with Adam so soon to return to the front, but at least they could reaffirm their love for one another. A sudden stirring of branches from across the road in the woods made her glance towards the trees. She thought of her first love, a gypsy boy named Kasan, and then flushed with guilt as she ran into the house.

'Did Adam invite Belinda as well?' Phoebe asked.

'No, no, Mother,' Belinda said in agitation. 'Rachel and Adam are engaged. I wouldn't wish to intrude.'

Phoebe sniffed disapprovingly. 'Should have a chaperone,' she muttered at which Belinda ran to her mother and put her arms around her.

'Don't be so old-fashioned. Of course Adam wouldn't want me hanging on, neither would Rachel if it comes to that.'

'I wouldn't mind,' Rachel said, but in her heart she knew she would. She loved her sister dearly but hadn't they spent all their early years doing everything together? Being thought of and treated as one for much of the time, except when Belinda was ill or too delicate to participate in whatever was involved. They were two such different people. Belinda's perfection made her feel quite inadequate.

As Rachel stood at the high window upstairs looking out as she brushed her hair, she drifted into a world of her own, wondering just what the future held for herself and Adam. The scene was a wintry one, yet she indulged in fantasies of being a free spirit. There were times when for some inexplicable reason she felt the urge to take off like a bird. To soar into the unknown leaving behind all rational thought and etiquette. The woods opposite looked drearily brown and lifeless but in her mind Rachel could visualise the colourful caravans of the Romany travellers dotted among the trees. How she envied them their freedom, and not only because she had happy memories of Kasan who had been kind to her. So far his lucky stone had proved to be just that. Her birthmark had disappeared and Adam was safe. She wished she had been able to give Charlie Mead a lucky stone as well. Perhaps, though, he was bet off out of the war. She tried to imagine how he would have reacted had he seen his mother in such a battered state. Poor dear Charlie who had caused Rachel such misery in her childhood and yet had become her friend. She was glad about that. She felt she had contributed to making his life a little more bearable.

When she thought about the Meads' home she experienced twinges of fear. How could she be sure that Adam or any man come to that wouldn't take to drink and become violent? But not Adam, he was too mild and courteous. The gypsies seemed to all outward appearances to be rough but having been helped by them Rachel believed them to be protective of one another, always ready to offer a helping hand with the utmost respect. She thought that they probably didn't wash very often or brush their hair. Most of them could neither read nor write, so she'd been told. They lived and loved freely with few cares. There was something wild and exciting about their lifestyle or so it seemed to her.

Rachel saw Adam approaching Calder Cottage so waited until he had knocked and Belinda had let him in. Then she went downstairs wearing her dark red woollen coat with the black velvet collar which she protected by wearing a fashionable silk scarf her parents had given her a year ago.

Belinda smiled up at Rachel as she stood beside Adam in the hallway. But was there just the tiniest hint of envy behind the sweetness of that smile? Rachel felt a pang of guilt at her own good fortune. Guilt that was rapidly forgotten as they set off down the lane, Adam's hand beneath her arm.

'Let's walk through the woods, Rachel,' Adam suggested. 'Where we can be alone to talk for a while.'

She looked expectantly at him. She was almost the same height as he in her high-heeled buttoned boots.

'How's your mother, Adam?' she asked. 'I don't want to keep you away from her – after all, that's why you're home.'

He sighed. 'Mother never stops complaining. She should be out there in France, then she'd have something to grumble about.' He stopped and turned Rachel to face him. She felt herself growing warm with anticipation. The sparkle behind Adam's dark eyes drew a loving response from hers. He held her arms gently and allowed his lips to meet hers. It was sweet and lovely but lasted only a brief moment. 'I want you to tell me, dear, exactly what happened that afternoon when you were visiting Mother,' he said. 'I know my father was not all he appeared to be. I expect you think our home was a happy one, Rachel, but I doubt that it was very different from the Meads'.'

'Oh, Adam, you mustn't say that. Everyone knows how Mr Mead drank too much. So many stories have been going round, who can possibly know the truth? Belinda and I were just leaving your house when we met Beth Cropper in a great hurry. It all seems so long ago now. I do think they should have got you home much sooner.'

'But that wouldn't have saved Father. Mother insists that Dick Mead killed him, but according to the death certificate he had a heart attack and died instantly. Did you see the fight they're supposed to have had?'

'I wasn't very close but your father pushed Mr Mead into the mill stream and then collapsed himself, I understand.'

'If only I could find Dick Mead or Beth Cropper they'd tell me exactly what it was all about, but they've vanished.' Adam held Rachel's shoulders with urgency. 'Rachel, I need to know – that's why I didn't call on you the moment I arrived home. I wanted to, believe me I did, but mother was being difficult, saying she wishes she was dead too, that she'd kill herself if I had to go back. I had to get the doctor to her. He sedated her and then I visited Mrs Mead. She wasn't much help though.'

'Poor woman, I don't suppose she was. She seems to be the victim in all this. Beth had been carrying on with Mr Mead for ages, but what happened that day to bring about such violent reaction I don't know. Beth seemed to blame herself and for a while went to live with her mother. She left the basket factory and no one saw much of her. Mr Mead did seem to have turned over a new leaf. He was working hard, doing odd jobs wherever he could find them. Unfortunately, so June told me, he worked for the Croppers and I suppose Beth called to see her in-laws. Suddenly no one knew where they'd gone. It's been quite a scandal as you can imagine.'

'But what's behind it all? Dick Mead has been a drunkard for years and Beth Cropper – well – we all knew what kind of woman she was. So why did it all blow up out of all proportion, and what did it have to do with my father?'

'Rumour has it that there was rivalry between your father and Dick Mead, but from a long time ago. What could it matter now after all these years? Surely your mother must know, Adam?'

'If she does she isn't telling, and I hate having this awful antagonism against dad. He's dead, nothing can bring him back now. I know there was some kind of feud between Dad and Dick Mead but I never thought it was serious any more than the fight Charlie and I had.'

'That was my fault, Adam. For having that horrible birthmark. You couldn't blame Charlie for taunting me about it. He'd been taunted enough himself for being a half-wit.'

'And he was nothing of the sort. Not very bright but he never had a chance, and what could you expect having a father like Dick Mead? Away from him Charlie changed as you saw for yourself when he came home.' Adam pulled Rachel towards a huge fallen tree trunk and they sat down together in the most secluded part of the wood. 'I fought Charlie because I couldn't stand by and listen to him making unkind remarks about you and calling you Strawberry Girl.' He kissed her firmly on her mouth. So hard in fact that she was forced to open her lips. In response Adam opened his mouth and the lesson in teaching Rachel how to express her love began.

The next few days passed by swiftly, Adam eagerly seeing Rachel at every opportunity, always there to meet her when the day's work was done at the basket factory. When she had a half day off they visited a jeweller in Fareham who made Adam's grandmother's ring a size larger to fit Rachel's finger. Christmas Day their engagement was made public and Rachel thought she must be the happiest girl in all of Hampshire, except that they had barely another forty-eight hours to spend together before Adam had to say his goodbyes.

Mrs Taylor refused all invitations to spend any part of Christmas with the Hunters.

'It isn't seemly to celebrate when I'm still in mourning,' she told Adam.

'Aren't you being just the tiniest bit of a hypocrite, Mother?' he said. He was realising that he was now the man of the house and needed to adjust accordingly. Being a corporal in the Army meant that he had learnt to assert himself and give commands on occasion. Although he felt profoundly sorry for his mother he was determined to show her that she was not going to dominate his life as she had in the past. 'You and Dad weren't exactly close, were you? He went out because you made his life a misery – what was it? – some kind of penance for his womanising?'

Lily Taylor looked at her son sharply. 'Who've you been talking to? What have the Hunters been saying? Filling your head with all kind of wicked rumours, I s'pose?'

'Mr and Mrs Hunter have been most considerate and sympathetic. They aren't the gossiping kind, but goodness knows, Mother, everyone knows what Dad was like. You haven't been a proper wife to him for years.'

'And what would you know about such things, my boy? A couple of years in the Army doesn't give you the right to speak to your mother as you like without respect. I've not enjoyed good health since the day you were born.'

'That's hardly my fault. Dad's gone now so you can stop putting on an act. You're not old. I expect Rachel's parents are getting on for ten years older than you. It's time you got out and about more. Mix with people, make them welcome here and when you get an invitation to go somewhere for afternoon tea then go and enjoy yourself.'

'Don't be so tiresome, Adam. You don't understand about a woman's problems in middle life.'

'Then you must have been in middle life for the past twenty years! I'm twenty-two, Mother, and you've always made your poor health an excuse for living like a recluse. Dad waited on you hand and foot. The truth is you've got into a rut. Has the doctor ever said there was anything physically wrong with you? Well, has he?'

'I don't hold with doctors. They don't care about old women like me, much less understand.'

Adam was losing patience. 'Mother! You are not old. I've got to go back tomorrow or I shall be classed as a deserter. As soon as this wretched war is over I'm coming home to marry Rachel and I want her to have a pleasant mother-in-law.'

'If she's coming to live here she'll have to tow the line and abide by my rules.'

'Then I'll ask Squire for a tied cottage.'

'No, Adam please – don't do that.' She began to weep and this time her tears were real enough. 'You're being deliberately cruel, Adam.'

'I . . . I'm sorry, Mother, but you don't help yourself. I shall worry about you while I'm away. I'd like to think that you had friends to keep you company sometimes. You aren't the only person who's in mourning, you know. Think of all the other women who have lost husbands and sons in the war. Give some sympathy to them and people might be more friendly.'

'Friendly!' she scoffed. 'No one has ever wanted to be *my* friend.' Lily Taylor considered herself a cut above the rest of the community having private means, so she didn't need friends.

'Why should they? Father had an unpleasant job to do collecting rents – he wasn't exactly the most popular or friendly person in the area. You have your small private legacy but what do you do to help those less fortunate? You can afford to have a woman help with the housework or washing but so far everyone who's ever worked for you has been subjected to some of your tasty tongue-pie – and people, however poor, will only take so much. I'm sorry, Mother, but you've done yourself a great disservice. But you're still young enough to make a fresh start, if only you had the inclination.'

'I never heard such rot, Adam Taylor. It's a good job your father isn't here to hear you talking to me like this.'

Adam only grunted. 'I'm going to see Rachel. It's our last evening to be together so I don't know when I'll be home. Don't wait up.'

He flung on his greatcoat and went off still buttoning it up. His loyalties were divided which didn't help his frustration. He loved his mother but she was a hard difficult woman whom few could get on with. Now local people had given up and if the truth were told avoided her as much as possible. The Hunters had offered her the hand of friendship, inviting her to Calder Cottage for Christmas Day and Boxing Day too, but she'd enjoyed playing the martyr which embarrassed Adam. He had spent as much time as decency allowed with Rachel and his future in-laws but now he was going to have to leave Wickham with some measure of guilt.

Rachel tried to soothe his troubled mind by saying, 'It may not be for long, Adam. Think of the future when you come home for good. That will please your mother – and we'll be together for always.'

They went for a walk along the crispy frosty bridlepaths, their last chance to be alone – for how long? Adam's brief sexual experience in

France had developed his virility and he found it difficult to keep his feelings in check. He knew he must. Rachel and the Hunters were respectable people – but Rachel had shown that she was capable of showing her affection with some degree of passion.

'Rachel,' he began hesitantly, thinking selfishly of what he needed from her to seal their betrothal. 'You wouldn't consider? No, I mustn't ask . . .'

'Of course I don't mind, Adam,' Rachel responded eagerly. 'I know your mother won't be easy to live with but I'll be as patient as I can and try to fit in with her ways. I'll visit her often while you're away and try to make her like me, even though I know she likes Belinda best.'

Adam felt as if someone had poured cold water over him. How could dear innocent Rachel have any idea what was in his mind? Girls thought only of pretty weddings, the frills and fripperies. Consummating the marriage would be merely a duty, he supposed, and that very definitely after the church ceremony. During his leave and many visits to Calder Cottage he had grown used to the talk of collecting items for a bottom drawer, flowers, bridesmaids, and every other thing which was to make their wedding day memorable, but now on the eve of his departure he thought how negative it had all been. He would carry back to the front a lasting picture of his fine fiancee, of the happy moments shared, the kisses, cuddles, even a little horseplay. If only Rachel realised how desperate he was for a more physical bond to remember her by.

'Goodbye-ee, goodbye-ee . . .' The paper boy whistled the tune of the hit song of 1917 as he delivered the morning news, reminding Rachel of her emotional farewell to Adam who was by now back across the Channel.

As 1918 was heralded in there was renewed hope that the war would be brought to an end as quickly as possible but when February snowdrops carpeted the woods hopes were dashed. By the end of March came an uneasy peace between Russia and Germany. The one thing the Allied Commanders had hoped to avoid was happening as troop trains began to travel west and new tactics were employed to devastate the Allied lines in France. Germany's Erich von Ludendorff looked as if he was to be successful in beating the British back to the Channel. The Allies lost 400,000 men in three weeks and the Kaiser was confident of winning the war.

Rachel waited and watched anxiously for news. Since Adam's leave the war seemed that much more real. He had given graphic descriptions of some of the events at the Front but counterbalanced the horrors by telling her of the way the men made their own amusements when they went back to quieter towns and villages for a brief respite. Here they could relax and there was always someone who was capable of organising a Follies Show to entertain the war weary soldier. But as the Meon Valley bore the first signs of spring with crocuses and daffodils in bloom the news was too gloomy even to think of men singing and dancing and generally enjoying themselves.

By the summer a crippling epidemic of influenza brought a month long lull in the fighting on the Western Front but when battle resumed with renewed ferocity the opposing army was at last halted and when the Allies mounted an offensive with some twenty divisions near Amiens the enemy collapsed. A black day indeed for Germany which changed the character of the war.

Towards the end of September the Allies were sweeping all before them regaining ground in Flanders where the war first began.

But a different war was raging around the world and millions of people were dying. The worldwide epidemic of Spanish Influenza was taking its toll everywhere, Great Britain included. Through the hardships of war people were undernourished and had little resistance to this virulent strain. No successful vaccine could be found to combat the disease which resulted in more US servicemen dying from it than from war wounds.

Those who survived though were jubilant when the Armistice was signed at Compiegne in November 1918 and the sound of gunfire ceased after four long years of war.

Wickham mourned not only for the war dead but the many local people who had been flu victims.

Mrs Waterstone, Nessie Mead's widowed mother, was among them. Wally Hunter became seriously ill and for a while his condition caused great concern, but with loving nursing by Phoebe and Belinda he made a good recovery.

Rachel took it upon herself to nurse her future mother-in-law. She was a difficult patient though not as seriously ill as many others.

'*Please* drink this juice, Mrs Taylor,' Rachel urged. 'The doctor says it's important to have plenty of fluids. Eating doesn't matter but I've brought you some broth Mother made for my father.'

'Leave me alone to die,' Lily Taylor moaned. 'My husband's gone and now Adam. There's nothing else to live for.'

'There's everything to live for, Mrs Taylor. I'm sure no news is good news and Adam will soon be home.'

She looked out of the window at the bleak mid-winter. A year ago Adam had been able to spend Christmas at home even though it was a sad homecoming after his father's death. The celebrations which followed the end of the Great War gave way now to counting the cost in human life. Many wives and mothers didn't know whether or not their loved ones were alive or dead. Those who did return told stories of horrific injuries – shell-shock, hundreds suffering from the effects of being gassed – what was Adam's fate?

Chapter Seven

Rachel and Adam hesitated outside the railway cottage which had been Mrs Waterstone's home for many years.

'Are we doing the right thing, Adam?' Rachel asked. 'We more or less promised your mother that we'd live with her after we got married. I don't like going back on my word, and it isn't characteristic of you either.'

He pulled Rachel closer to him and kissed her cheek. 'War changes people,' he said. 'I know Mother dominated me before I went away. She'd made Dad's life a misery, always grumbling – and I don't want to have my marriage ruined by her interference.'

'But she expects us to live with her. While we were waiting for you to come home she kept reminding me of your promises, and she'll surely blame me if we get this cottage.'

Adam hugged Rachel to him in desperation. 'I can hardly believe I'm home, darling,' he said. 'Thank goodness Squire was willing to write to my unit and confirm that my job was safe, otherwise goodness knows when I'd have been demobbed.' He glanced up at the ivy-covered cottage. 'I've always loved this little place. I came here with your dad to put up a new fence and gate for Mrs Waterstone just before the war. It's small but pretty and I know the old lady was happy here. I believe houses reflect the people who live in them.'

'Don't forget Beth Cropper was born here and lived with her mother until she went off with Mr Mead.'

'But she's the black sheep of the family, Rachel. The rest of them are all nice hardworking folk.' He held her at arm's length. 'But you're sure, aren't you?'

'About what?'

'About marrying me for one thing, and this cottage for another?'

'Oh, dearest Adam, you know I want to marry you more than anything in the world. It seems as if we've had to wait for ever.'

'But you're still only eighteen, Rachel. It's quite young . . .'

'But I shall be nineteen by the time we get married at Easter,' she interrupted him. 'And of course I love the cottage. A tent would have done as long as we're together, but this will be our very own. Well, yours to be exact.'

'Once we're married what's mine belongs to you too. I know I'm very fortunate having this money left to me by Dad, and we're so lucky that the rail company wanted to sell the cottage cheaply just at the right time.'

'Mm . . . all the same, Adam, I'm not sure that my parents will approve and it might make your mother ill.'

He laughed. 'It would if Mother thought it would make me change my mind, but it won't. When I was a child we had a grandmother living with us and there was always friction. I believe that's why Dad went out drinking so often.'

'But he wasn't a drunkard – not like Mr Mead.'

'No, he knew when to stop – and that was when he was under the influence enough to go and find some woman who was willing to oblige him.'

At that moment voices grew louder at the back of the house and a figure emerged from between bushy shrubs.

'You the new tenants then?' the gypsy woman asked in a gruff voice.

'Not yet,' Adam said stiffly.

'Newlyweds unless I'm mistaken.'

'Yes, you are mistaken. We aren't married yet. Not that it's any concern of yours.'

The middle-aged woman eyed first Adam then Rachel suspiciously, and Rachel was reminded of Merle, the woman who had told her fortune so many years ago.

'Take some white heather to wear on your wedding day, m'dearie – for good luck.' She thrust a sprig towards Rachel but Adam pushed her hand away.

'If she wears white heather then I'll buy it for her,' he said firmly.

The woman's face darkened. Rachel felt some foreboding at her expression and was suddenly afraid. When she'd walked into that gypsy encampment as a child she had felt no fear and they had been kind to her. Kasan had given her the lucky stone which had taken her birthmark away and she had dreamed romantic dreams about him. She must remember to ask Adam about her stone. An eerie feeling crept over her as if it was important to have her stone back to ward off the evil that was emanating from this woman.

'Take care, young man. All is not as it seems, believe me.'

'Of course I don't believe you. You can't frighten me just because I won't give you any money.'

'This house ain't yours nor never will be.' She stepped around Rachel cautiously. 'Be . . . be kind to the woman . . . yes . . . be very kind.' She hitched her basket of wares on her hip and hurried away.

'Whatever did she mean, Adam?' Rachel asked in a frightened voice.

'Goodness knows, but nothing for us to worry about.'

'Adam . . . she meant your mother. "Be kind to the woman" she said. She must have seen your mother's distress.'

'Rachel!' Adam sounded annoyed. 'Surely you don't believe all this good luck nonsense, and seeing into the future?'

'Well, yes, I do. My stone helped to take away my birthmark, didn't it? And it brought you back home safely.'

'No, Rachel, dearest. Your birthmark faded quite naturally, and I was one of thousands of others destined to return home.'

'You kept my stone, didn't you, Adam?'

'Yes, Rachel, I did. For almost all the war, and then at the last offensive when we had to go out into the trenches to try to save the poor devils who were cruelly wounded and many more gassed, it must have fallen out of my pocket. But losing it hasn't brought me any bad luck, has it?'

Rachel fell silent. She shivered with a sudden chill as the wind whistled round the side of the house, and when she looked up she saw Mrs Mead standing against the wall watching them. Adam followed Rachel's glance.

'Hullo, Mrs Mead,' he said with eagerness in his voice as he propelled Rachel forward. 'The gypsy woman wanted me to buy white heather for luck. Don't hold with such silliness myself.'

'Hullo, Adam, Rachel,' Nessie Mead said with a hesitant smile. 'I'm never quite sure whether it's safe to upset the gypsies. I suppose I've had enough bad luck in my time to make me cautious. I crossed her palm with silver in return for a sprig of white heather which I've put in Ma's living room – just in case.' Her smile broadened and she motioned them to follow her into the cottage. A few bags were propped by the doorway and one or two sacks in the yard awaiting disposal.

'I've cleared everything now except a few pieces of furniture which I thought you might be able to make use of. It's hard when you first set up home as everything costs so much, but you'll be able to make nice things, Adam, and I daresay Rachel's father will help.'

'We'll have a lifetime to get our home together, Mrs Mead,' Adam said. 'It's very kind of you to think of us though.'

'Not many folk round here can afford to buy a house or cottage, but it's the right way to start out and I hope you'll be very happy here. My parents were and we all had a happy childhood even though times were tough, especially for Ma after my father was killed on the railway.'

'How old were you then, Mrs Mead?' Rachel asked.

'Seventeen, and I was married three months later. I was the eldest you see. My Benjie was born a couple of months after my mother had our Esther. She didn't even know she was going to have another baby when Dad had his accident. Wonder she didn't lose it with the shock. Reckon that's why our Esther has always been special to her – *was* special to her. Can't get used to Ma not being around and it'll seem mighty strange not having to visit her here. Nearly forty-six years she lived in this cottage. Don't expect you'll stay here that long, though. Things are changing and young folk want to move into the towns.'

'I'm sure we shall love living in your parents' home, Mrs Mead,' Adam said. 'It'll be nice to remember her.'

'No, my dears, you must forget the past and start afresh. She'd give you her blessing, though, just as I do. Now I'll be on my way. I'll get our Benjie to come by and get rid of the rubbish and take these bags on to a jumble sale. Just be happy together.' She looked directly into the faces of the young people. Strange, she thought, how absurdly alike they were. Made for each other, Ma would have said, because their noses were exactly the same type. Noses could make or break a face. Some people had slightly crooked noses, while others were short, or long and thin. Both Adam and Rachel had good straight noses, almost perfect in shape. Reminded Nessie of someone, now who was it? Someone she knew well, someone she'd had intimate dealings with – why, of course Adam's father, Jake Taylor. She looked away guiltily, fumbling in her coat pocket for the key which she handed over to Adam.

'I'll leave you to it then.' She couldn't bring herself to look at them again but Adam and Rachel walked her to the gate, and with a slight inclination of her head Nessie Mead raised her hand half-heartedly as she hurried away down the path alongside the railway line.

'Did we say anything to upset her?' Rachel asked perceptive to the sudden change of mood.

'No, I don't think so. Mrs Mead was good to her mother and she's still grieving, I expect. She's sad that her mother has gone, and doesn't like to think of someone else living in the old family home.' Adam squeezed Rachel affectionately. 'And that someone will be us after Easter.' They almost danced back to the open doorway of the cottage and once inside they closed the door firmly against the outside world.

Nessie had a long walk back to her house at Hundred Acres. A long slow walk with things churning over in her head. Rachel Hunter and Adam Taylor looked so . . . so *together*. She couldn't get the uncanny likeness between them out of her mind. The Hunter twins were so unalike – supposing they weren't twins at all! But Nessie couldn't imagine Phoebe Hunter carrying on with the likes of Jake Taylor, and anyway the Hunters weren't locals so she wouldn't even have known him in her younger days. Fool, she told herself, if the twins shared the same birth date they could hardly both be Phoebe's *and* have a different father. As she walked other things came into her mind. Rachel was such a fine young woman now that the birthmark had faded. If her own daughter had lived, hers and Jake's, would she look as attractive as Rachel Hunter? Nessie's footsteps quickened in time with her thoughts. Stupid impossible thoughts, she told herself. But Rachel Hunter did have that birthmark and she was about eighteen now, just as her daughter would be had she lived . . . had she lived . . . had she lived? Oh, dear god, supposing she hadn't died? Nessie's feet fairly flew up to her front door where she let herself in and sank down in the nearest armchair in the front parlour. Her baby hadn't been baptised so had no name. She'd never seen a death certificate. There'd been no funeral. She'd hated the child until it had gone and then she loved it passionately and wished it back again, birthmark and all.

What had Dick done all those years ago? Given it away? It was possible. He was capable of anything, but no, that didn't make sense. If he knew that their daughter was alive somewhere would he have been so angry when Beth told him that the child wasn't his? He ought to have been pleased. No, the child wasn't important to Dick, one way or another. What had angered him was that his old rival, Jake Taylor, had been his wife's lover. What a mess she'd made of her life, Nessie thought now. Jake Taylor was dead, and her mother. Charlie too. Dear Charlie, her protector as he'd grown older. And that was another strange coincidence, she reflected with renewed interest. First Charlie had taunted Rachel Hunter when they had come to the area to live. Then in some ridiculous way they had ended up friends. Was it because . . . dare she begin to believe that it was because there was a blood tie? Both *her* children? Charlie, Dick's offspring, and Rachel, Jake Taylor's? Nessie got up suddenly and took off her coat, then she went through to the kitchen and made herself a pot of tea. She drank tea until every drop was drained from the big Brown Betty teapot. Silly fool, she reprimanded herself. What wishful notions she was conjuring up. Incredible, fanciful, unreasonable fantasies which could in no way be true or Adam and Rachel would not be permitted to marry. She tried to cast her mind back to the dreadful day when her last baby had been born. It was so long ago and a great deal had happened since, but hadn't Doctor Grant and Minnie Fletcher confirmed that her baby died soon after birth?

Still, it was not an unpleasant thought that Rachel Hunter might be a replica of the child she had borne. Rachel was a nice girl who'd been upset when Charlie was killed in the war and shown genuine compassion.

The Meon Valley seldom experienced the sounds and smells of motor vehicles but on this early March day heads turned and people ran out of their cottages to see the unusual sight of a 1912 Morris Oxford chugging its way through the narrow lanes. When villagers saw that the driver was none other than their beloved Doctor Grant home after service in the Army, he was besieged and forced to halt his journey several times.

I should have crept stealthily in by night, he thought with a wry smile as he admired new babies and listened to tales of goings on during his absence. It was early evening before he sounded his horn as he came into the Square at Wickham. It wasn't much like spring with the damp drizzle falling softly and no one appeared to be interested in his arrival here. He parked the car and switched the engine off. Nothing much had changed, he supposed. But he had. The bout of influenza he'd suffered had left him feeling persistently weary and depressed. He'd lost weight and at times felt as if he had no future. But it lifted his spirits to be back where he'd learnt to live again after being jilted. He loved the countryside and the people of Wickham especially.

He got out of the car and closed the door as quietly as he could. He needed time now to come to terms with his mother's death. His fate might so easily have been the same as hers since it had been a cruel strain of influenza. He wondered how the locals here has fared and how many of his old patients had survived. He needed a meal and he guessed his old housekeeper at the surgery would have one prepared as he had notified Doctor Barber of his visit. But first he wandered around, gazing with interest and many memories at the old buildings. The large Mill was just as he remembered. Built in 1820 it contained beams from the United States Frigate *Chesapeake* which was captured off the coast of Boston in 1813 by *H.M.S. Shannon*. Cyril Grant smiled to himself as he came to Dip Hole where steps led down to the river which enabled people who didn't have pumps to draw water. Living in Kent where the large town of Maidstone afforded better amenities had made him forget how these local folk lived. He passed the brewery and malt house which stood on the banks of the Meon and made his way to the Church of St Nicholas from where he could hear strains of organ music. The heavy iron-studded doors was unlocked so he went inside and sat quietly in the back pew to listen. He was lost in tranquility so didn't notice the Vicar coming through the aisle. A light touch on his arm made him jump to his feet.

'Vicar! How good to see a familiar face,' he said huskily.

'And I might say the same to you, my good man.' The Vicar hardly recognised the doctor who now sported a beard and was several stones lighter than four years earlier. 'How are you, Doctor Grant? Welcome home,' he said, offering a hearty handshake.

'Not as fit as I was a few months ago. This wretched 'flu hit me badly just when I should have been able to help my mother, but sadly she died.'

'I'm sorry indeed, and to hear that you're not feeling as well as you'd like to be, but a few weeks back amongst us will soon put you right, I'm sure.'

Cyril Grant sighed. 'Not back for good, I'm afraid. I suppose if I'm honest it's time to move on and there's still a lot of my mother's estate to attend to so I'm going to settle back in my old home town of Maidstone. I'm here just to finalise the selling of my practice to Doctor Barber who seems to have fallen in love with the area and people just as I did. I'm a bit old at fifty-one to be starting again but the town is growing and there's room for a new practice near the family home.'

'You do surprise me. You've been greatly missed and we've all been asking when you would return but Doctor Barber hasn't divulged anything of your plans.'

'Good! I'm pleased because I specifically asked him not to as I needed to come back and say goodbye to all my old friends personally. I daresay some of the young men didn't come back after the war and this 'flu has probably taken several of the old people off.' He patted the pew beside him. 'Do you have time to sit and tell me what's been happening hereabouts, Vicar?'

'I'll surely make time, Doctor Grant, but at least let's be civil and talk over a meal.'

'I think I'd better pay my respects to Alice who has no doubt prepared a banquet for my home-coming. I'm sure there'll be sufficient to include you.'

The two men returned to the centre of the Square where the doctor's house stood. After they'd admired his new acquisition standing proudly at the kerbside, Cyril rang the bell and both Doctor Barber and Alice greeted him enthusiastically.

An awkward silence followed through as both housekeeper and Doctor Barber were stunned by the change in him. When he removed his hat Alice noticed that what was left of a once fine head of hair was iron grey and his cheeks were quite sunken, giving him a gaunt appearance. But, as they sat round the table enjoying the appetising meal Alice had lovingly prepared, they quickly realised that Cyril Grant was still the kind, caring doctor everyone loved. Afterwards the men retired to the sitting room where Alice served port wine and the Vicar disclosed the names of the young men lost in the war.

'Poor Charlie Mead,' Cyril said. 'I can hardly believe he was suited to the Army '

'He changed quite dramatically,' the Vicar said. 'He was wounded twice and came home to recuperate after the first injury. It was difficult to believe he was the same boy. Getting away from his father and going into the Army made a man of him, and he vowed to look after his mother.'

Doctor Barber stood before the hearth to light his pipe, afterwards holding the edge of the high mantelpiece with one hand as he brooded over past events in Wickham.

'Which is more than that scoundrel of a husband of hers ever did.' The doctor gave a detailed account of Nessie's condition after Dick's beating and of the fight between Dick and Jake which ended in Jake's death.

'What were the two men fighting about?' Cyril Grant asked. 'I know they were once rivals but that was when they were youngsters, so Mrs Waterstone told me.'

'Something to do with Nessie Mead's sister Beth,' Doctor Barber said.

'But she married Harry Cropper and settled down, I thought?' Cyril said.

'Harry was one of the first victims of the war,' the Vicar explained. 'Beth's in-laws were a good influence over her and she seemed to have changed for the better, but when she went to work at the basket factory she began to flirt outrageously and I'm afraid her own brother-in-law was easy prey, though what their relationship had to do with Jake Taylor no one seems to know. Eventually they went off together and no one knows where they are,' Vicar said. 'Mrs Waterstone was shocked and angry. Fortunately she had Nessie to look after her until this 'flu saw her off.'

'Mrs Taylor didn't seem too upset by the death of her husband,' Doctor Barber said thoughtfully. 'She put on a show of crocodile tears to impress. I understand she has means of her own. To my surprise she doesn't appear to mind that young Adam is to marry

Rachel Hunter, though I believe there's some conflict as to where they'll live. She expects them to live with her but Adam intends to buy the railway cottage.'

Cyril Grant answered vaguely at first as he wondered how the delicate Lily Taylor would manage without Jake's strength to manipulate. Then the penny dropped as two names linked together filled him with utter shock and despair. Adam and Rachel. Half-brother and sister. They *couldn't* marry – but they weren't to know that! He couldn't admit to what he and Minnie Fletcher had connived to do nineteen years ago!

Voices floated over his head and thankfully the other two men thought he was overtired after his long car journey so suggested that he should retire He did so gratefully but sleep eluded him. Had he come back in the nick of time? Should he keep quiet and pray that they would have no children? It seemed an impossible situation but by dawn he knew that he had to see Adam and tell him that marriage to Rachel Hunter was out of the question. His head ached in anticipation of the questions he would be asked. Adam was no fool. He was going to demand to be told the truth, but that too was impossible. Whatever would Nessie Mead's reaction be to discover that the baby she thought had died was alive and had grown up right under her nose? Cyril searched his memory for the way things were before the war. Yes he remembered that Charlie Mead had enjoyed taunting young Rachel. He recalled seeing Adam and the two Hunter girls together but it had never crossed his mind that anything would come of it. Heavens, he thought, Adam Taylor, why couldn't you have chosen Belinda instead of Rachel!

He knew he needed time before he acted and whatever decision he took must be carried out with discretion. For the next couple of days he travelled round the villages meeting up with old friends and familiar faces to get the feel of the place again.

When he visited Phoebe and Wally Hunter he learned that Rachel and Adam were to be married at Easter and there was great excitement as preparations were made. It was to be a grand occasion when all the villagers would join in the celebrations. He didn't have much time to think out a plan so rode over to Beech Cottage only to find that Minnie Fletcher had moved away to live near the sea with her sister.

Cyril felt desperate. He visited Nessie Mead who was delighted to see him but she avoided any gossip about Dick and her sister. She was still mourning her mother as well as Charlie. The shock of what we did with her child would kill her, Cyril thought. She'd had a hard life and fate had dealt some cruel blows, how could he deal her another one? She might be glad that Rachel was her daughter but that would hurt Phoebe and Wally, not to mention the two youngsters themselves.

Cyril tossed all manner of ideas around in his head, and during the service on Sunday morning prayed for guidance to do the right thing. He greeted Rachel and Adam afterwards with courtesy, offering his warm congratulations. How could he do this to them? Better to stay out of it and hope for the best, but he was a doctor and knew the dangers. He had a week before the banns would be called. The longest week of his life.

Still no nearer to making up his mind how to do what he knew he must, he took a drive out to Romsey and then on to Winchester to see some old friends. The countryside was at its best on a rare bright sunny day and the small wild daffodils in the woods hinted at a hidden spring. His friends were overjoyed to see him though concerned about his health and it was late when he left the town to return to Wickham. He decided against taking the better road via Southampton and Fareham. When the moon got up there would be enough light to see his way back to Wickham through Bishop's Waltham and the Chase. The drive was pleasantly uneventful. He had passed the Hunters' cottage at Kingsmere when he saw a lone figure ahead of him jauntily walking back towards Hundred Acres. At least he could offer the young man a lift, he decided, then cowardice tempted him to pass by when he realised who it was. But wasn't this the opportunity he had prayed for so earnestly?

Adam turned when he heard the car coming up behind him. He knew who it must be and guessed the doctor would offer him a lift. Such opportunities rarely came his way in such an area as Wickham so he accepted gratefully.

'Just said goodnight to your fiancée, Adam?' Cyril Grant said.

'Yes. It'll be nice when we can be together in our own home, Doctor Grant.' Adam was more interested in the car and how to drive it than his forthcoming marriage, though. He smoothed his hands over the leather upholstery and admired the polished grain of the wooden dashboard.

'This is real luxury,' he said in admiration. 'Something I shall never be able to afford.'

'You don't know, Adam. I'd never anticipated progressing beyond doing my rounds on my bicycle. My mother, you see, owned a rather large family home which I inherited after her death. If I'd married and raised a family I'd have needed the house. Instead I've settled for a modest town practice and a new vehicle to go with it.'

'Yes, I heard that you were only back to visit us all. I'm sorry that you aren't going to return here to live, Doctor Grant, and I know Mother is disappointed.'

There was a moment's awkward silence then the doctor pulled in to a clearing in Bere Wood and they talked briefly about the war and its consequences.

'Lots of things have changed here, Adam,' Cyril Grant said gently. 'I know war plays havoc with people's lives both on and off the battlefield. I was sorry indeed to come home and hear about your father.' He turned in his seat to face the young man. He couldn't have it on his conscience that he'd let this opportunity to execute his duty pass by – a duty he must tackle sympathetically but honestly, yet without revealing more than he need.

'It didn't take long for someone to tell you all the local gossip then,' Adam said dispassionately.

'I knew that there had always been a difference of opinion between your father and Dick Mead.'

Adam was glad that it was dark. He knew people still gossiped about the fight and the reason for it but there had never been anyone who could tell him how the feud between the two men originally started.

'I only know what people say and Mother tells me it's all nonsense. Folk round here didn't think too highly of Dad because of his job, but rumours have it that it might have had something to do with Mrs Mead or maybe Beth?'

'Whatever the cause, Adam, it all happened a long time ago, before my time. I think perhaps your father was keen on Mrs Mead and Dick won the day. Better I daresay for Nessie Mead if she had married your father. Dick didn't do her any favours, did he? And now gone off with Beth Cropper.' Cyril Grant shook his head sadly.

'I expect both men were to blame for the fight, Doctor Grant, but it was the heart attack which killed Dad and no one can say different.'

'Very sad for you and your mother. She's lucky to have you and I hope you'll be good to her.'

'She wants Rachel and me to live with her after we're married, but I've put my foot down. She'd make Rachel's life a misery – any woman's come to that – and being that Dad left me some money, I can afford to buy Mrs Waterstone's cottage.'

'I admire you, Adam, I just which you'd chosen any girl but Rachel.'

There, it was out, now he had to justify his remark. Adam was clearly shocked. Cyril Grant could feel the boy's defensive reaction.

'But I thought you of all people would be pleased. I thought you liked Rachel?' he said.

Cyril placed a hand on his shoulder. 'No one is fonder of Rachel Hunter than me, Adam. I've watched her grow into a fine young woman, and life was pretty cruel to her in the beginning.'

'I know, I felt sorry for her with that awful birthmark.' Adam leaned forward. 'Is it because you think if we have children they'll have birthmarks too? Belinda didn't have one. They're not a bit alike and they're twins.'

'My dear Adam, I'm afraid this is a painful duty I have to perform but what I'm about to tell you must be in the strictest confidence. It seems fate brought me back to Wickham in the nick of time. You can't marry Rachel Hunter – you simply can't – and I'm so very sorry.'

'That's a dreadful thing to say, Doctor Grant! Why ever not?' Adam's tone was highly indignant.

'You know I wouldn't make such a statement without very good reason, Adam. The plain truth is that you're related and any affection you feel for each other is probably because you . . .'

'Related? Me and the Hunters?'

'Only Rachel. This is very difficult for me, Adam. I'm not at liberty to disclose certain events concerning Rachel's birth. Suffice it to say that I believe you share the same father.'

'But how can that be? Rachel is Belinda's twin sister and they –'

'No, Adam. They aren't twins at all. When Phoebe gave birth to Belinda she had only the one infant, much loved and wanted after many years of waiting. Rachel was born in questionable circumstances, unloved and unwanted. It was touch and go whether or not she would live. The Hunters lived miles away. No one ever thought they would choose to move to the very area where Rachel was born. Phoebe Hunter took the poor mite in and mothered her as if she were her own. They've been good to her and no one has ever suspected anything.'

'You're just telling me this – this fairy story. It's all a pack of lies! Is it because you don't want me to know what a rotter my father was? I suppose Mrs Hunter was another of Dad's fancy women? It seems he was well known for cheating my mother. I thought you were a friend. I'll walk home, thank you very much.'

'Calm down, Adam. It wasn't like that at all. I can confirm that you and Rachel share the same father. Beyond that I can reveal nothing. Even Phoebe and Wally Hunter don't know Rachel's real parentage so I must ask you to keep this knowledge to yourself. But you must see, Adam, that you cannot go through with a marriage to Rachel. Now, if it had been Belinda, everything would have been fine.'

'I never thought my father was capable of such blatant adultery, let alone with Mrs Hunter.'

'Adam, please try to think things through. If Rachel's real mother were Phoebe Hunter would she have allowed you and Rachel to marry? She has no idea that you're related which is why only you and I can share this knowledge. Please believe me, Adam. If there was any other way – if I had any doubts – but I know it to be true. You must have wondered why Rachel and Belinda are so different in looks and character?'

Adam sat with his head in his hands. 'I don't want to believe you, but I've never known you to be anything but upright and honest. Is it that you want Rachel for yourself?'

Cyril Grant placed his arm on Adam's shoulder. 'Now you're being ridiculous,' he said softly. 'She's a fine person – but she's not for you, Adam. She's your half-sister.'

'What can I do?' he cried in despair. 'What can I say? How can I tell her it's off?'

'You'll need to sleep on it for a few nights, I suspect. We can talk again if you like? I'm due to leave Wickham in a couple of days' time but I'd like to see this thing settled before I go.'

'You sound as if you feel responsible?'

'Only in as much as I saved the life of a child once, Rachel's, and found her a good home. Your father and her real mother believed she died soon after birth. To all intents and purposes she's the daughter of the Hunters. I can hardly believe that you and she – it's just incredible, Adam, a quirk of fate, if you like, but you must try to understand that I had no option but to prevent your marriage from taking place once I realised what was about to happen.'

'What if you hadn't returned here?'

'Then no one would be any the wiser – in a way I wish I hadn't, but I have a conscience. There would be risks, Adam.'

'Will you visit them with me?' he asked after a few minutes had elapsed.

'No. It might be better if I don't. Too much would have to come out into the open, and too many people would be hurt. The only way I can suggest is for you to say that you've changed your mind, Adam.'

'But I love Rachel, Doctor Grant, and she loves me.'

'Then if you really love her you know you're doing wrong in going through with this. I . . . I can't stop you, of course, though I know I should stand in church and forbid the banns. I don't want it to come to that, Adam. Think of your own reputation, your mother's, Rachel's and her family's. I know how much this hurts, believe me, and how much it's going to hurt Rachel. I was jilted myself many years ago, but there's no other way. Either you must engineer a quarrel to finish it or you must tell her that you've changed you mind. She's still young, only just nineteen, and you'll soon find someone else.'

Somewhere in the distance midnight chimed but Cyril Grant knew he must see the night through with Adam.

'Come back to the house,' he begged. 'We'll have tea and get warm while we talk – if it helps.'

'I don't want to go anywhere. Yes, I do, I want to go away as far as I possibly can, but there's my mother. I've got to confront her and see what she can tell me.'

'I doubt that she knows anything about the matter, Adam. She seldom took an interest in the doings of others. She was always too busy complaining about her health. I could never find much physically wrong with her. I fancy she feigned ill health to keep your father at bay. So, you can't altogether blame him for seeking satisfaction elsewhere.'

'In any vacant bed it would seem! Maybe we don't have to look too far to know which one.' Adam spat the words out angrily. It was all slotting into place now, but Cyril Grant lifted his hand in protest.

'No more speculation, Adam, please. It's all in the past and we don't want to hurt people unnecessarily, do we? I've always had reason to believe that you're a young man of integrity and I want you to think this over very carefully before you go to see Rachel. Who her real parents are isn't important any more. As far as she's concerned, Phoebe and Wally Hunter are her mother and father, and you must let her go on thinking that.'

'Doesn't she have a right to know the truth?'

'I doubt that any of us know the real truth, and how would it help her? The shock of hearing that she's not Phoebe's daughter, Belinda's sister, might be too much for her. It could turn her brain, Adam. Nothing can change the circumstances but you're not in a position to offer Rachel marriage now that you know that you're half-brother and sister. I'm sorry. I wish it didn't have to be me coming between you and Rachel, but professionally I must advise against marriage.'

'I'm beginning to wish I'd never come home,' Adam said suddenly. 'Then I'd never have known.'

'It might have come to light, sooner or later, and then think of the terrible heartache it would have caused.'

'T'would be easier if I went away but that would kill my mother just as the truth would. But I don't know how I can do this to Rachel! What a mess! Poor Rachel.' He thought of how she believed in good luck, that it had removed her birthmark and brought him back from the war. She would think so ill of him, her love changing to hatred, and she'd believe it was all down to his losing the lucky stone.

The two men sat and talked the matter over until the first light of dawn began to appear.

'You'll never be ready for your work, Adam. Can you go home to bed and for once tell a white lie and say you're ill?'

'No, Doctor Grant. I'll go home, have a wash and shave then get off to The King's Head where I'm working on some new outside tables. Thank goodness I'm not working with Mr Hunter at present. He's still suffering from the effects of 'flu so he has to work inside. I'll be glad to go to work to think out what I can say to Rachel and her parents. They aren't going to think too much of me, are they?'

'Better the upset now than in a few years' time when who knows what might happen. You've got a lifetime to prove to yourself that you've done what's right, Adam. It's hard. I know what you're going through and we'll hate ourselves for what we're doing to Rachel – but you must see, Adam, it's the only way.'

'I wish I didn't believe you but it ties up with things I know about my father. I'm sure you respect the Hunters and like Rachel too much to do anything to hurt them unjustly.'

'You won't do anything silly, will you?'

Adam shook his head, and as early morning farmhands and carters set about their morning's work, heads turned in surprise to watch the motor vehicle going through the lanes at this early hour.

Adam took his mother a cup of tea after he had washed and shaved with an unsteady hand as he couldn't pare away the shock of the night's revelation.

'You're up early, Adam.' Lily Taylor sat up in bed wide awake having been disturbed by the sound of the car engine. 'Where have you been all night?' One look at her son confirmed that he hadn't slept in his own bed. 'You haven't taken advantage of Rachel before the wedding, I hope? I thought I heard the doctor's car outside?'

Adam had decided against confiding in his mother just yet but she was a wily old bird and knew something was wrong.

'The doctor brought me home, Mum. I've been talking to him – you know, about the war and everything. The time just drifted by.'

'Time doesn't drift by unless you're up to no good. I suppose even the good doctor isn't above drinking to forget the horrors of war. You look awful, Adam, fit for nothing – I hope you're not taking after your father and soaking yourself in beer and whisky and the like?'

'I haven't touched a drop and neither has the doctor as far as I know,' he replied patiently.

Lily Taylor had never been an affectionate woman though in her own way she had coddled Adam and been possessive. He needed someone to confide in now. Going away to war had toughened him but the bitter blow he had received was just beginning to affect him and his chin quivered as the wound in his heart could only be soothed by tears. He suddenly knelt by his mother's high bed and buried his face in the quilt, sobbing.

'Adam! Dear boy! Whatever's the matter?'

He hated himself for his weakness but it all had to come out.

'Doctor Grant tells me that I can't marry Rachel, Mother. Dad fathered us both. Tell me it isn't true, please? Tell me he's wrong?'

The cup rattled in its saucer as Lily took in what her son had blurted out. Adam glanced up in time to see cup and saucer falling from his mother's hands as she sank back against her pillows. He managed to retrieve the china but the tea was spilt everywhere. His mother's cheeks were ashen as she cried. 'No! *No*! It can't be true. Your father was no saint, heaven knows, but not a bastard child – not here in Hundred Acres. You mustn't believe it, Adam. It's just vicious gossip.'

'But it must be true, Mother. You know Doctor Grant would never come between Rachel and me for the sake of vicious gossip.'

'It can't be true, I tell you. It isn't true!' She began to gasp and her cheeks turned from grey to bright red and then to purple. Adam ran for the brandy and held his mother close until she revived. 'Never speak to me of this again, Adam, nor anyone else,' she panted, clutching at the front of her nightdress.

'But if you know anything, Mother, anything at all, please tell me, for God's sake?' he pleaded.

'I know of no child, Adam. There have always been rumours about your father and his affairs but a lot of them to spite me because I had money of my own. Stupid jealousy, of course. People are so wicked and full of treachery.'

'But Doctor Grant wouldn't say such a thing if there wasn't some truth in it, would he?'

Lily lay back her eyes closed, her breathing spasmodic. To anyone else she could have been at death's door but Adam had witnessed such attacks all his life and no longer feared them.

'The Hunters came from several miles away in the New Forest so how could they have known your father?' she said after recovering. 'It's true the two girls are very different – I always suspected something fishy. Now Belinda is the one you should marry, Adam. She wouldn't object to living here with me. Gentle, quiet and sweet-natured, and I know she adores you.' She sipped more brandy. 'Rachel could be quite fiery, I should think, and you can't deny she chased you. She thought no one would look at her because of that strawberry mark.'

'Now you're saying unkind things, Mother, and I don't want to hear. I'd better get off to work. I need time to think.'

Lily pleaded with Adam to stay at home even if there was nothing she could say to console him. She was as shocked as he and the thoughts which raced around in Adam's head brought him nothing but confusion. He knew his mother would be delighted if the marriage were called off. He felt defiant yet the more he thought it over the more he realised that he had to do what Doctor Grant had insisted upon. He kept arguing with himself. Supposing there was no truth in the rumour? Then all this trauma was for nothing. But if it were true – and so much pointed to his father's disloyalty to his mother – he daren't risk the health of any offspring he and Rachel might have.

When Adam could stand the strain no longer he visited Calder Cottage straight after work before going home for his tea.

'Why, Adam!' Phoebe Hunter exclaimed. 'Rachel wasn't expecting you this early. I believe you're going to see the Vicar this evening?'

She looked at his work clothes with disapproval.

'I . . . I . . . need to see Rachel urgently, Mrs Hunter. We . . . we . . . won't be going to see the Vicar after all.'

'Oh dear, what's happened? Not your mother is it?'

'In a way. She's had one of her attacks. It's made me realise that I can't go through with buying the cottage. It wouldn't be right to leave her on her own.' Adam followed Phoebe into the living room where the meal had just been placed on the table. 'Oh, I'm sorry,' he apologised, 'I didn't stop to think. Your tea . . .'

'Sit down, lad and have some with us,' Wally invited.

Hurrying footsteps sounded on the stairs and Rachel came bounding into the room.

'Adam!' she said excitedly. 'I wasn't expecting you just . . .' She stopped and the pleasure faded from her bright eyes as she saw the solemn expression on his face. 'Is something wrong?'

Adam looked down at the cap he was twisting between hot sweaty hands. How could he say what he'd come to say? What right did he have to upset this harmonious family who'd never harmed anyone? Curse Doctor Grant, he thought venomously. But he had no choice.

'Something's wrong in a manner of speaking.' He dared to glance up at the faces waiting for an explanation. He realised that Belinda was home. He hadn't expected that and nodded by way of acknowledgement.

'I'm not going to buy the cottage, Rachel,' he blurted.

'But I don't mind, Adam,' she said with a nervous laugh. 'I told you I'd do my best to be nice to your mother. It'll be all right in time.'

'I . . . I'm sorry,' he stammered. He wasn't making a good job of this but there wasn't a nice way to do it, he knew. 'I'm sorry – this is going to come as a shock – but – I can't marry you, Rachel. It wouldn't be right.'

'Whatever d'you mean? Wouldn't be right?' Rachel's voice was high-pitched and demanding. His mother was right, she *did* have a fiery streak. He hadn't meant to say it wouldn't be right, he'd meant simply to state that he'd changed his mind.

'I shouldn't have let things go this far before telling you,' he said. 'But coming back from the war, there was an urgency in everything. Truth is, Rachel, I never meant . . .'

'Well, go on,' Phoebe urged with an edge to her tongue.

'It . . . it's Belinda that I love and want to marry. I'm sorry, Rachel, I never meant to hurt you, honestly. I felt sorry for you and you did chase me . . .'

'I think we'd all better sit down and have a cup of tea,' Wally said with a firmness unusual for him.

'Just as well to come to this conclusion before the wedding than afterwards, I s'pose,' Phoebe said haughtily.

'T'will be wedding nerves, Adam,' Wally said, trying to calm the tense situation. He went out to the scullery where the kettle was just on the boil over the stove. 'You've been through a trying time being away from home for so long and losing your dad. Postpone the wedding, why don't you? For three months to give you time to settle down?'

Adam shook his head. 'No, I'm sorry. Rachel – I hate myself and I won't blame you for hating me, but I just got carried away with it all. You made it seem so easy but I just can't marry someone I don't love.'

Adam despised himself. He lied too readily for he did love Rachel and knew that marriage to her would have been lively and full of fun.

She burst into tears and fled to the safety of her bedroom, throwing over her shoulder as she went: 'I hate all of you – *all* of you – and especially you, Belinda. You always get the best of everything.'

Phoebe went chasing after her which left Adam and Belinda facing each other.

'I've always been fond of you both,' Adam said. 'I know I shouldn't have let Rachel become so attached.'

'You seemed equally attached, Adam,' Belinda said quietly. 'Perhaps if you do what Father suggests and postpone the wedding it will be all right?'

'No, Belinda. I know my own mind. I didn't want to hurt Rachel but you and she are so different. You will marry me, won't you?'

'Oh, Adam, no. I couldn't – I just couldn't – it would be so painful for Rachel. And I love her too much to be so cruel.'

Adam left Calder Cottage feeling an utter failure. He crossed the road and disappeared into the woods where he walked until he was too weary to place one foot before the other. A new thought came into his head which brought a mite of comfort to his troubled mind. He had every right to love Rachel because she was, after all, his sister. Maybe that was why they had become friends in the first place.

Chapter Eight

The news soon spread round the villages, quickly followed by a rumour that Adam was secretly courting Belinda up at the big house.

Rachel looked pale, but her large dark brown eyes smouldered with humiliation and she refused point blank to go to work. Phoebe knew that she was ready to erupt and dreaded to think what might happen if she crossed paths with Adam Taylor or his mother. Not that it was very likely. Lily Taylor seldom left the house, and Adam had no cause to come to Kingsmere while he could see Belinda at the big house at Hundred Acres. Phoebe wanted what was best for both her girls, especially Belinda. It grieved her to think that Adam might have been playing one sister off against the other. He was a nice enough young man but his recent behaviour had shocked them and caused alarm, suggesting instability. Supposing he married Belinda and then changed his mind again!

'You've got to face people eventually, dear,' Phoebe said kindly to Rachel who was helping her with some baking one morning.

'And have them laugh in my face?' Rachel retorted. 'I don't need to go into Wickham or any of the other villages.'

'But your father can't keep you, and you can't do nothing for the rest of your life. You were very rude to Vicar when he came to see you. He might have been able to help you. No one blames *you*.'

'No, they just feel sorry for me and I don't want their pity. I've had that all my life. I never thought Adam Taylor felt so sorry for me that he'd actually get engaged and then break it off. I could understand it if I still had my birthmark, but I'm not that ugly now, am I?'

'I'm sure it's got nothing to do with whether you're ugly or pretty, Rachel, but you know you're very nice-looking, and I still believe that Adam is very fond of you and always will be. His mother's behind it, you mark my words.'

Rachel was kneading the bread dough vigorously. She paused, staring unseeingly at the copper pans hanging on the brick wall. Yes,

Mrs Taylor had shown a fondness for her sister. She preferred Belinda, that was it, probably considered it was a risk for her beloved son to marry a girl who'd had such a horrible disfigurement. She was thinking ahead to her grandchildren. Rachel had thought Adam was standing up to his mother but now she realised that he was very much under her influence still. With a painful cry she wiped her hands on her apron and ran up to her bedroom where she flung herself down on her bed and wept huge tears of despair.

Phoebe sighed but left her to drain her unhappiness with weeping. What else could she do? The situation was unpleasant, the atmosphere tight whenever Belinda came home now. It was Phoebe's turn to pound the dough. She could hardly believe it of Belinda when she'd asked that she might invite Adam home to tea on Easter Saturday. How was she going to break the news to Rachel?

'It's too soon,' Phoebe said to Wally when they were alone preparing for bed that night.

He found it difficult to deny his own true daughter anything.

'We've a lot to be thankful for that the two have been so close up to now,' he said thoughtfully. 'They've grown into fine young women, each developing her own character, and now must fashion their own destiny.'

'I don't know much about Shakespeare but didn't he say something like: "There's a divinity that shapes our ends, Rough-hew them how we will"?' Phoebe asked.

Wally grunted. 'Probably. What difference does that make? I'm sorry it's turned out like this, Phoebe. Given you a lot of worry. In a way I was glad it was our Rachel that was getting wed first. After all, we know nothing of her background and it would have been a relief to see her married and settled down. All I want is to see Belinda happy. If only Adam had had the decency to wait before switching from Rachel to Belinda. Can't think what came over the boy. He ought to have let Rachel down gently.'

'He was very unkind, I thought. She's taken it badly and I'm sure she'll not want to be here when Adam comes to tea.' Phoebe slipped the wide, high-necked winceyette nightdress over her head and buttoned the front opening. 'We could refuse, I suppose. And if they're thinking of rushing into marriage we can forbid it until Belinda is twenty-one.'

'Now who's being unkind?' Wally asked. 'Maybe we should have insisted on making Rachel and Adam wait until he'd been home from the war longer? I mean – we don't know what effects the war will have had on him. People change. They're exposed to all kinds of disease abroad. But, for the moment, we can't do anything much. If Adam can change his mind once, he'll as like as not change it again. We must try to persuade Belinda to be discreet and wait until this scandal has died down, though I suppose there's no harm in Adam coming to tea. Perhaps it'll break down some awkward barriers. If we try to stop it, Phoebe, they'll start courting in secret and we all know where that can lead.'

'But not our Belinda. You surely can't think . . .?'

'No, 'course not, she's much too sensible. She's shy and Adam wouldn't do anything to hurt her. Yes, I reckon t'will bring things out into the open if Belinda brings him home to tea on Easter Saturday, but you'd better warn Rachel in good time.'

Rachel accepted the news quietly. After copious weeping came days of morose solitude. During the quiet of an afternoon she took to walking alone through the woods. Subconsciously she was running away from things which had hurt her and looking for things long past which had brought her pleasure.

She followed sounds of children playing or dogs barking, anything which reminded her of the gypsy travellers, but the woods remained empty of such people. What a fool she'd been to give Adam her precious stone. Now she knew she'd never find Kasan again, let alone enjoy good luck. That myth was quashed – a merciless answer to happy expectation. She longed to be free of the noose around her neck. It was getting ever tighter as bitterness towards Adam and Belinda grew. How insensitive they were, she thought. She'd always thought that Adam was attracted to her sister, but to drop her and take up with Belinda immediately was the last straw. Well, Belinda was welcome to him. She could invite who she liked to tea but Rachel wasn't going to be made to feel small. She didn't know where she'd go but somehow she would escape any confrontation with Adam Taylor or her sister.

She told no one of her plan to go out on that Saturday afternoon. It was a crisp cold day with high winds and she wrapped up warm and took a small bag of sandwiches with her, planning not to return until well after dark. Her parents were in their bedroom getting ready so Rachel stealthily crept down the stairs, praying that they wouldn't creak. Once she had reached the back door it was easy. Her boots hardly touched the ground as she raced through the long garden, past the almost barren vegetable patch, skirting the fruit trees, brown and lifeless now. She ignored the indignant clucking of hens in their coops as she picked her way over the rubbish plot. When she reached the hurdle fence she had to hitch up her skirts, but long legs made it possible to get over without too much difficulty. Walking through the paddock wasn't quite as trouble-free though as the two horses put out to grass there were inquisitive and expected Rachel to have apples in her pocket. She stopped just long enough to talk to them and pat their noses and then took to her heels and ran the last few yards to the gate. She made certain that she secured it behind her and then made for the bridlepath near the river.

Rachel had no definite plans to go in any particular direction. It occurred to her that she could start walking towards her grand-parents' home in the New Forest. Something urged her to get back to her roots, to the place of her early childhood where she'd been happy with much loved grandparents to run to when in trouble. But when she reached the Waltham Chase Road it looked long and cheerless. Not one carter was in sight so there was no hope of getting a lift. It was Easter and after the solemnity of Good Friday when everyone excepting her had attended the Church Service in Wickham people were spending the time closeted by their own firesides. The north-east wind lashed at her cheeks so she turned back in the direction of Wickham through copses, over streams and ditches, always careful to avoid any rider or walker by keeping to the thickest part of Bere Forest.

She had no idea what led her to the Church of St Nicholas in Wickham but she turned the iron handle and went inside. She sat in a pew at the back admiring the mass of beautiful flowers which had been especially arranged for the Easter Day services. All the arrange-ments for her wedding crowded into her mind, disturbing the peace of this ancient building. Her mother had intended to supply the floral displays to decorate the altar and church for her wedding on Easter Monday. Hers and Adam's. Rachel stood up and walked slowly down the aisle imagining her father by her side, Belinda in her sky blue dress standing solemnly behind them carrying a basket of spring flowers. Everything had been arranged, even to the carriages and reception in the old school hall. Who had cancelled everything? she wondered. Her parents, or Adam. God, how she hated and despised *him*! What right did he have to treat her so callously? She felt her finger-nails digging into her palms as outrage filled her senses. Her whole body stiffened and then relief flooded through her as a gentle arm was placed on her arm.

'Rachel, dear?' Nessie Mead was shocked to feel the hostility in the girl's manner. 'Are you all right?'

'Yes, of course, why shouldn't I be?' She pulled free with irritation then lowered her head in shame. What had this woman done to offend her? A woman who had known pain and misery for as long as Rachel could remember. 'I . . . I'm so sorry. I didn't mean to be rude.'

'Shall we sit down and have a chat? I've been placing some flowers on my parents' grave and the bitter cold wind has chafed my hands.' Nessie laughed softly. 'Stupid, isn't it, to come into this cold church to get warm?'

They sat side by side and each silently remembered another time when they had sat together, to mourn the loss of Charlie. Rachel was filled momentarily with remorse. She had sat in this very place and prayed many times for Adam, Charlie, and other local men away at the war. Not that was all over, but life was far from peaceful.

'I was sorry to hear that your engagement to Adam Taylor was broken, dear,' Nessie said. 'I expect it feels like the end of the world, but remember there might be better times ahead.'

'I doubt it, Mrs Mead. Setting up home with Adam meant so much to me,' Rachel's voice cracked.

'I know it did, Rachel.' Nessie wasn't sure what to say to this grieving girl who obviously felt that she had lost everything. 'Perhaps it wasn't meant to be. We don't always understand why things happen and we rebel against life, but invariably things turn out better than we deserve.'

'How could he do it, Mrs Mead?' Rachel quelled the tears which threatened. She must be a woman and stand tall and proud for she had done nothing to be ashamed of. 'To break it off so suddenly and turn his attention to Belinda – how could he be so unfeeling?'

'I'm afraid that's the way of men, Rachel. If you find a good one – like your mother did – then you're a very lucky person. I must admit I thought Adam was a decent lad, but how can we tell what people are really like? I'm sure he didn't mean to hurt you and cause you such misery. You must remember that he's all his mother's got and I fancy she might have swayed him.' She shrugged. 'For some reason best known to herself.'

'I know she didn't like me very much, although I tried to please her. But I can't understand Belinda either. We've always been close and vowed never to quarrel or part from one another – how could she do this and not expect me to despise them both?'

'You're both grown woman now. How old are you, Rachel?'

'We were nineteen on March the seventh.'

'You're still young, my dear. You and your sister have to make your own choices and decisions in life now, and you've got a lifetime to find real happiness. I know you don't understand it at present, but one day you'll laugh at it all and be glad you didn't make a big mistake.' Nessie stood up to leave. She felt Rachel's dark brooding deeply. She felt compelled to share in her torment and wanted to do something to restore the girl's faith in human nature. As she stood looking down at the dark head she felt a ridiculous urge to invite her home where her own daughters might help to cheer her up. She could love this girl who might have been her own baby. She felt Rachel's need too keenly for comfort and was letting her imagination run amok. She must go and persuade Rachel to go home too. 'I must get back home. June will be in for her tea,' she said. 'It's lovely to have my family around me – and I'm sure your parents want you to be with them.'

Rachel allowed herself to be guided to the lych gate and in the lane beyond they said their goodbyes and parted. But Rachel only walked a few yards to the bridge, then turned back. The church was as good a place as any to hide away until her former fiancé had taken his leave of Calder Cottage. She idled her time away looking at the slabs of grey marble which marked the burial place of descendants of the Uvedale family. She knew the history of the church and most of the old families of Wickham off by heart from schooldays. The long walk in the cold had made her hungry so she huddled in a quiet corner to eat her sandwiches. Bored, her thoughts turned again to the reason for her solitude. Bitterness built up inside her with no outlet. She had been wronged and someone had to pay. Why was it she who had to leave the comfort of her home to avoid her sister's pleasure? Adam had used her to get to Belinda. Rachel could see it all clearly now and burned with a sense of injustice. It wasn't fair – it simply wasn't right! She hurled the wrapping paper across the grey stone floor which had been thoroughly swept ready for the services tomorrow. She'd have happily scrubbed them to make them look nice for her wedding day on Monday. But it wasn't going to happen, and all because Adam Taylor was too much of a coward to leave his mother. Hadn't she said that she was willing to live with her? Things wouldn't have been easy but she would have made the best of it.

Dusk was descending, the light coming through the high windows making the interior of the church eerie. She wanted to go home but knew she mustn't. They would all look at her with regret. Adam might try to make amends with soothing words but nothing he could do or say would pardon him for the misery he had caused her. Cold and unrelenting she paced the floor, hatred for the world at large mounting inside her. She kicked out at the nearest pew. That too was unrelenting. Made of good solid oak which had taken a few other knocks in its time, it now refused to yield to Rachel's sacrilege. Neat rows of hassocks lay beneath each pew waiting for worshipper's to kneel. No more would she ever kneel to pray, she vowed, picking up one after another and hurling them across the church. Soon the place was littered with hymn and prayer books, and such was Rachel's frenzy that she removed the large Bible from the lectern and hurled it towards the altar. A huge vase of flowers toppled and lay in an untidy mess on the carpet. Then, as if possessed by the devil himself, she dashed the rest of the flowers to the floor and trampled on them, giving vent at last to all the resentment which had been building up over the past three weeks.

At the door she turned and surveyed her handiwork. Her dark eyes glistened with glee and she let out a harsh laugh. Her dark hair, escaping from her hat, blew across her eyes and mouth. Her fury stimulated her and she tore around the church once more, kicking at everything in sight. Then, picking up her bag, she let herself out of the door and began to run.

Clouds scudding across the night sky quickly blotted out the moon and stars. Like a demented animal Rachel ran until her body weakened and she was forced to drop to her knees at the roadside. A grassy bank took her weight. It was wet and she realised that a slight drizzle had given way to torrential rain. She didn't care. She was free at last: free from pitying glances, free from obstacles which had shackled her from the day she was born. There was no one to answer to out here in the wild. She had run, walked, hurried along an unfamiliar road, but what did it matter? She began to laugh again, a high-pitched unnatural hysterical sound that came from someone else not her. Her head felt light, her sides ached, yet she revelled in the feeling of the rain as it cascaded down to mingle with her tears. The world was totally unreal. She was no longer Rachel Hunter but someone with no name, no identity. Her heart gradually slowed its frenzied pounding and she drifted into a state of exhausted sleep.

Chapter Nine

Rachel believed that her mother was standing over her trying to waken her, but it was a wet nose which nuzzled her cheeks and ears. An excited whimper, not the voice of a human, made her sit up sharply. The dog's urgent barks were music to her ears. He needed someone to love and she stretched out her arms to hug him.

'Wonder where you've come from and what your name is,' she said. He wagged his tail frantically, still talking in his own way, and then crouched down, scraping his paws backwards. When she didn't move he rushed at her, whining louder. 'You're as wet as I am,' she said. 'And if it's food you want, I haven't got any.' He ran round Rachel playfully and then, obviously annoyed because she wouldn't get up, began to bark his short urgent demands. Rachel was stiff, cold, and definitely not herself.

'I don't know where you want me to go,' she said, 'but I'm not going to get very far at this rate.' It was a painful struggle to pull herself up and she found it difficult to make her legs and feet work. They were quite numb, but with some perseverance she took a few steps, then one or two more, the dog chasing his own tail, going round and round her excitedly. 'Do stop,' she said, 'you're making me giddy. Come on, let's try to find out where we are.'

Her hat was too wet to put on her head and the water squelched in her boots. Rain and sleet had saturated her coat so that it was twice as heavy as normal. She walked a few yards. What was she doing out of doors before it was really light? Had she really stayed out all night? Where on earth did she imagine she was going?

Suddenly there was a noise behind her and she felt a heavy hand on her shoulder.

'And where might you be off to, young lady?'

Rachel turned to face a rough-looking man of about thirty. He was wearing an old army cape and a cloth cap.

'I . . . I'm just walking,' she said nervously.

'At this time of the morning? You mean you're stealing my dog.'

'No! No, I don't want your dog. He found me.' The icy cold rain enveloped her and she felt as if she were being swept away on the crest of a wave to somewhere where nothing mattered any more. She swayed . . . made a grab for the nearest support . . . felt herself being sucked down into a dark, ice-cold cavern.

Unfamiliar voices grew louder, stirring her from unconsciousness.

'She were stealing my dog, I tell you!'

'Stand back and let me have room to look at the girl.' Rachel felt warm breath against her cheek as if someone had bent over her. 'Her heart's beating all right, but she looks mighty pale. What's a nicely dressed girl like her doing out in this weather, and before six o'clock? Fetch me some weak tea with plenty of sugar.'

Rachel was too afraid to open her eyes. She wasn't sure that she could. Pain was attacking her everywhere. Each muscle felt like a tightened cord binding her.

'Come on now, dearie, open your eyes. Keep awake – don't faint off again. You'm quite safe. No one 'ere's going to harm you.' Rachel thought the woman's voice, although gruff, sounded kind. She opened her eyes slowly and it was as if she had come home. No, it wasn't home, not Phoebe's warm cosy place, but somewhere she'd sought refuge before, a long time ago. The colourful interior of the caravan shocked her back to life. Brightly coloured flowers painted on the walls and bow ceiling made her feel as if she were lying in a beautiful garden.

'Where am I?' she asked in a small voice. 'One minute I was talking to a dog, I think . . .'

''Tis my dog,' the young man retorted sharply.

'I think he found me,' Rachel said. 'I must have fallen asleep and when I woke he was nuzzling my face.'

'I think you'd better get out of those wet clothes, Missie,' the woman said. 'You'm soaked to the skin. Out, everyone, while I find som'at for the girl to put on.'

'You're very kind,' Rachel managed weakly. 'I don't want to put you to any trouble. Perhaps I'd better be on my way.'

The woman laughed. 'And where might that be? You ain't got no luggage. Even us 'as moves about 'as belongings.'

Rachel frowned. Where had she intended to go? Why was she on an unfamiliar road and in the middle of the night? From a long way away came the sound of church bells. She gasped and sat up, crashing her head on the roof of the van. The church, God's house, what terrible, wicked thing had she done? Blood rushed to her cheeks and she began to sweat as all the painful memories returned. She sank back on the bed.

'Oh dear Lord, what a dreadful sin I've committed,' she cried.

The woman insisted that she sipped her tea. It didn't taste very nice and Rachel made a face.

''Tis herbal tea and t'will do you good. We must get the chill out of your bones. You'm delirious, I reckons. A nice sponge down with warm water will make you feel better. What's your name?'

The woman bathed Rachel's face with a cold flannel first and then insisted on helping her to discard her sodden clothes.

'My name's . . .' she began vaguely. She was in disgrace. The police might be looking for her. What she had done must be a criminal act. 'I can't remember, and I don't know where I am or what I'm doing,' she said lamely and without conviction.

'I'm sure a nice young woman like you 'asn't committed no offence. S'pose there's a young man at the bottom of this?' The woman washed Rachel's body all over and she didn't have the energy to protest. Strange but sweet-smelling clothes were put on her and at some time she had the feeling that lots of pairs of inquisitive eyes were peering at her. Left alone she fell asleep, blissfully at first but then tormented by fierce and violent dreams. Someone was trying to catch her but she fought like a wild cat to escape. Occasionally a pretty little woman came to her and tried to calm her but then the woman was dragged away and beaten.

Rachel cried out with fear, flailing her arms around. Was it rain pouring down her face? The cool sponge tempered the fever. Someone insisted she should keep drinking from a china cup. Where was she? Who were these people? The agony seemed to go on for ever, and then a man's calm gentle voice lulled her to sleep, but it wasn't Adam or her father. Her grandfather's perhaps? Hadn't she set out to visit them in the New Forest? But her head felt as if it were in the clouds and she floated away, safe at last.

The sun poured in on Rachel's face. She knew by the smell of the fresh drying earth that it was a clear, crisp spring morning. She was herself again, all fever vanished, her body cool and free from pain. For a long while she lay taking in her surroundings. There was no sound of anyone about and it crossed her mind to get up and make a run for it. But she realised as she turned over on to her side that she simply didn't have the strength.

Something below her moved and she looked down from the berth where she had lain for what she thought must be several days and noticed that two cupboard doors stood open. She peered inquisitively over the side and saw bed covers spilling out on to the floor of the gypsy waggon.

Once she had been afraid of gypsies but now, with memories of Kasan returning to remind her of their kindness, she felt happy and contented, believing that she was safe among friends.

The waggon shook gently as the woman below her levered herself out of the lower berth and stood up, stretching with grunts and groans.

'Good morning,' Rachel said. 'I believe I must be in your bed. I'm sorry if I've put you to any trouble.'

The woman, short and somewhat overweight, turned to look at her uninvited guest. Her black hair was twisted into a thick rope tied with a piece of coloured material which she now tossed over her shoulder. A voluminous nightdress covered her completely and Rachel was amazed at the brilliant whiteness of it.

'Not trouble, Missie, exactly, but we had to delay our moving on 'cos of you. Me name's Sybil, what's your'n?'

'Rachel. I don't know how to thank you, but I'm afraid I can't pay you any money for taking me in.'

'Have I asked for any such?' Sybil retorted sharply.

'I didn't mean to offend you,' Rachel apologised. 'I mean, you've cared for me, given me drinks and dry clothes.'

Sybil grunted. 'No more'n we'd do for any other traveller. Now I'd best get washed and dressed. Then we'll see if you fancy any breakfast.'

At the far end of the van on the stove stood a pan of steaming water, and on the cupboard at the side a wide-topped bowl. Sybil moved towards it pausing to draw brightly coloured curtains across which divided the van into two sections.

Rachel sank back against soft pillows, eager to study in detail the interior of the caravan. Everything was bright and cheerful and spotlessly clean. She was surprised at its roominess with locker seats and cupboards, side windows as well as the one at the back above her bed. She sat up and drew back the chintzy curtains. Being tall she had to keep her head lowered where the bow top curved. When she moved too quickly she experienced a dizzy feeling, probably because she was weak. She wasn't sure how long she'd been here but felt sick when she realised the anxiety her absence must have caused her family. She hoped they hadn't made themselves ill with worry or that her father might have got a soaking if he'd gone out looking for her – but that was unlikely. They were only concerned for Belinda and Adam, and their future. Once word got out of what she'd done in the church it was unlikely anyone in Kingsmere or Wickham would want to set eyes on Rachel Hunter ever again. They'd know it was her because the last person she had spoken to in the church was Nessie Mead. Somehow Rachel knew that Nessie wouldn't deliberately tell on her, but being the kind person she was would want to help trace Rachel. The last place in the world anyone would look would be among a group of gypsies and Rachel smiled with satisfaction. She felt so much better and at home, and fervently hoped these good people would allow her to remain with them.

'But you'm a gorgio, Missie,' Sybil said when Rachel voiced her thoughts to the older woman later.

'Whatever's that?' Rachel asked with indignation. 'I'm sure whatever it is I'm not.'

Sybil threw back her round head and laughed. ''Course you'm a gorgio – you b'aint a Romany, that's certain.'

Rachel felt ridiculous and hung her head while Sybil continued to chuckle as she scrambled eggs in an iron pan over the stove.

'I wish I was a gypsy,' she said softly.

Sybil spun round. 'A young woman like you?' she said in disbelief. 'What would you know about the way we live compared with your easy life? Not that I'd change, mind you, oh no! Freedom's what us folks like.'

'And that's what I want to be, Sybil. Free. Free to smell the fresh air and do what I want to do.'

'And what might that be, may I be bold enough to ask, Missie?'

'Live near the sea with the wind and spray on my cheeks.' Then Rachel fell silent. Was that really what she wanted? Wasn't it a cosy cottage to share with Adam Taylor? But he'd deceived her, she recalled. Now she didn't feel she could trust any man. During the time she'd lain ill in this waggon, in moments of waking she'd had time to think, to relive the events of the past – was it days, weeks, months?'

'How long have I been with you, Sybil?' she asked.

'No more'n about five days, but who's counting?' Sybil put two warmed plates on the table and dished up the eggs. 'Now you get this down you and you'll feel stronger, Missie.' She broke chunks of bread from a large homemade loaf. 'Here, eat this, the dear God's grain which he provides, and may He set you up well and strong again to return to your folks.'

At first the bread tasted strange and was rough to Rachel's throat but she found the eggs appetising and was soon enjoying the bread too. She felt confused in her mind. Sybil talked of God which brought a guilty flush to Rachel's cheeks. She would be punished for what she'd done to God's house. There could be no escape and she shivered with fear.

'You cold?' Sybil asked bluntly.

Rachel shook her head. 'No. Someone walked over my grave, I expect.'

'Not for a long time yet, me dearie. What's ailing you, Rachel?' Sybil leaned across the small table and peered into her eyes.

'I . . . I've committed a terrible sin. You mentioned God and his goodness but He'll have me punished for what I did.' Rachel's voice cracked. She seldom cried but suddenly couldn't help herself and wept uncontrollably.

''Tis 'cos you'm weak. There, there, child – don't distress yourself. Whatever's ailing you can't be that bad. You didn't kill anyone, I'm sure of that. We'll talk about it when you'm stronger.'

'No, I must tell you now. D'you believe in God? I thought gypsies didn't. I thought you were a law unto yourselves.'

'We'm believers, same as other folks, Rachel,' Sybil said solemnly. 'Not all of us, you understand, but this family does and we've got a good spiritual leader who teaches our children and keeps us on the straight and narrer. He came to see you when you was in a terrible fever. He said a prayer and that seemed to quieten you down. Whatever's wrong, Missie, I'm sure Lemuel can help you overcome it.'

'I . . . I went wild, Sybil. My mother always said I had a wild streak, not a bit like my twin sister.'

'Now don't you go upsetting yourself again. There's plenty of time to tell us if you wants to.' Sybil wiped her mouth on the corner of her apron. 'We'm moving on today or tomorrow.'

Rachel felt the blood drain from her face.

'You're planning to leave me behind then?' she asked anxiously.

'In your state? Never! But if you was wanting to go home we could find a carter or someone to take you. Where d'you live, Missie?'

'Um . . . I'd rather not say, Sybil. And I meant what I said about wanting to stay with you. I'll work to earn my keep – do whatever you say, honestly. Just please don't leave me behind.'

'Best tell me honestly, young woman, what trouble you're in? Is it that you'm in the family way?'

'Good gracious, no!' A warm flush crept into Rachel's cheeks. She finished her breakfast and then faced Sybil dry-eyed as she calmly gave a brief outline of her story. Sybil was intrigued and leant her fat arms on the table as she listened without interrupting.

'So you see, I simply can't return home. I . . . I don't know whether they'd send me to prison for what I did, but my parents and Belinda must feel so ashamed of me.'

'There's such a thing as forgiveness, Rachel. Don't you think that by now your folks are beside themselves with worry? They'd be that pleased to see you safe and sound that I reckon they'd forgive you anything.'

'I'd like to believe they'd understand, Sybil, but I'd only hurt them all over again if I went home. And I don't think I could bear to see Adam and Belinda together. I hope they'll be happy, but people might pity me and I've had that all my life. I must go somewhere to find work. I'm quite good at figures so perhaps I could go to the town – by the way, where exactly is this? I've no idea how far I walked that night.'

'A deal too far, Missie, by the state of you when Davy found you. This is Portsdown Hill and we'm on our way to the Isle of Wight.'

'Portsdown Hill,' Rachel echoed. 'Did I really walk that far?' She remained thoughtful for several minutes, pleased that she managed to put so much distance between herself and Kingsmere. 'Please can I come with you?' she begged. She knew it was impolite to invite herself but this was too good an opportunity to miss.

'Oh, don't know about that. We'll have to see what Lemuel says.' Sybil seemed troubled by Rachel's request. She got up from the table and put a large shawl round her shoulders. 'I'm going to feed me horses to I'll leave you to clear and was up the breakfast things. If you feels faint, though, you sit down and rest.'

She put a large-brimmed hat on top of her hair which was now pinned up into a plump bun at the back of her head. The hat wobbled about and Rachel wanted to laugh, then she remembered her sister and wished she was here with her. How could she have felt so angry towards Belinda? They'd always had such a happy childhood together, and their growing up years had been amicable too – until now. They had shared everything, tears and laughter, until Rachel had fallen in love with Adam Taylor. And all the time he had really loved Belinda. It was so cruel.

'This is the washing up bowl, Missie. There's one for your clothes and a different one to wash yourself in. There's a kettle of hot water on the stove. Later on you can come with me to fetch some wood. Always plenty 'o work to be done, living' free like we does.'

Rachel worked with a willingness she had seldom shown at home. The sun was warm as it shone through the open doorway, breathing new life into her as she watched the gypsies going about their daily tasks. One or two of them eyed her suspiciously, some of the men nodded but it was with the children Rachel made friends first. They soon lost their shyness and before long about a dozen were vying for a front line view, so when the washing up was done Rachel sat down on the top step and chatted to them until they were called away.

'They 'as their books to read,' Sybil explained. 'Lemuel makes sure as 'ow each and every one of 'em can read.'

'Don't they go to school?' Rachel asked.

'How can they, dearie, when we'm on the move? If we stay long in one place then the school man comes and makes sure they go. But he can't fault the learning Lemuel's given 'em.'

'They're lucky to have someone like him then.'

'Yes, and you'll like Lemuel – he'll see you at noon.'

Rachel wasn't quite so confident after that. Sybil spoke of him with respect as if he were some kind of elder. Rachel envisaged a tall, severe man who would demand that she return to her own family. It wasn't likely that they would want her tagging along. She wasn't one of them and they didn't mix with gorgios.

But when Sybil took her across the field to a solidly made plain caravan the man she met was nothing like she had imagined. He was dressed similarly to a priest in a small-brimmed black hat. He was of medium height, his back rather bent, but when he lifted his face to look at Rachel his smile was friendly, his grey-blue eyes intelligent and sympathetic. He held out his hand and helped her up the steps, inviting her inside the van.

'Peace be with you, child,' he greeted her and Rachel felt calmed. He invited her to sit down. 'There's no need to look so worried, my dear. I hope you don't find me or my travelling friends frightening?'

'No, I'm very grateful for the kindness which has been shown to me. I don't know what Sybil has told you, but –'

'Sybil has repeated your story as best she could but perhaps it would be better if I were to hear it from your own lips?'

Rachel began hesitantly. Lemuel listened with such patient interest that she soon forgot any fear of being judged harshly, and her outrageous actions seemed less shocking as she sensed his understanding.

When she finished speaking she waited for some comment but he had his yes closed while he pondered her predicament.

He pulled on his goatee beard which was a soft shade of grey with white patches. When he opened his eyes he looked at her kindly.

'I believe you may have more affinity with us Romanies than you realise, Rachel. You have the – the –' He waved his hand in small circular movements until he found the right word. 'The spirit,' he said. 'Few people ever bother to discover who were are – the race we're descended from, the work we strive to do, and they know nothing of the way we live. A young girl like yourself, obviously from a happy home and well provided for, would normally have been scared of being rescued by gypsies. I know you were quite sick as a result of being exposed to the elements overnight but you showed no alarm at finding yourself in strange surroundings when you came out of the fever.'

'I met a group of gypsies once before when I was lost in Bere Forest. They were kind to me then and a young man took me home. I have cause to be grateful to you all. There's no reason to be frightened of you, and I'm really serious about wanting to remain with you – though I'll understand if you don't want me.'

Lemuel surveyed this strange young woman with misgivings.

'If we agree to your accompanying us to the Isle of Wight what then, my dear? Supposing you become homesick? This may seem like some kind of adventure, but you will probably soon tire of our way of life.'

It was Rachel's turn to remain silent. She couldn't deny that she had doubts, but she'd had plenty of time to consider her crime and the penalty she might have to pay. She missed her family, and a reminder of the vexation she had caused her mother made her chin tremble and tears fill her eyes.

'I do love my family,' she told Lemuel solemnly. 'I know what I did was wrong. I felt so betrayed which made me angry and vicious. Now I'm sorry, but I can't expect them to forgive me that easily. I can't go home, Lemuel,' she pleaded. 'I simply can't. If you won't let me stay with you then I must move on by myself.'

'I understand, Rachel. We all have to make up for our own wrongdoing and in time I pray that you'll find a way to redeem yourself.' His voice was soothing yet firm. He stroked his bearded chin thoughtfully as he surveyed her appraisingly. 'Travelling with us cannot appease your guilt. Only when you have said you're sorry to those you have wronged can you expect to feel pardoned, but here in the great outdoors you can begin to make your peace with God. A time of self-examination may be easier among strangers though I fancy you won't feel a stranger for long.' His smile gave her comfort and a measure of hope. 'One thing, however, I must insist upon.'

'I'll do anything – *anything*.' Rachel sat forward eagerly, but Lemuel raised his hand to restrain her.

'Not so fast. Thus committing yourself, my child, without knowing my condition could be dangerous. After all, you know nothing of me and the people here. Trust must be earned, Rachel. Oh, I know you're young and anxious to please and I have few doubts that allowing you to become one of our family will be anything but beneficial to us all, but hasty words and actions may be your downfall – a lesson already forgotten?'

Rachel flushed penitently. 'Impetuous,' she said humbly. 'That's what my parents say. How can I show you that I am really sorry? And what is your condition, please?'

'You may not like it,' he warned. 'Put yourself in your parents' shoes, Rachel. You cannot have the remotest notion of the desperation they've been feeling over the past week. Only a mother can know such anguish, so you must send word to them that you're all right.'

'But I can't do *that*!' she shrieked. 'They'll be able to trace me and I shall be forced to go home.'

Lemuel said nothing. Rachel was forced to submit to his impervious stare even though the devil inside her rebelled angrily. He wasn't offering her forgiveness, no one ever would, least of all her parents. How could she return home? This strange man seemed to be mesmerising her with a power even she was unable to break, and after the heat of revolt came tranquility. She sat with her head lowered.

'A picture postcard would suffice, my dear.' Lemuel broke the silence in a gentle but firm voice. 'Posted from the mainland with no suggestion of where we're heading. The first step towards reconciliation will have been made. Try to imagine their relief that you're safe.' He leaned forward and took both her hands in his with a force which gave her renewed strength. 'It will spark off many questions, I suspect, but at least they'll know you're alive and well. The first step across a precarious bridge for you too, Rachel, as you pen those precious words "I'm sorry".'

'Can I think about it?' she asked in a small voice. 'I . . . don't want to say I'll do it and then let you down. I'd like to travel with you as far as the ferry –'

'Perhaps you're thinking that you'd like to go home, after all?'

'Oh no!' She shook her head vehemently. 'I know I can't do that. I loved Adam dearly and found it hard to believe that he could treat me so badly. I never want to see him again – least of all married to my twin sister.'

'The passage of time will make the burden easier to bear, my dear Rachel. By all means travel with us to the ferry, but I meant what I said. My conscience wouldn't be clear if I allowed you to continue with us without word to your parents. If you decide to go on alone then I shall have to examine my conscience even further and may be obliged to inform the authorities.' Lemuel stood up, towering above her, a veritable gentle giant. 'Go back to Sybil and make yourself useful. She's not finding life too easy these days as her rheumatism gets worse. She had a daughter once.' Rachel looked up quickly, her expression curious. 'No – Sybil will tell you herself in her own good time.' Lemuel took Rachel's arm and guided her through the doorway to the steps. 'Think very carefully about what you should do.'

Rachel had plenty of time to think while she washed pots and scrubbed cupboards. She was kept busy all the time as they prepared their vans to move on, and all the rubbish collected was built up to make a huge bonfire which was lit on their last evening on Portsdown Hill. It made a spectacular sight, and Rachel felt she had been accepted as one of them as she joined the group singing songs while the men played violins and squeeze boxes, before Lemuel conducted evening prayers asking for safe passage to the Isle of Wight.

They were up at dawn next morning to complete packing crockery and utensils in storage boxes for safety. Food was placed in the built-in cupboards underneath the rear of each van. Rachel learned these were called pan-boxes and served as larder and kitchen cupboards. She was amazed at the orderliness with which the gypsies both lived and organised the travelling procession. The younger couples with children headed the convoy, each van closely followed by grand-parents and older relatives' waggons. Lemuel travelled fifth in line, followed by Sybil and Rachel, with one or two hawkers' waggons bringing up the rear.

Rachel quickly forgot the misgivings she'd had about leaving this part of the world behind. It was like embarking on a brand new adventure. Even the horses seemed to sense the excitement as they trotted along, manes flowing and shiny horse brasses jingling. By mid-day they had travelled the five miles to Portsea. Here they rested on a piece of wasteland and had a meal of bread with cold ham before the first few vans moved towards the ferry crossing at the south-western tip of Portsea Island. Sybil went with Rachel to a nearby shop and Post Office where provisions were bought and Rachel purchased a postcard and stamp.

'Take your time now, child, and think what you'd like to say,' Sybil said. 'I ought to persuade you to leave us and go home but I knows you won't do that. Maybe 'tis your destiny to come awhile with us.'

'Can you look into the future, Sybil?' Rachel asked. 'Can't you read my palm or something and tell me truly what's going to become of me?'

'We all makes our own destiny, Missie. You've a lot to learn yet. For instance, never knowingly harm other folks or cause distress – now you just make amends with your folks and give 'em some peace o'mind.'

Rachel went to sit on a low wall and rested the postcard on the pillar at the end. She wrote her parents' name and address in the space provided then in her neat handwriting she began: 'Dear Mum and Dad'. She sighed and changed that to 'Dearest Mum, Dad and Belinda'. After several minutes of composing and recomposing sentences in her head she was still sucking the end of her pencil. What could she say? How could she put into words both love and hate? How could she expect them to understand? Her message must be simple. She dared not say where they were heading or that she was living with gypsies. That in itself would probably cause one or both her parents to be ill. In an almost childlike expression of her thoughts she told them what she was feeling.

'I love you all so much and I am full of remorse for the things I have done and the pain I have caused you. It is better that I stay away for a while, but do not worry about me as I am staying with some very dear people.'

She wanted to tell them how kind the gypsies had been to her in looking after her when she was ill, but that might add to her parents' concern so she simply signed her name and quickly dropped the card into the post box.

Sybil gave her a hug as they walked down the road.

'You'll feel better now, dearie. You've done your duty and they'll known you'm safe. Even if they set about trying to trace you, 'tain't likely they'll look among us travelling folk.'

Rachel smiled to herself. If she happened to meet anyone she knew from Wickham they wouldn't recognise her wearing a brightly coloured woollen scarf round her shoulders and another silk one over her hair. It hadn't taken her long to realise that she would be more easily accepted by her newfound friends if she made the effort to dress the same as the other women, and Sybil had taken her under her wing in this respect. There hadn't been open hostility but one or two of the younger women had eyed her with great suspicion especially when the young men talked pleasantly to her.

Rachel had given little thought to the methods of transport available to the gypsies or any other travellers come to that in order to reach Ryde on the Isle of Wight. As they waited patiently on the jetty they watched Lemuel's van being pulled on to one of the barges by his faithful piebald mare, called Goldie on account of the golden streaks down her nose. Then Sybil's van was taken aboard, though her horse, Astra, shied at the shouting and noise as cars revved up to take their place alongside. When every space on the two barges was occupied the steamer gave the signal for the ropes to be cast off and they gently moved out into deeper water.

'Have you been to the Isle of Wight before?' Rachel asked Sybil.

'Gracious me, yes,' she answered with a gruff laugh. 'Fair held every spring and most travelling folk gets there if they can. 'Sides, Lemuel's chest ain't usually too good after winter so the sea air does 'im good. Meets up with all our old friends, we does – won't be much chance of anyone spotting you now, Missie.'

Rachel tried not to show her apprehension as the water slapped against the sides of the barges and she was grateful that the crossing was relatively calm and took little more than half an hour. The horses could smell land and needed no encouragement to get up the ramp and on to the country road away from the sea. They travelled south and soon caught up with those who had already reached a large field lying in a hollow between rolling downland hills, and by early evening the last of the brush waggons joined them. They made camp here where Lemuel suggested they remain for several days.

Rachel's first task was to go in search of sticks and suitable firewood with some of the older children. At least she felt free of the past, knowing that no one could come after her with the sea separating her from her family. After the evening meal the horses were put out to grass and most of the older members of the group retired early but Rachel wanted to explore.

'You won't mind if I have a look from the top of the hill, will you, Sybil?' she asked.

'As long as you wrap up warmly against the evening chill. You can hardly get lost on this island but don't stay out too long.'

Rachel put on her warm woollen coat and wrapped her brightly coloured shawl round her shoulders. She was hurrying across the grassy hill when a young woman called after her.

'Wait for me, Rachel. I'll come with you.'

Rachel turned to wait for Ena, a slim girl of about seventeen who was slightly shorter than herself. Her sallow skin and high cheekbones were complemented by a cascade of rich raven black hair, but there was something about the twist to her full red lips which made Rachel suspicious of her. Rachel had watched the girl from the window by her bed on several occasions darting to and fro between the waggons and even sitting cross-legged beneath the one she lived in with her parents and several children. They had never exchanged any conversation before but Rachel was often aware of being watched by Ena.

'Where are you going?' the girl asked.

'Just to look at the view. I wondered if we might be able to see the sea from here.'

'Haven't you seen enough of the sea for one day?'

'Don't you just love it? The salty smell, the sound of the waves, the vast expanse of it? It fascinates me.'

Ena grunted, unmoved by Rachel's enthusiasm. 'Sea's just something that stops folk from going places, as I see it,' she said. 'Where d' you come from, anyhow? Ain't you never seen the sea before?'

'Yes, once or twice, but I lived in the countryside and didn't visit the seaside very often.'

'Why did you run away from home then? Reckon you had it nice and comfortable. Did you do something real bad?'

Now Rachel understood why she was viewed with curiosity. Sybil had kept her secret which made the others sceptical about her motives.

'In a way,' she replied hesitantly. 'I didn't hurt anyone. I . . . I just wanted to get away by myself for a while. I got soaked to the skin and caught a chill so I'm grateful to Sybil for taking me in.'

'T'was Davey what found you.'

'Yes, I know – well, it was his dog actually.'

'You sure you wasn't trying to steal his dog?'

'No, of course not! Do I look like someone who'd steal a dog?' Rachel raised her voice indignantly.

'Thieves don't look any different from other folks, Rachel. But I reckons you must be all right or you'd have taken whatever you wanted and been gone by now.'

'Time, Ena. What's what I need, time.'

'Time!' the younger girl repeated. 'Time don't cost nowt.'

'The best things in life are free. There,' Rachel said reaching the top of the hill and turning round and round to view the landscape. 'This is free – the air, the wind, the sky, the sea. It belongs to us all and we can take what we need of it. Love is free too, but sometimes there's a price to pay for that.'

'You lost someone maybe. Your ma or pa?'

'In a way, yes. I thought I would have been married by now. We loved one another so much. I still can't believe my fiancé could change his mind at the last minute like he did. I'll never understand it.'

'You going to have a baby then? Is that why you can't go home?'

'Good heavens, no! While Adam was away at the war his father died. We got engaged and planned to get married when he came home for good. He was buying a cottage for us to live in . . .' Rachel's voice trailed away. She sat down on the grass and plucked at a daisy. She had wept all the tears she could; now it was comforting to talk with a girl of similar age. 'Then he suddenly announced that it was never me he loved but my twin sister.'

'You poor thing.' Ena's voice was full of genuine sympathy. 'Gosh, you must hate 'im and your sister.'

'Sometimes I feel that I do and at others I know I can never hate them. I just hope he's good to Belinda. Now you can see why I can't return home.'

'We-ell, I reckons that gives you good enough reason for staying with Sybil.'

Rachel got to her feet and gazed seaward. 'She's been very kind. I don't know what I'd have done if Davey and his dog hadn't found me.'

'Jes s'long as you ain't got designs on 'im, that's all. 'Cos I'm warning you, no gorgio's goin' to take one of our men!'

Rachel began to understand why she was viewed with such suspicion.

'Is Davey a special friend of yours then?'

Even in the growing twilight Rachel could see Ena's dark eyes glinting. 'Very special,' she said. 'We've got a secret as well.' She suddenly darted up to Rachel's side and, standing on tiptoe, reached up to whisper: 'I'm in the family way. No one but us knows yet.'

'Shouldn't you tell your mother, Ena?'

'Nah. She'll find out soon enough.'

'Are you planning to get married?'

'Gypsies don't always. Davey's saving up to get us our own waggon though. Trouble is, our families don't get on. When me ma finds out about me there'll be trouble. Reckons I'll tell her when we get to the Fair. Plenty of drinking then and the men'll be ready for a showdown.'

'But that's awful! Can't Lemuel stop them?'

'They'll fight it out away from the waggons. Lemuel's been teaching us about God and stuff, but our families don't go along with all that. They jest pretends they do to please 'im. Mind you, if we could get married I'd like it to be in a church with lots of flowers.'

'If that's what you want then you must work to get it. I'm quite good at sewing. I'll help you make a pretty dress. But first I think you should confide in Sybil or Lemuel. They could talk to your parents and Davey's. Get it sorted out sensibly by talking it over.'

'Gypsies only knows one way of sorting out disputes and that's with their fists.'

'Then perhaps we could help to change their minds. I could go with you when you talk to your mother.'

Ena laughed this to scorn. 'They ain't got a very high opinion of you as 'tis. Thinks you're after something. You must learn not to poke your nose in where it ain't wanted.'

'I'm only trying to help, and you must prepare for the baby, Ena.'

'Plenty of time for that. Now you go on back to Sybil and I'm going to wait until Davey comes with our supper.'

'Supper?'

'He's gone after rabbits. We'll have a canoodle in the woods first then take the rabbits back, skin 'em and cook 'em. Don't you tell on me, mind. You 'aven't seed me at all.'

Ena picked up her skirt and ran down the other side of the hill where she disappeared into a thicket of trees.

Rachel took a long last look at the fading view before she walked slowly back to camp. Now she knew that the gypsies thought she was on the scrounge and must be careful not to take anything for granted. She felt some pity for Lemuel, knowing that he was doing his best to educate these folk yet all the time they were only pretending to believe what he said. He couldn't be a real Romany, Rachel thought. He might have been accepted by them for helping them with their finances and teaching the children to read but she didn't believe he really belonged among them any more than she did. Maybe he had a skeleton in the cupboard too! Perhaps he had not always been so saintly. Was there something in his past which made him particularly understanding when others did wrong? She'd probably never know, and it didn't really matter as she felt she could trust him implicitly. He was kind and wise, a fatherly figure to them all but one Rachel valued as a friend.

Chapter Ten

During the next few weeks they travelled round the island selling clothes pegs, but as soon as the wild daffodils burst into bloom Rachel and the other girls spent each morning gathering them from the woods. Then with baskets laden with neatly tied bunches, they went from village to village knocking on doors. Rachel was amazed at how quickly the pennies earned turned into pounds, and any embarrassment she felt at hawking soon disappeared. She greeted householders with a nice smile and some looked surprised at how well-spoken she was.

'Tain't fair,' Ena complained. 'They buys from you much quicker 'an from me.'

'Well, you could try being pleasant,' Rachel said. 'I know you get a lot of back-ache, Ena, but people aren't likely to look upon you favourably when you've nearly always got a scowl on your face. You don't bother to wash your face let alone your hair. Tidy yourself up and be nice to people if you want them to buy your wares.'

'Hmph! S'pose you thinks yourself a cut above the rest of us? Jest 'cos you'm tall and slim and pretty – and I've got a big belly?'

'There's no need to be crude. Have you told your mother yet?'

Ena said nothing for several seconds and Rachel guessed that her mother was none too pleased with the situation which was why Ena was so bad-tempered.

'She guessed,' Ena said dismally. 'Right telling off I got an' all, but she ain't told me dad yet.'

'What about Davey's parents?'

'He's a man. Don't make no difference to 'is people. He can deny 'tis his if he wants.'

'But he wouldn't do that, surely? I thought you really cared for each other.'

'I fancy he's gone off the idea of marriage or setting up 'ome together!'

'Perhaps he thinks you're a bit too young. He is quite a bit older than you, Ena.'

'Yep. But he said that didn't matter. He liked me 'cos I was a young bit 'o stuff and I loved 'im all the more 'cos he was growed up, not soppy like the other boys. He treated me growed up as well.'

'I'm sure everything will be all right. Once your back doesn't ache so much and you don't feel so rotten first thing in the morning, he'll begin to look forward to the baby coming.'

'He still takes all he can get,' Ena stated crossly. 'Never mind how sick I feel or how much me back's breaking he's making the most of a good thing.'

'How old is Davey?'

'Jest turned thirty.'

'How long have you been going together?'

Ena sighed. 'Reckon I've always chased after 'im, since I were a nipper. 'Cos our families were always feudin' it seemed to make 'im more attractive. When he went away to war I wrote to 'im and when he came back – cor, there was no waiting for 'im. Never mind about the risks, never mind about not being married. "I'll make you mine right now," says he.' Ena laughed cynically. 'Great it were. Davey had money in 'is pocket and we had a good time without thinking about the consequences. Ma says I must confess all to Lemuel, but what good'll that do? Damage is done. Too late to have second thoughts, but I reckon Davey is.'

'Why don't you talk to him, Ena?' Rachel suggested. 'Tell him you want your baby to be born in wedlock.'

'He don't seem to want to talk about it.'

'Maybe he's worried about finding a van.'

'Don't think he's bothering about that either. No . . .' She looked directly at Rachel with anger flashing in her dark eyes. 'If you want the truth, Rachel, he's got his sights set on you. I wish to God you'd never joined us. Why don't you go back to your own kind.'

Ena began to weep, quite noisily at first, until her cheeks were streaked with grubby finger marks as she hastily dried the tears away. Rachel felt sorry for her.

'Davey means nothing to me, Ena,' she said softly. 'I was so grateful to him for finding me and taking pity on me. Please don't cry.' She placed her arms round the younger girl and took her basket from her. 'You shouldn't be doing this kind of work now. The baskets are too heavy in your condition.'

'And what would you know about my condition?' Ena snapped. 'Unless you've been in the same boat – and I wouldn't put that past you. How do we know you 'aven't had a baby and been turned out?'

'I swear to you I haven't,' Rachel said. 'And I swear to you I don't want Davey. He doesn't even like me – he thought I wanted his dog, remember?'

'He's changed his mind about that. Thinks you're posh. Likes the way you talks and dresses. Wants me to have nice clothes but how can I in this state?'

'I'll help you, Ena. We'll sew a pretty summer dress which will help to cover up – well, you know.'

'Say it, go on, my bulge. I never thought Davey would change jest 'cos I got big. He likes doin' it but he don't like the result. Reckons *I* should have been more careful, if you please. Goddammit, he never gave me time to get prepared! But he ain't goin' to get away with it. My brothers'll sort 'im out.'

'Now, don't be hasty, Ena. Let's get you prettied up and then see who he prefers.'

Rachel did all she could to help. As the weather grew warm with bright spring sunshine she insisted that Ena sat on the verge in the shade while she herself went from cottage to cottage. They spent their evenings sewing until Ena had a light floral dress to wear but although it hung loose from the shoulders nothing could hide her expanding figure.

The group travelled on to meet up with other gypsies where the Spring Fair was to be held. They set up camp and in the cool of the evening Rachel went to a nearby house to ask if she might fill her carrier with water. At the gate Davey caught up with her.

'Here, let me. I need some too so I'll ask if they'll fill both containers.'

'We-ell, thanks, Davey, but I don't mind asking.'

He was tall. He smiled down at her with the kind of smile which instantly put her on her guard.

'You've got the hang of the way we live pretty good, haven't you?'

'I expect when the winter comes I shall wish I was back home,' she replied. 'But I am grateful to Sybil for letting me stay awhile with her. I've enjoyed helping Ena too. She looks nice in her new dress, don't you think?'

Davey didn't answer immediately so Rachel looked up at him expectantly. She noticed that his sandy hair was recently washed and combed and his checkered shirt was freshly laundered.

'I don't think about anything else but you, Rachel. When we've got the water will you come down to the woods with me?'

She felt her cheeks burning, not from embarrassment but from anger. She snatched at her water carrier but Davey held on tightly.

'Let go! Let – it – go!' Rachel shouted. 'How dare you suggest such a thing, Davey?' They tussled for several minutes but he was the stronger so Rachel turned on her heels and ran back to the caravan.

'Didn't you get the water then?' Sybil asked.

'Davey's getting it. I . . . I'm going to have to move on or something,' she said despondently.

'Why? What's up?'

'It's Davey. He's got Ena in trouble and now he's after me.'

'I heard she was expecting. She's too young for Davey really but she asked for it. He's always been a bit of a lad and since he went in the Army he's worse. Thought there was trouble brewing between the families but Lemuel won't have none of it, you mark my words. Don't you take no notice of Davey.'

Rachel wished it was that simple but every time she left the caravan he was hovering in the vicinity. That night he knocked on the van door well after dark. Rachel saw him through the window.

'Go away, it's late and we're in bed,' she called.

'I've brought a rabbit for Sybil.'

She was standing before the mirror brushing her hair. She opened the top half of the door and leaned out.

'Now look here, young Davey, don't let me see you hanging round here again. Rachel don't want anything to do with you. You've got responsibilities to Ena. You put her in the family way – now go and look after her. If I'm not much mistaken she's going to have twins.'

'Twins?' he echoed.

'Your twins – not surprising really since your grandparents had two sets and your own parents got twin girls. You'll have a lot of mouths to feed so you'll do well to work a bit harder instead of chasing pretty faces. And I'm telling you, Davey Smith, we ain't going to stand any nonsense this year at the Fair. Lemuel's going to send your family and the Wellses back to the mainland if either one of you gets making trouble.'

'T'aint no business of your'n or Lemuel's what feuding we gets up to. I only wanted to thank Rachel for helping Ena with her work and making the dress.'

Sybil half turned. 'She's heard – and since when has us folks needed thanks for what we do to help one another? 'Tis my guess your family don't know about Ena's condition so I reckons you best get home and tell 'em smartish – before I do.' With that she slammed the door shut and Davey was left alone with his rabbits tied to a pole balanced on his shoulder. They heard his feet shuffling away and when Sybil had gone to bed Rachel peeped out of the window by her bunk.

There was a high, bright moon which showed clearly the outline of the different types of caravan. The horses were all tethered either to a tree or pegged to the ground near to the owners vans. An owl swooped low close by, evidently picking up a mouse or vole before flying off to its nest in the woods. Everything seemed eerily quiet and then Rachel spied figures moving about stealthily across the grass. As her sight became accustomed to the night gloom she could see Davey being marched along by his father, a short stocky man.

The caravan belonging to Ena's family was across the field and when Davey and his father reached it they stood outside, shouting and banging on the windows. Rachel was too far away to hear what was going on but suddenly the door of the van opened and Ena was pushed out and down the steps. Rachel forget about her head and banged it noisily on the roof as she tried to sit up to see what was happening.

'What you doing?' Sybil called from the lower berth.

'Sorry, Sybil, but I was looking out of the window. It looks like trouble between the Smiths and the Wellses.'

'There's always trouble between them two lots. Get off to sleep now and don't worry your head about them.'

'But I think Ena might be hurt. It looked as if they threw her out and down the steps. Davey's bending over her, best I can see. Maybe she's hurt. Should I go and see?'

'We-ell, maybe – but Lemuel usually sorts them out. Don't think he ought to be woken up though. 'Tis late enough.'

'I'm not afraid,' Rachel said. 'I should at least help Ena.'

'You might get a beating yourself – and you'm a gorgio, I daresay you aren't used to such goings on.'

'Poor Ena, she was so unhappy about Davey not wanting her as well as about the baby. Do you really think she's having twins?'

'Sure of it. And we don't want anything to happen to the babies, do we?'

Although Sybil didn't actually say so, Rachel felt certain she wanted her to go investigate so she got up and wrapped her shawl round her before unlocking the door and creeping out. She thought an element of surprise was the best approach so skirted the field, keeping close to the vans, but just as she reached the Wells' van another figure emerged from between two latecomers' vans. Rachel had watched them hitching their waggons earlier just as the sun was going down but didn't know who they were.

'What's all this noise?' the young man asked in the voice of authority. He was tall and of medium build, and all Rachel would distinguish in the darkness was that he had a mop of dark hair on his head and round his chin.

'What's it to do with you?' Davey's father snapped.

'Everything. We've had a long, tiring journey and we need to get some rest. Might have known it would be you two families, you're always arguing about something. We aren't going to put up with fighting any more so what's your problem?'

'Oh, hark at you, Kas Dolan, and who d'you think you are?' Davey scoffed.

Rachel clutched at the front of her nightgown and drew back into the shadow of the nearest van. Kas? Had she heard aright? Kas Dolan – was it possible that it was her gypsy boy from all those years ago? If it was it was a miracle seeing that Adam had lost the lucky stone he'd given her.

'We want some peace and we mean to get it,' Kas said shortly. 'What are you quarrelling about this time?'

A head appeared through the top half of the Wells' van door. 'Kas? Is that your voice I heard?' The door opened fully and a figure stood silhouetted in the half light. 'S'pose you might have guessed. Davey's got our Ena in the family way,' said Mr Wells.

'Is that all? Then the sooner they marry the better,' Kas said. 'But can't it wait 'till morning and we'll hold proper court with Lemuel?'

'Best settle it now with our fists,' Ena's father said gruffly. 'Davey Smith's no good and he's too old for our Ena?'

'Shouldn't Ena and Davey decide that?' Rachel's voice sounded cool and cultured in the evening air. All heads turned in her direction.

'And who the hell are you?' Kas said impatiently.

'Rachel – Rachel Hunter. Ena is expecting twins. I came to see if she's hurt. You had no right to throw her down the steps like that,' she added to Mr Wells.

Ena slowly uncurled herself and sat looking up at everyone. 'I'm all right,' she said in a small voice.

'Twins?' Kas echoed, then he laughed. 'As if there aren't enough of you lot already. You'd best get up and get back to bed. That goes for the rest of you. When I see Lemuel tomorrow morning I'll tell him there'll be a wedding to prepare for.'

Rachel was amazed to see them move quietly away to their own vans. Kas turned to face her.

'Why do I seem to think I know the name Rachel Hunter? Let me look at you. Come closer.'

'I doubt that you'd remember me,' she said softly. 'I was only a schoolgirl when we met several years ago. I was lost in Bere Forest. You walked me home and gave me a lucky stone.

With a firm hand on her shoulder Kas turned her into the moonlight. 'Mm . . . yes, now I recall. Yes, Rachel Hunter,' he said slowly and thoughtfully, 'the Strawberry Girl.'

Rachel felt herself blushing furiously and was grateful that it was semi-dark. She buried her face in her shawl.

'Fancy you remembering, though I never forgot you,' she said.

'But you're not a Romany or even a traveller. Come from that pretty little cottage somewhere – I know, in Kingsmere wasn't it? What brings you here to the island?'

Rachel sighed. 'It's a long story,' she said. 'Too long at this time of night, and you said you wanted peace and quiet.'

'You mean you're saying with the group? You've joined the Romanies?' His voice was filled with incredulity.

'I'm staying with Sybil – for the present anyway. I . . . I had to get away for a while, but like I said, that's a long story.'

Kas turned Rachel round and propelled her through the caravans away from the camp to the edge of a field beneath some trees.

'Suddenly I'm not tired any more. I want to hear this intriguing story. A gorgio living with the travellers. It isn't the first time, but not one of your sort. This story's got to be good.'

Rachel felt that he was mocking her. 'No, there's nothing good about it, Kas, and if you think it's amusing then I won't bother telling you.'

'A woman with spirit, I like that. You should fit in well with our sort. I'm sorry if you thought I was laughing at you, but you must admit a young woman from your type of background coming to rough it with travellers does sound highly unlikely.' They walked to the far end of the field where several horses were tethered. Kas patted each one in turn and then led the way up the wooden steps to his van. 'Come in for a few minutes. Night time is a good time for talking.'

Rachel shrugged and gabbled a few meaningless words, hesitant lest someone else might be in the van.

'No, Strawberry Girl, I live and travel alone, mostly. Since the war that is. Merle died in the 'flu epidemic while I was still away at the war and Josh died long before that.' He jerked his head towards the door. 'Come on, I won't bite. I can hardly believe it's you. The strawberry mark will prove it though.'

'No, it won't,' she replied. 'Merle was right about that, it faded – though sometimes a slight red patch shows. Your lucky stone helped I daresay.'

At that Kasan laughed. 'Come on, the kettle's boiling its head off. I make a nice cup of cocoa. Sybil won't even miss you.'

'But it's getting late.'

'I'm not that tired really. Had a long wait to get across on the ferry which I find irksome. Didn't feel I could handle a fight at this time of night. Any idea what it's really all about?'

Rachel followed him up the steps and into the van. It wasn't as colourful as some of the others but was tastefully decorated and tidy. He seemed less of a gypsy now than she remembered. Maybe going away to war had changed his lifestyle. She watched him mixing cocoa and milk in some dainty china cups before he added boiling water. She told him what she knew of Davey and Ena.

'They were all suspicious of me to begin with,' she said, gradually finding it easier to talk to Kas. 'I've tried to earn their trust and my keep, but now Ena says Davey prefers me to her.'

'And how do you feel – about Davey, I mean?'

Rachel looked at Kas fearlessly. If she'd had even the slightest inclination toward Davey, which she hadn't, she knew that Kas's arrival would have changed her mind. By the light of the lamp she realised how many years had passed since their meeting in the woods. It must be all of eight and they had both matured. Rachel was no longer a child but a young woman and Kas must be well into his twenties, she thought. His hair was cut much shorter than she remembered and his thick growth of beard made him look older, but his dark brown eyes still reflected the gentle warmth which had made her trust him when he walked her home.

'I don't have any feelings towards Davey,' she said. 'That's what my story is all about, Kas. Heartbreak, disillusionment . . .' She passed a hand across her brow as painful memories returned. 'Maybe the war had something to do with it, maybe it was misguided pity because of my birthmark – it was all so ugly.'

'I'm sorry, Rachel. I didn't realise. I shouldn't have asked – some other time. Drink your cocoa. We'll talk another time.'

She put her hands round the small cup. The pretty design on the china reminded her of home. Phoebe, Wally and Belinda . . . Now that they had received her card they probably seldom gave a thought to her or what she was doing. An ache crept up from the pit of her stomach, an ache of homesickness, and for a brief moment she felt the urge to escape, back to the safety of Calder Cottage and the people she knew and loved in Kingsmere.

'I was going to be married,' she began eventually.

Kas didn't press her to continue or try to stop her. He listened with the utmost patience until she finished. Then he remained silent as if there was nothing to say, no condemnation, no words of sympathy either.

'Thank you for telling me, Rachel,' he said softly. 'That is some story – and I feel it isn't over yet. This is just waiting time. Sooner or later you'll want to go back where you belong.'

'I don't think so, Kas. I'm happy here with Sybil and the others. Lemuel has been understanding in allowing me to accompany them but on the condition that I sent a card to my parents, which I did. They have no idea where I am, though, and it's best that way. It sounds silly but there's something of the gypsy in me, I believe, because I feel part of the group.'

Kas smiled warmly. 'I know exactly what you mean. I'm not a true Romany, neither is Lemuel, but we've been cared for by these good people and accepted. That makes them very special. They don't ask questions or make demands, neither do they condemn, but offer help and kindness – which is a good deal more than so-called Christian folk.'

'I'm afraid I was brought up to believe that gypsies were evil rogues but I soon found out that wasn't true.'

Kas laughed heartily. 'A little harmless poaching perhaps when we're hungry but most of us want to earn an honest living.'

'How was it for you in the Army?' Rachel asked. 'You shouldn't have given me your lucky stone.'

'It wasn't so lucky, was it. It brought you unhappiness.'

'Only after Adam had lost it.'

'We'll find another one. There's plenty on the beaches here. That's where I found the first one.' He sighed. 'War opened my eyes to lots of things. Living in the trenches wasn't as hard for me as many of the other chaps. Perhaps I was better equipped to look after myself than them. I felt as afraid as any soldier but I knew better than to show it. Yes, Rachel, I have to admit that on the whole, stone, or no stone, I was luckier than the poor blokes who got 'blighties'. At least I came back.'

'Was it awful?'

'War is needless, terrifying and cruel. I wish I could say it makes better people out of us, but I doubt it. When it comes down to it we all have to look after ourselves. No one owes us anything, Rachel. But we owe it to our own self-respect to be trustworthy and care for our fellow men.' He placed his cup on the side and took Rachel's from her. 'I hope we'll get to know one another much better while we're here. Now I'd better see you back to your van.'

The moon was up, lighting their way across the open field. 'I nearly didn't come,' Kas said. 'I mostly travel around on my own these days, never sure whether or not I'd like to get a decent job and live in a house. This is a waiting time for me too, Strawberry Girl, while I try to forget the war and decide what I want to do with my future. They put me in the cookhouse in the Army so I've even toyed with the idea of going abroad, to Australia or New Zealand, and getting hotel work.'

'My parents often said how difficult it was for men to adapt to civilian life again – maybe that's what changed Adam, I don't know. It was all so sudden, so unbelievable.'

'Would you still have him if he came after you?'

'He won't ever want me now that he's got Belinda. I can't honestly say that I don't still have some feelings for him, but I could never trust him after what he did. I don't know why I'm so different from Belinda either. She would never have behaved the way I did, and after being brought up in such a loving, respectable home why do I have this urge to be free of it all?'

'Perhaps you're just the outdoor type. At this time of year that's what I like about this life – and the horses, of course. In France, and I'm told Australia, there are thousands of wild horses.'

'I like horses, too, but I don't suppose I shall ever have one of my own.'

'I'll loan you one of mine – to ride, that is. I may buy another at the Fair. There's usually a bit of dealing goes on.' He looked up at the night sky. 'It looks as if we're in for some really good weather.' He put out his hand and touched Rachel's arm lightly. 'Goodnight, Strawberry Girl.'

'Please,' she said shyly, 'would you mind not calling me that? If people hear you call me that they'll copy and want to know why – and my mark has quite gone so it isn't really true any more.'

'I'm glad for your sake that the mark faded. It wasn't that bad – made you special, didn't it?'

''Specially bad, I expect,' she said with a light-hearted laugh. 'That's all in the past and I'm into a new life now. I never ever expected to see you again so I think I was meant to run away.'

'But you would go home if you felt you wanted to?'

'Maybe, one day, a long time from now.'

A lengthy silence ensued while Kas studied her thoughtfully, then he said: 'I'll be taking my horses to the nearest beach every morning for a dip. They love it and it gets them used to the sound of rough water. If you'd like to come, watch out for me about seven o'clock.'

'Thanks, I will,' Rachel said, and with a slight wave of her hand she tiptoed up the steps and was soon lying on her bunk. But sleep wouldn't come, she was too excited. She drew back the curtain and watched the moon hanging like a pale yellow balloon in the heavens. Shadows were everywhere and somewhere in close proximity was Kas, the boy she had dreamed of, now a man whom she regarded as a friend. She couldn't believe her good fortune that he still remembered her. She lay still, knowing that too much movement would disturb Sybil. Had she seen this meeting in Rachel's future? Everyone knew that Sybil had the 'gift', but according to Lemuel's teaching it was not for everyday use. But Rachel often caught Sybil watching her with a faraway look. What did she know of Kas? Rachel wondered.

At 6.30 a.m. Rachel was wide awake, still feeling excitement running through her veins. As softly as she could she slid from the top bunk and went through to the kitchen end of the van where she poured cold water into the bowl to wash herself.

There was a nip in the morning air as she unlocked the door and stood outside on the platform at the top of the steps. Most waggons had detachable steps but Sybil's had been specially made only to fold up over the staging during transit. Rachel stood listening and watching for movement across the field. There was little sound except the neighing of horses but then a man's voice heralded a fine black horse with Kas astride it, leading two more on a rope. As soon as he saw Rachel he waved and pointed to the gate at the far end of the field. She ran down the steps and reached the gate ahead of him to open it.

''Morning,' he called cheerily. 'Come on, you can take the mare.'

'I don't think I should, I haven't ridden for ages.'

'She's yours and you'll never guess what her name is?'

Rachel laughed up at him. 'Daisy? Blossom?' she asked.

Kas shook his head. 'Strawberry Girl, of course.'

'Oh, Kas, you've only just thought of that, haven't you?'

He leaned down from his great height and grinned. 'If I can't call you Strawberry Girl then it's a good name for No-Name. She's a bit high-spirited and not always obedient – like most women – but she deserves a name and I only got her recently so I hadn't christened her yet. We'll do it this morning. Come on, they're raring to go.'

'But there's no saddle.'

'So you ride bare-back like the rest of us. You'll soon get hardened to it. At least they've all got bridles.'

Rachel tried unsuccessfully to jump up on the horse's back.

'Come round this side and I'll help you,' Kas said.

After a great deal of laughing Rachel finally managed it, and with the rope attached to the bridle firmly in her hands they set off down the twisting lane.

It took several minutes to reach the path which led to the beach but soon they were galloping along the sea-shore with the feel of a cold spray on their faces. Although it was a fine spring morning the sea was rough, but that didn't deter the horses who were eager to feel the water splashing round their hooves. Kas made sure that Rachel kept alongside him, with the smaller pony cantering along behind. It was a small secluded bay and after exercising the horses and enjoying a paddle Kas cupped some seawater in his hand and splashed the chestnut mare with it.

'I name thee Strawberry Girl,' he said. He patted the horse and in return she lovingly nuzzled his neck and face. 'Now you be good to your namesake. I'm letting her adopt you while she's with us.'

Rachel sat down on the sand and put her shoes back on. 'Do you think I ought to be living with your people?' she asked hesitantly.

'Gypsies, Rachel. Gypsies. Never be afraid to call us what we are. I'm concerned for you,' he said. 'I know you've let your parents know that you're all right, but you came from a good home and while this may seem an adventure, how long is it going to last?'

In her heart she knew that it would last at least as long as he was here. Aloud she said with as much indifference as she could muster: 'Indefinitely. I don't want to make plans or decisions, Kas. I'm happy to be living free for the present.'

'But you will go back when you feel you should?' Why was he pursuing this question? He was the same Kas she remembered, yet he was different. So grown up, showing such thoughtfulness for her welfare. Was he still thinking of her as a schoolgirl?

'As I told you before, maybe one day,' she said impatiently.

An uneasy silence prevailed as they made the return journey.

The van door was open as they reined in outside Sybil's door and a delicious smell of frying bacon wafted to greet them.

'Come on in for breakfast, Kas,' Sybil called.

'How did you know it was Kas?' Rachel asked as she ran up the steps.

'Ah! Knew some'at was up, didn't I? You stayed out half the night and spent the other half day-dreaming, then up at the crack of dawn again? Saw Davey fetching water and he told me Kas had come. I guessed where you'd gone and I knows the sea air make a body hungry.' Sybil turned from the stove to hold out her arms to Kas. 'My, 'tis good to see you again, lad.'

He embraced her warmly and then sat down at the table which was already set for three. Rachel listened attentively as Kas and Sybil discussed recent events.

'Merle didn't suffer too long, Sybil,' Kas told her. 'Once the 'flu took hold t'wasn't long before she got pneumonia. It wasn't easy to gather the clan together so soon after the war but I honoured her wish that all her earthly belongings should be burnt along with her waggon. The Army gave me compassionate leave 'cos I'd put her down as my next-of-kin. Then the Armistice was signed so I never went back to France.'

'What've you been doing since? I sees you got a nice new waggon.'

'Merle and Josh left me all their money. It wasn't that much because they'd bought a couple of houses near Christchurch. Two joined together, not very large but smart. Reckoned they'd settle down as town dwellers eventually,' Kas laughed, 'but I knew better. Romanies don't settle and as long as they lived they wanted to be on the move. I bought me van with me own money I saved through the war. I used some of theirs to buy the horses. Thought that would please Josh. The chestnut mare's the latest and I want Rachel to ride her.'

'Friendship's going by leaps and bounds,' Sybil said with a note of disapproval.

'We met years ago,' Rachel put in quickly, and between them the incident was related to the older woman whose expression changed to one of understanding as if she now had a clue to some unsolved puzzle.

'Now,' she said to Kas, 'you were going to tell me what you've been doing since the war. Hawking on your own can't have been easy?'

'I'd learnt a bit about making cart wheels before I went in the Army and they showed me the rest. Gun carriages have to have strong wheels and there's a lot of maintenance needed on vehicles of all kinds. I did a bit of smithying, helped with the horses, learnt a bit about car engines too, so I reckon I can turn my hand to a few things nowadays.'

'Think you've come up in the world then, young Kas?'

'I'm still the same, Sybil, but there's no harm in trying to better myself, is there? Reckon I'm not so young either at twenty-six.'

'Who owns the houses at Christchurch now then?' Sybil asked. Rachel had discovered since living with the travellers that they were astute businesspeople, kept no secrets from one another, and few seemed poor.

'I do. They're rented out by an agent so I can't live in either of them unless the tenant dies or gives notice.'

'Still, it's nice to know you've got an income and property to sell one day if the need arises.'

'The income has to be used to keep them in good repair. Merle left it all tied up as Josh wanted. I won't misuse it, Sybil. They were good to me, probably better than my own parents would have been. I know I'm not a true Romany, no better than an Irish tinker if what they told me about my family is true, but I'll always think of myself as belonging to Merle and Josh. Who I was and what happened before they found me doesn't matter.'

Rachel listened with interest until she heard Kas say: 'Got to get this young woman back to where she belongs, don't you reckon, Sybil?'

Rachel stopped chewing. 'What do you mean?' she demanded.

'Living like this isn't right for you, Rachel.'

'Now hold on a minute, Kas,' Sybil said. 'Rachel was took poorly when Davey found her. We looked after her and helped her through a bad time, but I reckon she's old enough to make up her own mind. She can return home any time she wishes – ain't that right, Rachel?'

'Yes, of course, and no one's going to tell me when. I'm enjoying the life. I feel free –'

'All right, Strawberry Girl,' Kas laughed. 'I was just testing you, that's all. But I feel certain when winter comes you'll be back home like the shot out of a gun.'

'We'll see,' was all Rachel would say, determined to prove him wrong. Everything she ever wanted was here. The sea, freedom to come and go as she pleased, to live without too many rules, and now the company of her first love. That he had given her little thought over the past eight years didn't matter. She suspected he might be the one to move on first but meanwhile she meant to make the most of having him near.

Ena and Davey were married a few weeks later in a small church at Godshill, the prettiest village Rachel had ever seen.

'The old Romany custom was for the couple to join hands in front of witnesses,' Sybil explained. 'But Lemuel don't hold with it so he persuades the young'uns to go to a church if the parish priest will perform the ceremony. Nothing will ever stop the Smiths and Wellses from fightin' and feudin' but 'tis only proper that Davey should do right by Ena.'

They were sitting side by side in the beautifully decorated church. Davey, dressed in a smart blue suit, was standing beside Kas, his best man, down in the front right-handed pew. Rachel had helped with and supervised the sewing of a beautiful cream silk wedding dress for Ena, and pretty pale blue ones for two of her sisters who were bridesmaids. Rachel was surprised at how well-dressed everyone was but she had been warned that the wedding breakfast afterwards might end in some kind of affray.

As the service proceeded she looked round the church and the memory of the night she ran away came back to haunt her. How could she have done such a wicked thing? Rachel felt crushed with shame until Sybil patted her knee as if she knew and understood how she felt.

''Tis Ena's day,' she whispered. 'Be happy for her.'

Rachel did her best to forget the past and entered into th spirit of the celebrations, glad to help any way she could. She realised though, that despite its being his wedding day, Davey watched her every move.

Each morning Rachel went to the nearest beach with Kas to exercise the horses and afterwards worked all the harder to help Sybil keep the waggon clean and to make the pegs and hurdles which were their livelihood.

By the time the Spring Fair was in progress more travellers had congregated on the island and the authorities asked that the gypsies use a larger piece of spare ground between Newport and Brading.

After they had moved, each morning at dawn while the dew was still wet on the carpet of bluebells in the nearby woods, Rachel and some of the gypsy girls picked vast quantities of flowers which they sold along with other wares as they mingled with the crowds at the Fair. Shouts and screams echoed across the downs and through the valleys, and the organ-grinder kept up a continuous stream of tunes from his barrel-organ. It was a good time for business with everyone in high spirits, and in the evenings although they were tired Rachel and Kas returned to the fun fair to enjoy the bright lights and amusements.

Kas insisted that they have a go on the merry-go-round. The large wooden horses were painted and decorated in vivid colours and Rachel sat on one on the inside while Kas sat next to her on the outside. They were laughing happily, their voices drowned by the loud music as the horses went up and down on their poles and the merry-go-round circled round and round. Suddenly Rachel felt herself go cold. The colour drained from her cheeks. She caught a glimpse of a couple standing close by whom she recognised instantly as Beth Cropper and Dick Mead. Before they circled round again Rachel leant over the side of her horse away from Kas, keeping her face hidden. He caught her and pulled her up, thinking that she was feeling giddy and falling.

'You all right, Rachel?' he shouted above the music, and then a woman's voice reached her among the hub-bub of noise.

'Rachel! Rachel Hunter! Fancy seeing you here!'

Anyone but Beth Cropper, she thought. Anyone! But she was trapped and as the merry-go-round slowed and stopped, Beth came running up to her.

Kas looked first at Beth Cropper and then at Rachel, curiously. He helped her down.

'I hardly recognised you,' Beth said. 'Never expected to see anyone from Hundred Acres or Kingsmere here.' She searched Rachel's face then Kas's before letting her astonished gaze dwell on their clothes. 'You here for the day or on holiday or something? Never expected to see you dressed like a bloomin' gypsy!'

Rachel fancied Dick might have nudged Beth's arm to prevent her from saying any more. For this occasion, and to please Sybil, Rachel was wearing a brightly coloured floral skirt with a low-necked white cotton blouse, and round the scarf over her hair she wore a band of jangling coins.

'All part of our fancy dress for the evening,' Kas put in quickly. 'Now, if you'll excuse us, I have to see a man about a horse.' He propelled Rachel away among the sightseers while Beth and Dick looked after them in complete astonishment.

Chapter Eleven

Rachel hurried to escape from the fair, jostling people out of her way. Kas had difficulty in keeping up with her but when he did he held her back and drew her behind the fortune-teller's tent.

'For goodness' sake, Rachel, slow down!' he said angrily. 'Who were those people and why are you trying to run away?'

'Oh, you don't understand! You can't understand. They're from Hundred Acres and it was that man who beat his wife and nearly killed her. He's Charlie's father, and Beth is Dick's sister-in-law. I'd have rather have met anyone but them. Anyone!'

'What do you suppose they're doing on the island?'

'Goodness knows. Dick stayed with his wife for a while after the scandal but then he and Beth went missing. As far as I remember no one knew where they went.'

'Then perhaps they're hiding as well as you?' Kas suggested.

Rachel leaned against the tent pole and sighed miserably. 'You could be right, Kas,' she said thoughtfully. 'I don't think they'd want anyone to know where they are, so why did Beth want to talk to me? Once she'd recognised me you'd have thought she'd be the one to rush away.'

'It was a natural reaction at seeing a familiar face from home, I expect. You'd probably have done the same thing.'

'But I didn't. I was trying not to let her see me 'til you pulled me up.'

Kas began to laugh. 'I thought you felt giddy. I didn't want you falling off and hurting yourself.'

Rachel looked up into his dark eyes. He put his face closer to hers. 'I want to look after you, Rachel,' he said in a low voice. 'My gypsy girl – at least you really look like one of us now. Your friend thought so.'

'Not my friend,' Rachel said heatedly as she turned her head away. She wanted Kas to kiss her and felt certain he almost had but she was afraid. Afraid of feelings which were growing deeper every day. Afraid that Kas was only teasing, playing a game until he chose to move on alone. Afraid of the new situation she was in knowing that Beth and Dick were here on the Isle of Wight. 'Suppose they return to the Wickham area and tell my parents where I am?'

'Just suppose?' Kas echoed.

'You're only making fun,' she challenged him with flashing eyes and burning cheeks. 'They could come to find me.'

'I reckon you could make a stand for yourself. I know you're not twenty-one yet but you should be able to make up your own mind. We could solve the problem, of course,' he added mysteriously.

'How?' Rachel asked.

'You could go home voluntarily or . . .' he held his head to one side indecisively as he placed his hands on Rachel's arms '. . . you could marry me?'

The blood drained from her cheeks.

'Now you really are making fun,' she said, experiencing a cold sickly feeling in the pit of her stomach. 'I don't want to go home. I'm loving it here.'

'And the second alternative?'

She lowered her gaze thoughtfully. 'If I thought you were being serious it might be worth considering.'

'Then let's work on it together.'

'But you intend to move on by yourself,' she said.

'Who says? After the war and losing Merle and Josh, I needed some time to think out what I wanted to do. Like you, I love being a free traveller, Rachel. The climate here is kind. It's good for Lemuel and he's getting old and frail so I reckoned he might need someone to look after him. Sybil's not so young either. The war changed everything but there's time enough to make decisions. Little did I ever expect to find you here with our people, and I'm sure your friends will take a little time to get over the shock of seeing you here, especially dressed like that.'

Suddenly Rachel saw the funny side of it. 'Fancy dress indeed,' she laughed. 'That was good.'

'It wasn't bad at short notice. It was obvious you were upset at seeing them so I had to think quickly.'

'Thanks anyway. Maybe they're just here for the day, but I shall be on my guard from now on. Beth Cropper can never be a friend, she's a horrible person. I worked with her and she's hateful – you can't imagine.'

'Then we won't think about her any more. Have you had enough of the fun fair?'

She nodded. 'I daren't stay here any longer.'

'Let's go and fetch the horses and take a ride along the shore.'

Rachel didn't need a second invitation. She and the chestnut mare were now firm friends and she loved every minute she could be riding, or grooming her horse, as well as the opportunity to be with Kas.

They returned to the field and told Sybil where they were going.

'Just be careful,' she said, waving a warning finger at Kas.

'We shan't go far into the water and there's no sign of fog.'

'I wasn't thinking of those kinds of dangers. 'Tis the custom that if you'm walking a girl out, then you 'as a chaperone.'

Kas went up to Sybil and placed his arms round her shoulders.

'I'm over twenty-one. I know Rachel is younger. You should know me better than to think I would do anything to harm her in any way. I promise I'll look after her and bring her back safely to you before midnight.'

Sybil grunted, then gave Kas a shove. 'Be off with you before I gets me shawl and comes too.'

'You're welcome if you can bear to ride up behind me.'

'And I would if I were a few years younger. Midnight, mind, and not a minute later.'

Kas winked saucily at the older woman as he led Rachel to where the horses were tethered, and to the distant sound of music and laughter from the fair they trotted along deserted country lanes towards their favourite bay, leaving the merrymakers to their fun.

As they neared the cliff the horses began to show excitement at the smell of the sea. They quickened their pace, tossing their long manes with impatience. It was a steep run down to the beach and then the horses were allowed full rein. Kas galloped away on the great black stallion he called Kitchener, and although Rachel did her best to catch up, Strawberry Girl was not so fast. Before she could reach the other side of the bay Kas was racing back towards her. She turned her mare towards the cliff away from the water with Kas in pursuit. When he caught up with her he made a grab for her, pulling her off. With his large hand and an arm spanning her small waist he kept her dangling alongside his horse. For jew a few seconds he allowed Kitchener to ride on before he brought him to a halt and to the sound of Rachel's screams let her down on the sand. He jumped down himself and rolled her to the ground, teasing her before his lips met hers with almost brutal force.

'Quite a lot we can do before midnight, gypsy girl,' he whispered as he clasped her tight in his powerful arms.

'No, no, we mustn't,' Rachel said breathlessly. 'Sybil . . .'

'Sybil isn't a prude. She didn't think we were coming to the beach to say our prayers.'

'We could,' Rachel suggested provocatively.

'And what would you pray for, gypsy girl?'

She turned her head away from him, but she could still feel his warm breath on her cheek. 'I don't know.'

'For everything to be back to how it was three months ago?'

Rachel shook her head. 'No,' she said solemnly. 'Three months ago Adam told me he'd changed his mind. I wouldn't want to have to go through that humiliation again. There have been times when I've desperately wished I could turn the clock back to six months ago, but there's no going back. And now . . .' She looked into his face with a measure of uncertainty in her expression. His rugged handsome features made her breathless with apprehension.

'And now?' he prompted.

'Now I don't want any of this to change – ever.' She sat up and hugged him to her. 'Oh, Kas, I never thought I'd be so happy again.'

'Because of me?'

She nodded. 'I thought of you often in the past, and when I met up with the travellers on Portsdown Hill I felt comfortable with them. It's almost as if I am really one of them. I know I'm not, of course. My parents and grandparents are all thoroughly respectable . . . Oh, I'm sorry, I didn't mean –'

'Yes, you did. Gypsies and travellers have acquired a bad reputation, not always deserved. If it's true that I came from Irish tinkers then their reputation is even worse. But none of that matters. It's what we are inside ourselves that counts. When you suddenly find yourself away from people you've always known and in a frightening situation you have to develop a close bond with others in the same situation. While I was doing my Army training some of the chaps weren't very friendly to me, especially when they'd had a drink or two, but once we went across the Channel we were all on the same level, officers and men alike.

'Kas, it must have been awful for you and all the others, especially dear Charlie Mead who was wounded about three times. He was the village dimwit when he was young, and I dread to think of what he went through before he got drowned on his way home. Life can be cruel, can't it?'

'It can. But why are we being so morbid when all I asked was what you'd like to pray for?' Kas pushed her back on the sand and bent to kiss her again. 'This maybe? And this – and this . . .'

'Oh, yes please,' she whispered.

Each kiss was more fierce than the previous one. Rachel wasn't sure what was happening to her. She had thought Adam's advances had brought a glow to her body but now she felt as if she were on fire.

She clung to Kas, silently begging him not to stop, yet she wasn't sure what else there was to follow. His breathing deepened until with a groan he lifted himself away.

'That's enough. The horses . . .' He stood up, took a deep breath and went after Kitchener.

Rachel sat up, hugged her knees, watching Kas and realised just how much she loved him.

Next morning over breakfast Rachel hardly said a word until Sybil spoke.

'So, you've a great deal to ponder over this morning, Missie?' she said harshly.

'I . . . I'm sorry, Sybil. I was miles away.'

'Not so many, I fancy, young Rachel. I hope you and Kas behaved properly.'

'We were back well before midnight.'

'That's not what I asked.' Sybil leaned across the table. 'How well informed are you about the ways of men and women?'

Rachel flushed deeply. 'I only know what I feel, Sybil, and it's like a bubble inside which won't burst.'

'Then it's time we had a cosy chat, me girl. That bubble's not for bursting! You don't want to end up like Ena, now do you? She chased Davey, making up to him like some street woman, and look where it's landed her. You have to restrain yourself, Rachel. A man gets to the point where he can't no longer – that's the danger. Then it's mighty pleasant but there are consequences. Your reputation will be damaged for good an' all.'

'I wouldn't lead a man on, Sybil,' Rachel said, remembering the little her mother had taught her about such things.

'I should hope not. I sees you and Kas –'

'You mean you can see in the stars that we're right for each other?' Rachel asked eagerly.

'I don't hold with such things,' Sybil said with a haughty sniff.

'But you can't deny you have the gift?' Rachel went round to Sybil's side of the small table and hugged her warmly. 'You've been so good to me, Sybil. Please, *please*, I beg you, tell me if it's right for me to love Kas. Does he love me?'

'Ah, now that's some'at you'll have to ask 'im.'

'I think he does. Well, I'm sure he does or he wouldn't have asked me to marry him, would he?'

'Got that far, 'as it? Seems like I ought to have come with you last night.'

'We didn't do anything wrong, Sybil, honestly. After all, we don't know one another that well.'

'And talking of marriage already?'

Rachel kissed Sybil on her cheek. 'You know from the stars that it's right, don't you?'

'I have a premonition that it might be in your destiny – but marriage ain't always the answer to everything. Most marriages have 'appy times and sad'uns as well. Slow down, dearie, and get to know one another properly first. Work together, find out what it is you wants from life – it may not be the same thing.'

'Happiness is all I want, Sybil.'

'And your folks, your real flesh and blood? Where do they come into it?'

'Oh, why did you have to spoil it?' Rachel ran her fingers through her long dark hair. 'I'd forgotten – no, not about my family. I pray for them every night and think about them all the time. But at the Fair last night we met a couple from home.' She sat down at the table again and told Sybil about Beth and Dick.

After she had finished Sybil said,' If they're living together illegally 'tisn't likely they'll want to go back, let alone tell folk they saw you dressed like a gypsy. I daresay they have enough problems of their own without giving you much thought.'

'You're probably right, but it did give me an awful fright.'

'And did they seem happy?'

'I s'pose so. I didn't wait to find out. They've both caused their families so much distress. I know I did my parents, but now they know I'm all right I don't think they'll worry too much. I always got the feeling that they would have been relieved to get me married off but it was Belinda's future which caused them most concern. I suppose by now she and Adam will be married and living in the railway cottage. I'm sure Dad will have helped them to do it up nicely.'

'And was the cottage more important to you than the man?'

'No, Sybil. I honestly loved Adam very deeply – still do in a way – but now I know he can never be mine, I try not to dwell on all that happened. I just hope he's good to Belinda. I was even prepared to go and live with his awful mother. She always preferred Belinda. I suppose it was all her doing that he changed his mind.'

Sybil took Rachel's hand and after a few minutes she realised the old gypsy was smoothing it gently the same as Merle had done years ago. Sybil's face was solemn, her eyes glazed as if she had gone away somewhere a long way off. Rachel kept silent, and then Sybil began to mutter.

'Not so . . . not so . . . reasons, deep dark reasons.' She turned Rachel's palm over, studying it carefully before placing her hand down on the table.

'What do you see?' Rachel asked in a whisper.

Sybil opened her eyes wider and smiled. 'That happiness isn't so far away from you, child, and you could do a lot worse than love Kas.'

'Oh, I do love you, Sybil!'

'Ah, but wait on – I didn't say it would all be smooth sailing. I believe you're a very privileged young lady. The past is often clearer than the future but yours is shrouded in some kind of mystery. The future isn't clear either which means that troubled times may come, but in the main I believe with Kas you may find truth.' Sybil stood up and banged hard on the table. 'And now I've broke me promise to Lemuel. I must away to speak with him.'

'But there's no need to tell him what you saw.'

'I never saw nothing – 'tis jest a feeling, a sense I gets, and he must be told or I'll never sleep easy again. Get on with the chores, Miss, if you please.'

Sybil pulled her coloured shawl about her shoulders and hurried from the waggon. She was away so long that Rachel began to feel troubled but she worked hard, washing dishes, sweeping and scrubbing the floor. She was polishing the windows when Sybil returned.

'Get over to talk with Lemuel, child,' she said gruffly.

'Oh dear, is he very angry? It's all my fault and I'll tell him that,' Rachel assured Sybil.

'Bless you child, Lemuel angry? Never in a million years. 'Tis the wise one he is, and more amused than angry. All the same he feels a little talk might help you just now. Brush your hair first.'

Rachel did as she was told and then walked calmly across the field to Lemuel's caravan.

'Ah, Rachel, my dear. Come inside. It's going to be a grand day, a heat wave has begun. Not that I like the heat, mind you, it knocks the stuffing out of me, but it sets us all up for the winter.'

Rachel sat down a little nervously but Lemuel handed her a cup of tea and then chatted about everyday occurrences until the door opened and Kas joined them.

'I'm in no position to preach at you,' Lemuel said, smiling at both of them as they sat side by side on the window seat. 'But the relationship between you must be taken slowly and with caution. Your upbringing was so different. Rachel, you escaped what you thought of as an impossible situation. You've made new friends and been guided by Sybil while Kas had the unhappy experiences of war to contend with. I understand that you met several years ago and no doubt, Rachel, you were at an impressionable age. Kas became a sort of hero. Now, it may well be that destiny has brought you together again – you certainly make a fine couple, indeed, a handsome one –

but it would be wise to live from day to day, learning about each other before making a commitment. Legal marriage is not for you until you reach the age of twenty-one, Rachel, and although the Romanies observe their own rules, I believe you should wait until you come of age.'

'We both know this, Lemuel, and although I have asked Rachel to marry me I know we must wait until after March 1921,' Kas said. 'And even then I'd prefer that we have Rachel's parents' blessing.'

'If you truly love each other this will be a great strain on you both,' Lemuel warned with a kindly inclination of his head. 'Easier, though, if you honour and respect each other. I can't stop you if you want to go off by yourselves but it would please me if you remained with our group. Rachel has become like a daughter to Sybil and you Kas, having lived away from us for a while, have much to offer the warring factions among us.'

'I can't promise always to be able to keep the peace, Lemuel, and I've had the notion as you know to build up a reputation as a good honest horse dealer and smithy, but for the present I'm content to stay among you.'

'You have a worthy ambition, Kas, and I hope you'll realise it. You've shown wisdom in your thinking and you're clear-headed in making your plans so I can only wish you well. But for Rachel our way of living is an adventure and the day will come when she feels a desire to return to her family.'

'One day I may want to see them again,' she put in quickly, 'but I really do enjoy the life here and want to stay.'

Kas put his hand over Rachel's and squeezed. 'No one is doubting how you feel at present, but none of us can know what the future holds. Our way of life isn't always easy, you know. When the going gets tough I think you'll want to go home as Lemuel says.'

'I don't know that – and neither do you,' Rachel said firmly. 'It doesn't do to try to anticipate the future.'

'So for what reason did you want Sybil to look into yours?' Lemuel asked. Then with a smile he added, 'I understand, child. When we're young we all wish to know our fate, but if were meant to know we'd be born with this knowledge. The world might be a happier place but that's not how it is. Choosing the right path, making sensible decisions, knowing right from wrong, trying not to hurt others – isn't that what we should be concentrating on?'

'I didn't really want to know my future,' Rachel said, somewhat shamefaced. 'I only wanted to know whether Kas loved me as much as I love him.'

Lemuel looked from Rachel to Kas questioningly.

'Rachel, at this moment I love you very much,' Kas said, putting his arm round her shoulders. 'But how can we be certain that it isn't the joy of meeting up again, the situation we find ourselves in? I wouldn't have suggested marriage if I'd had any doubt, but we must learn more about each other first. A chance meeting in the woods, a lucky stone which turned out to be not so lucky, is not a basis for marriage. I'm sure what Sybil sees in our destiny is correct. She's wise, she uses her talent wisely. But let's enjoy our friendship first.'

Lemuel covered their hands with his own and blessed them before they left his van, arms entwined, heads together as they talked and discussed plans which might or might not be realised. Rachel was happier than she had ever been and throughout the summer indulged in daydreams as she worked to help pay her way among her gypsy friends.

As the weeks and months passed she forgot about seeing Beth and Dick Mead, presuming that they had been day trippers on the island. The people of the Isle of Wight seemed happy enough to accept Lemuel's group who chose to remain after many others had left following the Fair. Kas purchased two more horses and became a frequent visitor to the local blacksmith who admired Kas's expertise and allowed him to share the use of his anvil in return for assisting him when he was overworked.

Just before Christmas Rachel and Kas decided to go to the mainland by ferry. They visited the shops in Portsmouth where Rachel bought small gifts for her parents and Belinda, and enclosing greeting cards had them wrapped ready for posting.

'We can't post them here,' she told Kas. 'It's too risky as it'll be the same postmark as my last card. Could we take a bus ride to the next town to post them?'

'I've got a better idea,' Kas said. 'There's sure to be a ship in port bound for London and we can pay one of the seamen to post it for you.'

'Is that safe? He might go off with it?'

'That's a risk we have to take – or maybe we shall see a carter heading for a different county. Let's go to a cafe and have something to eat and drink to warm us up and we'll see who's about.'

They walked along the main road until they came to a suitable cafe. It was a miserable damp kind of day and they enjoyed platefuls of stew which was both satisfying and warming.

'We'll take a walk along the docks presently,' Kas said as he stirred his cup of tea thoughtfully, then he suddenly grabbed Rachel's parcel and dashed to the door with it. The driver of a Lyon's tea van was just about to close the door as Kas rushed up to him and began talking. To Rachel's surprise the driver got out again and the two men shook hands. They seemed to be enjoying a chat and then the driver touched his cloth cap and got into his van, driving away bearing Rachel's precious parcel.

Kas returned smiling. 'An old mate from the Army,' he said. 'He's on a delivery round which will take him all over the southern districts so he's going to post your parcel as far away from here as possible.'

'Do you think he'll do it? He might forget until he gets home and then it'll be too late to reach Kingsmere before Christmas Day. Where does he live?'

'Near Reading. It's his last delivery round until after Christmas so he's travelling all through Sussex and Surrey before going home. He learnt to drive in the Army and it's earned him a decent job now. A nice chap is Percy. He won't let us down. I offered him a tip but he wouldn't hear of it.' Kas lifted Rachel's chin. 'Happy now?'

She nodded, and although she smiled her eyes were moist.

'Missing your folks?' Kas asked gently. 'There's still time to get home, you know.'

'It'll be my first Christmas away from the family, but I don't mind. I've got you and Sybil, and the others. Ena should soon have her babies. She's scared so I'd like to be near to help if I can.'

'We don't need to rush back now. Is there anything else you'd like to do before we catch the ferry? Let's go back to the shops again. I want to buy you a present.'

They paid the bill and returned to where bright lights sparkled in the gloom and a band played carols for the benefit of shoppers. Kas bought a silver bracelet for Rachel, and small gifts were purchased for Sybil and Lemuel. When they passed a wool shop Rachel went in to buy white wool to knit matinee jackets for Ena and Davey's babies. As they walked down a side street which led to the ferry she bought a fine set of horse brasses for Kas from a small shop overflowing with all manner of treasures which kept them occupied until they realised that they would have to hurry to catch the Portsmouth to Ryde passenger ferry.

'It's getting dark already but I hope you've enjoyed the day?' Kas asked.

The journey back was uneventful and they were pleased to reach the cosiness of Sybil's waggon.

Christmas celebrations were like nothing Rachel had ever dreamed of. Everyone joined in to help cook the traditional fare, and the smell of chickens cooking over open fires whetted the appetite. Huge cauldrons hung above wood fires to steam Christmas puddings, and later others were used to boil fresh vegetables.

'Just as well it's not raining or snowing or worse,' Rachel said to Sybil as they warmed plates on the smaller stove in the van.

'Then we'd have had to each cook our own in the waggons. 'Tis part of Christmas to celebrate all together and I daresay you ain't never been to such a gathering as this before.'

Rachel agreed that she hadn't. Now she was so much a part of the Romanies' way of life she hardly gave a thought to how her family were spending Christmas. But after the day's exciting events Lemuel conducted special prayers in a nearby spinney which sheltered them from the winds and then Rachel was overwhelmed with homesickness. It was as if a heavy cloud descended on her and her alone as they sang softly, 'Holy Night, Silent Night'. The voices echoed through the cold crisp air tunefully reminding Rachel of the sing-songs round the piano at Calder Cottage, her father's fine voice complementing the women's. Were Adam and Belinda celebrating at Calder Cottage? she wondered. Had he managed to persuade his mother to join them? Were they missing her? Even after all the food she'd consumed she suddenly felt empty. Why was she here? What was she doing leaving all the comforts of home to live with a group of gypsies? Tears trickled down her cheeks and she hung her head, unable to sing another note. Kas held her close to him as he felt her trembling. He didn't need to ask what was wrong. He knew that however much she tried, Rachel Hunter would never be a true gypsy. For a while all this was appeasing her conscience but one day, maybe far off in the future, she would need to return to her people. He wanted to marry Rachel more than anything else in the world but were their worlds too far apart for a relationship to last? They had another fifteen months to wait before they could be married and a great deal could happen in that time.

Before the service had ended a loud wail echoed across the field. It came from Davey Smith's waggon and although they honoured Lemuel's attempts to continue his reading and prayers they were all uneasy for Ena. She had become so large that it had been difficult for her to get about much during the past few days. Her whole body seemed to have swelled to unsightly proportions. A special delivery tent had been erected with a makeshift strawbed prepared which afterwards would be destroyed as was the custom. Most of the old customs had been lost but Rachel loved to sit and listen to Sybil who related how women had once been considered *mochardi*, the Romany word for unclean. If in the presence of men, women should sit with their legs pressed tightly together, and always pass behind a man who was sitting down. Sybil still retained some of the old ways and insisted that Rachel must never let her hair down or brush and comb it in front of any man.

When the service was over the women moved towards the birthing tent where Ena screamed. They stood round, huddled together in small family groups, waiting anxiously.

'It must be awfully cold in there,' Rachel whispered to Sybil. 'Shouldn't she be in the waggon?'

'T'would be awkward because everything would have to be taken out of the vardo, the living waggon, or destroyed afterwards. A separate tent is best and let's hope those babes won't take too long a'coming.'

The night passed and Ena was given some herbal medicine to calm her and stave off the labour pains for a while in order to give her some rest until the babes dropped lower. But by early morning her terrified screams had resumed and could be heard all round the field. Davey came banging at the door at five o'clock.

'Sybil, Rachel, come quickly. Ma says some'at's wrong. She's bleeding bad.'

'All right, Davey,' Sybil called. 'Give me time to get me clothes on.'

Rachel dressed quickly and then tried to help Sybil who suffered a great deal of stiffness first thing in the mornings.

'Shouldn't a doctor be called?' Rachel asked. She wanted to rush to Ena's side but realised that she knew a little of such happenings. When they entered the delivery tent the sight of so much blood filled her with horror.

'I'm going for a doctor,' she whispered to Sybil.

'We don't hold with such things,' the old woman said but Rachel was quick to observe that no one attempted to prevent her from rushing across the field and saddling Strawberry Girl. It was Kasan who tugged at the mare's reins.

'And where d'you think you're off to?' he demanded.

'Ena needs a doctor, Kas. She's bleeding badly. She should be in hospital.'

'We don't use doctors and hospitals. Our women are well experienced in such matters.'

'I don't care – I'm not going to stand by and watch her suffering any more, Kas. Please, let go of the reins.'

'Rachel, listen to me. They won't thank you for interfering . . .'

She pulled on th reins and gave a click of her tongue. Strawberry Girl set off at a trot. It was as if she sensed the urgency and when Rachel asked her to jump a gate instead of their stopping to open it the mare cleared it with several inches to spare. Once or twice her hoofs slipped on the icy damp surface of the lane but as soon as they reached Newport Rachel made for the Police Station she'd noticed in the town. The sargeant on duty heard her coming and came outside to see who it was in such a hurry at this early hour, especially during the festive season.

'I need a doctor, Sargeant, urgently,' Rachel said. 'One of the gypsy girls is in labour and bleeding badly.'

'Humph! Not likely he'll want to turn out for them on a Boxing morning.'

'It may be a matter of life and death. Will he want that on his conscience?'

'You don't sound like one of them? What's it to you, Miss?'

'Oh, what does it matter, for goodness' sake. Please, help me, it's really urgent.'

'Doctor Grinstead lives down the other end of the High Street but I doubt that he'll be awake or sober enough to go anywhere.'

Another horse came galloping up to the door. 'Have you found anyone, Rachel?' Kas asked. 'I think you're right. Ena's in a bad way.'

'I'll telephone him while you bang on his door,' the sargeant said. 'Between us we might rouse him.'

Rachel spotted the brass plate on the gate of a large double-fronted house. She ran to the front door and began knocking with the heavy wrought iron knocker. Kas banged on the window where light could be seen through a chink in the curtains.

After a few seconds they heard a man's voice muttering as bolts were being withdrawn and when he opened the door he growled. 'All right! Damn you gypsies, all right. 'Tis Christmas, for God's sake, can't a man even have a bit of peace on one day of the year? What's up?'

'One of our women's in a bad way, Doctor,' Kas said. 'She's having twins and she's haemorrhaging. Come on, I'll take you on my horse and bring you back when it's all over.'

'I hope it won't be all over – not for the woman anyway,' the doctor grumbled. 'Twins are always trouble,' he said as he put on his overcoat and wrapped a thick woollen scarf round his neck.

'Your bag, Doctor,' Kas said impatiently.

The little man seemed bemused as he went off into another room to fetch his medicine bag, pulling his cap down firmly on his head. He was unsteady on his feet but not completely inebriated and the cold night air soon sobered him up as they galloped back to the field.

There were no screams now and Kas and Rachel exchanged worried glances as they helped the doctor down from Kitchener and ushered him towards the tent.

'Get some strong coffee, Rachel,' Kas whispered. 'God knows what will be required of him. At least we can keep him warm and hopefully in command of himself.'

But Rachel hesitated as Sybil appeared at the tent flap. 'She's all right,' she said, 'and one of the little'uns – but the boy's dead. I'll see to some'at for the doctor, Rachel. You best go in and comfort Ena.'

Ena was only semi-conscious. She had lost a great deal of blood and required stitches which Doctor Grinstead inserted with unsteady fingers.

'Lucky to be alive, this young woman,' he said. 'Should have had pre-natal attention.'

'But she carried well, Doctor, and we folks know a thing or two about having babies,' Ena's mother said. 'I've had seven of me own. T'weren't no need for you to be called out – Christmas an' all.'

'I'm going to give her an injection to prevent further bleeding.' The doctor proceeded cautiously and afterwards looked up quizzically at Rachel. 'I suspect you're responsible for sending for me, young woman. Whatever these good people think or say, it's a good thing you did. I couldn't have saved the one infant any more than they could, but if the mother had continued to bleed they wouldn't have been able to save her either. See that she gets rest and plenty of warmth. Get her into a waggon at once. I'll be back later on to see how she is.'

Kas took the doctor back to Newport while some of the men from the Wells and Smith families carried Ena gently into Davey's waggon. He was missing, so Sybil and Rachel remained with her while Ena's mother bathed the baby girl and dressed it in fine white clothes.

Much later, when Rachel was returning from the woods with kindling wood, she came across Davey hiding behind a tree.

'For Goodness' sake, what are you doing here?' she admonished. 'Ena and your baby daughter need you.'

'Daughter?' In spite of Davey's weight and size he held a fair resemblance to a troubled schoolboy. 'Is it all over then?'

'Yes, and you might well have lost Ena as well as your son. I'm so sorry Davey, every man wants a son, I know, but this time it wasn't to be. They couldn't save the baby boy.'

He emerged from his hiding place and fell on Rachel, sobbing like a child. 'T'were all my fault. I should never – she's too young to be saddled with infants, she's no more'n a nipper herself. I couldn't bear to hear her, Rachel. I never heard no one cry like that before.'

Rachel patted his broad back and then pushed him away. 'Come on now, Davey. Pull yourself together. You should be proud, you have a lovely little girl. She's small and sweet. You're going to love her, and work hard to provide for Ena and the babe. It's true she had a bad time but then lots of women do, especially when there's twins, but she's all right now and the doctor has treated her. She needs rest, plenty of it, but I'm sure she wants you to tell her how pleased you are that you have a daughter.'

'Oh, Rachel, dearest Rachel, you're so clever and wise. I wish it was you I'd married.'

'Nonsense,' she retorted angrily. 'Don't let me hear you whining such rubbish again. I'm certainly not clever or wise or I wouldn't be here.'

'You thinking of going home to your folks?' Davey asked, wide-eyed.

'No, not while I can be with Kas. I like being here with you all but if you say such silly things to me, I shall have to move on. You're Ena's husband. You were married in church and made vows which you must honour.'

They walked back to the camp in silence and when Rachel urged Davey to go inside his waggon Ena stirred. Rachel thought she looked quite lovely as she lay between fresh clean sheets but her big dark eyes were full of fear when she realised Davey was there. Rachel pushed him forward and then left them alone together.

Rachel shared nursing the new mother and baby with Sybil who was always ready with herbal tea and plenty of other remedies. The baby girl, weighing only four and half pounds, had a healthy enough cry and nothing would pacify her. Rachel cradled her in her arms at every opportunity, pitying her the loss of a twin which she knew all about.

'You're like me now,' she crooned softly. 'My twin and I are parted, but we'll make it up to you just as these good people have helped me.'

She sat for a long while nursing the baby until eventually she slept. During the next few days it was Rachel who bathed, dressed and fed her with plain boiled water until Ena could be persuaded to feed the child herself.

Ena gradually recovered from the ordeal, but in spite of Davey's attempts to show compassion and affection, she was quick to blame him for what she had suffered so it wasn't surprising that he appeared to become increasingly indifferent towards his little daughter.

'Why should I want to hold it?' he snapped when Rachel suggested he take a turn at nursing the baby.

'She's your child, she's adorable, and she needs to know you're her father.'

''Tis Ena's, not mine. Let her do the nursing and feeding.'

'A baby needs two parents, Davey. You're nothing but a selfish coward, running away just when Ena needed you.'

'That weren't no time for a man to interfere. Ena's got what she wanted – tricked me into marriage, she did – so she must take the consequences. Lucky one of 'em did die. At least we've only got one extra mouth to feed.'

'You hadn't better let Lemuel hear you speaking so indifferently about God's precious gift, or Kas either. The baby may be the consequence of your selfishness, Davey, but now she's born you must devote your lives to looking after her. I can't wait to be married and have a baby.'

'If you'd come to us a bit sooner it might have been you lying there,' he said in a low voice, nodding towards the bed.

Rachel felt indignant colour flooding her cheeks which brought an amused grin to Davey's mouth. She felt angry at his inference and hoped Ena hadn't heard.

'You sound like some love-sick young boy,' she spat at him. 'What makes you think I'd give you a second look, Davey Smith? Get off about your work before I tell your mother.'

He leered at her for a second and then slunk away. Among the Romanies a man was very much head of his household but it was the woman who did the lion's hare of the work to support the family as Rachel had discovered. There wasn't so much work to do now that the holly wreaths had been made and sold, and for a week or two life drifted by uneventfully while Ena's baby was cosseted and admired. Rachel and Ena became very close, but once Ena was on her feet again, even though she was pale and listless, Rachel made sure she left the young parents alone. Ena seemed relieved though when Rachel occasionally visited her and took over looking after the baby.

'She's going to give you so much pleasure,' Rachel said one day after she'd managed to lull the baby to sleep following what Ena described as days and nights of fretting.

'Brought me nothing but misery has that one,' the girl said dismally. 'Davey don't want nothing to do with her nor me.'

'He'll come round when she begins to grow and you feel more like your old self. It's early days yet, Ena. You must take all the nourishment you can and all the herbal medicines Sybil and your mother give you.'

'Davey don't want more babies so he won't even sleep with me. Might as well not be married.'

Rachel tried changing the subject. 'What are you going to call her?'

'Oh, they're all quarrelling over the name. The in-laws insist on Elizabeth after Davey's gran, Ma wants Mary 'cos she was born at Christmas, but I fancy Carol. That's Christmassy too, ain't it?'

'Carol is very nice. Why not all three – Carol Elizabeth Mary? But you and Davey must decide. Make him something special for his supper tonight,' Rachel suggested. 'Wash your hair, put on a clean dress or skirt and make yourself nice so that he can't help but notice you.'

'Mmm,' Ena mused, 'maybe I will. I want my Davey and so does Carol.' Then she turned on Rachel aggressively. 'You sure you ain't carrying on with my Davey? 'Cos if you are I'll scratch your bloody eyes out.'

'*Ena*!' Rachel exclaimed. 'I've got Kas, why would I want Davey? He's *your* husband, and I told him you were married in church and he must honour his vows.'

'So you've been seeing him behind my back?' Ena accused.

'No! I told him off for running away and leaving you when you were having your baby. I wish I hadn't bothered,' Rachel shouted impatiently. 'You're welcome to Davey, I don't even like him.'

She flounced out of the waggon and went in search of Kas.

Chapter Twelve

A few days later Ena came knocking at Sybil's door.

'Is that gorgio bitch here?' she called. 'My Davey's gone and I bet she's gone with him.'

Sybil opened the upper half of the door.

'If you mean Rachel, she's here, see for yourself, but you're not welcome to come inside if you can't keep a civil tongue in your head.'

Rachel glanced up from peeling potatoes. 'I haven't even seen Davey,' she said calmly.

'You ain't been over to see Carol so when Davey didn't come home last night I thought you'd gone off together.'

'The trouble with you Ena, is you've got a vivid imagination. I told you, I don't want Davey. He's probably gone to the other side of the island for some reason. Kas has gone to look at another horse. Maybe Davey went with him.'

'Got tired already of helping with the baby?'

'No, you know I love taking care of Carol, but if it causes trouble between you and Davey then I'd best steer clear.'

'She stops crying for you. She takes one look at me and bawls her bloomin' head off.'

'That's because she can feel your hostility. It's no use blaming her, she didn't ask to be born,' Sybil said. 'You played with fire, young Ena, and you got burned. You can't make a man love you. Just the fact he was a Smith made him attractive,' she went on. 'Well, now you got his child so be thankful for that.' She waved a warning finger at Ena. 'Look at yourself for reasons why Davey might have gone off, though I doubt very much that he has, and don't come 'ere accusing and blaming other folk.'

'I'm sure he'll be back,' Rachel said.

But Davey didn't and no one knew where he was. They assumed he'd taken the ferry back to the mainland but enquiries of people they knew revealed nothing.

'You wouldn't think anyone could lose themselves on a small island like this, would you?' Kas said as he and Rachel rode together across the downs one morning. Rachel remembered the shock of seeing Beth and Dick at the fun fair just when she was feeling safe. For weeks she was convinced that every door she knocked at would be opened by one of them but Kas had assured her that they were probably only day trippers.

In a secret hollow they let the horses roam freely while they lay on a blanket on the grass.

'It's possible Davey's found work on one of the farms,' Rachel said. 'Maybe he'd be happier living in a cottage with Ena and the baby.'

'Davey's a wanderer. He wants to get away from their families but he should have taken Ena and the child. He made a commitment so he should stick by it.'

Rachel turned to look at Kas. 'Do we have a commitment – a real, honest commitment?'

He pulled her into his arms. Rachel loved the raw earthiness of him. His sometimes unruly hair, the thick growth of beard round his chin and the smell of horses on his jacket and breeches. His mouth was moist and enticing on hers.

'I love you, Rachel Hunter,' he said huskily. 'Isn't that commitment enough: sometimes you tempt me beyond endurance, Strawberry Girl. I have a mind to jump the budget instead of waiting to do things the gorgio way.'

'What's jumping the budget? I know Romany marriages are recognised in English courts and it seems so easy, just joining hands in the presence of witnesses. Sybil told me all about that.'

'Jumping the budget is an Irish custom. You know the box I keep my tools in? That was the only thing Josh found belonging to my parents and that's what tinkers call their budget. We could hold hands and jump over my box and we'd be man and wife as long as there were witnesses from both families – but you don't have any family here, and neither do I.'

'Wouldn't Sybil and Lemuel do?' Rachel asked.

Kas laughed. 'You know damn' well Lemuel would never agree to such a ceremony, and neither would you.'

'I might be persuaded,' she taunted him. 'I rather like the idea of jumping the budget. Even if we get married in church we could still do that, couldn't we?'

'I shall insist upon it,' he said. He caressed the firmness of her young breasts, wishing that it was warm enough to remove some of her clothing. He could feel her bosom beneath her blouse harden to his touch and by the way she put her legs together he knew that she was as impatient as he.

'Unfortunately my darling, gypsy girls must guard their modesty. We shouldn't even be here without a chaperone – but oh, dear God, Rachel, I want you so badly.'

She wound her fingers through his coarse hair as they indulged in passionate kisses and when his moans became uncontrollable Rachel would willingly have given him her all but Kas rolled away in desperation.

He helped Rachel to her feet and they called the horses.

'A canter along the shore,' Kas said with a wicked grin. 'If only it were summer we could cool down in the sea.'

Their happiness knew no bounds as Strawberry Girl and Kitchener splashed through the white-foamed waves while Kas and Rachel laughed and chatted happily until it was time to return home.

There was still no news of Davey and a few days later Kas told Rachel he had to go away for a few days.

'Can't I come too?' she asked.

Kas shook his head. 'No. I'm not sure how long this business will take but I'll be back as soon as possible.'

He was gone for less than two days and when he returned he brought Davey with him. The men bore the marks of some kind of scuffle.

'Whatever happened?' Rachel asked.

'Davey was reluctant so I had to persuade him.'

'Kas, why should you put yourself at risk for him?' Rachel demanded angrily. 'He's got a father and brothers and I'm sure Ena's family would willingly have dealt with it.'

'That's exactly why I went, my darling.'

'How did you know where to find him?'

Kas tapped the side of his nose. 'That's enough questions for now. He's back, though whether Ena is capable of keeping him is another matter.'

Rachel could get nothing further out of Kas and for a while things seemed improved between Ena and her husband.

After wintry weather the grass showed greener and the freshness of spring blew in on the wind from the sea. Primroses and crocuses followed delicate snowdrops, and the goods the gypsies had industriously made all winter could now be hawked through hamlet and village.

At Easter the entire group went to church at Godshill where Ena and Davey's baby girl was christened, Rachel and Kas being godparents.

The gown Rachel made for Carol was much admired but the infant's crying was still a source of concern. But she always stopped for Rachel.

'I might almost think t'were you'n,' Ena's father said during the festivities which followed the service. 'If I didn't know what our kid went through to have her.'

'Don't you see, Mr Wells, it's because she's missing her brother?' Rachel looked at Sybil who was sitting nearby. 'Isn't that right?'

Sybil pursed her lips doubtfully. 'S'pose you could be right but I don't know about such things.'

'I'm one of twins and I know how close Belinda and I always were until . . .'

'Until she took your man from you, child. Now that wasn't a kind thing to do, twin or no. But I reckon it might be some'at like that with this 'un. Maybe she needs extra loving and 'tis Ena what ought to show her that.'

Rachel helped Ena with her dress and hat for the occasion and Davey did show some interest in both his wife and daughter but only for that Sunday. Then he disappeared again without a word.

Over supper that evening in Sybil's van Rachel begged Kas not to go looking for him again.

'No,' he said. 'I told him I wouldn't. He'll get more than a beating if Ena's family go in search of him so it's up to him now.'

'I can't understand him not wanting to be with Carol at every opportunity,' Rachel said.

'You don't know Davey,' said Sybil. 'He likes the women but he didn't want to get tied down. Ena's only got herself to blame. She threw herself at him and when you came on the scene she meant to have him before you did.'

'I was never interested in any of the men here,' Rachel said sadly. 'I was just looking for a safe haven – and I found it with you, Sybil. I can't ever repay you.'

'But you have, child. You do all my work now, or most of it. You might have been the daughter I lost.'

'A daughter – you never said?' Rachel questioned.

Tears came into Sybil's eyes, dimmed with age now yet still far seeing.

'I haven't talked about her for years. Pretty golden-haired child she were, and I was young too. We'd done well that year, me and my man, just bought a new van, so off I goes to market to buy new fripperies. No one will ever really know what happened but when I got back the van were burnt to the ground and –' Sybil sniffed and blew as tears streamed down her wrinkled cheeks. It was several minutes before she recovered and then she said, 'My little Kitty were burnt to death and me man died trying to save her.'

Rachel and Kas did their best to comfort her but she got up and indicated that she needed to be alone. From the doorway they watched as she walked slowly towards Lemuel's waggon.

'They seem very close,' Rachel observed as he opened the door to welcome Sybil.

'He's a great comforter, is Lemuel,' Kas said. 'A wise counsellor if any of us needs to talk things through.'

'Sybil's pretty wise herself. If she's got the gift why didn't she know what was going to happen?' Rachel asked.

'That's why she won't use her "gift" as you call it. She had an inkling of danger that day but was so enthusiastic about the new van she ignored the warning signs. She blames herself and needs to go to Lemuel for comfort.'

'It's all so sad,' Rachel said as she cuddled up to him. 'I feel so sorry for Ena too. I thought my troubles at home were bad enough and I always thought gypsies had a happy trouble free life.'

'But now you know 'tis a hard living.' Kas kissed the top of her head. 'Still want to stay or are you getting nostalgic for Kingsmere?'

She lifted her face to meet his loving gaze. 'I think about them all, of course, and then I'm consumed with guilt for the way I behaved. I want them but I want you more, and I have to prove I can live my life responsibly.'

'I think you already did that, by fetching the doctor for Ena and acting so swiftly while we all stood by wondering what the hell to do. I want us to be married and have children. I long for a son of my own, but I couldn't bear to see you going through what Ena did.'

'I interfered, and for what?' Rachel said thoughtfully. 'Ena's aunt delivered the babies with Sybil's help. The doctor may have prevented any more bleeding and he gave Ena iron pills afterwards, but he admitted that he wouldn't have been able to save the little boy. I acted on impulse, and now Davey's gone off and left her.'

'You just keep on acting on impulse, that's the way I like you.'

A whole year had passed since Rachel had joined the gypsies and as spring sunshine warmed to the longer days of summer she enjoyed the early morning rides whether across dewy downs or along the seashore with Kas and his horses. One of his new mares was with foal and as the time drew near he refused to be parted from her so Rachel peddled the besoms they had made through the winter, along with bootlaces and clothes pegs, with Ena. At last Carol was less fractious and the two girls took turns to push the rickety pram along dusty lanes leaving the other free to knock on cottage doors. Shabby the pram might have been but the baby was kept clean and fresh-smelling so that many a householder admired Carol and brought goods they didn't really want to help the gypsy girls.

At an isolated farmhouse they received no reply except for a fierce growling from a large Alsation dog attached to a long length of strong chain who guarded the premises.

'All in the fields, I expect,' Rachel said as she turned away.

'Look, there's a cottage right up there through the lane,' Ena said. 'Wonder if anyone lives there.'

'Bit of a long way to walk if it's empty,' Rachel said. 'Still, we might as well. Probably no one else thinks of going up there. Let's try – that's if we can get the pram along the rough track.'

They secured the besoms across the bottom of the pram and set off, hardly realising what a long steep incline it was up to the cottage door. The weather was pleasantly dry and sunny, and once past the farm buildings to the right they enjoyed a vista of ploughed fields and meadows with a fine display of wild flowers among which were a host of large red poppies. Rachel was reminded of the painting in Wickham's school hall and related the story to Ena of how Charlie Mead defaced it to depict herself and the ugly strawberry birthmark she'd once had.

'Can't imagine you being ugly,' Ena said.

'It wasn't very nice. When I was really little I didn't realise why everyone pitied me and paid much more attention to Belinda. I had a rude awakening when I went to school and had to defend myself against teasing boys like Charlie Mead. Poor old Charlie,' she added wistfully.

'Why d'you say poor old Charlie? He didn't have any sympathy for you.'

'Not at the beginning but he had this rotten father who drank too much. Charlie changed so much went he went into the Army. He was wounded three times and then the boat he was coming home on was torpedoed. I felt so sorry for his mother. She was heartbroken. It was her I talked to in the church before I . . .'

'Now don't start on about that again,' Ena said. 'I don't suppose you damaged anything that couldn't be mended or replaced.'

'But a church! I can't believe I was capable of doing such a thing.'

They struggled along in silence for several minutes. Rachel tried hard to forget her crime but every now and then it washed over her to make her feel utterly miserable and guilty again.

As they neared the cottage they could see that the windows were open and curtains were fluttering in the sea breeze. They hadn't realised how near to the coast they were.

'Just look at that view,' Rachel said. 'The sea looks so inviting.'

'Lucky sods who live 'ere. They've probably got a track down to the beach. Maybe we'll get a drink of lemonade if we're lucky.'

But there was no reply to their persistent banging.

''Tis no good, Rachel. All this way for nothing,' Ena moaned.

'We could sit in their garden and eat our bread and cheese though,' Rachel suggested with a giggle.

They were cautious as they went round the side of the cottage which appeared to be well kept. Beyond a small flower garden was a vegetable patch and a woman's happy laughter came from somewhere in the orchard farther on. As Rachel moved towards the sound she saw a woman bending over a brick well lowering a bucket. A man leaned against her, holding her still while his groping hands explored beneath her skirt. The girls watched with a mixture of embarrassment and curiosity the horse-play in progress as the man turned the woman over to bend her backwards over the edge of the well, but she struggled free and as they broke apart Ena gasped.

'Davey Smith!' she exclaimed. 'The swine! I'll . . . I'll kill 'im!'

Rachel held her back, alarmed and equally angry when she recognised the woman as Beth Cropper. They stood mesmerised as Davey hauled up the bucket full of water and the two lovers went into a clinch before realising that they were being watched.

Rachel heard a hidden oath from Davey, and Beth ran towards the two girls.

'Why, if it isn't the Strawberry Girl again,' she sang out. 'Now I know my eyes didn't deceive me before. You've become a gypsy girl.'

'And you've pinched someone else's husband,' Rachel retorted.

'Yes, *mine*!' Ena made to lunge at Beth but Davey got between them.

'You tricked me into marriage, Ena Wells,' he said.

'Not Ena Wells – Ena Smith if you don't mind! This is your child that I sweated and nearly died for. What sort of villain are you? Nothing but a cheating rat!' She beat against his chest while Rachel turned on Beth.

'And you've caused nothing but trouble all your life, Beth Cropper. You cheated on your own sister, not that her husband was much good but you never gave him a chance to get back with Nessie Mead.'

'Oh, hark at you, Miss Goody-two-shoes. For your information Dick has gone back to Nessie, so there!' She took a step nearer Rachel, menacingly. 'Why have you left Kingsmere anyway? What are you doing here on the Isle of Wight? If you go back and tell where I am you'll be sorry.'

'But you just said Dick has gone back to Hundred Acres so he'll tell that he saw me at the fair, and who cares where you are?'

As they squared up to each other Rachel could see that Beth's face was now deeply tanned from the sun and her skin was wrinkled. She looked well used and much older than her thirty-two years. A cry from Ena made Rachel turn in time to see Davey throw off his wife. She ended up on the grass.

'I don't want you,' he shouted. 'I never did. You're too young and nothing but a little slut. You chased me, remember – always begging me to get between your legs – and finally you got what you wanted. But you don't own me. Beth and I are happy together so it's going to stay that way.' He looked across at Rachel. 'Might have been different if you'd been willing,' he said with snigger. 'Toffey-nosed bitch, sending the mighty Kas after me. He didn't get off so lightly at the pub though. I only agreed to go back because you was threatening to kill your bloody self,' he added to Ena. 'Well, go on and do it for Christ's sake. This 'un'll take care of the babe. You never wanted 'er any more'n I did. You just want any man – whore!'

Suddenly Beth realised that Rachel might be a threat so smacked her face and without thinking Rachel reciprocated. For a few seconds the two women pulled each other's hair, bit and scratched, giving vent to the hatred which they'd always felt for one another. A shout from Davey brought a halt to the fracas as they realised that the pram was running away, but Ena was going the other way to a path that led down to the sea, her agonised cries echoing behind her.

'Go after her,' Rachel shouted to Davey as she tore downhill to catch the pram but not before it had hit a piece of rock and toppled on to its side. She slid the last few feet to reach Carol who protested loudly as she lay on the ground, thankfully protected by her clothes and the blanket she'd been wrapped in. Rachel caught her up in her arms to console her as Beth and Davey ran to her aid.

'I told you to go after Ena,' Rachel said.

'No, 'tis no good, Rachel. I don't want Ena and 'tis wrong to pretend. She'll have to wake up to the fact. I've tried to tell her often enough. I should never have wed her, but I let you, Kas and Lemuel talk me into it. If you won't have me then I shall stay here with Beth.'

'I wouldn't be too sure of that, Davey Smith,' she retorted. 'I've had enough of being used by useless men. If you want Rachel then that's it. You never told me you had a baby. You sure it's Ena's not Rachel's?'

''Tis Ena's all right,' Davey said calmly. 'I've always fancied Rachel, I don't deny it, but she loves Kas.'

'For goodness' sake stop going on about who wants who,' Rachel shouted. 'Go after Ena, I tell you.'

'No, she'll get over it – you go after her if you like.'

Rachel put Carol back in the righted pram. 'Ena's desperate,' she said. 'You watch the baby while I go after her then.'

Beth turned the pram round to return to the cottage while Rachel ran across the garden to find the path down which Ena had disappeared. All kinds of terrible consequences ran through her mind as she went. Ena was capable of doing something awful in her quest for Davey, she might even throw herself off the cliff, but when Rachel came to a clearing she could look down to the beach below and saw Ena making for the sea. Could she reach her in time? Would Ena really do anything so final?

Rachel realised that she really was determined and by the time she reached the sea shore Ena was in the water up to her neck.

'Ena! Ena!' Rachel called. 'Don't be silly, turn back – turn *back*!'

Rachel wasn't a strong swimmer, she didn't get to the seaside often, but as a child her father had made sure that his daughter was capable of taking care of herself. She knew she must rid herself of some of her clothing which would otherwise hamper her progress so she kicked off her shoes and the ankle socks she was wearing, also her skirt and petticoat and then ran into the water. In spite of the warm day the water struck cold and took Rachel's breath away momentarily but she managed to keep Ena's head in view for a while before she lost sight of her. Rachel went on until she was out of her depth so she knew wherever Ena was she was certainly out of hers. She turned to doggy paddle as she called Ena's name then to her dismay saw a head bob up for a few seconds. It was some distance away. Rachel swam to where she thought Ena had surfaced and thankfully was nearby when she came up again. The sea was fairly calm, but the expanse of it shocked Rachel as she grabbed the struggling Ena round the neck and began to pull her towards the shore which seemed deserted until a couple of fishing boats drew in behind her. Within seconds of reaching the beach the men were out of their boats and helping Rachel to drag Ena to safety.

'Turn her on her side, Miss,' one shouted.

'Pump the water out of her lungs, Jack,' another said.

'Ena! Ena! Come on,' Rachel urged. At last she spewed the sea water out. Rachel sat back on her heels exhausted.

'Well done, Miss,' the man called Jack said as he went to Rachel's side. 'Not many a young woman could a'done that. You all right, me dear?'

'Yes,' she breathed in a hoarse whisper. 'Will she be all right?'

'I daresay. Ought to call the authorities really. Can't have young women walking into the sea, t'aint right.'

'Please, don't do that,' Rachel begged. 'She's had a nasty shock, She's got a baby too. I'll look after her, I promise.'

Ena began to moan and cough so Rachel massaged her back until she had recovered. The fishermen went back to their boats after Rachel had thanked them for their help. The last thing she wanted was a fuss. She did her best to pacify the distraught Ena, uncertain how she was going to get her back home. Both girls were soaked and dripping but they weren't aware of how they looked until Beth arrived with blankets to put round them.

'Come back to the house. Can she walk?' Beth asked.

'We'll have to help her. Why didn't Davey come? He could have carried her.'

'He's up at the top with the baby.'

'Is she all right?'

'Yes, she seems fine,' Beth said. 'A hot drink and you'll both be fine too, I reckon.'

They didn't talk any more as they helped Ena up the cliff. It was a slow process and Rachel was aware of Davey standing at the top of the path without making any attempt to help.

'Now see what you've done,' Rachel accused when she faced him.

'Silly bitch,' he muttered. 'Out of her bloody mind, she is.'

Rachel pushed him out of the way and took the wailing Carol out of the pram.

'Here, hold her,' she said to Davey. 'Good job the pram is large. Ena can sit in it to get her back to the cottage. Mind her legs don't drag on the ground, though.'

Ena looked ashen and hollow-eyed, and they had almost reached the cottage before she recovered consciousness.

'Where am I?' she asked, then looking round her and seeing Davey carrying Carol, she closed her eyes again with a cry. 'No, no, why didn't you let me drown?'

'Don't talk silly, Ena,' Rachel said. 'Whatever would your family have said if I'd stood by and let you do that – besides Carol needs you.'

'No, she doesn't. You're better with her than me. I'm no good as a mother.'

'You should have thought about that before you took your knickers off,' Davey said.

'Oh, shut up the pair of you,' Rachel said crossly. 'Bad enough to be soaking wet without all this bickering.'

Davey put one hand on the pram handle and helped to push the last few yards to the cottage.

'Have you got any spare clothes, Beth?' Rachel asked. 'Anything so long as it's dry, just to get home.'

'Where is home?' she asked.

'Just off Pedlar's Lane, near Yarrow's Wood.'

'I might be able to borrow a cart from the farmer,' Davey said.

'There's no need. We'll get home all right. Ena will be fine when we've had a cup of tea.'

While Beth heated the kettle Rachel and Ena changed into the clothes Beth had found for them. Ena needed help. She seemed to have lost all her energy.

'You must move about to keep your circulation going,' Rachel explained.

'Come on, Ena, for God's sake stir yourself. 'Tisn't the end of the world. Rachel saved your life. At least you could show your gratitude.'

'Why didn't you save me?' Ena asked in whisper.

''Cos I can't swim. 'T'was lucky Rachel could.'

'Here we are, have some hot tea,' Beth said as she poured it from a pretty teapot and added two spoonfuls of sugar to each of the cups.

Ena cupped her hands round the cup and sipped slowly as she avoided looking at Davey. Rachel watched the two of them. It seemed such a shame that with a lovely baby like Carol a rift divided them. She glanced across at Beth who eyed her suspiciously in turn. After that they avoided eye contact. Of all the places to come, Beth and Dick had chosen to hide away on the island just as she had done. It was an incredible coincidence too that Davey had met up with them. As yet she didn't know how, but was he with them when Kas found him and made him return home? Would Kas have remembered them from the day at the fair? Davey was young-looking for a thirty-year-old and handsome. Beth would be about thirty-two now, Rachel guessed. If it wasn't ruled out by his marriage to Ena they might have been made for each other while poor Dick Mead, at least fifty she thought, had obviously outlived his usefulness. Rachel thought of Nessie, his ill-used wife. Would she take Dick back? No one would blame her if she refused after all she had been through, but knowing Nessie Mead, Rachel felt in her heart that she would soften just as she had when he was let out of prison.

Davey kicked the chair leg as he moved and everyone jumped. Rachel's gaze met his and she saw that he was about to say something to Ena. A shiver went through Rachel and she shook her head at him. Some presentiment warned her that whatever was on his mind, now was not the right time to make it public. Davey went outside, mumbling to himself.

'He don't want me nor Carol,' Ena said in an embittered voice.

An awkward silence filled the room then Beth said, 'Well, you are a bit young for Davey, dear. Not much more than a school girl and he's a grown man.'

'Not too much of a schoolgirl to lie a'bed with, nor suffer hours of bloody labour to bring his twins into the world.'

'*Twin*!' Beth was shocked.

'S'pose he never told you nothing about me, nor the babe, nor his responsibilities? Where d'you meet 'im? Didn't take you long to make 'im comfortable, did it?'

Ena was recovering fast and couldn't hide her aggression, but running footsteps made them look expectantly towards the door as Davey rushed in.

'Horse coming up the lane,' he said anxiously. 'And 'tis Kas. How the hell did he know where to find you?'

Rachel stood up and went to the window where to her relief she saw Kas on Kitchener riding up to the cottage door. Now she need not be afraid any more. He would sort them all out. He knocked before entering immediately. With his hand still on the door latch he looked from one to the other.

'What in God's name's been going on here? I came out looking for you, Rachel. One or two people saw you in this area and then when I went down on the beach a fisherman said that a young girl nearly drowned.' Again his searching eyes roamed the room, alighting on Carol sleeping peacefully now in the pram. 'Thank God you're all safe.' Then he glared at Beth. 'You again,' he said. 'You and Davey deserve each other. Wherever there's trouble you're in the middle of it, just as you were when I found Davey at the pub. Where's your other man?'

Beth stood up smoothing down her dress, the bodice of which fitted just that bit too tightly but showed off her figure to advantage.

'Gone back to his wife. Too old for me. I need a younger man like Davey. Or if you've come to take him back and you're available . . .'

'Shut up, woman,' Davey snapped. 'Don't cheapen yourself, same as Ena did. Kas has got designs on Rachel 'ere.'

'Mm, maybe I can change that,' Beth smirked. 'Come on, Rachel dear, you don't want to see this nice little family split up, do you? How about it? Why don't you go back to Kingsmere and I'll have Kas while the gypsy girl gets her man back to help her with the children?' She sidled round the table towards Kas, tantalising him with her full lips as she wiggled her hips.

'It's a good job for you I'm not in the habit of ill-treating women, Ma'am. Just one look at your face and I know what kind you are. Rachel and I will be wed next year and neither you nor the devil himself can come between us.' Beth's eyes glinted with anger but she turned her attention to Davey. 'Yes,' Kas went on, following her gaze, 'if it weren't for Ena and the child you'd be welcome to him. As 'tis I can't make you stick by Ena, Davey, it's got to be your own decision. But if you stay with this woman then don't think you can ever come crawling back.'

'Oh yes he can,' Ena shouted. 'I love Davey and he'll always be welcome in my bed. Davey, please come home with us – *please*.'

Kas appeared to have reached the end of his tether. He drew his hand through his thick mop of hair with impatience.

'You can have a ride back on Kitchener with me, Ena. But it's got to be now,' he said sternly.

'No, let her stay here,' Beth suggested, at which Davey paled visibly. 'I never wanted kids of my own, always had to look after Nessie's brood instead of having a good time. But I might quite like looking after Carol. She's yours, Davey, and she's sweet.'

Ena grabbed Carol in her arms. 'No, you bitch! You ain't going to touch my baby. I'd sooner Rachel had her than you.' Ena went to stand by Kas who led her outside. Rachel followed.

Kas helped Ena up on the horse and then handed her the baby.

'D'you mind walking, Rachel? Someone has to push the pram and I'd better lead Kitchener. I wish you could ride as well. One day we'll have a pony and trap.' He smiled at Rachel, despising Ena and Davey for involving her. It never ceased to amaze him how well she fitted in with their way of life when he would have expected her to be far too genteel for such a rough existence. The more he witnessed her strength of character the more he loved and admired her, yet he couldn't shrug off that fear that one day she would want something better. He was building up good contacts as a blacksmith as well as horse dealer, planning that in a year or two he could offer Rachel a decent home in a picturesque cottage here on the island or a town house if she preferred. But for now he was content to be with her at every opportunity.

Rachel fetched the pram. 'Thanks for the clothes,' she said to Beth. 'Well see that they're washed and returned.' She looked at Davey. 'You're making the biggest mistake of your life if you don't come home with us.'

'What's it worth, Strawberry Girl, to take Davey and leave Kas?' Beth said. 'You haven't told me how you came to be a gypsy. Fancy one of the Hunter twins falling in love with a gypsy boy! Do your folks know where you are and how you live? I'll keep quiet, though, if you persuade Kas to stay with me.'

'No contest, Ma'am,' Kas said firmly. 'Well, Davey, what's it to be? Your family won't be pleased.'

'And you'll take great pleasure in telling them where we are. Maybe we'll move on, back to the mainland, and head for London where no one'll find us,' Davey said. 'Just keep that wife of mine off my back. I've made my choice and I'll see to it that Beth here soon forgets you.'

'Good luck then – until she meets someone she fancies better,' Kas said.

Ena cried into the baby's shawl all the way back. There was no doubt that she loved Davey passionately and to have to leave him behind with Beth Cropper was more than she could bear. Kas and Rachel hardly spoke as they slowly walked the narrow lanes. Rachel could understand from her own experience exactly how distressed Ena felt and vowed to help the younger girl get over her heartbreak.

Over supper with Sybil and Kas that evening she expressed her concern.

'I know she's got her family, and her mother will help to provide for Carol, but she's so young to have to bear such a burden. Davey has been very cruel.'

'Now the Wellses and the Smiths will start feuding all over again,' Sybil said. 'A bad business, but that Davey Smith never was much good, only after one thing. I'm mighty pleased you put him in his place, Rachel.'

'I s'pose Davey will tell Beth how he came to find me when I ran away,' Rachel said. 'She'd take great delight in telling my parents where I am and what I'm doing.'

'But I doubt that she wants her people to know where she is,' Kas said.

'Dick's probably already told them. Still, after all this time I don't think anyone will come looking for me. I've sent cards and messages telling them that I'm well and happy, also how sorry I am for what I did. They probably can't understand how devastated I felt at being rejected so coldly, but I know just how much Ena is suffering, after the way Adam hurt me.'

'Maybe he hasn't married your sister?' Kas suggested. 'Perhaps if you were to go back . . .'

'Oh, Kas, dearest Kas,' Rachel said, clutching at his arm. 'I'm so happy now. Don't let's ever talk again about my going back to Kingsmere. I can't think of a single reason that I'd want to or be persuaded to.'

He kissed her lightly on her cheek and Rachel glowed with contentment. Sybil stood up abruptly.

'You'm looking tired, young Rachel. I reckon 'tis time we turned in.'

'Will Ena be all right on her own with Carol or should I offer to stay with her?'

'She's got family – and they'm none too pleased with you 'cos they think you've been a bad influence on Davey. I knows that ain't true, Davey don't need any encouragement, but best to keep things quiet for a while. Ena'll get over all this in time.'

Kas kissed both Rachel and Sybil goodnight and left. But Rachel couldn't sleep. The horror of trying to reach Ena in the sea kept returning to haunt her and she knew by the creaks and groans coming from the lower berth that Sybil was restless too. Eventually sleep came just before dawn but almost immediately they were aroused by a fierce banging on the door.

'I'll go,' Rachel said, instantly awake even after so little sleep. She pulled a wrap around her shoulders and opened the upper half of the door to find a distraught Mrs Wells outside.

'Is our Ena here with you? I only left her half an hour ago to get the family's breakfast and now she's disappeared. Don't tell me she's gone off after that scoundrel Davey Smith again?'

'We haven't seen Ena, Mrs Wells,' Rachel said. 'Not since we left her van last evening.' She recalled how Ena had hugged her fiercely before they'd left, and her own promise that they'd always be like sisters. Ena had wept and then pushed Rachel away, her eyes like steel. She had experienced a momentary pang of guilt that Ena still blamed her for Davey's cooling towards her.

Sybil came shuffling up behind Rachel. 'Best get out and look for her,' she said. 'Probably couldn't sleep no more'n the rest of us. There's trouble somewhere, I'm sure.'

'Oh, Sybil, I know you don't like "seeing" but for God's sake, 'tis my Ena and I'm afeared that some'at 'as happened, if not to her then to Davey or that wench he's living with. I stayed the night with her 'cos I was worried. She felt murderous towards that hussy. Please help me.'

Sybil frowned and turned away, not wanting to say what she sensed. Rachel knew the signs now and she too had an uneasy feeling about Ena.

'Please, Sybil,' she urged, 'can you tell us where to look for her?'

Sybil sat down heavily in the chair and rocked back and forth with her eyes closed. Rachel thought she looked many years younger. Was it possible there was something to this gift after all? Sybil couldn't help having it, Rachel thought with some sympathy. With a moan she sat upright. 'Try the spinney,' she said, and all the weary lines were back in her ageing features. 'Hurry.'

Rachel gave no thought to the fact that she was only dressed in her nightdress and shawl as in bare feet she raced across the field, with Mrs Wells following behind at some distance. Rachel's long legs carried her swiftly to the woods where even the birds were silent.

'Ena! *Ena*!' she called, but there was no response. Dry twigs crackled beneath her feet as she ran on. Which way to go? 'Where, Sybil, where?' she pleaded. Pausing for breath she wondered why the spinney. It was just such a place where Ena and Davey canoodled on many an occasion, she knew. Had Ena lost her reason? Did she think she'd find Davey here in the spinney waiting for her?

A cold shiver went through Rachel and she moved forward slowly, breaking the low branches of small young trees as she pushed deeper into a thicket, and then she caught at the front of her nightdress. Farther on between the leafy branches of a tree she could see two bare feet gently swinging with the weight of a young girl's lifeless body.

Chapter Thirteen

Rachel pushed her way through until she was standing, mesmerised, beneath Ena's limp body. Then she turned and ran back to halt Mrs Wells.

'No, no,' she cried. 'Don't look, don't come any closer. We must fetch Kas and some men to cut her down. I think –'

'It's too late,' Mrs Wells said. 'I know she's dead. I should never have left her on her own after what happened yesterday. If only I'd woken her and taken her to our van. She was sleeping so sound, and when the baby woke I took her with me to let Ena rest. God! Dear God! My Ena!'

In spite of her own shock Rachel did her best to console the older woman and they retraced their steps out of the spinney, but by now word had gone round and some of the men were already on their way. Rachel spoke briefly to Mr Wells before she led Ena's distraught mother to Sybil's waggon. Sybil gave them both some herbal tea and then Mrs Wells began to weep.

Rachel felt too numb to cry at first. Her body felt cold with shock and horror and she just buried her head in her hands and thought this must be the blackest day of her life. When the tears began there was no stopping them, especially when the men brought Ena's body out of the spinney. The next thing Rachel saw were policemen and a police surgeon, and later on she was questioned as to how she came to find the body. It was all so terrible – the travellers went into deep mourning, even though it was considered a crime to kill oneself.

'Poor Ena,' Rachel said to Kas as she leaned on him for support. 'I never thought she'd try it again. Perhaps it would have been better if I'd let her drown. She didn't struggle much so I didn't really think she was too intent on finishing herself off. How could she do such a thing?'

'She must have loved Davey more than any of us realised, dear,' he said. 'You did so much for her, and you did save her life yesterday –

today there was nothing anyone could have done. She'd made up her mind and sooner or later she'd have succeeded. Thank goodness Carol is too young to understand.'

'What will happen to her now? Will her family look after her?'

'I'm sure they will. But she'll want for nothing. We're her god-parents remember.'

Lemuel was a great comforter and Kas took Rachel along to his waggon during late afternoon where he consoled her and prayed for Ena's soul.

'It was all my fault,' Rachel sobbed. 'If I'd gone home when you wanted me to, Davey and Ena would have settled down nicely with Carol. I did my best to help Ena. I wanted us to be friends, and most of the time we were, but I know she still blamed me for intruding into the family group here.'

'You've done a great deal of good by being amongst us, Rachel, my dear,' Lemuel said in his quiet, soothing voice. 'Ena's mind was always a troubled one. Every other young woman she met was a threat. If only Davey had moved on before things went too far. He used her and she became too possessive.'

'I thought once they were married and had the baby things would be all right,' Rachel sobbed.

'Marriage is a partnership. It's not the means to get one's own way, Rachel. Davey may be thirty but in many ways he's very immature. I wasn't wholly convinced that it was right when they got married but for the sake of the twins Ena was expecting marriage seemed the sensible way. None of us was blind to his roving eye, especially where you were concerned. Let's hope he's going to settle down now with this other woman.'

Rachel falteringly explained who Beth Cropper was and the troubles she'd caused in Wickham, and Lemuel listened sympathetically.

'Kas, someone must go to Davey and tell him what's happened,' he said. 'Her family will arrange the funeral but he should attend. It's his duty and you can tell him I said so.'

After the inquest they were allowed to proceed with making the funeral arrangements. Davey reluctantly returned with Kas but he was morose, spoke to no one and hardly showed any sadness at what Ena had done, let alone remorse.

Because it was suicide many of the usual funeral rites observed by the Romanies were waived, but her body lay in state in a separate tent where relatives and friends could pay their respects. Three of Ena's elder brothers kept vigil as was the custom and a candle was kept burning at the head of the coffin day and night. Her bereaved family fasted on bread and water for the three days before Ena could be buried, then items of jewellery and a few trinkets which had been her favourites were placed in the coffin. At last Ena lay at peace and looked quite beautiful in her best clothes. A hearse drawn by four of the gypsies' best horses was followed by family and friends, either walking or on carts, all sombrely dressed in black. There was much weeping and wailing as the simple coffin was lowered into a corner of the local churchyard and then they returned to the field where a special meal had been prepared.

During this Lemuel announced that he had something to say. He said a special prayer for Ena before too much drinking took place and then he said, 'Ena left a letter to me. As you know she was no great scholar but her wishes are clear enough. She wants Rachel and Kas to take Carol and bring her up as their own.'

A gasp went up. Already the Wells and Smith families had begun arguing as to who had the legal rights to the child. Davey made it quite clear that he intended to return to Beth Cropper and wanted neither his waggon nor any of their belongings, much less take charge of the baby.

Loud murmurings went round the group while Lemuel stated that the remainder of Ena's belongings were to be burnt the following day, though anything which might be of use to Carol was to be preserved.

'I can't believe it,' Rachel whispered to Kas. 'Surely Ena must have known the trouble this would cause between the two families.'

'Not nearly as much trouble as if they had to decide between themselves who took charge of Carol if Davey wasn't prepared to, and Ena obviously knew he wasn't interested,' Kas said. 'That was what hurt her the most, to have borne him a child he cared nothing about.'

'Shouldn't we forgo it and let Ena's mother have her?'

'No, that would start a riot. It's in black and white and we must carry out her wishes. Don't tell me you don't want her?'

'No, Kas, I love her already as if she were my own, but I do have some sympathy for the families. It doesn't seem right.'

'Maybe not in the kind of lifestyle you were brought up in, but among these people things are different.'

After the drinking began so did the quarrels and although Lemuel did everything he could to maintain some order, begging them to respect the dead, the men took themselves off to the nearest pub and soon rumours came back of violent fighting spilling out into the streets.

Sybil and Rachel were jointly to take care of Carol until Rachel and Kas got married. The child settled down contentedly with them, unaware of the dreadful happenings of the past few days which had taken their toll on Sybil in particular. She looked drawn and was glad to get to bed. Rachel tidied round and was relieved to climb into the upper berth, though troubled thoughts kept her awake until nearly midnight.

In the early hours of the morning she woke up coughing and choking. The wagon was full of smoke. She almost fell off the top bunk, and holding the skirt of her nightdress over her nose and mouth, shook Sybil frantically, pulling at her bedding until the older woman scrambled out of her bed.

'We're on fire,' Rachel screamed as she gathered up the baby, bedclothes and all, and heaved at the door to get out. She ran down the steps and carried Carol to safety, laying her gently on the ground before shouting for help to anyone who might hear. Then she returned to the van to help Sybil.

Within minutes the place was alive with men carrying buckets of water, old blankets, and anything which would douse the smoke. As yet no one could detect the source of the fire and there appeared to be no flames. The horses were disturbed by the acrid smell and their whinnying and stomping had already roused Kas.

'God,' he breathed taking Rachel into his arms, 'thank goodness you're safe. And the baby too.'

'Sybil's safe though she's very shocked. Lemuel came and took her back to his van with Carol. Have we lost everything, Kas, I daren't look?'

The early morning mist helped to dispel the smoke and with the dawn light Rachel could see that the van, though blackened, was still intact.

'Why were there no flames?' she asked.

'Because this is arson. Whoever did this cowardly mean thing didn't mean to kill you, Sybil or the baby – just get their revenge.'

'Revenge for Ena's death you mean?'

'I'm afraid so. Her family were angry that Sybil couldn't foresee what was going to happen, they're a suspicious lot, and Davey's people felt slighted because Ena wanted us to have Carol. They blame you for everything. Stupid creatures should have realised that Sybil and Carol could have died from smoke inhalation, and then they'd be wanted for murder! You're young and strong, my darling. The person they most wanted to harm was the least likely to be affected. Thank God you're all unharmed. You acted bravely and promptly, Rachel. I'd been awake some minutes – I woke with an uneasy feeling. Have you noticed anything?' Kas pointed to two empty places in the group of waggons. 'They've up and gone.'

'Together?' Rachel asked in surprise.

'Probably not actually together. I daresay Davey's family will try to see him and persuade him to move on with them. They've taken his and Ena's van and when they find a suitable spot they'll burn it. By now the Wells family will have reached the ferry anxious to be first across.'

'All so needless and sad,' she said. 'Will we be able to live in Sybil's van again?'

'That's up to Sybil. She may want it destroyed or she may decide to have it repainted. Thankfully there'll only be smoke and water damage. Now I want you to get some sleep. I've got some investigating to do with Caleb Sanders.' The Sanders were a good family whom Lemuel had met and converted to the Christian faith several years earlier. They had six daughters and four sons and kept themselves to themselves.

Kas sighed. 'At least with those two families out of the way, we shall be a more harmonious group.'

'I feel so guilty. It really was all my fault for staying on.'

'You've become one of us now and you're here to stay – if you want to.'

'Oh, Kas, I want to more than anything and now I've got to, to care for Carol. That's what Ena wanted so we're committed to each other – for ever.'

He guided Rachel to Lemuel's van where Lemuel and Sybil waited with the baby.

'I suspect we shall find the evidence we need underneath Sybil's van,' Kas told Lemuel.

'It's a bad business,' he said. 'No amount of teaching could change their ways, always drinking and fighting, so it's best they go their separate ways.'

During the late morning Kas returned to Lemuel's van carrying a large galvanised bucket.

'As I thought, Lemuel,' he said. 'A bundle of damp rags, probably the remainder of Ena's clothes, mixed up with some very wet bracken. They must have set fire to it before they left – and they must have been preparing to go since before the funeral. What are you going to do, Sybil?' he asked. 'The van is wet now and will need complete redecoration.'

'Yes, I think I shall stay put for the time being. You and Rachel will be wed this time next year so you'll be wanting a new van, I daresay. T'will break the spell if I stay on – if I let it be destroyed it means that I've been burnt out twice. Third time maybe t'will be me as well.'

'When your time comes, Sybil, you'll have no say in how or when or where,' Lemuel said in his calm, wise way. 'If you take my advice you'll have your van all done up nicely ready for next year's wedding festivities.'

'I've got a suggestion,' Kas said. 'I'll do up your van, Sybil, and while I'm doing it, you, Rachel and Carol can stay in mine.'

'But where will you stay?' Sybil asked.

'Caleb's offered to help, and his two brothers, so it'll all be done in time for Christmas. I expect I can make up a bed of some sort for myself in your van.'

'You're welcome to stay here with me, Kas, until Sybil's is habitable,' Lemuel said.

There was no lack of offers of help. Most of the travellers were relieved to be rid of the Wellses and Smiths though no one voiced their opinion. While the women peddled their goods, the men spent a few hours each day repairing damaged wood, and Lemuel, who was an accomplished artist, painted beautiful pictures on the walls and the wood panelling for the new ceiling. Rachel helped Sybil make new curtains and bed coverings and by late autumn the van had been completely refurbished. Carol, who would be a year old at Christmas, was growing at a good pace and was too big for the small wooden crib passed down to Ena from her mother. Kas spent every spare minute making an iron cot where she could be safe when she reached toddler stage.

Gradually the traumatic events of that summer receded though were never quite forgotten by any of the group, especially Rachel. As Christmas drew near and she began to think about sending greetings to her family in Kingsmere she regretted that she was not able to see Belinda and share the experience with her. She doubted that her sister would have much sympathy with the gypsy way of life, but there were times when she missed her dreadfully and more often than not it was the happiness they had shared together which Rachel remembered rather than those final days.

Carol was looking more like Ena all the time and when Rachel recalled that she too was a twin she felt all the more pain of being parted from her own sister. But then her thoughts would move on to the way Beth Cropper had stolen Davey from Ena, a situation akin to her own when Adam had so insensitively announced that he had made a mistake and it was Belinda he loved. Rachel was happy beyond belief with Kas but recognised her love for him was different in a way she couldn't define from the young love she'd had for Adam.

Christmas was a happy occasion. Rachel was becoming very adept at cooking over outdoor wood fires in large pots hanging on a crane above, and the seasonal fare was eaten and enjoyed with relish. During the Yuletide evenings, while chestnuts were roasting in the embers, the families grouped around the camp fire singing carols and songs. Afterwards, Lemuel added a blessing which set a seal of friendship between everyone present.

The year 1921 promised to be special for Rachel. On March 7 she would celebrate her twenty-first birthday, and her marriage to Kas was arranged to take place on June 1 at noon. She and Sybil spent the long dark cold evenings sewing by the light of an oil lamp, making Rachel's wedding dress of cream lace with an underskirt of taffeta. Some of the women in the group were talented needlewomen and helped with the fitting and tacking. Caleb's wife Precious had a special aptitude for floral work and made some sample head-dresses with the first early spring flowers. Rachel was able to choose the design which suited her best, and this was to be made up on the day with pink roses to complement her dark hair which still fell forward in a beautiful wave on the left side of her forehead, the way Phoebe had trained it from birth. Attached to the head-dress would be a finely woven net veil, exquisitely embroidered, loaned to her by Sybil who had kept and treasured it since her own wedding day.

'I daresay your mother would have had something similar to lend you. "Some'at borrowed, some'at blue", says the old rhyme. My, oh my, young Rachel, I feels vexed for your folks that they won't be seeing you dressed up in your finery. We must get someone to take a picture, just in case you ever gets to meeting up with them one day.'

'I'm sure I will,' Rachel said. 'When I'm thirty maybe.' She sighed. 'Mum and Dad will be getting on, ten years from now. I think Dad must be turned sixty this year. I'd love to see them all, especially to wish Belinda a happy twenty-first birthday on March 7.'

'No reason you can't make your way there in time for that,' Sybil said, but Rachel smiled wistfully at the old woman who had been like a second mother to her and whom she loved almost as much as Phoebe.

'No, Sybil dear,' she said. 'My mind is made up. At first, I confess, I was very homesick but as the weeks and months have passed I've grown away from them and close to you, and here I stay.'

'Never thought so much could happen in so short a time. Our lives ain't usually so dramatic, believe me,' Sybil said.

'But always colourful,' Rachel answered with a bright laugh.

Sybil laughed heartily too. 'Yes, you could say that, dearie, and put like that it don't sound so bad.'

Kas took Rachel into Portsmouth just before her birthday and when she bought a gold pin brooch with filigree flowers at each end and the name 'Sister' across the centre for Belinda, he bought a lovely engagement ring with opals and rubies set in a cluster for Rachel. The shop gift-wrapped Belinda's brooch and afterwards they went to the Post Office and bought a registered envelope for safe posting. Enclosed with a card was a short letter from Rachel sending her special wishes and adding that she herself was to be married to Kas on June 1. She didn't include any address or whereabouts but used the Post Office as surety.

'Looking for you in Portsmouth would be like looking for a needle in a haystack,' Kas joked which put Rachel's mind at ease. 'I expect you feel sad that you can't celebrate your birthday with your twin sister?'

'I try not to think about it too much,' she said honestly. 'My feelings are pretty mixed up. Being twenty-one is rather special and I expect my parents thought they would be arranging a really slap-up party for both of us in the village hall at Wickham.' They were enjoying a mid-day meal in a pub, sitting close to a roaring fire. She set aside her knife and fork and stretched out her hand to cover Kas's. 'But what's in a party when I've got you and Sybil? I just know everything is going to work out well at last. I'm really happy and very excited.'

They toured the shops, buying any necessary items for the home they would share together in the summer, and on a street corner Kas stopped to buy matches from a beggar.

'We sell matches ourselves,' Rachel said, amused.

'And we're reasonably well off compared with him. He's blind, Rachel. Probably lost his sight on the Somme, poor devil. So many of them didn't have a chance. We're lucky. We can walk unaided, we can see and talk, we're not disfigured by burns. Two years on what have we to show for the appalling loss of life? Like Lemuel teaches we must never forget to count our blessings.'

Rachel squeezed his hand. 'You're such a good man,' she said. 'I must be the luckiest girl in the world.'

Kas put his arm around Rachel's waist, teasing her. 'Just you wait, my girl, until my Irish temper flares. You may not think you're so lucky then.'

But Rachel could never imagine Kas doing anything to hurt anyone.

There was a great celebration to mark Rachel's coming of age on March 7 and her official engagement to Kas, and then there was much to do in readiness for their wedding. Carol was toddling now. She was a pretty child with light golden hair, so unlike her parents who had the rich dark gypsy colouring. There were times when Rachel even wondered whether Davey was Carol's father after all or if Ena really had tricked him? Could he have had his own suspicions perhaps and that was the reason he'd been so indifferent to her and the baby?

Rachel wanted Carol to be a little flower girl so made her a dainty pale pink organdy dress which she smocked in pretty colours across the front. She looked a picture on the day with small white shoes, socks decorated with pink bows, and pink flowers in her hair and in the little basket she carried. One of Caleb's six daughters, Charity, aged sixteen, was Rachel's adult bridesmaid and also wore pink.

Rachel, looking radiant, travelled to the small village church on a decorated cart with Lemuel who was acting on her father's behalf. He had become friendly with the Vicar who had invited him to take part in the service by reading the lesson.

Kas, with his best man Caleb Saunders at his side, turned to look proudly at his bride as she walked down the aisle. He had feared that at the last moment she would remember her family back at Kingsmere and the occasion would become to emotional for her. But her large dark brown eyes smiled confidently at him and he admired her courage, knowing that somewhere inside a corner of her heart was stored a wealth of love for her family and a deep sorrow for the way she had vexed them. Her skin looked like porcelain beneath the transparent veil which covered her head and face. Kas remembered the strawberry mark and thought she would still have been very beautiful even if it had not faded, and he would have loved her just the same.

The ceremony over, the happy couple emerged into the sunshine where many well-wishers greeted them and showered them with confetti so that Rachel was hardly aware of the transport awaiting them. As their friends waved them off, back to the camp for the wedding breakfast, Rachel noticed that they were sitting on a brand new trap.

'Oh, Kas,' she breathed excitedly. 'Is this what you've been making when you've been going off secretly at night?'

'Well, I had to occupy my time while you women were busy with your needles and pins,' he said, kissing her cheek. 'I hope you like Bella?'

Rachel looked in front of the trap. It wasn't a pony. It wasn't a donkey pulling the trap, though both types of animals were owned by members of the group.

'She's a darling, Kas,' Rachel said. 'But what exactly is she? Pony, horse or in between?'

'A miniature horse, darling. My wedding present to you together with the trap. I know you like riding but it isn't easy with Carol to care for and with this you'll be able to take Sybil out and about as well, until we fill it up with our own children.'

'You're so thoughtful, Kas. What a wonderful day this is and a marvellous wedding present.' Their lips met in a passionate kiss heedless of onlookers as they travelled through the country lane.

'But I don't have anything so wonderful to give you,' she said.

'Just yourself – and that's all I want, until you present me with our first son.'

People waved and called their good wishes as the little horse, its fancy plumes fluttering in the breeze, trotted handsomely along pulling the trap with its happy occupants, attracting many an envious onlooker.

After the eating, drinking and merry-making Rachel had to be pulled away from Bella to join in the dancing, the music provided by Caleb's old squeeze-box.

'I think she's the prettiest little animal I've ever seen,' Rachel told Kas as they twirled in time to the music. Bella's coat was the colour of a young fawn, her sandy mane interspersed with white. 'We shall have to work very hard now to save some money. You must be broke, Kas, but I really appreciate how hard you've had to work already to make this day so extra special for me. I'm totally yours now, you don't have to be concerned any more. Suddenly I feel free of all that's gone before.'

'Together we'll reach the stars,' he whispered with a twinkle in his eye. 'And now, before we leave, we must observe a special custom to bring us good luck.'

Everyone made a huge circle and before the chief witnesses, Lemuel for Kas, Sybil on behalf of Rachel's family, the newlyweds held hands and jumped over Kas's special box to the sound of affectionate applause and cheers which echoed behind them as they set off in Kas's waggon to go farther south on the island to spend a week alone together.

When they reached a secluded corner of the field owned by a farmer Kas knew they tethered the two horses, Kitchener who had pulled the waggon and Strawberry Girl who had trotted alongside, to a nearby tree, and very soon the two lovers were lying together pledging their love anew.

The next few days seemed timeless as each morning they rode along the shore with the sun on their backs and the soft sea breeze wafting through their hair. Rachel's happiness knew no bounds.

On the quiet Sunday afternoon which she thought was the last day of their honeymoon, as she gazed out of the window watching for Kas to return from the farmhouse, she saw Precious and Charity coming into the field driving Bella and the trap. For a moment she thought something must be wrong with either Sybil or Lemuel but anxiety changed to delight when to her utter astonishment she saw all the other waggons following behind.

Rachel ran out to greet them all, at the same time calling to Kas who was coming from the other direction. 'Kas, Kas, the others are here!' She hardly knew which way to run first and greeted Kas with such enthusiasm that he nearly lost all the water from the canister. 'Oh, Kas,' she accused in response to his wicked grin, 'you knew all the time. You arranged for us all to move south – oh, I *do* love you,' she said earnestly.

Kas put the water down and hugged his wife to him. 'And I love you more and more each day,' he said as he kissed her hair. 'It was time for a change and I knew you weren't quite ready for the mainland yet so I scouted round the island and found this spot. The farmer grows strawberries so we shall all have work for the next few weeks at least.'

'The farmer doesn't mind so many of us?' she asked, waving to the gypsy families as they drew nearer.

'He needs extra help. It seems Beth and Davey have been working here recently but they've gone back to the mainland. He thought they were going to try their luck in London. Thank goodness they've gone. Lemuel called a meeting before we got married and there was a unanimous decision that it was best to put the past behind us and start afresh here after all that had happened. I hoped it would be what you wanted?'

'It's a lovely way to start our married life,' she said with tears streaming down her cheeks as she greeted Lemuel, Sybil with little Carol, and her other friends.

There was great jubilation at setting up camp in the field the farmer had leased them on an annual basis, provided those who could would work on the farm and in the fields when he required help. The spirit among the community was harmonious and Rachel could relax, knowing that Beth Cropper and Davey were not around to taunt her any more.

The weather throughout the strawberry season remained glorious, and when Rachel's back began to ache as she filled her basket she would look up at the blue sky and offer a prayer of thanks for a happier life than she could ever have imagined.

Later in the year haymaking and harvest kept the men busy while the women picked apples and plums, preserving what they were given by the farmer for the winter. By early autumn Rachel knew she was pregnant but no sooner had she got used to the idea of motherhood than she miscarried.

'Kas, I'm such a failure at everything I do,' she bemoaned.

'Darling, you haven't failed me and that's what matters. Yes, I hope we shall have a family of our own, every man's ideal is to have a son, but your health is more important so get strong before we try again.'

Carol was an active toddler who used up Rachel's energy and time, but she loved her desperately and often mourned the loss of Ena in such tragic circumstances. She felt guilty at her own happiness, especially when she found herself pregnant again, but for the second time, in spite of Sybil's herbal remedies and every precaution, she miscarried again and a year later lost a third baby.

Kas insisted that she visit a doctor for a thorough examination but no cause could be found for the miscarriages and the local doctor referred her to the hospital in Newport. The doctors there considered she was a healthy young woman who for some unknown reason simply was not ready to carry a pregnancy full term. Kas decided that for the next year or so they would forget about starting a family which depressed Rachel.

'I feel miserable now,' she confessed to Sybil one morning when the men were all out at work. 'Kas won't let me do any work at all.'

'You've got your work cut out with young Carol,' Sybil said. 'Forget your troubles, dearie, then it'll happen when you ain't thinking on it.'

'Look at me, Sybil,' Rachel said. 'Tell me what you see – please? Dare I hope?'

'You must always hope, Rachel. I ain't capable of seeing no more.'

'Years ago when I got lost in the wood and by chance met up with Merle, Josh and Kas, Merle read my palm,' Rachel recalled thoughtfully. 'I didn't ask her to, she just did, and said I'd find happiness then be unhappy. I wonder what she meant – what she saw?'

'We all 'as unhappy times and then happy ones again,' Sybil said. 'Don't you fret, child, t'will all come right in God's good time. You jest be a good wife to Kas, 'cos he's a good man to you and everyone else.'

'But how can I be good to him when I know he wants a son and I can't give him one?'

'Jest stop worrying yourself, and 'im as well. I knows you misses teaching the children but that can't be helped since we've stayed on the island longer than intended. The authorities were bound to put their foot down eventually and insist they went to school. Lemuel misses teaching the little'uns, and I fancy he ain't so well nowadays. You can always help him. Cleaning his waggon, cooking his meals.'

'Oh, Sybil you know he doesn't have to do anything for himself. There's always someone doing for him.'

'Then see if he needs help with writing and suchlike. He always has his head in books when I goes to see him. Goodness knows what he's up to.'

At first Rachel had no inclination to visit Lemuel but when she saw him taking an early morning walk she thought how much older he looked. He wasn't a man who accepted help readily so she had to be discreet. The summer of 1923 had been tiring and now, as autumn leaves fell, dropping their blanket of yellow, gold and red, the bitter north-east winds whipped them up again to fly like miniature kites across the island. Rachel could hardly believe she had been with the group of gypsies for over four years, and come Christmas Carol would celebrate her fourth birthday.

'You've matured in this time,' Lemuel said as Rachel reminded him how long she'd known him. 'And I've grown much older.' He looked sad but smiled in his usual way.

'Only four years older, Lemuel,' she said to cheer him.

'But four years is a long time when we're past our prime. I've had my threescore years and ten, and a few extra.'

'Maybe you're just a bit weary,' she said. 'The summer is tiring. Funny, isn't it, how all through the winter we look forward to spring and summer, and by the time autumn comes we're looking forward to sitting round the fire again?'

'That's why the good Lord gave us four seasons. "To everything there is a season", and mine are running out, my dear.'

'Are you ill, Lemuel? Shouldn't you see a doctor if you are?' Rachel asked kindly as she set the table in his waggon for his evening meal.

'My chest gives me some pain, and my sight is not as good as it was.'

'You've done too much writing, Lemuel. What is it that's kept you so busy?'

'I – well, I've had a fortunate life, Rachel. I wasn't born into this type of lifestyle but that of the privileged classes. My father had a government post in India and it was there that I first learnt of the Romany ways. I had a special interest in languages and so I studied the Romany language in particular.' He sighed, remembering his youth. 'I didn't always practise the Christian faith, Rachel. I enjoyed the good life, money and a good education, then the woman I thought I was going to marry helped me to lose my father's inheritance.'

'How?' Rachel asked.

'We went into business together. She and her accomplice embezzled quite a fortune, leaving me with nothing but the clothes I stood up in. My family disowned me.'

'Weren't they caught? Wasn't there anything you could do to get it back?'

'The love of money, my dear, is the root of all evil. It would take too long to tell you of my follies as well as hers. Suffice it to say that finding myself alone and penniless, like you, I found some gypsies who happened to be retracing the Romany journey from India across Europe to England. They took me in and in return I taught their children and wrote down much of what they could tell me about their ancestors and the true Romany way of life. I still haven't completed my manuscript, but when I have I hope to find a publisher – that's if I'm spared. Not many gypsies are Christians but their way of life taught me a great deal, and I feel I owe it to the world to tell future generations about these people.'

'Perhaps I could help you?' Rachel offered.

'That's kind of you, but you have Carol to take care of and she's at a demanding age. Perhaps when she goes to school you'll be able to spare an hour or two each day.'

'I'm sure Sybil or Precious Sanders would look after Carol, Lemuel. I'd like to help and I know Kas would like me to.'

Through the long winter days Rachel sat with Lemuel and wrote as he dictated. She became so absorbed in the story that all her own past disappointments were forgotten. Time became the important factor as she realised with regret that Lemuel's eyesight was failing and on top of that as the winter progressed he developed a bad cough.

When Rachel arrived at his van one morning and found him still in bed she became really concerned.

'It's al right, my dear,' he croaked. 'Nothing that a rest for a couple of days won't cure. The book can wait. In fact if I'm unable to finish it I shall pass it on to you to do as you think fit. You're young and you'll have a family soon, then when they're growing up you can bring the book up to date.'

Rachel sponged his hands and face and realised that he was running a temperature. She made him a warm drink and then went to tell Sybil.

The group rallied round to nurse him as they always did in times of crisis, for they knew that Lemuel was a very sick man.

'We should have returned to Bere Forest to shelter for the winter like we always used to,' Sybil said.

'But the climate seemed good here,' Kas said. 'And there's been work for most of us. The farmer has been exceptionally kind. Should we call in a doctor?'

'He'll mend,' Sybil said knowingly, 'but I think he's pining for the mainland. Maybe it's time to leave the island.'

Rachel went cold. She didn't want to leave this idyllic place where she had found happiness, except for having a baby.

The matter was discussed at length when Carol had been put to bed behind the dividing curtain and Kas and Rachel were quiet and alone.

'I think we ought to get a doctor to visit Lemuel,' Rachel said.

'I agree, but we have to honour the elders' wishes, and Sybil seems to think Lemuel wants to return to Portsmouth. I know the island suits us, but there is a bleakness about it in winter with those biting winds from off the sea. His cough is worsening and we don't want him to develop pneumonia.'

'Goodness, no,' Rachel said in alarm. 'But we don't have to go too, do we?'

Kas inclined his head with a wry smile at his young wife. 'I'm afraid we do,' he said. '"Whither thou goest I will go. Thy people shall be my people",' he recited. 'We stick together. I know you dread returning where you might be recognised, but everything has changed now. You're over twenty-one and you're my wife. Your family would be overjoyed to see you again, I'm sure.'

'But they won't acknowledge my having become a gypsy.'

'As long as you don't want to return to them, there's no harm in a visit just to test the waters.'

'If we go to Portsmouth it's for Lemuel's sake,' she said. 'I don't think I'll ever have the courage to return home even for a visit, though I'd love to know how they all are.'

'Once we're settled again you can write to them and give a box number for them to reply. And who knows?' Kas added 'You might have better luck with a baby somewhere else?'

The idea was attractive for that reason alone but Rachel voiced her misgivings to Sybil when it was confirmed that they were all planning to move back to the mainland.

'The worst of the winter is almost over,' she said. 'And Lemuel seems to be improving, doesn't he?'

'He's much weaker, Rachel, and wants to leave the island. There'll be no arguments, we do what's best for him. The bronchitis has gained a hold and our remedies ain't working.'

'I thought perhaps Kas and I could stay here?'

Sybil screwed up her ageing eyes and stared intently at her.

'I can understand why you don't want to go,' she said in a low voice, 'but in the end 't'will be best.' Rachel watched as her appearance changed. She looked younger, more aggressive, as she added, 'The past needs to be remembered – there may be changes . . .'

Rachel realised that for that brief moment Sybil was 'seeing' – but was it into the future or the past? Fear clutched at Rachel's doubting heart but in a moment Sybil reverted to her normal self.

The sea was choppy and rain fell heavily as the ferries carried the group two by two back to the mainland. Rachel was convinced that the journey was doing Lemuel no good at all. He was well wrapped up in his waggon but his racking cough could be heard distinctly. When she took her turn at tending him she realised that he was getting weaker each day and by the time they reached the outskirts of Portsmouth his condition appeared to be serious.

'I think it's pneumonia,' Kas said. 'Rachel, you and I will take him in his waggon to the nearest hospital and the others can hold up on some waste ground until we can carry on to Bere Forest.'

It was evident that they were not particularly welcome as they entered the grounds of the hospital but when Kas spoke to a doctor stretcher bearers were summoned and Lemuel was rushed inside where he was given immediate attention. Kas and Rachel sat on a bench in the corridor waiting for the doctor's verdict.

'Poor Lemuel,' she said gloomily. 'He's been so good to everyone and always known what to do in a crisis. It'll be awful without him.'

'Who says we're going to be without him? He's tough, and with the right treatment may make a good recovery.'

It seemed like hours before the young doctor returned to them.

'What a wonderful gentleman,' he said with a smile. 'I'd say you got him here in time. He's weak and exhausted but tells me that he's been very well looked after and that it's his own fault. He's been working to hard on his history of the Romanies.'

'But how his he, Doctor?' Kas asked.

'A touch of pneumonia but with plenty of bed rest and the best medication we have there's every chance Mr Davidson will make a good recovery,.' He glanced at Rachel. 'Perhaps you could fetch a change of clothes and his toilet things as we'd like to keep him in for at least two weeks, I should think.' The doctor smiled and Rachel felt annoyed that he seemed to find the whole thing amusing. 'A most convenient way of travelling round,' he went on. 'You have all his possessions on the spot. Your caravan is the subject of much enthusiasm. So charming and brightly painted – but I'm afraid you can't leave it here.' He actually looked apologetic but Kas assured him that they would remove it once Lemuel was settled.

Rachel felt quite relieved as she ran back to the van and collected some of Lemuel's possessions. When she joined Kas again he said, 'They're taking him to the men's medical ward and we can go along too so that we know where he'll be.'

Swing doors opened and a trolley bearing the much loved Lemuel appeared. Rachel held his hand. 'It's going to be all right,' she said affectionately. 'You'll be in the best place and we'll be able to visit you.'

Lemuel squeezed her hand, then she felt that she was being scrutinised. Looking up into the porter's face, the never-to-be forgotten Adam Taylor, the shock was too much. She closed her eyes, wanting to believe it was he yet willing him away as she slid to the floor.

Chapter Fourteen

When Rachel recovered she found herself in a small waiting room where a nurse was undoing the top button of her coat and calling her name. Kas was there too looking as shocked as Rachel felt.

'Are you all right?' he asked.

Rachel nodded and was grateful for the cup of hot sweet tea a young probationer nurse brought her. The doctor came in and felt her pulse.

'A bit fast, and you're very pale,' he said. 'Are you sure you're all right?'

'I'll be fine,' she said in a small weak voice. 'I thought I saw someone I knew.'

'You did, Rachel.' Adam poked his head in at the doorway. Adam, the man she'd loved and wanted to marry, the man she had run away from. She took a sip of tea but the cup rattled in the saucer as she trembled with emotion. 'I'm sorry if seeing me here was too much for you – but seeing you again has given me a shock too.'

He came further into the small room – the same old Adam, his features kindly and sympathetic, his smile warm as he studied Rachel as if unable to believe his eyes.

'Well, if there's nothing else we can do for you,' the doctor said, 'we'll get back to work.' As he turned to go he added, 'And when you've rested awhile you can visit Mr Davidson.'

The nurse followed him out and Rachel was glad to be left alone with just Kas and Adam.

'Rachel,' Adam said as he closed the door and walked towards her eagerly, 'I can hardly believe it really is you.'

'Dressed up like a bloomin' gypsy?' Rachel mocked defiantly. 'That was how Beth Cropper described me.'

Adam looked puzzled. 'Beth Cropper? You've been with her?'

She shook her head. 'No, but we did meet up on the Isle of Wight.'

'You've been on the island all this time?' Adam frowned as if he found this too much to comprehend.

'Yes. I joined some lovely people, Romanies most of them, and as they were going to the Isle of Wight they agreed to take me with them. I was ill, you see, Adam – after all that had happened, I just couldn't face going home. I felt so ashamed.'

'No one blamed you for anything, Rachel. It was all a mess, a horrible misunderstanding.'

The colour began to return to her cheeks. Misunderstanding indeed, she thought. Then she looked at her beloved Kas. His eyes flashed warning signals, his expression was troubled, and Rachel realised she should have introduced them.

'This is my husband, Kas Dolan,' she said. 'But you knew I was getting married. I wrote to Mum and Dad to tell them. I hope Belinda got my present and card for her twenty-first birthday?'

'Yes, she did. It was such a relief to them when you sent the first postcard. They – we were all worried sick about you, Rachel, and as Belinda said it wasn't you who should have run away. She would have moved out until we got married.'

'And when was that?'

Adam looked down at his feet nervously. 'We waited to see if you could be found. Your mother put a notice in the paper asking you to return but when you didn't and they received your card – well, at least they knew you had come to no harm, and so we got married the following July. We've got a little boy, Billy, he's over three now.'

'Rachel,' Kas interrupted, 'don't you think we ought to go to the ward to see Lemuel?' It was clear that he felt ill at ease and was anxious to break up the conversation with Adam. Meeting this man from Rachel's past was as much of a shock to him as it was to her.

'Yes, of course. That's why we're here.'

There was so much Rachel wanted to talk to Adam about, so much she wanted to know about the family. Adam and Belinda had a little boy, it wasn't fair – it just wasn't fair.

'I'll take you to the men's ward, but before I do there's something you should know, Rachel. Your father is in that ward. He's been very ill indeed this winter.'

'Dad? Here? What a strange coincidence,' she said, but the way Adam averted his eyes warned her that her father must be in a very bad way.

'He . . . he's going to get better, isn't he?'

'That's not for me to say, but I'm sure he'll be overjoyed to see you again, and I know your mother and Belinda will.'

Rachel passed her hand across her brow. 'I don't think I've ever fainted before,' she said. 'It was silly.'

'Are you sure you're all right now?' Kas asked, taking her arm to help her up.

'Yes, perfectly,' she said, with eyes shining happily. 'Poor Lemuel will wonder what's happened to us.'

Adam hesitated, meeting Kas's gaze uncertainly, then led the way through long corridors.

'I think we'll see Lemuel settled in first then we'll visit your father, Rachel,' Kas said. 'Perhaps you should be prepared for a change in him.'

When they reached the swing doors to the ward Adam pushed them open and went at once to the desk to speak to the sister in charge, then he turned back to Rachel and Kas.

'Your friend is here, on the left behind these screens. Sister says you can only stay a minute or two as rest is important for him. I've explained that you're Mr Hunter's daughter and haven't seen him for a while so she said you could see him for just a few minutes as regular visiting time isn't until this afternoon at three.' Adam lowered his voice. 'She's a bit of a stickler for the rules but she's an excellent nursing sister. When you're ready your father is halfway down the ward on the right hand side. He's better than he was when he came in but hasn't improved as much as they'd hoped. I'm sure seeing you safe and well again will work wonders.'

Adam touched her arm lightly, nodded politely at Kas and left the ward.

Lemuel was already dozing. 'You can relax now and concentrate on getting well again,' Rachel said softly. 'I think we should leave you in their capable hands, but you only have to ask if there's anything you need, anything at all, and we'll bring it in for you.'

Lemuel opened his eyes. 'I know, child, but I want for nothing. I have a warm bed, perhaps just a bit warmer than in my van, but I shall miss your company. Yours, Sybil's, and of course you, dear boy. You've all been so very kind. A little rest is all I need and I'll be up and about again in no time.'

'Of all the people to bump into here it had to be Adam, the man I was going to marry,' Rachel said with a hint of excitement in her voice. 'He's a hospital porter and I'm afraid you'll think me very weak, Lemuel, but at the sight of him I fainted. He was just as surprised to see me and he's told me that my father is in this ward. Now, maybe, after all this time, I can make peace with my family.'

'God works in mysterious ways, his wonders to perform,' Lemuel said. 'Perhaps it was the right time to come back to the mainland and my sickness is a means of reuniting you with your family. I'm happy for you, child. Everything is going to be all right.'

'And you're going to get well very soon,' Rachel said with a bright smile. 'And I'm sure you'll be most comfortable here.'

He closed his weary eyes and Kas led Rachel away. She hesitated. How ill was her father? Would he recognise her? Would he be pleased to see her? She clutched at Kas's arm.

'I'm not sure I can go through with his,' she whispered suddenly. 'Perhaps it would be better to come back another time after I've seen Mum and Belinda?'

A rustle of starch and the ward sister was at her side.

'Taylor says you're Mr Hunter's daughter? I didn't know he had another one. You live away?' She didn't wait for any replies but strode swiftly down the ward, indicating that Rachel and Kas were to follow to where an elderly man sat propped up on pillows. His eyes were closed but at a glance Rachel could see that her father had changed little except that his colour was poor and his hair maybe a little greyer. 'Mr Hunter.' Sister shook his arm. 'A surprise for you. Your daughter's come to see you.'

Wally Hunter opened his eyes expectantly and the sister began to walk away. 'Just five minutes,' she said brusquely, 'it isn't official visiting time until three o'clock this afternoon.'

'Thank you, Sister,' Kas said, 'we'll only stay a minute.'

Rachel bent over her father and gently kissed his cheek. 'Dad,' she whispered, her voice cracking with emotion. Oh, how she loved him, and how vexed she was with herself for hurting him, but she couldn't put into words all that was in her heart. He neither spoke nor moved and when Rachel peered into his eyes they looked back at her, uncomprehending. 'It's me – Rachel,' she said. 'I've missed you terribly and I'm so sorry you're ill. You must get well quickly now that I'm home.' In her eagerness to show him how pleased she was she sat on the side of the bed and took both his hands between her own. For a moment she fancied she felt him squeeze in response and then Sister was back.

'Please don't sit on the bed,' she said stiffly, 'and I think that'll be enough for now.'

Rachel stood up, reluctantly letting her father's hands go, and as she kissed him again she noticed that a solitary tear trickled down his cheek.

'This is Kas, my husband,' she said. 'I do so want you to be friends.'

Kas took Wally's hand in his just for a second. 'It's nice to meet you, Sir,' he said. 'I hope we can visit you again soon.'

Kas led Rachel away. Neither spoke, nor were they aware of curious onlookers as they drove away in Lemuel's waggon to join up with the rest of the group.

Inside Sybil's van Rachel wept unashamedly. 'I don't think he knew who I was,' she wailed. 'I thought he squeezed my hand but he said nothing and showed no sign of pleasure at seeing me.'

'Don't fret, Rachel,' Sybil said. 'I daresay t'were a shock and now he'll lie there and wait for you to visit again. I've got a bit 'o stew on the stove so as soon as you'm ready we'll sit and eat.'

'We'll take Bella and the trap when we go back to the hospital,' Kas said. 'It'll be nice to meet your mother and sister, Rachel, but I'll make myself scarce after the introductions.'

'But I want you to stay with me,' she said.

'We can't leave the pony and trap unattended in the hospital grounds for long. It's better that we have our own transport then we can get back to Carol.'

'She's no trouble,' Sybil said. 'Precious and Charity will take her for a while when I needs a nap.'

'I'd like Mum and Belinda to see her,' Rachel said. 'But she isn't mine – and it's no good pretending she is.'

'But you will have your own child one day. Our baby will come in its own good time.'

Sybil clattered about with pots and pans and they sat down to eat. Rachel watched the clock on the wall, apprehensive yet eager to return to the hospital.

'I don't think we should get there too soon,' Kas said. 'Let your mother and sister get used to the idea of you turning up first.'

'I'm sure Adam will have got word to them somehow by now. I wonder where they live. Kingsmere would be too far for him to travel daily to work.'

'Are you sure you feel all right?' Kas said. 'You could go back another day. How d'you feel about meeting Adam after so long?'

'It was a surprise, but he hasn't changed.'

'And you don't hate him any more?'

Rachel looked up at the unusually acrimonious tone in Kas's voice.

'Nothing will change what happened,' she said softly. 'But what good does it do to harbour grudges?'

''Tis time to bury the past,' Sybil put in. 'You're all older and wiser now – and families need each other. I jest knows you ma is going to be overjoyed to see you, Rachel.' She sniffed as she often did when something bothered her. 'Hopes your pa recovers soon.'

Rachel was too bothered by events herself to notice Sybil's uneasiness but as they drove off in the trap she felt a vague queasiness come over her. She prayed she wouldn't faint again. She'd never done so in her life before, why should she have done today? Concern over Lemuel, she supposed, added to which was the surprise of coming face to face with Adam Taylor as well as the unexpected blow of finding her father in hospital too.

By the time they reached the hospital Rachel knew that she was about to be ill and she had to make a dash for the nearest lavatory. She looked red-eyed and putty-coloured when she rejoined Kas.

'Rachel, you shouldn't have come, you look awful,' he said.

'It's all right. It's just the emotional shock. Let's get to the ward and get it over with. I . . . I can't help wondering . . . will they be pleased to see me?'

'Of course they will,' he reassured her as he put his arm round her, and they walked the long corridors in silence.

As they turned off the main corridor and went into the passageway leading to the men's medical ward Rachel saw her mother and Belinda outside Sister's office. Rachel disengaged herself from Kas's arm and ran forward. But a few yards short of them she stopped. Her mother was crying and Belinda was comforting her. Rachel's feet moved slowly forward in spite of her subconscious telling her to turn back. Then Belinda saw her.

'*You*!' she accused in a tight aggressive whisper. 'Why couldn't you stay away? On top of everything else, how could you do this to Dad?'

'Do what? Oh, Belinda, I've wanted to see you all so often – tell me what's the matter?'

'Dad's had a stroke – a really bad one. He can't talk or move – and it's all your fault! You should never have visited him without giving us a chance to warn him,' Belinda said.

Phoebe turned then and after staring at Rachel through tear-filled eyes held out her arms. Rachel, the unwanted child with the hideous birthmark whom she had accepted as a gift from God, and whom she still loved in spite of everything, fell into them with pitiful sobs. Neither was capable of speaking. There was so much mutual love and understanding in their hearts.

Belinda's gaze moved towards Kas. So this was Rachel's husband. Tall, dark and extremely manly, she noticed. But for the fact that he was a gypsy Belinda had to admit that her twin sister had done very well for herself. Or was he just a stop gap until such time as she could return to take Adam away from her?

'Mum, oh, Mum – maybe Dad'll get better,' Rachel said croakily. 'I'm sorry – really sorry if it's my fault.'

'I doubt if it's anyone's fault, Rachel. He was a sick man. Years of chest trouble had weakened him, and he had hardening of the arteries so the doctor said.' Phoebe dried her eyes as she held Rachel at arm's length. 'Just to see you again, my dear, *dear* Rachel – I can hardly believe it.' She wept again and Rachel wept tears of relief.

Then she took her mother's arm. 'I want you to meet Kas, Mum,' she said. 'He and Sybil have been so kind to me and we're very happy. Lemuel, the leader of the Romany group who found me, is quite ill. We brought him in yesterday. He's a lovely man. Little did I think that Dad would be here too, let alone Adam working in this hospital.'

Kas shook hands with Phoebe Hunter, a strong, warm clasp which gave her a measure of reassurance, but Belinda seemed reluctant to shake her brother-in-law's hand. All kinds of suspicions were racing round in her brain. Were they really man and wife according to the church or had Rachel lied to them when she said they were legally married? It wasn't Romany custom, she knew. If they weren't legally married . . . Belinda hadn't yet recovered from the shock of Adam coming home for his dinner with the exciting news of seeing Rachel again. He would never discuss why he had changed his mind about marrying her, and Belinda could never quite convince herself that his affections for her were genuine. But they'd been happy, especially when Billy came along – until now when she felt that their future was threatened.

'Rachel has talked about you always,' Kas was saying. 'I'm delighted to meet you both but I wish it was in happier circumstances.' He turned to his wife. 'I'll go to visit Lemuel in case he thinks we're not coming. You can join me when you're ready.'

'Why are you standing out here?' Rachel asked her mother when Kas had left them. 'Can't we see Dad? Visiting time will soon be over.'

'He doesn't know any of us,' Belinda said abruptly. There was a degree of guilt in her short-temper. Since she and Adam had moved to live near the hospital in Portsmouth their visits to Kingsmere had become much less frequent and she knew there was no valid excuse, while at least Rachel had a legitimate reason for running away from Kingsmere. 'The doctor is still with him,' Belinda explained. 'Dad had the stroke shortly after Adam returned after dinner. We were only allowed in for a couple of minutes.'

'Oh dear, this is terrible,' Rachel said. 'You're right, Belinda, I shouldn't have rushed to see him, though they only allowed me a couple of minutes this morning as it wasn't visiting time.'

'It would have been a shock to see you again whenever you turned up,' her sister said sarcastically.

'But I'm sure it pleased him to know that you came, dear,' Phoebe intervened.

'He wept,' Rachel said. 'I actually made him cry . . .' She sobbed again into her handkerchief.

'Crying won't help now,' Belinda said. 'I doubt that he was pleased to see you after all the heartache you caused Mum. Dad would never allow us even to speak your name after you desecrated the church and ran off.' She had no intention of letting her sister forget her shame.

Phoebe put a restraining hand on Belinda's arm. 'That's enough,' she said, softly but sharply. 'That's all in the past now. Naturally we were both grieved at what happened and we still don't know what caused such an upset. I doubt if any of us are entirely free from blame, Belinda. Your father loves you both and we must be happy that we're back as a family again.'

'As long as she doesn't expect us all to change into gypsies,' Belinda said scornfully.

Rachel could hardly believe there was so much hatred in her sister's voice when it was she who had fared best out of the two of them. Adam was evidently working hard to provide for his wife and child.

The swing doors opened and closed behind two doctors, the young one Rachel had seen earlier accompanied by an older dark-suited consultant. There was a serious expression on their faces which brought the three woman instant consternation.

'My husband,' Phoebe said falteringly, 'is he going to be all right?'

The older man placed his hand on her shoulder.

'I'm very sorry, my dear. There isn't anything we can do now. So sad, just when he seemed to be making a recovery. Strokes take people in different ways. Another one may follow quickly or he may linger, though he'll never be able to walk or do things for himself. For the moment we must just wait and see. By all means visit him, though, and talk to him. We can't be sure how much people can hear in this semi-conscious condition.'

Phoebe was too distressed to ask further questions and the doctors went with the ward sister into her office.

'Can we all go in?' Rachel asked.

'Of course, dear. It might help him to know we're beside him altogether.'

'She's the cause of all this,' Belinda hissed. 'I reckon it would be better if she stayed away.'

Phoebe put a hand on each girl's arm. 'We're here to help your father,' she said solemnly. 'Quarrelling won't do that. We must try to support one another.'

Rachel looked at Belinda apologetically but her sister glowered back. Phoebe went first and kissed the man she had married nearly forty years ago. He was a good man, honest and upright, a devoted husband and father, though he had never seemed quite the same after Rachel had disgraced the name of Hunter. Phoebe had pleaded desperately hard with him on the runaway's behalf for forgiveness, but Wally had accused her of spoiling Rachel at Belinda's expense.

Phoebe was sure she hadn't. Both girls had been treated the same but who else was there to try to make up to Rachel for that awful birthmark? They didn't know anything of her background or where she'd come from so couldn't be prepared for such an outburst as she'd displayed in Wickham Church. Phoebe blamed herself. Somehow she'd failed Rachel over the affair with Adam Taylor. It had all been a nightmare which had caused tongues to wag and Wally just hadn't been able to bear that. Now, just when things had quietened down and the past was forgotten, here was Rachel, looking more mature but very happy with her handsome husband. If seeing her again had brought on Wally's stroke it was a high price to pay to have this rebel child back, Phoebe thought as she gazed at her beloved husband. She felt so helpless, there was nothing even she could do for him now. He was there but not there, alive yet dead to all that was going on around him. He looked pale and drawn and Phoebe seemed quite unable to speak the words she had rehearsed.

Rachel stood aside to let Belinda kiss her father.

'It's all right, Dad,' she whispered close to his ear. 'We won't let anything else upset you. Just nod or lift a finger if you'd like her to go away.'

Rachel went cold and a sick feeling caught in her stomach. She watched for some sign of response from the father she loved so dearly but there was none. Belinda went on whispering and then with a sigh stepped back.

'Suppose it's your turn,' she said to Rachel, 'but if he doesn't acknowledge us, it isn't likely he will you.'

Rachel hesitated. How she wished it was just her and Kas here. Earlier today her father had acknowledged her and squeezed her hand, now she was afraid of causing any further agitation. The screens were round each side of the bed and as Belinda stood back to allow Rachel access to the bedside she was acutely aware of the heat of her sister's anger. But she bent over her father and kissed him on each cheek.

'It's me again, Dad – Rachel,' she said softly. 'I'm sorry to find you so poorly. We all want you to get well quickly. I know I have so much to thank you and Mum for, and I'm sorry I had to go away in disgrace. I hope you've forgiven me? You must know I wouldn't have hurt either of you for the world but I was devastated when Adam jilted me. I could have borne it if it had been for any other girl, but my own twin sister . . .' Rachel could no longer cry. She felt stronger now and able humbly to voice her case, as she knew Lemuel would wish.

Rachel lifted her father's frail hand and held it between her own. Yes, sure enough, his fingers moved. There *was* life there. She freed his hand so that she could cup his face lovingly and as she gazed down into his face his eyelids fluttered for the briefest of moments.

'I felt his fingers move,' she said, turning to her mother. 'And he's just fluttered his eyelids. He can hear us all right. Now he'll get stronger, I'm sure.' She pressed her cheek against his, willing him to fight, willing him to forgive her. 'Dearest Dad,' she murmured, 'get well again. Please, for me.'

It was Kas who gently persuaded her to leave. 'Let your mother and sister have the rest of the visiting time, Rachel,' he said quietly, sensing Belinda's hostility. 'We can come again. Lemuel is anxious to see you before the others get here.'

The others! Yes, Rachel had been and still was part of a much larger family than just the Hunters. She hugged her mother as she left her father's beside and after a few minutes with Lemuel who was much brighter and rested, Sybil and Precious arrived.

The nurses soon insisted that only two visitors were allowed for each patient, so Rachel and Kas went outside to find Carol and some of the other children who they looked after while the adults took turns to visit Lemuel. The time passed quickly and a loud bell echoed through the corridors when four o'clock came. Lemuel's flock gathered with much chatter over the welfare of their beloved leader, but when Rachel saw her mother and Belinda emerge from the main doors she ran to them.

'Did he respond to you, Mum?' she asked. 'Do you think he'll be all right?'

'You're deluding yourself, my dear,' Phoebe said solemnly. There's not much life left in his body.'

'But, Mum, it's his brain,' Rachel said. 'It's what's in his brain that matters.'

'Well, don't kid yourself that there are any kind thoughts for you,' Belinda said.

'I just want to get home and have a cup of tea.'

'How are you going to get back to Kingsmere?' Rachel asked. 'We've got a pony and trap. We could take you.'

Belinda scoffed. 'Pony and trap! You think Mum would be seen dead with a group of filthy gypsies!'

'Excuse me,' Kas put in as he joined them. 'True Romanies are never filthy. Because we choose to live a nomadic life doesn't mean we are any less clean and honest than you. I suggest you come and stay with Rachel and me to see for yourself. Mrs Hunter, you'd be most welcome to remain with us while your husband is in hospital.'

'Mum's staying with us,' Belinda snapped aggressively.

'And where is that?' Rachel dared to ask.

'Just a few roads away, within walking distance.'

'Who's looking after your little boy then?' Rachel enquired. 'I'd love to see him, Belinda.'

'Of course you would, dear,' Phoebe said in an attempt to pour oil on troubled waters. 'But perhaps another day. He's with a neighbour for now.'

'We'll see you tomorrow then,' Rachel said, kissing her mother's cheek. 'Lemuel will have to stay in hospital for at least another ten days.' She hesitated, not wanting to leave without some kind of reconciliation with her sister, but Kas tugged at her sleeve.

'If there's anything we can do, please let us know,' he said to Phoebe. 'We shall be making camp on Portsdown Hill while Lemuel's in hospital.'

Belinda guided her mother in the opposite direction. It was some while before Rachel felt calm.

The next morning while Kas was outside feeding the horses Rachel washed and dressed Carol. She was still experiencing a feeling of nausea and found Carol's exuberance difficult to handle.

'You'd better go and find Daddy,' she said as she lifted the child down from the table. 'A run before breakfast might burn off some of your energy and give you an appetite. Tell Daddy it'll be ready in ten minutes.'

Rachel helped Carol on with her coat and hat but when she opened the van door a surprise awaited her. Kas and Adam were a few yards away in earnest conversation.

'Daddy! Daddy! Breakfast in ten minutes,' Carol shouted eagerly as she ran down the steps and flung herself at Kas.

Rachel had to support herself on the framework of the van. Now Adam would believe that Carol was really their child – but what was he doing here in the camp at this time of the morning?

The two men exchanged glances when they saw Rachel at the door of the van.

'Come in, Adam,' Kas said as he hoisted Carol up in his arms.

'What brings you here?' Rachel said in a husky voice. She felt sick to her stomach and everything began to swim. 'How did you manage to find us?' She forced herself to go back inside the waggon and sit down. She closed her eyes, knowing there was bad news to come yet not wanting to believe it.

Adam went up the steps two at a time and stood inside, looking round, noting everything about the interior of their home.

'This is very pleasant,' he said. 'I'd no idea there would be so much room.'

'I'm afraid I haven't tidied round yet,' Rachel said. 'I was just getting breakfast.'

'Rachel,' Adam said, and came to stand directly in front of her, 'I'm here because the news is grave.'

'It's about Dad?'

He nodded. 'He had another stroke in the early hours and I'm afraid he died about five o'clock. I'm so sorry Rachel, but I'm glad fate intervened and brought you to the hospital. At least you saw him.'

'But . . . I . . . killed him.'

'No, of course you didn't,' Adam said quickly. 'He was a sick man. Your mother told me to tell you that you mustn't blame yourself. The doctors have said that it could have happened at any time.'

'But Belinda will always say it was my fault. If only Lemuel hadn't needed to go into hospital. Why didn't we go to Southampton, Kas? This might never have happened.'

'And we might not have met up again. It had to be, Rachel,' Adam said. 'And for your mother's sake too – perhaps most of all for her sake. She'll need you now.'

'She's got Belinda.'

'She'll need you both, Rachel.'

'Did Dad manage to talk – did he say anything?'

'No. There was no response while we were there. I'm afraid you must have imagined what you thought you felt and saw because it was what you wanted so badly. If you hadn't seen him when you did it might have been too late.'

Rachel buried her face in her hands and wept.

'Can I offer you a cup of tea, Adam?' Kas asked. 'I'm sure Rachel needs one. Darling, I'm sorry that this happened but your father was well over sixty.'

'That doesn't seem old though, does it?'

'His chest had bothered him for a number of years,' Adam said.

'Could the shock of what I did and then me turning up unexpectedly really have caused a stroke.'

'Most unlikely,' Adam said, trying to be as prudent as he could. 'I've got time off to help your mother and Belinda arrange the funeral,' he hurried on. 'You'll both come, of course? Mrs Hunter's expecting you to. What about the little one? I didn't know you had a daughter.'

Rachel looked at Kas.

'She's not really ours,' he said. 'We wish she was. Unfortunately Rachel has had three miscarriages, but her turn will come.' He smiled warmly. 'Carol's mother was a friend of ours. It's a sad story. When she died she left a note asking us to bring her up as our own which we've been pleased to do. One day our children will be her brothers and sisters.' The blackened kettle began to sing and Kas warmed the pot. 'Yes, we shall be at Mr Hunter's funeral if you're sure that's what Rachel's mother wants? No need to worry about Carol, there's plenty of our folk who will mind her.'

'Look,' Adam began, 'I'm sorry Belinda has been difficult. I hope you can find it in your heart to excuse her bad manners. She doesn't mean to be rude but she's been worried about her father and it was a shock seeing you again, Rachel – for all of us. It's your right to be at your father's funeral. I'll let you know as soon as we know the time.'

'Will it be at Kingsmere?' she asked.

'Yes. Mr Hunter's wish was to be buried in the churchyard at Wickham. Apparently a will has been left to be read by his solicitor after the burial.'

Rachel felt numb. It was all so final. Why couldn't it have been Lemuel who had died? He was older, there were no blood relatives who would mourn his passing, and no one would have blamed her. She blinked away more tears hating herself for such selfish, ungracious thoughts, but no matter how anyone tried to comfort her and exonerate her from blame she knew she must accept that she was partly responsible for her father's death, and the guilt would weigh heavily on her. Kas passed her a cup of tea and she took it without realising what was taking place around her. Kas and Adam talked amicably but after one or two sips of the hot sweet liquid Rachel had to rush outside to vomit.

'I'd better leave you,' Adam said as Kas led Rachel back inside the van. 'It's a rotten business, and I'm sorry to be the bearer of bad news. Belinda and Mrs Hunter need me, there's so much to arrange. I'll let you know about the day and time as soon as I can.'

'We shall be calling to see Lemuel every day,' Kas said. 'To save you coming out here again you can leave a message with him or we might see you there. It's hard work cycling up the hill.'

'Yes, I'll see you at the hospital, later today or maybe tomorrow.'

Rachel watched him walk away pushing his bicycle, with Kas in earnest conversation and Carol jumping alongside. The years rolled back. If only she could roll them back still further to when she and Adam had been happily engaged. But there was no going back. He was married to Belinda and she was married to Kas. Her mind spun like a top with confusing emotions. If only . . . if only . . .

It was a grey February morning, frost crackling beneath their feet and the sky overhead thickening with snow clouds as Kas secured black plumes on Bella's head. She stood quiet as if she knew that this was no joy ride but a solemn occasion. Rachel looked drawn and pale in her black coat and woollen shawl which she had draped over her black hat to protect her ears from the icy north-east wind. As she got up in the trap she turned to raise a gloved hand to Sybil and Carol who were watching from the window of Sybil's van. Kas got up beside her looking every inch the country gentleman in a thick dark coat and sombre grey trilby hat with a black band which he'd borrowed from Lemuel. He put a thick rug over Rachel's knees before they set off at a trot. Sybil had insisted that she have a bowl of thick nourishing broth, made with her usual concoction of herbs, to stave off the nausea which Rachel had experienced ever since their arrival in Portsmouth.

Sybil's mouth was tight-lipped as she let the curtain fall. She had sensed trouble for Rachel but happiness too. What was taking place was out of her jurisdiction but she feared that there was more trouble to come before the girl who had become like a daughter to her would be truly happy. She couldn't rightly say what emotion it was she saw in Rachel's dark eyes. A mixture of sadness, torture and longing – but for whom?

The tops of the hedgerows glistened with frozen dew as Rachel recognised familiar surroundings. Her emotions were mixed, not of sadness, torture and longing but a strange kind of relief at coming home. She saw barren fields, powdery white waiting for spring planting, trees with branches like horny brown fingers pointing skywards, and evergreen bushes and shrubs brightly coloured with red berries. As they neared Wickham the local flock of rooks was making the most of the wind to swerve and dive, chasing each other, cawing endlessly with their mournful chatter as if in sympathy with Rachel's grief.

It seemed ironic to Kas that he and Rachel's former fiancé could have become instant pals in these unexpected circumstances. Kas wished he had taken an instant dislike to Adam Taylor but the truth was he had felt an affinity with him at their first meeting. He searched in vain for some logical explanation for Adam treating Rachel the way he had but he seemed the most unlikely person to behave in such a manner. Kas was doing his best to comfort her in her sorrow. He was anxious for today's sad events to be over and done with, for Lemuel to get well enough so that they could travel on, but a sense of foreboding plagued him. Of course, he feared Rachel becoming too nostalgic about the past. He watched her and Adam together, so kindly disposed to each other, with no apparent rancour over what had happened four years earlier. It didn't seem quite natural to him. Surely Rachel should have experienced some embarrassment and bitterness at Adam's change of heart? But the only bitterness evident was between the two sisters. Kas could hardly credit how totally unalike they were in looks. Belinda was of slighter build and fairer complexion, decidedly pretty, but her round blue eyes could cut as sharply as the blade of a knife. He couldn't help wondering whether she hadn't played some devious role in past events. It was clear that she saw her sister's return to the mainland as an intrusion. Did she, like Kas, have reason to be apprehensive about the future? He vowed that he would do all in his power to get Rachel away from this area as fast as he could after today and spare her any more agony.

They had arranged with Adam that they would only travel to the outskirts of Wickham and await the funeral cortège down a small farm track which Rachel knew of, and it wasn't long before they heard the horses and carriages coming through the lane. Kas removed his hat as the procession passed and then urged Bella forward to join at the rear. He felt that Rachel at least should have been invited to travel with her mother and sister in their carriage, but she had chosen to be an outcast, a gypsy, and so must bear the consequences, he supposed.

The village church was full as the much respected and loved resident of neighbouring Kingsmere was brought inside by estate workers acting as bearers and the service commenced. Rachel felt quite faint as she once more relived her rebellious actions in this sacred place. She sat down quickly, pulling a veil over her face, but all eyes turned on her and Kas with curiosity. As she was tall there was no way of hiding. Perhaps word hadn't got out that she was going to be there? Her reappearance caused hushed whispers and a constant turning of heads.

The service over, family, local villagers and friends filed out to the open graveside. Phoebe kept turning round, trying to urge Rachel and Kas to move closer to the family, but Rachel kept her distance, her head bowed against inquisitive glances. A handful of earth was thrown on to the coffin. Rachel saw Adam place an arm round her mother's and Belinda's shoulders to support them, and then the family stood back as people paid their last respects. Rachel waited until last. She wanted to refrain from giving Belinda any cause for complaint. As they moved forward Kas took a small posy of snowdrops from his large pocket which Rachel held for a moment and then let slip from her fingers on to the coffin of carved oak. Her father would have been proud of it.

'I'm sorry,' she whispered as she bade him goodbye.

At Calder Cottage the tiny rooms were filled to overflowing not so much with relatives as friends. During Rachel's absence over the past four years her grandparents had passed away at a great age. Strange, she thought, that her father had died while still a comparatively young man, which only confirmed her belief that it must be her fault. A glass of home-made wine was offered but Rachel was forced to decline and could merely pick at the sandwiches and other delicacies which followed. A cup of tea went down gratefully and as time passed people began to forget the reason for Rachel's hurried departure. They were curious about Kas and word had soon circulated that there was a child. No one dared ask outright but Rachel suspected that there was speculation as to Carol's parentage. If it pleased them to think that she had been compelled to marry Kas because she was pregnant then she doubted that anything she said would make them think otherwise.

It was almost three o'clock when Phoebe diplomatically explained that the solicitor was anxious to deal with legal matters which involved just the family, and get back to his head office in Winchester. Belinda and her mother stood at the front door and thanked the visitors for coming. Rachel was buttoning her coat too.

'Can I come to see you, Mum?' she asked as she hugged her mother.

'This is still your home, Rachel dear,' Phoebe said. 'But you can't go yet, you're family too.'

'I'm sure I'm not needed so it's better if Kas and I leave now.'

'No, Rachel,' Adam intervened. 'Mr Fisher insists that we must all be here.'

'Kas too?'

'He's your husband, isn't he?' Belinda said sharply.

'Of course.'

'Well then?'

'I would much rather we didn't stay,' Rachel said. 'I feel positive there's nothing that involves me, and if there was Mr Fisher can always contact me later.'

'I have a letter your father expressly wishes me to read at this time,' Mr Fisher said. 'I have no knowledge of its contents but it is my duty to carry out Mr Hunter's requests.'

The solicitor was a small thin man. He was a pillar of the church and local community in Wickham but an unfriendly type. It was fairly evident that he didn't care for children or younger people and rumour had it that he had lost his job as a magistrate owing to the unwarranted harshness of his sentencing of young offenders.

The cottage seemed unnaturally cold and almost sinister after the other mourners had left. Phoebe sat with just her two daughters and sons-in-law, waiting with apprehension as Mr Fisher untied a sheaf of papers. He spread them out on the highly polished mahogany table and then looked from one to the other over the top of his spectacles.

'Most of Mr Hunter's estate goes to his wife, Phoebe Hunter. The property, Calder Cottage, which he purchased from Squire, and two cottages at Minstead in the New Forest which had recently come into his possession on the death of his own father are now yours, Mrs Hunter. All properties are to be bequeathed to your daughter, Belinda Taylor, to be equally shared between her and her offspring after your demise which I trust will be many years hence.' He paused to smile reassuringly at Phoebe before he went on, 'There is a bequest of three hundred pounds for you at this time, Belinda Taylor.'

Mr Fisher shuffled his feet nervously under the table as he then withdrew a sealed envelope.

'I will now read Wally's letter,' he said as if this might not be considered a truly legal document. 'It is specifically intended for his wife and daughters.' After coughing and taking a quick glance at the short letter in his hand his brow puckered in a frown. For a minute it seemed as if he couldn't go on and he visibly paled as he read aloud:

'My dears, anything I have been able to leave you has been obtained by sheer hard work. My life and love have gone into everything I have ever done for you both. Although I have become very fond of Adam Taylor as my son-in-law I would have wished for someone else for you, Belinda, after the scandal of his broken engagement with Rachel, but I trust he will be a good husband to you and will make you happy.'

Mr Fisher swallowed hard and tried to glance further along the page. 'Rachel, our wayward cuckoo in the nest, we took you in as a favour when you were just a few days old, doing all in our power to bring you up as a God-fearing, honest, hard-working young woman and look how you have repaid us. I was never able to love you as my own daughter though I did try for Phoebe's sake. Your mother did love and protect you, always loyal to the promise that she would treat you like Belinda's twin sister and she never thought of you as anything but her own child. Doing what you did and then disappearing for several days without a word caused your mother terrible anguish which I cannot forget. I hope someone will find you one day and pass this letter on so that you understand why you are not legally entitled to a legacy, and I cannot think of one good reason why I should make an exception.'

All eyes turned to Rachel. Phoebe gasped and cried into her handkerchief. Rachel's face went stiff, and turned the colour of stone.

Chapter Fifteen

No one heard the rest of the contents of Wally's letter. Even Mr Fisher was only vaguely aware of the words he read aloud as the painful silence seemed to drown his voice. Phoebe kept her head bowed as she continued to sob.

'How could Wally do such a thing?' she wailed after several minutes. 'We were never to tell anyone, least of all you girls.' She looked up with fear and pleading in her expression. 'What have you done?' she accused the solicitor. 'Why couldn't you have given me the letter first? There was no need for this to have come out – *ever* – let alone now. As if it isn't enough that Wally has gone . . .' She was inconsolable.

Rachel felt as if her brain had frozen. Even Belinda remained with her head lowered but Adam looked apologetically towards Kas.

'God!' he said. 'This is terrible. Kas, Wally was a good man, really he was. He probably wrote that letter in the heat of the moment when he was upset about Rachel running off. I'm sure he didn't mean to be so callous. It's so uncharacteristic of him.'

Suddenly Belinda ran from her chair and placed her arms round Rachel.

'We *are* sisters,' she exclaimed, 'we are! I can't believe this story. How can it be true?' She hugged Rachel as if she really meant what she was saying and kissed her cheek. 'Oh, my dear, *dear* Rachel, I'm so sorry for all the hurt we caused you. It was Adam's fault, he just couldn't wait. I'll share my legacy with you. Mother, I can, can't I? Dad was wrong, wasn't he?'

Mr Fisher stood up. 'I don't think there is any way in which I can be of further use to you, Mrs Hunter – not at this precise moment. I shall be available, of course, should you need any advice – any at all.'

Phoebe got to her feet and held on to the edge of the table. She felt weak and utterly weary. She and Wally thought they had put the past behind them skilfully after the retirement of the Fletcher sisters who were the only people in the world who knew that Rachel wasn't their own child. Whatever had possessed him to do this terrible thing?

'No, Mr Fisher,' she said quietly. 'I don't think I shall need your services again. I suppose I can't blame you, you did what you were asked to do – and a right hornet's nest you've disturbed!' She ushered him to the front door. 'Poor Rachel, so upset when Adam jilted her and now to discover she's not really Belinda's sister. Not my true daughter. Somehow I must make her understand that I love her just as much as the day I agreed to pretend she was mine.'

Mr Fisher hovered on the door step. 'It sounds to me as if you may have been persuaded into making an unwise decision many years ago, Mrs Hunter. Now if Rachel had been legally adopted by you and your late husband, she could have contested the will.'

'I don't think what we did matters to anyone but our family. I shall see that Rachel gets her share, don't you worry, and please, not a word to anyone, especially local people.'

Mr Fisher leaned closer to Phoebe. 'May I be permitted to ask – if it isn't too impertinent – who was Rachel's father?'

Phoebe very nearly spat in his face with anger at his inference. 'No, you may not! I don't know who either of her parents were and if I did I wouldn't tell you. Because of her disfigurement she was unwanted. That's what we were told when she was brought to us under cover of darkness. I had just given birth to Belinda after fifteen years of hoping. We made an arrangement to bring Rachel up as Belinda's twin sister, which we did. Where we lived then in the New Forest no one ever questioned anything so there's no reason for you to either, Mr Fisher. I didn't give birth to her and Wally was not her father. Whether or not she was illegitimate I cannot tell you. A poor wee mite born with a blemish and rejected. Maybe if they'd realised that the strawberry mark would fade in time they'd have kept her, who knows? I know nothing of her background or circumstances, and I'll thank you to keep this whole matter in confidence. Good day to you, Mr Fisher.'

Phoebe almost pushed him out of the way as she closed the heavy oak door with a resounding thud. She stood with her back against it, the force of her rage having exhausted her. Several minutes passed before she could return to the parlour where Rachel was pacing the floor. The other three were trying to pacify her.

'I don't care who your parents were,' Kas was assuring her, 'it doesn't alter the fact that you're my wife and I love you. Isn't that enough?'

'My birth certificate, Mum,' Rachel demanded. 'I need it. The real one. I managed to get a copy from Somerset House when I got married but it was just a brief one. There must be some details on the genuine one.'

'Rachel, I'm sorry, my dear. First the shock of seeing your father in hospital, dying, and now this. I don't know anything about where you came from except that you were brought to us shortly after Belinda was born. The births were registered together and you became legally Belinda's twin sister. That's what it says on your birth certificate and you must accept it.' Phoebe sat down in the nearest chair. 'I can't understand how your father could so such a thing. He never talked even to me about his financial affairs so I had no idea that he'd even written this letter let alone altered his will. I can't imagine when he did it. He never said a word. Well, he wouldn't because he would have expected me to try to persuade him not to. I was always convinced you'd turn up again one day, Rachel.' She covered her face with her hands. 'Now I almost wish you hadn't.'

Kas placed a gentle hand on Phoebe's shoulder. 'Aren't we getting this out of all proportion, Mrs Hunter?' he said. 'Money isn't important. I work hard to keep Rachel and Carol as comfortable as I know how. I had some property left to me, down in Christchurch. I don't use the rental money, it goes into the bank and is kept for repairs. It's an investment for us and our children.'

'I never want children,' Rachel screamed. 'My childhood was wrecked by that awful birthmark. I always wondered why Belinda was so much prettier than me, and now I discover that I must have been born out of wedlock to some unknown woman. What was I thinking of to marry a gypsy? I never stopped to think of what the children would think of their heritage.'

'Rachel, please,' he begged. 'This isn't like you. What you've heard today makes no different to us.'

'Of course it does,' she said impatiently. 'I've got to find out where I came from and who my real parents are.'

Adam went to the sideboard and poured some spirits into a glass. 'Here,' he said, compelling Rachel to take the glass.

'What is it?' she asked, sniffing.

'Brandy, it'll calm your nerves. And you must calm down, Rachel. This has been a shock to everyone.' Not to me, he thought, and please God she'll never find out who her real father was. 'You must put it right out of your mind,' he went on. 'It happened years ago. No one can know the truth of the matter so it's best that you try to forget.'

'How can I? How would you feel if you suddenly discovered that the people you'd thought of as your parents weren't related at all?'

'I was in that very position,' Kas said. 'Josh and Merle were not my real parents, and I know very little about my mother or my father but

I'm grateful to Josh and Merle for all they did for me. How can it help you to know who they were, Rachel? Surely it's more important to be grateful to the folk who love you and gave you security and a home than to worry about your true parentage?'

'But they may still be alive,' she persisted. 'And if they are, I'd like to meet them.'

'And cause them as much of a shock as you've had?' Kas asked. 'I do understand how painful this has been for you, but what good will it do anyone to delve into the past?'

'I – I *need* to know, Kas,' she said with feeling.

'We're going home now,' he said abruptly. 'It's been a long and trying day for your mother. She needs a little peace.'

'I'm going to stay with her,' Rachel announced. 'I *will* find out who I am – I *will*!'

'Mum's coming back to Portsmouth with us,' Belinda said. 'We'll look after her.'

Phoebe held up her hand to silence them all.

'I want to be left on my own,' she said softly. 'I need some time to be quiet, and you would all do well to do the same. I'm sure dear Wally never meant to cause such a stir. He must have had his reasons and I want to read his letter in peace to try to understand. He was never a vindictive man. Maybe he was wise in his thinking and anticipated some future trouble for Rachel, being that we didn't know anything about her background.'

'But it's what we are, Mrs Hunter,' Adam said politely, 'not where we come from that counts. Rachel has never done anything wrong in her life to deserve this.'

'Hah!' she scoffed. 'Only desecrated God's house and then run away, which led my father – or the man I thought was my father – to write such a letter. He's not only hurt me but you, Belinda, and Adam and Kas.'

'It's only surprised us, Rachel,' Belinda said, 'not hurt us. As Kas says it doesn't make any difference to any of us. He is your husband and if it doesn't affect him then why should it worry you?'

Rachel stared at her sister. Now she knew that her childish jealousies had not been without foundation. Belinda, the pretty one with golden sunshine hair and baby blue eyes. The delicate one who was always had the best of everything and the most attention. The one who had stolen the heart of the man she loved. Rachel's gaze moved to Adam. He wasn't as handsome or strong-looking as Kas but there was a genuine warmth in his expression which she felt sure was for her alone. It wasn't pity. His cheeks flushed at her scrutiny.

'You'll help me find my parents, won't you, Adam?' Rachel asked in a low husky voice.

He averted his eyes and shook his head.

'No, Rachel. It would be like looking for a needle in a haystack. Where would you begin?'

'You must put such ideas right out of your head this minute!' Kas's voice was loud and clear. 'We're going home, Rachel. Bella needs feeding and it'll soon be dark. The roads are icy enough as it is.'

'But someone should stay with Mum,' Rachel said.

'We can stay,' Belinda offered. 'Our neighbour will understand.'

'No,' Phoebe said. 'Can't I make you understand I want to be by myself. Tonight, tomorrow, and probably for several days after that.'

Belinda went to fetch their coats from the bedroom and they sheepishly prepared to leave, not entirely certain that Phoebe was capable of knowing what she wanted or needed at that moment.

Rachel hugged her mother as she wept for the umpteenth time that day.

'When can I see you again, Mum?'

'Give me a few days, dear,' Phoebe said. 'Perhaps you could all come to tea on Sunday? We shall have had time to calm down by then.'

'I've got a better idea,' Belinda said. 'Why don't you all come to our house to tea? Your little girl can play with Billy. They're about the same age.'

'Carol is not my little girl and I shall make sure she grows up knowing that,' Rachel said adamantly.

'Thanks very much for the invitation,' Kas said. 'We'd be pleased to come. We'll be visiting Lemuel in hospital in the afternoon anyway.'

'Is he likely to be there much longer?' Phoebe asked.

'He's making good progress. The rest has done him good so hopefully in about a week they'll let him come home. Come along, Rachel. Carol will be missing us.'

She was reluctant to leave her mother, and it was hard for her to think of Phoebe as anything but that.

'Your parents are the people who rear you,' Kas said as explanations were made to Sybil on their return to camp. 'It doesn't matter who gave birth to you. Mr and Mrs Hunter looked after you almost from the day you were born, loved you, gave you all the things you needed, clothed and fed you. Isn't that enough, for God's sake?'

'I can understand what a shock you've had, Rachel,' Sybil said, 'and it'll take time to grow used to the idea. But whatever the circumstances, nothing can change the fact that your parents were good and kind to you. They gave you their name and shielded you from the stigma of being illegitimate – if you were. Maybe your real mother died in childbirth. Who's to know the reason there was for you being given away. Think of the alternatives, my dearie. You might have ended up in an orphanage or in a home where there was no harmony – drunkenness, abuse, fighting for survival along with a dozen others. Maybe that's it, Rachel. Perhaps your real parents already had a large family and just couldn't make room for one more.'

She felt she had let Rachel down by not seeing some of this in her reading of the past. The plain truth was she had seen things she didn't want to see so had conveniently pulled a blind down on them.

Sybil had prepared a meal for them and although Rachel tried to show her appreciation she could only toy with the food on her plate and hardly spoke. Carol was as lively as ever and chattered non-stop. When she got no response from Rachel she leaned across and pulled Rachel's sleeve.

'Mummy, are you still unhappy?' she asked, gazing up into Rachel's face.

'I'm not your –'

'Careful,' Kas warned, and for the first time in her married life Rachel was afraid of the dark, angry expression in his eyes. 'Mummy has been feeling sad because her daddy was very ill,' he told Carol.

'I know – he's dead,' she said matter-of-factly.

'She asked lots of questions so t'was best the truth be told,' Sybil said. 'Children don't like being fobbed off with half truths.'

'But I was,' Rachel snapped. 'Why couldn't they have told me the truth when I was young? I always knew there was something. That horrible strawberry birthmark, and Belinda being so pretty.'

'Being pretty isn't everything,' Kas said. 'You have striking features – when you're your normal self.' He tried to smile, tried to cheer her up, but she was quick to retort:

'How can I be normal? What *is* normal? Evidently they didn't think I was normal when I was born or they wouldn't have got rid of me so quickly. Just two days old and my mother handed me over like some unwanted kitten.'

'You can't know that,' Sybil said in a firm low voice. 'It probably pained your mother a great deal to part with you.'

'Where is she now?' Rachel asked with a tremor in her voice. 'How can I find her? Please, Sybil, help me to find her?' she pleaded.

'You mustn't even think of trying to find her,' Kas said bluntly. 'Your parents lived in the New Forest at the time, so you could have been born in any one of a dozen places miles away. You can't think of them as anything but your real parents, Rachel.'

'Well, I mean to find out where I came from. I'll move heaven and earth to trace who I really am,' she said defiantly.

'Not with my help you won't,' he answered, equally defiantly. 'We've got our own little "cuckoo in the nest", as your father so delicately phrased it. We're going to see that Carol has everything in life that we were both given by substitute parents. I owe a lot to Josh and Merle just as you do Mr and Mrs Hunter.'

'But it isn't the same,' Rachel argued. 'At least you were told that your parents died.'

'And maybe yours did too.'

'I've got to know,' Rachel muttered.

Kas stood up and banged his fist hard down on the table, making the crockery jump. 'That is enough,' he shouted. 'I don't want to hear any more about it. Let's get home and put Carol to bed.'

Sybil pulled herself out of her chair too. 'Sleep on it,' she said. 'Don't let this come between you, Rachel. You've a good life with Kas. Knowing who your real parents were won't make any difference now, will it?'

'Yes, to me. Trust you to all stick together! At least let me have this legacy for myself. What sort of life have I had? Born with a birthmark, then loving a man who really wanted my sister, and now discovering that I'm not who I thought I was – oh, it's all too much!' She rushed out of Sybil's waggon, banging the door with wild fury.

She hurried away, darting between the trees just below Portsdown Hill where the group were sheltering from the cold weather. She unlocked their van door and inside lay on the bed, utterly worn out. Why did Lemuel have to be ill? Why did she have to bump into Adam of all people and what were they doing living in Portsmouth? He'd been an apprenticed carpenter before the war. She supposed there was more money to be earned as a hospital porter. It was regular work which was something to be thankful for in this day and age.

Rachel was full of remorse for the anguish she'd caused her parents. She had experienced regret many times before but not as deeply as she felt now. For her father to disinherit her she knew he must have been bitterly disappointed in her. Or had he been glad of the excuse to leave everything to Belinda eventually? Memories of her childhood came back to taunt Rachel. She remembered hearing him say, 'We won't let Rachel down,' when she'd been ill with fever. She had thought he meant he had some magic way of curing her measles but now she realised what he meant. That they were going to do their duty. Why had they agreed to take her in? she wondered. Who could the mystery couple be who had conceived her? Why? Why? Why?

She felt the draught from the open door as Kas brought Carol home.

'You might have stayed long enough to thank Sybil for her trouble,' he said. 'She's not a young woman to have the responsibility of a four year old.'

'I expect Precious or Charity helped,' Rachel said noncommittally.

'Well now you can help – get up and see to Carol.'

She slid off the bed. The stove was kept alight during the cold weather and a kettle was already full of hot water. She poured some into the washing bowl and began to undress the little girl.

'We'll take you to meet Billy on Sunday,' she said as she bathed the child's face. 'What have you been doing today?'

'I played with the others.' As Rachel rubbed her dry Carol stretched out her arms and hugged her. 'You won't cry any more will you, Mummy? Lemuel will soon be better, won't he?'

Rachel hugged her back as she fought against more tears.

When she had settled Carol in the iron cot, covered her with warm knitted blankets and a patchwork quilt she'd made herself, Rachel drew the dividing curtains across the middle of the van and sat on the couch in silence. Kas was sitting close to the stove in a wooden rocking chair reading.

'Where d'you think the Smiths and Wellses went?' she asked suddenly.

Kas didn't move immediately and then with a pronounced sigh he put down his book and looked at Rachel.

'How would I know? Why d'you want to know?'

'You were clever enough to find Davey. I think we should take Carol back to her grandparents. She isn't related in any way to us, Kas. Isn't it her right to know her real family? What is she going to think of everyone when she grows up?'

'In most cases a child would probably never know that the people they call parents aren't their real ones. What you've heard today has stunned you. I'm full of sympathy for you, but Mr Hunter couldn't have been thinking rationally or he would have realised the terrible shock he was inflicting both on you and his beloved Belinda.'

'You don't like Belinda? Everyone likes Belinda,' Rachel said.

'I hardly know her but she doesn't seem as open as you are. Still, you can't judge people by their looks.'

'You don't like her,' Rachel repeated. 'You don't trust her.'

'Like I said, I don't know her so how can I trust her? After what she and Adam did, how can I trust either of them?'

'You think she had a hand in Adam changing his mind?'

'Well, don't you?'

'I've tried not to blame her,' Rachel said thoughtfully. 'Perhaps they poisoned Dad's mind against me?'

'You ran away – and I can't blame you for that, even though it was probably a foolish thing to do.'

'I lost my temper in the church – that's what Dad couldn't forgive. I wonder when he changed his will? When he wrote that awful letter? I felt sure he forgave me when he was in the hospital.'

Kas went back to his book. Rachel's eyes burned, her throat was dry and she ached everywhere while her tired brain chased a variety of thoughts round and round.

'Once we've found Carol's people and handed her back I'll travel all over the Forest to find my people,' she said.

Kas threw down his book and stood up.

'Shut up, Rachel!' he yelled angrily. 'Stop whining, for heaven's sake. I know it's been a hell of a day and what you need now is sleep so I suggest you go to bed.'

Rachel stood up to face him. 'How dare you shriek at me?' she said. 'It's my life, my background that's in question, so if I want to find out who I am, I will!'

'We both know who you are – my wife, Carol's substitute mother. And one day we'll have children of our own – a new family. The past is over and done with. I shall be glad when you can see Lemuel on Sunday. Maybe he can talk some sense into you.'

'I shouldn't have run away, I realise that now,' she said.

'No, you probably shouldn't, and then there would have been no need for your father to write that letter, but what's done is done. It all goes back to Adam jilting you. That wasn't a very noble thing to do and I daresay your sister had some part in it. I would have expected your parents to have been more sensitive to your feelings.'

'So everyone's to blame? But it still doesn't alter the fact that I want to know who my parents were – or are. They could still be alive and often wonder where I am and what became of me.'

Kas ran his hands through his hair in desperation. 'Rachel, Rachel,' he said. 'Stop tormenting yourself. Please – go to bed.'

'You don't want me to know. You're sorry I ever met up with my family again.'

'I'm sorry for your mother. She's the one who's most hurt by this, so you must try to be understanding to her. She's lost her husband, she's still in shock and grieving. If you carry on like you're doing now she'll wish you'd never turned up again.'

'But I love her – I always loved her more than Dad. I never want to be parted from her again, Kas.'

'Then try to be forgiving, darling. Be there when she needs you. Don't keep harping on about finding your real parents or you'll cause her untold pain. Can't you see that you'll make her feel she failed you?'

—

Rachel knew that she could never lay that at her mother's door. Her parents hadn't failed her, but she had them. She went behind the curtain and prepared for bed. Carol lay sleeping unperturbed, unaware of who her parents were or had been. In her circumstances Kas was right. She must never be told that her mother had hanged herself and that her father was a womaniser, and it was up to Rachel and Kas to see that she never knew. Ena had left her in their care, trusting them to do whatever was right. However she turned out, whatever she did, whether or not she disgraced the Romany group, she was Kas's and Rachel's responsibility and they must do the same for her as they would for their own children.

Rachel lay on the bed but couldn't sleep and when Kas joined her, placing loving, protecting arms around her, she moved away. She loved him, of course she did, but seeing Adam again had aroused old memories of their courting days when she hadn't a care in the world.

Lemuel was up and walking around the ward chatting to other patients when they visited the hospital on Sunday afternoon. The weather had changed again and frost had given way to mild damp days but he assured them that he would soon be back among them. Two visitors only were allowed at each bedside so as Kas and Rachel were visiting Belinda's home afterwards they went in first.

'You look so much better,' Rachel said as she kissed the elderly man. 'But you'll have to be extra careful when you get home not to catch a chill. You'll need special care to build you up so that you're fit again by spring.'

'And I've no doubt that you and Sybil will see to that,' Lemuel laughed. He shook hands with Kas, and then took Rachel's hands in his. 'My dear, you look quite wan. I wish I could offer you some comfort in the loss of your father but only time will soothe the pain. It was such a cold bleak day for the funeral. Was it a dreadful ordeal for you, my dear?'

'You could say that,' she said. 'It was strange being back in Wickham again and people stared as we knew they would, but the worse part was going to Calder Cottage without Dad there.'

'I'm sure your mother was quite relieved to have you there, and I trust everything is well between you now?'

'It was a strained reunion, Lemuel, and none of us were prepared for the will and letter Dad left.'

A nurse had insisted that Lemuel should get back into bed during visiting hours so Kas fetched chairs for them to sit one on either side of his bed. Rachel told Lemuel all that had transpired and he listened, hardly able to believe her story. Even though sleep had eluded her she was calmer now, and determined to keep the trauma hidden from others.

'Life has treated you unkindly, my dear Rachel,' Lemuel said. 'It might have been better if we'd never come back to the mainland and I'm afraid I'm to blame for that.'

'No one's to blame,' Kas said. 'Naturally it seems that it was meant to be for Rachel to see her father before he died but no one can change events.'

'I'm pleased that you're going to spend some time with your mother and sister so I don't want to keep you this afternoon, Rachel dear,' Lemuel said. 'I expect the others are waiting to come in and after that I shall spend time considering what you've told me. It's quite a lot to take in for me so I can understand the effect the shock has had on you. As Kas says we can't change anything, but talking helps and I daresay you'll feel better when you've seen your family again today. As time passes the burden will get easier to bear, so go with peace in your heart, my dear.'

Rachel was eager to get to Adam and Belinda's home yet apprehensive too. If Kas wasn't going to support her in looking for her real family she hoped she could appeal to Adam. Didn't he owe her that much?

They joined the rest of the group outside the hospital grounds where the Sanders family were looking after Carol. Adam had told Kas how to find their house only a few minutes' walk away from the hospital so they were able to walk there, leaving Bella and the trap with Caleb.

The road seemed to stretch endlessly to the horizon but number seventeen, a well-kept terraced house, was only a few yards along and Adam opened the door almost before Rachel had let go of the wrought iron knocker. He was quickly joined by a small boy with fair hair and hazel-coloured eyes. At the sight of strangers he hid behind Adam but as soon as he saw Carol he forgot his shyness.

Rachel was surprised at the size of the house inside. It was clean and nicely decorated and in a corner of the square hall stood a tall jardiniere on which stood an aspidistra with shiny broad dark green leaves hanging over the sides. At a quick glance Rachel noticed the steep staircase with fine oak banisters, recently renewed, an example of Adam's craftsmanship, she guessed.

Adam showed them into the front sitting room where Belinda and Phoebe had been sitting by the fire.

'Take Carol up into the attic,' Belinda said. 'There are plenty of toys up there.' She smiled at her sister. 'That's one thing about a terraced house – it goes up three floors, and Adam has made the attic into a good-sized playroom.' She greeted Rachel with a light kiss on her cheek.

Phoebe hugged Rachel warmly, kissed her and held her for several seconds. 'Come near to the fire, dear,' she said. 'You look pinched with the cold. And how was your friend today?'

'Up and about. He'll soon be able to leave hospital, I expect.'

Phoebe held out her hand to Kas. 'I hope we're going to have a chance to get to know you better. There's a few years of catching up to do. It's been a sad business but it's such a relief to see Rachel again.'

'Adam,' Belinda said, 'why don't you show Kas round the house while Mum and I have a chat to Rachel.'

Rachel felt herself bristle with annoyance. Trust Belinda to want to show off her home, she thought. But if she hoped to make Kas envious Rachel knew she would be unlucky. The Romany way of life suited him and he was unlikely to change even though he had property of his own.

'Are you feeling all right, Rachel?' Belinda asked after the men had left the room. 'The past week has been eventful to say the least. I can't begin to tell you how sorry I am that at Dad's funeral you had to learn you didn't really belong.'

'But she does belong to us, the same as she's always done,' Phoebe insisted. 'I've had time to think, Rachel, and although what your father did seems hard-hearted, it was because he was upset that he didn't know where you went. How could he have known that you were so close to us all the time or that you were going to turn up like that at the hospital?'

'I won't deny it was a shock,' Rachel said. 'But all I want to do now is to find out who my real parents were. Isn't there anything you can tell me, Mum? Any clue at all?'

'You're nearly twenty-four years old. All I can remember is the midwife bringing you all wrapped up in blankets and – well, I'm sorry – but you looked a poor little thing.'

'You mean with that awful birthmark?'

'Not so much that, although it was something of a shock, but we were assured that it would fade by the time you went to school. It didn't, it's true, but just look at you now, not a blemish – a bit too pale but I reckon that'll be the worry of all that's happened recently.' She smiled almost proudly at Rachel which brought a lump to her throat.

'What else can you remember? Didn't anyone say where the midwife got me from?'

'She was getting on then and seemed mighty agitated. She brought you to me and laid you beside Belinda. We were so grateful to have a daughter of our own at last, two was a blessing indeed.'

'But didn't you ask any questions? Surely you wanted to know something about me?'

'I suppose I was fairly weak. It wasn't an easy birth and we felt so sorry for you. Reckon at first it was touch and go whether you survived, but I remember the old midwife – Nurse Edwards her name was – a widow, everyone called her Teddy. Big woman, round rosy cheeks and a hearty laugh, but she was good at her job. Without her help I don't think you would have made it. Love was what you needed most, Teddy said. Yes, 'tis all coming back. Unwanted, unloved, she said, but she'd never tell us anything more.

''Course, as time passed we quite forgot you weren't really ours even though you and Belinda didn't look alike. Folk commented but so far as I know no one ever questioned it. T'was lucky we moved to Kingsmere then. The secret was between us and Teddy. We promised never to tell a soul and we kept our promise, which is why it's so out of character for Wally to have written that letter.' Phoebe put her arm round Rachel's shoulders as she directed her to a chair near the roaring log fire. 'You never wanted for love and protection, dear.'

'Oh, I know that, Mum. I do understand that, although I always felt Belinda was Dad's favourite. But now that I do know I'm not really a Hunter, I feel I want to know about my family.'

'It might be better not to know, Rachel,' Belinda said. 'Dad wasn't really capable of making the right decisions when he made his will and wrote that letter, so Adam agrees with me that you must share my legacy.'

'Thank you, but no, I couldn't take anything, Belinda. Not all gypsy people are poor. We work hard to earn a living but Kas has had property left him. He was away in the Army during the war so he learnt to be a blacksmith and can turn his hand to many jobs. He made our trap for my wedding present and bought Bella, the little miniature horse, especially for me and Carol.'

'What brought you back to the mainland?' Phoebe asked.

'Lemuel wanted to return here. They don't usually stay so long in one place but there was work on the island and we were all happy there.'

When Adam and Kas came back into the room Rachel was telling them about the book Lemuel was writing. She was anxious to bridge the years they'd spent apart and her face became flushed from the heat of the fire as she talked excitedly.

The children were brought down from the attic for tea and when Belinda called them all to go into the back living room Rachel stood up quickly. She felt her head begin to swim so promptly sat down again.

'Are you all right?' Kas asked anxiously.

Rachel laughed. 'Of course. It's just the heat from the fire.' But as she tried again her legs gave way beneath her and the light at the end of the long dark tunnel grew smaller and smaller. No matter how much she tried to keep it in sight it was slowly receding until everything around her became enveloped in the blackness.

When she recovered she found she had been placed on the couch and Kas was encouraging her to take a sip of brandy. Phoebe was loosening the neck of her dress and Belinda was waving a fan in front of her face.

'That's the second time,' Adam said, looking down at her with concern. 'And it wasn't the shock of seeing me this time.' He smiled, lovingly, warmly, and Rachel felt her heart flutter with the spark of affection she'd known of old. He still had the tender and gentle manner which had drawn him to her when she was younger. How could he have deserted her? What had she done to make him change his mind? She tried to sit up but they were all making a big fuss, so much so that she suddenly announced impatiently, 'It's all right – I'm expecting again. It's nothing.'

The news stunned them, in particular Kas. It was only six months since the last miscarriage and he thought he'd been too careful for this to happen. They had been advised to wait for a year before trying again but their love was strong and feelings uncontrollable, and now he felt guilty.

'That's marvellous,' Adam said.

'I am too,' Belinda cried. 'We'll have our babies more or less at the same time. How exciting!'

But Kas didn't seem pleased. 'Rachel has had three miscarriages already,' he said in a low voice. 'It's too soon, we should have waited.'

She held out her hand to him. 'I'm sorry,' she whispered. 'I know this wasn't the right time to tell you but I thought you'd be pleased. I'm not sure that I am.'

'Why ever not?' Belinda asked.

'I want to know about my background before I have a baby,' she said. 'It's only fair to the child.'

'But you weren't worried before when you thought you were Belinda's sister,' Kas said. 'All I'm concerned about is your health. This time you've got to put your feet up and rest. The doctors at Newport warned you – the first three months are important and you must rest.'

But Rachel was already making plans. She had a mission. She didn't care whether she had to travel all over the south of England, she was determined to find someone who knew where the midwife got her from.

Chapter Sixteen

The one thing Rachel didn't plan for was the way everyone cossetted her. Although she returned to the waggon with Kas and Carol, her mother and sister persuaded her to join the medical aid club and Belinda introduced her to the local doctor under whose care she herself was.

'Doctor King would like to see us both,' Rachel told Kas when she returned to the common where they were camped.

'We don't use doctors as you well know,' he replied sharply.

'Not as a general rule, Kas, but there are times when it's necessary, like when Carol was born for instance.'

'And he admitted that the job had been done when he arrived.'

'But he treated Ena after she'd lost such a lot of blood.'

'Our folks have their methods too and they've been well tried over centuries.'

'But you were as eager as anyone else to get Lemuel to hospital,' Rachel said. 'Otherwise we wouldn't be here now and I wouldn't have seen Dad before he died.'

'That was different. Lemuel's getting on and wasn't making the progress he should have been.'

'Perhaps you don't want me to have this baby?'

'You know that's not true, Rachel. But we were advised to wait a year before trying again.'

She sidled up to her husband and put her arms around his neck. 'That was asking a bit too much of both of us, though, wasn't it?' She inveigled him into kissing her but after a few moments he pushed her away. 'Kas,' she pursued, 'we both want a baby of our own. I agree now isn't such a good time, and although I had my suspicions I didn't think I could be pregnant again yet. With so much happening with Dad and everything I put it right out of my mind. I thought I felt ill because of Dad and then the shock of finding out that I'm sort of suspended in limbo.'

'Don't talk rot,' he said impatiently. 'You're not suspended anywhere, let alone in limbo. Things have only changed if you want them to change. As I've said a hundred or more times, Rachel, we can't change anything and now we can't alter the fact that you're expecting. I'm quite happy for this doctor to keep his eye on you but I can't see why he would want to see me.'

'But you've always looked after me.'

'It seems I've been relieved of that job as your mother and sister have taken over.'

'Kas,' she pleaded, 'it isn't like that at all. I want you to be as happy as I am that I've been reunited with the family again, and it'll be nice for Belinda and me to go through this together. I think her baby is due about a month before ours.'

'And what if we move on? The others have been talking about going down to the New Forest near Burley ready for the summer?'

'Oh.' Rachel's smiles changed to a frown. 'I didn't know. When was this decided?'

'It's not definite yet, but the others think it'll be better for Lemuel as soon as he's fit enough.'

'But probably not for us,' Rachel said thoughtfully.

'Why's that?' Kas asked.

'We-ell, Doctor King is going to get a report from the hospital in Newport, but from what I've told him he considers I should be spending the next few weeks in bed. I explained about us being travellers and he wants me to go and stay with Mum.'

Kas stared at Rachel darkly. Whereas he had always been so kind and caring, of late he seemed moody and quick-tempered. Rachel had tried to shrug off his moods as the effects of recent events. Now she realised that he was sorry she had found her family again.

'So that's it?' he said. 'They don't want anything to do with you if you're a gypsy?' He sighed. 'I suppose it's understandable but we don't have to stay around to embarrass them. As soon as Lemuel is well enough we'll move down to the New Forest.'

'I didn't want to tell you what the doctor said, Kas. I thought he could have explained it much better than me.'

'Doesn't matter who does the explaining, does it? I presume you'd like to go and stay with your mother? Where does that leave me and Carol?'

'You'd come as well, of course.'

'No, Rachel. I have a living to earn and we'll pay our own way.'

'Please go with me to see the doctor, Kas?' she pleaded. 'You heard what the one in Newport said and you were sympathetic then. Why are you so angry now?'

'Because I feel your mother and sister are making all the decisions.'

'But they didn't come in with me when I saw Doctor King. The consultation was between me and him.'

'So how come he suggested that you stay with your mother?'

'Belinda gave him some of the background when she introduced us. He'd like to see us in a week's time when he's had the report from Newport.'

'We shall have to see what the others think.'

'It's got nothing to do with them,' Rachel said.

'Forgotten all about community living so soon?' She could hardly believe that Kas could be so unfeeling. 'Can't you see, Rachel, they're trying to entice you back into their way of life and I'm not prepared to let that happen.'

'No, Kas. What's got into you? It's just to safeguard our baby, that's all. Three months and then I shall be over the danger period.'

'And by then you'll be so much under your mother's thumb you won't want to come and live free again.'

'Oh, dear Kas, of course I shall. That's what I want for my baby. Don't let's quarrel, please, I *do* want to keep this baby – for you.'

Kas turned and left the waggon. Rachel watched from the window expecting to see him make for Sybil's van to fetch Carol but he went to where the horses were tethered and in a few minutes she saw him astride Kitchener, galloping away.

She remained alone for a while wondering why this was happening to them. They hardly ever quarrelled and she hated it. When she felt composed enough she walked across and knocked on Sybil's door. There was no sound of Carol's voice as she expected.

'Come on in, me dearie,' Sybil called. 'Carol ain't 'ere, she's with Charity. Gone to the woods to look for snowdrops with some of the other young'uns.'

'She's been all right, Sybil? Not too much for you?'

'When 'as any of 'em been too much for me? More to the point, Rachel, how did you get on?'

'Don't ask.' She sat down wearily. 'The doctor Belinda's introduced me to is writing to the hospital in Newport to get my records. In view of what I've told him though he suggests I ought to remain in bed for the next few weeks, and thinks it would be a good idea if I stayed with Mum.'

She looked expectantly at Sybil for her reaction but her ageing features showed none as she waited for Rachel to continue.

'I thought Kas would understand. He's always been so thoughtful, but we quarrelled and he's ridden off on Kitchener.'

'I know, I saw him go. I've known Kas a long time, dearie, and it takes some'at to disturb 'im. I knew by the darkness of his frown that some'at was up and I was afraid t'was you and the baby.'

'It's hardly a baby yet. I must have started morning sickness almost as soon as it was conceived. Because of the shock of meeting Adam and Dad I thought it was that. I think Kas is upset that it's happened again so soon. We wanted to wait but there's no going back now.'

'And you – d'you want this child?'

'Yes, Sybil, of course I do. I want Kas's baby more than anything in the world but I too wish it had waited – waited until I've found out who I am.'

'You'm a child of the Lord. That should be enough to satisfy you.'

Rachel looked away, sad, uncertain about her future, her life, past and present.

'I thought if I stayed with Mum for a little while it would help her, and I'd try to make up to her for losing Dad as well as recompense for what I did.'

'You can't make up to her for your father's death, child. That was his destiny. It'll be hard for her for many months to come but with your love and support she'll weather that particular storm. You must put the past behind you, Rachel. We can't change what's gone – 'tis up to you to get on with your life. I understands about the need for rest and we've a month or two of winter to get through first. T'would be more comfortable with your mother although you knows everyone of us 'ere would see to it that you was properly looked after, Kas in particular.'

'I suggested he could come with me and Carol too.'

'She's at a busy age. Always on the go, always asking questions, so I daresay t'would be best if she stayed with us. And Kas has his work to do. Then there's Lemuel we'll have to look out for when he gets home.'

Rachel brightened. 'I popped in to the hospital to see him after I'd seen the doctor. It was quite close. He's looking so much better, more cheerful and a much healthier colour. He's been moving round the ward talking to the other men. Sister said they were reluctant to let him go, he's been such a comfort to the other patients. But that's our dear Lemuel, always thinking of other people.'

'Ah, 'tis a good man he is. Now why don't you have a talk to him about things.'

'I was going to, but visiting time was just ending.' Rachel made tea with the boiling water in the tin kettle on the stove. 'I need to talk to him and I hope he'll talk to Kas. I feel guilty about keeping Carol when she has grandparents who are her real family.'

'We don't know where Ena's folk went and I doubt that Davey will ever want to recognise that he had a daughter. He won't take responsibility for her. Ena made it quite clear what she wanted, and that was for you and Kas to be her ma and pa, and you'd be letting Ena down if you tried to push her back on her grandparents.'

'I wouldn't do that, Sybil. Surely you know me better than that?' Rachel sat down opposite her with a sigh. 'I love Carol and until recently I thought of her as ours, but now I'm confused and only want to do what's right.'

'Then carry on as if nothing has happened, dearie. You'm reconciled with your mother and that should be cause for rejoicing. Let bygones be bygones.'

'Sybil . . .' Rachel broached hesitantly. 'You won't like what I'm going to say but I must say it all the same.' She sipped her tea, avoiding looking directly at Rachel. 'Tell me honestly if you saw any of the recent events in my future?'

'I don't "see" no more – I've told you that before, Rachel.'

Rachel reached across the table and held the older woman's hand. She knew well enough that Sybil fought with her conscience over her gift but Rachel was keenly aware that she couldn't help herself at times. Hadn't she told them where to look for Ena? That was for good, Sybil had excused, so now Rachel hoped she could influence her to help her find out the truth.

'I told you that there would be happy times and sad times, child,' she said, dreamily, then pulled herself up smartly. 'Now that could apply to each and every one of us, so don't make nothing of that.'

'But just a little clue so that I know where to look for my real parents?' Rachel begged.

She covered Sybil's hand with her free one and she felt her enclosed hand grow warm and supple as Sybil smoothed gently over the ball of her thumb.

Rachel watched closely as Sybil's eyes narrowed then close.

'Sisters . . . sea . . .' Her voice became so soft Rachel held her breath for fear of not hearing what the gypsy was saying. 'Sisters . . . babies . . . nothing but good . . . all for the best . . .' Sybil jerked and opened her eyes. 'Rachel, you hoodwinked me.' She shook her head in disapproval.

'I need to know, Sybil dear,' Rachel said, 'and I'm sure you could guide me.'

Sybil withdrew her hand sharply. 'Lemuel's our guide, you talk to him.'

'You felt something though, didn't you?' Rachel said. 'Sisters, you said. Was that Belinda and myself? Babies – was that us too, meaning that being brought up together was right? Nothing but good, all for the best. Please explain it, Sybil?'

'I talk a lot of rubbish, pay no attention, I ain't no good no more.' She stood up. 'Got to get me tea and then I need to rest, so you go home and do what's right for Kas and Carol. They'm your family now.'

'Come and have tea with us,' Rachel invited.

'So that you can cheat me into seeing again? No, Rachel. 'T'wouldn't be reliable anyway and I could send you off on some goose chase wasting everyone's time and energy. If Lemuel thinks I can help, he'll be the one to ask.'

Rachel knew it was no good trying to press Sybil so she left her and went to fetch Carol.

A large pot of scrag end of lamb with potatoes and onions had been simmering all day on the stove. It smelled good and Rachel felt quite hungry. When she had washed Carol's hands and face she sat her up to the table with her bib on. As she was cutting up the child's meat Kas came in.

'You must have smelled the dinner,' she said as light-heartedly as she could.

He came up to her and kissed her cheek.

'Yes, and I'm hungry. Nothing like a ride in the country to whip up an appetite.' He washed his hands in the bowl, dried them and sat down in his usual place. There was little opportunity for serious conversation when Carol was around. She chattered almost non-stop and her funny, appealing ways soon mended any rift.

When they went to bed that night Kas held Rachel close.

'I'm sorry if I seemed angry with you, my darling,' he said. 'The truth is, I can't bear the thought of losing you.'

'Losing me? Whatever d'you mean, Kas? I'm not going anywhere.'

'In a way you are. You're going back to your old home to live – and three months is a long time. Once you're settled in there will you ever want to come back to me?'

'Of course I will. You can come and spend time with us. Mum would like that, Kas. She wants to get to know you. Belinda and Adam do too. I've been part of your family for the past five years, now it's your turn to become part of mine.'

'I know that, but my main concern is for your health. You've lost three babies, Rachel, could you bear to lose a fourth?'

'Maybe this isn't such a good time to be expecting but if it's to be then everything will be all right. We must have faith, Kas. Isn't that what Lemuel will say?'

That was exactly what he did say when they visited him the following day.

'I've thought so much about all that you told me before, Rachel,' he said. 'Of course you want to know the truth about your birth but there's always the danger you won't like what you discover. Isn't that the reason your parents didn't tell you the truth earlier? Somehow I can't help thinking that your father didn't really mean to cause you such anguish. He was a sick man and when our bodies are unhealthy then our minds become confused too. Now you must decide what to do with this knowledge. How will it help you or your mother to discover who your real parents were? Have you thought about the emotional trauma you're going to cause Mrs Hunter as well as either or both your real parents should you find them and confront them?'

'I've tried to see it from everyone's point of view,' Rachel said solemnly. 'I know it may seem absurd to you, Kas and the others but I feel there's an urgency to seek out the truth. But for the moment I can't do anything as I'm supposed to be resting most of the time. There wasn't time to tell you yesterday but the doctor I saw suggested that I go to stay with Mum for the next three months.'

Lemuel stroked his beard while he took this in.

'And I daresay Kas doesn't agree with this idea?' he said slowly.

Kas shifted his feet uneasily. 'I know I'm being selfish, Lemuel,' he said. 'But I feel that Rachel is slipping away from me. Her family are taking over.'

'Then it's up to you to see that they don't. If Rachel doesn't go to her mother and loses your baby, I think you may well feel you're to blame, Kas. Rachel has been parted from her family for several years now. The Lord be praised that they've been reunited even if the circumstances were not entirely happy ones. Is three months too long to sacrifice for the sake of a baby? And to allow Rachel to spend this time with her mother?'

'It isn't as if we wouldn't see each other, is it? she said. 'You can always come to stay whenever you like?'

'We'll see what the doctor says when we see him next week. Then we'll discuss the matter with your mother,' Kas said. 'The others have been talking about moving down to the New Forest when you leave hospital, Lemuel. How d'you feel about it?'

'Whether she stays with her mother or not, the important thing is that every care is taken of Rachel this time. It might be sensible to stay within easy reach of the hospital.'

'Belinda did suggest that I stayed with them,' Rachel said. 'I declined the offer. She's being kind, I know, but underneath she dislikes my being a gypsy. I expect she'd like me to move away as far as possible. As Kas says, we don't want to embarrass them.'

'Then I think the better idea is for you to stay with your mother and we can move to Bere Forest so that we're all close. The time will soon pass, Kas. You must think of it as a time of reconciliation between Rachel and her family which I'm sure you wouldn't wish to deny her. There'll be plenty of time to go farther south by early summer.'

Rachel knew that Kas was not pleased about the decision but he recognised the wisdom of the elder of the group, and when he went with Rachel to see the doctor at the hospital he was assured that there was no reason for her not to carry the baby full term if they did as he advised.

Sybil made sure that Rachel spent most of every day resting in her van while Carol enjoyed being indulged by the other families and a week later, after Lemuel was discharged from hospital, the travellers moved in convoy towards Wickham. While the families made camp in a suitable copse on the western edge of the Forest of Bere, Kas drove Rachel in the trap to her old home at Kingsmere. She savoured every moment of renewing her acquaintance with the oak wood she had loved since childhood. After the Great War when so much timber had been felled, the newly formed Forestry Commission had taken over management of the forest and ordered that more conifers should be planted, but there was still a great variety of broadleaves left to be admired.

Phoebe was quickly at the door of Calder Cottage, obviously delighted at Rachel's decision to stay with her for the next three months.

'Adam helped me put up a bed in the front parlour,' she said. 'We thought it would be nicer for you to be near the window looking on to the road and the woods on the other side.' Kas carried in Rachel's belongings, noticing that the bed was a single one and assuming that he was not welcome to stay. Phoebe sensed his feelings. 'Now you feel free to come in at any time, Kas,' she said. 'My home is yours, and if you can stay overnight you can move up to Rachel's old bedroom with the bigger bed.'

'I'm sure this is putting you to a lot of trouble, Mrs Hunter,' he said.

'Nonsense. I can do with the company, and Rachel and I need to talk. We all want her to keep this baby. So sad to have lost three already. I know what it's like to want a baby. I thought I was never going to have a family at all. Belinda can't get here very often as it's too far to walk from the station at Wickham with young Billy, especially now she's expecting again. You can't always be sure a carter will be coming this way from the station, but Adam visits me when he comes to see his mother.'

'How is she?' Rachel asked. 'There's so much I want to ask and so many people I'd like to see. What about the Meads? Is Dick back with Nessie?'

'Yes, and they seem content to grow old together. Well, they're not old really. I think Nessie's about fiftyish and Dick'll be a few years older. They're enjoying their children and grandchildren and life's a good deal more peaceful than it used to be. Good job that Beth is out of the way. A real black sheep she was. As to Adam's mother, she's still a recluse and doesn't get out and about. But you must settle in gently and ask all your questions gradually.'

Phoebe made cocoa while Kas helped Rachel with her things.

'You will come to see me every day, won't you?' Rachel asked. 'Bring Sybil and Carol. The others are all welcome too.'

'You're looking flushed already, Rachel,' he said. 'I think the doctor really meant rest in every sense of the word. It isn't going to work unless you make the most of this opportunity.' He kissed the top of her dark head. 'Just remember that I love you very much indeed Strawberry Girl, and your health is what's most important.'

Rachel put her arms round Kas's neck and hugged him tightly. 'Thank you for everything,' she whispered. 'I love you too and we'll soon be back on the road together. I know this is a wrench for you. It's not so bad for me because I'm happy to have the chance to be with Mum for a while, and I think it'll help her so the sacrifice will be well worth it, I promise. We shall have time to talk, time to reflect on the past, and time to make up for lost time.' Rachel laughed happily. She had longed to be back in Calder Cottage, but her happiness was marred by the loss of her father and the knowledge that he had disowned her – her laughter died as she clung to Kas.

'Not too much talk, darling,' he said softly. 'I'm sure I shan't be able to sleep without you. Don't let the past come between us, please.'

'Dear Kas, as if I would. I shall sleep only because I'm weary.'

Phoebe came back in the room then with steaming cocoa and a plate of small cakes. She sat with them, listening to Rachel's chatter, observing the mental torment Kas was experiencing and wondering how a daughter of hers could have become involved with these travelling folk. But she had to admit Rachel appeared to be happy with such a lifestyle. She had done her best to give her a good start in life and Wally had been supportive. Phoebe still couldn't understand why Adam had behaved the way he had. He refused to enter into any dialogue on the matter, saying only that he had made a mistake. ''T'would be too late once we'd been married,' she remembered him saying by way of an excuse. ''Tis Belinda I want.' Want was one thing, love another, but they were happy enough, Phoebe thought.

Damp mild weather alternated with snow, ice and heavy frosts. The days were short, the nights long, but around teatime each day Phoebe and Rachel talked at length about everything. Rachel plied her mother with questions about the time she was taken to them at Minstead but Phoebe insisted she knew nothing except that the midwife was anxious to find a good home for her. Rachel had to be content with that, and when on the Sunday Belinda, Adam and Billy visited for afternoon tea she had a different set of questions ready. She was alone with Adam as Belinda was helping her mother prepare tea.

'Why did you go to Portsmouth to live?' Rachel asked.

Adam sat forward in his chair and twisted his long fingers together nervously.

'There was gossip, Rachel,' he said. 'I didn't want Belinda to be hurt.'

'Hm,' she said shortly, 'never mind how much I was hurt.'

'Rachel, I know it was dreadful for you, and I'm sorry, but as I told your parents it was better it happened then than after we were married. I – well, I loved you both.' He ran his fingers through his hair. 'Nothing I can say or do can ever make things right, but believe me it had to be this way. We're happy, and I can see that you and Kas are too. Isn't that enough?'

Rachel looked long and hard at Adam. She wanted to despise him, hate him, but his pained expression made it impossible. He seemed to be troubled and hiding something.

'Everything is all right with your job though, isn't it?' she asked with genuine concern.

'Everything is fine, really, Rachel.' He sighed. 'It isn't easy living in Portsmouth when both our widowed mothers are hereabouts.'

'But your mother is well?'

'As well as she'll ever be. She's younger than your mother yet she's always been an old woman. If only she'd take an interest in what's going on in the village, but she prefers to remain housebound so the less she does, the less she can. Perhaps life hasn't been kind to her, and maybe I should do more.'

'I thought it was all settled that you were going to live with her when you and Belinda got married?'

'Yes, but work wasn't too easy after the war. We stayed with her for several months and then I heard about this job at the hospital. I used to go on the train every day to begin with but then it seemed sensible to sell that cottage I bought and use the money to buy a house in Portsmouth.'

'It's all very nice. You've evidently worked hard on it.'

'That's one thing I was trained to do and I enjoy working with wood so it was easy. Wally used to come and help us during the summer months when he was well enough. Oh, Rachel, and to think you were just across the water.'

'You must have thought I was in Portsmouth when I sent the postcard to Mum and Dad?

'We . . . we guessed that you wouldn't stay there, but I always felt that there might be a possibility of seeing you there one day. It was just a gut feeling though I never expected to see you walk into the hospital, and with . . .'

'Gypsies?' she laughed. 'I saw Beth Cropper and Dick Mead on the island so I was sure they'd come home and tell everyone they'd seen me "dressed up like a bloomin' gypsy" as she said.'

Rachel told Adam how Beth had tried to entice Kas away from her, and how she'd taken Davey from Ena, and the subsequent events.

'Didn't you ever want to come home, Rachel?' Adam asked.

'Of course, quite often, especially at first, but Lemuel and Sybil were so kind to me that gradually I became one of them. I felt I had disgraced my family so I wouldn't be welcome back here, and I was right. Poor Dad, how he must have despised me.' Rachel's eyes were filled with tears when Belinda came into the room. She stopped short in the doorway just as Adam stretched out his hand to take Rachel's in his to console her.

'It wasn't really your fault, Rachel,' Adam said, not realising his wife was a witness to the scene. 'The circumstances were –'

'Were what?' Belinda challenged.

'Awkward,' Adam said, withdrawing his hand slowly. 'My mind was in such a turmoil after the war. You know, it wasn't easy to adjust – everything had changed.'

'And we'd all grown up,' Belinda said. 'At least now we know why Rachel and I don't look alike.' She studied her sister with steely blue eyes which slightly mocked as she added, 'Perhaps your mother was a –'

'Gypsy? You needn't be afraid of using that word.' Rachel stared directly at her. 'Yes, perhaps she was. Now why didn't I think of that? There were always gypsies in the forest.'

Phoebe came in carrying a silver teapot only used on Sundays.

'Mum?' Rachel said. 'Belinda's just suggested that my real mother might be a gypsy. There was a group in the New Forest, wasn't there?'

'Ouch!' Phoebe said as she scalded herself on the teapot which she almost dropped. 'I don't know much about them,' she said hurriedly. 'Travelling folk have been around for centuries. Like I've said, we weren't told anything, and we were so thankful to have Belinda safe and sound that it seemed only right to take you in.' She fussed about putting the teacosy on the teapot. 'I've made the tea. Kas and Carol are just taking their coats off.'

Conversation then centred around the two children who had become instant friends, and the two hours they were all together as a family passed very quickly. Kas was pleased to take the others to the station in the trap to catch the train from Wickham back to Portsmouth, and in the reverent silence of a winter Sunday evening Phoebe and Rachel watched pictures in the fire, each with their own memories.

After a few weeks the morning sickness which had plagued Rachel stopped. There were no more giddy turns and she began to feel extremely well, so much so that she persuaded Kas to take her mother into Wickham in the trap to buy wool and material to make things for the baby.

'I never got the chance to prepare much before,' Rachel said. 'But this time I feel different and it's such a waste of time lying here watching the world go by. I need to keep occupied otherwise the waiting will seem like an eternity.'

Rachel dozed for a while after dinner, then woke feeling restless for Phoebe and Kas's return. There had been method in her madness for although Phoebe kept her grief hidden for much of the time, Rachel felt that her mother too needed to something to fill the days apart from waiting on her hand and foot. Knitting or sewing would help her rest and relax.

Letters of condolence from people in neighbouring villages and towns continued to arrive each day as word was passed from place to place. Wally had been well thought of and respected wherever he went. Sometimes a letter would reopen the wound; another would bring Phoebe some much needed comfort. Quite a pile of such letters had accumulated, placed on a small table near Rachel's bed for her to read as and when she wanted to. Now she thumbed through them, knowing that to just take one out of its envelope would make her sad but would help pass the time. She looked first at the postmarks, villages she'd never heard of, and others from places like Romsey, Fareham, Winchester, Lyndhurst. And then Rachel looked and looked again. Minstead . . . Maybe the village where she'd been born even though her mother assured her that no other woman thereabouts had been expecting at the same time she was. The handwriting was neat, each letter perfectly formed on the thick parchment paper. Rachel glanced at the end to see who it was from and read a name she didn't remember – Grace Whitmarsh. The letter was fairly short, offering sympathy and adding that she hoped Phoebe would visit soon. 'I'm sure we can find some means of transport and you're welcome to stay a for as long as you wish. Your girls don't need you now so you're free to take a much needed holiday and soon the forest will be at its best.'

Rachel read and re-read the letter. She searched her memory. Was there ever an Aunt Grace? No, she couldn't recall one. A relative or friend? Then her imagination flew in all directions. Supposing Grace Whitmarsh was her mother? Perhaps she'd been in service, let down by her lover so that she had to give her baby away in order to keep her job. Rachel watched eagerly for her mother's return. Was she about to discover the truth at last?

Chapter Seventeen

Rachel dozed off and was soon dreaming of a reunion with a woman, not so much faceless as unrecognisable, and then noises in the distance brought her back to reality. She felt rather hot and agitated until she remembered the letter from Grace Whitmarsh. It was lying on the bedcovers but before Kas and her mother entered the room Rachel put it back on the small table. She suddenly felt rather foolish for having such unwarranted flights of fancy. Why on earth should a woman named Grace Whitmarsh be her real mother?

Kas came in carrying a bag. He went at once to Rachel, kissed her and held her tightly.

'Have you been asleep? You smell all warm and cosy.'

'Yes, I dropped off while I was reading some of Mum's letters. Dad was a wonderful man, Kas. How could I have let him down like I did?'

'Hey, come on. No more feeling sorry, either for yourself or for what you did. The past is irretrievable. The future is ours. Don't read any more letters if they make you feel sad.'

'Some of them make me weep,' she said. 'Dear Dad, I wish he were here now.'

'Look what we've bought,' Kas said, opening the carrier bag to cheer her up. 'Balls of white wool, lace and fine lawn for petticoats, your mother said. At least she'll have something now to take her mind off her loss.'

Phoebe seemed quite excited by her purchases and after they'd eaten and Kas had left she showed Rachel some new knitting patterns she'd bought.

'I want to knit something for Billy as well as something new for Belinda's baby,' Rachel said, echoing her mother's enthusiasm.

'I think Belinda already has a good supply of baby clothes she kept from when Billy was small. Adam's mother has kept her well supplied with beautiful garments she makes herself, and she's very fond of young Billy.'

'Difficult to imagine Mrs Taylor being fond of any child,' Rachel sighed. 'Poor Adam, his home life couldn't have been very exciting. Not to be wondered at that he should behave so strangely having such odd parents.'

Phoebe went to the scullery to wash up. She didn't voice her opinion to Rachel for fear of upsetting her but she had observed the covetous looks Rachel gave Adam when she thought no-one was watching. Phoebe had to admit that Adam was a good son-in-law, kind and thoughtful, and he cared devotedly for his own mother, but now that Phoebe was getting to know Kas better she discovered he had many good qualities to his credit. He had the stronger character which she felt was right for Rachel and she was certain they were immensely happy together. She wished with all her heart that Wally was alive to meet Kas. Gypsy or no he was a likeable man with honourable principles.

The two women settled down on either side of the fire. At this time of day Rachel sat out of bed to make a change, and now they happily discussed which pattern to use for which type of wool. Stitches were cast on but the clicketty-click of needles was drowned when Rachel asked her mother, 'Who's Grace Whitmarsh, Mum?'

'You wouldn't know her, dear,' Phoebe said. 'But surely you remember letters arriving from abroad? You always wanted the stamps. Not that Grace wrote very often. Her Christmas card and letter usually arrived in time for Easter.' Phoebe laughed. 'We went to school together. Her father worked for the East India Company so when Grace was about fourteen she and her mother went out to Singapore to join him. Although her mother didn't want to go they had a good life, and Grace worked for the government out there, something to do with Customs and Excise.'

'She's back in Minstead now then and wants you to go to stay with her for a holiday?'

'Not back in Minstead. We went to school in Lee-on-Solent, remember that's where I was born. Grace retired a few years ago and just after your grandfather died wrote and said she was back in England and was thinking of settling down in the New Forest. Your father was looking for a new tenant for the cottage his parents had lived in and that's how she came to move to Minstead.'

'You need a holiday, Mum. Wouldn't you love to go and stay with her?'

'Too right I would, but how can I with you and Belinda both expecting babies?'

'That's not for ages, and once I can get about again our group is going to move down to somewhere near Burley. You could travel with us.'

'Oh, my goodness, whatever would your father have said to that?'

Rachel lowered her head to hide her pink cheeks.

'I'm sorry, dear. I didn't mean to hurt your feelings but –'

'I know, nice people don't hobnob with gypsies,' Rachel said. 'But people criticise without really knowing them.' She went on to explain how she and Kas had first met in the wood just across the road from Calder Cottage, and how he had joined the group on the Isle of Wight.

'I have a lot to thank the gypsies for,' she said. 'I was quite ill after running away and being out all night in the rain. Sybil has the gift of seeing, but she tries not to use her gift. I know she can tell things about the past and future and I desperately wanted her to tell me what she could about my real mother. She went into a bit of a trance and said "sisters", which I suppose means Belinda and me, and "sea".'

Phoebe smiled gently at Rachel. 'Knowing doesn't always help, dear,' she said quietly. After a few minutes' silence she laughed. 'A gypsy came to the door before I knew I was going to have Belinda. I was a bit afraid of them, especially as Wally always told me to keep the doors locked when the gypsies were in the vicinity. Minstead as you know is a small village and our cottages were in an isolated spot in the forest. This woman had a basket of white heather and promised to tell my fortune if I bought some.' Phoebe put down her knitting and looked across at Rachel. 'I never did tell Wally I bought some, and in return this woman, whom I must admit was very pleasant, told me I was going to have a beautiful daughter . . .' Phoebe turned quite pale as she remembered. 'As she went out of the little wooden gate Wally had made she turned and gave me a lovely warm smile as she said, "Might even be two".'

'There you are,' Rachel said victoriously, 'she was right, wasn't she? Oh, Mum, I do wish you could remember more about me arriving.' Now it was her turn to laugh. 'D'you know, when I read Grace's letter I thought maybe she was my real mother.'

'I do assure you dear, it isn't anyone I know. Teddy brought you all rolled up in a blanket and said there was nothing we needed to know. I suppose we did ought to have asked a few questions, but there, that was all a long time ago, and it really doesn't matter now.'

Rachel had to be content with that. She felt she knew her mother well enough to know that she wasn't hiding anything, but there was always a flicker of doubt.

Early in March Rachel and Belinda celebrated their twenty-fourth birthdays. Doctor Barber from Wickham called in regularly to see how Rachel was and had pronounced her as fit and healthy as any other pregnant woman, but he agreed with the hospital doctor and advised caution until the first three months had passed.

Phoebe prepared a special tea for all the family and Kas took Bella and the trap to fetch Belinda, Adam and Billy. The evenings were drawing out at last and the weather was more spring-like.

Calder Cottage seemed hardly large enough for them all and the small kitchen was decidedly crowded when they arrived. Rachel insisted on getting up and dressed for the tea party. She had helped her mother with the preparations until Phoebe had made her go to sit by the fire with her feet up. The door opened and Adam was the first to enter.

'Ah, so you're up,' he greeted. 'Many happy returns of the day, Sister-in-law.' He went to her and kissed her cheek warmly. 'Are you sure you should be?'

'I couldn't spend my birthday in bed, now could I?' she said. 'And I'm not your sister-in-law. Stepsister-in-law maybe.'

He inclined his head. 'I hope you're not going to let this spoil the day, Rachel. You were brought up as Belinda's sister. Everyone accepted that so you must as well.'

The situation wasn't easy but she couldn't expect Adam to understand. Rachel wanted to despise him but when together they could still ignite the spark of attraction which had been so cruelly stamped out. In lonely moments during these inactive weeks she'd tried to cure herself of the 'what might have beens'. It was all fantasy, she had Kas now, but she knew deep down that Adam couldn't rid himself of his feelings either. Fortunately at that moment the children, freed from warm coats, hats, scarves and gloves, burst into the room and Carol fell on Rachel with great enthusiasm.

'Darling,' she said as she hugged the child and kissed her. 'Isn't this lovely, to come to Grandma's house for my birthday tea?' She felt vexed with herself for ever thinking that she would be able to part with Carol. The warmth of the child's love for her far outweighed any guilt at keeping her from her real family. Ena had wanted it this way. Kas and Sybil were right in honouring her wishes even if it meant that one day Carol might have to face the same truth that Rachel had. It was painful, it had stirred her emotions, unnerved her, and given her a mission even if no one else would help her find her real parents. In Carol's case it was different. Her mother had died and left instructions as to who she wanted her daughter to live with. One day she could be told the story if she wanted to know. But no one seemed to know anything about Rachel's parentage and it was the lack of identity which tormented her.

Kas and Belinda followed the children into the room bringing gifts for Rachel, and she stood up to kiss her sister and wish her a happy birthday. Between them Phoebe and Rachel had knitted a dainty bed-jacket for Belinda, also a pale blue jumper.

'Rather practical,' Rachel said. 'But the best we could do being stuck at home so much.'

Rachel noticed Belinda's response to her use of the word 'home'. Calder Cottage would always be her home as long as Phoebe continued to recognise her as her daughter, though now she could understand why Belinda might find her presence an intrusion.

'Kas took Mum into Wickham to buy the wool so we've been kept busy making things for the babies as well,' she added. 'I hope you like the colour.'

'It's lovely,' Belinda said, and then Adam pushed his way forward and handed small gift-wrapped presents to her and Rachel.

'But you've already given me my present,' Belinda said to him.

'Yes, I know, but this is a special occasion after all,' he said. 'My two special girls reunited,' he added with a broad smile.

Wife and sister, he thought and wished again that he could tell them all as much as he knew.

Rachel experienced acute embarrassment while Belinda's eyes showed her discomfiture. The presents were wrapped identically and inside the jeweller's boxes on a bed of cotton wool lay identical crystal necklaces.

'Adam,' Rachel exclaimed, 'you shouldn't have!'

'They must have cost the earth!' Belinda said sharply.

Adam held up his hands in surrender. 'It's all right, Belinda. You'll still get your housekeeping at the end of the week. I've been doing a carpentry job for an ex-patient in my spare time so I decided to treat you both to something special.'

'It's very nice,' Belinda said and shut the box decisively. 'Better get on with tea or it'll be time to go home before we've even sat down.'

'It's quite beautiful, Adam,' Rachel said. 'But you really shouldn't have included me.'

'I . . . I wanted to, let's leave it at that.' Then he turned to Kas with a worried frown. 'I hope you don't mind? I ought to have asked your permission first.'

Kas laughed. 'It's all right. I know it pleases Rachel. I think perhaps you should have asked your wife first, though.'

'I did it because I'm so thankful Rachel is back in the family circle. Grateful too that it was you who found her, and made her happy. We've all been grieving for Wally, but today I felt we should celebrate Belinda and Rachel's birthdays to make up for lost time.'

'I'm sure Wally is with us in spirit,' Phoebe said. 'He'd want both his girls to make the best life for themselves that they can and he'd be thrilled to have more grandchildren. We can't imagine what was in his mind to write the letter he did but now that Rachel is back he would want her and you, Belinda, to be best friends. He'd be glad for me that I've got you both, and two sons-in-law to care for us all.' She went back to the kitchen but in an instant returned carrying a vase full of beautiful flowers. 'It isn't *my* birthday as I've just told Kas but he's brought them for me for looking after you, Rachel. Such a kind and generous thought, thank you.'

Rachel reached out and took Kas's hand. 'That was a lovely idea, darling,' she said. 'Gosh, we are lucky, Belinda, to have such nice husbands.'

Belinda half laughed, half grunted and then went to the scullery to bring in the tea. Any awkwardness she had caused was quickly forgotten as the children enjoyed jelly and fruit and kept up a constant chatter.

'By the end of this month I shall be able to get about more,' Rachel said as Phoebe refused all offers of help.

'You're going to take it easy for the whole time,' Kas said.

'But I do feel it's going to be all right this time, and I'm looking forward to moving with the others down to the New Forest. Belinda, Mum's been invited to go to stay with an old friend in Minstead, did you know?'

Belinda looked across at her mother. 'You didn't tell me,' she said accusingly.

'I thought you'd read all the letters, dear,' Phoebe said.

'I didn't have time to go through all of them,' she replied. 'Not properly. How are you going to get to Minstead?'

'We're going to take her when we move on,' Rachel said.

'What a good idea,' Adam said. 'You need a change, Mother.'

'It isn't so much that,' Phoebe said. 'After all, I don't want to be away too long in case Belinda needs me, but there are matters to attend to with the cottages now that I'm the legal owner. Grace Whitmarsh is in the one Wally's parents lived in so I know she's a good tenant, but I'd like to see who's in the adjoining one. I fancy Wally was never too keen on the family. He thought they were rather destructive, but you know Wally, he was so careful and proud of anything he'd made.'

'How long d'you plan to stay away?' Belinda asked. 'And who will you be staying with?'

'Grace has invited me to stay with her. It'll be strange being back in the cottage where your grandparents lived but nice to see the few people in the area I know. It isn't all settled yet, though, we've got to see Rachel on her feet first, and if you'd rather I didn't go, Belinda . . .'

'Of course you must go,' Adam said eagerly. 'Such a good idea to travel with Rachel and Kas.'

'You needn't worry about me,' Belinda said pointedly. 'Everything is ready for the baby and I've got good neighbours to help me.'

'I shall be back long before your baby is due,' Phoebe said. 'I shan't stay long.'

Belinda made no attempt to hide her irritation. Rachel recognised all the signs of jealousy. For the past few years Phoebe and Wally had been able to indulge her with Rachel out of the way. After all, they had always known that Rachel wasn't really theirs so it was probably quite a relief when she ran away. But Rachel had little doubt that her mother was glad to have her back. Phoebe demonstrated her love in every thought, word and deed.

Belinda and Adam lived too far away for Phoebe to visit often or them her. Belinda thought of herself as a town girl now with her fashionable friends. From little things Phoebe said Rachel guessed it was Adam who was the more frequent visitor.

A few days later when Rachel was in the house alone after Phoebe had gone in to Wickham to put fresh flowers on Wally's grave, she heard a knock on the back door and a male voice called, 'Hullo?' She scrambled out of bed and looking over the banisters saw Adam in the kitchen doorway.

'What are you doing here at this time of the morning?' she asked as she pulled her dressing-gown round her.

'Sorry to make you get out of bed,' he said. 'Where's your mother?'

'Gone into Wickham to the churchyard. There was a bit of shopping she wanted to do at the same time. I'm glad she's getting out as she needs to meet her old friends and she's used to walking.'

'I expect she's walking back by the river. I didn't see her. It's my day off so I cycled in to see Mum.'

'Didn't Belinda come with you?'

'No, Mum can't take too much of Billy – and you know, mother-in-law versus daughter-in-law.'

'Your mother always preferred Belinda to me,' Rachel reminded him.

'Mother didn't really know Belinda properly. No one could ever have lived with Mum.' Adam laughed. 'Not even you – especially not you.'

'Why especially not me?'

'Because you're quite quick-tempered. Mother really is impossible at times. I haven't said anything to her about your not being Belinda's real sister.' Adam sighed as he followed Rachel into the living room. 'Belinda and I had words about it. She seemed to think the whole world could be told but I've sworn her to secrecy.'

'It doesn't really matter, Adam,' Rachel said. 'I expect Belinda is pleased to think she was an only child, and the "cuckoo-in-the-nest" is not her real sister. I've got used to the idea now and it doesn't hurt quite so much, but we mustn't do or say anything to make it difficult for Mum.'

'Then don't you think you should stop wanting to find out where you came from? Don't you realise how hurtful that is to her? She couldn't have been a better mother to you if she had been your own. It's a bit like slapping her in the face to want to delve into the past in the hope of finding someone else you can call "Mother". It's all too long ago, Rachel. Besides, I doubt that the woman who gave birth to you then gave you away wants to be reminded, let alone have you turn up out of the blue.'

'I expect you're right,' Rachel agreed. 'But it's only natural for me to wonder. You know I wouldn't do anything to upset Mum. We were very close, and I love her very much. I loved Dad too but somehow he always kept me at arm's length. Now I know why.'

'But he was a good father, Rachel, and gave you a wonderful childhood, better than I had. Count your blessings, then, like Belinda says, we must get on with our lives.'

'Does she know you're here?'

'She knows I'm visiting Mum.' Adam sat down near the fire and twisted his cap between his fingers nervously.

'You are happy with Belinda aren't you, Adam?' Rachel asked as she curled up in the arm chair opposite him.

'Of course.' He didn't look up immediately. 'I never imagined it was possible to love two women at the same time,' he said sheepishly raising his head at last. 'I hope you really liked the necklace. S'pose it was a silly thing to do, or at least Belinda thinks it was.'

'What was she supposed to think, Adam? What was anyone supposed to think? Some kind of consolation prize?' On impulse Rachel slid off the chair and knelt on the floor in front of him. 'I never stopped loving you, you know. There were times I hated you for what you did, but I never ever stopped loving you.'

'But you love Kas, and you've got a good man there.'

'You don't have to tell me that, Kas is one of the best, but like you, I didn't think it was possible to love two people so desperately, and I do. Oh, Adam, I do still love you just as much as the day you fought Charlie Mead at the fair.'

He stood up so suddenly he knocked Rachel backwards.

'Then you'd best stop ever thinking about me because the love I feel for you is quite different from the passion I have for Belinda. I behaved badly and nothing can ever excuse that. I was weak, too weak to tell you when I came out of the Army that I preferred Belinda and it was her I wanted to marry. I've seen the look in your eyes,

Rachel, and so has Belinda and you're coming between us. Like she says, the sooner you pack up and move on the better t'will be for us all.' He stopped to help her up. 'I'm sorry. I've caused you enough pain but it had to be said. Don't hurt Kas by thinking that you still have feelings for me. Only you can cure yourself of those, and you must be strong enough to do it, Rachel.

'I wanted to do something to try to show you my regret at what happened. Now I realise that I let you think there could still be something special between us, but that's over, Rachel. I want you to regard the necklaces as a kind of bond between you and Belinda. You were brought up as sisters and you loved one another so much, don't let anything change that. But love between you and me?' Adam shook his head vigorously. 'No, Rachel. The past is over and done with. You're my sister-in-law and Belinda's twin sister – nothing in the world can change the way you were brought up.'

'And nothing can change the way I feel,' she said, standing to challenge him as she felt she had a right to. 'No one will ever erase the feeling I have inside me that things are not quite as I'm expected to believe.'

'You've been living with the gypsies long enough to think you've got second sight like your friend, I suppose,' Adam said. 'Forget it, Rachel. You're a grown woman now. You should know there's no truth in such rubbish. Go back to your travelling lifestyle, and make Kas and your unborn child happy and proud of you. I shan't call again, but tell your mother if there's anything she needs to send a postcard. I hope all goes well with you this time. Once you've got your own baby in your arms, believe me, Rachel, you'll forget all about us, but if ever you're Portsmouth way come and see us.'

He made for the door.

'Adam, please don't leave like this. There's still so much to say,' she pleaded.

'Too much has been said already. I made a mistake five years ago, I've made another one now and I'm sorry. I should have thought and spared you any further hurt, or caused Belinda to think badly of me. Like she says, the sooner you've gone the quicker we can get on with picking up the pieces.'

He hurried through the back door as if the house were on fire. Rachel ran through to the front window anxious to call him back but as she watched him pick up his bicycle from the hedge outside and jump on it the determination in his expression made her pause. She shivered. Someone walking over my grave again, she thought, and went back to the fire.

Adam had accused her of slapping her mother in the face but he had been equally as cruel. Rachel could just hear Belinda saying that it would be better for all concerned when she moved on. She tucked her feet beneath her warm winceyette nightdress and became engrossed in her troubled thoughts.

She had to admit that she had been revelling in this time back home at Calder Cottage. How many times during the past five years had she longed to be here, though not without her father? She couldn't rid herself of the feeling of guilt that she had driven him to his death and she had stupidly thought that being here with Phoebe would help compensate. Idiot, she reproached herself. Coming here to stay had caused even more trouble, and now between Adam and Belinda.

Belinda wasn't the same sweet delicate girl Rachel remembered. In spite of being cossetted she had proved to be the stronger after all. One son to her credit and another baby on the way and not so much as one day's sickness. It didn't seem fair but maybe this was Rachel's punishment. Already three babies lost; she couldn't bear to lose yet another one. Being with her mother had seemed as if it would consolidate the situation but Rachel knew there was no guarantee. It was time she returned to her chosen family of gypsies. She had caused inconvenience and distress to them at first, now she was blind to the upset she was causing her own family. But they weren't *her* family! All the more reason for leaving soon, she decided.

In her mind's eye she could still see Adam as he'd told her that he no longer loved her in the way she imagined. That wretched necklace was the real cause of this outburst. Rachel had told the truth when she said that she had never stopped loving Adam in spite of the agony. She had felt convinced that he felt the same, but now he was trying to excuse his expressions of affection as 'sisterly', a different kind of love. He had to say that to nip in the bud whatever was ripening between them.

'Only me, dear,' Phoebe called from the kitchen. Rachel didn't answer. She needed to be alone. She didn't want to have to tell her mother that Adam had even called but she supposed she'd have to. 'I'll pop the kettle on,' Phoebe called again.

Rachel heard her mother go into the hall to hang her coat on the hall stand, a fine peace of furniture crafted lovingly by Wally's gifted hands. Footsteps sounded on the stairs.

'I'm down here, Mum,' Rachel said dully.

'Oh, not dressed yet then?' Phoebe said coming into the living room and warming her hands by the fire. 'It's not a bad day out, getting warmer I think.' She looked into her daughter's face. 'You all right, Rachel? You look a bit pale.'

'I'm fine. You sit here, I'll make the cocoa.' Rachel got out of the chair and went into the kitchen. She put milk in the saucepan, got out two cups and stood looking out of the small window, down the garden, remembering how she had run away without really considering the consequences. As she mixed cocoa, sugar and milk together her thoughts were just as mixed. Regrets at her wilful actions but none at living with the gypsies and marrying Kas, and now all she wanted to do was to return to the safety of the group.

Phoebe sensed Rachel's reluctance to talk so for a while they sat on either side of the hearth drinking cocoa in silence. Then Phoebe said, 'Nice bit of spring weather without too much wind, and the flowers will keep better in the churchyard. Guess who I saw today?' She hurried on when she received no response. 'Nessie Mead. She offered her condolences and asked after you and Belinda. Can't believe the change in that woman. She's spruced herself up all nice and tidy and I do believe she's filling out a bit. Dick seems to have settled down at last since he left Beth and came back to Nessie. Think she's a brick for taking him back really, but he's the father of her children after all. Nessie was telling me about them all.

'Benjie's over thirty now, married with three boys, and all three of Nessie's girls, Kittie, Susy and June, are married too. Kittie and her husband moved to Winchester and bought a little grocer's shop. Doing very nicely, Nessie said, but no family. Susy and June both married local chaps who work on the estate and they've each got a little girl.' Rachel lifted her head and smiled but she wasn't taking in what her mother was saying. 'Nessie sent her best regards and hopes you'll have the baby all right this time.'

'I'm sure I will, Mum,' Rachel said softly. 'Adam came in while you were out. He said to tell you if you want anything doing to send them a postcard.'

'Oh, must be his day off then. Suppose he came to see his mother. Sounds as if they aren't intending to visit again for a bit.' Phoebe sniffed significantly, picked up the cups and went to he kitchen. Rachel realised that her mother was feeling the distance between Kingsmere and Portsmouth more acutely now that her father was gone, and wished there was more she could do to bridge the gap. She went upstairs, washed and dressed, and later as they sat down to eat their mid-day meal said, 'How soon can you be ready to leave for Minstead, Mum?'

Chapter Eighteen

It was a bright April day when Kas, Rachel and Carol pulled up outside Calder Cottage. Rachel had been back with the gypsy group for a couple of weeks since Doctor Barber had pronounced her fit and over the danger period, and as she was feeling so well the group had commenced their journey in the direction of the New Forest a few days earlier. To spare Phoebe's embarrassment Kas and Rachel decided to fetch her in the trap.

'Oh, you haven't got your pretty little miniature horse,' she said as she locked up the front door of Calder Cottage, and with her bag full to overflowing closed the front gate behind her.

'The others are already well ahead, Mum,' Rachel explained. 'With three adults and Carol the trap would have been a bit heavy for Bella to pull. She'll be happiest riding alongside our waggon with Strawberry Girl. We've borrowed Caleb's pony for today.'

Kas took Phoebe's small case and strapped it under the trap at the rear and then helped her up to her seat beside Carol and opposite Rachel. Phoebe didn't look back, she didn't dare as her memories of Wally were in every stick and stone of Calder Cottage and she felt guilty at going away. Yet she knew she needed this holiday and it would be lovely to see Minstead again and her old friend Grace. There were no neighbours either to wave her off and she questioned whether she would be able to continue living in such an isolated area. Loneliness had descended on her like a menacing cloud after Rachel had returned to Bere Forest with Kas and Carol. Adam and Belinda had called to see her the previous Sunday, staying for tea but making no promises to visit again before the holiday. Phoebe admitted if only to herself that they had no idea what loneliness was like. But she didn't feel sorry for herself long as every sign of a warm spring was evident in the countryside through which they travelled.

They caught up with the gypsy travellers just outside Botley where they were resting. Phoebe was introduced to all the families as well as Lemuel and Sybil.

'You could have visited Rachel at home,' Phoebe told them. 'It was nice for me to have her with me for three whole months, and I'm sure she missed you all.'

'It was good for Rachel,' Lemuel said. 'We felt she needed that time with you. But we've certainly missed her. She's been a great asset to our family, helping with the children when our group was larger and, most important, a Godsend to me with my work.'

Phoebe was amazed at the cleanliness of the brightly painted waggons, and the camaraderie which existed between the families. She thought she would have been viewed with suspicion. Instead, in no time at all she became one of them.

Once past Southampton where they stopped to rest the horses and enjoy some refreshment they entered the New Forest with its rich variety of woodland, open parkland, trees, bracken and thickets, the sun reflecting on the diverse shades of green. After several stops along the way they left the main Cadnam to Ringwood road to the pretty secluded village of Minstead.

The few residents from outlying cottages came out to see the gypsies arrive. Phoebe had sent word to Grace as to her anticipated arrival and suspected the news had been circulated as the welcome was particularly warm and friendly. One of the foresters directed them to a clearing among trees where they could camp and be sheltered from winds or storms.

'This is a charming place,' Lemuel said to the forester. 'To think we've travelled the nearby road many times but never found this little corner of God's earth.'

'How long will you be staying, sir?' the forester enquired.

'A few days at most, and I can assure you the site will look as clean and tidy when we leave as it is now.'

The forester touched his cap and returned to his home while the gypsies unpacked the things they needed to heat the water over open fires and prepare the evening meal. Rachel went with her mother to two adjoining cottages about half a mile on the other side of the clearing where a woman in a wide-brimmed hat was waiting at the gate.

'Is this Grace?' Rachel asked in a whisper.

'It must be but it's many years since we met,' Phoebe said.

The woman waved frantically. 'Phoebe, Phoebe – it's so good to see you again.' She came running down the track with arms outstretched and for both women the years spun round like a top out of control. They hugged, laughed and cried together, while Rachel stood by to look on and appraise this old schoolfriend of her mother's. Grace Whitmarsh was elegantly tall and slim. Her face was elongated, but as Rachel looked into the woman's eyes she recognised at once that here was a woman of youthful exuberance and inner beauty.

'So this is Rachel,' she said, at last freeing Phoebe. She took Rachel's hands in her own and kissed her lightly on her cheek. 'I may not have seen your mother for several years but we have kept in touch. I'm so sorry about dear Wally. So very sad and it'll take time to realise he's gone, my dears. So the Romanies have adopted you, Rachel? I understand you've married into the clan. I hope I shall meet them and your husband. Come along into the house, tea's ready.'

'I'd better leave you then, Mum, and Kas and I will bring your things over later,' Rachel said.

'You come in whenever you like, my dear,' Grace said. She had a sharp turn of phrase which from anyone else might have sounded officious but from her exuded nothing but the warmest of invitations. Phoebe glanced round with a smile as Rachel left and Rachel felt instantly confident that her mother was in good hands.

Back in their own waggon where Kas had started to prepare the meal Rachel laughed merrily as she set the table.

'Grace is quite a character, I think,' she said. She went on to describe her, adding, 'By her size and tone of voice you'd think she was a school teacher but she has a lovely dimple in her left cheek and such a happy smile. She seems to sum you up with just a glance. I liked her at once.'

'That's really nice for your mother,' Kas said. 'She'll need a friend of her own age.'

'I hope she won't discard us though.'

'Never. Not your mother, Rachel.It's up to us to be there when she needs us, but we must remember not to intrude or take advantage of her. There'll be times when she'll seek company and others when she'll need solitude. I believe she's disappointed that Belinda and Adam live so far away. I got the impression that she doesn't see them often which is a shame. Children grow up so fast and once they go to school time is limited.'

'You're so sensitive to other people's feelings, Kas,' Rachel said, looking up into his face with admiration. 'It's lovely to all be back together again – and I did come back, didn't I?'

He leaned across and ruffled Rachel's hair, much to Carol's delight. 'There'd have been trouble if you hadn't,' he said in mock anger. Then, in more sombre mood, he added, 'I hope it helped your mother having you at home for a while. I know you think she wishes it had been Belinda but we must let nature take its course. One day Belinda may need your mother more than she realises. Maybe she hasn't experienced too many of life's disasters yet but you've been through troubled waters, and we've weathered our disappointments together, so we know what it's like not to have things all our own way.'

Rachel ate in silence. Life didn't stand still. It progressed, Lemuel said, and she was glad it did, but every now and then that last scene with Adam tormented her, washed over her, enveloping her in depression. Then she would find herself lying awake at night going over much of what had happened during their courtship and subsequent events. She'd never believe Adam didn't care for her. She remembered the railway cottage they were going to share and the gypsy woman who had warned them of some impending change in their plans. Adam had been quite rude to her but Rachel felt a certain respect and now recalled that the woman had said they'd never own the cottage. She'd said, 'Be kind to the woman', Rachel could remember that bit quite clearly. They'd thought it meant Adam's mother but now Rachel was left perplexed. Maybe her own mother? But there was no chance of them not being kind to Phoebe. The gypsy had warned that all was not as they believed. That bit had been proved right too – Rachel wasn't who she'd always thought she was! Adam had scoffed at any hint of fortune telling but Rachel knew better. She knew it didn't please Kas either to speak of finding out who her real parents were so she kept her thoughts private. Memories returned too of how she'd been taunted at school and called the Witch of Wickham because of the hideous birthmark. If for no other reason she desperately wanted to find her real mother to prove that she wasn't a freak and that the birthmark had faded. Rachel felt impatience growing but she had no idea where to start her search.

'We'd better hurry up,' she said while they were washing up. 'Or it'll be your bedtime, Carol, before we've taken Grandma's case and bag to her. I want to show you and Daddy where I lived when I was a little girl.'

It had been a long, tiring day and the light was beginning to fade as Rachel, Kas and Carol took the small path across the wood. No lights shone out from the cottage where Phoebe was staying with Grace, but next door a lamp was burning brightly in the window of the front room and distant voices could be heard.

'Oh that does bring back memories,' Rachel said as she stood still while she took in the scene. 'I was only seven when we left here but these cottages hold such precious recollections of our childhood.'

'And your grandparents lived in the adjoining one?' Kas asked.

'Yes. I believe my great-grandfather built them. Seems he had a bit of money. He was a builder, my father and grandfather both master carpenters. It was great fun having them live next door. If we got into trouble with Mum or Dad for any reason we would sneak next door and get given sweets.'

'What made your father want to move?'

'There wasn't enough work about, I think. Grandfather was too old to work and Dad heard about the Squire needing a carpenter at the Manor House at Wickham, with a tied cottage included. I remember the grandparents weeping when we left. At some time Dad must have been able to buy Calder Cottage but I don't remember exactly when. Maybe it was when Mum's parents died. We only visited Lee-on-Solent in the summer. Grandma was left on her own for several years but I think I remember something about some money being left to Mum when I was still at school. Maybe they bought Calder Cottage then.'

Behind the lace curtains Rachel could see movement as the lamp was lit and an eager hand waved them to come inside which they did.

'Can I take your case and bag upstairs, Mrs Hunter?' Kas enquired.

'I'll show you where,' Grace said. 'You can come too, Rachel. I expect you've forgotten about your grandparents' old home. I haven't had time to do much to the place except new wallpaper and a bit of varnish here and there. I love the fresh air so the garden takes precedence over housework. There's a tidy bit of garden too but I've got it all well planted with spuds and the rest. Hope we don't get any late frosts, I took a chance.'

Everywhere smelled either of carbolic soap or lavender polish. Rachel wondered if it was all for her mothers' benefit but considering Grace claimed to prefer the great outdoors she had certainly made her mark on the cottage. Downstairs was clean but more cluttered with Grace's memorabilia from abroad, and the time flew by as she related story after story about each item which intrigued her visitors.

'Now I want you to come every day for as long as you're staying in the woods,' Grace said when Rachel insisted it was past Carol's bedtime. 'Your mother and I are going to have fun catching up, and I do want to get to know you better before you go off travelling again.'

Even Kas had to agree that Grace seemed a kind person, and after all that had happened she just had to be the tonic Phoebe needed.

Carol too was much taken with Auntie Grace and eager to return to the cottage next day. The long garden was exciting to explore and as it was a lovely warm day Grace brought lemonade and a pot of tea outside.

'So what's Kas doing today then?' she asked.

'The men are out hawking round the houses. They take advantage of every opportunity,' Rachel said.

'D'you help too?'

'Of course. I have to help earn my keep the same as the others, but not just as the moment as we really want this baby.'

'Phoebe said both you and Belinda are expecting. Such a shame Wally won't be here to see his new grandchildren.' She poured the tea. 'I suppose you'd have liked these two cottages for the girls, Phoebe?' she said thoughtfully.

Phoebe glanced at Rachel quickly and she knew by her mother's look that Grace had been told nothing about her father's will and letter.

'If you haven't told Grace yet, Mum,' she said, meaning that she wasn't really Belinda's twin sister, 'you may as well.'

'Grace was the only person in the whole world who knew that I didn't give birth to twins, dear,' Phoebe said, slowly. 'When I got over Belinda's birth and grew stronger I realised what an enormous responsibility it was to take in someone else's baby, and Grace, being thousands of miles away in Singapore, was the best person to confide in.'

'Can you remember any details of what Mum told you, Grace?' Rachel asked eagerly.

'Heavens, no! How old are you now? Twenty-four? My memory isn't that good, I'm afraid, Rachel. I used to keep all the letters I received, but I wasn't very good at writing back, was I, Phoebe? The life was so exciting and hectic.' Grace paused and leaned forward in the whicker chair. 'But you know now, Rachel? I thought it was to be a never-to-be-discovered secret, Phoebe?'

She sighed. 'It was,' she said solemnly, 'and we didn't ever tell anyone but you. Moving to Kingsmere when the girls were seven it faded from our thoughts for much of the time, especially when the birthmark disappeared. Wally's death has been more tragic than you know, Grace.' She went on to tell her friend about the will and letter.

'Phew!' Grace exclaimed as she sat back in her chair again and sipped tea. 'That was a bit below the belt, wasn't it? You poor dear, Rachel. Such a revelation was enough to turn your brain.'

'It was a blow, but well deserved after what I did.' Rachel stretched out her hand and squeezed her mother's. 'It doesn't alter my love for Mum, and I do appreciate all she and Dad did for me. I was hurt that Dad disowned me, I can't deny that, but like Kas says, money isn't important, it's people that matter.'

'I'd like to buy this cottage, Phoebe,' Grace said. 'That's one of the reasons I wanted you to come to Minsted. I can afford it, and as I've no relatives of my own I could leave it to Rachel.' She laughed. 'Won't be for a long time yet though, m'dear.'

'Wally left everything tied up in such a way that the cottages, all three of them, can't be sold until I die,' Phoebe explained. 'And then the proceeds have to be shared between Belinda and her offspring. If only we'd adopted Rachel legally she could have contested the will.'

'But could you have done that? Adopted Rachel, I mean?' Grace asked. 'I thought at the time you said you had no idea where the child came from?'

'That's true . . .' Phoebe began, but Rachel interrupted quickly.

'I mean to find out where I came from, and who my real parents are or were,' she said. 'Oh, I know everyone thinks I'm mad to rake up the past and I don't want to bring trouble to any family, but I *need* to know. Can you understand that, Grace?'

'But that's some task, dear, if Phoebe doesn't know anything.'

'I do wish Rachel could let the matter drop,' she said a trifle impatiently. 'I've told her all I know which is that Teddy, the midwife, brought her to us very early in the morning while it was still dark. No one in Minstead knew or suspected, not even Wally's parents. By the time we let them see the babies there were two, and when they saw Rachel's birthmark they assumed that was why they hadn't been allowed in. The truth was that Wally's mother was a bit of a ditherer and I couldn't take too much of her so Wally kept them away for the first few days.'

'And the midwife?' Grace asked. 'Where is she now? Dead, I suppose?'

'She and her sister retired during the war, I think. Nurse Fletcher was the elder, a spinster, and lived not at all that from the Calder Cottage strangely enough, but Teddy lived at Cadnam. She was a widow with three children and had to go back to work as a midwife after her husband died, to keep herself and her three children. I believe they went to live by the sea somewhere, Christchurch or Bournemouth it might have been.'

'Surely someone round here would know?' Rachel said, but her mother shrugged and remained silent.

After dinner Phoebe said that she wanted to visit the family next door. 'I expect you'd like to come, Rachel. After all, that's our old home. They're complaining that the roof leaks and a few other jobs need doing so I'd best get it over and done with.'

'How long have they lived there?' Grace asked.

'Ever since we left nineteen years ago,' Phoebe said. 'They had seven children so the cottage has taken a bit of a beating during the years. It used to grieve Wally to see the woodwork scratched and the' windows broken but I suppose they're much like any other big family.'

Rachel listened eagerly. 'If they've lived there ever since we left,' she said, 'then surely the same midwife would have delivered some of the seven children?'

Grace laughed. 'I was thinking much the same thing, Rachel, but didn't dare say so. I expect your mother is right and it's better to let sleeping dogs lie, but I do understand how you feel. As if you don't belong – as if you don't have any identity – but your husband is right to say it doesn't really matter because you can't change anything now. If it wasn't a legal adoption you might be getting someone in trouble on top of everything else.'

'I wouldn't want to do that,' Rachel said, 'but I'd dearly love to talk to the midwife, if she's still alive.'

'There's not a lot I can do to help you, Rachel, but I'll ask around to see if anyone knows where the midwife went to live,' Grace offered.

But Rachel didn't want to accept help from anyone else and after she'd helped with the dishes went with her mother to the cottage next door.

From what Phoebe had said Rachel expected to find the woman of grubby appearance, but considering she had a family of seven children she looked surprisingly youthful and nicely dressed.

'Mrs Hunter,' Emily Young greeted. 'It's nice to meet you at last. And this must be . . .?'

'My daughter, Rachel.'

'Yes, we heard a rumour that you were coming with the travellers.'

'I've come about the repairs that need doing,' Phoebe hurried on to hide her embarrassment about Rachel being a gypsy. 'I'll have a look round whenever it's convenient to you, Mrs Young, and then see what we can do.'

'It's convenient now, Mrs Hunter. I've only got Lucy at home today. Michael and Leslie are at school and the others are out at work. You've just missed my Alec, he's been in for his dinner and gone again. Come along in.'

Upstairs in the small bedroom a little white-faced girl lay in bed.

'I was sorry to hear about Mr Hunter,' Emily said quietly. 'Very sorry indeed. I know it's early days yet, but we was wondering, my Alec and me, if there'd be any changes?'

'None that I can think of, Mrs Young,' Phoebe said. 'As tenants you have certain rights, but of course without a man now I shall have to watch my expenses so I'd be grateful if you'd take as much care as you can of the house.'

'Well, we had a talk and we understand the situation so my Alec said I was to say that he and the boys will do what repairs they can themselves if you can provide the materials, same as before.'

'Hullo, you must be Lucy,' Rachel said to the little girl. 'How old are you?'

'Seven, Miss,' Lucy whispered.

'I lived here until I was seven,' Rachel said with a smile. 'Aren't you well?'

'A bit delicate, is Lucy,' Emily said. 'Picks up every germ that's going, she does. Doctor thinks she might have a heart murmur but I daresay she'll grow out of it and be as boisterous as the rest. She's the last of the brood so my Alec spoils her, I daresay.'

Rachel saw an opportunity not to be missed.

'Did you have all your children here in this cottage, Mrs Young?' she asked.

'Yes, came here soon after we was wed. Alec got a job on a farm near Cadnam and he's still there now. Had my Esme within the year, we did. Poor Nurse Edwards almost lived here for three or four days, my labour was so long.' Emily Young laughed heartily. 'Wasn't long about after that, though. More I had the quicker they came.'

'Don't suppose you happen to know where Nurse Edwards is now?' Rachel ventured.

'Retired a long time ago, but she remembers Esme's birthday even to this day. Thought she'd have to get the doctor to me for her, but Teddy wouldn't give up – and I couldn't.' She laughed again. 'My Esme's married now and living in Wiltshire. She'd have the address but I do know Teddy lives near the sea somewhere down Bournemouth way. In a home for retired nurses, I believe.'

'She delivered my – um, me too,' Phoebe said. 'She must know this cottage very well, though I only had Rachel and Belinda.'

'Reckon Teddy knows every stick and stone hereabouts. Couldn't have done without her, none of us.'

Lucy began to cough and her mother gave her a drink. After Phoebe had surveyed the damp patch on the ceilings of two of the bedrooms they went over the rest of the cottage while Mrs Young showed them where repairs were needed. Phoebe promised to do what she could, and as they left and returned to the cottage next door Rachel said, 'Wasn't in too bad a shape, Mum. What did you think?'

'They invited me in for a cup of tea the day I moved in,' Grace said, 'and I must say everywhere appeared to be clean and tidy. Quite a hard-working couple, I should say.'

'I daresay Wally coveted this place and saw damage where there wasn't any,' Phoebe said. 'Besides, the children are all growing up now. Not too much to do. I'll have to find a workman somewhere.'

'I'll speak to Kas, Mum,' Rachel offered. 'Travelling folk have to do their own repairs and most can turn their hand to anything. Grace, I've found out that the midwife who took me to Mum is living in a home for retired nurses somewhere on the coast.'

'She's still alive then?'

'Yes, so at least I know where to start looking.'

'Shouldn't be too difficult to find then, but whatever you do, Rachel, dear, don't rush into anything.'

'Kas won't let me,' she said dismally. 'I doubt very much that he'll agree to my searching for Nurse Edwards in Bournemouth or anywhere else.'

'If I were you I'd get your confinement over and done with before you continue with the search,' Grace said.

'But by then the sisters might be dead. They must be pretty old as it is,' Rachel said.

At the close of the day when Kas and Rachel were relaxing in their own van and Carol had been put to bed, Rachel told Kas what she had learned. As she had predicted the response was negative.

'Your health is what matters and after you've had the baby, Rachel, you'll have your work cut out looking after it. Should we ever find ourselves on the coast then you can make enquiries but we aren't making a special journey to Bournemouth where gypsies aren't received very cordially.'

Rachel knew that she had to accept his decision however difficult that was. But nothing could prevent her from thinking and planning. When they reached Burley the distance wouldn't be so great and it might prove to be her only chance. She would discuss the matter with Lemuel and Sybil and solicit their help.

As soon as she mentioned the repairs required by the tenants of the cottage, Kas offered to look into it at once.

'We didn't reckon on staying here more than a couple of days but if there's a job to be done we must see to it,' he said. 'If the others want to move on we'll stay here alone while I do the work.' He smiled, his dark eyes twinkling mischievously at Rachel. 'I know you'll find it very irksome to have to while away the days with your mother and her friend.'

Rachel tossed the nearest cushion at him. 'It's my guess,' she said, 'that the others will want to help too. I'd like Lemuel and Sybil to have time to get to know Mum and Grace better.' Rachel laughed. 'Poor Mum, it was quite obvious that she wasn't keen to be seen having anything to do with gypsies but I do believe she enjoyed travelling with us.'

Kas watched Rachel anxiously as the days passed. She blossomed in a way he couldn't describe and once the repairs to both cottages had been completed the group began to prepare to move on. He half expected Rachel to want to remain with her mother for longer but on the other hand he guessed that she was eager to move nearer the coast, while he planned to travel back towards Wickham once the time drew near for their baby to be born in late August. Although the gypsies were well experienced in childbirth he wanted what was best for Rachel, and knew that it would please her mother to be on hand, but he said nothing to his wife as he wanted it to be a surprise. After all that had happened with Ena he also felt he would be happier in close proximity to a doctor and hospital.

Their last evening at Minstead was a fine, dry, balmy one and with caravans packed and ready to move early next day a huge camp fire was lit. The forester had presented them with several rabbits as a token of his appreciation for not causing any undue noise and litter during their stay. In turn he and his family, along with Phoebe, Grace, the Youngs and any other neighbours who wanted to, were invited to join in the final gathering. Plenty to eat and drink, a joyous sing-song accompanied by Caleb's squeeze-box, and, to everyone's surprise, Grace's guitar, brought romanies and gorgios together in harmony for a feast they wouldn't easily forget.

Grace was a woman of the world, nothing shocked or surprised her, and she entered into the spirit of the happy occasion with gusto.

Rachel said her goodbyes after Lemuel had finished prayers.

'We'll see you again before too long, Mum,' she said emotionally. 'When August comes perhaps you can come to stay with us?' Then she turned to Grace. 'I can't tell you how pleased I am to have met you, and I know Mum is loving every minute of her holiday with you. You've been very kind.'

'Nonsense, Rachel,' Grace said. 'It's been my pleasure, and your mother and I are going to see a great deal of each other from now on. I'm hoping to go and stay at Calder Cottage so we'll meet again one of these days. Naturally I'm anxious to meet Belinda, Adam and Billy too.

Rachel slept in Kas's arms that night full of contentment.

The dew had hardly dried on the grass verges when they set off southwards next morning, and when the first signpost to Bournemouth appeared at the roadside Rachel was filled with renewed hope.

Briar Hill near Burley was a good site, and they prospered financially by selling their wares among the local people who treated them kindly. Weeks passed in rapid succession, Rachel disappointed because no mention was made of travelling farther south to the coast even though she had hesitantly suggested to Lemuel it might be good for him. Kas was just relieved that Rachel continued to keep well.

'I know I shouldn't worry,' he said one morning after he'd been to fetch water, 'but I shall feel more secure if we're near your mother and a doctor or hospital when the time comes.'

'It's ages yet before I'm due,' Rachel said, vying for time. 'It's nice here and I expect Lemuel would like to move nearer the sea. I thought perhaps one Sunday you and I could take him in the trap to Christchurch or Bournemouth.'

'Nice try,' Kas laughed. 'You can't fool me, you should know that, but it's quite a way and we don't want to travel out of our way in your condition.'

Rachel had been advised similarly by Sybil and Lemuel and was downhearted, but tried to keep her spirits up by promising herself that once she had her baby she would go to Bournemouth by herself on the train from Wickham. She might even persuade her mother to accompany her.

On a wet miserable June morning as Rachel and Carol sat inside the van doing a jig-saw puzzle while Kas was feeding the horses a strange noise distracted Carol.

'Oh, look, Mummy,' she called from her kneeling position on the window seat. 'A motor car – oh, and look, it's Grandma!'

With great excitement she ran to the door and looked out with Rachel, now rather too large to move quickly, hastily following.

'A car!' she exclaimed. 'It's Mum and Grace!'

The car chugged its way close to the van and Kas came running across the field greatly intrigued. He looked the shiny vehicle over enviously before helping Phoebe and Grace out.

'Come along in,' Rachel called. 'What a marvellous surprise.'

Phoebe and Grace ran in to avoid getting too wet. 'Just had to come to see how you all are,' Phoebe said. 'Oh, Rachel dear, I have missed you. That's the only thing I have against you living like this – we don't have any way of keeping in touch.'

'I assumed you would be back in Kingsmere,' Rachel said while Kas put the kettle on. 'And what's this – a borrowed car?'

'No, m'dear, 'tis all mine,' Grace said in her usual abrupt manner. 'I drove all the time in Singapore, well, everyone did, and now my finances are straightened out I decided to make life easier by being able to go where I want to, when I want to.'

'Grace came to stay at Calder Cottage,' Phoebe said. 'We had a lovely time and went to visit Belinda and Adam. He's talking about getting a little car one day.'

'I'd already made up my mind before that so we went to a reputable garage in Portsmouth, and here we are.'

'You haven't chosen a very nice day for travelling around,' Kas said.

Phoebe cast a cautious look towards Grace who said fearlessly,

'That's the whole point, Kas. I know you aren't too much in favour of Rachel pursuing her parentage, but Phoebe and I feel that she'll never settle until she knows. It's quite an intriguing story, after all. And as Rachel says, you do know a little about your roots but she knows nothing.'

'And what she doesn't know can't hurt her,' Kas said sternly.

'You have a valid point there, dear boy. But we thought as it is such a miserable day I could drive down to Bournemouth and take you all for a spin. It's June, after all, so it might buck up later on. Rain before seven, shine before eleven, isn't that right?'

Grace was not so much persuasive as coercive. Rachel couldn't believe her luck and for once was totally speechless. She could hardly bring herself to look at Kas but when she did his dark eyes melted her apprehension.

'OK, you win, I suppose,' he said with a lop-sided grin. 'I won't pretend I like the idea at all. I'm afraid of causing distress to some poor unsuspecting middle-aged couple. I don't want you to get hurt, darling. You must be prepared for disappointment. Even if you find the midwife it doesn't mean she'll be willing to betray a confidence.'

'Don't you think I've had time to think all this over a million times?' Rachel asked. 'I realise that I've only got a slim chance of finding out who my parents were but I feel compelled to try.'

'Grace and I have talked a lot about it too,' Phoebe said. 'It may be that after all these years Wally felt we'd done something not above board by taking you in without legal advice. He'd evidently given the matter considerable thought and it's possible he was of the opinion that he owed it to you, Rachel, to tell you the truth.' She pulled a scrap of paper from her bag. 'Mrs Young's daughter Esme sent her this address. I don't know that we'll be able to find the place though. It's on the outskirts of Bournemouth near a river.'

'We can stop off somewhere at a newsagents and get a map,' Grace said. 'Or we've got tongues in our heads, we can ask.'

'Well, I wish you the best of luck,' Kas said.

'But you're coming as well. I might need you to help me start her up,' Grace said, 'or change the wheel if we get a puncture.'

How could Kas rebel against such a command without appearing ungallant? Grace's Morris Oxford was a big attraction, and although with Rachel's extra bulk she and her mother had some difficulty squeezing in the rear seat with Carol, they managed comfortably, Kas riding in the front passenger seat as navigator. They journeyed through country lanes to Bransgore and Christchurch before heading towards Bournemouth at over twenty miles per hour, Grace assuring them that they could travel fifty miles on one gallon of petrol.

By noon the clouds had scudded away and the roads were quickly drying in the June sunshine. They stopped near a small shop and received directions to some brick buildings enclosed in green-painted iron railings where a board near the gate announced that these were the homes for retired nurses and midwives.

'We've found it so easily,' Rachel said.

'Yes, and done it in good time,' Grace said proudly. 'In fact it may be a good thing we've got here before dinner time. Elderly people often have an afternoon nap so you might catch her now if she is still here. But I hope you'll agree with me, Kas, that it might be better for Rachel and Phoebe to go it alone from here?'

Kas agreed readily and they decided that he and Grace would take Carol for a walk along the river bank which was close by.

Phoebe led the way up the path, admiring the well-kept lawns and flower borders before entering a door marked 'Office'.

A grey-haired gentleman was sitting at a desk but stood up as they entered.

'Good afternoon,' he greeted politely. 'Can I be of help?'

Rachel opened her mouth but nothing came out. She felt as if she had been struck dumb and Phoebe looked at her with concern. Then she took the matter into her own hands.

'We've come to enquire about a lady named Mrs Edwards,' she said. 'She lived at Minstead in the New Forest where she was midwife for many years. We understand she came here to live with her sister Miss Fletcher – Minnie Fletcher. She was midwife in the Wickham area.'

The gentleman offered his hand to Phoebe has he introduced himself.

'Sydney Cox,' he said. 'I'm sorry to say dear Miss Fletcher died a few years back, but her sister, Mrs Edwards – yes, she's very much with us. Does she expect you?'

'No,' Phoebe said. 'We've come from Minstead and picked my daughter up near Burley. It wasn't arranged, you see, an unexpected opportunity – I don't want to upset Nurse Edwards.' Suddenly Phoebe had cold feet.

'I'm sure she will be delighted to have unexpected visitors. She's getting on, you know, well over eighty. Miss Fletcher was eighty-nine when she passed away but they enjoyed several years of happy retirement together, taking every opportunity to visit the seaside. Now if you take the path which leads to the rear of this building you'll find the little dwellings all have numbers. Mrs Edwards lives in number twenty-three.'

He escorted them to the door and showed them which path to follow.

The solid doors were all painted green as were the small high windows but most looked attractive with frilled lace curtains. Rachel went ahead of her mother in her eagerness to find Teddy, but as they reached the door marked twenty-three she held back.

'What are we doing?' she whispered. 'Suddenly I'm afraid I won't like what I hear, or cause the old lady to have a heart attack or something.'

'She may not be prepared to tell us anything,' Phoebe whispered. 'We can't be sure what state of mind she's in so say we're just visiting my old midwife for old times' sake.'

Rachel knocked on the door and it was opened surprisingly quickly.

'Yes?' the elderly woman croaked, peering first at Rachel then at Phoebe. Then she threw her hands in the air and opened the door wider. 'Well, 'pon my soul, if it isn't Phoebe Hunter.'

'Hullo, Teddy,' Phoebe said, smiling broadly. 'I wasn't sure if you'd remember me.'

'Not remember you? 'Course I do – and that cottage at Minstead. Delivered another seven after yours. But don't stand out there, come along in. And let me see . . . is this your girl?'

As they went inside, carefully brushing their shoes on the doormat Phoebe said, 'One of them.'

'Ah, yes, there were two – 'tis all coming back.'

By the time they were all inside the living room Nurse Edwards' cheeks were rather flushed. She sat down in a high-backed chair near the window and Phoebe sat opposite. The old nurse appraised Rachel's condition.

'Long to go? Couple of months mebbe?'

'The end of August, Mrs Edwards,' she said. 'I've had three miscarriages though.'

'Mmm . . . 't'will be all right this time by the looks of things. Once you get over three months, should go full term. Well, fancy that, you coming to see me,' she mused as she stared hard at Phoebe.

'An old friend brought us in her car,' she explained. 'My husband Wally died at the beginning of the year.'

'I'm sorry, my dear. A good man was your husband, and such a wonder with wood. He couldn't have been all that old?'

'No, not even sixty-five, and his parents lived to well in their eighties.'

'Ah, well, that's one thing we can't arrange to suit ourselves.'

Phoebe went on to explain about Wally's illness, and then, looking down at her trembling hands, continued nervously, 'I'm sure dear Wally didn't mean to upset the apple cart, Teddy, but he left a letter explaining why he couldn't include Rachel in his will – because she isn't really Belinda's twin sister.'

'That wasn't the real reason though,' Rachel put in. 'I was jilted by my fiancé who then said he'd made a mistake and wanted to marry Belinda. I couldn't bear it so I ran away. Dad couldn't forgive that. I . . . I joined up with some gypsies. They're really nice people though.'

'I ain't got anything against gypsies, my dear. Helped a few of 'em out in me time when they had bad deliveries. It's always the few who give the rest a bad name. Mostly they're kind, clean and helpful.'

'I'm married to one,' Rachel said with a smile.

'Kas is an exceptionally good man,' Phoebe said. 'But he's not too happy about us bothering you. Neither am I if it comes to that.'

'But I *must* know, Mrs Edwards. I must find out who I am and where I came from. I hope you understand?' Rachel pleaded.

'You're Rachel Hunter as I recall,' Mrs Edwards said slowly, then pursed her lips and frowned. 'I could tell you that I don't know anything either. After all, t'was my sister who brought you to me – how do I know where you sprang from?'

'But you do, Mrs Edwards, don't you?' Rachel said in a soft persuasive voice.

'Let's have a cup of tea. You must be tired after your long journey and talking always makes me thirsty.'

'Can I help?' Phoebe offered. 'We don't want to put you to any trouble.'

Rachel was surprised at how spritely Teddy was for her age. She was keen-eyed and mentally alert, with no sign on senility.

'I don't get many visitors these days,' she said. 'Minnie and me wondered whether we'd done the right thing to move away from people we knew, but we love the sea and enjoyed our days together.'

'I'm sorry she passed away,' Phoebe said, following Teddy to the tiny kitchen. 'She was well-loved and remembered in her parish, just as you were and still are in yours.'

Teddy laughed heartily. '"Parish" is good,' she said. 'T'was like that for the both of us. We knew everyone for miles around and watched the children grow up, get married and have babies of their own. 'Tis the kind of job you miss, but Min and me, we had our memories to live with and we exchanged our stories – yes, and we often talked about you and your girls, Mrs Hunter.' She turned from the table and put her arm round Phoebe's shoulder, whispering, 'D'you really want the girl to know the truth? I've kept Min's old records and I've read 'em through so knows 'tis all there. Remember it like it was yesterday – better'n what happened yesterday.'

'Do we have an option, Teddy? Doesn't she have the right to know, having been told this much now? We promised never to tell anyone and Wally and I kept that promise. I don't know what came over him to change his will and write the letter he did. It was pure chance that Rachel met up with Adam Taylor at Portsmouth hospital or she might not have seen her father before he died.' Phoebe found it difficult to talk about those unpleasant days, but she told Teddy the full story.

'Suppose in a way she blames herself for Wally's death then?'

Phoebe nodded. 'Poor Rachel, life wasn't very kind to her having to grow up with that horrible birthmark, but at last she does seem happy now, even if it is with gypsies. Wally's letter was a dreadful shock for her but she isn't going to let it rest until she knows the truth, Teddy.'

'But what does she plan to do if I tell her?'

'Best ask her,' Phoebe said.

The tea made, Phoebe carried the tray into the living room where Rachel sat patiently waiting, though inside she was churning with a mixture of excitement and fear.

'If we're keeping you from your dinner, Teddy, we could come back another time?' Phoebe suggested.

She nodded towards Rachel. 'That wouldn't please you now, would it?'

'I'm not here to cause trouble,' she said. 'I'm anxious to find the truth, even if I don't like it.'

'Oh, bless you, child, there's nothing you won't like. But I'll get Min's record book out and we'll see what it says.'

Rachel felt impatience growing as Teddy first poured a cup of tea each and offered them biscuits then went into the hallway where a huge oak blanket chest stood. She returned a few minutes later with a black notebook conspicuous by its red spine.

'Now I must warn you that once I've told you, Rachel, this book will be burnt. I should have done it after Min died, but something niggled in the back of me mind and I couldn't bring myself to. This isn't the official record book, you understand. Min had a feeling that one day someone might come asking questions. Once she'd died, o'course, no one need know anything, but now that you know a bit you might as well know the rest.'

'Oh, *please*,' Rachel urged.

Teddy put her spectacles on and turned the pages. 'Very meticulous was our Min over details of her work.' She paused, skipping down the page, then read aloud, 'Because of the birthmark the man of the house, a man given to over indulgence in strong drink, threatened to kill this female infant. The mother had a difficult time, wasn't a strong woman after giving birth to five children previously. She had no interest in the sickly child and so in the interests of the baby the doctor present and myself decided to fake the infant's death.' Teddy glanced up to see how Rachel was accepting the story. 'We then colluded with my sister who was also a midwife and had recently delivered Phoebe Hunter of a female infant to give her the unwanted child and pass it off as a twin. They were duly registered officially as twin daughters of Phoebe and Walter Hunter of Minstead.'

'But the name of the woman – my mother,' Rachel asked anxiously.

Teddy's glance reverted to the top of the page. 'Case notes of Agnes Mead, wife of Richard Mead of Hundred Acres near Wickham.'

A deathly hush filled the small, stuffy room.

'*Nessie Mead*?' Phoebe cried, putting her hands to her throat. 'Heavens above! I can scarcely believe it. We took you back to within a couple of miles of where you were born, Rachel.'

Chapter Nineteen

Rachel sat white-faced with shock. Then she began to laugh.

'I'm Charlie Mead's sister!' she exclaimed. 'I've got another brother and three sisters. I'm one of a large family and Nessie is my real mother.' Her lips were dry and she drank almost greedily from her cup. It was almost too incredible to sink in. So many questions to ask Nessie and Dick, and perish the thought – Beth Cropper was her aunt!

'I would never have guessed in a hundred years,' she said. She stood up as discomfort compelled her to. A moment of giddiness possessed her.

Teddy and Phoebe fussed over her and gave her a drink of brandy. The colour returned to Rachel's cheeks and she blinked. 'I'm terribly sorry,' she said. 'Whatever came over me?'

'Quickening, I shouldn't wonder,' Teddy said. 'About five months, you say? Baby's turned all right then and it'll be plain sailing all the way now.'

'I don't know what to say.'

'You wanted to know, my dear, and now you do. Remember, this Mr and Mrs Mead think their baby died so it has to be your secret as it's been ours for this past twenty-four years. I never knew the Meads but Min told me all about them. I suppose she and the doctor could have been prosecuted for what they did, though as I told Min, with a good lawyer the authorities would have accepted that what was done was done in good faith for the sake of the child. Your parents gave you a good home, Rachel,' Teddy patted her hands. 'Now you be a good parent to your family, and may they all be healthy children.'

'Sisters – the sea,' Rachel muttered with a faraway look.

'What's that, dear?' Phoebe asked.'

'Oh, nothing. Something I remembered.' She recalled something else too, when she and Adam had been at the railway cottage. The gypsy there had said, 'Be kind to the woman.' Yes, Rachel thought, I've always had a warm feeling for Nessie Mead. I can understand why she didn't want me and I'll always be kind to her, just as I'll try to be extra kind to Mum.

They left Teddy and went to find the others. Kas and Grace listened with interest to Rachel's story while Carol announced with some impatience that she was hungry, so they travelled on to the cliff-top road and down to the promenade where they stopped for refreshment in the cafe there. Afterwards, while Rachel mused over what she knew and discussed it fully with Phoebe, Kas and Carol made a sandcastle on the beach and they allowed Carol to paddle in the water.

It was late afternoon when they returned to Mrs Edwards' home to present her with a bunch of pink carnations and a cake they'd thought she might like from a local bakery. From a fruit stall along the way they purchased a small basket of fresh strawberries for her. This time, Kas, Carol and Grace were introduced to her.

Teddy kissed Phoebe warmly as they made their goodbyes and then hugged Rachel. 'You've turned out a fine young woman, my dear. I hope all goes well when your time comes. Now, remember, that book never existed and there are no records left from my sister's work so the past is dead and buried too. Min wouldn't have wanted any recriminations, and when I'm dead and gone won't be any good anyone coming looking for evidence.' She tapped the side of her nose. 'What you know is your secret now.'

Rachel kissed Teddy warmly. 'You've been so helpful,' she said. 'I appreciate that you didn't have to tell us anything, but I'm so relieved and grateful that you did.' They waved goodbye, promising to visit if ever they were that way again. The journey back to Briar Hill seemed to be over as if by magic but only because Rachel couldn't stop talking.

There was an emotional goodbye between Rachel and Phoebe after they'd eaten together.

'You'll always be my real Mum,' Rachel said, giving her a hug. 'I'm glad it's turned out to be Nessie. It puts so much into place, like the friendship between me and Charlie. Not sure that I like the idea of Dick Mead being my dad, so I'm quite content to be a Hunter.'

'We shall be moving towards Wickham now, Mrs Hunter, during the next few weeks,' Kas told his mother-in-law.

'I shall be anxious for Rachel,' Phoebe said, 'and Belinda as well. I want to be on hand when my new grandchildren arrive.'

For the next few weeks of summer Rachel had much to brood over and discuss with Sybil and Lemuel. She wrote often to Phoebe, and even wrote to Belinda as well, hoping that she was well and saying that they would be seeing them fairly soon. She knew Phoebe planned to tell Belinda and Adam the true story in an effort to put an end to any speculation. It couldn't be the end for Rachel though. She desperately wanted to get back to Hundred Acres if only to see Nessie Mead from a distance. Kas, in his quiet, wise way, knew what Rachel hankered after and openly forebade any communication with the Meads except for polite greeting if they met by chance.

'The shock of discovering her baby didn't die, plus the fact of the doctor and midwife faking your death, might be very cruel to her,' he said.

'Yes, I know,' Rachel agreed. 'I've always felt so sad for her somehow, and I wouldn't ever do anything to hurt her, but I would like to see her – just to look at her and think, "You're my Mum".'

'It isn't likely that you'll ever meet up with people from that area again,' Kas said. 'After our baby is born we shall have to think seriously about the future, darling.'

'Why? Having a baby isn't going to change anything,' she said a trifle indignantly.

'Our group has split up a good deal since the war,' he said. 'We're a much smaller family now, and Lemuel and Sybil are not young travellers any more. I've been giving the matter some thought and I wondered how you'd feel about living in Christchurch?'

'Christchurch? Why Christchurch?' Rachel asked.

'Not for some while, but perhaps when our child gets to school age. As you know I own two cottages there. I thought we might take a trip down to see them before we move on. If they become vacant at any time we could live in one, and Sybil and Lemuel in the other.'

Rachel stared at Kas. 'It's a wonderful idea,' she said after thinking about it briefly. 'But would they want to? They've been travellers for many years. I'm sure it would be better for their health, but I'm not sure they'd approve of the idea.'

'Lemuel was talking about returning to the Isle of Wight. Sybil wasn't so keen, I felt. It's just an idea, Rachel, we must think carefully about it for the future.'

'How old are the people who live in the houses now?'

'An elderly couple live in one. They lost two sons in the war and I don't think the woman has ever recovered from the tragedy. A widow lives in the other one, but she's often away staying with her married daughter who lives in Poole. I can't turn them out, they're protected tenants, and I wouldn't want to, but we must be prepared for the houses to become empty one of these days.'

'It might not happen for years,' Rachel said. 'But I like the idea, Kas. It would be good to be more settled if we're to have a family.'

He wrapped his arms round her. 'Let's bring this one into the world safely to start with,' he said, cuddling her and their unborn child.

A month later and the travelling gypsies had regrouped in the Forest of Bere. It was pleasant for Rachel to be able to spend time with her mother as Kas, Caleb and some of the younger men found temporary work on local farms. The strawberry season had all but ended, and the fields needed to be cleared and ploughed ready for the following year. Rachel felt happier than she had done for a long while, and with the bloom of motherhood came contentment as she entered into the final phase of waiting.

'I'd feel easier in my mind if you'd let a doctor give you a check-up,' Kas persuaded her. 'I know nature takes its course but Doctor Barber knows the situation and would be glad to confirm that everything's all right. Bring the trap to the farm at 5 o'clock and we'll go into Wickham – please, Rachel, time is getting short.'

She laughed at Kas's concern but eventually agreed to do as he wished. She knew he was taking precautions for her sake and she appreciated the care he took of her, but doubted that any doctor could offer any better advice than Sybil and Precious. All the same, in spite of her well-being she had many moments of apprehension. Everyone was a tower of strength and did their best to reassure her, but too much had happened to Rachel since the day she had walked out of Calder Cottage and into a completely different lifestyle not to feel that fate might be waiting round the corner with some unexpected bombshell. At times she felt there must be some kind of jinx on her. First the strawberry birthmark. What had Nessie and Dick Mead done to cause such a blemish, she wondered? None of the other Meads had such a mark. Then Adam jilting her, and much later her father disowning her. She was afraid of what else there might be in store for her and tried hard to press Sybil into seeing into the future, but all she would say was, 'Happy times and sad times Rachel, and we all 'as to accept those.'

There was an early autumn feel to the late afternoon when Rachel set off alone in the trap drawn by Bella. Rachel and Carol had been to Calder Cottage to have dinner with Phoebe. Carol and her grandma were the best of friends so Phoebe was pleased to have the child's company while Rachel went to meet Kas.

'I've picked some of the best of the gladioli and roses,' Phoebe said. 'Perhaps you could take them to your father's grave before you come home?'

Wally would have been proud of his garden. Phoebe had worked hard to keep everything just as he'd always done, and the flowers had been particularly colourful and plenteous this year.

Rachel took the Wickham road towards the farm where Kas and the others were working, and when she reached the open fields pulled in at the side of the track. Her back ached from the bumpy ride so she climbed down and looked about her. Huge black rooks their glossy plumage shot with purple and green, tumbled in the sky before descending on the ground to scavenge whatever was going, making a noisy pantomime. She decided to walk about to try to ease the pain low in her back. In the near distance she could see the neat brick houses of Hundred Acres. I was born in one of those, she thought, and with her own confinement so close now tried to imagine the scene on the day she opened her eyes to the Mead household. There was no sign of Kas or any of the other workers yet. The church clock struck five and she guessed that Kas was washing up in the outhouse at the farm in readiness to take her to the doctor's. Rachel turned to go back to Bella and saw a woman coming along the track by the hedge. It was Nessie Mead.

As Nessie approached Rachel felt her bosom swell with admiration for this woman who she now knew was her mother. She'd had a hard life, Rachel knew, but Nessie looked younger than she remembered, still slim but somewhat more rounded. Her well-brushed chestnut coloured hair shone in the sunlight and her pretty green eyes sparkled with happy recognition.

'Hullo, dear,' Nessie said.

Rachel wanted to speak, there was so much to say but the words wouldn't come. 'I'm your daughter,' she wanted to shout from the rooftops, but how could she cause Nessie such a shock?

It seemed they stood and regarded each other for ages and then Nessie said in a low voice, 'I know what's in your heart, Rachel, dear. I think I always knew there was something special between you and me.'

'You . . . you . . . know?' she gasped.

Nessie nodded, and her eyes filled with sad tears. 'Adam came to see me.'

'He had no right,' Rachel said, suddenly angry. 'It's none of his business. The last thing I wanted was for you to be hurt, Mrs Mead.'

'It's as much Adam's business as anyone else's dear,' Nessie said. 'I'm not hurt – rather glad – to think that the baby I felt was a curse on me survived, and had such a good home with wonderful parents.'

'How long have you known?' Rachel asked, perplexed.

'Looking back I realise there was always some doubt about my baby. I wanted it to die, God forgive me, and afterwards when I thought it had, oh, I longed to have it back again to love, blemish and all. I've only known the truth of the matter since Adam came to see me a couple of weeks ago. After you'd discovered I was your real mother, and Adam was told, he was afraid you wouldn't be able to help yourself but come to see me or blurt it out if we met. He felt I should be warned.'

'It must have come as a dreadful shock, Mrs Mead. Adam didn't have the right to interfere though. He's Belinda's husband, my brother-in-law. He shouldn't have taken matters into his own hands.'

'I'm glad he did. It's best for the truth to come out and be done with. Rachel, his father was yours too!'

'Mr Taylor, my father?' she was stunned. 'And Adam knew all the time?'

'Don't you see? That's why he couldn't marry you,' Nessie went on. 'If you'd gone through with marriage, it would have been against the law. It was fate intervening that brought Doctor Grant back to Wickham after the war in time to prevent such a terrible mistake.' She placed her hand on Rachel's arm. 'It was a terrible shock for Adam then and he couldn't share it with anyone. He thought he'd have to live with the secret for the rest of his life. He had a notion that I might be your mother from rumours he'd heard. He was devastated when he had to treat you so cruelly.' She looked into Rachel's face anxiously. 'I think you'd best sit up in the trap, dear. I'm sorry if this is all too much for you.' Nessie got up to sit beside Rachel and took her hand in hers.

'Why ever couldn't Mum or Adam have told me the rest of the story once they knew that I knew who my mother was?' Rachel asked.

'Mrs Hunter doesn't know that Jake was your father. She and Belinda think you're Dick's child. Adam hasn't told anyone else. He doesn't want his mother upset. Being that you're in the family way and not living in the district, he felt I should know, but asked that we keep our secret.'

'Another brother,' Rachel said slowly as the truth finally dawned and everything became so much clearer. How could she ever forget the fight between Dick Mead and Jake Taylor which caused – her father's death? And all over her, she supposed.

'*Half*-brother, just as Charlie and Benjie are, and my girls are your half-sisters,' Nessie explained.

'But . . . but how . . .' Rachel shook her head. Perhaps this was one question she shouldn't be asking.

'How did Adam's father come to be your father too?' Nessie asked the question for her, then looked away, her lips twisting in a wry smile. 'Rivalry,' she said bluntly. 'Jake wanted me to marry him.' Nessie sighed. 'All our lives might have been very different if I had, but Dick was a bit wild and made sure a shot gun wedding was necessary. I suppose Jake never forgave him for that. He married Lily on the rebound. Life was hard for me with Dick being too fond of the drink and I couldn't always pay the rent, so when Jake became rent collector for the Manor he suggested I could pick strawberries during the season to help out.'

Nessie put her workworn hands to her face at the hurtful memories.

'He forced himself on me,' she said with trembling lips. 'I was used to rough treatment, but after five children I was thin and weak so had no strength to deal him the blow he deserved. It all happened so quickly, here in this very field,' she said softly. 'Doctor Grant found me. He wanted me to prosecute Jake, but I didn't want Dick to know for fear of what he'd do.' She turned and looked at Rachel with alarm in her eyes. 'He found out from Beth eventually. That's what the fight was about all those years later. He was furious that Jake got me in the end, but he knows nothing of your being that baby. There's no reason for him to know.'

She put her arms round Rachel and hugged her. 'I'm so grateful to Doctor Grant and Minnie Fletcher – glad that your life was spared. And I'm sure you're all the stronger for having had to endure the taunts over that strawberry mark. You're such a beautiful woman now, Rachel. I'm proud that you're my daughter, and Jake would have been too.' She laughed. ''Tis no wonder you thought you were in love with Adam – but now that you know you're half-brother and sister, both you and Belinda will be able to understand and accept the situation better.'

'I could never understand why I felt sorry for you, and for Charlie too,' Rachel said. 'I think I must always have loved you.'

'But think what you owe Mrs Hunter – never forget that she brought you up and gave you more than I ever could.'

'Be kind to the woman,' the gypsy's warning echoed in Rachel's ears, and when she saw Kas coming across the field she got down from the trap and went eagerly to share the story with him.

The flock of rooks took off on their flight of fancy to weather storms, mate, nest and prepare for the next strawberry season.

Epilogue

Through the window of the van Rachel marvelled at the enormous orange harvest moon. Another season over; a new and very special one just beginning for her and Kas. She looked down at the month-old baby girl she was cradling in her arms with its mass of rich black hair, navy blue eyes, round and trusting, which Rachel knew would be almost black in a few weeks time. A tiny eager tongue, still milky-white from the last feed, peeped through a dainty rosebud mouth. Rachel glanced back at the moon and offered up a silent prayer for the perfect infant entrusted to her and Kas, though she wished she could have borne him the son he longed for.

'Next time,' she promised with a warm smile. Three times Kas had stood up to go to settle the horses for the night but he hadn't been able to pull himself away from watching Rachel with his baby daughter at her breast.

'The important thing is that you're all right,' he said softly.

'I was beginning to think I'd never be able to give you a baby,' she said. 'And then to have such an easy birth.' Rachel crooned lovingly to her baby. 'She's so beautiful – not the tiniest blemish anywhere. No one will ever be able to call her names, will they?'

'Blemish or no, she'd still be perfect in our eyes,' Kas said. 'Just as I'm sure you were to your parents. But just think, darling, without that strawberry mark Mrs Mead might never have been convinced that you were the baby girl she had.'

Rachel gently touched little Mary's pink cheek. 'I wonder who she'll take after? The Mead girls are all nice-looking, and Adam is too.'

'She's *ours*, and we aren't that bad, are we?'

Rachel laughed. 'I s'pose not. I hope life will be kind to her. We'll try to be good parents, little Mary.' She pulled the exquisite knitted shawl up round the baby's head, wrapped the two ends across in front and laid her in the crib. 'It's a lovely idea to have little Mary and Douglas christened at the same time,' she said after she'd pulled the dividing curtains across the van. Kas already had the kettle on.

'I thought you were going to see to the horses?' she said.

'I'll make us a cup of tea first.' Kas poked the boiler until the coals showed red and then stood with his arm round her. 'Your mother is so proud of both new babies. Now we have two daughters and Belinda and Adam have two sons.'

'She's so pleased that the group has decided to stay on here in the Forest of Bere for the winter.'

'And she'd not the only one,' Kas said, kissing the top of her head.

'Suddenly everything in the world has come right. No more wondering why Adam behaved the way he did. I understand now how awful such a discovery was for him, though I can't imagine how he managed not to tell anyone. Perhaps it made it easier, when I ran away. At last I feel much more contented now that I know the real truth, and it's lovely to be back on friendly, easy terms with Belinda again. We're special to each other – chosen sisters.'

'As Lemuel says, you must regard the past twenty-four years as an era, one which has ended satisfactorily. And as Sybil says we can look forward to the happy times now. No more jealousies, no more misunderstandings.'

Rachel sighed. 'I just wish Dad had lived long enough to know all the answers.'

'You might never have known the truth of your parentage if your father had lived, Rachel. I'm sure wherever he is he knows, and he'll be your guardian angel. Belinda's as well. He'll also know that his letter was meant to be written, and his blessing is on us all, I'm sure.'

While Carol and little Mary slept Kas and Rachel sat outside on the steps of the van, watching the moon rise in all its majesty amidst a myriad of stars.